AUSTRALIA

A ROMANCE ANTHOLOGY TO BENEFIT FIREFIGHTERS AND WILDLIFE

A romance anthology with over THIRTY original, never-before-seen stories from bestselling and award-winning authors. Each piece was written for this anthology to benefit firefighters and wildlife in Australia. AUSTRALIA is only available for a limited time, so one-click your copy before it's gone.

AUTHORS INCLUDE: Penny Reid, Meredith Wild, Carly Phillips, Sierra Simone, Emma Scott, Susan Stoker, Kennedy Ryan, Willow Aster, Skye Warren, Kylie Scott, Aleatha Romig, Willow Winters, AL Jackson, Julia Kent, Rebecca Yarros, Tijan, Giana Darling, Emma Hart, Chelle Bliss, Noelle Adams, A. Zavarelli, Jenika Snow, Dylan Allen, Audrey Carlan, Robin Covington, Mary Catherine Gebhard, Melanie Moreland, Parker S. Huntington, Nana Malone, Jewel E. Ann, Annabel Joseph, Celia Aaron, Michelle Heard, Brighton Walsh, Tamsen Parker, Pam Godwin, Kayti McGee

All royalties from this project will be donated to relief funds in Australia, with 50% going to a firefighter charity and 50% going to a wildlife charity. We aren't affiliated or endorsed by these charities. We are simply authors who want to support an important cause.

THE LAST SONG

SKYE WARREN

1

Samantha

The search of the hotel suite takes fifteen minutes.

Fifteen minutes of standing by the door clutching my violin with an armed guard while Liam and another man search every door and window and cabinet with guns drawn.

"Clear," comes the voice from the balcony.

"Clear," comes a tinny voice through Elijah's headset.

Only then does Liam return from the bedroom. "All clear."

I wade through the plush carpet and fall on the leather sofa with a sigh. Thirty-six hours on a plane has made every joint in my body stiff, especially the ones in my lower back. Some women become radiant when they carry a child. I'm the opposite of radiant. A black hole.

Masculine murmurs track the progress of settling in an entourage and security team to the five-star hotel. I wish the precautions weren't necessary, but I can't argue with them. Not after the man I love was shot protecting me. Threats come from my past. They come from being in the spotlight. They even come from natural disasters, like the one we're here to fight.

I gave my last performance a month ago.

As soon as I found out I was pregnant, I stopped booking concerts. The bushfires in Australia brought me back into the spotlight one more time. It shouldn't feel so final. Motherhood doesn't have to end a career, but I have this secret fear that it will.

Liam unmolds me from the sofa, tearing the violin case from my arms.

Orange light presses against the windows. I'm not sure whether it's dawn or dusk. I'm guided into the bathroom, which features an oversize Jacuzzi tub. Liam goes instead to the walk-in shower with dark slate tiles. He tests the water with his hand until it's right.

Then he reaches for my slouchy sweater. "I'm not in the mood," I mumble as he takes it off. I'm unresisting as he gently pulls the tank top over my head. My nipples peak in the steamy air.

"I know," he says, his voice grave, his expression solemn.

That's the thing about Liam. He does know. I could refuse him every day throughout eternity, and he'd still be here, undressing me, bathing me, taking care of me with his every breath. There's something not-right about this level of devotion, something I would never give up.

"I didn't mean it," I say, a tear slipping down my cheek. Not sadness, that tear. Exhaustion, maybe. And pregnancy hormones. I've been a mess for months now. My jeans slide down my legs, and I step out of them, pliant and almost numb. "I do want you. I'm just grumpy and jet-lagged."

My panties come off last. Liam tugs them down with a brisk, businesslike movement. I could almost believe he's unaffected except for the very large bulge in his black tactical pants.

I'm standing in front of him. Naked.

That would have been enough to make him hard, naturally. It's different now that I'm pregnant. Even breathing is enough to make him hard. It's like I'm exuding some kind of sex-drive chemical. What do I know about reproductive science? Maybe I am. It makes him want me nonstop, until I'm chafed between my legs, tender in the most secret places, until I wince when he pushes inside.

He isn't pushing inside now. No, he's got himself wrapped up tight. Like a punishment. I let him move me under the hot spray, but I don't let go of his hand. Two hundred and twenty pounds of pure muscle. I couldn't move him if he didn't want to be moved. He lets me pull, pull, pull him under the water until he's half-drenched and fully dressed.

His brow lifts, sardonic. "Do you want me to shower, too?"

Hot water plasters the black fabric of his T-shirt to hard muscle. That's another thing that changed since I got pregnant. Five a.m. runs and three-hour workouts. Those are typical things for Liam North, ex-military, CEO of North Security. Now he's training even harder, even longer. As if maybe this baby will be a hundred fifty pounds and need to be bench-pressed.

I reach up to place to a kiss on his bristly jaw. "Join me, Liam. Please."

He's stripping off his soaked T-shirt before I can finish begging. He's hard edges and deep shadows. There's no other word for it. He's ripped. Droplets cling to the coarse hair across his chest. His cock rises in the spray, ruddy and rude. It should be awkward, his cock and my belly, these pieces where we don't fit together. That's how it feels a foot away. Then he closes the distance. Skin to skin, we fit together perfectly. No space between us. Only heat and sensation and that special familiar electricity.

"I'm sorry," I say, breathless, though I don't know why I'm sorry.

It seems like the right thing to say, because he laughs. A break in the clouds, that laugh. A brief reprieve of the severity with which he protects us both. "You are perfect and sweet. And most of all you're tired. I'm supposed to be washing your hair."

A drop of water falls from his eyelash, and I'm helpless. This strong man uses every ounce of muscle to protect me. He's like the water wrapping around the earth. I want to soak him into my skin. "Wash my hair," I say. "Later. I want you now. Liam, I want you."

Those green eyes darken. "You should rest. And I should—"

"Do a perimeter check?" It's not fair to tease him about this, but he needs the teasing. He needs something light and playful in his life. "I need my perimeter checked."

Emerald glints down at me. "East? West? North?"

I take his hand and drag it lower. He's my very own Atlas, holding up the weight of the world. It's my job to make that load a little lighter. He lets me pull his hand between my legs. A light, watery touch makes me gasp. "South."

He rubs my intimate places with blunt, casual strokes. "There does seem to be some weakness in your defenses." Two fingers invade me, sandpaper on velvet. "Here."

I'm gratified by the roughness of his voice, by the dark look in his green eyes. I'm spread open to him, vulnerable and wet, impaled on his fingers, but he's affected, too. Hurting with it. His cock presses against my hip, heavy, insistent—hotter than the water that streams over my skin.

He moves his wrist. I feel the subtle shift in muscle and tendon against my skin. One second later, his finger brushes over a sensitive place. Darkness clouds my vision, pinpricked with light. The careful lover evaporates in an instant. Liam becomes merciless, driving me toward climax with knowledgeable caresses, fighting my body for a fast climb. I clasp his wrist as if to stop him, to tell him it's too much, too hard, but I don't have the strength to make him stop. It feels too good.

The orgasm rips through me like a tornado through a town, tight spirals of pleasure that feel almost like pain, leaving devastation in its path—trees torn out of the ground and buildings split in half. That's how my body feels once it's over. Every muscle seizes and goes limp. I would sink to the warm tile floor of the shower except that Liam catches me. I'm boneless in his arms.

Liam

I towel her dry. She lets me move her this way and that, unresisting. When I set her down in bed, she curls into the pillow. "What about you?" she mumbles, looking at me through glazed, half-lidded eyes.

She's asking about having sex. Or maybe giving me a handjob. Something that would be fair, considering I got her off. I don't give a fuck about fairness. That's not why I touch her. This isn't a goddamn trade negotiation. The flights exhausted her, but she still had a jittery energy. That's why I forced that orgasm out of her—so she could relax enough to sleep easy. Well, it wasn't entirely for that reason. I also love touching her. Making her come is the best thing I know how to do. These hands know how to fight and work and kill, but they can also make Samantha come so hard she almost passes out.

"Rest," I say, pulling the blanket under her chin.

It's always a little disconcerting when I tuck her in, the reminder that I was her guardian before I was her lover. Those two roles are entirely different, except for one thing—that I can take care of her in both.

The suite features a balcony with a view of the Sydney Opera House. Night fell in the span of a shower. Water and night create a dark tapestry. The white arcs of the theater glow against the backdrop. In the safe bubble of the hotel, we can't feel the extreme heat from outside. The smoke that hangs is temporarily sieved from the air due to a light shower this morning. Hard to believe that in the same state firefighters still battle bushfires.

Outside the bedroom my brother Elijah waits at the gleaming dining table. We have men and women working for North Security. One of them stands in the hallway. Another's in place on the living room balcony. More are positioned around the hotel. I hired and trained most of them myself. I'd trust any one of them with my life. But Samantha's life... that's different. For that I'd prefer to have one of my brothers on duty.

"She asleep?" Elijah asks, his voice and expression casual.

Of course he'll know what happened the next room over. It's not hard to deduce, and Elijah's a skilled operator. "Out like a light. Hopefully she'll stay that way the whole night. It'll help with the jet lag."

"But you're not going to join her."

"I need to hit the gym. All those hours in a tin can."

My brother snorts, aware that our tin can was a large Gulfstream with plush leather seats and a private room with a queen-size bed. "God forbid you go for twenty-four hours without pummeling your body in punishment for... for what, exactly? I've never been sure."

"Don't start," I say, crossing the suite to the bar area. I twist the top off an ice-cold bottle of water and gulp it down. That's the problem with brothers. They know too damn much about you.

"Still feel guilty about Sam? You should."

Elijah's the youngest North brother, which makes him closest in age to Samantha. They had more of a friendship. I was the one who met with her teachers and set the curfew. Elijah was the one she talked to about... hell, I don't know what they talked about. Boys she had a crush on?

Now she's all grown up, a celebrity violinist and soon-to-be mother of my child.

"Don't worry about my shit. Worry about yours," I say, which is a low blow. That's brothers for you.

"She doesn't need you to have an eight-pack. Being able to survive three months in a desert isn't going to make you a better husband." He points to the bedroom. "Go back in there. Sleep."

"You don't give the orders around here, little brother."

"I should," he mutters.

Hell. "If you were in charge, North Security would have gone up in flames years ago. We'd have done some heroic rescue, probably saving a bus full of nuns from a grizzly fate. Not all of us want to be heroes, Elijah. Some of us just want to survive."

We stare at each other. I'm breathing hard. This is maybe the most honest I've ever been with him. We were raised like a litter of stray dogs, the three

North brothers. Each of us went into the military and forged our own path. You don't go into battle and walk away without scars.

I don't judge my brother. He's right about me. Guilt? I don't need a single reason. There are a hundred. I think of them when I go downstairs and run fifteen miles on an inclined treadmill and do hundreds of reps at the bench. Every time Samantha's feet hurt or she can't sleep. Every time she has morning sickness. My fault, because I made her pregnant. I fucked her without a condom again and again and again. I wanted her to have a child so I'd bind her to me, so I'd make her mine.

And in doing so I may have ended her career.

Samantha

The charity concert was put together quickly. Major pop stars and bands have flown in for a single night. We don't have time to rehearse or plan any kind of smooth transition, but it doesn't matter. The koalas and the kangaroos need our help. The people here need it, too. Money will go to the local volunteer firefighters and a wildlife rescue organization.

When my last tour ended, I didn't know it would be the end.

I didn't know that two months later I'd pee on a stick and see two pink lines.

That makes this concert different. It's the last time I'll perform in front of people… for how long? I'm not sure. I grew up being dragged by my father from one country to the next, more like a piece of heavy baggage than a child. I won't do the same thing to the baby growing inside me.

How long until I'll feel comfortable leaving him or her? Five years? Eight? Ten?

It's something that isn't written in the *What to Expect When You're Expecting* book. Being a solo violinist isn't the kind of job you can leave and come back to. In ten years no one may buy a ticket with my name on it. Most likely they'll forget about me in two years. There's an endless line of talented, ambitious violinists waiting to take my seat.

A limo takes us the short distance to the Sydney Opera House.

My violin case rests in my lap.

Liam sits across from me, wearing a tux and a grim expression. "Nervous?" he asks.

"The usual." Every crowd brings its own energy to a concert. Some are boisterous and engaging. Others are pensive and serious. It interacts with the notes in a way I can't predict. Live music is fundamentally more raw, more expressive than when its recorded. I've played this song a thousand times, but in a couple hours, when I play onstage, it will become brand-new.

"The Paganini?" he asks.

It's one of the pieces I often play when I'm in a lineup of modern music. It can feel like a drag to go from an upbeat hip-hop song to a slow classical piece. The Paganini has energy and melody that feel accessible, even if someone doesn't usually listen to the violin. I shake my head.

"One of yours?"

I've been exploring my own compositions. "A new one."

That sharp green gaze takes me in. "When have you been practicing?"

By the time you see someone play the piano or the cello or the violin onstage, they've practiced that same song until they hear it in their sleep. They know the precise fingering they'll use. They've breathed every single beat. Liam would have heard me play a piece before I perform it, but he hasn't heard this one. "When you're working, usually. Or when you're working out."

The admission sits between us, thick as butter. It's a secret. Not the first secret that's been between us. Not the most dangerous or illicit secret, but the first one since we've been married. There's a cushion-cut five-carat ruby on my finger surrounded by pavé diamonds. Unconventional as wedding bands go, but it's perfect for me. For us. It wasn't about secrets. We'll always have those. It's about love. Unconditional love. The kind Liam North showed since I stumbled my way into his life.

He leans forward. The back of his fingers brush my knee. "Did you think I wouldn't like it, sweetheart? You don't have to hide anything from me."

My hands clutch the wood violin case, knuckles turning white. "It's... a present."

"A present?"

"For you."

"For me." He waits with infinite patience. The world might fly off its axis, and he'd still be sitting across from me in the limo, waiting for me to explain.

"I know you're worried about me, about the end of my career."

"It doesn't have to be the end. I'll go with you anywhere. I'll take care of the baby while you play—"

"That's no life for a child. Neither is having armed guards check your hotel room before you walk inside. This has to be the end, but that's okay, Liam. That's what I'm trying to tell you."

Green eyes turn dark with turmoil. He wants to argue with me. It kills him to think the baby might deprive me of this—career, fame, money. But that's the thing about feminism. It gives us the right to work when we have children. That's a choice. Which means I can make the other choice. I want to stay home with my child. And I'm lucky enough to have that option.

I struggle with the words when it's so much easier to speak with my fingers and the strings of my violin. "I wrote this to show you how I feel, that it's okay, that you don't have to worry, that I *want* this. You aren't taking anything away from me. You're giving me a family."

A grunt that's mostly refusal. "You don't have to make the decision now. Wait until you've had the baby. Wait until you've recovered. Then you can decide—"

"We'd only have this argument later instead of now." I look down at my violin case with its gentle curves and its antique locks. "Maybe you'll understand when you listen to the piece."

Emerald eyes narrow. "What's this piece called, Samantha?"

"'The Last Song.'"

Liam

When I got custody of Samantha Brooks, I swore to the legal system that I would care for her. It was nothing compared to the promise I made myself. She would have the best education, the best clothes, the best food. She would never suffer a single second if it was within my power to stop. I would move the sun and the stars around to suit her.

For years it seemed like I had almost kept that promise. Then she turned eighteen. She looked at me, not only with trust in those beautiful brown eyes, but with lust. And I was gone. No matter how hard I fought it, I gave her my heart and soul. I gave her my body.

Now she has a round belly and an aching back. There are shadows under her eyes.

I did that to her. Maybe an ordinary man would be proud to see the result of his virility. I'm not an ordinary man. I've spent the past decade trying to atone for my mistakes.

It will never be enough.

I wait with her while we watch a performance of a major pop artist that includes thirty backup dancers and pyrotechnics. The backstage bustles with the lighting and stage crew, with costume designers and makeup artists. The performer onstage rips off her sequined dress to reveal a fire-colored bodysuit that makes it looks like she's on fire and naked at the same time. The crowd goes insane.

That must be some kind of signal because the director with his earpiece and iPad gestures to Samantha. "Ten minutes until you're on."

"I'm ready," she says, sounding calm and collected. Only when he walks out of earshot does she let her nerves show. "How am I supposed to follow that act? My God."

"You're the greatest violinist of this generation, Samantha. You don't follow anyone. They open for you."

That pulls a laugh out of her. "And the performers going after me?"

"The encore." When she smiles, it makes her glow. Like a goddamn light source, that's her. She wouldn't appreciate me telling her that, though.

"I'm the token classical musician. So they can say they featured twenty different kinds of music." She makes a face. "And probably the token Asian here, too."

I pull her into my arms until she's facing away from the stage. Her eyes hold a hundred sleepless nights. A thousand worries for the future. I can't protect her from what's inside her head. For a brief moment, I set aside the idea of protection. I set aside the idea of guilt. What I want most is to kiss her, and so I do, a brief brush of my lips against hers, the smallest taste, a single breath.

She's the one who deepens it, grasping the back of my neck. Her tongue flicks against mine, playful the way she can be sometimes, almost aggressive when she lets herself, and I growl my approval.

"You're up," comes the voice of the director.

I have her plastered against me, my fists gripping her arms, my cock hard as steel between us. Pure force of will allows me to set her aside. Jesus. "Break a leg," I tell her.

She looks dazed. "It's time?"

"You're the star of the show," I tell her, pressing one last kiss to her forehead. Lord, but I love this woman. Maybe she was invited from some inclusivity checklist, but I don't give a damn. She's been the best violin player in the world since she was six.

An impish smile curves her lips. "I know."

She takes a step back, and another, and another, before she whirls and almost skips onto the stage. I'm awed by her. Brought to my knees by her. She's a goddess, and the audience seems to know it. A hush falls over them.

They should be blinded by fire and deaf from heavy bass, but they seem to know they're in the presence of greatness.

Samantha steps to the microphone, her simple black gown making her pregnant belly plain. "Good evening," she says, her voice low and a little husky. "I'm Samantha Brooks."

There's a rumble that might be a greeting from the audience.

She smiles. "I'm guessing most of you don't know me. Don't worry. I don't know most of you, either. We're strangers, but we both showed up tonight for a common cause."

There's clapping and a whoop from the back.

"We both showed up tonight because we love this planet too much to let it burn. We love the animals too much to let them suffer. We love our fellow humans too much to let them go through this alone. It might feel far removed from the fires, being here in your beautiful clothes, drinking champagne during intermission, but it's not so far away. We're making a difference as surely as someone applying salve to a koala or dousing a house in water. This is how we help, by doing what we can, by giving everything we've got, and most of all, by showing up. This is how we save the world."

Applause sweeps over thousands of people as she takes her seat.

Her violin comes out of the case. She touches the strings the way she does every time she plays. In practice, in performance. It always starts this way, with a gentle *hello* from her to the instrument. And then from the instrument to her.

She does not do anything so obvious as glance at me, but I feel her attention focus on the side of the stage nonetheless. My skin prickles with awareness, as if it were a physical caress.

That's the only warning of what's to come. *The Last Song.*

Samantha lifts the violin. She positions the bow. And when the first strains dance across the air, I suck in a breath. This is energy completely unlike the dancing, beating, fire-breathing of the performance before. This is electricity running through my veins. It's a whisper down my bones.

Refusal tightens my stomach. How can this be the last song? How can this be the end?

The melody lifts, sudden, unexpected, a joyous sound. It's almost impossible not to smile, hearing that. Almost impossible not to hope for more. The irony makes me ache.

The Last Song. No.

The song lasts an eternity. It's over in a second.

It tells a story, this last song. A story of searching, stumbling, losing. Of needing love. Of finding it. Enough, enough, enough. It tells a story of finally having enough. There's almost surprise, when you've gone so long without. A sense of disbelief. It feels like you have more than you deserve.

It feels like someone's going to come and snatch it away.

It's her story, and it's mine. We both had broken childhoods and a sense of guilt. We both can't help but doubt the happy ever after we've been given. The one who won't have guilt and doubt... the baby nestled in her stomach, listening to the music from the best seat in the house. The baby will know he's loved from the moment he's born. From right now. We've broken the pattern. That's when I finally understand the song. The last fear. The last hunger. The last pain.

It's not a song about endings. It's about a new beginning. *The Last Song.*

The final note rises higher and higher, buffeted by the clouds, like a balloon floating away.

Silence. And then the opera house erupts in applause. Adulation. It's completely deserved, this praise. I can't even bring myself to clap. She does a slow, elegant curtsy. Then she walks off the stage. Our eyes meet. There are a thousand differences between us. Our ages are too far apart. I'm a fighter. She's a musician. There are so many reasons she's not right for me, except one. Love.

She runs to me, and I'm waiting to catch her, always here. Always hers.

Samantha

I'm waiting in the dark. The hotel hums with quiet efficiency, keeping out the heat of the season, making a cocoon for me. I've been alone for hours now. Liam has been working out. That's never going to change. It's part of his career, for one thing. It's also part of his strength. I've come to see, too, that it's almost like the hours I spend practicing the violin. A meditation.

A soft click from the door. Light skates over the smooth white bedspread and then disappears. He's soundless as he moves across the room. Only a faint rustle as he closes the bathroom door behind him. The shower almost sounds like a dream through the walls. It feels like a dream when I put my feet onto the carpet. I follow him into the bathroom, where steam has already clouded the mirrors.

He pauses when he sees me. Water drips down his temple, his jaw. It streams down his chest. He might be a Greek god bathing in some waterfall.

I take off my nightshirt and let it fall to the floor.

He doesn't move as I open the shower door and step inside.

Strange how water that's so hot can feel cold when you're inches away. The spray makes my skin pebble and my nipples turn tight. He drags me close to him so the shower hits me fully, and I gasp at the heat—the hot water, his body. A combined furnace that raises my temperature, boiling over.

I raise my eyebrow. "Do you want me to shower, too?"

He runs a square-tipped finger across the slope of my breast. "Please."

It would be so easy to let him take over. So pleasurable.

Instead I push him until his back hits the wall. He doesn't flinch, not my soldier, but the tile must be cold on his skin. He's already hard and pointing in my direction. His cock looks swollen and red, almost as if it's been hard for hours, never gone down since we landed in Sydney.

"What are you doing?" he murmurs.

I grasp his cock in my fist. "Taking care of you."

"You don't have to—"

A finger to his lips. "I don't have to, but I want to. It makes me feel good to make you come. To give you relief. To make your knees weak. The same way it makes you feel good when you do it to me."

He leans his head back against the tile. His arms spread as if to say, *Have at me.*

Of course it's easy to talk about making his knees weak. The reality is a little more perplexing. When I squeeze him gently, his whole body jerks. When I stroke him, he grunts. I touch two fingers beneath his heavy cock, to the soft, tight sac underneath, and he grits his teeth. His body is like sheet music; it tells me the notes to play. I follow them across the staff up and down, playing a song that means desire, that means trust, that means gratitude.

"Thank you," he says, his voice low as gravel.

"For what?"

"The present. The song. It was beautiful. Beyond beautiful."

"Oh." My cheeks feel warm. A smile plays at my lips. "You're welcome."

"Of course you didn't tell me we were exchanging gifts. I didn't get you anything."

I sit every day and play the violin for hours. That hasn't changed even while I'm pregnant. It probably won't change when I have this baby either.

It's part of me, the same way his late-night runs and weight lifting are part of him. They're the way we experience the world. A form of worship. "You did get me something," I say, walking my fingers down the ladder of tightly defined abs. "Yourself."

And then I show him how very nimble and strong my fingers have gotten from years of daily practice. I show him how much I appreciate his taut, muscled body. I show him that there's love and lust and laughter, even after the last song has been played—that there's music, even after the last note goes dark.

* * *

PASH, NO RASH

PENNY REID

"I've always wanted to learn how to surf. Maybe I'll learn how to surf. That won't chafe the thighs, will it?" Using the condensation my whiskey sour glass had left behind, I drew a surfboard on the surface of the bar. "But really, thigh abrasions aside, how likely am I to learn to surf?"

I didn't lift my attention as I asked this question, didn't check to make sure Patty the bartender was still listening. I'd known Patty for just two hours, but I liked her. She'd served me *several* drinks, offered me a room upstairs should I become too inebriated to walk back to the lodge, and didn't seem to care that I was fuck-all good at small talk. Basically, she was now my closest friend.

Though, I doubted she was within earshot at present.

Didn't matter. I wasn't talking to her, not really. I was talking to myself, as I was prone to do in moments of panic, excitement, or melancholy. I'd been talking to myself quite a lot today.

First, when I thought my alarm hadn't gone off this morning, as follows, "Holy shiitake mushrooms, Audrey! You are so fired. Your third business trip and you oversleep? And on a team building retreat. What is wrong with you? Pull it together! Where the hell are your pants?"

As it turned out, my panic was all for naught. The hotel's digital clock on the nightstand hadn't been adjusted after the end of daylight savings time last week. I hadn't overslept, I hadn't been late. I'd made it to the team building breakfast thirty minutes early and therefore was forced to wait in the lobby until it started. But I'd impressed the big boss by being the first from Research and Development (R&D) to arrive.

Unfortunately, the second person to arrive had been Mr. Fallon, who I considered the Australian version of Darth Vader. Well, he hadn't technically *arrived.* He'd strolled through the lobby in a sweaty, tight, black workout shirt and dark gray workout shorts, both of which looked like wrapping paper around his gorgeous body.

He didn't notice me, of course. He never noticed me. And you know what? I was really okay with that. Elias Fallon only noticed people right before he eviscerated them. So, no thank you. No me gusta. Nein. Nah. Nope.

I'd stepped behind a large fake bush while he passed, his dreamy yet eternally distant and dismissive brown eyes fastened to his watch. It was one of those watches I refused to buy, the ones that knew more about you than you knew about yourself—sleeping habits, social media stats, calories ingested, burned, steps taken, hopes, wishes, dreams, sex positions attempted. I didn't wish to be watched, especially not by my . . . watch.

But back to me talking to myself.

Later, after the team building breakfast and the ropes course, as I was on my way back to my room for a quick shower, I'd discovered a ten-dollar bill in the front pocket of my pants while fishing for my key card.

!

!!

TEN DOLLARS?!

HUZZAH!!

There's not much that gets me as excited as found money, therefore the words spilled out, "Ten dollars?! Holy shirt, this is great. This is the best day ever. I am officially having the best day ever. Mark it down, Audrey. Take a note. Let the record sh—"

The sound of approaching steps ended my excited monologue and I glanced over my shoulder, finding none other than Mr. Elias Fallon striding down the hall. This time in a suit instead of workout clothes, but again in shades of black and gray, befitting his monochromatic soul. Stuck in startled mode, my eyes moved over him. He was a tall man, lean but solidly built, his hair thick and jet black. And yet, he wasn't classically handsome. *At all.* Definitely not pretty.

Rather, his face was interesting. Every time I looked at it, I discovered something new. For example, the two halves were not symmetrical. His pronounced jaw was crooked, like he'd slid his bottom teeth slightly to the side and they were stuck there. Or maybe it just looked that way because his full lips slanted down on the left more than on the right, giving the impression he was either perpetually grimacing or twisting them in wry disapproval. He also had several dark freckles on his left cheek, scattered like a constellation beneath his eye, and at least one, albeit small, brown mole on his upper lip. On anyone else I might've called it a beauty mark.

But I found his eyes the most interesting, he was the only person I'd encountered who could convey an encyclopedia of unspoken words with barely a look. Usually, it was disdain or impatience, but the magnitude of it —with no shift in his features but a slight flicker of his stern eyebrows, a narrowing of his eyelids—registered on the Richter scale. When he was pissed, the earth shook. Or so it had felt that way to me over the last year as I'd observed the man.

And right now, he's looking at you, Audrey.

The realization had me coming to myself and I hurriedly whipped my head back to my door, fumbling as I shoved the key card into the lock apparatus and gulped a measure of air. The LED light on the device turned from red to green, making a telltale *eeer-eek-err* noise as it unlocked. Pushing the door open, I darted inside and closed it behind me, pressing my back against it as I strained my ears over the sound of my racing heart, waiting for his steps to pass.

Why I'd done this, I had no idea. But I always did. The few times we'd crossed paths back at corporate outside of scheduled meetings, in a hallway or on an elevator, I would always, *always* turn and speed-walk away.

Instinct maybe? Perhaps some part of me recognized or detected something in him that warned me to steer clear, a subconscious undercurrent wresting this inane, immediate reaction. Or maybe a pheromone? Maybe it was an ingrained, biological process making my mouth dry and my chest seize, and a shock travel up my spine at the mere sight of him.

Preservation instinct...

"Why do you do anything? Mystery for the ages," I mumbled at the memory of hiding in my room earlier this afternoon. Presently, I whispered my lament to the water sketch on the bar, which resembled a crescent moon more than a surfboard. So, I guess I was talking to the moon.

My curriculum vitae said I was a content expert in my field, an impressive human who was extremely competent at her job. I should've been more self-assured in social situations, and I'd honestly been trying. But how does one improve at prosaic greetings and idle chitchat? How was that accomplished? I couldn't practice. If you suck a chitchat, no one wants to talk to you.

"Tell me, Mr. Moon. Tell me how to excel at small talk. I sincerely wish to know." Unless people were discussing a subject where I was an actual content expert—like fluid mechanics for example, or the process of harvesting honey from bee boxes, or maybe *Nick at Nite* TV shows from the early 1990s—my skills were the equivalent of steaming dog poo on the pavement of life.

I stank. And made things weird. Which is what had happened earlier in the evening at the corporate "mixer."

One of my contemporaries from the marketing team had asked me if I liked to travel and I'd made the mistake of being honest. "Not usually. The TSA always wants to touch my hair and my right boob. Never the left, always the right. There's something about it that sets off the wave scanner. Maybe I should get a mammogram."

. . . Crickets.

After a few minutes of conversation misfires, I'd faded to the periphery of the discussion, the topic being how much everyone else loved to travel and all the fantastic, unusual, adventurous destinations they'd visited. When the woman to my right mentioned that she loved to climb mountains and documented her adventures on Instagram to the extent that now she was an Instagram Influencer with over fifty thousand followers, all I could think about was altitude sickness, thigh chafing, and the horror of having fifty thousand people reviewing my vacation photos.

Another thirty minutes passed, me sitting quietly as harsh reality set in: I had nothing in common with these people. They were all interesting and fascinating, turning small talk into something bigger, insightful, and at times humorous, living their interesting and fascinating lives. Meanwhile, here I was contemplating thigh chafing.

Listening awkwardly and not contributing, I excused myself when my glass of wine ran out and went in search of another drink. That's when I discovered the lodge had limited us to one drink per person, and *that's* when I asked the kid refusing to serve me another where I could find a bar nearby that would serve me drinks.

He recommended Genie's Country Western Bar ten minutes up the road.

Here I sat, talking to the water-moon on the bar about my dearth of surfing ability.

"I'll never learn to surf. I'll never climb mountains. Do I want chafed thighs? I don't even know. I'll just continue to be boring in every possible way except my left-handedness. That's the only thing interesting about me—my inability to use scissors and can openers." And that was about as interesting as listening to my nana talk about her collection of Epsom salts.

"What'll you have?" Patty the bartender's voice asked someone from somewhere close behind me.

I eyed my empty glass and heaved a sigh. Pushing up from my slouched position on the bar, I decided I should catch Patty after she took the mystery person's order. I would have one more drink. Just one more something before returning to the Donner Lodge.

But then, just as I'd straightened on my stool and decided on the efficiency of straight whiskey over the frivolousness of another whiskey sour, a deep male voice speaking in an Australian accent said, "I'll have what she's having."

My head turned of its own volition and I was strangled by surprise because there he was, sitting on the stool next to mine, his interesting face in profile, the full force of his attention on Patty the bartender. How she managed to hold his gaze, I had no idea. *Your old friend Patty is a tough cookie, that's how.*

Lord Vader himself. At a country western bar. In Tennessee. Sitting next to me.

My heart climbed up my esophagus and the discomfort of hyperawareness ignited a sudden hot flash beneath my skin. I was still staring at him as he turned to face me, his movements unhurried, easy, graceful. But a split second after our eyes connected, I flinched back, dropping my chin and studying the wooden bar.

What is he doing here? And why is he so close? There must've been twenty other free stools. It was a Tuesday at 6:30 p.m. He could've sat anywhere. He could've—

Wait a minute.

Am I about to be eviscerated?

"Well?" Patty's friendly voice cut through my diatribe of confusion and I affixed my stare to her smiling expression. "What're you drinking this time, sugar?"

"Whiskey?" I squeaked.

Her grin grew and she nodded once, glancing quickly at my inexplicable companion and then back to me. "Top shelf, right?"

"Of course," he said, the juxtaposition of his cultured Australian inflection against her adorable southern twang befuddled me.

I opened my mouth but couldn't bring myself to speak. To my ear, I had no accent. Which meant *I* sounded like I had an accent to both of them. He was cultured, she was adorable, but what adjective would they use to describe me? Generic American tedium? Flat Midwestern dullness? These thoughts made my brain stumble.

Patty winked and skipped away, presumably in search of top-shelf whiskey.

Meanwhile, I watched her go, watched her reach for the top shelf—who knew they actually kept "top shelf" liquor on the top shelf?—and pull down a bottle of amber liquid, pause and chat with another bartender, all the while feeling the weight of Mr. Elias Fallon's attention on the side of my face.

"You can't use can openers?"

My lashes fluttered at the deep tenor of his voice, and I slid my gaze to the right, discovering he'd turned completely, one of his feet on the bottom rung of my stool, his other long leg stretched out behind me.

I successfully fought a shiver and shrugged. "It can be challenging, depending on the type of can opener." I'd managed to keep my tone flat.

"Challenging." His elbow on the bar, his thumb beneath his chin, the side of his index finger brushed against his top lip. He appeared to be completely at ease. But then, he always appeared to be completely at ease, even when he eviscerated people.

"You have to, uh, turn the crank with your right hand." I peeked at his face again. He watched me with a forceful yet inscrutable expression. I blurted, "I'm left-handed."

"I know."

I looked at him squarely. "You know?"

"Yes."

"That I'm left-handed?" I felt my forehead wrinkle.

"Yes."

I searched the bar beyond him. "But you don't—"

"Don't what?" He leaned a smidge closer.

You don't know who I am.

I couldn't say that, because he did.

We'd been introduced several times last year when I'd first been recruited to take over as lead design engineer at headquarters. Every time, he'd shaken my hand in a firm grasp, freezing me in place with the expressive intensity of his gaze, and said, "Dr. Bello. We're glad you're here."

No. He knew who I was, he knew my name. I'd given presentations at meetings where he'd been present. He'd asked questions and I'd answered them plainly. That kind of interaction hadn't flustered me. Like I said, when talking about subjects where I'm a content expert, I have no problem.

So instead of saying *You don't know who I am,* I said, "You don't know me."

Analyzing him and his unwavering yet oddly warm—*is that warmth?*—gaze, I ignored the tight, prickly sensation in my chest and licked my lips. They still tasted like the sour mix from my earlier drink, sweet and tangy.

Elias Fallon's focus wavered, dropping to my mouth for two beats of my racing heart, and he spoke slowly, as though measuring or counting every word. "You take notes during meetings in your composition notebook instead of using a laptop or your phone."

"It's so I can sketch designs as they occur to me."

"You could do that with an iPad or a tablet."

"But then they'd be the property of the company. I buy my notebooks myself. Not all my sketches are for corporate." What I didn't say, because it was none of his business, was that I often sketched people during meetings —him included. *Especially him.*

Which made me a weirdo creeper. Yeah. I know this about myself, okay? But what could I do? His face was so *interesting*. I liked looking at it, but only when he wasn't looking back.

"And you always use a felt-tip pen."

"If I used ballpoint or pencil, I'd smudge them with the side of my hand."

"Makes sense." Elias Fallon placed his palm flat on the bar in front of me. "You also always sit at a corner seat, so no one is sitting on your left."

Disarmed and distracted by this last observation, I threw caution to the wind, met his arresting gaze squarely, and set my elbow on the bar a few inches from his fingers so I could rest my chin on my hand. "Do I?"

He nodded once, warm eyes tracing slowly over my features. "Yes. It makes finding a seat next to you very difficult."

"Why would you want to sit next to me?" I asked mechanically, too distracted by the glamor of Elias Fallon up close.

"Perhaps I've been hoping for an opportunity to talk to you."

I sunk into the depths of his amazing eyes, swam in them. "About what?"

He shrugged lightly. "Just small talk."

That broke the spell. I flinched back, blinking away. "Oh, then you'd be disappointed. I fail at small talk."

"Then big talk." He bent his head, moving back into my line of sight.

His words pulled a confused smile out of me. "Big talk?"

"Yes. Of shoes and ships and sealing wax."

"Cabbages and kings?" My grin widened and I gave him another glance, surprised by his Lewis Carroll reference. "Big fan of *Alice in Wonderland*? Or, I guess more precisely, *Through the Looking Glass?*"

"Big fan of that poem, *The Walrus and the Carpenter*." Something mischievous glinted in his gaze, though his face remained poker straight.

"Those poor oysters." I tutted. "Thinking they're just going for a walk, and instead they end up being eaten."

Elias Fallon inclined his head and whispered darkly, "Don't feel too bad for them. I've never met an oyster that didn't enjoy being eaten."

A spike of heat, with the suddenness of a gunshot, spread throughout my entire body followed closely by a rush of jittery confusion. We stared at each other. Just stared at each other. And I got the sense he was waiting for me to catch up, to realize something, to give him some sort of clue or sign or answer.

What . . . what is happening?

Before I could respond—or figure out how I wanted to respond—Elias glanced beyond me as though distracted in the distance. Not a second later, two shots of whiskey were placed between us. Sliding his arm back, his long fingers curled around one of the whiskey glasses as I collected the other. Before I could bring it to my lips, he clinked his glass against mine.

"To pleasant walks and pleasant talks," he said, eyes now definitely warm. Something warmer than warm. And definitely unnerving. "And finally knowing each other."

Knowing each other? Finally?

My hand suspended in air, I watched him take a drink from his shot glass, watching him toss his head back and swallow easily, which made me wonder—

"How much have you had to drink?" If he were drunk, it would certainly explain the warmth in his eyes. It would also explain why he was speaking to me in the first place (either tipsy boredom or horniness) and the lack of evisceration (thus far).

Maybe it was my imagination, maybe it was the whiskey sours, but I could've sworn the side of his mouth hitched upward. "This is my second of the evening."

"How big was the first glass?"

A rare flash of teeth as both sides of his mouth curved. His dreamy, velvety, impossibly expressive eyes arrested mine, and I felt my breath catch as I swayed an involuntary inch forward. Right now, they looked so different than I'd ever seen them, so soft and inviting.

Inviting.

Yes. That was the word. Like a blanket and a warm fire on a cold day, his eyes were drinking chocolate without the frothy accoutrements. No sprinkles, no marshmallows, just the promise of delectable, straightforward satisfaction.

Yeesh. How many drinks have I had?

"My first drink was smaller than that one." He indicated to the shot still in my hand, answering my question.

"Hmm." My stomach fluttered and I lifted my glass, downing my whiskey in one swallow. This was either my third or fourth. Or sixth.

When I finished, he'd resumed his earlier position, his hand flat on the bar in front of me. Except now he seemed even closer. Or perhaps I'd moved closer. Never mind. I was too preoccupied by the green and silver flecks in his irises to be alarmed by our proximity.

His eyes are my favorite.

Elias Fallon still seemed to be gauging my reaction to . . . something. "Audrey—"

"What else do you know about me?" *And why am I whispering?*

He paused, took a slow, deep breath. His continued, pointed attention felt like hooks, or industrial strength Velcro. Or rare earth magnets. Whatever. I felt stuck, rooted in place under his inspection.

My tipsiness took advantage of his slowness and I spoke before he could respond. "Because I don't think I know anything about you, besides that you enjoy children's rhymes, you're brutally competent, and you're a little scary."

He straightened, flinching, the curve of his lips falling. "I'm sorry. Am I making—am I scaring you?"

For some reason, I leaned forward at his retreat. "What? Now? No. Not really. No. Actually, not at all. Not in the way you're inferring. Just, at work, when someone does shoddy work or fucks up, you are quite effective in expressing your dissatisfaction without doing or saying much at all, and that can be intimidating." My hand had decided to lay itself on his forearm, and then my fingers decided to squeeze said forearm.

Goodness, that's a quality forearm. Maybe his forearms were my favorite.

Elias glanced between my hand and me. "But I don't intimidate you."

I hesitated.

As executive leadership, we were at the same meetings, briefings, and so forth. We had to interact, I had to watch him make difficult decisions, take action, and he'd watched me do the same. Elias may have had seniority over me—being there longer—but he wasn't my boss. We weren't even in the same division. And yet . . .

"Not on purpose," I finally answered.

His eyes frowned. Not his face, his *eyes*. A subtle swirl, a shift. His other features did nothing at all.

Swallowing, this time with seemingly more difficulty than when he'd thrown back the whiskey, he said quietly, "I'm sorry to hear that."

Oomph.

My heart gave a painful tug at his words, his tone, the unhappiness in his gaze, and I leaned even closer. "I don't think you can help it—intimidating people—it's your gift."

He lifted an eyebrow a scant millimeter or two. "Making people uncomfortable is my gift?"

"Unsettling them." I nodded. "You're exceptionally good at it. Take right now for instance."

"Right now."

"Yes. I am unsettled."

The frown intensified, now tinged with disappointment.

I soldiered on, fueled by whiskey and a building sense of aimless, and therefore, reckless purpose. "My cheeks are hot, see?" I captured his hand and held it to my cheek. His eyes widened, following the movement. "And so is my neck." His lashes flickered, his chest rising as I slid his hand down to my neck, and then lower between my breasts. I pressed his fingers against my left rib cage just above my abdomen "And my heart has been beating out of my chest since I realized you were here. Speaking of which, why are you here?"

"I wanted—" He started, stopped, licked his lips. His eyes were darting everywhere—from mine to my neck, to my breasts, to where I held his hand over my heart—visibly disconcerted. Good. I'd never seen him disconcerted. "You never stay still, at the office. I don't want to waste your time, but I want to know you."

"Why?"

"Isn't it obvious?"

Again, I was close enough to spot those baffling specks of green and silver. In fact, my face was so close to his, if I moved a centimeter or two forward, he'd be blurry, and our noses would bump. What would that be like? To bump noses with the fearful Elias Fallon?

My chin lifted in the absence of my brain instructing it to do so and I slid my nose against his. Our breath met, our lips almost, and a wonderful, gentle, hazy warmth expanded within my abdomen. He smelled like expensive cologne and whiskey, and apparently I'd lifted my hands to touch him when I'd leaned forward because his shoulders were suddenly beneath my fingers and felt wide with strength and muscle.

Question answered: bumping noses with Elias Fallon was quite nice.

Oh. Whoops. I hadn't meant to do that. But he didn't pull away. In fact, a second after I'd brushed my nose against his, both of his hands were on my body, gripping my sides at the indent of my waist as though holding me in place. He was blurry, I couldn't see him, but I could feel the singularity of his attention on my lips, the catch of his breath, the dig of his fingers, and just before my mind realized his intent, he lifted his chin and kissed me.

And I was wrong. His lips were my favorite.

They were velvet softness, but not a blanket or a warm fire on a cold day. More like a fast car ride, taking turns too quickly. I lost myself to the momentum—acceleration and force and speed— and my center of gravity dropped to the pit of my stomach, hot and twisting and *deliciously* unsettled.

A stool scraped—mine or his—and we were both standing, his head angled over mine, his hands now on the center of my back, pressing me more firmly to him. His mouth worked, lavished, and consumed while I dug my nails into the back of his neck and did the same. We devoured each other until I was absolutely breathless, but he tasted so good, the slide of his talented tongue provocative, I wanted so much more. Wound so very tightly, I felt dizzy when he pulled away, like he'd spun me in circles.

Dipping his chin to his chest, which separated our lips but kept our foreheads connected, I listened to his harsh breathing for a moment before I realized the sounds came from both of us. We were both breathing hard and holding each other. Actually, if you want me to be precise, we were wrapped in each other: my arms twisted around his neck, his arms completely encircled my torso.

It was at this point that Elias Fallon's eyelids lifted halfway. His inebriating gaze, now *legit* smoldering, lingered on my mouth until he leaned back, evading my seeking lips, intensely focused eyes scrutinizing mine.

His lips parted and remained open for several seconds before he finally spoke. "How many drinks have you had, Dr. Bello?"

"Now I'm Dr. Bello? A moment ago, I was Audrey. How interesting. What will you call me if we kiss again?" *Shoot.* I'd meant to think that rather than speak it out loud.

His lips curved upward, giving me the impression that my words pleased or embarrassed him or both, and he liked them. "How many drinks?" he asked once more.

"Three." I lied. This was the best chitchat I'd had in my life. I mean, look at all I'd accomplished! No way was I letting him know I was almost drunk.

Perhaps alcohol was the solution (pun intended) to my small-talk problem.

Brilliant brown eyes turned assessing but no less amused. "You've had more than three."

"Four."

"Four?"

"Five."

He laughed. And it did something totally amazing to his eyes, which in turn did something totally amazing to my insides.

I wanted him to laugh again, so I said, "Six if you count the shot."

"Dr. Bello—"

"Mr. Fallon."

His eyelids seemed to flicker as his name left my lips and a breath whooshed out of him. "You are incredibly sexy," he murmured suddenly, his voice rough and deep.

"Am I?" I asked, tilting my head to the side to see him better. "It's the uptight librarian look, right? Some guys like that." And, honestly, it was fun in bed to play the role. *Waaaay* easier than being myself.

A flash of some emotion I couldn't place ignited behind his eyes, turning them almost black, and they moved between mine. "It's so many things. All of which I'd be happy to describe in *explicit* detail—" Elias Fallon's arms around my body loosened, slackened, and to my eternal sorrow, they slid away "—when you're sober."

My face scrunched at the withdrawal of his warm, hard body. I let my arms drop as well, my heart and abdomen giving a protesting pulse as air filled the space between us. But then our surroundings came sharply into focus, especially my old friend Patty the bartender in the distance, pretending to dry glasses while watching us.

What are you doing? You're at a bar, *Audrey. Kissing Australian Darth Vader. A man who terrifies people by glancing at them. This is problematic behavior. It's time to reevaluate your life choices.*

My stomach swirled and I removed myself another step, the back of my neck prickly and hot. "Uh, you know what—" a tittering laugh tumbled out of me and I yanked my eyes from his smoky, searching gaze "—maybe you're right about me being drunk."

"I didn't say you were drunk." Elias Fallon caught my fingers, brought my hand to his chest like he was holding it hostage or keeping me from retreating further.

"You implied I wasn't sober."

"Not the same thing." His small grin was crooked. *Roguish,* my brain told me, and that descriptor paired with his now cheeky sounding accent did little to settle my swirling stomach.

Or was it twisting? Or what the heck was that? And why did my body react so forcefully to this man?

"Even so," he continued conversationally, except his voice was too wonderfully deep to ever be anything as mundane as conversational, "I'd like you to be in full possession of your faculties before we have this conversation."

"What conversation?"

He pulled a fifty out of his pocket and placed it on the bar, leading me forward with his other hand. "The one where I ask why you think you'll never learn to surf."

Uh. Crap.

I stumbled, gaping. "You—you heard all that?"

"Oh, yes. I could teach you how, you know. And the thigh chafing comment, in particular, is of great interest to me. So many questions." He slid an arm around my back, his palm settling on my hip. Elias Fallon bent his head to nuzzle my neck, hot breath falling beneath my ear. "Have you ever heard of a pash rash?"

"No. What's that?"

"Hmm. Have your thighs ever been chafed, Dr. Bello?"

This time when I shivered, I didn't fight it. "I, uh, can't say that they have."

"Pity," he said, and then nipped at my earlobe. "When you're sober, we'll give it a try."

"That's presumptuous of you," I said, the effect of the words ruined by how breathless I sounded because, goodness, I was quite forcefully turned on.

"I meant surfing, Audrey." He leaned away, his features impassive except for—of course—those bedroom eyes. And they communicated loud and clear that he *had not* meant surfing.

"Hey! Wait." Patty the bartender's shout had me turning, but the suspicion-laden glare she was sending Elias had me glancing between them. She marched up to where we hovered by the long stretch of bar, her hands on her hips, her gaze softening as it moved to me. "Do you want me to take you home?"

I opened my mouth to respond but Elias spoke first, sounding haughty and dignified, "I'm taking Dr. Bello back to the lodge, to her room, so she can recover properly."

Patty didn't acknowledge him, just stared at me. "I can drive you back, or —like I said—you can stay here."

"It's fine." I sent her a reassuring smile, impressive since I was still hot and bothered. "He might sound and look like a pirate, but he's actually just a CFO."

"You think I look like a pirate?" he asked, the question a mixture of perplexed and pleased.

Meanwhile, Patty asked, "CFO?"

"Chief Financial Officer," he supplied, then mumbled to no one, "Which is basically the same as a pirate."

Patty the bartender appeared torn. "Why don't you let me take you back?"

"Why?" I tilted my head to the side in question.

Her attention flickered to Elias, and then back to me. "I'll drive you."

Elias made a short sound, one of disbelief. "I assure you, my designs on this woman are long term. And, regardless, I would never—"

"It's his eyes, right?" I knew my smile had probably turned wistful.

Patty's own eyes narrowed, still focused on me. "They're penetrating without giving anything away."

"Right?" I nodded, relieved she saw it too.

Elias Fallon cleared his throat.

"Like two damn magnets." Patty ignored him, continuing, "They're disarming, those soulful eyes. I know the type."

"The *type*?" A hint of offense colored his words.

She shook her head, as though frustrated. "I shouldn't have given you that last drink. I just don't want you to do anything you'll regret."

Oh, Patty. I was going to have to return in the afternoon tomorrow and thank her for being a good person.

Sensing Elias's body stiffen at my side, I glanced up at him and found those too expressive eyes pointed at me, a potent blend of concern, desire, hope, and vulnerability hooking into my brain and body. Elias Fallon dug me. He dug me *hard.* How long had this been going on, I had no idea. But the truth of it was right there on his magnificent, interesting face.

An answering warmth bloomed once more in my stomach. "I don't think I'll regret it," I said quietly.

I heard Patty breathe out followed by a short grunt. "Okay then." She gestured to the door, waiting until we turned and walked a few steps together before calling out to our backs, "But if there's chafed thighs in the morning, don't say I didn't warn you."

For the first time in my life, I hoped maybe—if not tonight, then perhaps quite soon—there would be.

* * *

Do you want more of Penny Reid?

One Click TRUTH OR BEARD now!

THE RULE OF ALWAYS

IZ + CALLIE

KENNEDY RYAN

1

ISRAEL

It's the worst time to lose my train of thought.

Shit.

Around two hundred people crowd the Rare Book Room of New York's Strand Book Store. All eyes on me, but *my* eyes lock with hers, and the thoughts hiccup in my head. Dark eyes, that much more arresting because of their intelligence. Knowing eyes. Had the person seated in front of her not bent and shifted, I might never have known Callista Garcia came tonight.

"Um, what I think Dr. Hammond was trying to say," Marlon "Grip" James offers in my trail of silence while I stare back at Callie. "Is that when we decided to write this book, we both approached it like a love letter to hip-hop and some of our heroes."

He angles a pointed look at me asking if my head is in this game.

"Certainly." I clear my throat and adjust my glasses. "Grip's exactly right. *For the Culture* examines the intersection of activism and hip-hop. And we say hip-hop, but there is a rich tradition of marginalized musicians leveraging their platforms to speak out and shine light on issues that are uniquely ours through music that is uniquely ours, but reaches everyone."

"Agreed," Grip chimes back in. "I named my daughter Nina in honor of Nina Simone, who said an artist's duty is to reflect the times. As a musician, I count myself lucky to follow in footsteps like hers."

"And on that note," the moderator interjects, apology in her voice. "We have to end our time. Dr. Hammond, Grip, thank you so much for being in conversation here at the Strand tonight. They'll both be available to sign books after. Thank you for coming."

"What was that?" Grip murmurs, setting his handheld mic down on the small table between our leather seats. "Where'd you go there at the end?"

He and I have found a rhythm on this tour. When discussing this book, music, activism—all of it—we can practically finish each other's sentences now. That came in handy tonight.

I make sure my mic is off and lay it down beside his. "I got distracted. Thanks for stepping in."

"You know I always got your back." A sly grin takes over the face I grudgingly admit is handsome as he glances over my shoulder. "I was about to ask what distracted you, but I think my answer is headed our way now."

I turn to see Callie picking her way through the knot of people preparing for the signing. The staff asked attendees not to come up right after, but to give us time to settle at the tables and save their comments for the line. Callie, of course, is not the general pop. The semester I taught at NYU, she was my teacher's assistant and Grip was my student. In the five years since, she has occasionally volunteered with some of the tours and community programs Grip and I sponsor. We have history, the three of us. She is one of the few people who, in a room with Grip and me, always seems to be looking at *me*. She's a fan of Grip's music. Even has a tattoo of one of his lyrics, but as she approaches us, she's not looking at him. Her warily defiant gaze fixes on me.

"I've never seen a man so determined to deny himself exactly what he wants when it's offered to him on a platter," Grip says. "But hey, your blue balls, not mine."

"Don't start. You don't know shit."

"Not only do *I* know." He slants me a cocky grin. "But so does *she*, and you hate it. She can read you like a book."

Before I can dismantle his bullshit, he steps away from me and toward the petite woman walking to us.

"Callie!" He stretches his arms and enfolds her. "How the hell are you?"

"I'm good." She laughs up at him, tilting her head back so dark, wavy strands of hair stream over her shoulders, stark against the scarlet wool of her coat. "Congrats on becoming a *New York Times* bestseller."

"All thanks to Dr. Hammond here," Grip says, releasing her and smiling at me over her head. "I'm just riding his coattails."

I roll my eyes and release a scoffing breath.

Lies.

True, my first book, *Virus*, sat on the bestseller lists for months, but anything Grip touches turns to platinum. He could have written a treatise on the history of gardening in hip-hop, and everyone and their mama would have bought it.

"We all know you would've done well on your own," Callie says, shifting her eyes up to meet mine. "But working with someone as esteemed as the professor couldn't hurt."

The first time Callie called me "the professor," my dick calcified to solid bone in my pants. Very uncomfortable, highly inappropriate at the faculty mixer under the scrutiny of a hundred onlookers.

"It's good to see you again, Dr. Hammond," she continues, her voice the same low, honey-smooth provocation it's always been.

"Good to see you, too." There's no trace in my voice of the turmoil stirring behind my zipper. "You look good."

Motherfucker.

I didn't mean to bring up the way she looks. She *has* to know how she looks. She *has* to know that I hate how the way *she* looks makes *me* feel.

Hungry.

Out of control.

If there is one thing I prize, it's my control.

"Why thank you." Her thick brows lift, a simple gesture, but as knowing as the smirk she used to wear when she'd catch me eyeing her ass. "I didn't want to come slummin' to see my favorite activists."

"I didn't know you were still in New York," Grip says. "You visiting or—"

"I live here actually. I've been bouncing around but settled here for the last year or so." She shifts her glance back to me. "You still in Philly, Iz?"

"Uh, yeah." I burrow my hands into the pockets of my dark jeans. "This is actually the last stop of the book tour, and then I can finally head back home."

"Nice," she says. "Bris and the kids with you, Grip?"

"They're always with me." He grins, obviously a man besotted by his family. "I think Bris took them up the street to a toy store or something.

Believe it or not, at three and one, they aren't exactly fascinated by Daddy's deep musings. They kinda showed out at the last signing."

He and I share an amused glance. Horrified when her children started screaming and crying at the event, Bristol fled her post at the back of the room before they brought the house completely down.

"I still haven't met Martin," Callie says wistfully. "Any chance I'll get to see him?"

"Sure, and Bris would love to see you," Grip says. "They'll be back once we've finished signing if you'll still be around?"

I hold my breath, shoulders tense, half hoping she *will* be around and half hoping she won't.

"I'll be here for a bit." She side-eyes me, and it feels as much threat as promise. "Maybe there will be time to chat."

"Maybe," Grip agrees with a smile. "Rhyson and Kai are in town, too. We're meeting them for dinner."

"How are they?" Callie asks. "I caught her show on Broadway a couple years ago. She was fantastic. Did I hear she's in another one?"

"She is," Grip replies, smiling. "Opening night was last week. Rhyson's managing their two little rugrats. The cousins love seeing each other every chance they get. You're both welcome to roll."

"I can't," I say with decisive relief. "I'm meeting that reporter C.G. Holmes from the *NY Daily Register* for an interview after."

The moderator steps up and clears her throat. "So sorry to interrupt, but are you ready to sign?"

I glance beyond her to the long lines forming at our table.

"Oh, hell," Grip mutters. "Sorry. Of course."

He leans down to kiss Callie's cheek. "If you're still around at the end, make sure you come see Bris and the kids."

I wish I'd walked off before he did. Once he's gone, a tight little silence clamps around Callie and me.

"Well, uh, I guess I better get—"

"So will *you* be around for a few minutes after, too?" she cuts in softly.

"No." I take off my glasses to clean them on the hem of my shirt. "Like I said, I have that interview."

She watches me cleaning the lenses. It's one of my tells when I'm nervous or discombobulated. Callie always has that effect on me, but I used to be better at hiding it. With no time to prepare for her reappearance, I guess my defenses are weaker. I stop circling the glasses with my shirt and shove them back onto my face.

Her full lips quirk to an ironic angle. "No time for an old friend?"

I allow my eyes to hold hers, something I didn't do often when she was my TA. Her steady stare is and always has been dark, depthless waters. A man could drown there.

And this brother never did learn to swim.

"I better get to the table." I skirt her question and gesture toward the long line of people waiting. "Good seeing you again, Callista."

"So formal," she says dryly.

I ignore that and head for the table. An hour later, we're signing the last book. Grip and I exchange a relieved look, both releasing a deep breath when the moderator tells everyone we're done for the night.

"That's a wrap on the tour," Grip says, standing and extending his hand. "Nice doing business with you, Iz."

I accept the proffered hand and stand, too. We're dressed similarly, but I'm wearing one of my many Malcolm X T-shirts and elbow-patched blazers, while he wears a hoodie under an army jacket. Where I sport shell-toe Adidas, he wears a pair of vintage Air Force Ones from his extensive tennis shoe collection. When I found out a "rap star" would be in my class at NYU a few years ago, I had no idea this deep bond would form between us, or that some of the most meaningful work of my life and career would be in partnership with him. And this after I offended him colossally. At first, I didn't think she was the right woman for him. I misjudged Bristol, and I insulted Grip.

And yet here we are.

The more I got to know them both, the more my views evolved. As if to remind me just how wrong I'd been to question their relationship, Bristol walks into the room. Grip gets this look on his face whenever he sees his wife. I don't know how to describe it other than absolute contentment, peace. Every look and touch they share testifies that the love I always thought a myth, is real. At least for them it is. I have a divorce under my belt as a reminder that it doesn't happen that way for us all.

"Iz," Bristol greets me warmly, her silvery-gray eyes smiling. "Sorry I missed the last stop, but these guys got restless."

Grip takes his son, Martin, from her hip and drops a lingering kiss at the corner of her mouth. She gives him a slow smile that makes promises for later and grips her daughter's hand. Nina, the three-year-old, blinks up at me through long lashes, her eyes the same bright silver as her mother's.

"Hi, Uncle Iz," Nina says, her voice soft but already confident.

"Hey, Nina Meena." I drop to my haunches to look at her directly and push a clump of caramel-streaked unruly curls away from her face. "We missed you tonight."

"Mommy was afraid Martin would be loud," she shout-whispers into my ear. "He's such a baby."

We adults laugh, though Nina's face remains serious.

"Well, he won't be a baby forever," I say, glancing up at her little brother's chubby cheeks. "Enjoy him at this age because one day he'll be bigger than you."

"Mommy's gonna have another baby," Nina says with a careless shrug. "So it's okay. I'll have a backup."

Bristol closes her eyes and shakes her head, but Grip's grin is wide and proud.

"Guess the cat's out of the bag, so to speak." He kisses the top of Bristol's head, and she leans into him.

"We were trying to make it through the first trimester before telling people," she says, looking at her daughter with pointed affection. "But someone forgot what *family talk* means."

"Congratulations." I pull Bristol into a hug and kiss her cheek. "You guys making a basketball team or something?"

"She can't keep her hands off me," Grip deadpans. "It's a curse."

Bristol is so used to Grip, she doesn't miss a beat or even roll her eyes but nods soberly, lips twitching. "It's true. He's such a good sport putting up with my amorous ways."

"Mommy, what's 'amorous' mean?" Nina asks, eyes stretched and waiting.

Nina is notoriously curious and absorbs everything even vaguely profane or salacious like a little sponge.

"It means Daddy loves Mommy," Grip says, leaning down to kiss her head, "and Mommy loves Daddy."

"I knew that," she preens, smug and adorable.

"Sure you did," Grip drawls and glances at the aged plastic black watch I've never seen him without, a sentimental gift from Bristol. "Ready to see your cousins?"

"Aria!" Nina squeals, clapping and jumping up and down.

"And Ronan," Bristol reminds her. "We've barely seen him since Aunt Kai moved back to New York for her show. You have *two* cousins now."

"But he's just a baby like ..." Nina discreetly tips her head toward her little brother curled sleepily into his father's neck. "That one."

I stifle another laugh. Nina promises to be a handful.

"We need to go," Grip says, scanning the room. "Callie was here, Bris, and wanted to see you guys. I forgot she hasn't met Martin yet."

"Ahhh, the beautiful, brilliant Callie." Bristol gives me an appallingly knowing look. I glare at Grip because I've obviously been the subject of some serious pillow talk.

"What?" Grip feigns innocence. "I didn't have to tell her. It's obvious being in the same room with the two of you for even a minute."

"What's obvious?" Nina asks.

"Uncle Iz knows," Bristol says with a laugh, adjusting the baby bag on her shoulder. "If she's not here, Grip, we may have to see her next time. The car's double-parked waiting to take us to Rhys and Kai for dinner, and we're already late."

"Yeah, I don't see her anywhere," Grip says, looking around and shifting Martin, who has fallen asleep on his shoulder. "Where's this reporter you're supposed to be meeting, Iz?"

"He said in his e-mail he'd meet me here after the signing." I assess the thinning crowd. "Old boy's got five minutes. My hotel is a block away, and I'm ready for a steak and a bed."

"Well, we gotta go," Grip says. "My dude, we'll be in touch. I think the bail fund charity concert in Miami is the next time I'll see you."

"Yup. Sounds right." We dap each other up and dole out hugs all around.

"See you soon," Bristol adds with a smile over her shoulder as they leave.

I pull out my phone to recheck the reporter's e-mail. It says what I thought it did. He'll meet me after the signing here at the Strand. I've given it a few more minutes when Callie's signature citrusy smell reaches me. Her words aren't far behind.

"Did I miss Grip and Bristol?"

After a moment and a deep breath, I lift my head to find her standing right in front of me, the red coat tied tight at her waist, her dark hair blown around her face, lips the color of pomegranates.

It annoys me how fucking beautiful she is.

"Uh, yeah. Sorry, you *just* missed them. He said they'll catch you next time." I frown down the foot of height that separates us. "Do you need a cab, an Uber or—"

"So eager to be rid of me, huh?" She tightens her mouth, making a bitter line of the soft curves.

I pause, dropping my glance to the stilettos she's wearing, flimsy straps of leather with a precariously high heel. The elevation stretches the already sleek muscles of her calves to even sexier.

"Those shoes are a hazard," I mumble.

"You're not a pleasant man. Anyone ever tell you that?"

"I think you did once or twice when I required you to do your actual job as my TA."

"More like indentured servitude requiring me to sacrifice my social life and personal studies."

"You knew where the door was. You could have used it at any time."

"You would have liked that, wouldn't you?" She folds her arms under the curve of her breasts. "If I'd given up on you?"

"Given up on *me*?" I cock an imperious brow, falling into our old tempo of parry and thrust. "You were an employee of the university and there for the program, not for me."

"Every student in that class, Grip included, was there for you. I was no different. I jumped at the chance to study with you. No one warned me about the stick lodged up your ass when I did everything but sell my soul to TA for the great Dr. Israel Hammond."

"I'm sorry you were so disappointed."

"You know I wasn't," she says, her tone softening. "It was the worst and best semester of my life."

Our eyes lock, and the people milling around us, the books lining the shelves of the Rare Book Room, fade. The searing stare transports us back to campus, behind the closed door of my shoebox office. The memory of our last day on campus rises between us like steam—visceral, vivid. That damned *her* smell—lemons and tropics and lust. The curve of her neck—sun-warmed velvet. The hot, slick interior of her mouth. How her ass overran my palms—lush, full, firm. The fragility of her rib cage encased in the roughness of my hands when I lifted her onto the desk. The spread of her thighs and the scent of her desire enticing me through her panties.

Fuuuuuck.

"I need to go," I say abruptly, pulling my blazer closed to cover a burgeoning erection. "I'm waiting for someone."

She smiles and slides her hands into the pockets of her red coat. "Are you really?"

"I am really, yeah," I snap, irritated with her and with C. G. Holmes for being an uncommunicative, tardy bastard. "I have an interview, so if you'll excuse me."

"I won't excuse you."

"Look, I'm sorry for what happened between us the last time we saw each other."

"I'm only sad you didn't finish what I started."

"It wasn't appropriate. You were my TA, not to mention you're young enough to be my daughter."

"Your daughter? Please. You would have gotten a very early start."

Ignoring that. "I would never take advantage—"

"Take advantage? *I* kissed *you*, Iz."

"Would you lower your voice? For fuck's sake, Callie, what will it take for you to realize I'm not interested in pursuing this with you?"

"When you can be in the same room with me without being aroused, without watching my every move like a hungry hawk."

"I'm leaving now," I grit out, my jaw tight. "This reporter isn't coming, and I want to go to my hotel."

"Oh, what's your room number? I'll meet you there."

Eleven fifteen.

The numbers bounce around in my head, and I have to lasso them before they make it past my lips. I suppress the image of Callie at the door of my hotel room.

"It really was good seeing you again," I say, taming my tone into politeness. "But this reporter hasn't shown and I'm leaving."

"Hasn't shown?" she asks mildly, a smile spreading warmth across her face like sunbeams. "I'm right here, and I've done everything but throw myself at you. I tried that once, and I see where that got me."

"Huh? I don't follow."

"Oh, sorry." She grabs my hand, shaking it and caressing the back of it with her thumb. "C. G. Holmes at your service."

2

CALLIE

It was worth it.

Begging my editor for the assignment to interview Dr. Israel Hammond. Being so careful to cloak my identity so he wouldn't bolt as soon as he realized I was the reporter. Putting up with all the defenses I knew he'd erect when I walked into the room. Splurging on these shoes and the dress hidden beneath my wool coat. All worth it to see the brief unguarded moment of shock skitter across Iz's face.

"What'd you say?" His eyes narrow behind the square black lenses.

He looks even better than the last time I saw him. The same severely sketched bone structure. The thick wing of brows over black-brown eyes, framed by a tangle of long, curly lashes. The sinful curve of his mouth, at turns stern and sensual. There's actual gray at his temples now and sprinkled into the stubble kissing his granite jawline.

So fucking hot.

How am I still standing? By all rights, I should already be on my knees sucking this man's dick through his pants. If he takes those glasses off and polishes them on his shirt again, I will combust right here in the Strand's Rare Book Room. Israel Hammond is nerd porn. He's bookish and brawny, his ideas straining the limits of his mind, his arms straining the sleeves of his jacket.

And I've wanted him since the day we met.

"*I'm* C. G. Holmes." I caress his thumb again, grinning when he jerks his hand back like I scalded him.

"No, it's a guy, and—"

"I never said I was a guy in my e-mail," I remind him.

"Yeah, but—"

"You assumed I was a man." I shake my head and tsk. "And here I thought you were a feminist."

"You used a fake name to maneuver me into this?"

"Not maneuver and not a fake name. It's my byline. Callista Garcia ... Holmes. My father's last name is Holmes, but I dropped it legally years ago."

"Why?"

"I'm supposed to be asking the questions here."

"Are you? Is this some kind of joke?"

"Not a joke. My job."

"Your job?" A harsh laugh erupts from him, and he eyes me skeptically. "You expect me to believe you're a hack for the *NY Daily Register*? You graduated with honors from Yale at eighteen and were a damn Rhodes scholar. You're a PhD with a trail of fellowships behind you and can do anything you want."

"Exactly. Anything *I* want. And apparently what I want is to interview rude assholes who refer to me as a hack. Now you said in the e-mail your hotel was nearby and we could conduct the interview there. You ready?"

Wariness sifts into his gaze. The thought of having me in his hotel probably sets him on edge. God knows it's got me burning to think of us that close to a bed. I start walking toward the exit, pausing to look over my shoulder when he doesn't follow.

"Coming?" I ask, loud enough for anyone listening to hear. "Or you scared I'll kiss you again?"

A scowl jerks his thick brows together. "Dammit, Callie. Would you ..."

He draws a deep breath, marches his fine ass over, grabs my elbow and ushers me to the door. I lean my head into his arm, breathing in that clean, masculine scent. He frowns down at me and drops my elbow.

"Don't smell me," he grumbles, holding the door open for me to pass ahead of him.

"Like I can help it if you bathe in cologne."

"You don't like it," he says, walking ahead, setting a too-fast pace. "Don't inhale."

I scramble to keep up, not a simple task considering these heels are nose-bleed high. We clomp along in silence for the block to his hotel. The sounds of the city, the press of the crowd, do little to distract me from the big man beside me. Even in heels, I don't clear his shoulder. To be crushed beneath his weight while he comes into me. He'd probably snatch my breath with one thrust. The power of his body ...

I'm hot. I'm wet. How does he *do* this to me? Reduce me—a scholar who has prided myself on having my shit together my entire life—to this throbbing, horny girl who just wants to wrap my legs around him and *hump*?

"Why the hell are you writing for the *Register*?" he asks, the suddenness of his deep timbre startling me.

"I told you. It's what I want to do right now."

"You're a PhD, Cal."

"No, I'm not." I glance up at him, showing him defiance but secretly wondering if he'll judge me.

"But you were just a few credits from your doctorate when you were my TA."

"Never too late for a gap year," I joke faintly. "Or five."

He doesn't stop, but his steps slow, and he finally watches me for more than a few seconds. "What's going on with you?"

This is the part people miss when they quick-judge him as broody, moody, aloof. I mean, he *is* all those things, but they miss what I saw in him every time he stayed long after class to answer students' questions or to challenge their worldview, to stretch them into considering something new.

He cares.

"I've been in school my whole life," I say. "Whatever the world has told you about intense Asian parents who pressure their kids to excel, at least in my case, it's true. There are, of course, exceptions, but my mother was not one of them."

"Your mother is Japanese, right?"

"Yeah."

"And your father?"

"Columbian. They met in college." I huddle deeper into my coat against the cold night air. "They weren't together long."

"He left?"

"He died. Car accident," I sigh and shrug. "I think he would have tempered her some if he'd been around, but when she saw my IQ scores and my teachers urged her to skip me ahead a couple of grades so I would be challenged, she pounced. And hasn't looked back since."

"So this is some kind of delayed act of rebellion?"

"No, this is me as an adult woman figuring out what the hell *I* want to do with my own life. Yes, I've been to Yale and Oxford and have a pile of prestigious fellowships, but I haven't enjoyed much of it. I want to enjoy something."

"And posing as a reporter does that?"

"I'm not posing. If you remember, I double majored in undergrad."

"Public policy," he says, nodding with a stiff little smile tugging the full, sculpted line of his mouth. "And journalism."

"Bingo. So not that much of a stretch. I've just always focused more on public policy. The last few years have been about what I want to do. I've traveled and met new people and wasted time, a luxury I've never had. And, yes, I'm freelancing to support my quarter-life crisis."

He stops in front of his hotel and I stop, too. We stand still as the revolving doors spit out a stream of people exiting the building.

"So you're serious about this," he says.

"I am."

He watches me through a length of curled lashes before nodding and gesturing toward the hotel entrance. The lobby, luxuriously understated, hums with activity, and a low murmur of voices drifts from around the corner. I assume it's a restaurant because a mix of tantalizing scents tease my nostrils and make my mouth water.

"Have you eaten?" he asks. "They do a great steak at this restaurant, if your tastes haven't changed."

"I still love steak," I answer, shooting a hesitant glance up at him. "But I think it would be better to conduct the interview somewhere private."

"Let me guess," he drawls, a wry twist to his mouth. "My hotel room would work better?"

"It would, yes." I lick my lips, nervous in case he refuses. "I typically conduct interviews in private and use my phone to record. I think I laid out the terms in the e-mail, and you agreed."

"Yeah, but that was before—"

"Before you knew it was me?"

He doesn't answer but starts for a bank of elevators nearby. "Let's go."

"Um, u-up?" *Am I really stammering right now?* "Up to your room, you mean?"

Consternation and possibly irritation jerk his brows together. "Isn't that what you said you wanted?"

If he could hear my thoughts about what I want from him, he would take the stairs two at a time and bolt his door.

"Yes, that's great," I say, composing myself and suppressing any whorish urges.

"You hungry? I'm starving."

"Starving," I agree and follow him into the elevator. It fills up, and I find myself pressed to the back wall with Iz standing in front of me. The blonde beside me runs acquisitive eyes over the regal set of his head, the wide stretch of his shoulders, the broad plane of his back tapering to his waist. He takes up more space than everyone else. Not just the big body, but his *presence*. He lures you to look and then holds you in thrall. I stare at her until she feels my eyes on her. When she drags her stare from the vicinity of his ass to meet mine, I tip my head toward him and bare my teeth at her. I run a finger over my throat with a slitting motion, and her eyes widen.

I lean toward her and whisper, "Just kidding."

But I think I might for real cut a bitch over this man.

When we reach the eleventh floor, he steps off, looking back to make sure I'm following. I wave at the blonde.

"Lucky bitch," she whispers with an envious grin.

I offer a "what can I say" shrug and totter after Iz before he changes his mind.

He's scanning his door open when I catch up to him. I step into his suite, inspecting the sitting room furniture and the well-appointed room. Bed must be in the back. I offer up a silent prayer to the goddess of hookups that I find out before the night is over. Phase one of my plan—the element of surprise—wasn't flawless, but it worked. Now for phase two.

The Dress.

"Is there somewhere I could hang my coat?" I let the sleeves slither down my arms. The wool pools at my feet, and I hear his sharply indrawn breath. I know what he sees. There's no back. Nape to waist, just naked skin. The dress is the thinnest leather imaginable. So thin it almost feels like satin, and it molds my ass. My Columbian father may have died when I was very young, but I've met his mother. And I inherited *Abuela's* ass. I bend over to retrieve the coat from the floor, and he groans softly.

Good.

This man has made me suffer for a long time. He should suffer, too. While I was his TA, he never saw me in anything but T-shirts and leggings and jeans and hoodies. I kept my hair short and wore almost no makeup. Face is fully beat tonight. My hair, pulled over one shoulder now, swings to my elbows. More than once I've imagined him pulling it while he fucks me from behind.

I've been such a good girl, Santa. Just this one early present, please.

I turn, brows lifted. "Closet? Hanger? Should I just toss it—"

"I got it." He steps forward and takes the coat with the tips of his fingers, avoiding contact. His stare drops to my breasts. The dress has long sleeves that cling to my arms, but the front plunges. It's not immodest, but shows the girls at their full, perky best. It's a little cool in here, and my nipples peak, pressing against the fabric, visibly budded. He looks at them and away quickly, expelling a harsh breath.

"I'll hang this up," he says, turning away with my coat and hanging up his jacket, too. "The menu's on that table. We can call for food and get started while we wait. I don't want to keep you."

Yes, you do, Professor. You've wanted to keep me since the day we met, and tonight I'm going to show you why you should.

We order steak and salad. I'm not sure I'll be able to keep food down with the knots in my stomach, but my hunger dictates I at least try. With that behind us, we settle at the coffee table in the center of the room, me on the couch and him in a seat across from me that looks almost too small to contain the powerful breadth of him.

"There's plenty of room over here." I gesture to the ocean of space on the couch beside me. "If you want to—"

"I'm fine over here, Callie."

"Yeah, you are," I agree with a husky laugh.

The glance he shoots me is sharp, but I detect the tiniest press of his lips like he's squelching a grin. He just rolls his eyes, though, and slumps in his seat. "Begin."

I lean forward to place my phone on the coffee table, well aware that my breasts are near to spilling from the bodice of my dress.

"Is that your usual interview attire?" he asks, eyes zeroed in on the flaunted décolletage.

"Oh, this?" I point to the dress and offer a tinkling laugh. "I had an event beforehand and didn't have time to change."

His skeptical look calls me a liar; my innocent smile dares him to prove it.

"I'm recording." I press the red button on my phone and dive in.

I ask him the usual questions about *Virus*, his groundbreaking bestselling book, about his formative time at Morehouse College, his foundation for criminal justice reform, the bail fund program he and Grip have been raising money for through a college campus tour. He's the most fascinating man I've ever known, and I could ask him a thousand questions and still have a thousand more buzzing in my brain. Every time I'm near him, I feel smarter, stronger, stand taller. He has that effect, stretching you, challenging you into the absolute best version of yourself. It's why his class was overflowing to wait-listed when he was the visiting professor at NYU. It's why I did everything short of auctioning my virginity (*which was by then, alas, long gone anyway*) to win the coveted spot as his TA. His combination of rare intellect, sincere compassion, irrational modesty and an immutable sense of right is irresistible. Moth to flame. Bee to honey. Iron filings to magnets. Whatever you want to call it, I'm inexorably drawn to this man and tired of resisting.

Our food comes halfway through the interview, and we both eat with relish but keep talking. The beer he ordered with his steak seems to relax him. The muscled slope of his shoulders loses some of the tension, and soon his deep laugh that always unleashed butterflies in my belly warms the room. I start asking outrageous questions just to make him laugh more.

"I'm sure your readers don't care if I'm over or under on the toilet tissue debate," he says, a low-timbred chuckle rumbling from his throat.

"Favorite color," I press on.

"Black," he says with a wink that on a lesser man would be creepy, but totally works for him.

"Should have known." I laugh and chew on a straw. "Favorite revolutionary."

"Shit, that's impossible." He blows out a breath. "I'll do in the last sixty years. Female, Angela. Male, Malcolm."

I nod to yet another Malcolm X T-shirt hugging the width of his chest. "I should have guessed. What do you love so much about him?"

He sketches a brief shrug and sips his beer. "He was brilliant. The natural kind that formal education only refines. The elasticity of his mind fascinates me. How he was incredibly, almost obstinately principled on one hand, but allowed his views to evolve as he learned. And it never feels like a contradiction. Just a man asking questions and metamorphosing as he finds answers. I respect that kind of growth. I hope I can keep growing and evolving that way."

I allow his words to settle on my skin, sink into my pores, to *water* me. I haven't been around him in so long, and as much as my heart is pounding behind my sternum and my whole body feels on high alert, it also feels like home. We only had a semester together, and he has basically avoided me at the events where I've volunteered since, but when I'd catch him staring, like he does now, it always felt like I'd come home.

"Favorite person in the world?" I continue softly.

"My daughter, Cecily." His quick grin is affectionate, wistful. "She's the best of my ex and me. I'd trade everything for her."

I've never asked about his ex-wife, and now doesn't seem the best time to start. I remember him flashing pictures of his beautiful daughter on his phone.

"Last question," I say, reluctant to end it but sensitive to how long this day has been for him. "What would you want your legacy to be?"

His thick brows rise and then collapse into a thoughtful frown. "Hell, I don't know. I don't think like that. I started speaking out when I was in college about the bullshit happening to marginalized people because it needed to be said. By as many of us, as many times, in as many ways as possible. Next thing I know, people are asking me to come speak. And then I have a foundation. And then I have a book deal. And now you ask me about legacy when I was always just putting one foot in front of the other. Just doing what needed to be done right then. It was the urgency of the moment that pulled me onto this path, following the urgency of *every* moment."

He contemplates his beer and shrugs. "I guess that's part of it, not ignoring the things that need to be said or the people who need to be protected. Doing what's right, what's required right now. The rule of *right now* is how I got here, and I guess it's essentially what I'll leave behind."

He clears his throat and stands up, nodding toward the debris of our meal. "You done?"

"Sure. Yeah. Thanks."

He gathers our plates and glasses on a tray, striding over to set it outside the door. When he walks back, his gait is less assured. His steps seem to drag, and some of the wariness I hoped food and libations chased away returns to his eyes.

"So you got what you needed?" he asks, not sitting down. He hovers there like a thundercloud, like he's waiting for me to stand, and my heart plummets to my overpriced shoes. The dress, the stilettos, the hair and makeup, the stimulating conversation, the undeniable sexual tension sparking between us whenever we're together—none of it was enough to make him want me. Oh, he *wants* me, but it wasn't enough to get him past whatever holds him back. I'm not his TA anymore. Hell, I wasn't when I kissed him the last day of that semester at NYU. Is it the age gap? What's fifteen years between rabid lovers?

"Is that my cue to leave?" I ask, turning off my phone's recorder. I stand, tugging at the tight line of the dress across my hips. A deep swallow bobs his throat, and he looks away.

"You do that on purpose, don't you?" he asks quietly, resentfully.

"Yes," I reply, not bothering to play dumb.

The thick sweep of his lashes lifts, and his eyes narrow. "Why?"

"Because I like watching you want me." I bark a harsh laugh. "It's the only evidence I have that you don't hate me."

"You know I don't hate you, Callista."

I step around the coffee table until I stand right in front of him, so close the heat of his body warms the bare skin of my chest. "Show me then."

"Show you what?"

"That you don't hate me."

He runs a hand over the back of his neck and huffs an impatient breath. "What do you want from me?"

I stare up the long distance separating us. Not the foot or so difference between our heights, but the distance he has imposed since the first day I walked into his office. Nothing has worked. I've pretended I didn't want him. I've played hard to get, running off only to realize he wasn't chasing. I've thrown myself at him, and he didn't even try to catch. I kissed him our last day of class, and when he kissed me back, my pussy *melted*. My soul quaked, cracking open, inviting him in. And ultimately my heart broke when he pulled away and pretended nothing had happened. I've tried everything except just asking for what I want. So I'll shoot my shot. This last hope shot.

"What do I want?" I step even closer, so close my nipples tighten, pressed against his chest. "Kiss me before I go."

3

ISRAEL

If I kiss her, she won't be going anywhere.

I know that and so does Callie.

"I don't think—"

"Don't think, Iz," she whispers, lips trembling, eyes pleading. "Whatever it is you *think* that keeps you from doing this, from taking me, tonight, don't think it."

"Callie, find someone your age. Find someone else."

"I tried that."

My teeth grit at the thought of her with another man. Of course, she's been with someone else. *Elses*. A woman who looks like this, is as brilliant as she is, there would be as many *someone elses* as she wanted. I want to ask who. How many. How many times, but I have no right to those answers, and they would only make me miserable.

"Oh, yeah?" I finally reply. "You did?"

"I was actually in a relationship for three whole months not long ago."

"Why didn't it last with him?" I force myself to ask.

"Her." She smiles at my surprised look.

"I guess your tastes *did* change," I say wryly.

"Not really." She shakes her head, and a sheaf of black hair slips between her breasts. "I've known I was bi since high school."

"So why didn't it work with *her* then?"

Callie shrugs carelessly. “She was awesome. She was smart and creative. A graphic designer in Chelsea. Fantastic in bed.”

Erotic images of some chick with her head between Callie’s legs springs my dick rod straight.

“You like that?” She glances down to my crotch.

I don’t like the thought of her with *anyone* else, but that’s irrational since I won’t take her myself. “Red-blooded males tend to get excited by the thought of two women together. It’s predictable.”

“When I was with her, the guy before her, the girl before him,” she says, her gaze earnest, “I imagined you every time.”

“Callie.” I gulp down a groan. “Don’t tell me that.”

“It’s true.” Her bitter laugh hangs between us. “I could never come until I imagined it was you.”

“Fuck, Callista.” I drop my head, a mistake because I smell her. She presses her tight, curvy body into me.

“One kiss,” she says huskily, raising up on her tiptoes to whisper in my ear. “And I’ll leave.”

“You know it won’t go down like that.”

“Say *go down* one more time,” she groans. “And your dick will be in my mouth so fast your head will spin.”

I stifle a moan, and the dick in question twitches to rock level, begging me to accept her offer.

“I want this, Iz. You want it. Take it. Take *me*. Why the hell not?”

Why the hell not indeed? Before I was conscious of my position, of her as my TA and the power dynamic. Then there’s the age gap. What does she want with an old man like me?

“Callie, you’re in your twenties.”

“Barely.”

“And I’m in my forties.”

“Barely, and who gives a damn? You keep throwing rules up between us, rules I don’t care about. What about *your* rule? The one that got you where you are? The rule of right now?”

She leans into me fully, and her sweetly scented softness is my undoing. I palm the curve of her waist, warm through the thin layer of fabric covering her small body.

“You’re so tiny,” I say, almost wonderingly. “I feel like I might break you.”

“With a kiss?” she asks teasingly. “Or are you already thinking ahead? If so, I can assure you, I won't break when you fuck me. I'm trial tested, Professor."

Professor.

The rule of right now.

I lower my head swiftly before I talk myself out of it, and I take what I've wanted since I first laid eyes on Callista Garcia. *Everything.* I leave nothing in her mouth unlicked, unsucked, untasted. Her lips, her tongue, the sweet, addictive lining of her mouth. Every fantasy I've had about this woman begins with a kiss just like this, but it's so much better than I imagined. It's so much better than the one time she kissed me in my office because now I know we won't stop. Whatever lie I told myself, whatever thing Callie said to get us started, this can't stop. Not until I'm buried balls-deep inside her. I slide my hand into the low-cut neckline of her dress and palm her breast.

"Jesus," she gasps into our kiss, leaning into my hand. "Please, Iz."

I appreciate the weight of her breast for a second, the soft firmness, and then I knead it reverently and brush my thumb across the nipple. She breaks the kiss, lowering her head to my chest.

"Don't stop," she begs, easing her shoulder and arm from one sleeve, baring her other breast. She's breathtaking, a plump berry-brown nipple crowning her breast. In the cool air, it peaks, tightens. I slip one finger beneath the dress at her other shoulder and coax the fabric down until her neck, shoulders, breast, waist are all on display. I go to my knees, tug until the dress slides over her hips and legs, gathers around her ankles. She steps out, the silky gold of her body bare except for a tiny nude-colored thong. There's a dark spot on the front of the miniscule panties. I touch it, finding it wet.

"God, Callie." I groan and press my lips to the dampness. "Already?"

"Are you kidding?" She laughs breathlessly, cupping my face between her hands and looking down at me. "I've been wet since *hello*, Professor. I literally carried spare panties in my backpack that semester. I'd be soaked by the end of every lecture."

"Shit."

I cup her ass and suck her through the panties. The wetness christens my lips, and her flavor explodes in my mouth. It's galvanizing, the taste of her, the sweet musk of her. I jerk her panties down and press my face between her legs, matching the rhythm of my tongue and teeth around her clit with rough squeezes of her round ass. She's so compact and lush and full and tight. I'm overwhelmed by her scent and taste and the gorgeousness of her breasts and belly and pussy. She lifts one leg onto my shoulder, spreading herself and squeezing my shoulder to the point of pain as I eat her ravenously.

"Keep eating," she pants, her nails digging into my neck. "Oh my God. It's just like I …"

She sobs, her voice breaking as she comes, her body offering a stream of passion across my lips. She bucks into my mouth, reaching up to squeeze her breasts, pinching her nipples. I could do this forever, watch us both bring her pleasure so intense, tears stream from her eyes and her beautiful mouth opens on a silent scream. The tight plane of her belly trembles with ragged breaths, and her breasts heave. Her hips continue pumping against my mouth for long seconds until she slows, stills, sags, and I think she may fall. I stand, picking her up, bringing her chest level with my lips, and suckle her breasts. She's completely limp, deadweight, but so light it's no strain at all to carry her to the bed. I lay her gently on the cool sheets.

"I made it," she says drowsily, her lips swollen from kisses. "I made it to the bedroom."

"What?" I laugh, pulling the shirt over my head.

She sits up, naked and completely unselfconscious, and places her hands over mine at my belt. "Let me."

Her fingers are deft, efficient torture, brushing against my stomach as he undoes the belt, against my hip bones when she slides the jeans down. And then deliberate provocation, gripping me through my briefs. I choke back a needy sound and swallow, trying to maintain some semblance of command. Her hands slow when she tugs the briefs down, and her eyes scorch, they're so hot on me.

"Oh, this is very impressive, Professor," she says, licking a smile onto her pretty lips.

"I, um, haven't had any complaints."

Her fingers close around my naked shaft, squeezing and pulling.

"I wouldn't advise that," I groan, staying her hand. "If you want this to last for any amount of time."

"I don't care if it's fast." She raises her lashes and teases me with her stare. "We've got all night."

"Maybe you overestimate my virility." I chuckle, pushing at her slim shoulder until she falls back onto the bed, naked and, at least for tonight, completely mine.

"I don't think so." She crosses one slim leg over the other, hiding the cove between her thighs from me. I nudge her legs open, and her sly smile says I've done exactly what she wanted.

"This, Professor," she says, opening her legs a little wider, "is what I call a carte blanche lay."

"And how does that work?" I ask, struggling to keep my eyes on her face while she's talking, and not straying to everything below.

"You get whatever you want. Any hole you want. Mouth, asshole, pussy. You name it, it's yours." She laughs huskily, naughtily. "Hell, I have a strap-on back at my place if you want me in any of *your* holes."

"Nah." I laugh. "I'm, uh, good on that score. My holes are fine, and I'm much more interested in yours."

"They're interested in you, too." She swallows, some of the humor leaving her expression. "I'm interested in you. Have been for a long time."

"Well, I think we've waited long enough." I reach down to the floor, pulling a condom from the wallet in my jeans pocket.

"Tell me how you want it."

She's quite the adventuress. From her confident pursuit over the last five years, I suspected she would be. I can be adventurous, too, but tonight, I just want to look in her eyes when I'm inside her for the first time. I don't voice it but come over her, resting my weight on my elbows, afraid I'll crush her petite frame. I bend, taking one nipple in my mouth, grinning against her areola when she moans and links her ankles behind my back. I reach between us, slipping my middle finger inside the tight sheath of her body. She draws in a swift breath, her hips matching the invasion and withdrawal of one finger, then two, then three.

"I'm ready." She moves fitfully beneath me, squirming, eyes squeezed shut and head thrown back, her slim neck exposed. I nibble at the satiny length of her throat, and her fingers stroke the back of my head gently. I'm so much bigger than she is, when I slot my hips between her legs, it spreads her wide open. I look up the length of her, a runway of curves and silky flesh, until our eyes connect. Hers are surprisingly sober.

"Finally," she whispers, a single tear skidding over her cheek. "I won't have to pretend it's you. This time it *is* you, Iz."

I ease in, unsure of how her small body will receive me, but it's tight and hot and wet and unbearably perfect. I drop my head to the curve of her neck, holding myself still for a few seconds, savoring this initiation of our bodies together.

"This feels so right," she says, her breath stunted and ragged in my ear. "No one else is you. Don't hold back. I want it all."

"Are you sure?" I kiss her neck, behind her ear, push the tumble of dark hair away from her face.

"All."

I loose the reins on my legendary control and thrust so deep and hard into her, she moves up the bed, and the headboard knocks against the wall.

"Fuck," she says through clenched teeth.

With every thrust, my mind spirals away from my body until I'm lost in mindless possession. Nothing but animal instincts and bliss. Berserker fucking where my thoughts blur and we fall into a trance of coupling that is nothing I've known before. The sheets pull free of the mattress corners with the vigor of our bodies. Our skin slickens with sweat the longer I go, and I lose track of time. God, she must be raw by now, but I can't stop and I can't come. I'm trapped in this bottomless well of pleasure that seems to have no end. And she's right there with me. She grips my ass, pushing me in deeper. She claws my back and clamps her legs around me as if I might get away. She shudders around me with her release, raining kisses over my face and shoulders, begging me not to stop, not to leave her. I want it to last forever, but when I come ... God, I roar. I stiffen. I dig my knees into the mattress, scoop under her knees with my elbows and hammer into her, the release, seemingly infinite, but when it's over, completely satisfying.

This is why I stayed away. I knew this would happen. Nothing else will ever compare to this.

To her.

4

CALLIE

He'll have to kick me out.

I'm limp as a noodle and naked under the sheets. Iz's powerful chest rises and falls beneath my cheek. I want to stay here, curled into him while he sleeps. I trace the ridges in his abdomen with the tip of my finger, watching his belly clench. His biceps and legs are corded with muscle, every line and sinew finely crafted. Israel Hammond is a work of art. I toss my leg over him as if that will hold him with me when I know in my heart, nothing will. One night. One time.

Well ... multiple times.

My body does ache because he is not a small man, and fucking him is like riding a wild bronco. But by God, I stayed on.

"You okay?" he mumbles, kissing the top of my head, his words muffled in my hair.

I scoot even closer, eliminating the few inches left between our bodies. "I've literally never felt better."

"You're not sore?" he asks, concern in his voice.

"Only in the best way." I lift my head, straining to make out his roughly carved features in the pre-dawn light of the hotel room. "I could go again."

"God, how many times have we—"

"Not nearly enough." I reach for his dick, pulling on him, caressing the head with my thumb. "Fuck me again, Iz."

He stills, realizing I'm serious. He runs his hand over my ass, up my back, spears his fingers into my hair. When I see his swift nod, I push the sheets back and climb on top of him, my thighs stretched over his hips. He's already hard, and I guide him inside. We gasp in unison. His hands find my ribs, wander up to my breasts, pluck at my nipples while my hips roll into a wild rhythm. I raise my hands to my hair, lifting the long, heavy strands from my back and shoulders. I look down at him, clenching my inner walls around him possessively.

You're mine, Professor.

I may not say it with my words, but my body tells him. He grips my hips, taking control of the tempo, lifting his knees so my back rests against his legs. I lay back and just ride until our hoarse cries mingle, our bodies tangle in the sheets, and the sun rises on a new day.

We drift off to sleep in each other's arms, and when I wake, I'm alone. The smell of coffee tempts me to sit up. Grabbing the smaller of the two hotel robes from the back of the bathroom door, I pad out into the sitting room. Iz wears just jeans, the top button still undone. Silver domes dot the coffee table, and he lifts them to reveal eggs, bacon, fruit.

"This looks delicious," I say, sitting beside him on the couch and dropping my head to his naked shoulder. I brace myself for the usual rejection. For him to stiffen, pull away, flee, but he doesn't. He lifts my hand to his lips, linking our fingers and bending to kiss my lips.

Thank God.

"I wasn't sure if you'd have regrets this morning," I admit softly.

"Only that we didn't do that sooner," he says, his smile more open and easy than I've ever seen it. "And that the night wasn't longer."

"There'll be other nights," I say like it's nothing. Like I know there *will* be a next time, when I really have no idea. "It wasn't so bad, was it? Sex with me, I mean."

His startled bark of laughter bounces off the walls. "Um, no. It wasn't so bad."

The humor fades, and he kisses my forehead. "It was beyond everything I had imagined, Callie, and I'd done a lot of imagining."

"Well, what took you so long?" I demand, dropping the pretense of breakfast and giving him my undivided attention.

He takes another bite of his toast before setting it down and wiping his hands with a cloth napkin from the tray. "I told myself a dozen reasons why I shouldn't give in to the attraction between us. At first, you being my TA. Then it was the age difference. Everything but what it probably was."

"And what was that?" I'm not even breathing. My heart rate accelerates, but my chest is still while I wait for his answer.

"Do you know why I divorced?" he asks. I frown and realize I don't. People divorce all the time.

"I assume irreconcilable differences. You guys seemed to get along fine and have a good arrangement for Cecily."

"She cheated on me," he says softly, eyes fixed on the eggs on his plate.

"What?" I can't even imagine someone looking elsewhere with this man at home. "Are you kidding?"

"No. I like to think I'm a great dad, but I know I was a trifling husband. Completely absorbed by my work. Disinterested and distracted a lot of the time, especially when I was writing or traveling, which was all the time. I was angry when it happened, but I can't really blame her."

I can. Bitch.

"I've had my defenses up ever since. It was never an issue because I wasn't tempted to let anyone in. Not really. Fuck? Yes, but no more than that." He pulls a swathe of my hair free that's lodged under the collar of the hotel robe. "From the day you walked into my office at NYU, I knew you'd be more than that."

"Am I?" I ask with shaky hope. "Am I more? Do we get more than just last night, Iz? Because I know I said just last night, but—"

"I'd like more, too." He grins ruefully. "If you can put up with a workaholic who tends to lose himself in whatever cause has him on his soapbox of the moment."

"I love your causes," I say, meaning it. "I love your compassion, even when you're surly."

"I'm not surly."

"God, you so are."

"Okay, I'm surly."

"But I don't mind." I lean forward and kiss him, speaking against the firm, sensual lines of his mouth. "I love how hard you work for the people and things you believe in. I'd just like to be there with you, and to be the one you rest with. The one you play with."

"I don't play very much," he says with a brief laugh.

"I'd like to change that." I tilt my head. "What's next for you? Where do you go from here?"

"Back to Philly." He runs a large hand over his face, a gesture that is weary even though the day has barely begun. "I owe my publisher my next book in two months. Lots of work still to be done on it."

"But you could work from anywhere."

"Theoretically," he agrees cautiously. "What are you getting at?"

"Maybe you could come with me on my next assignment," I say in a rush before I chicken out or he can turn me down. "Hear me out. It's Brisbane."

"Australia?" he asks, his eyes brightening.

"Yeah. I'm covering a climate control summit there. It's a week, but I was going to stay for two. Would you consider coming with me?"

He sits back, leaning into the couch, his long legs stretched out in front of him. A dark, languid lion in repose. The most beautiful man I've ever seen. "A week ago I would have turned you down flat."

"I'm aware," I say dryly. "You've been turning me down flat for years."

"Ahhh," he says, grabbing my hand and linking it with his across his chest. "But that was before I started applying the rule of now to my personal life."

"And this," I say, gesturing with my free hand between us, "is now?"

He watches me, affection and something deeper entering his sober eyes. It's a look I've seen many times before when he's watched me, but he's letting me see what's behind it. It looks like what I feel inside. From the moment I met him till last night when I took him into my body, into my heart, into my very soul. His words may say this is for now, but that look, what we had last night, feels like *always*.

"Let's start with now," he finally says, kissing my fingers one by one. "And see where it goes."

I smile, falling forward until I'm on his chest, pressing him into the couch.

"You better be careful," I tease, reaching up to grasp his high cheekbones between my palms. "Once I have you, I may not let you go."

His slow smile warms the eyes I once thought cold but never indifferent, at least not to me. "Maybe you should be careful. I may not let *you* go."

I whisper a kiss across his lips and pull our twined fingers to my heart. "Professor, I'm counting on it."

* * *

Do you want more of Kennedy Ryan?

One click FLOW now!

BE THERE WITH ME

A NEW ADULT ROMANCE

GIANA DARLING

1

The plane ticket was getting damp and wrinkled against my breast, where it was stuffed between the skin and the heavy material of my borrowed black cotton dress. I was trying to figure out if the scanner would still be able to read my sweat-soaked ticket, but it was kind of hard to concentrate when the guy on top of me kept murmuring sweet nothings in my ear.

"Hey, Jake, shut up, would you?" I asked.

To ease the sting of my words, I scratched my nails over his buzzed skull and grabbed his ears to pull him away from my neck so that I could nibble on his lip. His hot hands raced under my tank top and around to my back to undo my bra. I quickly peeled the sweaty plane ticket off my boob and dropped it on the bedside table behind me.

"I can't believe I'm hooking up with you," Jake groaned when I bit down on his mouth a little harder than necessary, but he didn't get the message. "I'm actually hooking up with Darcy Noble."

"Oh my God." I pushed him back by his ears and whipped off my shirt and bra before he could continue. "Jake, please just shut up and take off your pants."

He stared at me for a moment like an untrained puppy, his huge brown eyes glistening with confusion and desire. I felt like a predator playing with my food before I ate it but there wasn't any big game at the party throbbing outside my closed bedroom door and Jake had always been cute in a baby animal kind of way.

I stood up to peel off my tights because I wanted to get this show on the road. Jake followed my lead, scrambling out of his jeans while his eyes remained glued to my topless form. I stuck a finger under the black thong string and followed it from one hip to the other and back, watching as I hypnotized Jake.

He may have been a bumbling virgin, but sometimes all you need is an audience to turn your own crank.

I laughed when he lunged for me, bumping me into the wall almost painfully in his haste to get his hands on me. They were gentle and ardent as they traveled over my gymnastics-toned curves. He cradled me against his body with one hand easily because of my small stature while he cupped my face with the other. It was sweet and perfect for a high school romance. But I wanted more.

I wanted to be ripped apart, pieces of myself flying across the room in shards and fragments so jagged, so small it would be impossible to put me back together. I wanted to be bitten and fucked and destroyed because in my heart I knew I deserved it. In my gut, I wanted it.

I groaned and tilted my head back when his lips brushed against my neck. There was a small red clock on the desk across the room, and I spent a few minutes squinting, trying to read the time in order to pass the time. Jake was on my breasts when I realized his attentions just weren't going to cut it.

I pushed him away with a knee to his hip, ignoring his panted protest. There was a nearly empty bottle of vodka on my bedside table, and I finished it off without class. The burning liquid dripped down my chin.

"Lick it off." I beckoned at Jake with the empty bottle before tossing it to the other side of the room, where I heard it crash.

A frown flittered over his sweet face, but I was on him before he could wonder if I was too drunk to fuck. I was, probably, but that was the point and I didn't want him to ruin it. I pushed him onto the bed, stifling a giggle when his erection bobbed wildly with the impact, and climbed on top of him. His hands found the curves of my waist when I wanted them on my ass. I decided to move them there myself and was rewarded when he squeezed them passionately.

Jake wasn't what I wanted, and hell, he wasn't even what I needed to appease the banshee inside me, screaming in pain and railing for impossible justice. If I couldn't ease the grief or bring my mother back, I figured I might as well distract myself with a pretty boy.

And Jake was one of the prettiest, with the kind of lashes girls would kill for atop deep, Byronic eyes. He was a nice guy too, gentlemanly in a sweet, old-fashioned way that seemed so out of place in Los Angeles. It was too bad he wasn't a good fuck.

Afterward, he lay beside me like a hardworking billows, air gushing from his heaving lungs so forcibly that it actually wafted across my skin from where I lay, as far away from him as I could. It wasn't that he repulsed me, he was cute even when panting, sweating and satiated, and I wasn't disgusted with myself even though I wondered if I should be. Instead, I felt deeply apathetic. My entire body felt numb and heavy, like something too often used and wrung out. My heart was still, barely hiccoughing, and my mind was empty. It wasn't much, but it was a hell of a lot better than the cacophony of regret that had been banging around under my skin for the last ten days.

"That was amazing," Jake said, turning his head to look at me with those puppy-dog eyes.

I grunted and rolled over the bed, grabbing my discarded clothes as I crossed into the bathroom. I closed the door on those puppy-dog eyes and the muffled noise of the party that still raged throughout my house. The silence was painful in its own way, but I could bear it for the few minutes it took for me to smooth my barely rumpled waves and wipe the smudge of eyeliner from under my bloodshot eyes.

There was a picture tucked into the frame of the mirror over my sink, and even though I studiously ignored it at first, inevitably, I ended up plucking it from the seam. My mother stared back at me, an older version of myself with lustrous, thick waves of caramel hair and large green eyes ringed in dark lashes. The shape of our smiles was the same, the constellation of freckles over the bridge of my nose the only thing I'd inherited from my father.

I didn't need a photo to remember my mother and I never would. I'd only need look at my own face in the mirror, and even though I knew that would bring me comfort in the future, it only made my chest pull tight like a coiled spring.

I'd been planning to change into the short, sequined number hanging on the back of the bathroom door, but the crush of emotions in my chest had me rethinking.

Maybe I'd give Jake another chance to distract me.

* * *

The day I met Tennessee Clark, I nearly drowned.

He was the new kid at school, with a molasses southern accent to boot, so obviously everyone wanted to be his best friend. I was the sole exception, and there wasn't even a good reason for it. He was just so at ease with everyone, instantly making jokes and relating to people in a way that my seventh-grade self simply could not comprehend. Sure, I had friends, but only a few that I could really stand. Most people made me violent or apathetic, and it took a lot of work on my part to maintain a cool, calm facade for the world.

But not this kid. No, Tennessee Clark epitomized good old-fashioned southern charm, and by the end of his first day at school, everyone freaking loved him.

To make matters worse, when a group of us headed to the beach after class like we always did, he followed. I ignored him as we gathered on the cool caramel sand, and I also ignored the fact that it was nearly the same color as his tanned skin. I ignored him when I stripped off my denim shorts and caught him staring over at me, his stupid thirteen-year-old face still round with youth. But I could not ignore him when he bragged to Joe Monroe that he had been the best swimmer at his old school.

To Joe's credit, he snorted, because everyone knew that *I* was the best swimmer at this school.

To stupid baby face's credit, he caught on pretty quick. His blue-gray eyes —the same color as the Pacific waves rolling into shore under a cloudy sky— swept over me lazily, completely unthreatened and only vaguely curious.

I bristled so furiously the pain of phantom thorns breaking through my skin was almost real. I fisted my hands on my hips and waited for him to taunt me, bet me to race him and thoroughly beat his ass.

But he only stood there, with his hands in the pockets of his faded khaki shorts. He was barely taller than me, which was normal at that age when girls like me matured and left the boys behind for another couple of years, but despite his lack of height, I could feel him looking down at me. He didn't move a muscle, didn't make a sound, but the emptiness of his reaction only made me angrier.

"Strip," I ordered. "And get ready for the race of your stupid little life."

It was a pretty weak insult and I regretted it immediately, but luckily, Tennessee obeyed without a word. I swallowed a laugh as he tugged off his shirt to reveal a scrawny, browned chest, but I couldn't help the snort that escaped when a few of my—traitorous—best girlfriends cooed over the sight.

If he noticed their admiration, he didn't show it. His gaze swiveled slowly between the ocean and me, back and forth like the rhythm of the waves. I watched his body move like that too, his limbs flowing through the air with a heavy, masculine grace that was at odds on a teenager.

He cleared his throat, and I jumped, shame curdling in my stomach as I realized he'd caught me staring at him.

"You move slow," I taunted to make up for my moment of weakness. "Not sure how you can expect to beat me."

"Slow and steady, Freckles," he drawled before winking at me and turning to address some of the guys who were goading him on.

I scowled and stomped to the water's edge to wait for him. I knew we would swim to the pile of sleek black rock jutting out of the surf about one hundred yards offshore because it was a swim most of us had been making for years and one that I did nearly every week. Usually, the thought of submerging myself in the sea made me tingly with delight, but Tennessee's presence was like static at the back of my mind.

"He *winked* at me," I complained when I felt Brighton come to stand beside me.

Brighton and I had been best friends since we were in diapers, so he knew me well enough to say, "He's a little shit."

"Totally."

"I think you like him."

"Oh shut your face, Bright," I snarled, bumping him a little too hard with my hip. "As if."

"It's not a crime to *like*-like boys, you know? I mean, you are a girl," he reminded me.

"Whatever. Maybe if he was Iker Cassis or Justin Timberlake," I said, thinking of my favorite soccer player and the sexiest N'SYNC member. "But *this* guy is just a scrawny little nobody."

I was always a little aggressive when someone had me on the defensive, but Brighton just rolled his eyes. "You're a scrawny little nobody too, Darce."

I stuck my tongue out at him. "You going to cheer me on or what?"

"If I do, you have to promise not to blow it. I can't be that guy with the loser best friend, you know?"

I turned on my heel, careful to kick sand up at him as I did, and stormed toward the water where the others huddled off to the side, eager to see the race. A few people were betting on the results, and I shot them a cocky wink just to stir the pot.

When I looked over at Tennessee, he was watching me with a completely blank expression, cute and poker-faced like a mannequin.

"What're you looking at?" I asked, channeling my inner Pony Boy.

He squinted at me like James Dean, which made me really angry because I freaking loved James Dean. "You."

"Scared?" I taunted.

His blink was long and slow. "I'm not scared of anything."

I scoffed at him and gestured toward the waves of steel being crushed into pieces against black rocks farther down the beach. "If you aren't scared of this, then you're an idiot."

He shrugged one bony shoulder, and I noticed the smattering of freckles there. "Never been in the ocean before, figure it can't be much different from the wave pool back home."

I threw my head back and laughed at the cloudless sky. I was so going to whoop his ass.

"Let's make this interesting," I said casually, trying not to betray my glee. "If I win, you never talk to me or my best friends again."

He frowned, and like every other stupid thing about this stupid boy, it was an unhurried and thoughtful expression that only made me wonder what the hell he was thinking.

"Now, I don't know about that, Miz Noble. Seems pretty unfair to me. See, as I understand it, you don't have any friends at all."

My teeth clenched together until I felt they could break. "You're one to talk, newbie."

"Give me a week and I'll be the most popular kid in the grade. Hell, even the entire school."

"Yeah, well, not if I win this race, which I'm obviously going to. And right now, I'm the most popular kid in school, so good luck having friends."

I was being a raging bully. The kind of person that parents warned their kids away from. I mean, I couldn't have been less welcoming if I'd stolen his lunch money. But Tennessee Clark just stared at me with those pretty eyes and shrugged.

"If I win, you teach me how to surf."

"What?"

He just tilted his chin down and rocked back on his heels.

"You'd want me to teach you how to surf?"

"Why not? I don't have the money for lessons, and I hear you're the best in your class." I almost flushed with pride before he added, "Of course, it makes sense seeing as who your daddy is."

I scowled at him. "Don't talk about him."

His eyes narrowed on my face, reading something that I could have sworn I hadn't written there. I shifted uneasily under his scrutiny and was surprised when he finally smiled, the left side of his mouth crooked up in a grin.

"Do we have a deal? If you're too afraid, I'm sure no one will make fun of you for more than two or three weeks, tops."

Jerk face.

"Deal," I agreed, taking his surprisingly large hand in mine. I squeezed as hard as I could, but I had a feeling it hurt me more than him.

"Ready?" Misha called from the group of spectators.

We both nodded and assumed our running positions. The ocean planted frigid kisses against the tips of my toes as I crouched low to launch myself forward into the waters that I loved more than my own life. I laughed before I could rein it in and looked over at Tennessee, who was smiling too.

We looked at each other, grinning like loons just as Misha shouted, "GO!"

I leaped into the sea, jumping over the waterline to avoid the weight of the current. When it lapped at my waist, I slipped under and began to swim in earnest. I didn't know where Tennessee was, but honestly, I didn't really care because as soon as I was in the water, I forgot everything else. It was just me and the cold blue world of the Pacific. My limbs were numb in under five minutes and my eyes stung from opening them underwater, but I felt invigorated by the adrenaline pumping through my blood, the push and pull of my muscles working to sluice through the churning surf.

The waves were deep and choppy that afternoon but it was nothing I wasn't used to and honestly, I should have seen the net but I was so busy wondering if I was beating that stupid boy that I wasn't as diligent as I normally was. I forgot that the sea didn't play silly games.

I felt the tug as the twine locked onto my toes, but I didn't think anything of it until it jerked me to a stop just as I was going to resurface. Flipping onto my back, I looked down to see the coiled black webbing twisted around my left foot. It wasn't unusual for fishermen or prawners to cut their nets if they got caught on ocean bottom debris, and I reached down to fix it without worry. But I was close to those black rocks now and the crashing waves made the water murkier than usual. I cursed my numb fingers for their clumsiness and then I cursed myself for not have my diving knife with me because I was almost out of air and I couldn't get the discarded fishing net out from between my grasping toes. Panic built in my belly, obliterating everything as it swelled bigger and bigger. Black spots flirted with my vision, coupling with the salty sting of the water until I couldn't even see the net.

I'm probably going to die, I thought as my lungs burned, *and I'm most definitely going to lose that stupid race.*

Just as my mind began to float away like an unhinged buoy, two hands appeared from out of the murkiness and made quick work of the tangled net with a small blade. A moment later, I was free and bursting through the surface of the malicious sea with a voracious gasp.

Tennessee's round face bobbed beside me, his face blank but those ocean eyes turbulent with concern. He didn't speak as I spent a good thirty seconds swallowing deep handfuls of briny air, and I was thankful for it. I couldn't have handled the ribbing, however good-natured, not when I was still shaken by how close I'd come to an idiotic death.

Finally, when I could breathe calmly through my nose again, I blinked water out of my lashes and locked eyes with him.

"This doesn't mean we're friends or anything."

The words came out of my mouth before I could dream of harnessing the attitude. I was a sassy girl, verging on bitchy, most of the time, and the adrenaline coursing through my body only added higher voltage to my electric tongue.

Tennessee blinked, then shrugged one bony, freckled shoulder. "Whatever you say, Freckles. We don't have to be friends, but you're sure as hell gonna be my surf instructor."

"Whatever," I scoffed, starting to swim back to the shore where all our friends waited.

"Yeah, whatever," he agreed easily. "If I gotta put up with your attitude, might as well do it while you're wearing a bikini."

2

"What the hell, Darcy?"

I crinkled my eyes shut and kissed Jake harder.

"Darcy, get off him."

Someone tried to lift me off Jake by the shoulders, but I locked my knees around him, for once thankful for my athleticism. It bought me a few more seconds to bite Jake's lip until the tang of blood hit my tongue like a percussion note.

The next second, I was in the air, supported baby-style under my armpits by huge hands. I wanted to struggle out of the hold, but when a familiar fresh oceanic scent washed over me, my body betrayed me by relaxing instantly. Tennessee's hands adjusted easily, scooping me up against his chest as if I weighed nothing.

Cade and Brighton were busy yelling at Jake, who was now naked, flaccid, and trapped in the corner of my bedroom. I felt badly for him because I had been on the other end of the boys' wrath and it was not a cozy place to be. But my mouth felt like the inside of an old slipper and I had been drunk for so long that my body was failing, growing heavy and weak. So, I didn't protest when they ripped into Jake, even though I should have told them it was my fault entirely.

"I'm going to get her out of here," Tenn said, already turning away from the scene.

The boys mumbled their agreements, but my ears had lost their focus as soon as the muffled percussion of Tenn's beating heart vibrated against my cheek. I had always been an awful sleeper, trying white noise machines, herbal remedies, meditation, and a glass of hot milk before bed, but nothing had ever worked so well as that seemingly eternal pulse.

He opened the door of my bedroom, and immediately the cacophonic swell of party noise flooded in, punctuated at the moment by the low cheer of "chug, chug, chug!" There was a couple on the stairs, half-naked and lying at an awkward angle in their haste to hook up. They didn't even flinch when Tenn stepped competently around their writhing forms.

"I should have hooked up with that guy instead," I said, envious of their total absorption.

Tenn's dark blonde brow rose, but otherwise, he ignored me.

A few people called out to us as we powered across the foyer and through the main doors onto the equally packed front lawn where over a dozen people were playing Beer Bat. I didn't respond because my job as a hostess was over; I had supplied the booze, the location and the people, so I figured it was up to them to keep the party going. Tenn didn't respond either, but that wasn't really surprising. He was the strong, silent type, especially when he was pissed.

I scratched the short hairs at the nape of his neck and tipped my head back to look up at the light-polluted sky of Los Angeles.

"Are you mad at me, party pooper?" I asked.

He snorted.

"You know, Tenn, you wouldn't be such a party pooper if you drank a little more."

He shifted my weight onto one arm so he could open the door to his ancient Jeep, and I adjusted by wrapping my legs and arms around him like a baby koala bear.

"You'd probably be a little pudgy," I continued, "with that little freshman-fifteen pouch every other student in the world but you has at one point or another."

He rolled his eyes, but I wasn't insulted because I lived for those dexterous slate-blue eyes. They were more the lenses through which I viewed the world than my own eyes were.

I waited for him to buckle me in, close the door, and walk over to the driver's side before I started in on him again.

"Sometimes, I think that you do the whole silent, broody thing just to annoy me," I said, narrowing my eyes at him.

His firm mouth twitched, but otherwise he remained unmoved as he started the car and the deep growl of the curmudgeonly engine rumbled to life.

"Oh, I get it. I totally cockblocked you, didn't I?" I snapped my fingers, but in my drunkenness, I misjudged my enthusiasm and hit my hand against the console in the follow-through. "Tenn, you should go back right this second. Leave me here to rot in peace and go get laid."

"I'm taking you home," he said, his eyes on the road and his hands perfectly placed at ten and two on the wheel.

I snorted. "I think *you* might be the drunk one. If you haven't noticed, we're speeding away from my house as we speak."

"We are not speeding. And don't play the pretty, vacant cheerleader with me, Darcy. I'm taking you home and putting your drunk ass to bed."

"You know, if anyone knew *half* the nice things you did for me and the boys, your bad-boy image would be totally ruined."

I reached over and flicked the silver barbell through his thick right brow and was rewarded with a scowl. I snickered and curled my legs up in the big, comfy seat. My tiny dress rode up over my thighs, but Tenn didn't even notice; he'd seen it all before over the years, and I turned him on as much as a juicy steak did a lifelong vegetarian.

"So says Malibu Barbie," he said.

He had a point. Both Tenn and I had worked hard to perfect our personas. So what if the Darcy Noble everyone thought they knew was only a mirage?

I was plastic perfection on the outside, and if it was good enough to make Barbie popular with all the kids, it was good enough for me.

I knew the Hollywood game.

You couldn't have a famous surfer-turned-inspirational-writer father and a silver-screen starlet for a mother without being instilled with some kind of intuition and briefed with some kind of intensity on the inner workings of celebrity.

And my father was my father, so I knew more than most.

He'd gone from an impoverished surfer sleeping on the beaches of Byron Bay, Australia, to one of the most celebrated surfers in the history of the sport. As if that wasn't enough, he'd written an inspirational memoir about his trials and then, together with my mother's father, turned it into a cinematic masterpiece.

Enough was never enough for Hamish Noble.

Unfortunately, he'd passed that trait on to me.

I had money, an early acceptance to one of the most renowned universities in the world, good friends, even better looks, and I wanted to flush it all down the toilet.

I cursed under my breath as I realized I'd left my plane ticket, damp and crumpled as a used condom, on the floor beside my bed. The electronic version was in an app on my phone, but there was something about having that inconsequential slip of paper in my possession. It was a symbol of everything to be devoured outside of Los Angeles and the existence I had already carved out there.

It was freedom.

"You're thinkin' awfully hard over there, Freckles," Tenn drawled as he rolled down the window before lighting the cigarette tucked into the corner of his pouty lips. As a kid, before we'd become friends, that full, sullen mouth had irritated me to no end. I didn't think it was fair for a man to have a mouth like that. Something so sensual, so filled with certain temptation should be on a girl.

Now, whenever I looked a little too long at Tenn's beautiful lips, I just thought they suited him in an odd way. Everything about him was hard—his long, wide-shouldered, narrow-hipped frame, the callouses on the ridges of his palms and the tips of his lean fingers, the angle of that strong, stubborn jaw. Everything but those pale pink lips like the full bloom off a rose and those eyes so changeable a blue they altered more than the sea.

They were the windows to a soul he kept locked up tight, and I'd grown to learn over the years to watch them if I wanted to know his truth.

He occupied them both now, with smoking and his gaze on the road, and I knew it was because he knew I was watching and he didn't want to give anything away. Not until he was ready.

I didn't need to watch him to know he was mad at me though.

Truthfully, I was *happy* he was mad at me.

Someone should be.

And my numb heart and soul didn't remember how.

"Jake, huh?" he asked finally, smoke curling in a caress over his cheek before sliding out the window into the night.

"Yep," I said, popping the *p* because I knew it would annoy him.

"He's wanted you for years."

I shrugged a shoulder. Lots of guys had wanted me for a lot of years. I didn't really care about it except for the fact it made me popular with the girls, especially because I never actually went for any of the boys in our grade. I just lured them to the group like bears to honey so the scavengers could have their fill.

"Feel good? Finally losin' it?" he asked in that long, slow voice that pulled words apart like taffy.

I shot him a glare, but he either didn't feel the heat of my gaze or chose to ignore it.

"Shut up."

"You're shuttin' up enough for the both of us," he countered. "Haven't said more than a handful of words since this afternoon."

That wasn't true, and even though I didn't want to talk about it *at all*, I'd never been good at keeping quiet when there was a wrong to right.

"I made a speech, didn't I?"

"Was that you up there?" he mused, and even though his tone was casual, his intent was utterly cruel. "I didn't recognize you up there."

I closed my eyes and turned my head away from him, biting my lip to keep back the sudden, uncharacteristic flood of hot tears burning my lids.

Unbidden, my mind conjured up the funeral, the nauseating scent of lilies, and the iron tang of wet earth from the ground they'd dug up to make way for her casket.

"Darce, you're up."

I stared up at Tenn as if from a great depth, his familiar features distorted by waves of waxy southern heat and my own disorientation. In that moment, for the life of me, I couldn't remember where I was.

"Darcy." Tenn leaned down into my face, and he suddenly snapped into focus, golden and handsome enough to make me blink. "You need to get up there."

"Where are we?"

He sighed and shifted his weight from foot to foot, a nervous habit that made me frown because I couldn't remember why he should be nervous. He stared at me hard for a moment. "We're at the funeral."

Reality pushed hard at my temples, drilling poles of truth into my skull. I gritted my teeth against the agony and wondered in my pain-induced delirium if I looked at all like Frankenstein's monster.

"For Alice," I confirmed.

He nodded curtly.

I couldn't even call her mom.

The speech that followed had not been Byronic or even eloquent. It was waterlogged in my memory with the tears I hadn't shed, but I knew it'd been trash.

I had been trash.

Plastic and broken like a thrown-out doll.

I hadn't called her mom, hadn't spoken about all the many ways she'd protected me in this life, how often she'd loved me or how she did it so fiercely I'd never doubted it for even one second of my existence. I hadn't talked about the way she'd always smelled like citrus even though she didn't wear perfume, because she was enamored with the orange trees that grew in our backyard and I could always find her out there, peeling the fruit before she'd even plucked it from the limb. I didn't tell everyone there to mourn her that she wouldn't have wanted them to mourn because she was the happiest, most positive person I'd ever known. That they should dance and laugh and smile to commemorate her because that was the kind of farewell a woman like Alice Jenson would have wanted.

I didn't say any of that. The words sat in my heart unheard and unattended to, but aching and throbbing with a pulse of their own until they thundered in my ears even stronger than my heartbeat.

Tenn was right to castigate me.

I hadn't been truth to my mom in the very moment she most deserved it. In my fog of bereavement I hadn't been able to summon the courage to expose my rawness to the hundreds of people gathered for the much loved actress's funeral.

Tenn knew it, and he wasn't even judging me for it, not really.

He was highlighting the issue because he knew me well enough to know, even only hours later, it was *haunting*.

"Leave it be, Tennessee."

"Never." When I turned to look at him, he was ready with his cool-guy shrug. "I'm serious here, Darce. There will never be a time in our lives when I 'leave it be,' not if it's sittin' in you like a poison that needs to be sucked out at the source. You've got to know by now, if you won't purge it, I will."

"Who gave you that right?" I snapped.

"You did. You made me the kind of friend that's family, and there's nothin' family won't do for one of their own if they're hurtin'."

I snorted.

The great and wonderful Hamish Noble hadn't even been able to make it home from his latest movie in order to see his wife die...

Tenn's big, hot hand landed on my thigh and squeezed so hard it made me wince. "Hamish isn't the kinda family I'm modeling this after. I'm talkin' about the good kind, the right kind. That's *me* for you, Darce. I know you don't have anyone else now, not really, not actual blood. But I'm tellin' you right now and you're goin' hear it even if I gotta talk until I'm blue in the goddamn face, you will *always* have *me*."

My throat went hot with imminent tears, but I swallowed them back because I knew with terrifying clarity that if I gave in to them now, I wouldn't stop until my body ran dry.

"You suck," I told him on a threadbare whisper.

His lips twitched, but he inclined his head in a slight nod because he knew I needed to be mean to him to counterbalance his kindness.

He always knew what to do with me, a powder keg of a girl dressed in the latest designer fashions.

We didn't speak again as we cruised out of Beverly Hills and onto the highway to Malibu where Tenn lived with his fashion-designer mother. I stared out the window at the bright lights sweeping past in neon smudges and wondered if I would miss it, all of it, when I got on the plane heading for Australia in the morning.

At some point, I must have fallen asleep, because when I next opened my eyes, they latched on to the tight fit of a gray T-shirt over a muscular chest. Tenn's sea-salt-and-sandalwood scent and the warmth of his big body cradling me to his chest instantly made me melt farther into his hold.

A soft chuckle vibrated against my cheek. "Like a kitten when you're sleepy and a cat with unretractable claws when you're awake."

"Rawr," I murmured drowsily as I snuggled my cheek into his hard pectoral and tried to remember when his teenage boy's body had turned into a man's.

I felt his nose in my hair, heard the deep breath he dragged in and then the light *hum* of approval he gave my scent.

"You're the animal," I teased. "Sniffing me like that."

His shrug jostled me as he moved through the dark house and up the stairs to his bedroom. "Like the smell of you, always have."

"Sunscreen and sweat?"

"Sunshine and sea brine," he corrected as he pushed open the bedroom door with his shoulder and moved to the bed with easy precision despite the darkness.

I slid under the sheets like a puddle of melted butter, made soft and tender by the closeness of the night and the warmth of Tenn's big body. I wondered idly, almost drunk on my delirium and grief, what it would feel like for Tenn to care for me in other, more intimate ways. How it might feel for the rough pads of his fingers to play over my tight curves and carved, muscular edges. Would he find sensuality in the body I'd worked hard to hone into an instrument to play over the waves? Or would he think, as I sometimes did alone in front of the mirror, that I was unfeminine and therefore undesirable?

How might it feel to have all his considerable manliness under my touch? Would it counterweight my insecurities enough to make me soft and pretty, fragile in a way that I knew intrinsically was its own strength?

Tenn watched me from his seat on the edge of the bed, his eyes shimmering even in the low light from the partially open curtain. I couldn't tell what he was thinking as he studied me with salacious, unusual thoughts in my mucked-up mind, but I was suddenly self-conscious.

My hand went up to brush the hair back from my forehead, but Tenn's beat me to it, those rough fingertips I'd just been thinking about coarse and tingly against my skin.

"Haven't been sleepin'." He told me something I already knew. "You'll sleep tonight."

His arrogance broke the strange electricity between us, and I scoffed at him as he moved away to ditch his clothing for pajama pants.

"Yes, sir," I quipped even though I felt closer to sleep than I had in months just being in his familiar bed.

Over the years, I'd spent countless nights at Tenn's house with him and sometimes Cade and Brighton. I was one of the boys, and my mother was cool enough to know our relationship was both vital to me and platonic.

My eye caught the glimmer of a condom wrapper lying on the bedside table as I turned to my other side to watch Tenn brush his teeth through the open door to the bathroom. My throat went dry as I thought about that condom and Tenn using it, my eyes now glued to the wide triangular plane of his back arrowing into his flannel sleep pants.

Stop it, you perv, I scolded myself. *This is Tennessee you're getting all hot and bothered over.*

I closed my eyes and decided sleep was my only escape from my new and broken reality. One where my mother was dead and Tenn seemed to be the answer to all my lonely woes. I kept them shut even when I felt his body depress the other side of the bed, when his leg rubbed over mine as he settled, and then still when a strong arm curled around my hips and pulled me back against his chest so my ass settled in the bowl of his lap.

"You'll sleep, because I'm going to lie here and hold you until you do," he said softly into my ear before pressing a kiss to the hair over it.

"You're something else, but you're not magic. You can't turn off my brain."

There was silence for a moment, and then, even before the noise hit my ears, I felt the vibration of his humming tune reverberate from his chest through mine.

He was singing.

I held my breath as the sound as his molasses voice poured warmth over my injured soul. Tenn hadn't sung for years even though he had one of the most agonizingly beautiful voices I'd ever heard. I had no idea why, only that one day shortly after our fourteenth birthdays, he'd stopped and refused to start again.

But here he was, singing for me now when nothing else could have pulled my focus from my pain long enough to lull me into slumber.

I closed my eyes as he crooned "Adore You" by Harry Styles into my ear, and let his words carry me away into the sweet oblivion of sleep.

* * *

Panic woke me just as the sun was cresting the horizon, the first hazy rays of white light filtering into Tenn's bedroom and falling across my face like a physical alarm.

I had to get up and get out before he woke.

Which would be a fucking feat because his large, hot body was sprawled over mine like a weighted blanket, his torso pinning mine to the bed, one of his heavy legs tangled with mine. Lord, he was fucking difficult to move. I tried to wiggle out from under him, and the effort made me sweat enough to finally slip him off my back.

Holding my breath where I crouched on the floor beside the bed, I studied his face for signs of wakefulness and, not finding any, quickly scampered down the stairs.

I could hear his mother puttering about in the kitchen and quickly changed course for the office at the back of the house where I knew I would find an old-fashioned house phone. After tapping in the number for a taxi company, I slipped out the back door and waited down the street for the cab to pick me up.

My house was a complete disaster when I arrived. People still sprawled asleep over the furniture, and sticky remnants of beer pooled over the hardwood from tossed-about red solo cups and beer cans.

I didn't take the time to worry about it, let alone stop to clean up. It wasn't my first party; I'd hired a service to come at nine a.m. to clean up.

I wouldn't be around to do it, and neither would my father.

My bedroom was empty, at least, and my suitcase already packed and tucked away in my closet. I collected it, my huge purse, and the crumpled plane ticket before descending the stairs and waiting out on the front stoop for my Uber.

The driver helped me carefully stow my luggage and my surfboard before we took off.

I didn't think about the house or the life I was leaving behind.

I didn't dwell on the fact that I hadn't even said goodbye to Cade, Brighton, or, most of all, Tennessee.

I just stared out the window, listening to music through my headphones, until the car pulled up at the airport.

I was just struggling through the automatic doors with my haul when a coarse shout halted me in my tracks.

"Darcy!"

Fuck me.

"Darcy fuckin' Noble!"

I squeezed my eyes shut, then turned slowly, hating it, to face the man behind the voice. Tenn was bounding across the pavement, his face contorted with rage, his body tight with adrenaline.

He was a beautiful sight even though I knew all that anger was directed at me.

I didn't say a word until he was right in front of me, his heavy breath fanning over my face, his hot hand reaching up to clutch my shoulder and give it a little shake.

"What the hell?" he asked me, and when I didn't respond in a timely fashion, he barked again, "What the fuckin' hell, Darce?"

I tried to shrug, but it didn't dislodge his hand. "What?"

"What? That is your brilliant response? What?" I'd never heard him angry, his words staccato and chewed off at the edges. "Were you really just going to take off the day after your mother's funeral when everyone would be worried fuckin' sick about where you'd run off to? Were you really going to leave without tellin' a single person goodbye? Without tellin' fuckin' *me*?"

I tilted my chin pugnaciously and glared at him. "I'm a strong, independent woman. I don't need anyone's permission to do anything. I'm eighteen and graduated."

"Christ, you're actually doin' this," he muttered, looking skyward as if appealing to God. "My bad, I forget sometimes how selfish you can be."

"Selfish?" I sputtered. "For going about my own life?"

"Selfish for not realizing you're not the only one who lost your mom!" he cried. "For not realizing she was a parent to Cade, Bright, and me too. For not even trying to understand how fuckin' *wrecked* we would be if you disappeared on us like this."

I swallowed convulsively, trying to force the boulder suddenly taking up residency in my throat back down to whence it'd come from.

"She was my mom," I argued even though to say so wasn't fair.

She'd been a mum to my boys too. They'd needed her just as much as I had, with the parents they'd been born to.

I was selfish. It wasn't news to say so. I was an eighteen-year-old girl born to wealth and status.

It wasn't exactly unusual.

What was unusual, and totally unfair, was the disrespectful way I was choosing to leave my friends behind without a care.

My heart burned in my chest like a single piece of coal, a failing, foul source.

Tenn brought his face down on mine, so close our noses brushed, and those oceanic eyes were all I could see.

"Speech I gave last night about you bein' family, did that mean nothin' to you?"

His closeness befuddled my resolve. I couldn't think straight with his scent in my nose and his warmth on my face.

"Of course, it did."

"Yeah? Yet, you do this in the mornin'. Christ," he cursed again, stepping back to run agitated hands through his hair so the dark blond strands stuck up everywhere. "*Fuckin' Christ.*"

"I'm going to miss my flight," I told him because I didn't know what else to say.

No, I didn't know *how* else to say the things that still sat unharvested in my chest.

I'm sorry.

Thank you for being the best friend in the whole wide world.

I love you, I love you, I love you, but please, God, let that stay in a box so I could move on with a life without feeling, at least for a while.

Tenn glared at me through his fingers, then dropped his hands to his hips and stared up at the sky again. "Fuck me. Okay, let's get goin' then."

"Excuse me?"

"You're not fuckin' excused," he muttered, stalking forward to take my surf board and suitcase from me and then starting into the terminal. "Keep up. You said yourself you're going to be late, and I need time to buy a goddamn ticket."

"Excuse me?" I repeated, following him on instinct while my mind rebelled.

"Keep up, Darce," he bit out as he bypassed the line, ignoring angry travelers, and slapped my suitcase onto the baggage scale beside the desk. "A ticket to..."

He looked over his shoulder at me, and when I didn't answer, he shook his head and snatched the ticket out of my hand. "One ticket to Sydney, Australia, please."

The attendant looked between the two of us and bit her lip before giving in to Tenn's sudden smile and asking, "Any baggage?"

"Hers."

He didn't have any stuff, only the clothes he wore and the wallet he pulled out of his back pocket.

"You don't have your passport," I whispered.

My chest was a tornado of emotions, so chaotic I couldn't even begin to see through the storm of them to what I really felt about the situation unfolding around me.

Tenn glared at me again and produced the blue passport from the back pocket of his jeans. "Called your housekeeper, Magda. She told me you'd booked a trip for the day after the funeral, but she didn't know where. How do you think I found you here?"

"You don't have any stuff," I argued irrationally.

"Jesus, Darce, I don't have any luggage because this phone call happened about an hour ago when I woke up to an empty bed and a bad premonition. Now shut your mouth and let me sort this out."

My mouth shut with a clang that rattled my jaw, and I watched bemusedly as Tenn bought his ticket, then ushered my things through the baggage drop-off. Only when he was done did he tag my hand and haul me through security, dropping it briefly through the metal detector, and then to our gate. He shoved me gently into a seat there and then stalked off without a word.

I sat there.

I sat there and tried not to think because I could feel the tsunami of emotions threatening to break against me and drown me in endless confusion and sorrow.

My gaze found a clock on the wall across from me and tracked the progress of the second hand across its face to distract me.

I lasted forty-eight seconds.

Forty-eight.

Fucking pathetic resolve.

Of its own volition, my head tipped forward into my waiting hands, and tears sprang from behind my lids like oil from a geyser. They seeped between my fingers, ran down my arms, and sank into my lap, darkening the fabric of my orange sundress.

I didn't care.

I couldn't care.

Not that I was losing it in such a public place or that my tears were staining my crotch like I'd had an accident.

Nothing.

All my focus had to be on breathing through the sobs suddenly racking my entire frame, robbing me of breath.

I'd gone from human to dangerous weather pattern, a tropical storm in less than a heartbeat, and now I just had to weather it until the water ran dry.

Through the haze, I recognized two warm hands sliding down the wet on my forearms before moving under my pits to cart me into the air. I let myself be maneuvered because I was out of it, but not enough that Tenn's sandalwood scent went unnoticed.

As soon as he had me in his lap, I curled tightly into a ball and pressed my leaking eyes into his shirt.

"Hush," he told me through the hysteria of my tears. "Hush, Darce. I'm here with you. I'm here. Not lettin' you go."

At one point, someone asked him if I was all right, and he said, "She will be. I'll make sure of it."

Which only made me cry harder.

But this time, cradled in his arms—a place I hadn't known before yesterday and a place I'd never before thought of coveting—the tears changed.

It wasn't a tempest any longer, but a purging, a spring rain that cleansed my ragged spirit of the poison Tenn had spoken of last night.

I was sad.

So fucking sad and so fucking angry, but I couldn't focus on the fury any longer. I couldn't let it harden me so I'd be forever calcified by the tragedy of losing my mother to heart disease too soon.

I had to allow myself to be sad if I had a hope of surviving this with any trace amounts of the Darcy Noble of before. The girl who had loved few, but powerfully. The girl who had loved to tease and joke, to challenge herself and others. The girl who was all steel and angles on the outside, but secretly, so secretly, soft as kitten fur on the inside.

I wanted a chance for some of her to remain within me.

For me, and also for Tenn, because I knew he needed that just as much as I did. I didn't know exactly why Tenn mattered more than anyone else, or if I had to spend time thinking about the why and how much of it, but the simple fact was that now my mother was gone, there was only one other person left that I loved more than my own life.

And he was currently letting me make a mess of his T-shirt with my tears.

So, I cried.

And when they announced it was time to board the plane, I tilted my head up to lock eyes with Tenn, who was already looking down at me, and I fought to put a trembling smile on my lips.

When that didn't really work, I put my hand on his face and traced the steep angle there.

"Be there with me," I asked him, even though I didn't phrase it as a question.

Even though I knew he already would be.

"Always," he promised, leaning down to press his forehead to mine. "Fuckin' always, Darce."

* * *

A PRETTY PENNY

MEREDITH WILD

PENNY

Penny lifted a glass of tea to her lips and drank it down eagerly. The liquid had gone warm over the course of her shift, but the sweetness made it tolerable, almost refreshing. Despite the springtime heat and the sweat dampening the curling tendrils around her face, she began to cool as she rested.

Down the street, the steady murmur of patrons and passersby was broken by the occasional hoot or holler. In other places of the world, the nighttime brought peace. Dark, quiet peace. In the heart of New Orleans, the night brought an excited, visceral kind of energy that few could resist once in its midst.

Drink. Skin. Colors.

Debauchery. Pleasure. Lights.

And music—the loud, soul-pounding instruments celebrating each intoxicating minute to the world.

Adding to the sensory rush of the French Quarter, the essence of truffle oil and *pommes frites* wafted off the rush of entrees being prepared in the kitchen inside, overpowering the less appetizing smells of the alley behind the restaurant.

Penny checked her thin leather watch just as the second hand marked the end of her break. She didn't relish the end of her shift, even if it meant spending a few more hours on her feet. Staying busy and making money were a welcome distraction from other realities. She stood and straightened the black apron across her hips.

Pushing through the back door, she nearly collided with Cybil.

"Sorry," the other waitress said quickly. "I was just coming to get you. That big table of suits wants another bottle of the good stuff."

Penny lifted her brows. "The Penfolds Grange?"

Cybil shrugged. "The Australian Shiraz. Two thousand eleven I think they said?"

"I don't even know if we have another bottle. They're eight hundred dollars a pop."

"I'd go hunt for it, but I'm on break. Plus the guy at the head of the table was asking for you." Cybil winked before slipping sideways past Penny and out the back door.

Penny headed for the small wine cellar, trying not to think about the dark-haired, gray-eyed man whose gaze seemed to follow her every time she came to check on their table. She'd already pegged him for the boss. Who else would be ordering bottles of wine at eight bills each? Having a party of guys in suits on a Friday night was a score. If she could keep them happy, the tips should be considerable by the time they finally ambled out for the night.

"Yes." She hissed out the whisper when she located the last bottle on the rack. With the towel that hung from her apron, she brushed off the dark curves of glass so it shimmered.

The second she turned into the dining room, the man's gaze found her and she felt a little current of satisfaction. She was that much closer to a fat tip. She quietly reassured herself that the ripple of warmth didn't have anything to do with the heated look he was giving her—a look that felt like warm silk over every inch of her skin.

God, it had been a long time since she'd allowed herself to appreciate a man, and to be appreciated in return. She pushed those thoughts to the back her of mind where they belonged and approached the table with a polite smile. She presented the wine for the man to approve before going through the performance of opening it with just the right amount of show.

"Would you like to taste it?"

His eyes were on her lips then. His were soft and wine-stained. Delectable really.

I wouldn't mind tasting you, gorgeous man.

The words bolted across her thoughts faster than she could reel them in, faster than the awakening of the rest of her senses by being in close proximity to him again.

He shook his head slightly, allowing her to redirect her concentration on pouring his glass full.

"Do you like your job?" He delivered the question with a rasp that felt almost personal.

Thankfully, Penny didn't need to lie. "I do."

"You like serving people? Like these jokers on a Friday night," he said, gesturing to the others who were animatedly involved in a conversation about someone's legendary bachelor party.

Penny smiled. "I think you've all been perfect gentlemen."

The man returned her smile with a devilish grin that did more unwelcome but exciting things to her insides.

"I can see why you like your job. You're good at it. You must make a fortune in tips."

She lifted her shoulder. "I'm not sure if fortune is the right word. But I get by."

She placed the bottle and its cork in front of him. Part of her wanted to stay there, sidled up beside him, flirting and basking in his looks. But she had other tables, and if he thought she was buttering him up for tips, she might not get one at all.

She turned to leave but was held in place by a warm hand cuffing her wrist. Anticipation and months of craving contact created an explosion in her chest as she struggled to take in her next breath. When she turned back, he was staring at her again. This time she had no doubts his thoughts had taken a dark turn and that they were directed only to her.

He dragged his thumb down until it rested in her palm. "What time do you get off work?"

She glanced around, grateful that none of the other servers seemed to notice his possessive clutch on her.

"The restaurant closes at eleven. Why?"

That was hours away. Even if he was interested in her, he and his comrades would probably find a dozen reasons to forget her after a few more rounds at the bars.

Plus, she wasn't in a position to be accepting propositions from customers. Or anyone. Not with the mess her life had become.

"Let me buy you a drink when you finish up. I can meet you at the bar across the street."

Penny knew the place and the bartender well. It was her typical last stop before the long walk home. She tucked her lower lip tightly between her teeth to keep from accepting. She'd be there anyway. Unwinding. Hiding. Waiting out the night.

What could it hurt?

"I'm Rich, by the way."

She closed her eyes and let a small chuckle leave her.

"What's so funny?"

"Nothing. Just..." She turned her hand so their palms met in a less intimate shake. "I'm Penny."

His eyes glittered as he gifted her with another sexy smile. "I'll see you at eleven then, Penny."

RICH

Rich sank into the black leather booth while his friends carried on loudly over the music. He'd stopped caring about what his colleagues had to say the second Penny had presented the first bottle of wine, offering the barest glimpse down the front of her white collared shirt.

Nothing but nude lace and flushed skin underneath. Her cheeks had been pink from hustling around the tiny restaurant too, setting off the ocean blues in her eyes. Even with her blonde locks cinched into a low chignon, he'd had an urge to tunnel his hands through the shimmery strands, angle her exactly how he wanted her, and kiss her until she moaned.

Pretty Penny. Even with all the tanned and tawdry flesh sauntering around the strip club now, all he could think about was the clock and getting back to the waitress who was as stunning as she was hungry for tips.

Rich worked with money every day. It was the currency of his life and his livelihood. Investments and returns. Past Penny's practiced smile and shaky pour, he could see plainly that she could use some more green in her life. So he'd tipped her handsomely, hoping she'd follow through with their rendezvous as well.

Joey bumped his shoulder hard into Rich's. "Man. You gonna hook up tonight or what? They told me you just pay for a private dance, and you can ask for whatever you want. Throw down enough cash, man, anything goes."

Rich brought a tumbler of sparkling water to his lips and swallowed. "Not tonight. Not here anyway."

"Argh." Joey bumped him again. A too-relaxed smile slanted across his face. His eyelids seemed to sink lower after his last blink. He wouldn't last much longer. Not with the expensive wine and hurricanes curdling in his stomach.

Rich lifted his wrist to check his watch. Wouldn't hurt to be early, just in case Penny finished up before eleven. He fished out his corporate card and dropped it on the table.

"Have all the fun you want. If I see any charges past three a.m., you're paying me back for the whole night."

Joey blinked with new alertness and nodded rapidly. "Got it. Three a.m."

"Not a minute later."

Joey nodded again. He was a good kid. Spent a little too much time crunching numbers and not enough time having a social life, but he'd earned tonight's celebration just as much as anyone. He wasn't much of a closer, but the work he did behind the scenes at the company was just as valuable. He and the rest of the team at the firm would be hating themselves come morning, but that's what this city did to people.

Rich tried to pick his excesses more carefully. He texted his driver, Giles. Ten minutes later they were pulling up to the open-air bar on the corner. Penny was there, perched on a stool in her tight black pants, laughing with the man behind the bar as he served her a glass of wine.

Rich rolled some of the tension from his shoulders. No point getting possessive over the woman. Even if she ended up in his bed tonight, she wouldn't be there long. Not wanting to dwell too much on the inevitable end of what he hoped would be a very enjoyable night, he made his way to her. He touched her shoulder gently, prompting her to spin toward him. Her eyes lit up, then softened, like she was tempering her reaction to seeing him again.

"Did you think I wouldn't come?"

She laughed nervously. "I didn't know what to think."

Rich took the seat beside her. "You must get people asking you out at the restaurant all the time."

She grinned and spun her glass by its delicate stem. "It's happened before. I can't say I've ever taken anyone up on their offer."

Rich was well aware of his assets. He'd lucked out with classic good looks and a natural charm that served him well in both social and business affairs. That he was obviously wealthy too didn't hurt. Unfortunately, it was a circumstance that complicated the things that mattered. Money changed everything.

Still, he allowed himself to enjoy a surge of pride that Penny had taken a chance on him.

He tipped his chin toward her wine. "What are you drinking?"

"I'm not sure it would suit your palette."

"You think I'm a snob."

Her pink lips thinned with a grin. "I think you have exceptional and very expensive taste."

"You're not wrong." Rich motioned to the bartender. "I'll have a glass of what she's having."

A moment later, he was clutching a twin glass of cabernet. The bar crawl with the guys had eaten up his earlier buzz. Not that he needed one, but he had a feeling Penny might after a long night on her feet.

He sniffed the deep red and took a sip, holding it on his tongue a moment before letting it slide down his throat.

"Not terrible."

She laughed. "Why, thank you. Not terrible and under ten bucks is my go-to vintage."

"Doesn't matter how much it costs. The experience is all that matters."

She held his gaze, a flash of mutual intrigue arcing between them. She was trying to figure him out. She never would.

Rich swirled the liquid in his glass. "Black currant. A little earthy. Maybe a hint of truffle."

"I think that's me. The truffle anyway."

It was Rich's turn to laugh. "Well, if I'm going to pick up a girl, I prefer if she smells like delicious French cuisine."

A flush of color worked its way up her neck and into her cheeks. "Are you trying to pick me up, then?"

"I definitely am," he answered without hesitation.

She acknowledged him with a slow, tentative nod. The decision seemed to weigh on the air between them. Rich had devoted too much of the night to torrid thoughts of her. He couldn't let her slip away.

"I don't make this a habit either, if you were wondering. I just couldn't take my eyes off you tonight."

She took a long sip of her wine and licked her lips. "I noticed."

"Did I make you uncomfortable?"

"Yes, but...not in a bad way."

He felt her giving in subtle shifts. Longer looks. Shorter breaths. She'd let her hair down since he saw her at the restaurant. Now it fell in short, messy waves and kissed her shoulders. He felt the need to tug on it. The very thought brought everything below his belt to life. Hell, he needed to know what she tasted like. How she'd sound when he made her come.

"This is going to sound a little forward, but I'd very much like to spend the night with you."

She jerked her stare up to meet his. Her eyes were wide, her breathing fast, which drew Rich's attention to her chest. He remembered her lacy bra and the supple flesh there. His palms itched to slide over her breasts.

Unable to keep from touching her any longer, he reached up, brushing his thumb softly over her full bottom lip. Everything about the small touch pumped the lust harder through his veins.

"Does that surprise you?"

"No. I just...I wasn't expecting you to come right out and say it."

"It's been a long night. And I've been thinking about you for most of it."

"Same," she uttered softly.

She was so close, but he was anxious to have her in his arms. Under him. Arms and thighs wrapped around him as he drove into her with abandon.

"Do you live nearby?"

She looked down into her glass. "No. I mean, I do. But...my place isn't good."

Rich paused, giving himself a moment to consider her discomfort on the subject.

"Family?"

"No, it's just not good." The quick answer was punctuated with a healthy swallow of wine.

Rich could sense her cooling, turning inward thanks to whatever upsetting thing was "home."

"Secrets are fine. I was just curious," he offered gently.

She answered with a soft hunch of her shoulders. "Sorry."

"Nothing to apologize for. We all have them. I even have a few of my own. So your place is no good. I'm uptown."

He should take her to a hotel. The Quarter was filled with them. Plenty of places to grab a room for a quick, sweaty romp. But now something else tugged at him. Something protective made him want to bring her home with him. And he wasn't planning to take no for an answer.

He slipped off the stool and stepped closer. He slid his hand into her hair, tilted her face, and bent to touch her lips with his. She braced her hand on the bar, the other on his chest while he took what he wanted. A kiss that was both tender and firm. Unapologetic. Determined as hell.

Somewhere in it, Rich hoped it communicated his commitment to take care of her tonight, in every way. In ways that wouldn't be gentle and nurturing but would be satisfying nonetheless. When he finally tore away, she drew in a ragged breath. Her eyes simmered with new warmth.

"Come home with me," he whispered, still holding her against him.

She drew her touch lower until it rested just above his belt. God help him, he was ready to find a dark alley to have his way with her. She had to give in to him. Now.

"Penny... I don't know what I'm going to do if you say no."

"I'm saying yes."

PENNY

Even with Rich's fingertips dragging across her scalp, his other hand creeping up her thigh in the back of the darkened car, Penny couldn't totally block out the fact that Rich's driver was a couple of feet away. His *driver*. The wordless man behind the wheel of the sleek Bentley that slid up to the curb to carry her off to the one-night stand she badly wanted.

"I'm going to rip your clothes off the second we get through the door," Rich whispered against her ear.

"Okay," she answered breathily. Sounded like a good plan.

"We just have to talk about something first."

She stifled a moan and shifted restlessly when he began sucking the sensitive skin below her ear.

"I thought we were done with talking."

"It's a small thing. Small but important to me."

The driver turned the car onto a quiet street and parked in front of a row of beautiful historic homes, which Penny only noticed when he smoothly left them alone in the vehicle, the motor still running. She refocused on Rich, whose lips she couldn't wait to get more acquainted with. His kisses were savage, like she imagined the rest of him would be once they got into bed.

Why weren't they headed that way already? Then the lust-haze cleared enough for Penny to remember where they'd left off.

"What do you need to talk to me about?"

He cupped her face, brushing his lips against hers again. "I want to pay you."

He kissed her again, and it was almost enough to distract from his words. She pulled back and stared up at him. Even in the dark, his eyes glittered. He was a beautiful man. But she couldn't let that cloud her thoughts.

"You want to what?"

"Compensate you."

"Why? Do you... Do you think that's what I was expecting?"

The mere suggestion was horrifying to her. She'd never want him to think she was with him because he had money.

"No, I never thought that about you. But it'll make me feel better if you give me tonight and let me thank you that way."

She pushed herself farther away, anxiety cooling her flaming need. "I'm not a prostitute."

"I never said you were, nor would I pass judgment on you if you were. It's just a transaction. Clear expectations."

Penny shook her head slightly, like she was shaking herself out of a dream. "Is this what that ridiculous tip was about? Did you think I'd sleep with you if you gave me enough money?"

"No, I did that because you deserved it, and you clearly need it."

Penny's jaw fell, pride and fury storming over the affections she was foolishly feeling toward this man. "I clearly *need it?* Not everyone is riding in style like you are, *Rich*, but that doesn't mean that everyone needs a helping hand."

"Don't you?"

"*No*. And it's none of your damn business anyway. I met with you because I liked you. I'm attracted to you. I wanted to just forget..." She pressed her fingertips to her forehead, refusing to expose herself any more to him. "This was obviously a mistake. I'm not the person you think I am if you think I would take money from you for sex."

"You took my money at the restaurant. What's the difference?"

"The difference is my dignity!"

"Call it what you want, then. Fuck, call it a gift. A loan that you never need to pay back. I don't care. Let's not ruin the whole night over it."

"For the record, *I* haven't ruined anything. And I'm leaving." She reached for the handle, already begrudging the fact that she'd have to dip into her tip money to get a ride home. On a Saturday night, traveling back through the throngs of traffic and tourists wouldn't be a cheap ride. The walk was too long, even if it did eat up half the night. She'd be exhausted by the time she got back, and she had another busy shift tomorrow night.

Rich tugged her back, cuffing her wrist the same way he had in the restaurant, only this time with enough force that their chests clashed. Oh, but she loved the contact even as she was growing to despise the man and his cruel words that rang with too much truth.

Of course, he was disgustingly rich in his silky suit that fit like a dream. And true enough, she was waiting tables every shift she could get to make ends meet. She had no choice. He didn't have to throw her circumstances in her face. She tried to wriggle away, but he kept her close. The pleading in his eyes was enough to get her to relent, at least for a moment.

"Penny."

He breathed affection into her name that didn't belong there. Not after moments in each other's arms. Still, she relished it, like a chocolate melting on her tongue that would disappear forever.

"Please," he said. "Stop for one second and listen to me. I have my reasons."

She rolled her eyes so hard it hurt.

"I don't think less of you," he pressed.

"Maybe you wouldn't, but I would. I have to live with myself."

He sighed and loosened his grasp on her. Disappointment flooded Penny because she knew it was the beginning of him letting go entirely. She had no idea how he could regain the ground he'd lost, but she'd desired him just as badly as he'd desired her. Their magnetic attraction had kept her thrumming with anticipation all night through the end of her shift. To lose a night with him this way was a torture all its own. She wanted him, but not like this.

"I'd ask you to hear me out, but I think we're probably past that." The resignation in his voice was a deeper cut. Almost worse than the loss of his heat and touch.

Somehow Penny was the one feeling guilty now, a turn of the tides that didn't sit any better with her than taking the man's money for a tangle in the sheets.

"I think you're right," she said, unable to meet his eyes.

"I'll have Giles take you home."

"I can walk."

"You can, but I brought you all this way. At least let me give you a lift home. I'll ride along if you want."

Penny shook her head, staring out the tinted window to the motionless driver and his wide stance on the sidewalk several feet away. Neither man made her feel unsafe, but now everything was confusing. Refusing money from Rich was suddenly lobbed into the same bucket as refusing the arguably chivalric gesture of making sure she got home safe. Penny didn't know what to think about any of it. Only that she was suddenly exhausted.

She sighed heavily and rested back against the seat. "Fine." Her voice was small and sad, and she didn't especially care if her mood added to Rich's guilt. She wasn't sure he felt any guilt at all, and she clung to that likelihood as he brushed one last kiss to her cheek and left her.

RICH

After a tumultuous sleep, a long run at daybreak, and a fairly distracted day poring over numbers that didn't need attention until Monday, Rich messaged his driver to pick him up at five thirty, which would get him to the restaurant right as they started serving for dinner. He dressed down, in jeans and a simple dark-gray shirt that molded attractively to his muscular upper body. He figured a thousand-dollar suit might not charm the woman who had turned him away last night.

There was a rather long list of women who would have chosen differently. The truth was pizza delivery could take longer than luring one of them to his doorstep for a Saturday night rendezvous, after which he would send her merrily along with an envelope of cash to seal the deal. Unfortunately, he didn't want any of them. He had eyes only for Penny, and she didn't want any part of his arrangement.

Was it strange that it wasn't normally a hard sell? He could usually explain he was a busy man who needed to sort all his affairs into tidy boxes, like cells in a spreadsheet that always balanced things out just right. And a friendly offering of cash was insurance that he wouldn't get too attached to anyone, and his bedmates knew the terms. Fucking was as cold and calculating as anything else in his life. And for the first time in a very long time, he wondered what kind of person that made him.

The problem was that as long as he had buckets of money to his name, any woman he slept with, dated, or courted would factor that into their relationship. Money was something he liked having, and he intended to keep having it, but he wasn't interested in falling in love with someone who loved his money more than they loved him.

Unfortunately, he'd reasoned a long time ago that most everyone did, and would. Even though Penny had refused his offer, he hadn't misread her circumstances. Giles had dropped her off at a run-down shotgun house in a neighborhood that wasn't exactly known for its low crime rate. She could use the help yet turned both a night of pleasure and money away.

He was determined to make things right with her, even as he doubted whether it was possible. Penny was beautiful and competent, and the way she responded to his touch made him instantly hard, but she was also headstrong. Perhaps too much for a man like Rich, who was used to challenges but also used to getting his way.

When Giles arrived, Rich settled in the back seat of the car. As much as the promise of seeing Penny again was pulling him to the restaurant, something else tugged at him.

"Take me to her place."

Giles answered with a curt nod. Several minutes later Rich was staring at the dilapidated front of the house Penny called home. He sized up the neighborhood a moment longer before walking up the steps to the door and knocking.

Several seconds passed before the door opened. A tall, unshaven man greeted Rich, squinting at the fading sunlight pouring into the otherwise dark house.

"What do you want?"

Rich paused, considering his words. "I was wondering if Penny was around."

"She's not home. What do you want?"

Rich shot the man his best disarming smile. "Sorry, I didn't catch your name. I'm Rich."

"Sandy."

"Are you her husband, or...?" Rich held his breath, hoping Sandy was buying all of Rich's ploys to get information out of him without sounding like a creep.

"Boyfriend."

Rich clenched his hands into tight fists. Secrets indeed. "Oh."

"Ex, actually," Sandy added, peering over Rich's shoulder to check out the sleek car idling nearby. "We haven't been together for a while, but we went in on this house together before we broke up."

"So...you're still living together."

"Until she can buy me out, yeah. I can't work. Asthma." Sandy gestured to the air like it was the invisible culprit.

Other than looking and smelling like he'd held down a couch for a solid week, Sandy appeared otherwise able-bodied. He certainly didn't look like someone who deserved a woman like Penny, but Rich suspected there was more to the story than her odorous ex was supplying.

"So what do you want?" Sandy pressed. The television blared loudly in the background, and he seemed like he was eager to get back to it.

Rich cleared this throat. "I had talked to her about working a private event for me. I thought I might catch her here, but I'll try the restaurant."

Sandy nodded, scraping his palm across his almost-beard. "Yeah, man. She's at Martine's almost every night. And she waits tables at the little diner down the street most weekday mornings."

Rich's gut tightened at the other man's almost bored rundown of Penny's nonstop schedule, the fruits of which no doubt went toward more than earning her half of the household expenses. Rich suspected she shouldered all of them.

Rich thanked him and headed back to the car. So that was home for Penny. A deadbeat ex-boyfriend who added nothing but financial pressure to her life every minute she wasn't hustling to keep a roof over their heads. Rich planned to get the full story eventually, but he couldn't help but hate the guy.

Knowing more about her situation didn't change Rich's plan for the night. And for Penny. If anything, he was more focused than before.

The hostess at the restaurant greeted him and led him to a small table by the window. Penny appeared moments later, her expression bright and her steps sure until she recognized her first customer of the night. She clutched the thick menu to her chest as she approached, cautiously, like there might be consequences for getting too close. Rich wasn't sure if she was worried about her willpower or his. All he knew was that one look at her had his blood singing with need again.

Her dark pants hugged the curves he'd had the pleasure of running his hands over. And her soft lips, parted and glossy pink, reminded him of the deep, languishing kisses they'd shared. The drive had been long enough to thoroughly enjoy every velvety sweep into her sweet mouth.

Rich clenched his fist and bounced his knee, a weak attempt to distract himself from the force of the visuals running rampant through his mind. They were so much better than the glower Penny was casting down on him now.

"What are you doing here?"

Her nostrils flared, which did nothing to ease his attraction for the fiery blonde.

"I'm here for dinner."

She dropped the menu in front of him and took a step back. "Very well. Cybil will be here shortly to take your order."

"She won't, because I'm good friends with the owner. And I requested you, so I'd rather not make a big deal about you refusing to serve me."

Penny seethed with an angry sigh. "Fine. What do you want?"

PENNY

Rich rattled off his choices from the menu. Penny took his order by memory, noting the expensive bottle of wine she'd have to go to the cellar to fetch for him. As she searched the racks, she cursed him. Cursed his wealth and his flagrant display of it on the heels of highlighting her financial struggles, which apparently were more obvious than she'd realized.

She shoved down the rest of her mental vitriol and brought the dusty bottle to Rich's table. She began uncorking it for him, not bothering to offer it for his appraisal first. He didn't seem to notice. In fact, he seemed distracted, pensive even, as she went through the motions of serving him. His gaze roamed over her body, then shifted to the goings-on outside the window, then back to her.

She searched for signs of gloating or some mannerism that would help her hate him more. But she came up empty. He looked different tonight.

More real to her. Like under those clothes he had a heart, and perhaps some piece of it wasn't all that happy.

The restaurant slowly filled, and the night began to darken outside. She brought Rich's courses out, impressed with his appetite but more surprised that he wasn't making a scene every time she came to him. Perhaps this interlude didn't really mean anything. Maybe he was just trying to clear the air. If he was friends with the owner, she and Rich might run into each other from time to time. No need for unnecessary tension.

"I hope you have a nice night, Rich," she said, forcing herself to give him a genuine smile. She wanted to be nice. She just wished last night had gone differently. So much differently.

He gave her a smile that didn't reach his eyes. "You too, Penny."

After a lap around her other tables, Penny saw Cybil at the beverage station.

"This is off your table." The other waitress grimaced as she handed the little tray off to Penny and disappeared back into the dining room.

Penny glanced down at the ticket. Rich's dinner was nearly a grand by the time he was done, after all the courses, the bottle of wine, plus dessert. She wasn't sure what to expect, but the line drawn through the tip field and the shiny penny sitting in the middle of the tray wasn't it.

Where she'd been willing to forgive last night's indecent proposal, she was fuming anew. She marched into the dining room only to find it empty of its worst customer. Its rude, arrogant, spiteful customer... The names kept coming as she spotted him through the windows walking to the bar across the street. She walked outside and followed him, not caring about the other tables she was neglecting.

"Excuse me."

Rich turned at the entrance to the bar, having the audacity to look surprised to see her. "Penny."

"That's right. And you can have yours back." She threw the nearly weightless coin at him. It bounced off his chest and landed with a dull ting on the sidewalk.

Blood rushed to her face, making it impossible to hide the embarrassment of her underwhelming display of anger. She felt no satisfaction, only rising frustration at this man who'd managed to work his way under her skin in such short time.

He tucked his hands into his pockets casually. "Why are you so upset?"

She answered first with a shocked laugh. "Well, I'm sure you've never had to work a hard day in your life, but in my world, when I bust my ass serving someone a four-course meal with a smile, it's customary for that person to show thanks with a gratuity. It's the decent human thing to do. *FYI.*"

Her shouting had attracted the stares of some of the bar's patrons, but Rich seemed unaffected, a circumstance that enraged Penny all the more.

"After last night, your position was very clear when it came to the exchange of money between us."

"That was different. When you walk into a restaurant wanting to be served, the expectations are clear."

"I made my expectations clear. How is that different?"

"It's sex," she hissed, lowering her voice.

"Some people say that eating French food is better than sex. I disagree, but still, I fail to understand your reasoning. You provided a stellar dining experience and you expect at least twenty percent as thanks. I have no doubt that last night would have been incredibly satisfying for both of us, but the idea of any money passing between us ruined every possibility of that."

Penny was breathing hard through her nose, struggling to form her argument, especially because Rich's seemed so sound. She hated him for it. Why did he have to come here tonight?

"So you want to tip me for sleeping with you. Is that what you're saying?"

Rich fought a smile. "I have a lot of money. I like to spread it around." His smile faded as if his thoughts had taken another turn. "And I want to help you."

He came closer. Penny moved to step away, but he caught her by the waist and cinched her tight against him.

She glared up at him. "Are you happy now? Now that you've made your point?"

He lowered his mouth to her ear. "Not really, but this is the happiest I've been all day. I can't help it if I want more. Every inch of you."

She breathed heavily, her resolve slipping the longer he held her this way. He smelled heavenly. Like expensive soap. God, he even smelled rich.

"I won't take your money."

He dragged his nose along her cheek. "Humor me. Please. It's stupid, I know, but I haven't been able to talk myself out of it yet. And I sure as hell can't leave you alone now. I'll come here every night if I have to until I break you down. Until you give in to me...because I know you want to."

She melted into him a little more. "You're infuriating."

"I'll admit that I am. Also that if you come home with me tonight, I'll make damn sure you won't regret it."

She didn't speak. She didn't know if she could. Last night had left her rattled, yet here she was in the man's arms again, ready to let him take her away with promises of bliss. And his irritating money.

He tipped her chin up to meet his stony gaze. "I'll have Giles pick you up at eleven, all right?"

She pressed her lips tightly together, refusing to give him a verbal answer. Meanwhile, inside, the part of her who was aching for a man's touch was singing to the tune of *Yes! Excellent! I'll be there!*

RICH

Tonight could be a disaster worse than the previous night. Or it could be a dream. A tiny voice—the bitter, jaded person Rich had listened to for so long—warned that the whole plan was idiotic. That he'd grown too attached to this woman he barely knew. Somehow, despite all his preoccupations with the almighty dollar, he suddenly had an urgent need to part with as much of it as would secure Penny's happiness.

And Rich couldn't believe that a single day in her house could be a happy one. He had to change that. He had to try. She might never speak to him again, let alone sleep with him again, but maybe it'd earn him more nights with her.

He pulled at least a dozen bottles off the wine rack, studying them, unable to decide which one might be perfect for tonight. Something sensible. Not pretentious. Rich mussed his hair, yanking the short strands with a groan. This woman had mixed him up in record time. That much he knew.

When he heard a knock at the door, he decided the bottle in his hand would have to do. He took it with him, too eager to see her. He opened the door, and there she stood.

After years in the investment business, Rich had learned to trust his gut. Numbers can look good, but numbers can lie. Then you're fucked, and you wish you had bet on your instincts instead.

In the five seconds between opening the door and her stepping through the doorway, Rich's gut had already announced that Penny was worth the bet. Thank goodness, because he already felt like he'd gone all in.

"I like your place," she said in a quiet voice.

"Thanks. I had it renovated a few years ago."

Her expression brightened, only to dim a second later. Rich hated that he knew why.

"What is it?"

She answered with a smile, nodding to the bottle in his hand. "What's that?"

Rich lifted it and squinted at the label. "Mollydooker Gigglepot Cabernet."

Penny laughed, and Rich felt the sound in the marrow of his bones. If her laugh was a bouquet, it'd be joy, sunshine, and probably the truffle oil he could smell off her work clothes. He didn't mind one bit.

"You laugh, but this is more than decent."

She lifted her eyebrows. "More than decent. Hmm. That sounds a little rich for my blood, but I'll give it a try."

"You'll like it," Rich muttered playfully, ushering her inside and into a sitting room where he located two large-bowled glasses. He poured the wine and decanted the rest of the bottle, even though he could feel her judging him as he did it. "How was work?" he asked, hoping to keep things light.

"It was fine. Had this really good-looking fellow seated in my section. Unfortunately, he stiffed me on a thousand-dollar check."

"What a prick," Rich said, delivering her glass to her.

He sat on the perfectly worn leather couch and coaxed Penny down beside him. She didn't shift away, which he was glad for.

"I hope that didn't ruin your whole night," he said, taking advantage of her closeness to massage up and down her calves, slipping off her shoes along the way.

She moaned breathily and melted against the leather. "No, I suppose not."

"I'm sorry for that, by the way. I plan to make it up to you."

She lifted her eyelids, casting a wordless stare toward him. He kept massaging her, which helped steer his mind off all the ways this could go wrong. He wanted so much for it to go right.

"The first girl I fell in love with broke my heart. Eighteen years old. Heart crushed into thousands of tiny, bloody shards." He took another fortifying gulp of wine and soldiered on. "My parents hated her, of course, because we were upper crust and my mom had it in her head that Kassie was after me for the wrong reasons. She was convinced I was just too lovestruck to see it. Kassie and I were together for two years in high school. Even kept things going into college until I found out she cheated on me. Then when there wasn't anything to lose, the truth all came out. My family had been right. She'd even lied about being on birth control to try to get pregnant. I guess I got pretty lucky."

A frown marred Penny's features as she listened. "That's unthinkable."

"I know. Really messed me up. I didn't want to be in relationships after that. I gave it a go a couple of times. But after Kassie, I started to see the signs. A lot of little things that would add up over time."

"Like what?"

"Like caring a lot more about what my lifestyle afforded than me." Rich peered into his wineglass and gave it a swirl. "So instead of fighting it, I decided to go with it. Make it about money no matter what. I guess it was my way of saying, 'Fuck it.'"

Penny was quiet for a long time. So long that Rich considered saying more, until she broke the silence.

"You know, love screws all of us. And we build these walls around ourselves that we think will protect us, but sometimes they end up hurting us in different ways."

Rich focused on drawing tiny circles around her ankle, absorbing her words. "I'm beginning to think you're right." He lifted his gaze to hers after a long moment. "I don't think you're like anyone I've ever met, and it wasn't fair for me to expect you to play this stupid game I've designed to keep myself from caring about anyone too much."

Penny reached out and toyed with the hem of his sleeve. "I'm glad I know why. You said you had secrets… If that was one of them, thank you for trusting me with it."

Rich tried to ignore the knot of worry that formed just then. He knew some of her secrets too. She'd either hate him for it, or they'd find a way past it. He should tell her. Just spit it out, and she could leave him high and dry if that's what he deserved.

But before he could get the words out, Penny set her wine on the table and took his glass to do the same. She straddled him and pressed her palms flat against his chest. She did nothing but look at him for a long time, like maybe she was memorizing new details about him that she could see this close.

"I like you more than I should," she finally announced.

Rich smirked. "I think you like me just the right amount, then, considering what an idiot I've been, which is all motivation to make you like me even more."

She pursed her lips with a suggestive hum.

In that moment, Rich let the worry fade into the background. He couldn't remember when he'd ever desired a woman more. As they drew close for a kiss that was searing and urgent, he swore he wouldn't let her go until she was past reason. Until she was screaming his name. By the time they were through, she'd more than like him. God help him, he wanted to make her fall in love with him too. It was a crazy thought, but one that felt oddly right.

He lifted her, keeping her legs wrapped tightly around him as he carried her up the stairs to his bedroom, where he planned to fuck her properly.

"I hope you don't have to work tomorrow," he muttered, tearing off her shirt and making quick work of her bra. This one was white lace, and underneath was the most perfect set of breasts he'd ever had the pleasure of uncovering.

"A rare day off, actually."

She giggled when he nudged her to the bed and commenced to sucking and nibbling at her sweet skin.

"Thank God. I need hours with you. And you're going to need hours to recover."

Her next laugh was breathier, nearly a whimper by the time he'd stripped them down the rest of the way. He looked her over with something like awe. His muscles twitched with the need to touch her. To invest every ounce of energy into loving her. When he thought of the place she called home, he came to her with fresh conviction flowing through him. He settled his body over hers, taking the space between her thighs.

"My pretty Penny," he whispered, nipping at her lips. "You're beautiful. So beautiful."

Her eyes fluttered closed, as if the words were hitting her harder than the blazing chemistry between them. He feathered kisses all across her skin—warm and slow and patient, even though he was feeling anything but patient.

Finally, when she was clawing at the sheets and he was dizzy from holding back, he rolled on a condom and spread her wide for him. He could hardly breathe for wanting her so badly. He slid the tip through her wetness, then higher over her clit, until she was trembling from the pleasure.

"Please," she whimpered.

"Anything for you." He meant every word as he pushed into her, a journey made smooth by her desire.

She locked her ankles behind his back, urged him farther and faster, and he was more than eager to oblige. More than happy to measure her gasps and sighs for how much she could take and what made her go wild.

When he didn't think he could go any deeper, he held her hip as leverage to punch forward harder. A throaty cry tore from her, matched by the firm clench of her core as he repeated the motion again and again. She dragged her nails down his shoulders when he tugged her hair, giving him access to suck and bite his way along her neck.

With every moan of his name on her lips, he drowned in her a little more. He was a blur of sensation, and every sensation was her.

Penny. This gorgeous, sensual creature who had managed to shine a bright light on everything that had been missing from his world for so long.

It was more than sex.

Already he knew that Penny had a place in his life. He cared for her and was driven to make her dreams come true, even if she'd hate him for it later.

As her cries went higher and body went tighter, everything in Rich flowed toward one point. Making Penny happy as long as she'd let him. Starting with the orgasm that rocked them both until they were boneless and wonderfully sated.

Rich didn't want to leave the bliss of her body, but he forced himself away to the bathroom, returning to her seconds later. She let go of a contented sigh as he nestled her close to him.

He should tell her. He didn't want to ruin this perfect moment. But what if they could have so many more?

"Rich..." She lifted her chin so it rested on his shoulder.

"What is it?"

"What are you thinking? You feel far away all of a sudden."

He smiled weakly and threaded their fingers together. "I really enjoyed that."

"Me too. If there's a heaven, I hope it's made of orgasms like that. It's never been like that for me." She sighed softly again. "Sorry. I don't want to sound like I'm getting attached. I just wanted you to know how incredible it was."

"I don't mind sounding attached. In fact, I don't mind *being* attached if that's something you might want."

She was quiet a moment. "I think I would like that." Her jaw set. "But no money."

"Right. I just owe you for the tip, that's all. No money."

She smiled and nuzzled into him again. "I think we're even. You can stiff me on the tip whenever if I can come home to this." The second the words left her, she slapped her hand over her mouth. Then she lifted herself to sit, the horror plain on her features. "I'm so sorry. That's not what I meant."

Rich followed her up, reassuring her with a tender kiss. "It *is* what you meant, and I'm not arguing."

She frowned. "No, but I'm not trying to get anything out of you. Or edge my way into your life. I have my own life. My own problems."

"Your own home."

She pressed her lips together and looked away. "Yeah."

"I stopped by." The confession felt like a brick leaving his chest, being replaced immediately by another one. Until she knew the full truth, he couldn't rest easy. Not even after the mind-blowing sex they'd just had.

She blinked up at him. "Where? My house?"

"Your house. I figured you were working, but I'll admit I crossed a line and wanted to see where you lived. Giles drove me to where he dropped you off."

The silence was filled with the sounds of Penny's soft breaths. "And?"

"And I met your good-for-nothing ex-boyfriend."

She nodded. "That's accurate."

"You're footing all the bills, aren't you?"

"He has—"

"Asthma. He told me."

"It's more than that. He has some health issues, but I think he's depressed too. And I don't think he's come to terms with us being over. He's a total dick one minute, like you'd expect a live-in ex-boyfriend to be, and then trying to joke with me and be friends the next, like maybe we can work things out if he does this hot-and-cold routine enough times. It's just the house..."

"You need a way out."

"I'll get there. It's just taking a long time. If you don't want to be with me because I still have him in my life—"

"Stop. Forget that. All of that. I've already decided I want you in my life. And I still owe you."

Penny rolled her eyes. "You don't really owe me. It was a real jerk move, I'll give you that. But I'm not going to hold it over your head."

"Let me make it up to you."

She shrugged. "Whatever."

"Promise," he said.

"Promise what?"

"Promise that this one time, you'll let me do something nice for you, no matter what it is, consequence-free. And you should have zero concern that it constitutes an unfair or indecent exchange between us since we're sleeping together now and I clearly don't want to stop."

Penny studied his features, her own expression skeptical. "This is beginning to sound like a very involved contract. Something that's maybe more your area of expertise, and I might be at a disadvantage."

"Do you trust me?"

"Not remotely."

Rich smiled. "What if I said 'please'?"

Penny let herself fall to her back with a dramatic sigh. "Fine."

"Do you promise?"

"I promise!"

He lay beside her, propping himself up with his arm so he could gaze down on her. He lost his train of thought when he realized that so many more hours needed to be spent in uninterrupted worship of her body. So many more hours...

"Rich. Spit it out. What is it?"

"Let me buy him out, immediately, on my terms, after which you can buy me out when you can, or let me be your co-investor on the property, which comes with its own advantages. And I want you to stay here until it's all sorted. If it's under renovation, you shouldn't be living in all that anyway."

Her eyes grew into wide saucers. "*Rich*."

"*Penny*." He smirked and wiggled his fingertips at her side. "Just say yes."

"You already made me promise!" She slapped him on the chest.

"Exactly right. And it's a great plan if you'll let me help with this." He bent to kiss her on the nose. "And I really, truly want to help. But I don't want to make you feel trapped into something with me. I think you've had enough of that already."

She softened in his arms. "I haven't had nearly enough of you, though."

"Are you saying you want more?"

She leaned up, catching his lips in a kiss that was soulful and promised many more to come. "I definitely want more."

* * *

Want more of Meredith Wild?

One click HARDWIRED now!

WHERE THE CURRENT TAKES YOU

EMMA SCOTT

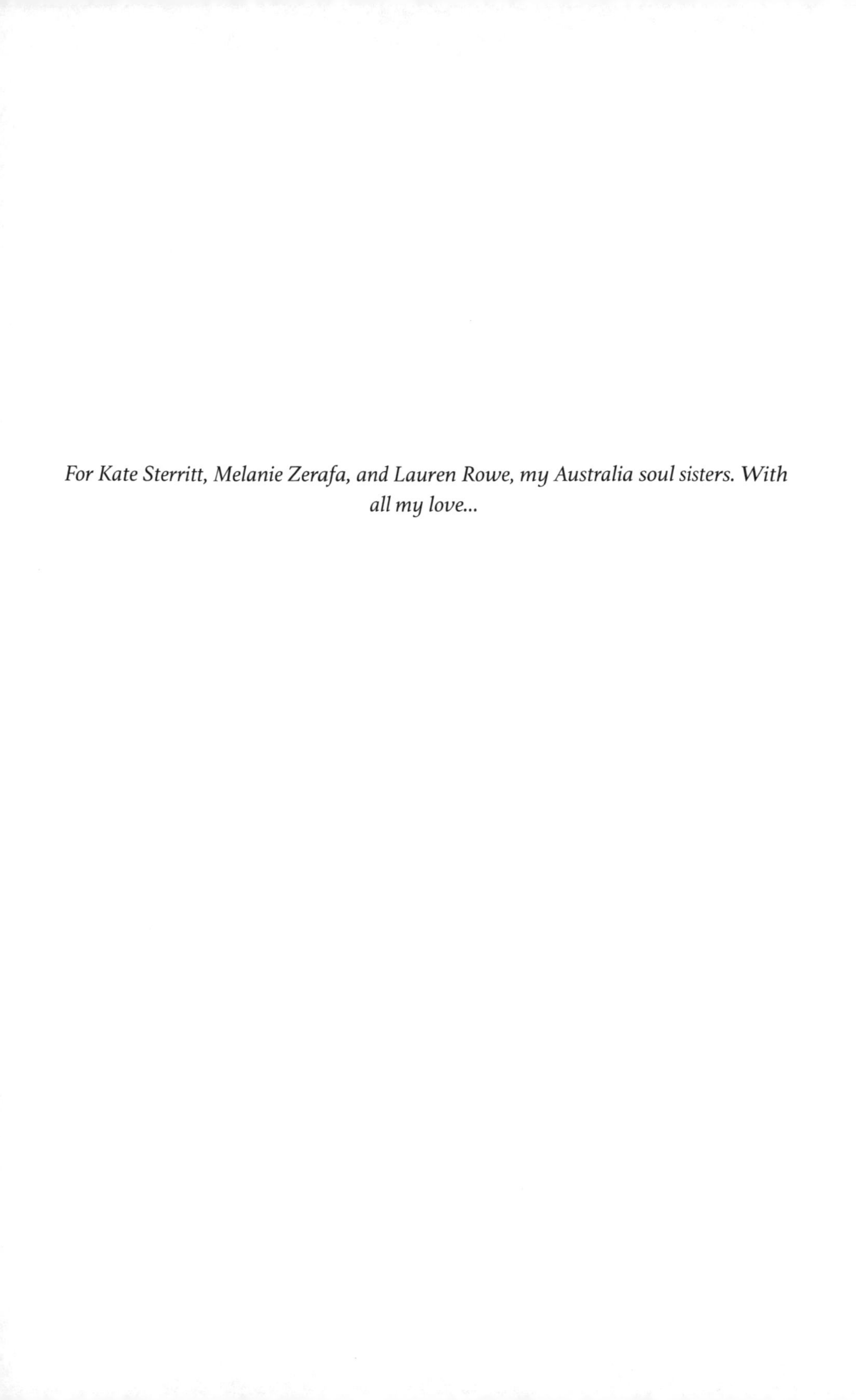

For Kate Sterritt, Melanie Zerafa, and Lauren Rowe, my Australia soul sisters. With all my love...

1

"What do you mean, you're still going?"

My best friend, Amaya, was wearing that *are you crazy?* look of hers. I'd seen it frequently during my whirlwind relationship with Phillip over the last six months. When I told her that he and I were engaged and going to elope to Vegas after five months of dating, she wore that *are you crazy?* look almost daily. She'd never liked Phillip and had told me frequently she didn't trust him.

I shouldn't have trusted him either.

"I paid for the trip," I said, throwing my brand-new white string bikini into the open luggage on my bed. "I may as well not let it go to waste."

Amaya humphed. "Of course, you paid for it. A shorter list would be what you *didn't* pay for with that bum."

"Not helping."

"Sorry, hon. It just pisses me off."

I smiled in gratitude. What Amaya lacked in subtlety, she made up for in loyalty. And she was right. Again. I'd paid for nearly everything when I was with Phillip. At only twenty-eight years old, I was one of the premier biologists at the San Diego Zoo Safari Park. I had a comfortable salary, I owned both my car and small ranch house, and dutifully contributed to my 401K. Phillip, on the other hand, had been "at a career crossroads." He'd been taking time off to "find his passion."

Amaya saw the truth before I did: he was a lazy grifter trying to score a free meal ticket. The last straw for me was when the bank called to confirm his application for a joint checking account *before* we were legally married.

Luckily, our whirlwind wedding was so rushed that the only thing I'd paid for was our honeymoon to Australia's Gold Coast. I'd put the airfare and hotel on my credit card.

Like a dope.

"Are you sure you're okay to do this? Alone?" Amaya asked, sitting in the window nook with views of Lake Hodges.

"I'm more than sure," I said, shutting the bulging suitcase. "Phillip swooped into my life, swept me off my feet, and would have swept my bank account clean had I not come to my senses a mere week before the wedding. My equilibrium is shot to hell, to put it mildly. I need to get away for a while."

"Yeah, I can see that."

"And it won't be all painful reminders of the Honeymoon That Never Was. The Park has work for me at the Brisbane Wildlife Conservation Association. I'm supposed to meet a Dr. Jonathan Somebody to discuss a partnership between our institutions in order to take in koalas displaced by the bushfires."

"Koalas are considered pests in Australia," Amaya said, examining her fingernails.

I shot her a look. "They've been burned out of their homes."

"I'm not saying they're not cute as heck..."

"No, you're right. Deceptively cute pests who sleep up to nineteen hours a day. Sound familiar?" I willed the tears back. "I don't know what I was thinking with Phillip. I'm a scientist. Scientists aren't supposed to be impulsive. But that's what drew me to him, I think. How he didn't play by the rules. I don't even know that I was *in* love with him. I was in a rut and needed a change."

"Most people would get a new haircut or redo the kitchen," Amaya said dryly. She moved to me and put her arm around my shoulders. "I'm sorry. Do what you need to do. But if you meet some hunky Australian, promise me you won't marry him."

I rolled my eyes. "I'm only going for ten days."

"Exactly."

* * *

The plane left San Diego at eight p.m. and arrived in Brisbane at six a.m., two days later. A Friday. My brain was just as confused as my heart about where and what I was doing. My boss in the bioresearch department at the Park gave me that Friday and the weekend to do what I pleased, promising the business with Dr. Jonathan Somebody—the paperwork said his name was Barnaby—wouldn't take up much time anyway.

She'd said all this with a pitying look and a pat on the arm. I'd been getting a lot of those lately. All my colleagues in the department had been shocked to hear that I, Kate Collins—the gal who put her name on her food in the communal fridge so no one would steal it—was planning to elope to Vegas with a guy I'd met six months ago. Which is partially why I did it, I think.

I'm so predictable that even my attempts to be unpredictable predictably fail.

After a quick power nap at my beachfront hotel, I changed into my bathing suit, threw a sundress over that, grabbed my towel, sunglasses, lotion and beach bag.

"I was doing just fine being boring," I muttered to myself, fluffing out my shoulder-length blonde hair. "Lonely, maybe, but at least I wasn't on the verge of having everything I'd worked so hard for stolen out from under me."

I sighed at my reflection.

"And now I'm talking to myself."

Brisbane, Australia, in January was a different kind of hot than anything we had in the States. A friend had warned me to use sunscreen nonstop, and she was right. The sun bore down on the beach with an intensity I'd never experienced before. My plans to spend the day sunbathing, reading, and taking an occasional dip in the water were thrown out the window. After spending most of my waking hours in a research facility, my skin didn't know what "sunlight" was, and in Brisbane the sun felt like it was a thousand miles closer.

Because it sort of is.

The beachfront was ringed with fun water-sport booths and tours for tourists. I saw a paddleboard rental and decided to give it a shot. I might fall off every other minute, but the water would feel nice in this heat.

I stowed my stuff in a locker, rented a board and paddle, and headed out to join a few dozen other swimmers, paddleboarders, and the surfers who were taking easy rides on the mild swells.

I paddled out beyond the waves to where the water was smooth and flat.

A dozen yards away, a cluster of surfers sat straddling their boards, talking and laughing, as I self-consciously climbed onto my board, willing myself not to wipe out in front of them.

No such luck.

I wiped out on my first two tries to get to my feet. Humiliation burned my skin hotter than the sun as I tried for a third. In my haste to get up quickly, I slipped hard, and the board shot out from under me. I fell face first into the water with a spectacular belly flop. Only the cord tethered to my ankle kept the board from shooting away from me. My paddle, on the other hand, drifted out of my reach…straight toward the small conglomeration of surfers.

Naturally. As if half the Gold Coast didn't hear me smack that water.

"Need a little help?" asked the nearest surfer in a clear, accented voice.

I brushed hair and water out of my eyes as a vision of the quintessential Australian surfer materialized in front of me. Ruggedly beautiful with a mop of shaggy blond-brown hair, scruff of a beard, tanned skin over lean muscle, and an accent that was designed to disarm unwitting tourists.

Like me.

He wore board shorts and a T-shirt made of tight-fitting wet-suit material that clung to him, highlighting the muscled contours of his body. Intelligent, laughing blue eyes the color of topaz watched me with amusement but not ridicule, making him even more handsome for his lack of derision.

I had to wipe out in front of the most beautiful man in all of Queensland.

"Uh, yeah. Thanks."

With the paddleboard still tethered to my leg, I doggy-swam toward the guy who had wheeled around on his surfboard and was using my oar to paddle toward me like a canoe.

"Quite the splat. You okay? Anything hurt?"

"Besides my pride? No."

He chuckled, flashing a smile of brilliant white teeth. "Wounded American pride is a dangerous thing."

"Very funny," I said, unable to keep from smiling back. "I'm not dangerous, I promise. The exact opposite."

"I don't know," the guy said. "Maybe I should hold on to this oar a little longer."

"Keep it forever," I said. "I'm done."

"Already? You just started."

"I have half the Pacific up my nose. I'm good."

He chuckled and his easygoing manner set me at ease too.

I folded my arms on the side of my board, swaying my legs beneath the water lazily. "I think I'll just drift out here. The water is too nice."

"Aye, bloody perfect." He jerked a thumb at his friends. "My mates and I do more yakking than catching waves at this beach."

"Are you a professional surfer?"

"We're all pros, aren't we, boys?" he said, craning around on his board.

"Oi. Lookee," said one. "Natey-boy found himself a chickadee."

"Took all of five minutes," said another.

"Slow day, mate?"

"Rack off," the guy said, laughing as he turned back to me. His smile slipped, and he coughed at my arched brow. "They're just messing."

"Right," I said. "Natey?"

"I'm Nate, but we Aussies add an *ee* sound whenever possible. It's part of our charm. Tell me your name, and I'll give you the Aussie translation."

I bit back a smile. "Kate."

"Too easy, *Katy*," he said and ran a hand through his hair in a thoroughly distracting manner.

"I never liked Katy," I said.

"Kate it is, then. Kate and Nate. We rhyme." His smile somehow grew even more brilliant. My heart fluttered as he offered me his hand. "Good to meet ya, Kate."

I put my pale hand in his tanned one that was lightly roughened, likely from spending all day in the surf. He gave it a warm squeeze, his eyes never leaving mine but regarding me with a question. *What do we do now, Kate?*

My sensible self (that had apparently taken a vacation around Phillip) answered: *Not get involved with beautiful men who live across the Pacific from you and spend all day lounging on surfboards.*

"I'll take that paddle now," I said, withdrawing my hand. "I'll lose my deposit if I don't bring it back in one piece."

"Going in already?"

"Don't want to press my luck. There are sharks out here."

"Stingers are more likely to get you than a shark."

My eyes widened, and under the water, I drew my knees up to the board I was hanging on.

"You here on holiday?"

"Yes and no," I said slowly.

"What's that mean?"

The last thing I wanted was to talk to this beautiful man about my broken engagement. I'd already made a fool of myself on the paddleboard, thanks very much.

"A little bit of work, a little bit of vacation. What about you? Are you from Brisbane?"

"Aye. Native. Locally sourced, beer-fed, and hormone-free."

Goddamn it, he's adorable.

"Well, it was nice to meet you, Nate, but I should get back."

"Hold on, fancy some brekkie?"

"Some what?"

"Australian for breakfast." He glanced at his impressive—and expensive-looking—all-weather watch strapped to one tanned wrist. "It's only ten. And even so, there's never a bad time for brekkie."

He held that question in his clear blue eyes, and even the sensible side of me started to cave.

Stay strong! Think of Phillip. Remember him? The guy who convinced you to marry him after six months?

Having breakfast wasn't quite in the same league as eloping to Vegas, but I couldn't take any chances. Nate was too beautiful, and I was too jet-lagged to think clearly.

"I don't think so," I said slowly. "But thank you for the offer."

Nate's smile slipped, and genuine-looking disappointment flashed over his face before it righted itself back to his stunning smile. "Nice to meet you, Kate."

"You too, Nate."

We rhyme...

I took the paddle from his hand with no small amount of disappointment myself and headed back to shore. Nate returned to his mates. The round of boos and good-natured joshing they gave him helped erase the idea that I was making a mistake. Nate had failed in picking me up, and given his friends' reaction, that didn't happen often.

He's a player. Same type of guy, different continent. Moving on...

* * *

I returned the rented paddleboard equipment and then lay out on the beach to dry off. It took all of fifteen minutes for my suit to lose its dampness. Despite layers of sunscreen, my skin felt on the verge of burning. Not to mention, my stomach was growling for "brekkie" after all.

I found a cute pancake place that smelled of syrup and fresh-brewed coffee with surfing memorabilia on every wall.

"Just yourself, love?" the hostess asked.

I started to nod when my eye caught Nate and three of his friends at a nearby table.

Shit. Shit. Shit.

I started to back out of the restaurant when he saw me. How his face lit up as our eyes met made my stupid heart skip a beat. He quickly down-shifted to satisfied amusement, raising a questioning eyebrow.

The hostess cleared her throat. "Miss?"

"Uh, right. One."

To back out now would be too obvious. My face flamed red and then redder as the hostess led me to a small two-person table only a few feet down from Nate's group. He gave me a knowing grin as I passed him. I started to scowl but rolled my eyes and laughed instead.

Damn him.

I sat and quickly lifted the menu to barricade myself from the sight of Nate dressed in board shorts and a T-shirt, his hair now a thick, unruly mop on his head—brown streaked with gold. A few seconds later, I heard the scrape of a chair, and my small, rickety table tilted.

I lowered my menu to see Nate sitting across from me, that ridiculously beautiful face a foot from mine.

"Can I help you?"

"You're stalking me," he stated.

"I'm not..."

"Clearly, you are. Either that, or you're rubbing my brekkie invite in my face." He frowned. "Should I be flattered or devastated?"

"The second one. I'm not stalking you."

"What a pisser."

"It's the opposite, actually. You're stalking me."

"Me?" He batted his eyes innocently. "How do you reckon? I was here first."

"True. But if you looked more like Harvey Weinstein and less like a model straight out of a surfing magazine, inviting yourself to my table would seem a lot less charming."

"Point taken."

Nate stood up, pushed in the chair, took a few steps backward, then approached again.

"Miss Kate. May I join you?" He indicated the chair he'd just vacated.

"Won't your friends miss you?"

"Desperately."

I cocked my head. "How much money is riding on you succeeding in picking me up? Ten bucks? Or is it *buckies* in Australian?"

"That's not a word." Nate's expression turned serious. "And there's no wager. I just...want to talk to you."

"Why?"

"If you let me sit, I'll explain," he said. "You got me hanging in the wind out here, Kate."

I sighed but it came out more like a laugh. "Sit."

"Much obliged." Nate sat and a fresh whiff of sunscreen, ocean water, and salt wafted to me pleasantly. His skin was tanned like caramel, remnants of the ocean still clinging to him.

That's what he is. Salty-sweet. I'll bet he tastes like salted caramel too...

The thought sent a flush of heat up my cheeks.

Get a grip, woman...

"So," I said, clearing my throat. "Explain yourself. I'm not the kind of girl who gets hit on by random men very often."

"Random?" Nate clutched his heart as if I'd stabbed him. "I'm merely random, am I? And here I thought I was a real bloke, flesh and blood."

"You know what I mean."

"No, I really don't." His clear blue eyes scanned my expression. "I find it hard to believe you're not approached on the regular." He waved his hands at my arched brow. "Yes, I'm aware that literally everything I've said so far sounds like a pickup, but there's something about you, Kate." He shrugged. "I just...want to keep being near you."

A blush crept up my cheeks against my will.

"Crikey, that sounded even worse," Nate said. He started to push his chair back. "I'll leave you be, love."

"Wait," I said, the word bursting out of my mouth before I could stop it.

What are you doing? Let him go. You don't need...whatever it is he's offering. A roll in the sack? You're leaving the continent in ten days. This is stupid...

Nate froze and his eyebrows went up expectantly. "Yes...?"

"I don't know what I was going to say."

He cocked his head, grinning. "You were going to invite me to stay and have brekkie. Because I look like a model who stepped out of a surfing magazine."

"Don't use that against me. I was trying to make a very serious point about misogyny."

"Uh-huh. By commenting on my looks. Seems legit." Mischief glinted in his eyes.

The waitress came by to take our order, saving me from having to respond.

"Short stack of pancakes and coffee, please," I said.

She turned to Nate. "For you, love?"

"My food's back there." He jerked a thumb to his table of friends, one of whom held Nate's plate of blueberry pancakes aloft and motioned his hand around it like a QVC model.

The waitress glanced between Nate and me, a knowing smirk on her face.

"I'll just put it in the warmer for you until her food comes?" she asked Nate.

"Perfect."

I hid my face in my hands. "God, now the entire restaurant is in on this pickup."

"Will you stop calling it that?" Nate said and leaned back in his chair, arm outstretched, hand reaching toward his table. One of his friends obliged and handed him his glass of orange juice. "I told you," he said, settling back into his chair. "I'm not picking you up. We're just talking."

Because he wants to be near me.

"What are we talking about? Our jobs? Allergies? Favorite color...?"

"Boring. How about this: We ask each other three questions, and if you like the answers, by the time your food arrives, we have breakfast together."

"Okay," I said. "What kind of questions, if not about what we do or what we like?"

"I'm talking about real questions that get to the heart of who we are as people."

"Sounds deep."

"I'm nothing if not deep, and I have only until your pancakes are ready." Nate held up his hands. "Go ahead. Ask me anything."

"No, you start. Give me an idea of the parameters here."

"Okay, Miss Kate. If you had one billion dollars to give to charity—but only one charity— which would it be?"

"That's easy," I said. "Whatever charity is doing the most to combat climate change."

Nate's eyes widened slightly, and he offered me his hand for a high five. "I cannot think of a more perfect answer."

"You care about climate change?" I asked, feeling as if the entire restaurant were watching as I high-fived him.

"Definitely. Take the Great Barrier Reef, for instance," Nate said. "Up the road from us a bit? It's dying. It's fucking dying, and it breaks my goddamn heart."

I felt my own heart softening at his words. "Okay," I said after a short silence. "My turn. What's your favorite book?"

"That's not an enticing and unique question, Miss Kate," Nate said.

"I beg to differ," I said. "It's a loaded question."

"Oh, I see. If I say *none at all,* then you know I'm a bonehead who doesn't read and that's a black mark against me, yes?"

I shrugged and smiled. "Answer and find out."

"Well, it just so happens I do read, and my favorite book is *The Giving Tree* by your bloke, Shel Silverstein."

I frowned. "The kids' book?"

"Some of the best literature out there is for kids," Nate said. "Because kids are still willing to learn and haven't yet become jaded arseholes."

"Okay, but that's your favorite? Even now?"

He took a sip of his juice. "There are millions of amazing books out there. That one punched me in the gut the hardest." He grinned mischievously. "Did that dispel your idea that I'm a blockhead surfer with more salt water between his ears than brains?"

"I never thought that at all."

"Lying liars who lie..."

I laughed. "I am not."

"And yet you boldly referred to me as someone who might walk off a surfer magazine."

I rolled my eyes. "You can't get over that, can you? Have you considered that I said that because when I met you, you were—in actual fact—sitting on a *surfboard?*"

"Touché. Okay, my turn. Question number two. Why are you here alone?"

I toyed with my water glass. "That's a very personal question."

Nate spread his arms wide as if to encompass the entire restaurant and beyond. "Why are we here if not to get personal? Life is short—too short—to have pointless, boring chitchat instead of a real conversation."

I guessed Philip hadn't killed the impulsive yearning to break free of the confines of my own rules, because I heard myself say, "This was supposed to be my honeymoon."

Nate reacted as though I had tossed cold water in his face. He blew air out of his mouth, and his eyes widened. "Crikey, now that's some real shit, isn't it?"

The waitress dropped off my coffee, and I busied myself with cream and sugar. "As real as it gets."

"Bloody hell, what happened?"

"Is that your question number three?"

Nick wrestled with himself for a minute and then said finally, "Yes. I have to know what kind of bonehead does that to a woman like you."

"You mean a woman who is gullible and silly? I met a handsome, charming, lazy man who swept me off my feet, tried to break into my checking account, and convinced me we should elope to Vegas."

Nate narrowed his eyes. "What an arsehole."

"Indeed," I said. "And now that I've completely humiliated myself in front of a virtual stranger, I'll ask my second question. Why did you really come and sit down at my table?"

"You want the truth?"

"That's the rules, isn't it? Your rules?"

"Aye. All right, I'll tell you. I watched you try to paddleboard and fail. I watched you get up again and again. You kept trying. There was something in your expression that I liked. Here is this beautiful woman"—he held up his hand—"don't argue with me. Here's this beautiful woman with a little bit of sadness and a whole lot of determination on her face, and when your oar skimmed straight to me after that spectacular wipeout, I felt it was like an arrow pointing at me."

"Cupid's arrow?" I said dryly, trying not to show how much his words touched me.

"Let's not get carried away; we just met," he said with that charming grin of his. "I don't believe things happen coincidentally, is my point."

"Okay, well, you're out of questions, but I have one more."

"I'm ready."

I sucked in a breath. "What do you see happening next? Between us?"

Nate's face lit up, and he was so devastatingly handsome, he was nearly blinding.

"This is my favorite question, and I'm so glad you asked. How much holiday do you have left?"

"This weekend only. I work on Monday. I arranged to turn my Honeymoon from Hell into a work thing so I wouldn't feel so pathetic." I arched a brow at him. "How's that for honesty?"

"Lovely," Nate said. "And I have to work Monday too. But let's not talk about work. Not for a minute. We have two days. Let's have them—really have them—and on Monday we'll go back to being responsible, contributing members of the human race."

"What do you mean, *we* have two days?"

Nate rubbed the scruff on his chin thoughtfully. "I mean, we only have the rest of today, Saturday, and Sunday, so we'd best make the most of them." He started ticking items off on his fingers. "First thing, we fly to Cairns, to the Great Barrier Reef. I know, I know, airplane flight is fucking horrible for the environment, but have you ever been?"

"No, but—"

"Then you have to go before there's nothing left of it. I would drive us there, but it's at least twenty hours to the good parts and we don't have that kind of time. So we fly to Cairns, we snorkel the Great Barrier Reef, we have dinner, and after that...?" He shrugged. "We'll see."

"You want me to fly with you up to Cairns?"

"Aye. That's what I want you to do."

"Why on earth would I do that?"

"Well, for starters, you have a history of agreeing to fly off to random destinations with men when they ask..."

I threw my napkin at him. "Oh, hush up."

He laughed but it faded fast. "I just feel like you came all this way under really crappy pretenses, so you may as well make something beautiful out of it. See the Great Barrier Reef. Hell, I don't have to go with you if that makes you feel awkward. But you should go."

I narrowed my eyes. "Are you using reverse psychology on me? Where the lighter the touch you use, the more I trust you?"

"A tad paranoid, aren't we?"

"I have a good reason to be."

"This is true." He put a hand over his heart and raised the other. "I swear on the life of the Queen, I have only the noblest and purest of intentions." He shot me a rakish grin that I bet he was famous for. "Unless you would prefer me to be slightly *less* than pure, in which case, I'm willing to make adjustments."

I laughed and felt lighter than I had in weeks. Lighter even than when I was with Philip at our most blissful. I realized that kind of happiness felt forced. Like I was trying to make something happen. Being with Nate was so damn easy. And the part of me that wanted to live in this world that I was fighting so hard to preserve had me nodding my head.

* * *

Saturday morning, I checked out of my hotel and met Nate, Last Name Unknown, at the Brisbane Airport. Amaya had sent me a check-in text, and I told her I was going to the Great Barrier Reef to do some snorkeling. I left my impromptu travel companion out of the conversation.

My travel companion... God. Nate showed up at the airport in ripped jeans, a loose white button-down linen shirt, and a shark-tooth necklace—white against his tanned skin around his neck. I tore my gaze away from the lean, muscular perfection of his body and looked up to see him drinking me in, in my yellow sundress. He jerked his eyes to mine, and we both smiled awkwardly.

"You made it," he said. "Good on ya. I was afraid you'd change your mind."

I grinned. "Come to my senses, you mean?"

He laughed. "I'm just glad you're here, whatever mental contortions you had to do to spend the weekend with a bloke like me."

"I'm not spending the weekend with you," I said. "We're going to be on the same plane, we're going to stay in the same hotel, separate rooms, and we might share a dinner table. That's all."

"Plane and dinner, for certain. Let's put the 'separate rooms' on the maybe list."

I rolled my eyes. "Not going to happen."

His grin never faltered. "If you insist. I'm glad you decided to come, anyway. The Reef shouldn't be missed, and the fact that it's slipping away..." He shook his head, and his bright blue eyes were momentarily shadowed. Then he brushed it off and flashed me one of his megawatt smiles. "Shall we?"

We took the short, two-hour flight, chatting comfortably the entire time. Aside from his ridiculous sex appeal, Nate exuded comfort. Safety. For all his Aussie surfer-dude looks and charm, he was a genuine person who cared about the natural world. He was out in it, he told me, every chance he got—seeing Ayers Rock, hiking, sailing, snorkeling, while I felt closeted in a lab back in San Diego.

In Cairns, we checked into a beachside hotel, to separate rooms with plans to meet up at the Pier at midmorning.

We have one full day together. Make it count.

I don't know where the thought came from or what it meant, but I steadfastly ignored it. It was crazy enough that I was on this side trip, given why I was in Australia in the first place.

If that's not getting back up on the horse, I don't know what is.

As I unpacked in my room, I took mental inventory of my emotions and realized what was worse than Philip trying to drain my money was how I'd been willing to bind my life to a man I didn't love. I'd expected I'd spend this Australia trip nursing a broken heart, and instead, I just felt ashamed for being so gullible. It was as if my heart had decided it wanted nothing more to do with the Phillip mess and was now running happily alongside Nate, tugging me behind.

* * *

The Pier was a huge shopping complex and marina, bustling with tourists in the brilliant January sun. Nate met me at a chartered tours shop, and we rented snorkeling gear. As we waited on the front cushions of our ship for it to fill with passengers and depart, Nate slipped off his T-shirt and began putting sunscreen on his chest and shoulders.

He's doing that on purpose, I thought, my gaze trailing over the tight cut of his abs, the smooth planes of his chest, and the rounded curves of his shoulder muscles.

"Little help?" he said, offering the bottle to me. "We'll be on our stomachs in the water." He batted his eyes innocently. "You don't want me to get burned, do you?"

I rolled my eyes and laughed, trying for nonchalant, when in fact my hands were itching to touch him. I took the sunscreen—a reef-safe brand that wouldn't poison the coral—and smeared it over his broad back. His skin was as warm and soft as I imagined, with powerful muscles lurking beneath.

"Now I do you," he said.

I fumbled and nearly dropped the bottle. Nate laughed.

"Let me rephrase: I will now apply sunscreen to your epidermis. It's not a come-on, I swear. The sun out here is not to be messed with."

I already knew that to be true, and besides, now my body was tingling with eager anticipation at the idea of *his* hands on *me.*

"Thanks," I said and removed my tank to reveal my white bikini top. I lifted my hair off my neck and held it up as Nate's lightly calloused hand roamed between my shoulder blades, then up over my shoulders and down the backs of my arms. Despite the heat, my skin broke out in gooseflesh as my mind imagined his hands on other parts of me, all over me...

"Thanks," I said and let my hair drop.

I turned to see Nate quickly conceal an expression of unmistakable want, and my heart thudded in answer.

The boat skimmed the blue waters that were the same color as his eyes, the wind rippled through his brown-streaked-with-gold hair, and I found myself having to tear my gaze away from him again and again. The beauty of the topaz waters and the curve of the coastline were in constant competition with this man beside me.

As the captain of the boat circled to find the right spot for snorkeling, Nate glanced at his expensive watch, and I was reminded of the fact that he'd insisted on funding the snorkeling trip (I'd paid for my own flight and hotel room, though Nate had tried his best to cover both). He refused to talk about work or our jobs, and I had to wonder if he wasn't just a surfer but a professional surfer. Possibly famous.

I put it out of my mind, because what difference did it make? After Sunday, I wasn't going to see him again.

Right?

"Are you ready?" Nate asked, again flashing me one of those million-dollar smiles.

"I think so." I sat on the edge of the ship's rail with my flippers on and set my mask on the top of my head. The strap was loose, and the mask kept sliding.

"Let me." Nate reached his hands toward either side of my face, and for a split second, I wondered if he was going to kiss me. His eyes met mine and then dropped to my mouth, my lips slightly parted.

"Someone should give me a medal," he said, his voice low under the hum of the boat engine and the chitchat of the other passengers.

"For?" I breathed.

His hands moved to cup my cheeks. "For *not* kissing you in this moment." He cocked his head, his eyes searching. "Would it be so terrible if I did?"

I knew it would probably be the exact opposite of terrible, but one of the ship's crew announced it was time to swim, sparing me having to answer.

"To be continued," Nate said, his rakish grin returning.

We both put our masks over our eyes and tipped backward into the water that was lukewarm, like a cooling bath.

I was transported into an entirely new world. Aside from my own breath moving through the tube, there was no sound. Only a light blue topaz infusion of water and a riot of color from the corals and anemones. And the fish. Thousands of stunning fish in shades that took my breath away. As if Mother Nature decided to use every color in her palette for these creatures. They swarmed around Nate and me, or glided away, tilting long, vertical bodies through the water, or darting horizontally like little arrows.

I felt Nate's fingers on my hand to draw my attention to a beautiful clump of black sea urchins. Orange fish darted between their spines.

A few moments later, a stingray shuffled under the silty sand beneath me, and it was my turn to grab Nate's hand to show him...and I held on.

He didn't let go.

We swam like that, hand in hand, visitors to this place. I felt a strange sense of gratitude to the fish around us for allowing me into this world, and to Nate for bringing me here in the first place.

We were both quiet on the boat ride back, exchanging small smiles now and then. When we disembarked, Nate found some of his old humor and jostled my elbow with his.

"Well? Was it worth the price of admission? Having to hang out with my ugly mug?"

"It was perfect. Thank you." Without letting myself think too hard, I leaned over and kissed his cheek.

Nate's voice was low and deep. "You're welcome, Kate."

I said nothing but savored the salty-sweet taste of him that lingered on my lips.

After some sightseeing along the beachfront, we returned to our separate rooms in the hotel. I showered and changed into a white sundress and clasped a white shell bracelet on my wrist. My blow-dried blonde hair settled rather prettily around my shoulders, I thought.

"Pretty" was how most people would describe me. I wasn't a great beauty. My nose turned up a little while my chin retreated slightly. My large blue eyes were my best feature, and while I wasn't trying to be super hard on myself, a guy like Nate could have his pick of any woman he looked twice at.

Why me?

An ugly thought turned over in my mind.

Because you won't sleep with him. He likes a challenge.

But that thought didn't match what I knew of him. Or rather, what I felt from him. But how could I trust my feelings when they'd nearly led me to disaster?

Nate met me in the lobby for our dinner at a vegetarian restaurant a short walk from the hotel. He wore pants, not jeans, and a silk version of his loose white button-down shirt that was open at the collar and rolled up at the sleeves. His hair was still wet from the shower, and the smile that lit up his face when he saw me eclipsed his handsomeness. Or maybe added to it.

Either way, I was in big trouble.

"You look stunning," he said. "Am I allowed to say that? Now that you're not wearing a bathing suit, I feel I should be able to make at least one comment about how beautiful you are."

"Thank you, Nate," I said. "You look very nice too."

"Nice," he said, tucking his hands into the front pockets of his pants as we strolled out onto the street. "*Nice* is the word you would use to describe cozy slippers or an afternoon reading to Grandma."

"I've already called you a surfer model, and you got a swelled head," I said. "Figured I better play it safe."

"So you're hiding your true opinions about my astonishing good looks," he said. "I get it. I'm a lot to take."

I laughed and all my jumbled thoughts and feelings fell into a comfortable place. He was beautiful, and he thought I was beautiful.

We rhyme...

We ate a delicious vegetarian dinner on a balcony overlooking the ocean, a candle in a small cup glowing on the table between us as twilight fell.

"That's another thing we have in common," Nate said, gesturing his fork at my plate of charred onions, walnuts, and ricotta under a balsamic honey glaze. "No meat."

"Well, when you work with animals as much as I do—"

"Hold up, we're not talking about our work, remember? Strictly holiday. Although now I'm intrigued. You work with animals?"

"Not directly. I work animal-adjacent," I said, thinking of Safari Park, which stretched out around my offices like a mini-African savannah.

Nate shook his head, spearing a green bean on his fork. "It all just makes so much sense."

"What does?"

"Why that oar of yours went straight for me."

"Okay, look," I said, setting my own fork down. "Before we get any further with this dinner or this evening or this whatever it is, we have to talk about parameters."

"Parameters," Nate said with a frown. "That's a very unsexy word."

"I live in the States; you live in Australia. Thousands of miles away. After tomorrow, I have to go to work, you have to go to your job, whatever that may be. Even if we hung out after the workday, I'm not here long enough. And despite the fact that you are very attractive and sexy—"

"True on both counts..."

"I'm not in the right mental place to have an affair, given my situation."

"Pardon my forwardness, but I think being jilted by a scumbag puts you in the exact right position to have an affair," Nate said, grinning. "However," he added, "I get it. You never did strike me as a one-night-stand kind of gal."

I frowned. "So why bring me here?"

He shrugged. "Don't know. Felt like the right thing to do."

"I don't—"

"Look," Nate said, leaning forward. "This might sound crazy, but I spend a lot of time in the ocean, the Reef, the Outback when I can get there, and in the rainforests of Bali every chance I get. And what I've learned is that there are harmonies and rhythms to life. Currents and tides. Humans add all kinds of shit to everything, always trying to make things be the way they want them to be, instead of just accepting them for how they are. Including their own feelings. Nature just *is*. And that's how I flow, too. I listen to my heart, my gut... I don't let my mind fill up with useless, bullshit noise."

"That sounds...really good," I said. "I feel like I overthink everything."

Except with Phillip, when it counted.

"It's quiet," Nate said. "And in the quiet, I listen. And something told me to ask you here." He shrugged and forked another bean. "Whatever happens or doesn't happen, I'm happy now."

"Me too," I said, the words slipping out before I could grab them back.

Nate smiled. "Then maybe that was the entire point."

* * *

On Sunday, we rode in a cab to the airport for our flight back to Brisbane. On the plane, our conversation felt a little stiff with our impending separation.

Ages-old society expectations had me feeling guilty I hadn't slept with Nate in Cairns. I had to remind myself I didn't owe him anything, never promised him anything. That was one lesson Phillip had taught me: there shouldn't be a price for affection or love. Nate had taken me to the Great Barrier Reef, but I could've gone there on my own. Even so, I felt like I was letting something precious slip through my fingers with every passing second.

What am I supposed to do? In a week, I'll be thousands of miles away.

The plane touched down in Brisbane, and Nate frowned, looking unsettled.

"Airplane takeoffs and landings generate the most CO_2," he said. "This just might be the last flight I'll ever take."

Translation: He's not coming to visit you in the States.

I hardened my heart that wanted to stay as close to Nate as it could. And it was impossible.

Neither one of us had packed much for Cairns; we skipped the baggage claim and went out to the cabstands. To go our separate ways.

"Thank you, Nate," I said. "It was a beautiful trip, and I'm glad I went."

"Me too," he said, his eyes watching me with longing.

"And it was very nice to meet you."

I offered my hand, and he looked at it with a perplexed frown. He took my outstretched hand and pulled me to him. Our lips were inches apart, our eyes locked. I was sure he could feel my heart pounding against his.

"Something told me I can kiss you right now," he said, his voice low and gravelly.

Before I could stop him, he kissed me. And I realized in that same instant, I didn't want to stop him. The last thing in the world I wanted was to stop as Nate's mouth captured mine in every way—light brushes and deeper sucking pulls, like an ocean tide receding from the shore and then coming back stronger. Taking more and more of me into him with every touch.

I was right, a voice whispered in my mind as we kissed. *He tastes like salted caramel.*

The salt of the ocean and the sweetness that was inherent in him filled my senses along with the bittersweet realization that I was exactly right to have not slept with him. If I could sink this deeply into him with one kiss, what would one night have done to me? Or two? Or ten? Because this kiss made me want more. More of him, more talks, more of his cute slang, his humor and his beautiful accent, and it was impossible.

Wasn't it?

Nate didn't seem to think so. He broke away and held my face in his hands, his eyes studying mine.

"Goodbye, Nate," I whispered.

A confident, soft smile bloomed over his lips as he let me go and began to walk away. "We'll see."

* * *

The following morning, Monday, I dressed in my lightest possible business attire for the summer heat—a white linen skirt and silky short-sleeved blouse in blue—and made my way to the Brisbane Wildlife Conservation Association. My meeting with Dr. Jonathan Barnaby and his team was to be held in a small building downtown—a satellite office for their big complex that was a little farther west of Brisbane.

Reception directed me to a conference room on the second floor. There, a half dozen people in far more casual attire than me were chatting, drinking coffee, and passing around a plate of croissants.

Standing among them, looking ridiculously beautiful in a loose button-down shirt, slacks, and shark-tooth necklace was Nate.

We locked eyes from across the room, and again that smile broke out over his features to see me.

A thought streaked across my stuttering heart: *A second chance...*

He left his colleagues in mid-conversation to meet me at the door. In those few seconds, my mind and pulse raced. This wasn't supposed to happen. I'd spent all last night at the hotel trying to reconcile myself to the fact I was never going to see him again. And now he had the audacity to be standing right in front of me, turning my insides into tangled knots of confusion.

And lust. Don't forget that.

I fumed. "What are you doing here?" I asked before he could say a word.

He stopped at my angry tone, and his smile faltered for a second before he regained his composure. "What am I doing here? I work here."

"Who...who are you?"

He rocked back on his heels. "Holiday is over, isn't it? Suppose it's time to introduce you to my professional self." He stuck out his hand. "Dr. Jonathan Barnaby, at your service."

I blinked. "Jonathan? You said your name was Nate."

"It is. Nate is short for Jonathan."

"*Since when*?"

"Jo*nathan*, Nathan, Nate." He gave me an amused look. "You're one to talk. My paperwork said I was meeting a Dr. *Katherine* Collins."

"Kate is the universally acknowledged diminutive of Katherine."

"I think the Kathy's of the world would beg to differ," Nate said with that maddening twinkle sparking in his eyes.

"Stop teasing. You're telling me you had no idea?"

"None. I swear. Though I had a feeling..."

I crossed my arms. "You had a feeling."

"Yes. When you said you worked with animals. I was tempted to peek at your driver's license when you went to the restroom at dinner but decided to leave it up to fate. And I was right."

"This isn't fate and it's not funny. I have a presentation to give and now I'm completely..."

"Flustered? Flabbergasted?" He shot me a wink. "Turned on?"

I punched him lightly in the bicep. "This is all your fault."

"Mine? How do you reckon?"

"Because who flies to Cairns and never tells the person their real name?" I said in a hissing whisper.

Nate/Jonathan looked perplexed. "You, for one. You seemed fine with relative anonymity, especially considering how the last bloke you hooked up with tried to take you for all you're worth."

Crap.

I hated that he was right. Keeping things as separate as possible with a total stranger, paying for everything myself, and never sharing anything of my identity had felt like a safer option. Now, I just felt foolish.

"Come on," Nate said. "Let's get this presentation over with and then let me take you to dinner."

"No."

"Why not?"

"You know perfectly well why not." I stiffened and mustered the will to tear my gaze away from his handsome face and wrench my mind away from the fact that six more days—five more *nights*—with Nate just fell into my lap. "This is just...business."

"Is it?" Nate mused. "Somehow, I doubt that."

"What is it then? More of your fate nonsense?"

"Why are you pissed?" Nate asked, lowering his voice. "I'm happy to see you. I thought you'd be happy t—"

"We'll talk about this later," I said, feeling the eyes of the others on us.

"Right. Over dinner."

"*No.*"

"Brekkie?"

He was wearing that irresistible smile that made me want to both smack him and kiss him.

Somehow, I made it through the presentation with my dignity intact. I switched into scientist mode and explained to the men and women assembled how the Brisbane WA and the Safari Park at the San Diego Zoo could begin a partnership for the care of koala bears displaced by the bushfires, their eucalyptus groves turned to ash. The severity of the situation and gravity of the damage done made it easier to focus, and Nate, I was happy to see, took it just as seriously.

And, listening to him talk, I had to add *incredibly intelligent* to the growing list of things that made him irresistible.

After the meeting adjourned, the others started to file out, but Nate called after me.

"Dr. Collins? Can I have a word?"

I gritted my teeth and shot him a glare. Once the others were gone, his expression softened. "Kate..." he said.

"Please don't."

"You don't even know what I'm going to say."

"Whatever it is, it'll be something good or sweet or sexy, and it's just going to make things harder."

He moved around the conference table to stand in front of me. "You know something's happening here, right? You know there is a reason the universe or fate or whatever keeps throwing us together."

"Yes, it's called coincidence."

"There's no such thing," Nate said, and the power of the conviction in his voice stirred my blood.

"What are we supposed to do?" I asked. "I'm only here for one more week, and then I go back to San Diego. Are you going to visit me?" I put my hands on my hips. "I think a steamer ship from Brisbane to San Diego will only take about *four months*. Or am I supposed to move here? So we can...do what? I've only known you for three days."

"I don't know," Nate said with an easy shrug. "I don't know what's supposed to happen, but what I do know is that I've never wanted to be with someone more than I want to be with you. And yes, that includes sleeping with you, but it also includes *not* sleeping with you. It includes just talking to you and being with you and eating meals with you and watching you wipe out on paddleboards." He grinned, though there was a softness in it. "Maybe we're supposed to have this week and that's it."

I was already shaking my head. "This was supposed to be my *honeymoon,* remember?"

Nate leaned against the conference table. "Did you love him?"

"I don't know," I said. "I think I loved the idea of being spontaneous and breaking out of my lab, and now here you are, the very definition of spontaneous..."

"I get it," Nate said. "Part of me wants to punch that bloke—what's his name?"

"Philip."

"Part of me wants to punch Philip in the face for hurting you, and another part of me wants to shake his hand for sending you here. To me."

"No one *sent* me..." I sighed. "Look, I'm going to my hotel. Maybe we can...talk later."

"No doubt," Nate said, an assured smile returned to his face.

"Okay, great. Do you want my number?"

"Nope."

"You don't."

"Nope. It'll happen." He laughed when I rolled my eyes. "I'm going to start calling you Scully."

"Who?"

"From the *X-Files?* I'm Mulder and you're Scully. I'm the believer and you're the skeptic."

"That's not a great basis for a relationship."

He cocked an eyebrow. "We have a relationship now?"

I sighed and shouldered my bag. "I'm going. I'll talk to you later. Maybe. If fate decides it."

"Yep."

He looked so confident—and damn sexy—watching me go.

He's not the sun, and I'm not some hunk of rock stuck in his gravitational pull. I have free will.

The whole fate notion was ridiculous, and I went to prove it by heading straight to the hotel. But another doctor stopped me on the way out to ask a few more questions. When I was free again, I hurried out and stepped into the elevator with a handful of other scientists deep in discussion. One of whom was Nate.

You're kidding me.

He shot me a wink, and I steadfastly kept my eyes averted.

Then the elevator stopped, and every single person got out except for him and me.

I shot him a look. "You don't need to join your group?"

"Not my stop."

I fumed. "Of course it isn't. Doesn't prove anything."

The doors shut and the elevator began to descend, then came to a lurching stop. A ringing alarm began to sound.

I whirled on Nate. "What did you do?"

He held up his hands, laughing. "I'm just standing here."

This isn't happening. This is crazy.

And yet, being alone with Nate in the confined space only served to erase my conflicting thoughts and replace them with everything that was him: his easy sex appeal, his handsome face, his scent, and his smile...

"Everything okay in there?" came a voice through the little speaker.

Without taking my eyes off Nate, I moved to the panel and pushed the speaker button. "We're fine."

"Aye. Sorry for the bug. We'll have you out in a jiff."

The silence thickened between us. Nate's smile melted away, and the glint in his eyes darkened to want. I felt my resolve weakening.

Nate moved to stand in front of me. "We have only a jiff."

I nodded, my eyes on his mouth that was about to take mine. "Yes..."

"We'd better make it count, then, eh?"

And that was the last straw. The last brick in my defense crumbled away, and he saw it. Nate reached out and hauled me to him and then we were kissing. Hard, deep, delicious kisses that set my skin on fire and burned up the hesitation—and caution—that had battered me for the last few days.

Maybe he only wants to sleep with me but screw it. I want to sleep with him too, so...

And that was the last coherent thought I had while Nate's mouth captured mine, devoured me, possessed me with kisses I'd never experienced before. Even more intense and beautiful and perfect than the kiss at the airport. It erased days of overthinking about what—if anything—should happen between us, and I simply let it happen.

I let us happen.

The elevator lurched again, sending Nate against the wall and me against him. Then it began to resume its descent. The doors opened before we could smooth our rumpled clothing, but I didn't care about that either. I didn't care about anything but being alone with Nate somewhere...and quickly.

Leaving the complex was a blur; Nate led me by the hand to his car, a hybrid SUV.

"I'm not gonna lie," Nate said as he drove, weaving expertly in and out of Brisbane traffic. "I've been fantasizing about taking you home on a hot rush of adrenaline-fueled lust. I just didn't think it would be yours."

I bit my lip and squeezed my legs together. "Just drive."

Nate's house was a modest little bungalow tucked into a beach community. Inside, he shut the door, and I had a second to glance around at his place decorated with Polynesian art and photos of him with his family or friends from his trips to Bali and Fiji.

"Would you like anything to drink or—?"

I pulled him to me and kissed him. I kissed him hard, leaving no question as to what I wanted. With a feral growl of want, Nate took over from there.

He pressed me back into the door, his mouth devouring mine. God, to have his hands on me, touching me... Back in the elevator, I'd thought I was merely giving in to the undeniable attraction between us. But the more his hands sought my skin under my clothes, the more perfectly right everything felt. Puzzle pieces clicking into place, one after another, moment by moment.

Nate's hands slipped under my blouse, found my breasts while I unbuttoned his shirt, fumbling in my haste.

"I want this so bad," he said, growling against my neck. "I want you so goddamn bad..."

I nodded wordlessly, falling into a delirium of his touch and hands and heat.

Take me, have me, use me...

I pushed his shirt off his shoulders, and that body of his—tanned by years in the sun, taut from hours likely spent at the gym—was all mine. I managed to get my blouse over my head, and Nate immediately put his mouth between my breasts. I cradled his head, his hair brushing my chin. I arched into him, pressing his mouth against me.

"Aye, bloody hell, I can't take it anymore..."

Nate lifted me off the floor, his arms wrapped around my waist. He tilted his head up, and I brought mine to meet him in a hard kiss. Without breaking our connection, he navigated down the short hallway to his bedroom.

I was briefly aware of a large bed in a spare, brightly lit room. Nate laid me down on the bed in a shaft of sunlight and stripped me out of my skirt until I was left in my panties and bra.

"Kate..." he whispered thickly, his dark eyes drinking me in. "I have to put my mouth on you. Have to taste you..."

My body shuddered in anticipation as Nate, stripped down to his boxer briefs, knelt over me on the bed. He kissed my mouth wetly, sweetly, and then trailed down between my breasts, down to my stomach, down to the hem of my panties.

He shot me a final, sly grin and put his mouth over my core, breathing hotly against the silk of my underwear.

I arched off the bed. "Nate... please."

He peeled my panties off and tossed them aside. His large hands slipped under me, lifting me to him, bringing me to his mouth.

I gasped at that first touch. Electric currents raced along every nerve in my body as Nate expertly worked me to a fever pitch. I gripped the sheets in both hands to anchor myself to the bed because I felt I was about to float away...until the orgasm crashed down over me like a wave. One that I wanted to drown in.

"So good," he said, laying kisses along my inner thigh. "But I need more."

I nodded and sat up enough to remove my bra while he reached in the nightstand drawer for a condom. I watched him remove his boxer briefs, and the sight of him, huge and hard and perfect, sent another flash of heat to the center of me that was still throbbing.

He finished sheathing himself and then knelt over me on all fours again, kissing me deeply, reverently.

"I'm so glad you're here."

"Me too," I said. "But God, I want you *now*."

"You want me inside you."

"Yes."

"You want me to fuck you."

God, those words. In that accent.

"Yes," I said, more of a moan.

Without another word, he lifted one of my legs over the crook of his elbow and drove himself deep inside me.

"Oh my God," I managed as the sensation of him, thick and heavy, filled me with a sweet ache of deep pressure.

Nate's eyes darkened and then squeezed shut. A growl issued from deep in his chest.

"God, you're so bloody beautiful," he said, moving slowly, in and almost all the way out of me. "So beautiful..."

I reached for him and brought his mouth down for a biting kiss while our bodies moved in sync. Finding a rhythm. A perfect tandem. As if they were attuned to one another. I didn't have to do a thing except let it happen, spread myself open, and offer everything to Nate because I couldn't imagine anything as perfect either.

Nate's thrusts came faster, harder, and I gave myself up to it, to him. The crazy ideas he had about fate, destiny, or whatever had brought me here came true, because this was exactly where I wanted to be. With this man working his body over me, taking pleasure from me and giving so much in return.

My second orgasm was a thousand times stronger than the first—a tsunami of sensation that swept through me, tossed me in its heated waves, and then left me dazed and drained. Nate came a few seconds later, his body tensing over mine, and I reveled in his release and the grunting sounds of it—so masculine and raw.

He slumped onto his back beside me, both of us breathing heavily as if we'd been shipwrecked on a shore. After a few moments, he rolled over to hold me close to him. He kissed my forehead, each eye, my nose, each cheek, and then my mouth.

His eyes held me with such reverence and care, but then a sly grin slipped over his lips.

"So. Believe me now?"

"About what?" I teased.

"This. Us. Meant to be."

"Oh, stop. You got lucky is all."

"Did I ever," Nate said with a laugh, and then he brushed the stubble of his cheek against my shoulder while I toyed with his hair for a few quiet moments.

"What happens next?" I asked.

"Do we have to know?"

"No," I said with a smile. "I don't think we do."

He grinned and kissed me softly and then deeply, and we fell into each other again for that afternoon and the rest of the week. We worked at the Conservation Association during the day, while nights were spent in heated bliss in Nate's bed and in long conversations over dinners and "brekkies" where we unfolded ourselves to each other, sharing personal dreams and nightmares, hopes and heartaches.

We only had a week, but I refused to think about it. I let those currents take me where they wanted to take me, because—after all—they had brought me to him.

* * *

Nate drove me to the airport on my last day in Australia. *What happens next?* was on my lips a hundred times, but I never gave it breath.

"What should happen, will," Nate said as if reading my thoughts. "Though if *what happens* is that you decide to stay, I'll be the happiest bloke in Queensland."

"Don't say that," I said, smoothing down the front of his shirt and toying with his shark-tooth necklace. "It just makes it harder to go. And I have to go. I have a job, a house..."

"I know," he said. "Go on then."

With a long, lingering, parting kiss, I went. We'd made no plans to call or e-mail or stay in touch in any way. And as I moved into the terminal and farther away from Nate, the more my doubts started to creep in. That his notion of us being fated or somehow cosmically planned seemed sillier with every step I took away from him. I began to suspect him. Even after so many intense conversations, I began to suspect I'd been played. Again.

It's easy to fake being interested in order to get someone into bed. But our talks? The private things we shared?

Phillip had really messed up my self-esteem and ability to trust, since all the overthinking I'd stopped doing in the last week swooped in as I waited in line at the Qantas terminal to check my bag. I was early for my flight because even the thought of running late to anything gave me hives, and I was first at an empty desk.

"Where are you heading, miss?"

"The one-fifteen to Los Angeles, then on to San Diego."

The woman frowned before I finished speaking. "That flight has been canceled. Did you not get the text alert?"

"Canceled? No, I..." I checked my phone. "It's not here. It's really canceled?"

"I'm very sorry for the inconvenience. There is a huge weather system over the flight path, and all flights have been grounded for twenty-four hours. Shall I help make arrangements for a hotel?"

I muttered a "no thanks" and quickly hurried back outside. Nate was likely long gone. No reason to stay, and security wouldn't let him loiter anyway. Even so, I rushed through the doors, my rolling luggage banging at my ankles.

And there was Nate, leaning against his car, chatting and laughing with an aforementioned security guard.

My heart thundered in my chest at what felt like an absolute luxury to have him for one more day.

But does he want me?

I strode forward. "Nate."

He turned, and his expression lit up without a second's hesitation to see me—no shock, no disappointment, no quickly masked irritation that I was still hanging around after our week of no-strings sex had ended.

Maybe there are strings after all. Connecting us...

He strolled to me, slowly, casually, but when we were close, he grabbed me in his arms and spun me around. "I knew it. You changed your mind? You're staying?"

"Um, not quite..." I said, overwhelmed that this was his first thought. His first hope. I vowed then and there to stop second-guessing him. Or myself. "My flight was canceled. Can't leave until tomorrow."

"Oh." Now the disappointment found him, but he brightened again. "Well, if it's only one more day, I'll take it."

"Might be time to move along?" the security guard said with a friendly smile for me. "But good chatting with you, Nate."

"Aye, Mick. Good to see you again," Nate said and turned back to me. "If I hadn't run into my old buddy, Mick, I'd be long gone. Have to turn around. Come back and get ya. Now we have all those minutes back." He pulled me closer, his voice dropping. "Do you believe me yet, Miss Kate, that you and I...?"

"I don't know," I said, touching my fingertips to his lips. "I might be coming around."

"That works for me."

He kissed me and then started to take my bag to put it back in the trunk of his car when my phone rang.

"It's my boss at the Park," I said. I put the phone to my ear. "Sharon? Hi..."

I listened to her talk, my eyes widening, my heart thumping, and my head shaking.

"You're kidding, right?" I glared at Nate, who was shutting the trunk. "Did a certain Dr. Barnaby put you up to this?"

"No, this is coming from the head office," Sharon said in my ear. "Glad I caught you before you jumped on a fourteen-hour flight. They want to fill the spot fast. So? What do you think?"

"What do I think?" I murmured and pulled Nate to me. "What do I think about taking a position in Brisbane, working in the field instead of in a lab for six months with the possibility of making it permanent?"

Nate's eyes widened, and then he laughed soundlessly before shooting me his now infamous *I told you so* look.

"That's the offer," Sharon said. "I know it seems like it's coming out of left field..."

I shot a glance at Nate. "You'd be surprised."

"Well?" Nate said. "Give the woman an answer, will you? I have plans to take you out tonight to celebrate, starting now."

I shook my head at him, marveling at this man who'd fallen into my life. Or maybe I fell into his. Or maybe it was what he said; we were fated from the start. Our destiny.

Because we rhyme...

"Yes," I said to Sharon, but I was looking at Nate. "Yes, I'll stay."

"Wonderful," she said. "I—"

Whatever else she was going to say was lost as Nate took the phone out of my hand and kissed me. A kiss so deep and pure, it left no doubt as to his intentions. His happiness. Then he pulled back, a triumphant smirk on his face.

"Don't say it," I said. "Don't you dare."

"Who me? I'd never."

"You would—"

He kissed my words away, his mouth moving sweetly and deliciously over mine. Then he stayed close, our foreheads touching, our eyes locked and filled with possibilities.

"Kate..." he said, his lips brushing mine.

"Yes, Nate?"

He sucked in a breath, held me closer, and then that smile of his spread slowly over his lips.

"Told you so."

* * *

I MEAN, IT'S COOL

TIJAN

1

I'd loved Cut Ryder all my life.

Okay. That's a lie. And I didn't even love him.

I'd only known him for this last year, and if I was being fully, fully honest here, I've only talked to him a handful of times.

I'm lying again.

I mean, I've seen him loads of times. He's Pine River High School's star hockey player, and we're a school where hockey isn't that big of a deal. Football and baseball are. But when Cut started playing for the team, everything changed.

I mean, that's what I'm told. I actually didn't go to school there until this last year, but it felt like I'd been there all my life. Just like I felt like I'd known Cut all my life. The real, real truth is that he's my brother's best friend, and see, that's why I thought I'd known him all my life. Except I hadn't. Just like I haven't really known my brother either.

I mean, not until this year. This was the first time I came to stay with my father.

But I just felt like I'd known my brother all my life. And after I moved here, I saw Chad a lot. That's my brother's name. He's the same age as me.

I mean, there were Sunday family dinners when he was there. Well, he was *told* he had to be there, but he totally was. I mean, I overheard our father telling him on the phone that Sunday dinners were required, but I think it should be more his effort that counts. Or the follow-through, I mean. Because he was there. Every single Sunday. And I smiled at him the whole time.

I mean, he didn't really talk to me.

He didn't talk to me in school either.

I got a ride to school from my stepmother (his real mom), and sometimes Chad would be there when we arrived because Natalie (his mom) needed to talk to him or ask him to do something. And Cut was there with him most of the time. Or some of the time.

Okay. Cut only came to the car twice the whole year, but it didn't matter.

I was sure he knew who I was.

I mean, I was his best friend's sister. Or half sister. Did it matter? We were siblings.

And yeah, Cut never really looked at me. He frowned at me once, in a hallway, when I yelled out, "Hey, Cut!" And he passed me right by, but there was a flicker in his eyes. He so knew me.

See? We were friends. We were tight.

Or we were in my head.

I guess, when I think about it, a lot of things this past year only happened in my head.

Like that I had loads of friends at Pine River. The truth is I didn't, but it was because everyone knew Chad was my brother. He'd told them not to befriend me. He was trying to protect me.

And he was super good at it, because he only talked to me once that year in school. It was at my locker. I was there, shutting it, and I knew Natalie was supposed to pick me up because I had to stay after for a meeting about my mom. Chad shoved a stocking cap at me. "Here."

He didn't wait for me to grab it, so it fell to the ground, but I scrambled—a big smile on my face—and I looked up. "Hey! Than—"

He was already walking away, looked like he was kicking at the floor. He was carrying his big hockey bag, and Cut was at the lockers with his own big hockey bag at his feet. A couple girls were standing with Cut, but he looked at me.

See? He did know me! I totally forgot about that time. There was no frown that time. Just his eyebrows pinching together, and he looked from me to Chad. Actually, now that I think about it, he looked kinda confused.

I mean... What was that about?

Chad had told him about me.

...

Hadn't he?

No way. Of course he had.

I mean, how do you not tell your best friend about your sister?

I mean, your half sister.

I mean, even though my dad didn't know about me until I was eleven. And that was five years ago. And yeah, there had been minimal phone calls or birthday cards. It wasn't my dad's fault. I heard him calling. Or more specifically, I heard my mom fighting with him. Like, all the time.

Then again, that's all my mom really does.

She fights with people, then she smokes up. She likes to lock herself into her bedroom.

And there was one time where she was in there for a long time, like a full week.

I knocked and asked if she was okay. Sometimes she'd yell at me to go away. Sometimes she didn't say anything, but she always got mad when I went in to check on her. And I didn't think she'd eaten that week or had any water, so I left sandwiches outside her door, and I stole a couple bottles of water from the neighbors. I always hated doing that, but if I was being honest, I don't think I was really stealing them. Mrs. Johanson saw me take a water one time, and she didn't say a thing. There were two bottles there the next day. Sometimes I swiped them, but I didn't like to. And it was only if I was in dire straits. But I didn't like being like that, so I spent as much time at school as possible. The water fountain was free, you know?

But anyways, back to Cut and how much I loved him.

Because I did. A lot.

I mean, he's gorgeous. He has this dirty blond hair, and he keeps it shaved on the sides of his head. He lets it get a little longer on top, and he's always running his hands through it. It looks messily rumpled, and it's just so adorable.

I wasn't the only girl in school who thought so.

Cut and Chad were both popular. I mean, they're hockey players, so of course they were popular. But Chad was grumpy a lot of the time. Or at least he was grumpy to me. You know, when he actually did talk to me. But not Cut. He was always grinning or joking, and everyone loved Cut.

How could you not?

Plus, he was going into the NHL. Everyone knew it. I heard Chad talking about it to our dad one night at the house. It was one of the few times he was there. At first I thought that was weird, but then I heard Natalie mention to one of her friends that they thought it was best if he stayed at Cut's house while Donna's kid was staying with them.

That's how she said it; those were her words exactly.

I mean, I knew she was talking about me, but it made sense.

I was Donna's kid.

I mean, I was also Deek's kid. So that meant I was Chad's half sister.

So even though Natalie didn't like calling me her stepdaughter, that's what I was. Actually. Technically.

But yeah, everyone's been great to me this whole time I was at their house.

The food was great every night.

I could drink water any time of the day, and get this—it was endless, coming out of their fridge. I just had to grab a glass and push it against the button, and voila: instant water. And it was good water too, so I didn't need to stay at school that long after school ended.

But back to the family, because it was the last day I was there, and I found out that I had another little brother. Can you believe that?

I had no clue where he'd been. Maybe like me, he'd been sent somewhere else while they needed to take care of me? Oh man. I hoped I hadn't put them out, or him out, or used his room? That'd be awful if they brought me in and sent him away because I took his room, but that didn't make sense.

Their house was epically big.

I mean, Chad could've stayed there, and I probably wouldn't have even seen him that much.

Though, thinking on it now, Natalie was gone a lot. There were a ton of nights when it was me at the house and Deek was working in his office. I mean, yeah, I spent time with my dad. That was super, über cool, you know? We had meals together a lot. And he talked to me about my mom, but when he did, he'd get all tense in the face. His words would come out clipped, but I got it. I really and truly did.

Donna is...well, let's just say Donna is a lot.

I'm her daughter, and she only talks civilly to me after she's been away at one of those clinics. She stays there a long time. This time was the longest, and my dad thought it'd be best if I spent it with them, but usually I stayed at my uncle's house. I like my aunt, and I love my cousins and uncle, but this time was cool. It was like seeing how the other half lives.

The high school was cooler too. There weren't gangs at Pine River.

Can you imagine? How Chad would be at my normal school? With the gangs there? I started laughing, just thinking about it, and then I thought about Cut, and then it wasn't funny anymore. *Shit.* Cut would've still been popular and pretty, but he probably wouldn't have joked as much.

That's sad.

"Ryan."

Crap. They're talking to me.

"Ryan." My counselor leaned over, putting her hand on my arm. "This is important. You need to focus on being present with us."

They're always preaching that. Being present.

What does that even mean?

So what if my mind wanders? So what if I'm hyper and sometimes so hyper I miss what's going on around me? I mean, I think you would be too if you grew up where I did, the way I did, and yeah, maybe you'd let your mind wander a bit too.

Being present sucks, especially now. I mean, more so now than ever.

Can we go back to talking about Cut?

"Ryan."

Shit. That's my dad talking.

I gotta go. Be back soon.

"What?" I looked at him. He was frowning at me, sitting in the corner with his arms crossed over his chest. Wow. He dressed up for this meeting—a business suit. And Natalie, she's here too, heaving a sigh, like she usually does when she's around me. I've noticed she doesn't do that when Chad is around. I couldn't say how she is around my other brother, because I don't know him. I don't think they know that *I* know about him.

Let's talk about that.

Why *haven't* they told me?

It's not like I'm this horrible person or something.

I didn't do anything. I mean, the worst I do is think, think and talk to myself, and yeah, be not present—which I could see my dad knew I was doing again.

He gets the same look on his face every time he's exasperated with me.

His mouth flattens. His nose wrinkles a little, and it looks like he had to take a crap but couldn't. Now he's uncrossing his arms, rubbing a hand over his forehead. He does that a lot when I *really* frustrate him.

"Ryan."

Aw crap. It's the counselor again. She's more insistent now, and I know I really do need to focus. If I don't, she'll get mad. Then I'll be asked to leave, and nothing good is discussed when I'm not in the room. I know because I like to eavesdrop, and I am good at doing *that*.

"Yeah?"

She was trying. I could see the effort, but even her face was tight and rigid. She nodded toward Deek and Natalie. "Your father is wondering if you feel comfortable enough to return to your mother's care?"

Yeah.

That.

I felt a knot coming up my throat.

I knew I didn't want to come to this meeting.

Deek cleared his throat, leaning forward and resting his elbows on his knees. "You've been at our house for six months, and we've made accommodations and changes so you'd feel comfortable there, but if you choose to remain, we do need to discuss bringing Chad and Hunter back into the house."

Hunter! That's his name.

I didn't think my dad realized that was the first time he'd told me about him or referenced him. I mean, I think...

Natalie wasn't looking at him. She had that same blank and somewhat peeved look directed at me. Thinking on it now, she looks similar to my dad whenever they have to deal with me. It's kind of funny.

I mean, maybe they had mentioned the other brother before, but I think I would've remembered. Hunter. Now I knew his name, I was never forgetting it.

"Ryan."

I messed up again. My counselor sighed.

It isn't my fault that I'm like this.

But it's on me to control it, so okay...

I had to really concentrate here.

A deep breath in.

Hold—that shit never worked for me.

"My mom's good again?" I asked.

Crap. That was a question, not a statement from me. I messed up there too.

The counselor looked relieved. I was participating. She always got less snippy when I responded to her.

"Yes, Ryan. She's graduated to the halfway house, and she'll be able to leave as early as this week. She's reached out and requested to see you."

I frowned. *Why?* I shrugged. "Nah. I'm good."

All three adults shared a look at that.

See! I'm so focused here. Noticing everything.

"What do you mean, you're good? You don't want to see your mother, or you don't want to live with her?"

See her. Duh. It's always the same. She comes out of those places all happy and hippie and seeing rainbows and talking about angels. She'll be nice, promising to keep with her yoga and meditation and the rules. Always the rules. And life will be decent, for a while.

But either she'll get lonely and start smoking again. Or she'll meet a guy and start smoking again.

Same old, same old.

And I'm not talking the cigarette kind of smoking.

"I'm good with living with her, but can I come back to Deek's the next time?"

A look flickered in my counselor's eyes. She knew what I was talking about.

Natalie's voice hitched high. "Next time? What does she mean, 'next time'?"

Oh boy.

That answered my question. Natalie looked all panicky at the thought that I might be coming back. But it was cool. I could stay at my uncle's. My cousins like me. They think I'm funny, and they understand me too. Plus, I wasn't scared to walk from my room to go get water there, though they didn't have the fancy fridge water that Deek's house did.

Still. It was all cool.

I'd miss looking at Cut.

Gah.

I loved Cut. I think I loved him all my life.

* * *

So I went back to live with my mom.

And it was cool, for a while.

She was nice, like I knew she would be.

Until she got bored, like I knew she would get.

Then she found a new guy, like I knew would happen.

So, the same old, same old happened.

That time, I knew not to ask Natalie, so I went to my uncle's.

Things were good, until they weren't. (Once again.)

Same old, same old. (But turns out, not this time.)

* * *

I couldn't believe they came for me.

I was more grounded this time. I mean, it was a whole year later. I was going into my senior year of high school, and this time I was with the normal kids. They got me meds. My uncle got me in to see a therapist that worked with me. There was group therapy, and yeah, okay, they sent me somewhere for a bit. But I came out, and it was like the world was shining brighter.

I mean, I've never felt like this.

People say things, and I understand them. I respond, and they reply.

I feel like one of them, you know?

If you know, you know. If you don't, that's cool. That means you're blessed.

Anyway, the place said I was misdiagnosed, and my symptoms are because my mom was a junkie. And I got all that. It made sense, but it was awesome. I mean, it wasn't. The reason I was there and all of us were there wasn't cool at all.

Though, can I tell you a secret?

I was relieved. And I feel bad saying that, and I'll never admit that to anyone else, but I was.

There were no more ups and downs, threats, screams, violence, cops, or fostering. From the time I lived with my dad and the times I've been with my uncle, I get that I need structure. And it says a lot that a kid like me gets that. Like, it says a *lot*.

"Ryan."

Oh, boy. My dad. He looks wary to talk to me, as if I might crumble.

"Hi, Dad." Crap. Did we have this talk? Can I even call him that?

He smiles, and it's bright, and I see him blink quite a few times before he comes the rest of the way to where I'm waiting.

He must've liked that. I think I'll keep calling him that then.

He reaches for me, and like a normal person (who can read that this is what he wants), I move in, and he hugs me. I hug him back, and it's cool.

It's all so cool.

Then Natalie is here, and she's smiling at me with all this gentleness. Whoa. Who knew she could be like that? Not that she was *mean* mean, but she was at least slightly bitchy mean. If that makes sense? And holy crapola I'm-gonna-crap-my-pants crap! There's a little dude next to her, and he looks just like Chad.

I think Natalie was reaching for a hug, but no way. I drop to my knees, smiling wide at this little guy, and I reach for him (because I can now, because I'm a normal person now—there are so many cool benefits to hanging in the normal, cool crowd), and he *comes to me!*

And screw it.

"Hey, buddy." *Keep it quiet, Ryan. Calm. Don't scare the little dude away*. "I'm your big sister."

"I know!"

I'm almost bowled over by his excitement.

"Hunter," Natalie reprimands him.

I don't know why, but he blinks at her and then he must remember.

"Oh." He lifts his arms, winds them around my neck, and squeezes me tight. Well, not me but my neck. He says in a rush, "I'msorryaboutyourmomI-heardshewasn'tnicebutI'mstillsorry."

Okay.

I replay it back silently, put in the spaces, and I've got it.

I ease back and hold up my pinkie finger.

He's watching me. Wide eyes. Then, grinning, he lifts his pinkie, and we lock pinkies.

I say, "Put it there, dude."

Can I tell you another secret? I don't like talking about my mom or why everyone's here. There's sadness, and I'll feel it, but right now I'm riding the wave of having my dad here, and Natalie. Now I've not only met Hunter, hugged Hunter, but we pinkie-duded each other. It's way cool.

Little Dude leans forward and whispers in my ear, "Do you like koalas?"

I lean back, giving him the biggest and brightest smile ever. "You serious? I love koalas!"

His whole face lights up. "Me too."

I look up, but no Chad. Or Cut. (I was really hoping Cut would come.)

As if reading my mind, Natalie coughs. She gives me another sad smile. "Chad's at a hockey camp where he's going next year."

I stand, but I gotta squeeze little dude's shoulder. He looks up, bumping into my leg, and I'm calling it. We're going to be the best koala-loving friends.

Then he moves over to his mom, and I get that too. She seems pretty chill this time.

"Silvard, right?" I ask.

Natalie's eyes get big.

Me. Normal. I'm loving it. "You told me last year that's where he's going. Early acceptance, right?"

"Yeah." She blinks some more, then shakes her head. "Uh. Yeah." She regains her footing, and her smile is more genuine. "Cut got a ride there until he goes to the NHL. Chad doesn't think he'll make the team. He's not as good as Cut, but he's hoping for one last year with him."

I got it. I'd want one last year with Cut, too. I still love the guy, though I've realized he had no clue who I was that year and we never actually talked. Like, ever. I was a bit delusional that year.

"That's cool." I'm bobbing my head, acting just like what I said.

It's my new favorite word, if you hadn't noticed.

Deek clears his throat, suddenly all serious. "I've talked to your uncle, and he mentioned the agreement we worked out. Is that—I mean—is that what you want?"

I knew what he was talking about, and I nod. "Yeah. It's chill. I'll stay with my uncle. I like my cousins a lot, but I'm guessing you want me to go to Silvard next year?"

He relaxes. His shoulders lower, and the lines of tension in his forehead ease at my words.

"Yeah. We're figuring since Chad will be there, you might want to get to know your brother a bit."

Now that I'm better...

Now that my mother isn't...

Now that I'm a normal.

"That'd be great." I wink at Little Dude. "But only if The Hunter and I can hang sometimes."

He giggles at his name, and Natalie laughs lightly.

Deek grins. "That sounds like a great plan."

The agreement he and my uncle struck is that since I basically and mostly grew up with my uncle's family, they want me to remain with them for my last year of school. With a clearer head, it turns out that I'm smart, and I might even be a little super-duper smart. I've gotta work hard and work a lot, but I'll probably get to graduate like another one of those normals. The agreement is that if I'm staying with my uncle, my dad wants to pay for my college at the school of his choosing.

My uncle thought I'd be pissed about that, but I'm down.

I'm not like one of those girls. I don't have plans, dreams, or Pinterest boards about what college I'm going to. I'm just happy to be able to go to college, and Silvard is no slouch school. They're D1 and pretty fancy-pants. I know it'll be hard, but as long as I keep current with therapy and meds, I'm down for the pound. I can so totally get a degree, and whadda ya know? I might get a decent job at the end of all this.

I see my uncle approaching, and it's time we get this shindig going.

My dad hugs me, and I think I hear a sniffle. It's like they forgot why they were seeing me and now they're remembering. It's all good though. Everything will be all good. I just know it.

Natalie hugs me and whispers, "I'm so sorry for your loss, Ryan." She smooths my hair, her hands falling to my shoulders, and then Little Dude is hugging my knees.

I don't tell anyone, but my shoulders tingle after that touch from her. My mom used to be nice like that, but that was a long time ago. Like, ages ago. Like, I can't remember now, but she must've been at some point.

All moms hug their kids, right?

But I don't want to deal with that all. I got my Little Dude here.

I crouch down and hold up my pinkie again. "We're gonna hang, right?"

He steps forward, all serious. He wraps his pinkie around mine and nods. "Hell yeah, we're gonna hang."

"Hunter!" his mom says.

But he just laughs, and I laugh back, and it's all good.

I mean, it's cool.

* * *

Do you want more of Tijan?

One click ENEMIES now!

DATE FOR HIRE

NOELLE ADAMS

1

"He show up yet?" My brother, Weston, sticks his head out of his office to ask the question.

I try not to roll my eyes since it's a harmless inquiry. But I've been jittery for almost an hour now, so it takes work to keep my voice and expression calm. "Not yet. He said twelve thirty."

"All right. Just checking. Let me know how it goes, Roar." He disappears back into his office without another word.

He's called me Roar all his life, his childhood shortening of my full name, Aurora. I find it rather funny, since I'm a quiet person and roaring isn't in my nature. Weston is five years older than me, and we weren't close until we became adults. He's normally not concerned about my social life, so I'm not sure what precipitated the questioning today.

He must know I'm nervous about Mike O'Dell stopping by.

I don't like anyone knowing I'm nervous. I've cultivated a manner that's cool, composed, organized, and in control, and it bothers me when someone recognizes that it's often an act. Don't ask me why it bothers me. Ever since I was a kid, I've hidden all my fears, anxieties, and confusion from the rest of the world.

I breathe deeply in an attempt to slow my racing heart and turn back to the spreadsheet on the computer at the reception desk of the office suite. We have an assistant who greets visitors, answers the phone, and does basic administrative tasks, but she works afternoons and evenings, when most of our calls come in, so Weston and I take turns staffing this desk in the mornings. We haven't had any calls this morning except for Mike confirming that he was coming in. Right now, I need to finish this spreadsheet. It's almost tax time, and Weston and I have worked too hard to make Companions for Hire a success to get in trouble with the IRS because of cute-guy jitters.

I'm thirty-four years old. I shouldn't be so nervous about talking to a man.

But I am. And no matter how many times I envision this conversation in my head—imagining myself acting casual and appealing as I offer a certain proposition and (hopefully) have it accepted—I'm still scared to do it.

For the next twenty minutes, I spin my wheels, pretending to work but not getting much done, until the door to the office suite opens at exactly twelve thirty and a man walks in.

Mike.

He's who I've been waiting for.

He smiles when he sees me. "Hey, Aurora." Mike is about four inches taller than my five-six, and he's lean and fit with thick, wavy brown hair and vivid blue eyes. He's just finished teaching a class at a local university, and he's dressed in an appropriately academic outfit. Jeans, brown sports coat, and slightly wrinkled shirt with no tie.

As far as I'm concerned, men don't get any more attractive than him.

"Hi." It feels like my cheeks are flushed—as they do whenever I feel emotion of any intensity—but I hope they're not too noticeable. "Thanks for stopping by."

"Of course. Did you have a good weekend?"

"Yeah. It was fine." It was actually a pretty good weekend. I stayed in for most of it, binge-watching a vampire show on television. "How was yours?"

He makes a face. "I had papers to grade."

We chat for a few minutes, talking about the paper he assigned in his zoology class and then shifting into the show I was watching and then Weston's attempts to install a new shelving system in my closet (still not completed).

It's always easy to talk to Mike. He asks real questions and seems to genuinely listen to my answers. That's not true of everyone.

In fact, most people seem to go through the motions of conversation when they really want to be talking to someone else or checking their phones.

When we fall into silence after a few minutes, I hear myself saying, "Thanks for coming in." Then I remember I already said that.

"Well, you said you had a new job for me. Since clients aren't exactly beating down my door, I'm not going to pass it off."

Companions for Hire is a service that provides exactly that. Companions. If you can pay our fee and any incidental expenses, we can provide a companion. Need a last-minute date to a wedding? A partner for a ballroom dancing class? A history buff to escort you through New England battlefields? A fluent French speaker for your trip to Paris? A fake boyfriend for a high school reunion? Companions for Hire can deliver—without any complications and without the underlying expectations of an escort agency.

The one kind of companionship we don't provide is sex.

In my experience, if you want to hire someone for sex, those services are readily available. What's harder to find for a fee are other kinds of social partners, and that's the gap that Companions for Hire has filled for the past few years.

Five years ago, I needed a date to the yearly banquet of the nonprofit I worked for back then. I'd just gotten divorced from my husband of seven years, and I didn't have the mental energy for dating yet. The friends I might have asked weren't available, so I ended up attending the banquet with my brother. The whole evening, I complained about how there wasn't a reputable service that provided partners for hire for such events. I'd done exhaustive searches in the Atlanta area and far beyond, and I'd found nothing I'd be comfortable using. All the agencies I could find were either geared toward men or clearly a front for sex work, and neither of those options worked for me.

I had money to spend, and I needed a man to wear a suit and sit next to me for one evening so that I didn't have to go to a big banquet alone. I should have been able to pay for what I needed, but there was nothing out there to provide me the service.

On the way home from the banquet, Weston and I brainstormed the concept of Companions for Hire. A week later, he called me up and said he'd put together a business plan for the company. He was bored of his corporate marketing job. He wanted to do something different and be his own boss. And since my skills lie in administration, he thought we could make a success of it together.

We did. A huge success that now brings in quite a bit of money. Most of our business is centered here in Atlanta, but our companions will travel all over the world for jobs—as long as the client will pay expenses—so we get calls from all over. We carefully vet every client before we pair them with one of our companions, so we end up turning down more clients than we accept.

Being selective works in our favor. We've got a waiting list for dates with some of our most popular companions.

Mike isn't one of our most popular ones. He isn't as drop-dead handsome as some of the men who work for us—he's more regular-guy cute—and he doesn't dance or romance clients. He's working on his PhD in wildlife conservation science, so we use him when someone is specifically looking for a companion who knows about animals or ecology. He's gone on several hiking trips with clients, and he took one sweet old lady to Africa for a "wildlife safari." But he doesn't get jobs all the time. The work he does for us is a good supplement to his income, which at the moment consists only of his teaching assistantship, but he's not making six figures like our top earners.

He's been sitting on the leather chair next to the desk, and now he leans forward toward me with his forearms on his knees. "So what's the job?"

I clear my throat. Try to remember the words I've mentally rehearsed. "The client is receiving a service award for volunteer work at a nonprofit. She needs a date for the awards banquet—which is actually a brunch on a Saturday morning. It's in New York, so you'd fly up with her on Friday afternoon and then come back on Saturday afternoon. Just the one event. In New York."

Okay. That wasn't quiet as smooth and lucid as I'd mentally planned, but it wasn't too bad.

Mike's thick eyebrows draw together. "Why are you asking me for this? Don't you have guys who specialize in those kinds of dates?"

"Yes, but she doesn't want someone like that. She wants someone who would be a... a better fit for her."

His thin, mobile lips soften into a smile. "Ah. I see. Since I'm not as good-looking as your other guys, you naturally thought of me." He's teasing. His eyes are warm. He's obviously not offended.

But I get roused into defense anyway. "You are too good-looking!" When his eyes widen in surprise, I remember my normal composure. I drop my eyelashes and say in a softer voice, "I mean, we wouldn't have hired you if you weren't attractive. But she's looking for more of a regular guy than a fantasy date. Anyway, that's what she wants, and you're the first person I thought of."

"Okay. It sounds easy enough. Thanks for thinking of me. So who's the client?"

He clearly has no idea. No idea at all. His expression is questioning, innocent.

So I swallow hard and get it said. "She's... me."

It takes a few seconds for this to process. Mike is very still for a moment. Then he gives a slow blink.

"It's me," I hurry on, hoping to finish my spiel before he can voice any objections. "I usually just skip the yearly banquet, but I'm getting this service award so I need to go. And I'm not dating anyone right now. I'd just take Weston, but he's got a trip planned that weekend. Events like this really stress me out, and I don't want to do this thing alone. So I thought maybe I could just hire you, if you're willing."

He's surprised. His lips are turned down in a thoughtful frown. "Wouldn't you rather ask Jackson or Rick? They'd be way better at this sort of thing than me. Or maybe Damien? I know he's busy writing his dissertation, but he would probably—"

"I told you. I don't want someone who looks like them." Jackson and Rick are among the most popular of our male companions. Both of them could have been models. And Damien might as well be a hero from a historical romance. He's cut way back on jobs for us, but he's still highly sought after by women looking for an evening of fantasy romance. "I want someone who might come closer to... to fitting with me."

If you haven't figured it out yet, I'm not exactly a beauty queen. I'm pretty enough in a round-faced, pink-cheeked, very curvy way. I have brown hair, brown eyes, and a big dimple on the right side of my mouth. I'm sure plenty of people could find me attractive. But I'd be very uncomfortable hiring a man who looks like a cover model to be my date. I'd feel like everyone who saw us together would know it isn't real.

"So you really want to go with me?" He still looks kind of confused, like he's trying to put pieces together that aren't making a coherent whole.

"Yes. I do. So if you're available the weekend after next?"

"I am free. I'll go with you. But you don't have to pay me for it. I can just—"

"I don't want it to be a favor." This is very important to me. All my life I've fought against feeling like a charity case, and I'm not going to start now, even though my interest in Mike goes far beyond a paid service. "I'd rather pay for it."

His eyes hold mine for a long moment. I have no idea what he's thinking, but his expression gives me weird shivers. "Okay. If you want me, you got me. So what are the details? And why didn't you tell me you're getting a big award? You're amazing."

I let out my breath, pretend he didn't just give me a compliment (since I'm terrible at responding to those), and start to explain.

2

Two weeks later, on a Friday afternoon, Mike and I get out of a taxi in front of the Manhattan hotel where we'll be staying for the weekend.

My stomach is churning with discomfort after the flight, airport, and long cab ride, and I vaguely wonder—as I always do whenever I visit this city—why I do this to myself.

I could have said no to this trip, but I didn't.

When I see Mike giving me a sidelong look, I force a smile.

"You all right?" he asks, obviously not convinced by my attempt at nonchalance. He puts a hand on my back as he guides me into the chaotic ground floor of the hotel.

"I'm fine."

He doesn't argue, but he also doesn't believe me. There's concern on his face as we head upstairs to the check-in desk, which requires maneuvering through random crowds of people whose only purpose seems to be getting in our way.

There's a line to check in. Of course there is. There are way too many people in this one space, and it's making me tense. As always, I try to hide it, keeping my eyes down and breathing deeply.

We stand in silence in the line for just over a minute, Mike's lean body only inches from mine. He's wearing khakis and an untucked green and brown checked shirt. Just slightly wrinkled, as all his shirts seem to be.

He leans in and mutters against my ear, “Tell me what the hell is wrong with you right now.”

I blink at the gruff authority of his soft voice. “Nothing,” I begin. Then I see his expression and add quickly, “It’s really nothing big. I just don’t… don’t like New York.”

“Why not?”

“It’s too many people. Too many buildings. All crammed together. It makes me… anxious.”

His eyebrows lift. “Really? Atlanta is a pretty big city. It doesn’t make you anxious?”

“Not like New York does. Particularly Manhattan. It’s just too much, all squeezed together on a little island. I feel trapped here. Like the buildings are closing in on me. Like I can’t get away. Like the whole thing is swallowing me up. It’s not a major phobia or anything. It just makes me… anxious.”

The line is moving. Mike steps closer to me, putting his hand again on my back. This time, he leaves it there, his palm pressing gently just between my shoulder blades. It’s strangely comforting. It lessens the churning of my stomach. “Why didn’t I know this about you?”

I sniff. “Why would you?”

“I don’t know. We’ve known each other for three years. I thought we were…” He clears his throat. “Aren’t we friends?”

“Yes! Yes, I think so.” Because I’m suddenly worried that he’s hurt, I start to ramble, which is something I rarely let myself do. “I just don’t tell anyone. I don’t know why. All kinds of things make me anxious, but I don’t tell anyone about them except Weston. It just feels like… I always try to put on this front of having it all together. I’ve done it all my life. And now I… I don’t know how to be anything else.”

He meets my worried eyes. His are thoughtful. Terrifyingly observant. Like he might be able to see past the composure I’ve cultivated for so long—maybe as far down as my soul. “Well, it’s worked,” he murmurs at last.

“What’s worked?” So maybe my mind is spinning from the look in his eyes. I’m not thinking as clearly as I should.

“Your act. The way you pretend to always have it together and be completely in control. I was… I was fooled.”

“You were?”

“Yeah. And I’ve got to say it was damned intimidating.”

“What?” (Definitely not thinking at full capacity here.)

"It's intimidating. Believing you were really like that. Like you didn't really need..."

His trailing off is incredibly frustrating, since I'm leaning into what he's saying, but I don't get a chance to prompt him to continue because a clerk calls us up to check in.

Our rooms are next to each other, and they're exactly the same. King-size bed with white coverlet. Walk-in shower. Expansive view. I'm surprised when, after we identify whose room is whose, Mike follows me into mine.

My eyes widen, and I stop myself from blurting out a confused question about what he wants.

"So what's your plan?" he asks, his eyes surveying the clean, polished furnishings.

"What plan?"

"What do you want to happen this evening?"

I gulp. Is he asking this for real? There's no way I'll be able to admit what I really want to happen this weekend—that Mike would fall deeply, miraculously in love with me. "W-what?"

He gives a soft huff of amusement and cocks his head. "I know we have the brunch tomorrow and then we fly home. But do you want me to make myself scarce for the rest of today? I'm happy to do that, if you want to do your own thing. Or did you want to..." He makes a weird throaty noise and drops his eyes. "... to hang out with me or what?"

I suddenly understand what he's asking. My heart gives a ridiculous gallop at how adorably self-conscious he looks. "Oh. I see. Well, the truth is I don't have any plans. But all you need to do with me is the brunch tomorrow, so you don't have to keep me company today unless you..." My cheeks warm.

He laughs for real—low and warm and husky. "Okay. I think I've got it. So let me lay it out for you. I've got nothing to do here this evening. If you want to be alone or spend time with other people, I'll be perfectly happy to hang out in my room. But otherwise consider me available for anything you might want."

His tone shifts at the end of his last sentence. I'm sure it's not intentional on his part, but the timbre becomes just slightly gravelly. Incredibly sensual. It makes my skin flush and a pressure tighten between my legs.

Because there's one thing I definitely want that he could provide.

Before I let myself get carried away with this idea, I remind myself that

I'm paying him for the weekend. Good money. Of course he's going to want to make sure he provides the best service, which in this case is his company.

He doesn't mean what I want him to mean.

I know some of our companions have sex with clients, and some of them probably get paid extra for it. What happens between consenting adults is their business, as long as it's entirely off Companions for Hire's books. But I don't get the sense that Mike sleeps with his clients, and I'd definitely not be comfortable with that arrangement.

I want him in an entirely different way.

"Okay," I manage to say. "I guess I'll need to eat tonight, so if you want to..."

"I'll be needing dinner too, so I'd love it if we can go together."

I smile, feeling silly and fluttery and ridiculously happy. "Okay. Good. Let's do that."

"Around seven?"

"Sounds good."

He looks around the room again. I have no idea what he's looking for, since it's exactly as it was on his previous survey. "I guess I'll leave you alone to unpack and take a shower or whatever you want to do until then."

I giggle. I'm not by nature a giggler, so it surprises me.

"What's so funny?" he asks with a frown.

"Nothing. Just that what I plan to do is bury myself under the covers for a while."

The corners of his mouth turn up just slightly. "Bury yourself?"

"Yes. It makes me feel better. When I've been anxious or jittery or something. I like to cover up. It makes me feel safe."

His smile broadens. Takes my breath away. "Yeah?"

"Yeah. What's wrong with that?"

"Nothing's wrong with it. I like it. I just didn't know that about you. Why have you been keeping all this stuff from me?"

"I haven't been keeping it from you!" That's instinctive defensiveness, and we both know it's not true. So I add, "Okay, fine. But I told you before that I don't tell this stuff to anyone."

"Well, you could have told me at least."

"Aren't you anyone?"

"No, I'm not just anyone. And I want to know all of it." He takes a step closer to me, his gaze never leaving mine.

"All... of... it?" It's a miracle I manage to get a coherent sentence out, given the way my heart is hammering. I'm a little scared to imagine how I look right now—all wide eyes and flushed cheeks and parted lips.

"Yes." His eyes heat up for a moment—or maybe I imagine it. But I definitely don't imagine the way his gaze flickers down to my chest and lingers on my neckline for longer than it should.

I've got a very curvy figure—so curvy that I used to always be on a diet until I finally accepted that this is my body—and my boobs are probably my best feature.

For one thrilling moment, I'm sure that Mike is noticing their appeal, a respectable amount of cleavage set off by the V of my top.

But then he gives a dry quirk of his mouth. "For instance, I would have been much less intimidated by you for all these years had I known you were secretly a groundhog."

It's like a blow to the gut, the sudden shift in mood. "A groundhog?"

"Yes. I didn't know the world made you anxious and you liked to burrow down and hide yourself from the world. I would have liked to know this earlier."

"I get that, but do you really have to compare me to a groundhog?"

"They're pretty cute. What would you prefer?"

"I don't know. A more interesting animal. Like a wombat."

He's grinning warmly. "Wombat. That's perfect for you. They're great burrowers." He works on his phone for a few seconds and then hands it to me. I stare down at a photo on the screen. It's Mike—dressed in dirty jeans and a gray T-shirt. He's kneeling on the ground with his hand on a large, furry animal with a very cute face. "That's from when I was working in Australia several years ago."

"Oh, I love him!"

"I thought you would." When I look up, Mike's eyes are soft on my face.

I gulp. "He looks very cozy and huggable."

"Well, it takes some work to get wombats to trust you, but it's worth the effort."

For a moment, I can't look away from him. It's not clear who he's even talking about now. Afraid all my composure is being melted away by his warmth, I make myself say something casual. "Okay. I'll admit it. I've always secretly been a wombat. I'll try not to keep such things from you again."

"Be sure that you don't."

He leans toward me, suddenly closer than I realized. My breath hitches as I think he's going to kiss me.

He doesn't. He gives a weird little jerk and then flicks a stray piece of my hair. "I'll see you at seven, Aurora."

He's gone before I can get another word out.

3

I spend an hour or so under the covers in bed—not sleeping, just recovering emotionally from the trip and my talk with Mike. But I make myself get up early enough to shower, shave, lotion, pluck, dress, and apply makeup far more carefully than I usually do.

I've got good skin—clear and smooth—and my eyelashes are naturally dark, so I usually don't bother much with makeup beyond a little powder and gloss. I don't normally wear pants as sleek and sexy as the ones I put on or tops with such a revealing neckline. And I definitely don't make a habit of more than a cursory shave a couple of times a week. But I want to look as good as I can tonight. While I know rationally that there's not much chance of anything happening beyond dinner and conversation, a little sliver of my heart isn't convinced.

I'm hoping for more, so I want to be ready just in case.

Mike knocks on my door at exactly seven—he's always been surprisingly punctual for such a laid-back man—and I can't help but smile when I see him. He's changed into an untucked black button-up and nice gray trousers. He looks more put together than normal.

As if he made an effort the way I did.

"You look great," he says, his voice a bit gravelly like it was earlier this afternoon.

"Thanks." I'm staring at the floor because I'm too embarrassed to look him in the eye. I'm not used to feeling this way. It's thrilling and terrifying and frustrating.

I'm never going to be good at flirting, but the least I can do is hold my head up and have a halfway lucid conversation. So I wrench up my chin. "Ready?"

"Been ready for a really long time."

I have no idea what that means. I know what I *want* it to mean, but that's very likely my hormone-afflicted imagination. I open my mouth to reply. Smooth. Witty. Light. Natural. Like the Aurora of all my daydreams.

Instead, I make a ridiculous squeaky sound.

His mouth twitches slightly, and he puts a hand on my back to get me out of the room.

Shit.

This isn't going well at all.

Is he laughing at me?

My cheeks are burning when we reach the elevator. I focus on the illuminated numbers above the doors.

"Y'okay?" he asks.

I turn my head to see he's peering at me.

"Yes." I elevate my eyebrows in an attempt at cool inquiry. "Why?"

"Because. You're tense. And flushed. Do you feel okay?"

I know for a fact that Mike isn't clueless. He's smart and observant and intuitive, so evidently I'm hiding my flustered nerves better than I realized.

This knowledge relieves me. I give him a real smile. "Yeah. I'm fine. Just bracing myself. For being out there with all those people."

"Oh. Of course." He's relaxing too now. He rubs my back gently. "We don't have to go out. We can just grab something to eat here—"

"No, no. I'd like to go out. It's not a huge deal. I mean, it makes me tense and jittery, but it doesn't keep me from doing things. If you understand what I mean. Once I'm at a table in a restaurant, I'll be just fine."

"Okay. Great. I made reservations at a place a friend recommended, but we can go somewhere else if you'd rather do—"

"That sounds great!" When he blinks, I temper my tone. "I mean, that was a good idea. I'm not picky about food, so I'm sure whatever your friend recommended will be perfect."

The elevator finally arrives—stuffed full of people from the higher levels of the hotel—and I take a deep breath before I make myself step on.

I hate crowded elevators and will often walk if it's a reasonable amount of stairs. We're too high for that right now, so I have to get on.

It's actually not as bad as it could have been. Mike maneuvers us against one of the walls and uses his body to block me from the surrounding passengers. Maybe he's not doing it on purpose, but it's nice just the same.

It feels protective.

Other than my brother, no one has ever really protected me before.

We walk six blocks to the restaurant and only wait a few minutes for our table. We talk about New York as we get our drinks, and we talk about Mike's PhD program while we wait for our food, and we talk about my family and my growing up years and my hopes for the future while we eat.

As soon as we sit at the table, I relax enough to talk naturally. And it gets easier and easier as the meal progresses. Mike answers my questions honestly, and he asks me real questions in return—ones he seems to genuinely want to know answers to, ones that require me to be more open about my real feelings than I almost ever am.

When dessert comes—a piece of chocolate caramel cheesecake that we share since we're both pretty full from our pasta dishes—my head and heart are both buzzing with a kind of excitement I haven't felt in years.

Maybe this is real.

Maybe this isn't just in my imagination.

Maybe the warm look in Mike's eyes is exactly what I'm hoping.

Or maybe not.

I don't want to get ahead of myself and end up crushed when I discover the reality. That he just thinks of me like a friend. Or he feels sorry for me and is giving me one fun night out on the town.

It's possible. Maybe even likely. I've been invisible to men most of my life, so there's no reason to assume that the man of my dreams will suddenly be attracted to me. My ex-husband was a decent man and one of the few who ever really seemed into me for a while. We were hot for each other for a couple of years, but once the heat faded, so did everything else between us. Eventually, it felt like we were strangers. We were both relieved when we got divorced. But Mike feels different. It's not just heat. It's like something more—something deeper—is drawing me toward him.

So maybe...

All this to explain why my head is spinning from wine and good food and a lot of feelings far more intoxicating than alcohol when we get up to leave.

I'm not in a fit state to maneuver through the crowded sidewalks or cross traffic-filled streets. I keep as close to Mike as possible, occasionally grabbing for his arm. Eventually, he takes my hand so that we don't get pushed apart.

I tell myself it's practical. Nothing but a commonsense strategy to keep us from being separated.

But he doesn't let my hand go even when the sidewalk clears a little.

I like it so much. The feeling of being connected to him. Like he's claiming me as his by the simple gesture.

We're quiet as we enter the hotel and ride up to our floor. He lets go of my hand in the elevator, so we're not touching as we walk down the hall toward our rooms. When we reach them, we stand silently, staring at each other in front of my door.

"Well," I say at last, since one of us needs to say something.

"Well."

"Thanks for tonight. You should have let me pay."

"I wanted to do it."

"Okay. Thanks." I look down and then up again. His blue eyes are soft and hot both.

So soft. So hot.

I can barely breathe.

"You're welcome," he murmurs, low and husky.

I suck in a breath. Let it out. I see him do the same.

My hand is shaking as I unlock my door and turn the knob.

I step in. Look back. Find the courage to begin, "Do you—"

"Yes!" He steps into my room and pulls me into his arms.

4

As soon as Mike's lips touch mine, a fire ignites inside me.

A fire like I've never experienced before.

I've had good sex before. My ex-husband and I were great in the bedroom for a couple of years. I've been turned on. I've been excited. I've felt like I could explode from the intensity of my lust.

But this is more.

This is different.

This fire isn't simple desire—at least not as I've ever felt it before. The heat spirals out from my heart and overwhelms my whole body as Mike's mouth moves against mine, hard and hungry and urgent.

He turns me around and steps me against the entryway wall, the door to the room falling shut on its own. I hear the click of the latch—a strangely freeing sound. It means we're safe in this room. Alone. A locked door standing between the two of us and the rest of the world.

I have no idea why this is a thought that passes through my mind, but the idea materializes and takes hold as Mike pushes me against the wall with the strength of his kiss.

His lean body is hard and warm against mine. His hands are moving greedily, feeling me all over. As if the deep curves and valleys of my body are his and his alone.

Desire pulses between my legs, and it's swallowing up all my normal reserve. I'm rocking shamelessly against him, trying to feel him exactly the way I need him.

He's making hungry sounds into the kiss, and they're the hottest things I've ever heard. He's turned off all his inhibitions, and it makes me want to do the same. I claw at his back through the wrinkled fabric of his shirt. I need to get it off. I want to feel his bare skin.

Maybe he reads my mind. He suddenly breaks the kiss and fumbles to unbutton his shirt. I help him—or maybe slow him down in my clumsy eagerness—but we eventually yank off his shirt and then pull off the undershirt he has on beneath it.

I'm about to grab him again since I can now get my hands on his skin, but he doesn't give me the chance. He pulls my top off over my head and stares down at my breasts in my black bra (as sexy a bra as I can find in my size while still doing the job I need it to do).

His blue eyes blaze. "Oh fuck, baby. You're so gorgeous."

I'm not sure which surprises and thrills me more, the endearment or the compliment. Before I can respond, he's kissing me again, and soon I can't form any words at all beyond repeated gasps of "yes" and "please."

Eventually, his kisses move from my mouth to my neck and then even lower. I arch helplessly against the wall as he nips lightly at one nipple and then the other through my bra. I'm so turned on that I raise one leg and wrap it around his thighs. It's not the most stable of positions, but I need stimulation on my aching arousal, and I need it now. He's just as turned on as I am, if the hard bulge I feel at the front of his pants is any indication.

I have no idea how long this lasts, since my mind has become nothing more than a heated blur. But eventually I become aware of the fact that Mike is moving us toward the bed without ever letting me go.

I'm so excited by this development that I bump into the corner of the bed frame and fall forward, taking Mike with me. We end up in a messy tumble.

He's chuckling as he turns me over and climbs on top of me, evidently unconcerned by the fact that we're at the foot of the bed, my legs hanging over the side.

His eyes are so hot that I'm surprised when he pauses, propped above me. He cups my cheek gently. "Tell me you want this, Aurora."

My lips part. My heart hammers. My cheeks blaze. "I want this." I should just stop there, but I can't. I've always been good at holding back my words, hiding my heart from the world. But it spills out now before I can stop it. "I want *you*."

He makes a weird gruff sound and kisses me again, and nothing stops us after that. We kiss and roll around and clumsily take off each other's clothes until we're naked on top of the coverlet, still hanging partway off the side of the mattress.

When we've gotten his underwear off, I grab for his erection, not caring if it makes me look shameless. He groans as I stroke him, his head falling backward as my fingers move down to his balls. He doesn't let me play with him for long, however. "I don't think you realize how far gone I am, baby," he murmurs, pulling my hands away. "You do that anymore, and this will be over before it's started."

No way not to like hearing that. I beam at him rather foolishly.

Something in my expression makes him chuckle and kiss me softly. Then his eyes move up and down my naked body, getting hotter as they do. "What did I do to deserve this?" he breathes, so softly I barely hear him.

But I *do* hear him. My heart gives a dramatic flip-flop, and I can't get any words out in response.

He's parting my legs when I remember something. "Should we use—"

He blinks. "Oh. Yes. Of course. Shit, I almost got carried away. I've got something with me." He hefts himself to his feet, finds his trousers of the floor, and pulls a condom packet out of the pocket before he rips it open and rolls it on.

Relieved that preliminaries are taken care of, I pull him back on top of me again, spreading my thighs to make room for him. He's so tense he's almost shaking with it as he aligns himself at my entrance and pushes in.

I make a silly sound of pleasure and surprise at the tightness of the penetration. We take a minute to adjust to each other before he starts to thrust. His motion starts slow and steady, but it doesn't last that way for long. We're both pretty far gone, and soon we're rocking together vigorously, shaking the bed and jiggling every part of my body in uninhibited enthusiasm.

It feels so good I can't hold back the sounds I make every time he pushes in. At first, they're little gasps. Then cries. Then helpless sobs as the pleasure coalesces and then crests in a hard orgasm.

He's right behind me, bellowing out his release as his body shakes and jerks against me.

We collapse together, hot and sweaty and breathless and replete.

Maybe it wasn't the longest or most creative sex I've ever had, but I can't remember anything ever feeling better than this. I feel *with* him. Connected. Like his body isn't just tangled with mine.

We're *one*.

I relax into the feeling, closing my eyes and snuggling against him. He's rolled us onto our sides so his weight isn't all on top of me. His arms are tight around me.

Soon, he'll need to let me go so he can take care of the condom, but he hasn't let go of me yet.

5

Nothing feels awkward between us until Mike finally gets up and walks to the bathroom naked.

I watch him go. His long legs. Tight butt. Red marks on his back from my fingernails.

For one moment, I'm happy. He looks like mine. Feels like mine. And we just had great sex.

Maybe he can be mine for real.

But as soon as I process this thought, all my normal anxieties force their way back into my mind in a painful rush.

I'm paying Mike for this weekend. That's the only reason he's here with me. And while it's obvious that he enjoyed the sex, he probably would never have gone to bed with me had I not been paying for his services.

He's brilliant and funny and kindhearted and incredibly hot. He could have any woman he wanted. I'm not going to be stupid about this. I'm not going to act like a naive, clueless girl who doesn't understand the realities of the world (even if I sometimes feel like that's who I am).

I'm going to be smart and mature and not get carried away.

I might be in love with Mike O'Dell, but he's not in love with me. If he were even the slightest bit interested in me, he would have asked me out months or years ago.

He never did. He never did anything more than chat with me until I paid him for this weekend.

Maybe he's expecting extra money for the orgasm he gave me just now.

The thought makes my stomach churn.

I hear the toilet flush in the bathroom.

Slightly shaky, I get up to grab an oversize T-shirt from my suitcase and pull it on, since I don't want to be naked anymore.

I want to get under the covers and pull them up over my head, but I manage to resist that impulse. Instead, I sit on the bed and wait until Mike comes out.

He smiles when he sees me, his expression softening in a way I love. "Hey."

"Hey." I smile back at him, reminding myself not to melt into a puddle of goo just because this man is looking at me in that way that feels special.

"That was amazing," he says, sitting down beside me and reaching over to take my hand.

"Yeah. It was really good." I swallow hard and respond to a flood of nerves by mentally chanting *Don't be stupid* over and over again. "Th-thank you."

He blinks twice. "Yeah."

Something in his tone sounds off, and I quickly try to fix whatever I messed up. "I mean, it was great. You were great. Thank you."

Okay. Perfect. I haven't fixed a single thing.

Being me, I try again. "I… I had a really good time. Thank you."

Shit, shit, shit, shit, shit.

He stands up, letting my hand slide out of his grip. "You don't have to thank me again. I had a great time too."

I lick my lips. "Okay."

He pulls on his clothes and then leans down to give me a soft kiss. "I'll see you in the morning."

He walks out of the room, and I burrow under the covers, pulling them over my head in a futile attempt to keep out the rest of the world and the mess I somehow managed to make just now.

* * *

The next morning, Mike texts to confirm the time I want to go down to the brunch, and he shows up at my door exactly on time and looking heart-stoppingly handsome in a suit and tie. His shirt is a little wrinkled, which would normally make me smile.

But I don't feel like smiling this morning because Mike's manner is perfectly appropriate. Polite. Friendly. Accommodating.

And the real him—the one I've come to know and love over the past three years—is entirely absent.

He's withdrawn in some indescribable way. I know it for sure. And I hate every moment of his civil smile and empty eyes.

I go through the motions as best I can, even quieter than normal. I'm not even as nervous as I normally would have been about being the center of attention because I'm so upset about the change in Mike and what it means.

I receive my service award, and I give a three-minute thank-you with perfect composure. I don't care about any of it. I just want to fix things with Mike—go back to how we were before.

I never would have slept with him if I'd known it would mess things up. Better to have him in my life in some small way than to have nothing but this vacant shell of the man I knew.

I'm trapped by fear and indecision, and it doesn't get better as the brunch ends, we return to our rooms to pack up, and then we take a taxi to the airport. Mike takes care of me as we go. He keeps a hand on my back as we walk, and he makes sure to keep us away from the worst of the crowds. I admitted to him yesterday that I hate making my way through New York, and he hasn't forgotten that.

I'd be touched if I weren't so upset about everything else.

My instinct when I feel this way is always to hide. To bury myself deep inside. I'm a wombat, after all. So I'm almost entirely silent on our trip home to Atlanta. I know I need to say something as soon as we touch down and make our way through the airport.

We're getting different rides back home.

This is the end of the trip.

And it might be it for us too.

I'm fighting to hold back tears, so I keep my chin raised as we stand on the curb and look at each other.

"Thank you," I manage to say. "I really appreciate your coming with me."

"You're welcome. It was my pleasure."

I bite my lower lip, unnerved by the sober way he's watching me. "Okay."

"Okay."

"Do you..." I trail off, unable to complete the question. I'm not even sure what I was trying to ask.

Something flickers in his expression. "Do I what?"

"Do you want..." I trail off again, the words completely trapped in my throat.

"Do I want what, Aurora?"

Oh God, I'm cornered now. I have absolutely no idea what to say. So I blurt out, "Did I give you enough money?"

That is not—*not*—what I wanted to say.

He freezes, something in his eyes chilling the flutters in my heart. "Yes," he says at last. "You were very generous. Thank you."

With that, he turns around and walks away.

* * *

I'm pretending to work in my office early on Monday morning when Weston finds me.

"Shit, Roar," he says after a normal greeting. "What the hell happened?"

I blink and force a smile. "Nothing. I'm fine. What are you talking about?"

"Why the hell do you try that with me?" he demands, yanking my side chair an extra foot from my desk before he drops into it. "You look like hell. You think I don't know you."

Of course Weston knows me. Better than anyone else. Our parents were decent but distant in our childhood years, and they moved to Florida ten years ago to basically begin a new life. We still call them weekly and visit a few times a year, but for a long time we've been the only real family the other has.

"Oh, I don't know," I admit now. "It's all a mess. I messed it up."

Weston's bearded face is mostly impatient, but his brown eyes are sympathetic. He looks a lot like me, but quite unjustly the solid frame and wide face look a lot better on him than on me. Women have always liked him. Even the dimple he tries to hide with the full beard has done more for him than it's ever done for me. "What did you do?"

"I don't know. I got anxious and uptight, and things are weird between us now."

He's frowning as he thinks for a minute. "Okay. I'm not too good at nuances, but can't you just call him up and fix things?"

"Yes, I could. But what am I supposed to say?"

"Tell him the truth."

Weston is always like that. Cut through the bullshit (his word, not mine) and get done what you want to get done.

"Right. I'm just supposed to call him up and blurt out that I... that I..."

"That you're into him. What's wrong with that?"

"What's wrong—" I'm almost sputtering in my outrage. "Are you serious? You do know who I am, right?"

"Yes, I know who you are. That's why I'm saying this. If you want something, you have to take some real steps. You've always been good at that with everything but relationships. If you're happy on your own, then it doesn't matter. But it seems like you're not."

"I am happy."

"Okay. But you could be happier. So why not take a real step. Call him up. How bad can it be?"

"It can be terrible!" The words come out as a wail.

"How much worse can it be than right now?" He stands up. "Do what you want, Roar. But guys are clueless a lot of the time. And I guarantee there's a good chance he has no idea how into him you are. So why not give him a chance?"

He doesn't wait for an answer before he leaves, closing my office door behind him. I stare at the door, my mind whirling and my heart starting to race.

Maybe Weston is right. Things didn't fall apart between us until I got scared. My first instinct was to assume Mike had emotionally retreated from me because he didn't want me and felt awkward about it, but he was actually really sweet after sex. He didn't pull away until I started trying to protect myself.

And even if he doesn't want me, what's the worst that can happen? He could tell me no. It's not going to feel any worse than I feel right now.

I pick up my phone and find Mike's number. I breathe in and out slowly, trying to work up the courage and mentally plan out what I can say. I haven't gotten very far when there's a knock on my office door.

"Not now, Weston," I call out, unable to keep the frustration out of my tone. "I'm trying to call, and I don't need any more pep talks!"

To my astonishment, the door opens. Weston's voice says, "You can put down your phone."

I stand up, ready to give Weston a good talking-to for invading my privacy this way (something he's never done before). But before I can get a word out, a man steps into my office.

Not Weston.

This man is a couple of inches shorter. Less broad across the shoulders. No beard except a thick five-o'clock shadow from going a day too long without shaving. He's got blue eyes. A thin, intelligent mouth. And he's wearing a very wrinkled blue shirt under his jacket.

"Mike?" The one word comes out in an embarrassing squeak.

His eyes are sober as he comes closer to my desk. "Yeah. Sorry for just busting in like this, but Weston said he thought it'd be all right. I wanted to talk."

"You did?"

"Yeah." Now that he's close, I can see deep shadows under his eyes. He looks like he hasn't slept in two nights.

Neither have I.

"O-kay." My plan is to sit back down, but I kind of collapse into my desk chair instead.

Mike pulls the chair that Weston moved away from the desk closer and sits down in it. "I don't know if you want to hear from me. I thought you'd made it really clear that you just wanted what happened to be a one-time thing. And if that's what you want, I'll respect it. I promise I will. I'll leave you alone if you tell me to." The words are coming out in a hoarse rush, which isn't like him at all. "But I can't... I can't just let it go like this. I've wanted this for too long, and it seemed like... Maybe I let my hopes run away with me, but it really seemed like we might... we might... work."

I stare at him, so shocked I can't move or speak.

He swallows hard. "When you pulled away after we had sex, I told myself to live with it. At least I had one amazing night with you that I can... I can hold on to. But it's not enough. It's never going to be enough. I want... more."

If it were possible for a head to explode from an excess of surprise and excitement and pure joy, mine would be exploding right now. "You want... more?"

He nods. "I want more. I want everything from you, Aurora. I've been crazy about you for years now, but you were always so self-contained that I assumed you'd never give me a second look. But this weekend I saw another side of you. A side I… I love. And that's the woman I want. The whole thing. The real you. So if you think you might want to… to try…."

"Yes!" Being me, my response isn't entirely socially appropriate. It comes out way too loud, and I punctuate it by throwing myself into his arms without warning.

He manages to hold on to me, laughing as he gives me a tight hug. "Really, baby? You want me too?"

"I've never wanted anyone more. I just got scared. Afterward. But I'm crazy about you too." My voice wobbles slightly, but I don't even care.

It's impossible to regret anything when Mike is gazing at me with his deep, warm heart in his eyes. "So you want a real relationship with me?" he asks. "A serious one?"

"Yes. As serious as it gets. That's what I want with you."

I could probably tell him more. I could probably tell him I love him. And if his expression is any indication, he might even say it back.

But we have time for that. We have time for everything.

After all, we haven't even had our first real date.

* * *

Do you want more of Noelle Adams?

One click PART-TIME HUSBAND now!

KENNEDY'S AUSSIE

NANA MALONE

1

The sound of my heels on the polished marble made a click-clacking sound. I mentally went over everything for my meeting.

Pastries had been ordered.

Presentation materials all laid out, and all other preparations are done.

I loved this feeling, the hum.... the excitement... *A new client.*

This was where I shined. Bringing them into the London Lords fold. Making them part of our brand. I loved every moment of it.

I didn't know much about the new client except that Ben was prepping the handoff himself, which meant it was a potentially huge client. Good, because frankly, Ben owed me.

He'd taken my best executive assistant. I'd been grooming her for something bigger. I wanted her to follow in in my footsteps. She might have just been an assistant, because that was the position I had open at that time. But she was smart. Bright. Fun. And I liked her on a personal level. But she was also shrewd. She knew how to handle a client and was so organized, it made me weep on occasion. Before I could even ask for something, she'd already anticipated it and laid it out, given me my pros and cons, made a list for me, and all I had to do was choose.

But before I could really groom her, Ben had poached her for himself.

It was fine. He did own the place, after all. Ben Covington, East Hale, and Bridge Edgerton were the London Lords. Cocky. Arrogant. So handsome that they'd make the devil weep. They were rich beyond imagining. And they paid me handsomely.

I rounded the corner, gently smoothing the lines of my burgundy sheath dress I knew played well on my olive skin. I was in charge. I could do this.

My little pep talk was all part of the routine. That little boost of energy and confidence before I walked in.

I plastered a smile on my face that said *warm* and *welcoming* but also *shrewd* and *not to be dicked with*. I'd been working on that particular smile for years.

I opened the door and saw Ben first. He gave me a broad smile, then stood. And when I pushed the door open farther, there *he* was, leaning back in his seat like he owned the place. Slightly mussed dark hair, a lock falling over his brow. Emerald green eyes that were cunning and mischievous narrowed at me. And I froze.

My brain did a quick mental calculation. If I continued inside, I would be forced to deal with him. Forced to acknowledge what I'd done. Forced to acknowledge what *he'd* done. Forced to wrestle with the ghosts of my past.

However, if I ran, I might not even have to see him again.

Somewhere in the far recesses of my mind, rationality tried to beckon. Tried to talk me down. *Yes, but if you run, how do you explain that to Ben? You won't be doing your job. Your job is who you are.*

At thirty-one, I had friends, a family who loved me, but no romantic love on the horizon, no children. I had hobbies, but nothing I loved as much as my job. I had often tried to get more balance, but nothing gave me the same kind of electrical charge.

That's not true.

Okay, fine. Jax Kincade had always given me that kind of electrical charge. But, he was a liar, a cheater, a conniving, arrogant alpha—

Make or break time.

The fight-or-flight reaction was strong. I couldn't help it. I could fight. I could run. Sweat beaded on my skin. *Choose. Choose. Choose. Choose.*

And I did. The heavy glass door didn't make a sound as it closed behind me. But heels sure did in a fast *clickity-clack, clickity-clack, clickity-clack* as I ran down the hall.

I didn't give a shit what Ben thought. No way, no how, was I sitting through a meeting with Jax Kincade.

* * *

Jax

I had known she would run. I'd expected nothing less. After all, the last time she saw me, she'd left me handcuffed to a bed. I, like a fool, had expected her to come back.

But she hadn't. It had taken me hours to get free. I'd had to break the damn headboard and nearly dislocated my shoulder.

And through those hours, I'd had time to stew about why she would have left me like that, why she'd walked out on me. Why the woman I'd fallen in love with against my better judgment, would disappear from my life.

I'd gone through all the stages. Denial. Anger. I hadn't hit acceptance until I'd seen the magazine article that had been just under the television with me and Alicia on the cover.

And then I'd known why she ran. I had known why she walked out and never came back.

That was two years ago. I had been deserving of her leaving because I'd lied to her. Or rather, I hadn't told her the *whole* truth. If I had, she might not have believed me at first, but I would have made her believe me.

And if need be, I would have had her talk to Alicia, to let her know that our marriage had been just for show. One of convenience so Alicia could inherit from her very traditional father. But I hadn't had a chance to explain then.

I had tried calling, only to find out she'd very quickly changed her number. And then, when I went to her office to try and speak to her, desperate to explain, they told me that she'd unexpectedly quit.

Her apartment, much the same. Cleared out unexpectedly. She had gone to the States. It had taken several months for a private investigator to find her. It had taken enough alcohol to embalm a body to try to let her go. But that hadn't worked. And then I had set my plan into motion.

First, I'd had to deal with the Alicia thing. We'd had to wait the appropriate amount of time until we could actually separate. But as soon as the papers were signed and I found Kennedy, I'd formulated a plan. It had to be a good one, because I'd only have one shot at it.

And I'd known she'd be mad. I'd known she'd run.

Like now.

I pushed up on my feet. "If you'll excuse me for a while, Ben."

Ben Covington's brows rose. "I'm so sorry, Jax. It's unlike Kennedy. She probably forgot something."

"Yeah. No, no problem. I'm actually going to take the opportunity to hit up the loo."

Ben nodded. "Yeah, go ahead. I'll, um, try and reach her office and see what's going on."

I nodded. "It's fine. I could use a couple of minutes myself."

"Right."

Kennedy was faster than I remembered. Hopefully I could catch her before she made it out of the building. What was she going to do, quit this job too?

When I met her a few years ago at Morrison Hotels, they'd been working to broker one of my luxury villas and make it part of the Morrison brand. Kind of a younger, hipper version of the hotel. In the end, the deal had fallen through and it hadn't been the right move for me.

But London Lords, they were right in the brand wheelhouse. They felt like me. And as an added bonus, Kennedy was their Vice President of Client Acquisition. Wasn't that handy?

I yanked the door and ignored Ben when he asked if I needed to know where it was. “Nope, thanks, mate.” I knew what I wanted.

The sound of her shoes clued me in to which way she'd gone. And I made quick work of running after her.

I caught her in the stairwell.

She was in the process of shoving the door behind her as she ran, but I held it open easily.

Her dark eyes went wide. Russet hair fell off her shoulders as she backed up. "Leave me alone."

"I'm sorry, love, I can't."

"Oh, but you can. You're just choosing not to. I swear to God, I will scream."

"You will scream, guaranteed. But not because you want to get rid of me."

"I hate you," she snapped.

She had a right to. I had fucked up. But I was here now. And I was going to make it better.

"I know. I know why you ran too."

She narrowed dark eyes at me. "Because you are a lying, conniving, son of a—"

I slammed my lips over hers.

There wasn't finesse. There wasn't a slow glide. I had come all this way to claim her. To make her mine. And I was impatient. The blood hummed under my skin. It had been so fucking long since I'd tasted her. I didn't want to wait. I couldn't. All I had dreamed about was this moment. Two years ago I'd vowed to get her back. And that was what I was going to do. But I knew this was going to take some convincing.

Her hands pushed at me, but her tongue slid over mine.

I shoved my hands into her hair, tugging just a little bit, the way she liked, and she made this low keening sound in her throat. I backed her against the concrete wall and then tore my lips from hers and kissed along her jaw. When I reached the shell of her ear, I whispered, "Scream all you want. Let them see you come."

"I am not coming. Get your hands off me."

With a gentle tug, I angled her head up so I could stare into her chocolate-dark depths. I wanted to be sure. She was mine. But I wanted her to feel safe.

Oh, there was anger there, for sure. But also, her pupils were dilated. Her lips were bruised and parted. And she was panting.

"You know the word to use if you want me to stop."

She glowered at me and lifted her chin. "Asshole."

I grinned. "That's not the word, sweetheart." This time I was slower with my kiss. A gentle glide as I licked her mouth with my tongue. The heat to my cock was instant. And I couldn't lie, it nearly buckled my fucking knees when my legs turned to jelly.

But this wasn't about me. *None* of this was about me. I wanted to show her that I was sorry. So, as much as I was dying, desperate to sink deep inside her and never fucking leave, this was more about making her remember. I knew my words wouldn't be enough. There was no way she would forgive me with just words. I had to make her remember what we were like.

I slid my hands over her hip and the soft material of her dress. I bunched it up quickly, pulling it higher along her thighs until I slipped my fingers under the fabric. She moaned softly when I grazed the edge of her panties.

Against her lips, I whispered, "Say the word. Go on. You remember it, don't you?"

"You Aussie prick."

I chuckled as I kissed her again. Those weren't the words either. I slid my fingers along her slit, and she gasped, allowing me more access so I could kiss her deeper and pull a response from her. Get her to give me what I wanted, what we both needed.

She was soaking wet. My fingers had a slippery glide along her folds, and then I gently dipped one in. Her hips rocked slightly, and I growled with satisfaction. Yeah, that was it. She remembered.

It was so easy with us. Volatile. Combustible. I switched my angle and then grabbed the cotton of her panties and yanked them hard, pulling them down, giving me better access. When she was bare to me, I slid a finger all the way in.

Her breath hitched as I gently rubbed my thumb on her clit.

Jesus Christ. She shook. And all I wanted to do was open my trousers, free my cock and slide it home. And no, this time, I wouldn't be fucking using condoms. I would slide into her bare, praying to God she wasn't on the pill. I wanted everything from her. She'd be mine. And she would never run from me again.

Easy, prick, she had a reason to run.

The problem was, my rational brain warred with that caveman part of me that wanted to grab her by the hair and drag her back to my cave. She was mine. *Had* always been mine from the moment I'd laid eyes on her in that first meeting.

She'd been new to Sidney, and I had offered to show her Australia. She clocked me right away as a player, playboy, an arrogant, wolfish jerk, and she'd said no.

And then, as luck would have it, I happened to overhear that she had booked herself on tours. So I booked tours along with her.

In the end, it hadn't been the arrogance or charm that had worked with her. But being real. I showed her parts of Australia that she may never have seen. Our guide had been excellent. We had spent our days with a group of two other couples, seeing as much of Australia as we could. From Sidney to Perth to Melbourne, and then spent three days in the outback, camping.

She hadn't loved camping. But it hadn't even been a real camping. It had been glamping. It was one of those fancy tents with a shower included.

But under the stars, I'd broken through and she'd been mine.

And then you ruined it.

I pulled my finger from her, and she whimpered. I knew what she needed. I sank two fingers into her and then rubbed slow, gentle circles up her clit. And there it was, the shaking, the slight quivering as I increased the movements of my fingertips. Slide. Retreat. Slide. Retreat. I needed to be quick, because despite what I'd said, that I wanted everyone to see that she was mine, what I could make her do, she worked here. And I knew how she felt about her job. She loved it. She always said that she *was* her job. I wouldn't want her to be embarrassed. I wouldn't want anyone else seeing what was mine. But I needed to cement our bond and do it quickly. I dragged my lips from hers, sliding my nose against her jaw and then up her neck to her ear.

"Hurry up and come. You know you want to. Hate me all you want, but know that this is good."

Her lips pressed against my neck, and she bit me as she broke apart on my fingers. Soaking them. Fuck, yes.

Both of us panting, I pulled my fingers from her and slid her panties back up. She shoved at me, and this time, I let her.

She smoothed down her dress and glared at me. "I hate you."

Gaze pinned on her, I licked my fingers, relishing her taste. "I know. But what do you say we go back to that meeting? Because your boss is waiting, and I have a proposal for you."

Her brows furrowed. I could tell I'd struck a nerve, because now that she wasn't running and now that I'd made her come, her rational brain had started to kick in. She still had a job to do at the very least, until she could get out of here without raising too many eyebrows.

"I'm not working with you."

"Why don't we see about that?" Then I watched her shakily stride in front of me to the door, swinging it open.

She turned briefly to meet my gaze over her shoulder. "You put your hands on me again, I'll break your hand."

I grinned then. "Uh-huh. Is that what you call that just now? Breaking my hand? I'm here for it."

"God, you're a prick."

"I know, but I'm your prick."

2

Kennedy

Well that had gone well.

If "well" meant I'd completely fucked up and embarrassed myself in front of my boss.

Also, if "well" meant having a hot-as-sin hate finger-bang with someone you despised.

I could barely walk. My knees wobbled, and my breaths came in shallow pants. But I needed to make this happen. I hated Jax Kincade. I loathed him. He was a liar. But my body apparently didn't get that memo. So I was going to take that up with her because what had just happened in the stairwell could never happen again. I was embarrassed. Mortified. Humiliated.

But I was a goddamn professional. I was going to walk into that boardroom, do my thing, and *then* run. I might never even have to work with him. I could say there was a conflict.

As if Ben would buy that. I'd never asked for anything before, though. In the two years since I'd started working with London Lords, I'd been on my shit. Poised. Cool. Controlled. I never had a problem. Maybe just this one time, he'd let me get away with it.

Coward.

It was embarrassing to think that I was willing to run away from this. But hey, sometimes you had to do what you had to do.

I marched into the boardroom and didn't bother waiting for Jax. I knew he was right on my heels. I could feel his heat. I could still hear that panty-burning growl he made in the back of his throat. Why did he think he could just own me? I wasn't his.

Oh yeah? Way to tell him that too.

When I marched in, I gave Ben a broad smile. "I'm so sorry about that. I forgot something for the slide. It's updated now."

I didn't care if he bought that excuse or not. He just watched me with a raised brow. Was something wrong with the way I looked?

And then I remembered the way Jax had fisted my hair. Now it probably resembled a helmet.

God, I really hated him.

Jax marched in with his smooth and easy confidence. "Found the loo. I ran into Kennedy here in the hallway. We were just getting acquainted."

Ben gave him a broad smile. But then, his gaze jumped back and forth between us, as if he knew. As if he understood exactly what was happening here.

He needed to mind his own damn business.

"So Mr. Covington, if you're ready, we'll get started."

As it turns out, my brain was able to put away some of the angst and survive the meeting. Somehow I managed to say the important things. Things like, *new client. Partnership. Branding potential. Opportunities.*

It was like I was watching myself from afar, watching myself perform, but I wasn't present. The present part of me was still dealing with the fact that Jax Kincade had just had fingers *in* me.

At one point during the meeting, I could have sworn I'd seen him with his fingers pressed against his lips, and Jax, the jackass, licked them. The slight smirk told me that he was thinking about what he had just done with those fingers.

Nevertheless, I finished the presentation. When all was said and done and hands were being shaken, I managed to give everyone my business no-nonsense smile. "So Mr. Kincade, I'll have my office drop off some of the paperwork that will need to be filled out. You can have your director or marketing do them, have product engagement, whatever. It doesn't matter. We just need to get your vibe of who you are."

His emerald-green gaze pierced mine. "Well Kincade Properties has been going through a bit of a rebrand. Changing who we are. Growing up a little."

Uh-huh. I didn't believe it for a minute. But if he wanted to tell that lie, far be it from me to correct him in front of Ben.

"Well gentlemen, this has been terrific. It was really productive." I needed to get the hell out of here.

But Jax just wouldn't die. He was like that zombie in video games that craved more. More torment. More torture. Just more.

"Actually, Miss Bright, if you have some time to sit with me, I'd love to go over some of our plans again in more depth. I'll be staying in London for a while. So I'd love to get a jump-start."

I froze. What was he doing? We'd just had an hour-and-a-half-long meeting.

I couldn't even form the words. But oh, lucky me, there was Ben agreeing for me.

"That's a fantastic idea. Kennedy, anything you've got on this docket tonight, let's move it so we can make this happen."

I glowered at my boss, and his brows rose. He'd never been on the receiving end of my *are you fucking kidding me?* expression. And he seemed slightly terrified. That gave me, at least, some form of satisfaction.

"Um, right. I did have some things to take care of. Remember, I have Paris to deal with tomorrow? So I was hoping for the evening to tie things off."

"Yes, of course. But it's just dinner. It's not too long. And you're not going to Paris until the afternoon tomorrow, yes?"

"Yes, I have my flight at three."

"That's fantastic. The sooner we can get started on this, the better off it is."

I gritted my teeth. When I turned to Jax, he was grinning like an idiot. God, I would never escape him. The one man I'd let myself love. I was never ever going to escape him.

Oh yes, you are. You were different before. Then you were weak. But not anymore.

* * *

Kennedy

As I took my luggage ticket for the Eurostar, I couldn't help that niggling sense of guilt.

Well it wasn't my fault. It was *his*. Honestly, to be fair, he'd refused to listen when I said I couldn't meet with him. He'd insisted that we were going to meet; that was his problem. I already told him I was unavailable. Just because he and Ben had chosen not to listen to me, wasn't something I could control.

Your flight wasn't supposed to be until tomorrow afternoon.

Yes, this was true. But frankly, it was always best to go early and be over prepared.

Coward.

Fine, I was a slight coward. But after what had happened in the stairwell, there was absolutely no way I was going to sit across a dinner table from Jax Kincade in mood lighting, candlelight, soft music, and the tension between us coiling and spooling, tightening us together. *Nope.*

I was a total coward. I was running. But hey, sometimes when it came down to fight-or-flight, flight worked better.

When I had first seen that magazine article right under the television in the hotel, my heart had been eviscerated on the spot. I'd been in love with him. I was willing to stay in Australia and move my whole life for him. And there he was on the cover of *Business Entrepreneurs* with his wife for a magazine cover shoot, fresh that month. His fucking wife.

There was no amount of apologies or lies that could assuage that burn, that constant chafe. That flayed skin. And yes, this afternoon, things had gotten out of hand. He caught me when I was lonely and vulnerable. And it sucked. I had completely caved. But I wouldn't be caving in again.

I would not be *alphaed.* When he'd met me, I was naive. Soft. I was not that same woman. He couldn't just steamroll over my life. Roll in and tell me we were going to be together. What woman actually fell for that? The women I knew didn't let the men dictate to them.

I smiled at the attendant and asked where the business-class cabin was. He pointed it out, and I lifted my purse higher on my shoulder as I steered on, satisfied that at least I would get a few more days of reprieve to think through a game plan. I had a stack of résumés that I needed to go through for a new executive assistant. I also probably really needed to hire an operations position.

I found the cabin then took a step up into the train, except the journey would be technically overnight. I had secured one of the private rooms. But at the very least, I could stop and have a drink and get something to eat. I had been in such a hurry to leave and hadn't wanted Jax to find me at my flat, so I had left as soon as humanly possible.

I rolled into the dining car, eased myself onto a stool and smiled at the bartender. "May I have a rum and pineapple, and then see a dinner menu?"

He nodded, slid me a menu, and then went to get my drink. From behind me, someone said, "You didn't think you were going to get away that easy, did you?"

I whipped around on the stool, nearly falling off.

Jax reached out and grabbed me, securing me on the stool.

"What the fuck are you doing here?"

"You keep acting like I don't know you well. I knew you'd run. You should have known that I would chase you."

3

Kennedy

"Stalker much?" I ground out.

"You're angry. You have a right to be angry."

I glowered at him. "Of course, I'm angry. I told you I didn't want to meet. You insisted on us meeting. And much like the handcuff thing, I left you with your dick in your hand."

"Actually, that would have been preferable, but you see, I couldn't touch my dick because my hands were handcuffed to the headboard."

I conjured up resting bitch face expression number three. "I'm sorry. Except I'm not."

He shook his head, his emerald-green eyes flashing. His dark hair falling forward, curling slightly. I remembered that boyish look, the sweet smiles, and the way he made my skin sizzle. How I couldn't help but love him, and he'd torn me apart.

"I didn't want you to follow me."

"Sweetheart, when are you going to realize that there is nowhere on this earth that you would go that I won't follow?"

There he was again with those words. The words that made me believe things. But I knew better than to believe that. "Oh yeah? Took you two years to come find me. I guess you were looking real hard."

The muscle on his jaw ticked. "There were some things I had to do first."

"You know what? I don't care. I don't even want to engage in this conversation."

"But you *are* going to engage. But before you engage, I have to apologize to you."

I didn't owe him a thing. "God, I just want you to go away."

"Not until you listen."

He wasn't going to back down. I knew how stubborn he was. "If I listen, then will you leave me alone?"

"I will stop haranguing you to listen." He answered carefully.

"Okay, say what you have to say."

"Look, I spent hours angry with you for the handcuffs, but then I got free and I understood why you'd left. And I realized, all that anger should have been directed at myself. I lied to you."

"Lied? That's an understatement."

"Fine. I'm sure it felt like a betrayal."

"You're getting warmer."

"I'm not going to stand here and tell you what to do. What I want to do is club you in the head and drag you back to London with me. Even better, back to Australia. But I owe you more than that."

"You think you can drag me back? I'm not that same naive girl. I'd fight you every step of the way."

"I know that. I'm not going heavy-handed with you because I want to control you. I'm going heavy-handed because we belong together."

"Oh, awesome. Another man come to tell me how I *belong* with him and I'm *his*, and oh yes,... Of course, how I need to be *dominated*. You can take that patriarchal bullshit and shove it. Don't believe everything you read in romance novels. Those fantasies are great, but in real life, you dominate me and it's going to end up kicking you in the arse."

* * *

Jax

One slight miscalculation. This afternoon, I thought after what we'd done on the stairwell, she'd realize that we had unfinished business. And so, while she was angry with me, she would comply. I thought she wanted closure, just like I did.

Except you don't want closure.

No, the fuck, I did not. I wanted her as mine. Beneath me in bed. Where she fucking belonged. Fighting me in the boardroom where she fucking belonged. Never backing down from me when I got a little too high-handed, where she fucking belonged. Point-blank, I just needed her with me. And I thought she felt that.

Well we've all been wrong once.

I would not underestimate her again.

After we'd left the office, something told me to give her a ride to dinner to make sure she got there.

I had arrived at her place because I hoped we could speak. But then I had seen her with bags and getting into a taxi.

When she didn't head toward the restaurant or Heathrow, I had a feeling she was headed for a train. I made some quick calls, got myself tickets, and made arrangements in Paris. After all, she was supposed to be there tomorrow. I just never figured she wouldn't actually face me head-on.

Well you hurt her.

I had hurt her. The problem was, I couldn't apologize if she wouldn't let me. But this wasn't about me. This was about her and her willingness to accept that I was back and that I wasn't going anywhere. Whatever she needed, I was giving it to her. I would open up a vein and bleed for her. And I would continue trying because I hadn't tried hard enough then. Because I hadn't told her all the truth that I needed to tell then.

She was a fighter, the moment something pricked her sense of injustice, she fought bitterly. Maybe I hadn't told her the whole truth because I had known she would balk at being with me, even if I *was* just married on paper. Maybe she would tell me she'd wait until I could actually be with her because she was the kind of woman that deserved everything. I had loved her, and I had let her down. But it was time to fix that.

Her drink arrived and the bartender stared at her expectantly. She gave him a smile, slid him her credit card, and turned back to face me. "I'm so sorry. I have lost my appetite."

He brought her card back, and she signed for it. "I need you to leave me alone. I'm going to take my drink to the room."

I followed after her and she looked like she was wanted to fight my following her, but then she just let me.

God, this woman!

When we reached her cabin, she used her phone to unlock it and stepped in. It was pretty lush. They'd managed to squeeze a full bed in there. It looked like a high-end hotel. Except it was tiny.

I closed the door behind myself.

"You really thought I wouldn't come after you?"

"Why are you here?"

"We had a meeting scheduled."

"You know what, you're like a bunion that won't go away."

I laughed then. "God, do you know how long it took me to get out of those bloody handcuffs?"

She grinned. "Well you probably shouldn't let a woman tie you up."

"Fair enough. But you and I, we're doing this.

“Here we go again with that domineering bullshit.”

I chuckled softly. "I have no intention of dominating you. That would be stealing your shine. I would never want to do that. You're fire. You spark. That's what I love the most. I want you to fight me a little. It would be interesting to see who wins. Look, sometimes I'll be an asshole. Sometimes I'll be an alpha asshole, but guaranteed, I want you to call me on it. I intend for you to be my match. I intend for you to leave a few bruises. Hell, if you want to spank me, spank me.”

And then the fool that I was, I went over to the bed and started unbuckling my trousers. Her eyes went wide as they roved over my body. Thank Christ she wasn’t immune.

I dropped my trousers, showcasing trim black boxer briefs hugging my arse, and well, there was no hiding how hard I was. "Want to spank me? Go ahead."

Her lips quirked as she tried to hide her smile. But then the laugh bubbled forth. "What are you doing?"

"I'm showing you. I’m not trying to subjugate you in any way. That isn't what this is about. What this is about is, I love you. I haven't stopped loving you in the two years since you've been gone. I do think you're mine, *but,* I'm also yours. I missed my partner. I missed you fighting with me. I missed you calling me on my shit."

"Oh yeah? You missed me so much that you came after me?"

"I couldn't come after you. Not at first. Because you were right about so much; I had a few things to fix before I came to you.”

"I can’t do this.”

"Yes you can. Because you and I have unfinished business."

4

Kennedy

"Jax, you don't get it. You can't just waltz back into my life as if nothing happened. As if you didn't hurt me. As if everything is just as it was."

He stood, strode to me, and I backed up. But there wasn't anywhere to go. Just the window of the train and its gentle rocking movements.

"I know I don't have any right, but I also know that from the moment you walked out, I hadn't been able to think about anything other than getting you back. I messed up by not telling you things. It wasn't what you thought."

"It doesn't matter now, Jax. It's over. You and I are over. Have been for a long time. I just want to move on."

He leaned in, the heat of him searing my skin, sinking in under my pores, threatening to light me ablaze. I turned my head. No! I had to remain unattached. Calm. Deep breaths.

Except, when I inhaled, his spicy scent worked its way inside me, heating me up from the inside, causing a low pulsing tug in my core. Everything about him was pure sensuality and seduction. And those emerald-green eyes, with the wicked hint of a smile, the mischievous dance in them. My mother would say, he had the devil's own charm. And he did.

I wanted to believe him when he said he was here for me. I wanted to believe him when he said he was sorry. *I wanted to believe him.*

You want to believe him because he gives good orgasms.

But that wasn't enough. I needed more than good orgasms.

How about we start with good orgasms first and move forward from there?

"Kennedy, just let me explain. Let me show you how much I've missed you. Let me show you I'm sorry."

I stiffened. I tried to shove him away. But he was already there. He'd always been there. Deep in my soul. Wedged. A connection like I'd never had with anyone else. One I'd been chasing for the last two years, unable to quite grasp. Always fluttering through my fingertips like fog on a dewy morning, ethereal and not quite there.

But Jax was here now. He was real. I could feel the heat of him. As I backed up, he pressed in. His nose skimmed up the length of my neck and I shuddered. I was complete trash for that sensation of him teasing before the kiss. I couldn't trust my own body.

Or maybe your body knows just what you need.

"Jax, why are you torturing me?"

"I'm not torturing you. I want to give you exactly what you want. Just tell me yes and I'll do the rest."

The smart part of my brain said no. Hell, no. It was the same part of the brain that I'd completely ignored yesterday in the stairwell. Because who wouldn't do that thing where they listen to their rational brain?

You. You do. You like rational. Rational saved you. Rational is safe.

But maybe it was time to stop being safe. He was here in front of me, wanting to give me orgasms. What the hell was wrong with me that I wouldn't take them?

Take what he has to offer. Worry about the rest after.

I turned my face toward him, and he was watching me with the kind of intensity that made me clench. "What do you want, Kennedy? Just tell me."

My mouth was too dry. I couldn't focus. I couldn't think. "You. I want you."

"I want you too." And then his lips were on mine. They weren't gentle. They were harsh, brutal, claiming. A desperate meshing of two souls that had been kept apart far too long. His tongue slid over mine, demanding a response. Sucking. Tugging. Teasing. Every slide of his tongue, every nip of his teeth, my body arched into him and I couldn't move. I didn't want to leave the strength of his embrace. I wanted to climb into his heat. I wanted to have it incinerate me.

His hands moved over my hips, pulling me against him. The rigid length of him nudged my belly. Hot and intense. We panted, teeth clashing, desperation forcing us to tear at each other's clothes, hands sliding over each other, pulling off buttons.

Once I gave myself permission to want this, to need this, I started to yank off his jacket, and he accommodated me. He smoothed his hand over my ass, hooking his thumbs in my leggings. He tugged them down, having to break our kiss to make them work. After a shuffle and kicking and wiggles, he had me bare.

I kicked my leggings aside and went for the belt of his trousers, but he knocked my hands away and knelt before me.

Before I could even process what was happening, he parted my thighs with his strong hands and planted his mouth directly on my sex. Jax was an expert at going down.

It had been two years, but he hadn't forgotten what I liked. Licking my slit with the flat part of his tongue in a strong, firm stroke, but only teasing the clit, never a direct pressure, gently fucking me with his tongue and then moving to suck on my clit. Hard. Pulling a response from me. Demanding that I give him everything. I dropped my head back against the glass of the window of the train, unable to move away, unable to even process what the hell was going on. But God, I couldn't say no. I didn't want to say no. I wanted this to go on for—

With a muffled groan, he glided two fingers inside me. Sliding and scissoring them out, widening me, preparing me. And then, while he sucked on my clit, he found that spot. That sweet, sweet spot. And he pressed. I cried out and bucked my hips. He was ever so helpful, rubbing that spot, sucking my clit, and a slow retreat of his fingers to come back and rub that spot for me again. I clamped around his fingers, wanting to keep him there. Keep him inside, to make sure this continued forever and never stopped.

I cried out, "Jax!" breaking apart on his fingers and his tongue.

My legs shook. My breathing came out in erratic pants. I couldn't even lift my head off the glass. I was weak. Exhausted. But still, Jax sucked. His fingering gentled though. Slowing in easy slide and retreat. My body still tried to pull him in. Keep him there. Refusing to let him go, as if completely understanding that he could never leave me again.

You left him.

I shoved away any thoughts. Now was not the time for thinking. Now was the time for enjoying. There would be plenty of time for regret and mistakes and running later. But for now, now Jax Kincade was mine.

He's always been yours.

Gently, he pulled away and slid his fingers out of me, kissing the insides of my thighs and then my hip bone up to my belly button, up to my torso. He paused at my breasts and licked one nipple, drawing it into his mouth. And I cried out, "Jax, oh my God!"

He released it with a light *pop* sound. He murmured against my skin as he continued kissing his way up. "I remember how sensitive they are after you cum. If I tease you just right, tugging on them, pinching them a little, you might cum again."

"Holy hell..." Was all I could manage on a shuddering breath.

He kissed me long and deep now, pouring emotion into the kiss. His hands cupped my face, sliding into my hair. The gentle massage on the nape of my neck had me feeling like jelly. But then, he turned me around so now my bare breasts pressed against the cold of the glass. His body warming mine, and there was a rustling of clothes. He was getting naked. He pulled my top off, unstrapping my bra. He leaned against me and whispered at the shell of my ear. "Are you still on the pill?"

"Jax, what are you—"

"Are you still on the pill, Kennedy?"

Oh God, I knew what he was asking, and I needed it. I wanted it. I wanted to feel him inside me. "I-I am. I haven't been with anyone else."

That one cost me. Saying I hadn't slept with anyone else in two long years, admitting that, took a slice out of my heart.

"I haven't been with anyone either. It's been two years, Kennedy. We have a whole lot of making up to do."

The thick length of him pressed against my ass. I shuddered from the cold, but also from anticipation. I wanted this. I wanted all of him.

He dipped his legs slightly and nudged the thick, broad tip of his dick against my slick entrance. "I want to go slow. I do. But maybe a fast one first. It's been so long."

"Jax, hurry."

He knew what I needed all right. With one swift thrust, he slid home, and I gasped from the shock and the sudden fullness. He cursed in my ear and held himself perfectly still. "You're so fucking tight. God, I missed this. I missed you so much."

He held me like that for several long moments. His hand slid up my belly to cup one of my breasts. He was pure heat compared with the icy coldness of the window. "You think anyone out there can see you? See your tits pressed up against the window? Know that I'm fucking you?"

Oh God. Everyone could probably see me. Although we were traveling at a lightning pace, someone out there was seeing him screw me against the window, and I didn't care. I just wanted more.

He started to move his hips. My breath caught. His dick just rubbed against that spot. That spot I needed so much. Before I knew it, I was pushing back against him. One hand pinched my nipple, molding my breast to fit his palm, and the other rubbed over my hip to the apex of my thighs and then sucked on my clit. His finger rubbed short, tight circles. This was no gentle glide. This was meant to get the job done. To drive me to the peak and then shove me over.

I needed just that. Relentlessly making love to me. Pushing me. Whispering dirty words of, "God, right there. You're so fucking tight. I miss fucking you. You're holding me like a glove. I can't wait to fuck your ass."

It was the last one. The way he said it combined with his teeth sinking down into my shoulder—I flew apart. Giving up all pretense of being able to resist him. I came. Pushing back against him, thrust with thrust. Needing more. Seeking more. But he wasn't done. He kept driving into me. When I started to go limp, he slowed his pace but didn't stop. God, no! No stopping. He shuffled us to the bed without leaving my body. "Put your hands on the bed."

I did as I was told, and he kicked my feet apart. Both hands now on my ass, palming, squeezing. "Do you know how long I've been dreaming about this?" One hand lifted and came down with a resounding crack.

The sting made me grunt but also made me so damn wet. "Jax..."

"I knew it was my fault. I knew right away when you left, it was my fault." Another crack.

Another sting. Another groan from me. He lifted the other hand. I expected another crack, but then his finger gently pressed against my ass and I moaned. "Yeah, I remember how much you like this. You like the idea of two dicks inside you, don't you?"

"Oh my God, Jax."

When his thumb gently pressed in, I could feel it. That deep quivering. That internal orgasm. The holy grail of knock-you-out kind of bliss.

His other fingers pressed over to my clit and started the onslaught. And I knew it. He knew how to play my body. He knew how to make me melt. He knew me so well.

"Oh my God, Jax. Oh my God, I'm—"

"Fuck! Ken, I can't hold it—"

And then we were coming together. The sparks of explosions rocketing through my body, shaking me, shaking us. My arms couldn't hold me up anymore, and I started to slide. With a final drag of his hips, he locked himself inside me, picking me up so I was facedown on the bed, with him on top of me, still inside. He gave me two more sharp, quick thrusts and groaned. "Fuuuck!"

I could feel him, the pulse of him coming inside me, the kick of his dick.

I knew this feeling. It was homecoming.

* * *

Jax

I held her tight. At some point, in the middle of the night, we rolled over. I still spooned her. My dick nestled up against her ass. But maybe twenty minutes ago, she started to wiggle. She always did. And of course, now I was hard.

But I couldn't fuck her again without us talking. I needed her. I had to have her. And if I fucked her again and she rejected me, if she still wouldn't listen, how could I ever let her go again?

I was serious when I told her I wasn't leaving her behind. If she would have me, I'd be her partner. Constantly there. I knew she couldn't resist me, and so I would have to work harder. I just hoped she'd listen now. She wiggled again. "See now, I know you're awake."

"How could I not be? There's a giant slab of salami poking my ass."

"Oh, you'll know it when I'm poking your ass."

Something that sounded like part whimper, part moan escaped her lips, and I nuzzled her neck. "You're not helping. Before we make love again, we need to talk."

"Is that what you call that? Making love?"

I ran my teeth over her shoulder where I'd bitten her before. There was a light hickey there, and it gave me an odd sense of male pride. I really was dragging her to my cave. "Ken, look at me."

For a long moment, she didn't. She stayed nestled in my arms. I pulled the sheet over us and tried to help her roll over. When she did, she kept her gaze averted. "Look at me. This won't hurt, I promise."

"I don't know what this means." She finally lifted her gaze to me. The chocolate-brown eyes that I loved so much were finally seeing me.

"Hi."

She gave me a shy smile. "Hi."

"Sweetheart, I just put my thumb in your arse. Don't be shy now."

Her face flamed, her skin matching her russet locks. "Oh my God."

I grinned. "When we get to Paris and we have a bed and nothing but infinite amounts of time, I'm going to fuck that beautiful ass with my tongue. And my dick. So you're going to get used to it."

She shivered and then bit her bottom lip. "Jax."

"You keep saying my name like that, and we'll do that now instead. But we need more lube than I have for that adventure."

Then her face really flamed. "Stop it."

"What? It's true. It's in my bag."

"Well I see you travel prepared."

"Only for you." I licked my lips. I needed to do this now. I had no idea how to start though. "That night, the magazine you saw, *Business Entrepreneurs...*"

Her gaze dropped down, and then I tilted her chin up so she could see. "That was Miranda Lock. And she *was* my wife."

Her body went rigid, and I held her stiff. My hand slid to her ass and pulled her close. She wasn't running now.

"Let me go."

"No. You're going to listen. And if after that, you want to run, you can run."

She narrowed her gaze at me, and I could feel her muscles loosen. "Fine, continue."

"Our families had been best friends since before we were even born. And she's one of my closest friends. Her father was old-school, and she was a bit of a wild child. All she ever wanted her whole life was to run his business. But he thought she needed tempering. He thought being married would do that. A husband who would take her and guide her, which was bullshit."

Kennedy frowned. "That's archaic."

I shrugged. "He didn't necessarily want her husband to run the business because he thought that should always be in the family name. But he wanted her to have someone to take her a little. Make her the kind of daughter he wanted. And he was dying. So it was her or one of her cousins. Because she wasn't married, he wouldn't leave it to her."

She frowned. "So seriously, you married her?"

I nodded. "We were friends. It was more of a laugh really. We were at a conference in Vegas. I was looking to acquire a new property to build something in the States finally. So I had some meetings. We were there, and we just got married. It was on paper only. But then, her father was so pleased. He wanted a big announcement. A big wedding. The whole thing. We hatched up a plan. Stay married for a year, and then quietly annul and separate. We never consummated the marriage. It was never a marriage in any way, shape, or form. We never even lived together. Not for a day. She was just a friend I was helping out. And then I met you."

"We met when I moved to Australia for the hotel job."

"Yeah, that was about three months after I was married. I told her all about you. How I'd met someone and we thought maybe we could separate, but her father was still happy and he was handing over the reins. And so we had to wait until at least that had happened. You and I, I thought we were just— I didn't know what it was, but by the time I did, it had been six months. I needed to tell you. That's why I took you to Sydney for that weekend. To tell you. Miranda was going to meet us. And I was going to tell you with her. She was going to reassure you that we weren't really married. The crazy part was, she'd met someone too. Someone she wanted to be with. But he was someone her father didn't see as a suitable match. He didn't have a penny to his name at the time."

"So you just didn't tell me?"

"I know that was a mistake. It was the worst thing I've ever done. It was so stupid, I should have just said it. I should have said it on our first date. Drag you over to Miranda's and be like, 'This is her. We're not really a thing. Just a marriage of convenience.'"

Kennedy grinned then. "Like one of my romance novels?"

"Exactly like that." I frowned. "Wait, they shag in those books, right?"

She nodded.

“Then, nope, we're not like that. Literally, just for convenience. Hers not mine. At least not when I met you.” She nodded slowly. "Okay, but then, why did it take you two years to come and find me?"

"Well, when you quit your job, it was a little difficult to find you. And then I had to extricate myself from the actual marriage. I knew when I came back and found you, I couldn't be in the same situation. Then I had to figure out an angle so you'd talk to me."

"So you're not doing a property that you're going to merge with the London Lords brand?"

"Oh, I am. Once I found out where you were and where you were working, I needed to build a scenario where I would have time to talk to you. Even if you said no, I needed one where we'd have time to get to know each other again. Where I might be able to show you that the man you loved is still here."

"You did all this for me?"

I nodded. "I'm sorry. I never anticipated that you'd find it out like that. But I have spent every minute trying to make it back to you."

"I want to believe you, but I'm not sure I can do that. I never want to feel like that again."

"Give me two days. Just two days in Paris. If you still feel this way, I'll woo you the slow way. I'll take my time. We'll work together and you'll get to know me again. But I'm not giving up. I'm not just walking away from this."

"You really are a persistent jackass, you know that?"

"Oh, I know. But like I said, we belong together. You just have to remember why."

* * *

Kennedy

I had given him two days. And in two days, I barely slept. Yes, around my meetings, we spent a ridiculous amount of time in my bed. But we also spent time walking in Paris. Holding hands. Talking. Not so much talking about our split. Why it happened. How it happened. The reasons around it. Like we were tap-dancing around the elephant that had to be dealt with. Point-blank,

I could choose to believe him. Or maybe I was a fool by going that route. I wanted to believe him, but the question was, if I did or didn't.

This morning the sun streamed in, and I groaned thinking how I had to pack for my flight.

"What time do you have to leave?"

"Two."

I could almost feel his smile against the nape of my neck as he kissed me. "Thank you for the two days."

"Thank you." It was all I could say really. Because I wanted to say, *God, I miss you so much. Come back with me.* I wanted to say, *I'm still in love with you.* I wanted to say all kinds of things. But I knew better because I didn't want to get hurt again.

"You're still unsure?"

I nodded. There was no other way to go except honesty.

"I understand." But that didn't stop him from kissing my neck and shoulder, rolling me over and sliding his hands over my belly and then my breasts. I didn't stop him from cupping my face and gently kissing me. I didn't stop him from groaning and then hitching my leg over his arm as he slid inside me.

He made love to me tenderly, and took his time. The kind of lovemaking with slow kisses, prolonged eye contact, intertwined fingers. The intertwined fingers were my favorite part. The kind of making love that said, *I am in love with you. And it's not going to end.*

But it had to end because I had to go back to London and he was going back to Australia. He claimed he was going to stay, but I didn't really see how this was going to work. It would hurt, but at least I had some closure.

You're a fool. You're in love.

I probably was a fool. To think I could dance this close to flame and not get my wings singed. Forget singed, they'd been burned off when I'd flown too close to the sun. Several orgasms later, after I turned off the shower, my muscles still achy, I wrapped myself in a robe. I paused at the bathroom drawer when I heard two voices in the living room. When I stepped out, I frowned. There was that woman. That pretty brunette from the cover of the magazine two years ago. The pain lanced through me quick and hot.

She smiled when she saw me though. I would prefer not to meet my husband's ex-wife when I was wearing not much else but a robe and a smile.

"I'm so sorry. I'm early. I didn't mean to interrupt you two."

I set my jaw and stared at her.

Jax stood. "Ken, this is Miranda. Miranda, this is her."

Miranda grinned at me. "You're just as beautiful as he said you were."

"I'm sorry, but why are you here?" I couldn't find it in my soul to be friendly.

She sighed and nodded. "I understand. I asked Jax if I could meet you. He said it wasn't a good idea, but I needed to clear my conscience a little bit."

My brows lifted. "Your conscience?"

She nodded. "I knew about you, and I begged Jax not to tell you."

I crossed my arms then. In just my robe, there wasn't much shielding to be had so I needed that small comfort. "Oh really?"

"Yeah, I was thinking about my company. And I was worried about my father and what he would think or say or take away from me. I didn't really give much consideration to what Jax was feeling or needed. Or the fact that you would feel betrayed or lied to."

"And now you're here, so what?"

"I'm here to apologize. I know Jax said that he was trying to win you back. And I wholeheartedly support this."

I frowned at her. "I'm not sure what to do with that."

She nodded. "I get it. But I do want you to know, everything Jax said is true. We were never married in a traditional sense. And while I can see women find him attractive, I am not one of them."

She lifted her hand and showed me the stunning diamond ring and wedding band. "I married the love of my life, who I met nine months after I'd married Jax. It was complex and complicated. I wouldn't have met him if I hadn't married Jax. And so I am grateful for that. Just plain old marriage of inconvenience, we call it."

My gaze flickered to Jax, who nodded. "The two of you were really not married?"

He shook his head. "No. I know there's a part of you that believes me. I just— I wanted you to hear so there would be no doubt."

Miranda nodded. "Well my part here is done. Jax, I'll see you next time I'm in Melbourne."

She nodded a goodbye to me and then strolled out. It was hard not to like her. She had a directness I appreciated. And she was beautiful. Obviously. But there was also an inner kindness that I could see in her eyes. I wanted to hate her, but that was irrational.

With her gone, Jax shrugged. "She was supposed to meet us at lunch. I'm sorry. When she realized we were here, she wanted to see us. I guess she wants to get back home to her husband."

"You didn't have to do that. I don't need hard evidence."

He walked over and wrapped his arms around me. "I will give you whatever you need to make you feel comfortable. I will give you whatever you need to make you feel safe. And for you to know that I am never leaving your side."

"How are you so sure?"

"I have done nothing else but spend the last two years trying to get back to you. If you need more time, I can wait. But I'm not going anywhere. I'm not going to run to Australia while being out of sight, out of mind. You take your time. I'll be right here."

I searched his gaze. "You mean it, don't you? You will be right here until I come around."

He nodded. "Yup. I love you. It's that easy. That simple. And I want to keep loving you. Even if you think you don't love me anymore. How I feel won't change."

It was only then that I relaxed into his hold. “Jax.”

"With everything that I have. I will keep loving you. All I need is to be with you. I am serious when I said I was moving to London. I want to be close to you. I can do my operations there. That doesn't change."

He was serious. Could I grasp it? Or was I going to choose to be scared? I lifted my gaze to meet his. "I never stopped loving you."

He grinned. "Oh, I know. You were just being stubborn."

"*I* was being stubborn?"

He laughed and slid his lips over mine. "I never stopped loving you."

"You're really moving to London?"

"Yup. You're not going to be rid of me. Not today. Not in two years. Not for eternity. So get used to it. Whether or not you allow me to give you orgasms. That's entirely up to you. I mean, who doesn't want orgasms though?"

I laughed. "You are the most stubborn, obstinate, irritating man I know."

"Are you sure about that? Because I feel like your boss, Ben, is right up there."

"Fair point. But he's not the one I love."

"Nope, I am."

"Did I mention arrogant?"

"Yup, you sure did. So what do you say? Are you mine? Forever?"

I relaxed into his hold, nestling into that spot, inhaling the spicy scent that I had longed for. "I'm yours. I always have been. Always will be."

* * *

Do you want more of Nana Malone?

One click Big Ben now! >

JUST JANE

JEWEL E. ANN

1

Just Jane

Jewel E. Ann

2

My good friend Jane's getting married in Perth, Australia. My first time there, and I couldn't be more excited.

I had two best friends until I met Jane in college. She informed me "best" is singular. There can only be one best friend. Did I mention she made this announcement in front of those two *best* friends?

Thankfully, at the time, all parties were deliriously tipsy in celebration of my twenty-first birthday. No feelings were hurt when I declared Avril as my best friend, since we had been friends from the first day of third grade. Erin took second place as my *better* friend. Avril and I befriended Erin in high school. Then the three of us met Jane in college—University of Iowa, pre-law.

Good. Better. Best.

Jane slid into my last available friend slot. The "good" friend.

After a delayed flight from Chicago, I arrived at LAX and now wait to take a later flight to Sydney, where I'll catch another plane to Perth for Good Friend Jane's wedding.

I haven't seen Jane in two years. She traveled to Australia for a three-week vacation, met a guy, and stayed two years. I get letters ... paper letters from her. She claims she has a cell phone and a computer but only uses it for work. I have a landline number for her.

A landline!

Good Friend Jane thinks the Internet is the beginning of the end of the world.

"Is this seat taken?" A dirty-blond man in a disheveled blue plaid suit blows his shaggy hair off his forehead.

"Nope. My bag can go on the floor." I move my handbag between my feet, giving the man a smile.

He attempts to return the smile, but it sags like a flat tire stuck to his scruffy face. My gaze slides along his ... *situation*. That's what I'd call him. A situation. A complete disaster. Only sleeping in a suit could impart that many wrinkles. I'm pretty sure the brown splattering on his lavender, partially unbuttoned shirt is coffee, and the smudge on his eggplant tie resembles mustard. I'm not sure why he's wearing the tie. It's loose enough to fit over the head of a rhinoceros.

"Rough day?" I release a tiny chuckle, attempting to be friendly but not nosy. Honestly, I don't even know why I asked that question. I made a similar mistake in Chicago, and a guy, probably twice my age, talked my ear clean off the side of my head. Scruffy's gaze meets mine, catching me observing (really judging) his appearance as he folds his tall body into the chair.

He makes his own visual assessment of me. I think I still look put together. That will not be the case after my twenty-six-hour flight to Perth.

He has beautiful amber eyes and sharp features. A mess, but a handsome mess. My cheeks fill with heat as his gaze sluggishly makes its way from my white Adidas shoes, along my high-waisted denim carpenter jeans, over my black Aerosmith fitted tee, pausing on my face just long enough to make his own decision on my eye color (blue or slate). I cling to blue. Who wants gray eyes?

He observes me tucking my black, chin-length hair behind my ears. I dried it straight for the flight, but most days I add a few curls to give it attitude like me in a courtroom.

"Rough *several* days," he says on a sigh, meeting my gaze once again. I think his sluggishly slow assessment has less to do with appreciating anything about my body and more to do with lack of sleep.

"Sorry. Hope things get better for you soon."

"Thanks." He drops his backpack at his feet and scoots down in the chair, running both hands through his hair as he tilts his head back. "It's really my own fault. I've willingly been bumped from one flight to the next. I've earned several round-trip tickets to anywhere in the world, along with two thousand in cash. Just playing the plane game."

"A travel hacker." I scroll through my e-mail.

He chuckles, eyes closed. "Not usually. No time for that. But I made time. I guess I'm in no hurry."

"What's that like?" I laugh.

"What's what like?" He continues our conversation with his eyes closed.

"Not being in a hurry?"

"Make a date with the end of your life, and you'll be in no hurry. I promise."

I glance over at him, squinting as he peeks open one eye and smirks. "Don't worry. I'm not dying."

"Good to know." I return my attention to my phone.

"So where are you headed? I've heard a lot of interesting stories over the past two days. What's yours?"

"Wedding. Australia. It's the fourth wedding I've attended in two months. I'm ready for wedding season to end."

"Have you been to Australia?"

"No, but I've always wanted to go there. I had a koala bear obsession as a little girl."

He grins. I catch it through the corner of my eye, but I don't give him the satisfaction of knowing how much I like his smile.

"Have you had a wedding?"

I laugh again. "You mean am I married?"

"I don't care if you're married. Just asking if you've had a wedding."

Resting my phone on my crossed legs, I turn my head to gage his level of true interest. He folds his hands on his chest over his loose noose tie, head canted toward me.

"I *planned* a wedding."

"You're a wedding planner?"

I shake my head. "I planned *my* wedding. The groom never showed up."

His eyebrows crawl up his forehead, but he says nothing.

On a shrug, I glance around the lounge, avoiding his wordless expression of pity, shock; I'm not sure what it says. "It was a small wedding. Honestly, I appreciated the phone call over him choking at the altar in front of friends and family."

"What did you tell the guests?"

"My best friend told everyone that Cary was deathly ill and that the wedding was canceled until further notice."

"That was your problem, right there. You were about to marry a man named Cary."

I don't want to grin, but I can't hold it back. "You don't like the name Cary?"

"Too feminine for my taste. But I'm sure he was a manly man."

I reach for my nearly empty glass of red wine—my second glass.

"Is," he corrects. "I'm sure he's not dead." He narrows one eye. "Or is he? Did you kill him? Did he die from the deadly illness?"

My wineglass hides my smile as I drain the last few drops. "No. No one died. I heard he finally made it to his wedding, just not *our* wedding. He has twin girls and a dog. A doodle of some sort. My mom still keeps in touch with his mom."

"Do you hate him for being happy?"

Resting the empty glass on the arm of the chair, I stare at his folded hands. Large, calloused hands. They don't fit the suit. Okay, they might fit the condition of his suit—his *situation.* "No. I don't. I loved him. Really loved him. When you love someone that much, you want them to be happy, even if it's not with you. Don't get me wrong." A tiny smile pulls at my lips. "I did some damage to his vehicle and gave away all his belongings that were at my apartment, which were a lot. I sank a lot of time and money into planning that wedding; there had to be some sort of ..."

"Revenge?"

I slide my gaze to his mischievous eyes. "Balance."

"Mmm ..." He closes his eyes again.

"Have you ever had a wedding?" I ask, seeing no ring on his finger either.

"No. But I've been to Australia. It's lovely. Plenty of snakes, but lovely snakes."

"There's no such thing as a lovely snake."

"Clearly, you haven't been to Australia."

"Let's stop talking about snakes."

"Fine by me. What shall we talk about?"

"Nothing. I'm going to get another glass of wine. You should take a nap. You look ..." I trap my lower lip between my teeth.

"Tired?"

"Sure. That." I wink.

When I return with my third glass of wine, Mr. Disheveled's eyes are closed, lips parted, releasing even breaths. I settle into my chair and sip more wine while attempting to focus on an e-mail from a client instead of focusing on the handsome man next to me.

"I look like shit."

I snap my attention back to my phone when he speaks. Jesus, I thought he was asleep.

"You wanted to say I look like shit. Not tired."

"No judgment here. I'll look worse by the time I get to my final destination."

"I don't think you could look like shit."

I ignore him. At least, most of me ignores him. It's been a while since a man has flirted with me. So really ... he might not be flirting with me at all. I can't tell for sure. I really should get out more often.

"Where are you headed?"

He chuckles, eyes still closed while rolling his head side to side. "I don't even know anymore."

"So you're just going to keep pocketing money and miles then ... what? Get your car out of long-term parking and drive home?"

"Maybe." Opening his eyes, he sits up and rubs his hands over his face. "I need something. Beer or caffeine?"

"If you're driving home, I think caffeine is the way to go." I gesture to my wineglass. "If you're getting on a plane in the next few days, alcohol is the way to go."

He studies my wineglass. "You feeling a buzz?"

"Maybe." I return a flirty grin. Why? I don't know. Third glass of wine? Sexy guy trying not to look sexy but failing miserably? Fourteen months without sex? Take your pick.

"I'll get a vodka and Coke. Covers both bases." He saunters off.

I watch. I keep watching. And I don't even blink when he returns.

"So ..." He takes a seat again. "Are we going to exchange names?" He sips his drink.

"Monica."

"Oh, thank God ..." He laughs. "I feared you might have a masculine name since your ex has a girl's name."

"Cary is not a girl's name. It's spelled C-a-r-y. That's the masculine spelling."

"Nope." He shakes his head, keeping his gaze on his drink as he swirls the ice a bit. "Spell it however you want to spell it. It's a chick's name."

"And what is your name, Mr. Masculine?"

"Magnus Steel."

I spit out part of my drink, earning me a scowl from the older lady sitting across the way. "That is not your name."

"Optimus Prime." He winks at me.

Yes, he's definitely flirting.

"Axel." He brings his glass to his lips.

I inspect him through narrowed eyes. "That's not entirely unbelievable."

He swallows. "Good. Because it's my name. So this Cary guy ..."

"No." I shake my head, grinning. "Let's talk about anything but him."

"So we *are* going to talk. Great. The woman he married, did he fall in love with her? Is that why he didn't marry you?"

I laugh on a slight headshake. "You're quite forward."

Axel shrugs. "Direct. Curious ... bored. That's it more than anything. I've been here too long and I'm bored."

I eye him as he inspects his tie and the stain on it before taking down half of his vodka and Coke. Seriously ... he's a mess. Bored? Yeah, I can see that.

"He met her two weeks before our wedding. She applied for the receptionist position at his office. He's a chiropractor."

Axel grunts, rolling his eyes. "A chiropractor named Cary. How did you get yourself into that mess?"

It's not funny. Okay, it's a little funny, just not in the way Axel's implying. Cary's not as tall as the *situation* beside me, but he's all muscle. He played football in college for two years before injuring his knee and rerouting his career to chiropractic medicine.

"Dating app. Two right swipes. A match."

"Not a match, a mess. He screwed his secretary."

"He didn't screw his secretary."

"He married her. Trust me, he's screwed her."

The absurdity. I giggle. "Let me rephrase, he didn't screw her before our wedding."

"You know this for a fact?"

Angling my body toward Axel's chair, I pull one knee toward my chest. "My gut tells me he didn't. My gut is usually right. However, I think she's the reason he called off the wedding. Even if he didn't know if he wanted to be with her, something about her made him question being with me. At the time, she was a game changer. He dated two other women after he called off the wedding before he ended up with her."

My lips twist to the side. "I envied her. I know ... it's crazy. But imagine being the person who makes someone rethink their entire future. Like a near-death experience. That aha moment."

"You want to be the woman who breaks up a marriage?"

I drink the rest of my wine, feeling the perfect buzz for my flight, which boards in forty-five minutes. "No." Closing my eyes to still the spinning in my head, I chuckle. "Maybe." Peeking open one eye, I cringe. "Is that terrible?"

His eyebrows slide up his forehead. "Uh ... yes. That's truly terrible."

"I'm kidding." I'm sort of kidding. "I don't want to be that person. I just want to feel. Ya know? Feel the excitement of impacting someone's world in such a profound way." I cup my hand at my mouth. "Jeez ... clearly I've had too much wine."

Axel studies me through narrowed eyes, rubbing his lips together. It makes me feel warm all over. Okay, that's probably the wine, but his gaze intensifies the sensation.

He scratches his scruffy jawline. "I'm going to go brush my teeth."

With a soft chuckle, I nod slowly. "O ... kay."

Axel hikes his bag over his shoulder and saunters off toward the restroom. Fifteen minutes later (and what I assume are really clean teeth), he makes his way toward the empty chair beside me.

Stops halfway.

Chews on his bottom lip.

Turns around.

Walks in the opposite direction.

Turns. Three steps. Chews on lip. Walks away.

He repeats this four times.

I'm ... well, I don't know what I am. Confused? Amused? Curious ... I'm *beyond* curious. Really, what is his deal?

Needing to stand and walk a bit before boarding the plane, I slide my purse over my shoulder and follow Axel. I find him around the corner at the bar, downing hard liquor like a sports drink after a long run.

"You okay?"

He turns toward me, eyeing me again. Eyeing all of me. "No."

"Oh." I frown. "Sorry. Anything I can do?"

Axel sets the empty glass on the bar and runs both hands through his hair as he paces a few steps away from me and back again. Towering over me, he cringes. "I purchased a massage." He looks at his watch. "In two minutes."

I glance over his shoulder toward the entrance to the exclusive spa. "That's ... nice." Squinting one eye at him, I try to read his *situation*. "Right?"

He lifts a single shoulder. "Perhaps."

"Okay. Well, enjoy your massage. It was nice chatting with—"

Grabbing my hand, he pulls me in the direction of the spa. I nearly trip trying to keep up with his long strides.

"I have a plane to catch."

He ushers us into a tiny, dimly lit room with a single massage table and shuts the door behind us. His hands run through his hair again, yanking at it. "I paid a thousand dollars for a massage, minus the massage and the therapist."

I gulp. This is ... I don't even know. "Sounds like an expensive nap." My voice shakes like the rest of my body.

"I brushed my teeth, paid for the room, and bought condoms. Am I crazy?"

Taking a step backward until the door hits my back, I nod a good ten times.

He chuckles, dropping his chin to his chest and shoving his hands into the front pockets of his pants. "You can go. I didn't mean to scare you. I have no idea why I did this. I'm feeling exhausted, confused, and clearly irrationally impulsive."

Yes. Yes. Hell yes.

"Y-you did this for me? You thought we ..." I clear the nervous disbelief from my throat. "You thought I would have sex with you? A stranger. In an airport?"

"I don't know," he whispers to the floor.

"Do you do this a lot?"

Why? Why am I still standing here? Any rational person would run. Did the wine steal my rationality? I'm an educated person. I have a law degree. What is wrong with my sense of safety and self-preservation?

"No." He chuckles. "I don't do this *ever*."

Say all rapists and murderers.

"Have a safe flight. Watch out for the snakes." He reaches for the handle, but I don't move. I can't move.

WHY CAN'T I MOVE?

"Where's your toothbrush?" I murmur, staring at his tie.

Axel lets go of the doorknob and retrieves a travel toothbrush and small tube of toothpaste from his right pocket.

"And the condoms?" I force my gaze up to meet his.

He blinks a few times, neutral expression, before pulling a three-pack of condoms from his left pocket.

I grin. This isn't happening to me. Things like this don't happen to boring prosecutors from Chicago—probably because boring prosecutors know how reckless behavior ruins lives.

My heart.

This is what it feels like to commit a crime for the first time. The fear. The adrenaline. The out-of-body sensation.

"I can't believe I'm doing this," I whisper.

Axel grins. I feel it everywhere. I feel him everywhere, and he's not touching me.

"Don't make me feel like a hooker. Don't ask me how I want it. Don't tell me to get on my knees. Don't—"

He grabs my face and kisses me. A nice kiss. He tastes like fresh mint as our tongues slide together.

What am I doing? What am I doing? What am I doing?

He steps back, leaving me breathless as he discards his tie and his shirt. I just ... watch him because ... I can't believe I'm doing this.

Fuck me ... he's sexy.

I gulp once ... twice ... and snap out of it when he relinquishes a cocky grin. With shaky hands, I peel off my shirt and reach for the button to my jeans.

"Turn around," he says in a thick voice.

On the verge of hyperventilating, I turn around, pressing my hands flat to the door as he unhooks my bra. Calloused hands slide over my breasts as his hot mouth ghosts over my shoulder.

"A perfect handful." His lips pull into a grin over my skin as the pads of his thumbs graze my hard nipples, causing my knees to buckle.

Yes, it's been *way* too long.

He hunches behind me, dragging his mouth down my bare back as his fingers work my button and zipper. Planting his mouth at the waistband to my pants, he kisses each inch of newly exposed skin as he works my jeans and panties down my legs—sucking my skin and teasing the curve of my ass with his teeth.

A stranger is undressing me. A stranger is undressing me. A stranger is undressing me. And ... I have a plane to catch.

Toeing off my shoes and stepping out of my jeans, I turn around. Axel grins again, or maybe he hasn't stopped grinning. I know I haven't stopped panting.

Really ... so pathetic.

I glance at my watch.

"You have a plane to catch."

Wrinkling my nose, I nod once.

Axel stands as his gaze violates every inch of my body. "If you're an early boarder. Or if you want to grab snacks ..."

He can't be serious. I'm naked. He's half-naked. And we're talking about early boarding and snacks?

"Shut up." My hands make quick moves to unfasten his pants.

He chuckles again, that arrogant, he-knows-he's-sexy chuckle. Before I push down his pants, he grabs the condoms, opening one while I gawk at his tented boxer briefs.

"Pull them down." He tosses the condom foil aside.

The deafening pulse in my ears makes his words sound distant. Maybe they are distant. Maybe this isn't happening. If not, I swear it's the best dream I've had in ... forever. And I will wake up with a sheen of sweat along my body and most likely my hand between my legs.

"Tick-tock ..." He inches his briefs down his hips because I'm not able to talk or move in this dream. After he rolls on the condom, he kisses me.

This kiss is more urgent, like he's losing control, or maybe he's making sure I'm able to board early and get snacks.

Such a gentleman.

A gentleman who grins when I say his name after he buries himself inside of me. A gentleman who whispers, "Sounds better than Cary, huh?" A gentleman who leaves imprints of his teeth in my nipples. A nice souvenir from LAX.

The next few minutes—seven minutes to be exact—pass by in a blink. A slow, intoxicated, I-need-that-orgasm blink.

As we piece ourselves back together, sharing nothing more than wordless, flirty smiles, I formulate a speech. I mean, we have to talk about it, right?

"Try the Vegemite. Either you'll love it or loathe it, but you have to try it." Axel hikes his bag onto his shoulder as I run my fingers through my hair.

Vegemite? That's his postcoital topic of conversation?

I retrieve my bag from the floor and open my mouth to speak, but nothing comes out.

"It's fine." He leans down and presses a soft kiss to the corner of my mouth. "I don't really know what to say either. Have a safe flight. And …" He stands straight again and opens the door. "You're definitely a game changer."

I wince. "You're getting married?"

He shakes his head and straightens his tie. It's the most put together he's looked since I met him. "No." He heads toward the men's room right as they announce the boarding for my plane.

"Wait!"

It was sex. Let it go. Let him go.

Axel turns, head cocked to the side a fraction.

Fishing a business card from my purse, I hand it to him. "If you ever need legal advice or … if you're in Chicago and need a tour guide." Or really hot sex again. "Call me."

He stares at my card. "Monica Smith. Why does that name sound familiar?"

I roll my eyes. "Because it's so common?"

Axel shrugs. "Probably." He slides the card into the inside pocket of his suit jacket. "It's been … fun."

"Fun …" I echo with an impossible grin.

A million years later, I make it to Perth and catch a cab to the hotel where most of the wedding guests are staying. My body clock is thoroughly fucked at the moment.

"Monica!" Avril and Erin set down their drinks at the hotel bar and run toward me.

We hug it out. I haven't seen them since our girls' trip to Mexico last year. They both moved to New York after graduating law school.

"You look exhausted. You should have come last week like we did." Avril takes my suitcase from me and leads us to the elevators.

I yawn. "I had to be in court, just like I have to be back in court in four days. How's Good Friend Jane?"

Erin laughs. "Psycho. Let's all be glad she only has a maid of honor and it's her sister."

We step onto the elevator. "And wait until you see Wendell's brother, Devin, the best man. I've already called dibs on him." Avril fans herself with her hand.

"Pretty sure you have a husband at home, right?" Erin shoots her the hairy eyeball.

"A girl can dream."

The doors open.

"We can dream," Erin says. "Monica is the only single one of us, so she can do more than dream."

Dreams ... I like dreams. And sexy guys in airports with too much money to waste on a room just to have sex with a stranger.

Yeah, that makes me sound like a whore.

Erin opens the door to the hotel room we're sharing. "Drinks? Food? Exploring? What do you want to do?"

I collapse onto the first bed. "Sleep. Wake me up when it's time for the wedding."

I don't sleep until the wedding, just the day before.

"Get out of the shower! Someone wants to see you," Avril yells, knocking on the bathroom door as I rinse the conditioner from my hair.

"Just a sec!"

After I dry off and wrap one towel around my body and the other around my head, I slide open the door.

"Monica!"

"Good Friend Jane!" I hug the bride-to-be.

"Watch the hair." She releases me.

"Oops!" My towel falls from my body.

"Oh my God!" Avril points at me before I get completely covered up again.

"What?" Good Friend Jane turns back toward me after checking her updo in the full-length mirror.

"Monica, what happened to your breasts?" Avril shoots me a wide-eyed expression.

"Nothing." I tighten the towel around me.

"They had ..." She grabs my towel and tries to tug it off me again.

"What are you doing?" I angle my body away from her.

"You have bruises on your breasts. They looked like ..." Avril's eyes shoot up her forehead as I sigh.

"Bite marks." I roll my lips between my teeth. No big deal. Right?

"Bite marks?" Good Friend Jane's jaw drops to the floor.

Erin tucks her curly blond hair behind her ears and crosses her arms over her chest. "You have some explaining to do. When I messaged you two weeks ago, you said you weren't seeing anyone."

"I'm not." I tip my chin up as if that will give me (the only naked person in the room) some dignity.

"The marks are red ... They're new." Avril squints.

Closing my eyes, I own it. I own my actions. "I met someone at the airport."

"And you let him bite your boobs?" Good Friend Jane presses her hand to her chest.

"No." I cringe. "Sort of. We met. We talked. We drank. And then he brushed his teeth, bought condoms, and paid an insane amount of money to use a massage therapy room in the private lounge so we could ..."

Nothing.

Three sets of eyes stare at me, unblinking, but no words.

"Please don't judge me. I don't know why I did it. It was so not me." My whole face contorts into fear. Fear of being judged by my good, better, and best friends.

"Was it good?" Avril winks.

"Best sex of my life." My cheeks burn with hot flames just like the rest of my body.

"When are you seeing him again?" Good Friend Jane asks.

"I'm not sure I am." I nibble my bottom lip.

"What?" She gasps. "You just ... screwed some stranger in an airport, and you're never going to see him again?"

"Probably not. Good Friend Jane, please don't judge me." I smirk at her because she can't keep from giggling every time I call her that.

"Fine." She huffs. "No judgment. I'm too excited about my wedding to worry about your misbehavior."

Someone knocks at the door. Avril opens it as I hide behind the corner.

"Jane, your groom is MIA," a male voice says.

"What do you mean?"

"He wasn't at the airport."

"Was his flight delayed again?"

"Your sister said you should check your phone. Five missed calls."

I peek around the corner as Avril mouths, *That's the best man.* But I can't see him.

"Have you talked to him?" Good Friend Jane asks in a panicky tone.

"Just ... call him," the best man says right before the door shuts.

She walks into the room again and stares at her phone, swiping her index finger over the screen like someone who doesn't ever use a cell phone. After she brings it to her ear, we all wait in silence. "Axel, where are you? Call me back right away. I'm worried." She presses end as my brain snags on his name.

"Axel?" I whisper before clearing my throat. "I thought his name was Wendell."

Good Friend Jane closes her eyes. "His middle name is Axel. He hates his first name."

"Was his middle name on the wedding invitation?" I ask.

She opens her eyes. "Yes. What is your fascination with his name?" Her words are laced with exasperation. "Gah! Where is he?"

"Where was he flying in from?" I cringe ever so slightly.

It can't be. There's no way.

"Los Angeles," Avril answers.

It's okay. It's still okay. It's a big world. There are many Axels in the world. There were probably several hundred guys named Axel at LAX.

"What's your deal?" Erin cocks her head at me. "You have sweat along your brow."

I wipe my brow. "It's just ..." I shake my head slowly. "The guy ..." I continue to shake my head. "It's ... a coincidence." Sitting on the bed, I take a deep breath.

"What's a coincidence?" Erin prods.

I glance up at Good Friend Jane. "The name. That's all."

"Axel?"

I nod. "Yeah. The guy I ..." I give her my guilty slut wince. "Well, you know ... anyway, his name is Axel."

"At LAX?" Avril asks.

I nod with a tight smile.

Good Friend Jane stares at her phone, clearly not bothered by the coincidence. A good sign.

"That would be really awkward if Monica had sex with your fiancé." Avril laughs.

Erin laughs too.

Good Friend Jane? Not laughing. "Axel's marrying me tomorrow. He's loyal to a fault. He's everything. Tall. Handsome. Sweet. I just wish he would call me back. He missed several flights from delays. The upside is they compensated him quite well. But he needs to get here. Why didn't he get on Monica's plane?" She frowns at her phone screen, like if she stares at it long enough, he will call.

"Do you have a picture of him?" I ask. I *have* to ask.

"Oh for fuck's sake, Monica. You didn't screw my Axel." Good Friend Jane tosses her phone aside and digs through her purse. "I have a picture of him somewhere."

"Seriously?" Erin laughs. "You don't have a picture of him on your phone?"

"Of course not. I hate that thing." She pulls out a small photo album. "Here. This is from our trip to Spain last year." She hands me the small photo album.

I open it.

Jane and Axel at a winery.

Jane and Axel kissing on a beach.

Jane and Axel in front of Casa Milà.

"He's not coming," I whisper.

"What do you mean?" Avril asks slowly because she knows. She knows the look on my face and the tone in my voice. It's the same look and tone I had when I announced Cary would not make it to the church to marry me.

You're a game changer.

"That's him?" Erin asks, complete horror taking up residence on her face.

My gaze slides from the photo album to Good Friend Jane. She waits ... lips parted, eyes nearly vacant. "My ... no." She shakes her head. "*My* Axel did not do that to your ..." She nods her head toward my chest.

I deflate as tears fill my eyes. What are the chances? How does something like this happen? "Good Friend Jane—"

"NO!" She takes several steps back like someone punched her. "Just Jane. I am *not* your good friend."

Habit. I call her that out of complete habit. It's possible, even fair, that I should no longer call her that.

The door slams shut.

I bear the full weight of Avril's and Erin's judgment. Well, judgment mixed with a smidge of sympathy. After all, they know.

It's not my fault.

If *Just Jane* weren't so anti-technology, anti-social media, I would have seen these pictures from Spain online. I would have known Axel's face at the airport, and I would have talked him into getting on the plane instead of letting him bite my boobs and fuck me into another dimension.

Whoever says technology is the ruination of mankind is dead wrong.

The following day, I make a quick exit to the airport with my best and better friends. They keep me in line until we make it back to LAX, no screwing random strangers.

"Get on your flight to Chicago. Don't look for him." Avril hugs me before she and Erin head to their terminal to catch their flight to New York.

"Yeah, that would have been really awkward. Asking *Just Jane* for his number, huh?" Erin winks before hugging me goodbye.

It isn't funny, but after hours on a plane and nausea from jet lag—flat-out punch drunk—sets in, I find everything funny. Anything to keep from vomiting or passing out.

The pathetic part? I look for him at the airport, as if he's still here. I check my phone every few seconds for weeks after returning to Chicago. Eventually, I let that *situation* fall from my mind.

I immerse myself into work.

I send a long apology letter to Just Jane.

I start swiping right again.

Until ... *he* shows up at my office.

I have fifteen minutes before my next appointment.

Axel's wearing a black suit this time.

A crisp, *clean* white shirt.

Red tie perfectly knotted.

He still sports a day's worth of stubble.

"Wendell." I sit up straight in my leather chair and fold my hands on my desk.

He smirks, rubbing his jaw. "So ... you went to college with Jane. You were on your way to ..." Axel drags his thumb along his bottom lip.

"Your wedding. Yes."

"See any snakes?"

I grunt a laugh and shake my head. "Nope. Just the one at the airport in LA."

"Touché." He chuckles.

"So what do you do, *Wendell*?"

"Axel."

"What is wrong with me? Why am I attracted to men with rather blah names?"

"So you're attracted to me?"

This Axel is different.

Confident.

Controlled.

Dressed like a million dollars.

Nothing like the man at the airport.

I close my eyes and drop my head, rubbing my temples. "I let a stranger with mustard on his tie screw me at the airport."

"I brushed my teeth."

I fight to hide my grin.

"I'm the CEO of a communications company. I met Jane on vacation in Perth. And I stayed for … too long." He shrugs. "The honeymoon ended before the wedding. I had to fly back to LA the prior month. And in that time, I felt … free. I didn't miss Jane. I don't even know why. I didn't want to get on the plane. So I took every opportunity I could find to not get on the plane. Then I met you."

"Then you met me," I whisper.

"I agonized over those actions that I knew would end things for good."

I remember. The pacing. The hair tugging. I remember it all too well.

"But you did it anyway."

Axel nods several times. "You were a game changer."

Taking a deep breath, I glance at my watch and stand. After making my way around to the front of the desk, I sit on the edge of it. "Sometimes game changers are nothing more than a change in tide, a sudden gust of wind, that sends us in a new direction."

Axel steeples his fingers at his chin. "True. And sometimes they *are* the new direction."

* * *

Do you want more of Jewel E. Ann?

One click A PLACE WITHOUT YOU now!

FIREWORKS

A SPARROW WEBS WORLD SHORT

ALEATHA ROMIG

WINNIE

My eyes fluttered between open and closed as the streets of Chicago passed outside the taxi's windows. I could be waking in my own bed, showering, and making my way to the airport. Sometimes I wondered what that would be like, to wake each day in the same place, and then I'd realize the amazing opportunities I'd been given and acknowledge this was the life I wanted, or most of it.

Today, or should I say last night, I made the executive decision to take the red-eye, arriving in the Windy City earlier than scheduled. With a jam-packed week of travel and nothing holding me back, I decided to get a head start on what was ahead.

The end result was that now I was here—in Chicago, the first of my many stops.

Shaking my head, I lowered the window to the back seat of the taxi.

Lifting my face to the cool spring air, I closed my eyes, allowing a fine mist to prickle my flesh. The invigorating breeze did more than wake me—it restored my smile to my face.

Yes, I was tired and had a long week before me. And yes, I loved every minute of it. My personal life may be the shits, but professionally, things were moving in a steady upward direction.

Long nights and traveling were exactly what I'd signed up for when I accepted a one-third partnership in an up-and-coming company—Sinful Threads. Sinful Threads was a specialty boutique that sold to only the most exclusive stores. Currently, we were only United States-based, but I had a vision for...yes, world domination. The possibilities were endless.

Who would have turned down the opportunity to play a significant role in an all-female company?

Especially one run completely by friends.

The day I applied for and accepted the offer to work as an assistant to two friends with a dream was the day I'd made the best decision of my life. Granted, things had been shaky here and there.

There was this one time with the FBI...but that was before, and things were now running smoothly. Those two friends were now also my friends, and with their help and encouragement, I'd moved up from assistant to active partner.

The names of the founding partners were Louisa and Kennedy. Right out of college, they'd started Sinful Threads as an accessory manufacturer. From accessories—scarves, pins, bangles, etc.—they later expanded into the clothing market, specifically dresses. That decision was a huge boost to the Sinful Threads brand. It also came at a time of personal upheaval for both women.

Kennedy decided to leave Boulder—our home base—and move to Chicago. Things were a bit wild. When the dust settled, Kennedy became Araneae Sparrow.

Trust me, it's a great story for another time.

While simultaneously, Louisa Toney and her husband, Jason, welcomed their first child, little Kennedy, named for Louisa's best friend. Little Kennedy was now older and the proud big sister to their newest family member, Dustin. It went without saying that Louisa was busy, and with her parenting responsibilities, traveling was no longer her priority. The same was true for Araneae, who with her wealthy husband enjoyed travel of the more secretive and leisurely variety.

Cue where I came into the upper fold. Sinful Threads needed a face at each location, one that meant oversight, and upon whom all the regional managers as well as manufacturing and distribution executives could rely.

That person was now me.

While Sinful Threads was still centered in Boulder, I traveled throughout the country to check in personally with all the branches of our company. I also made face-to-face meetings with well-known buyers like Nordstrom's and Saks Fifth Avenue, as well as exclusive boutiques located in renowned locations such as Rodeo Drive.

My jet-set life was truly everything I never imagined.

Business for Sinful Treads was continuing to grow. The newest premise had been Araneae's idea, and it was fantastic. While customers were willing to pay five-hundred dollars for a dress that they wore once, she surmised that for a product they would spend one-third of their life enjoying, they'd gladly pay much more.

Sinful Threads had ventured into the world of bed linens, with Sinful Threads bed sheets.

The bed sheet prototypes had only recently been showcased at the midwinter New York show, and now orders were coming in from all over the country.

Our newest endeavor was why I was currently in Chicago, to meet with Jana, our assistant at this office, and go over the new manufacturing and distribution schedule for the area. The bed linens were being manufactured outside of Chicago, where square footage for the needed space as well as wages were more economical for our company.

Araneae's husband was a real estate guru with the uncanny ability to obtain Sinful Threads remarkable bargains on real estate. Take the office I was about to enter. With little notice, Sinful Threads had scored six rooms on the twenty-sixth floor of a prestigious building on South Wacker Drive near the canal in downtown Chicago.

While our office view wasn't the best, the deal was still a steal.

After a day or two here, my schedule had me moving on to New York, New Jersey, Atlanta, and Houston before making it back to Boulder. Next week I'd be headed toward the West Coast.

It didn't take a genius to see why my personal life sucked.

Oh, I adored spending time with Louisa, Kennedy, and Dustin or seeing Araneae and Jana when I could.

That didn't mean I didn't dream of being whisked away to Sydney, Australia, to a yacht, sipping fine wine while fireworks rained down from the Sydney Harbor Bridge, or even sitting on the patio of the famous Opera House.

It was strange, but my fantasies weren't without a companion.

His sexy, firm body, quiet yet fierce disposition, and panty-melting blue stare were truly the things an active imagination could take to the next level. The thing was that I barely knew him. We'd only met a few times through the years. Nevertheless, whenever he was present, my skin warmed and insides twisted. I had no idea if he even knew my name.

However, in those daydreams, he knew more than my name. And his was the one I whispered in the dark of my bedroom—it was the closest my dreams came to reality.

Perhaps that was Garrett Givens's appeal. I didn't know enough about him, other than his strikingly handsome physique, stunning blue stare, and impeccable choice of well-fitting suits, to assess any negative traits. In real life, he'd always been polite and reserved, nodding and addressing me as Ms. Douglas.

With his current position working for Araneae's husband in some sort of security capacity, I doubted Garrett had noticed me much more than in passing or that he had the freedom of an impromptu trip to Australia.

I didn't either.

Living a fantasy like that wasn't my life.

Daydreaming it was.

My real life was living out of suitcases and traveling from city to city.

As the taxi pulled to a stop outside the building housing the Chicago Sinful Threads, I peered out onto the world beyond the windows. The sun had not risen, yet the city was coming to life. Securing my coat, I reached for my satchel and travel bag. Stepping onto the sidewalk, I stood for a moment as the cool breeze teased my auburn hair away from my face. Windows high above the street were popping to life, appearing like dots of light, as workers began their routines.

I pulled my phone from my coat pocket to check the time.

Shit.

In my sleep-deprived state, I'd forgotten to take it out of airplane mode. Switching that mode off, I entered the building and pushed the *up* button for the elevator. As I stepped within the empty cubicle, the phone woke from its slumber with dings and pings.

. . .

MISSED CALLS – 3
TEXT MESSAGES – 5

Oh, the exciting life of an executive.

Text bubbles appeared, dot after blinking dot.

Unfortunately, the reception in the elevator was crap. It wasn't until I began to unlock the door to the Sinful Threads office that I saw who the messages were from: ARANEAE SPARROW.

I hit her first text message.

"WINNIE, SORRY. I HOPE I CAUGHT YOU IN TIME. WE WILL NEED TO POSTPONE YOUR TRIP TO CHICAGO. GO ON TO NEW YORK. I'LL EXPLAIN LATER."

Second message:

"HEY, PLEASE LET ME KNOW YOU GOT MY MESSAGE. IT'S EXTREMELY IMPORTANT."

Third message.

"OKAY. WE FOUND THE EARLIER-THAN-PLANNED FLIGHT YOU BOOKED. CALL ME AS SOON AS YOU LAND."

That was what the people around her did, discovered anything and everything.

. . .

Fourth message as I pushed the etched-glass door open and stepped into the Sinful Threads entry.

"PLEASE, WINNIE, WHATEVER YOU DO, DON'T GO TO THE OFFICE."

WINNIE

My steps stilled just inside the door as the exit sign gave the front office an eerie red hue.

The phone in my hand began to vibrate as the shrill ring cut through the otherwise silent air.

Upon the screen I saw a familiar name: *PATRICK KELLY.*

Also part of the Sparrow world, he was tall, blond, scary, and yes, attractive. Not as attractive as the man in my fantasies, but honestly, no one I'd met through the Sparrow world of either real estate or security was bad on the eyes.

The reality of Araneae's text settled around me as my phone rang again.

PLEASE, WINNIE. WHATEVER YOU DO, DON'T GO TO THE OFFICE.

"Hello," I said after hitting the green icon.

"Ms. Douglas, this is Patrick Kelly."

"Yes, I just read Araneae's messages. What's happening?"

"Ma'am, you're safe. We have the Sinful Threads office monitored, and no one else is there."

My hands began to shake as I turned a complete circle, taking in the entry containing Jana's desk, computer, and pictures of her son. Along the perimeter were doors to the various offices, conference room, and workroom, as well as a bathroom.

"Patrick, what is going on?"

"Listen closely," he said, his voice calm. "Lock the door to the hallway. Once it's locked, go to your office and lock that door. We have a man on his way to escort you from the building."

My head shook. "Escort me where?"

"You may have been seen or associated with Sinful Threads. It isn't safe for you to travel until we have this threat contained."

I placed the phone between my ear and shoulder as I secured the outer door's lock. "It's locked. Patrick, this is crazy. What threat?"

"I can't say, Ms. Douglas."

My trembling hand reached for the doorknob to my Chicago office space, turning it, I pushed the door inward and flipped the switch. "Patrick, my name is Winnie. If you're telling me I'm being targeted by someone or more than one person, I think you could use my first name."

"I'm not saying you're targeted, Winnie," he complied with my request. "I'm saying you may have been seen. We have reason to believe anyone or anything connected to Mr. Sparrow could be under an increased threat."

I scanned my office.

It was exactly as I'd left it a few weeks ago, complete with my tan sweater draped over the back of my leather desk chair where I'd accidentally left it. Shaking my head, I made my way to my desk. "I'm in my office."

"And you locked the door?"

"Shit," I replied, walking back to the door and twisting the small latch within the doorknob. "Now it is."

"I can stay on the phone until Garrett arrives," Patrick offered.

Garrett?

He was the one, the one I imagined pouring wine into my glass as we floated in Sydney Harbor. His dark hair, blue eyes, and what I could only imagine was beneath his custom suits were what I saw when my eyes closed and I took things into my own hands.

"How much longer?" I asked.

A knocking sound came from the front office.

"Oh," I said, "I think he's here."

"No, Winnie."

My breath caught. "What?"

"Don't go to the door. I have the entrance security camera on my screen. That isn't Garrett."

The pounding grew louder.

"What do you mean?" I asked, my eyebrows knitted together. "It's not even seven in the morning. Who is it?"

"The man in question is wearing a delivery uniform. Garrett has a key. He won't knock."

My body jolted with each pound against the reinforced glass door.

"Oh my God. You're saying that this man isn't really a deliveryman?"

"Winnie, stay calm. This doesn't concern you, and we don't want it to."

A memory came back. It was from when I'd first become accustomed to the workings of the Sparrow world, the one Araneae was now a part of. There'd been a kidnapping and threats. "Shit, Patrick. I just came here to do my job."

"And we're doing ours."

My nerves grew taut as the pounding ceased.

Was the man gone?

Was he simply a persistent deliveryman?

Was he trying another way to get into the office?

I fought the urge to go out and look, to see for myself.

"Winnie," Patrick began while at the same time, new noises erupted beyond my office door.

Grunts and the sounds of fighting.

Oh shit.

"Winnie, do not open your door."

Sliding from my office chair to the floor beneath my desk, I brought my knees to my chest. "What's happening?" My voice cracked with the overload of fear rushing through my bloodstream.

Could I survive what others had?

A kidnapping.

I didn't want to find out.

"Patrick."

There was no response.

"Patrick?" I called his name once, twice, and a third time, yet he didn't respond.

The noise from the other room ceased, leaving me beneath my desk as the thumping of my own pulse echoed in my ears.

The doorknob to my office rattled.

"Patrick, someone is coming in."

No response.

Click.

Creak.

If only I had a weapon, anything.

A letter opener or scissors.

I couldn't see from my position under my desk as the door opened farther.

I held my breath.

"Winnie," Patrick's voice was back.

I hit mute before pulling the phone to my chest, hoping the intruder wouldn't find my location.

Clip, clip.

Shoes moved toward my hiding place, the sound of their steps magnified in the otherwise quiet of the office.

Large black shoes peeking beneath dark gray slacks came to a stop around the desk.

GARRETT

Blue eyes the size of saucers stared up at me as I hunched down, lowering myself, allowing my gaze to take in the woman hiding beneath her desk. "Ms. Douglas." I offered her my hand.

Worry and anxiety slipped away from her expression as the tips of her lips curled upward.

"Oh, Garrett," she said, reaching for my hand.

I folded my long fingers around hers, enveloping her petite hand as she moved from beneath the desk to standing all of five feet three, nearly a foot shorter than I.

Letting go of her hand, I cleared my throat. "I was going to introduce myself."

"Um, Patrick said..." Her eyes stayed fixed on mine. There were too many emotions swirling in their blue depths. I couldn't separate one from the other.

"You're safe."

Her head shook as auburn hair brushed her petite shoulders. "What is happening? Patrick wouldn't tell me."

I scanned her from head to toe, her frame still covered by her long coat. At least color was returning to her cheeks, bringing a glow to her quizzical expression.

When our gazes again met, I asked, "Are you hurt?"

She took a step back. "No, I'm not hurt. I was frightened and now I'm mad."

I stood straighter as a grin threatened my mask of indifference. "You're safe and now you're mad?"

I'd heard Mrs. Sparrow remark that Winifred Douglas was five feet, three inches of spitfire, and now, standing close enough to touch her, I had to agree.

"Yes, I'm mad. What the hell is happening?"

"Ma'am, it doesn't—"

She lifted her hand to stop me. "My name is Winnie. Stop with the 'ma'am' and 'Ms. Douglas' shit. You make me sound old."

She wasn't old.

She was more than likely close to my age, a bit younger. That was my guess, but as a member of the Sparrow outfit, I knew danger when I saw it, and discussing a woman's age was a surefire trap. "Ma'am, you're not old."

"Winnie," she corrected again. "And when I ask what's going on, I don't want to hear that it doesn't concern me." She pointed to the floor beneath her desk. "I was under there. It concerns me."

"Winnie." I attempted a change in subject, noticing the satchel and overnight bag near the wall. "Are those your things?"

Her arms were now crossed over her chest, her neck was straight, and lips pursed. "Will you tell me what's happening?"

"I am supposed to get you to safety first."

Her head shook. "I'm not leaving with you until I know what's happening."

Sounds came from the outer office.

Winnie's blue eyes grew round. "What is that?"

I stepped to the partially ajar door.

"Get rid of him," I said to the two men comprising the Sparrow cleanup crew.

"Yes, sir, Mr. Givens. We'll have him out of here."

"Take him to the tower for questioning. He should regain consciousness sometime later today."

A hand came to my back as Winnie peered around my frame. Quickly, I turned, closing the door and keeping the sight of the man I'd laid unconscious out of her view. Winnie's chin rose.

"What did you do to him?"

"It's better if you don't know."

"Don't know what?" she asked, her voice growing louder. "I don't know what you do here or what any of the people around Mr. Sparrow do. It seems all cloak-and-dagger. Are you the good guys or the bad guys?"

My cheeks rose as I gave in to the smile I'd wanted to show since the moment I found her curled under the desk. "My job is to insure your safety. I would suppose that to you, that makes me a good guy."

Her gaze narrowed as her words slowed. "But to others?"

"To the man out there who was attempting to break in to Mrs. Sparrow's office, I would be a bad guy." I shrugged. "But so would he, so it's subjective."

With her arms crossed over her breasts, it was Winnie's turn to scan me up and down, and for a reason I couldn't come to terms with, I hoped she liked what she saw. I certainly did—liked what I saw in her. I not only liked what I saw, I enjoyed the way Winnie took on life, whether it was her increase in responsibilities at Sinful Threads or questioning a six-foot-four-inch man who came to save her.

Yes, I'd noticed her over the years, watching her from afar.

Until today, I hadn't had the chance to speak to or spend time with her. As it was, that was my assignment, and when Mr. Kelly had called, I didn't argue. Hell, I would have volunteered if I'd been asked.

Instead, it was fate.

Her pretty face tilted. "How bad?"

My forehead furrowed. "How bad am I capable of being? Now, Winnie, that seems like a loaded question. You're Mrs. Sparrow's partner and friend." I turned and opened the door wide enough to assure myself that the Sparrow cleanup crew, and man with questionable intentions, were gone. "My job is to insure your safety until the threat level is lowered."

"But I have work to do." She reached for her satchel.

"Let me," I said, reaching for both bags. "During times like this, Mrs. Sparrow and Mrs. Norman work from home. They communicate via teleconferencing."

"Mrs. Norman? Jana, yes."

"You can do that once I have you settled."

"I've worked with them that way," she said, walking about the office. "But they never said it was because of an increased threat."

"They wouldn't because it didn't affect you."

She stopped with a huff as her balled fists came to her hips. “Stop saying that. I’m affected.”

“Today,” I agreed.

“So this happens…often?”

I let out a breath. “Ms. Douglas…I mean, Winnie, may we continue this conversation away from Sinful Threads?”

“Where are you taking me?”

“Your reservations were for the Palmer House. Since you may have been connected to Mr. Sparrow by the wrong people, that wouldn’t be safe. Mr. Kelly found you a suite in another hotel.”

“Who will know where I am?”

“Mrs. Sparrow, Mrs. Norman. It would be best if no one outside the Sparrows knew, just until—”

“The security threat is lessened,” she interrupted. “So, you’ll let me call Araneae and Jana once we’re settled?”

“You may text Mrs. Sparrow now. She’s aware of what’s happening.”

Winnie pulled her phone from her pocket. “Oh,” she said, lifting the phone to her ear. “Patrick?”

A beautiful smile filled her face. “Yes, he’s here. And it’s safe to go with him?” She nodded. “Okay. I want to touch base with Araneae.” Her lips came together as she listened. Finally, she replied, “All right.”

She disconnected the call and looked at me. “He said you’re safe.”

I smirked—if only Mr. Kelly knew my thoughts.

Winifred Douglas would meet no harm in my presence. That was not to insinuate she was safe. Because if it wouldn’t mean my job, I’d strive to learn what exactly was under her long wool coat and whatever she wore beneath that.

Her phone buzzed as she looked down at the screen. “It’s from Araneae.” With her blue gaze alternating between the screen and me, she read her text.

WINNIE

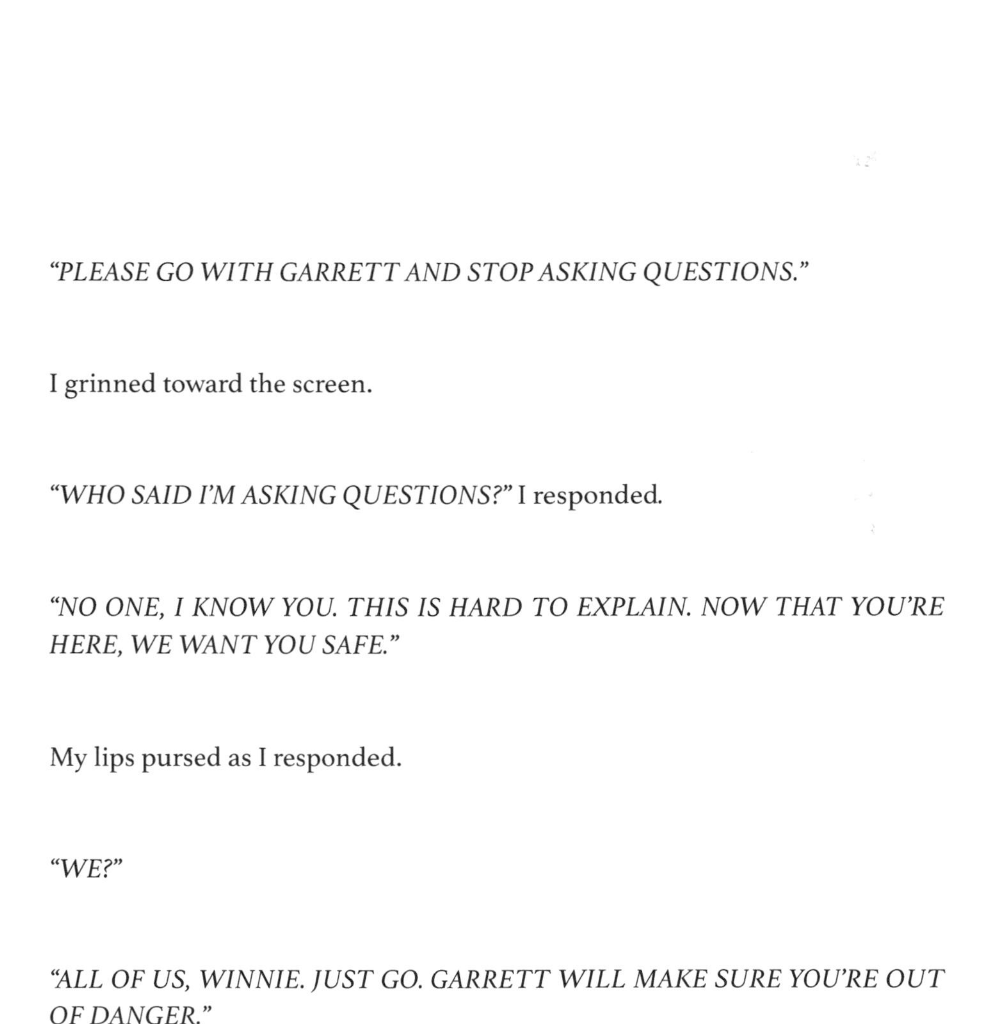

"PLEASE GO WITH GARRETT AND STOP ASKING QUESTIONS."

I grinned toward the screen.

"WHO SAID I'M ASKING QUESTIONS?" I responded.

"NO ONE, I KNOW YOU. THIS IS HARD TO EXPLAIN. NOW THAT YOU'RE HERE, WE WANT YOU SAFE."

My lips pursed as I responded.

"WE?"

"ALL OF US, WINNIE. JUST GO. GARRETT WILL MAKE SURE YOU'RE OUT OF DANGER."

. . .

I looked back up at the man before me. "She agreed with Patrick, saying I should go with you. She also said I should stop asking questions. Did you rat me out?"

His smile came back to life. "No, I wouldn't do that."

I took a deep breath. "I really don't have a choice in this, do I?"

"I find it makes people feel better if they think they have options."

I could think of worse people to be secured with until the threat rating lowered. Without trying to hide it, I did one more scan of the man before me. While I hadn't seen what he'd done to the man trying to enter the office, I had no doubt Garrett Givens could keep me safe.

"Okay, what are my options?"

Garrett's eyes shone. "You may go with me and I'll carry your bags, or you may go with me and carry your own bags."

My head shook. "So I'm your job?"

"Yes, ma'am...Winnie," he corrected, "you are."

"And what exactly does that mean?"

His cheek twitched as if he was losing a battle against another smile. "First, we need to get out of here."

"Take me away, Mr. Givens." I reached for my satchel. Tipping my head toward my overnight bag, I said, "My choice is for you to carry that."

A few minutes later, Garrett had the Sinful Threads office secured. Walking away, we took the elevator, not to the street level but down to the garage. As the elevator doors opened, a black car pulled up. Garrett opened the door to the back seat and gestured for me to enter.

"Um, are you going too?"

"Yes," he said with a nod.

Soon we were both within the back seat as a man named Romero drove us out into the daylight. I took in the view, realizing how strangely normal the city's streets appeared. There was no sign of upheaval. No sirens blaring or red lights flashing. According to Araneae, Patrick, and Garrett, we were in danger from an unknown threat.

Well, it wasn't completely unknown. There had been a man caught trying to break into Sinful Threads after I'd entered.

The point was that while according to all of them, danger lurked in the nearby shadows, on the surface, all looked ordinary.

"Aliens?" I whispered to Garrett. "That's it, right? It's like the old *Men in Black* movie."

"As in from outer space?"

I nodded.

"No, this isn't about aliens. And if I had that light thingy, you wouldn't be asking."

I let out a sigh. "I have so much to do, Garrett. This detour doesn't exactly fit into my schedule."

"Have you ever considered slowing your schedule? Taking some time to enjoy life?"

Within the confines of the sedan, his woodsy cologne filled my senses as his knee flirted close to mine. I turned his direction. "Tell me, do you...enjoy life?"

He shrugged.

"You do?" I asked.

"I like what I do. I respect who I work for. It's a commitment that requires dedication, and I'm proud of what I've done."

"Mr. Sparrow?" I clarified.

"Yes. He cares deeply about this city, about causes that seem too large to tackle, and about the people who mean the most to him." Garrett's blue eyes came to me. "That's why I'm here. You matter to Mrs. Sparrow. Mrs. Sparrow matters to Mr. Sparrow."

"How about you?"

"What about me?"

Romero didn't appear to be paying attention to our conversation, and as Garrett and I conversed, I wasn't paying attention to the direction we were traveling. My mind was on the man beside me. The one talking more than I'd ever heard him before, the one with the deep voice that stirred something within me that I'd thought had died, or at least retired to a warmer climate.

"Do you have someone who matters?" I asked.

"The people who matter to Mr. Sparrow..." He shook his head. "That's not what you're asking." He looked at me, really looked at me. "What about you?"

I shrugged. "I mean, I have friends, great friends. I'm lucky that they're also my colleagues. I care about them—very much. This whole thing reminds me of a time with Louisa and Jason...I think I was more frightened when it was them than now."

"Why?"

"Because I didn't know what was happening to them. Not knowing is worse than knowing."

"That's how Mrs. Sparrow felt this morning when she couldn't reach you."

A long sigh came from my lungs as I turned to the window. I hadn't thought of it like that. I hadn't considered how my actions affected those I cared about.

The car entered another parking garage.

How had I missed the name of the hotel?

"Where are the signs?" I asked.

"This garage isn't for patrons. This is private," Garrett responded.

Taking my bags, he helped me from the car. As we rode the elevator upward, a new wave of exhaustion came over me. I leaned against the wall.

"Are you all right?" he asked with genuine concern in his voice.

"I took the red-eye last night. I guess I'm tired."

The elevator doors opened to an empty hallway. Garrett led me to a door with 2756 on the plate to the side.

"Who knows we're here?" I asked as he unlocked the door.

"Everyone who counts," he replied.

He opened the door to a suite, complete with a large living area and an attached kitchenette. The drapes were open, revealing Chicago's skyline and a now cobalt-blue sky. After dropping my bag upon the sofa, I ran my fingertips over the furniture and made my way to the large windows. "This isn't the type of room I usually get on Sinful Threads' budget."

Garrett smiled. "Mrs. Sparrow said only the best."

"And what Mrs. Sparrow says goes?"

"Yes," he answered.

Removing my coat, I saw my wrinkled blouse, the one I'd put on last night before the flight.

I eyed another doorway and walked closer. Pushing the door open, I took in the bedroom with a king-size bed and more large windows. "Are you staying?" I asked.

"Yes, you're my assignment."

"Is there another…?"

"Bedroom?" he completed my question. "I will stay out here between you and the door."

"To be sure I don't leave?"

"To be sure no one else enters."

I nodded. "I think...I think I want to rest and maybe freshen up."

Garrett nodded. "I'll be out here."

"You never answered my question," I said.

"What question was that?"

"Do you have a special someone, someone you care about, not because they are an assignment, but who you actually care about?"

"I'd like to. It's difficult with my schedule and responsibilities. I never know where I'll be from day to day."

I nodded and turned to enter the bedroom.

"Winnie."

I turned back. "Yes?"

"The blue dress you wore at the Sinful Threads holiday party has never left my thoughts."

Warmth filled my cheeks. "You noticed me?"

He nodded. "It matched your eyes. It wasn't the first time I noticed. I believe the first time I saw you was before Mrs. Sparrow was Mrs. Sparrow. You came to town to help with Sinful Threads."

Bashfully, I looked down and back up. "I made some mistakes back then."

"Don't we all?"

I recalled my reasoning. It was the cause of most troubles throughout my life. It was a man. "I always want what I shouldn't have," I confessed.

"I have the same problem."

What did that mean?

Was he as interested in me, as I was in him or were we discussing abstracts?

"I'm going to lie down."

"You can rest. I won't leave."

Closing the bedroom door behind me, I bit my lower lip.

What were the rules in a situation like this?

What if I made a move or allowed him to make a move? What would happen when the danger was over?

GARRETT

"Well done," Mr. Kelly said on the other end of the phone conversation. "Mr. Pierce is with the man now. If he knows anything, we'll know it soon enough."

"He's conscious?" I asked, leaning back on the sofa, the city of Chicago before me. I'd removed my suit coat and rolled up the sleeves of my shirt. Since I wasn't going anywhere, it seemed that a bit of comfort was allowed.

"Yes," Mr. Kelly responded.

Visions came to mind centered upon what I knew about Mr. Pierce and his interview techniques. I wouldn't want to be on the receiving end and didn't know anyone who would. "Ms. Douglas is resting."

It had been over an hour since she'd disappeared behind the door.

Was it locked?

Was she asleep?

"We have capos swarming the streets," Mr. Kelly said, bringing my thoughts away from the woman behind the door and back to the dangers threatening our city.

"She should be able to travel to New York tomorrow," he continued, "but don't make any promises yet that we might not be able to keep. Mrs. Sparrow won't allow Ms. Douglas to leave the hotel suite if there's a chance of danger."

"Yes, sir."

I didn't want to tell Winnie she could go. I was content with the way things currently were.

"I'll contact you with developments," Mr. Kelly said moments before the call disconnected.

The door to the bedroom opened, and Winnie came out. Her hair was tousled, her face freshly washed, and her clothes had been replaced by a fluffy white robe, complete with the hotel's emblem upon the breast pocket. Her feet were bare, and from what I could see as she walked toward me, so were her legs.

"Is everything all right?" I asked, standing.

"I was thirsty." She passed me on her way to the kitchenette. As she did, the slight fragrance of flowers caught my attention.

Bending down, she opened the refrigerator, pulling out a bottle of water.

When she turned around and stood as tall as she could, her eyes were wide. She twisted the cap on the bottle. "I was thinking about our conversation."

"You were. Which one?" I knew what I'd been thinking about.

"Maybe if two people are both slaves to their jobs, jobs they love and don't want to lose..." she added quickly. "Hypothetically, maybe even though they weren't looking for someone to care about, but fate stepped in and presented an opportunity...?"

My mind told me to stay back, that this was against the Sparrow rules, yet my feet found me moving closer. It was as if she were a magnet and the attraction was too strong to fight.

Only inches away, I fought the urge to reach out and pull her petite frame to me, to feel her body against mine. Even the thought redirected my blood in an uncomfortable way.

Winnie looked up. "I don't know what rules you have. I don't understand much of anything about the world Araneae pulled us all into. I know that men like Mr. Sparrow, Patrick, and you have not only saved Louisa and Jason, but now me too. You see dangers people like us can't imagine, and yet you do what you do and remain calm. I know, I've noticed and watched you too. I don't know what any of this means." She shook her head. "I have a history of making poor decisions when it comes to men."

"If I were to kiss you," I said, my voice growing deeper, "would you make a poor decision and kiss me too, or would you make the right decision and slap my face and call Mr. Kelly or Mrs. Sparrow and have me fired?"

Her breathing had changed, growing more rapid as her breasts pushed against the robe, each breath parting the neckline just enough to see the tops of her round globes. Her cheeks grew pink, and her tongue darted to her lips as she stared my way. "I'm afraid I'd make the poor decision of kissing you too."

I reached for her waist and pulled her hips toward me. "The way I see this," I began as her back arched and face tilted upward. "We both essentially work within the same realm. You are a partner in Sinful Threads. I work for Sparrow. The two worlds are connected and will be for as long as Mrs. Sparrow retains her part in Sinful Threads. I can't offer every night or every day. The powers that be would strongly disapprove. However, I am dedicated to this city and you make your way here on a routine rotation..." I ran my finger over her soft cheek. "And when you do, we could try—"

Winnie rose higher on her tiptoes, lifting herself higher. Her lips brushed mine.

My hands went to her hair, tugging back as my mouth took hers. One step and another and she was flush with the wall. The space between us no longer existed.

Tasting her, feeling her, was the rush I'd imagined and more. Explosions set off nerve endings as heat warmed my skin and blood to my erection. Soft moans flowed from her lips as our tongues tangled together.

When we finally pulled away, her lips were reddened and her cheeks flushed.

"Garrett?"

"Poor decision?"

"Definitely," she replied. "Did you see them?"

"I saw you."

"The fireworks, just like over the Sydney Harbor on New Year."

My cheeks rose as I brushed hers with my finger. "I did. But I think it was only the beginning. I don't believe they're done."

Winnie's smile bloomed. "I hope not."

Our hands came together as I led her toward the bedroom. "Hold on tight for the grand finale."

The rest has been left to your imagination...

* * *

Do you want more of Aleatha Romig?

One click SECRETS now!

3, 2, 1

PARKER S. HUNTINGTON

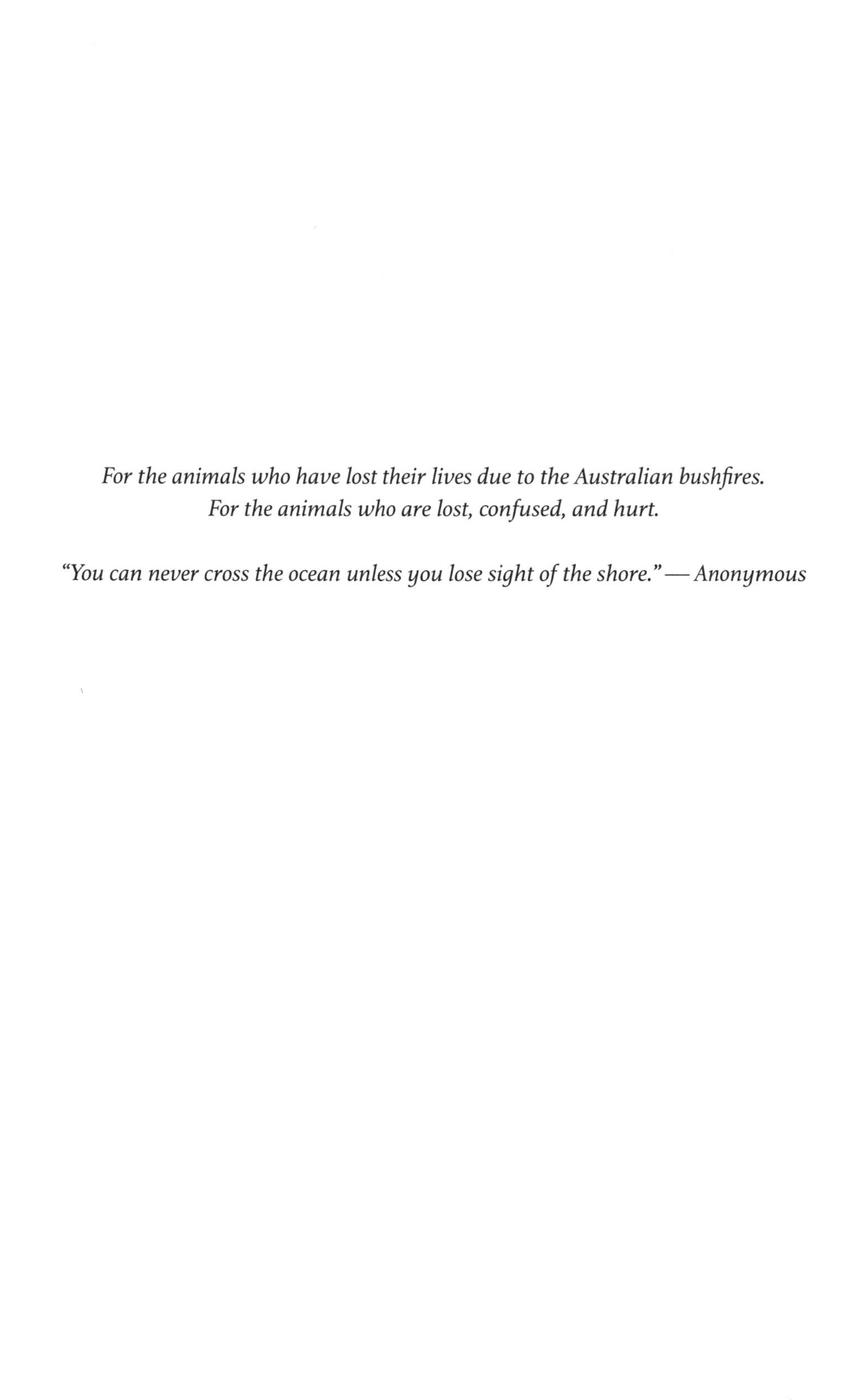

For the animals who have lost their lives due to the Australian bushfires.
For the animals who are lost, confused, and hurt.

"You can never cross the ocean unless you lose sight of the shore." — *Anonymous*

PROLOGUE

Bellamy

Bellamy, 22; Liam, 22

Betrayal tastes like blood.

I release my lower lip from between my teeth and swipe my tongue across the surface. Okay. That's actual blood. But I'm sure that, if betrayal had a flavor, it would be blood.

The mattress dips as I slide off it, clutching my dress to my bare chest. Flicking a glance at the man sleeping on the twin XL dorm bed, I slip the fabric over my head as quietly as I can and slide on my Chucks.

You can stay, I lie to myself, tucking the letter I wrote yesterday under his pillow. *You don't have to do this. You don't have to leave Liam.*

Except I do. We both have dreams that will take us to opposite ends of the world if we let them. I can't be trapped in Clifton, Alabama, watching Mom work three shitty jobs to make ends meet. The journalism internship in New York is a once-in-a-lifetime opportunity that will eventually provide for both of us.

And Liam Conners? He's a rising star athlete, intelligent on and off the field but loyal to a fault. He would follow me to New York, even if it meant declining the pro rugby offer in Australia.

This is the only way.

Stumbling over my graduation gown, I steady myself on his desk. When my fingers hit the doorknob, our entire childhood together flashes before my eyes. Late nights stargazing in the tree house Dad built before he died. Sneaking behind the football bleachers and stealing kisses. Hiding in the Clifton Zoo past closing and spending the night beside the koalas' enclosure.

I blink back tears and whisper, "In three years, I'll come for you, Liam."

It's a promise I intend to keep.

1

Liam

Three Years Later

For the record, I didn't kill anyone.

Still, Coach looks like he's ten seconds from shipping me a bulk pack of diapers to go with my team-management-certified babysitter.

Coach glares at me from across the locker room, eyeing the blood staining my rugby uniform. "I want a clean season, Conners."

He means off the field, where my life has become a shit show. On the field, I hold the record for the most tries this season—the only American to ever earn the honor in Rugby Australia.

The locker room emptied out hours ago, but given the fact that I supposedly KO'd some douche at a bar last night, it could be worse than a three-hour lecture and some suit tailing me twenty-four seven.

"Yeah." I swipe the sweat from my crew-cut hair and strip out of my yellow practice jersey. "Practice. Game. Home. I know the drill."

Except last night, when I went with my neighbor Craig for drinks at the bar below my flat. He threw a punch at some mouthy fucker, and next thing I knew, I was taking the blame for something I didn't do.

I don't have a savior complex, but Craig is on parole. The last thing I need is his wife yelling at me for taking him out for drinks and getting him arrested.

Coach remains unfazed by my nudity as I grab a towel, wrap it around my waist, and enter the showers. He follows me, stopping just at the edge of the room. "Tyson will shadow you for the remainder of the season."

I know Tyson. He's driven and a stickler for the rules. He'll be a pain in my ass, much like the clause in my contract that requires me to maintain a squeaky-clean image.

I am Australia's golden boy. The Southern transplant with the all-American smile, blue eyes, and dirty blond hair. Slap me shirtless on a billboard, and whatever I'm advertising will sell out, including the vegemite-flavored milk commercial I booked prior to obtaining an agent. (Lesson learned.)

Slinging my towel on the hook, I step under the showerhead and turn the spray to its hottest setting. My brow quirks at the sight of Coach hovering by the door, brows furrowed and fingers flying across his phone's keyboard. "Anything else or are you here to watch me shower? If it's the latter, get in line."

"Actually, yeah. There's one more thing." He ignores my attitude and pockets his phone. "Management set up a feature for you with some no-name American journalist from *Sports Net*. *Rugby Mag* agreed to distribute it here. We'll make it a cover feature."

Translation: You fucked up, so we scheduled a puff piece and chose an American sports journalist to write it because they don't give two shits about rugby and won't dig deeper.

I give him my back and dump shampoo on my head, wondering if *she* still works at *Sports Net* before dismissing the idea. Sports journalism was never her endgame.

"Got it," I finally say, but the water drowns my voice.

I'd get the interview over with, deal with Tyson for the next three months, and get my life back. And next time, I'll remember not to have drinks with someone who hallucinates aliens while drunk.

2

Liam

I know I'm fucked the second I see her.

It's like looking down the barrel of a gun, knowing I'm in danger, that I should move, and still being frozen to the spot.

In three years, Bellamy Davis hasn't changed. Her hair still matches the colors of the rainbow, starting with violet on the top and ending with a faded red on the bottom. She wears a ripped band tee tucked into tight skinny jeans that make me want to sink my teeth into her ass.

Kicking one Chucks-covered foot in front of the other, she leans against a couch in the lobby of the Prescott Hotel in Sydney. Her front teeth nibble her bottom lip, a nervous tic of hers.

I can't see it from here, but I remember the small gap between her front teeth. The memory halts me by the rotating doors.

I'm fifty feet from Bellamy with Tyson trailing behind me like a well-trained dog. He stops beside me and adjusts his red tie, which looks more and more like a dog collar by the second.

Everything about him is opposite of me. He wears a suit; I'm in a team tee and gray sweats. His black hair has been carefully slicked back; my blond hair is so short I haven't seen a comb since I was five.

He's also hopping around like he's going through withdrawals. In reality, he's waiting for me to make a mistake. Ten seconds ago, I would have laughed at the idea. Now, I'm not so sure.

I know what Bellamy's doing. I've seen her do it before when she worked for our college newspaper at Clifton University. The jeans, tee, and hair make her look approachable, but she's a viper, dedicated to finding the truth and turning it into a weapon.

So much for a puff piece.

The second she spots me, her lips part. I close the space between us, noting the gap between her teeth is still there, unfixed and proud. Her time in New York hasn't physically changed her, which only reminds me how fucked I am, because if she's the same person she was three years ago, I'll fall again... just for her to leave.

A-fucking-gain.

She extends a hand, a light smile tilting her lips up. "Nice to meet you, Mr. Conners. I'm Bellamy Davis, but you can call me Bell."

My eyes narrow, wondering what she's getting at as she pretends we haven't known each other since we were born.

I ignore her outstretched hand and yawn. "As in the thing farmers attach to a cow's neck? No, thanks."

Tyson's alarm-filled eyes dart between us before he clears his throat and slides his palm against Bellamy's. "I'm Tyson, Mr. Conners'—"

"Babysitter," Bellamy finishes for him, extracting her fingers from his clutches.

He freezes, and it's almost enough to make me laugh. This is clearly not going how he thought it would. "No, I'm his—"

"She doesn't care," I cut him off, but I know Bellamy gets what I mean. They're the words I would have told her three years ago if she'd had the balls to say bye to my face instead of in a letter.

She ignores my words, swiping at a stray strand of hair with the vigor of a pissed-off hooker. (The rugby position, not the job occupation.) "Tyson, it was a pleasure to meet you. I've booked a conference room for the interview. I'll have Mr. Conners back in an hour."

Her meaning is clear—this interview is between us only.

"But—" Tyson swallows his protest, at the mercy of the five-foot-one, rainbow-haired girl rocking a Barbed Wire Condom band tee. "I'll wait in the lobby."

I pull the media packet Coach gave me from my back pocket and shove it into Tyson's hands. "Later."

The second I have Bellamy alone in the elevator, I let loose a snort. "You pretended you didn't know shit about rugby to get this gig, didn't you? Once a liar, always a liar."

She doesn't rise to the bait, instead scraping her hungry eyes across my body in a way that makes me want to pull at the collar of my tee. It's so familiar it's almost as if we're back in Alabama. Except Australia is my home now, and it sure as shit has treated me better than Bellamy Fucking Davis.

Her head cocks slightly to the right, eyes fixated on me. "You're still angry."

She's right.

Have I stopped being angry since that day? Maybe the real reason I took the rap for hitting that dude at the bar was because if Craig hadn't, I would have. I've been spiraling, taking my frustration out on the turf like it's my personal battlefield.

I don't tell her any of this, giving her the cold shoulder I reserve for the media. "Is that a question, Ms. Davis?"

The doors slide open on the fifth floor, but she blocks my exit with a palm against my chest. "I pretended I didn't know you so your babysitter wouldn't report it back to your bosses. It wasn't an attack. I was trying to protect you."

My gaze dips to her hand. I could push past her easily, but I don't. I step into her touch, enjoying the way her eyes widen at the feel of my muscles.

That's right, baby. You might look the same, but I don't. I'm not that starry-eyed kid you screwed over either.

Ten hours of daily training has sculpted my body into granite that towers over her tiny frame, over a foot shorter than me.

"Why are you here, Bellamy? And no bullshit lines about protecting me. I want the truth."

She ignores my question. "You've changed." Her nose wrinkles up in distaste, bitterness tingeing her voice.

The Bellamy Davis I know isn't bitter. She's innocent and daring. Adventurous yet reserved. Somehow sweet despite the thorns. The knowledge that I don't know her anymore pisses me off.

Shaking my head, I scowl at her. "Don't pretend you know me."

I step around Bellamy and head toward the conference room my team has booked in the past. A woman manning the door opens it for me, barely managing to stutter a starstruck greeting.

I am fully aware I'm being an ass, but I'm too distracted by Bellamy to care. One week of her shadowing me, then she'll be gone forever again.

That's what I want, right?

3

Bellamy

My pen breaks in my clenched grip, squirting ink all over my shirt. I mutter a curse, swiping the ink on my jeans.

Liam remains seated on the conference room couch, not bothering to offer help. We've been sitting in silence for a solid minute.

I ignore the stain, toss the pen in the trash, pocket my notepad, and pull out my phone. Opening the recorder app, I lean back on the couch across from his.

"Do I have your consent to record this conversation?"

"You always do what you want anyway."

"I'll take that as a yes." I press the green record button. "I have begun recording this interview with your consent. Is this correct?"

He drags out a breath and runs his thumb across his sharp jawline. "Yes."

I clear my throat and begin the interview, though all I want is to explain why I left. That first year, he declined every phone call, left every letter unanswered, and blocked me on social media.

Mom overheard the Conners complaining that Liam never returns to Alabama, too. He flies them to Australia for visits.

"Mr. Conners, may I call you Liam?"

He doesn't answer.

I grind my teeth together. "*Liam*, in three years, you've taken your team from last in the league to first. After three consecutive championship wins, how do—"

"I feel?" he finishes for me. "Original."

I want to ball up the approved interview sheet his team's GM e-mailed me and throw it in his face. Liam is made, and for good reason. But I don't recognize this jaded man. Three years. I promised us three years.

I never considered the possibility that we'd change in those three years.

"That bad, huh?" Faking a laugh, I move on to the next question. "The Central Coast Rays are your next match. What are you doing to—"

"Prepare for the match? That fancy New York gig has sharpened your reporting skills."

His dig hits harder than I'd like to admit. In three years, I've had one promotion, which isn't exactly impressive considering it was from unpaid intern to the second-lowest-paying gig.

At my silence, he taunts, "Why don't you ask me a real question? Anything."

"Fine." I lean forward as far as I can without falling off the couch and keep my voice level. "Do you still love me?"

Silence.

"Fuck that." Liam's fists clench at his sides, his neck so coiled I can see the thick curvature of his muscles. "You come to me after three years, pretend you don't know me, then have the balls to ask if I still love you?"

I should be embarrassed. The phone continues to record us, and I have to send the interview tape to my boss in the morning, but I don't give a damn about the article.

Liam will get his puff piece, no interview needed.

I know every Liam Conners stat.

Every play.

Every try.

In the past three years, I've watched every televised game of his despite the time difference. Late nights spent up, heart in my throat every time the ball touched his hands. That week I took off work after his leg injury, and the only updates I could get were thirdhand from Mom.

Truth is, I'm not here to interview Liam.

I'm here for *him*.

"You told me to ask you a question. Anything. I did." I tuck a strand of colorful hair behind my ear, aware of the way his throat bobs at the movement. He misses me. I know he does. "Answer the question, Liam."

He opens his mouth to speak.

I brace for his words, but they never come.

Instead, he mutters a curse and leaves.

4

Liam

Sports therapy isn't erotic.

It's painful.

Luna is a twentysomething sports therapist, who paid her way through college by modeling. That's the last thing on my mind during my sessions, which I mostly spend with gritted teeth as she jabs my supposedly healed hamstring in ways that have me questioning whether she minored in torture.

Today, Bellamy is propped on a chair in the corner, hounding me with stupid questions our GM gave her. Questions I've answered in literally every interview I've ever given.

Puff. Fucking. Piece.

"I started in football and turned to rugby during college," I explain for the millionth time. The less fight I put up, the faster this week of her shadowing me will go.

She nods her head, looking distracted as she bites her lip and watches Luna's hand slide up my thigh near my groin.

Fuckkkk.

Bellamy needs to stop looking at me like she wants me inside her. I think of smelly socks and Grandma clipping her toenails to get my dick under control.

"Six more days," I mutter.

I almost wish Tyson hadn't stayed outside.

"What was that?" Luna asks.

"I said a little harder."

She nods, and Bellamy continues with the questions. I rattle off practiced answers. Ten minutes later, Luna tosses my shirt at me, says bye to Bellamy, and leaves us alone in the small massage room.

The air instantly thickens.

I stand, moving to slide the shirt over my head, but Bellamy's startled gasp stops me. "What?"

"Your tattoo."

Fuck. Me.

I'd managed to skip the shirtless photoshoots for years to avoid any prying questions from gossip rags, yet here I am, slipping up in front of the absolute last journalist who should see the tattoo.

The cold tips of her fingers hit my back. I freeze, muscles tense at her touch. She traces the tattoo.

5

What she wrote in that note she slipped under my pillow the night she left. I had the tattoo artist ink it in her handwriting.

"Why?" Her breath fans my back as she speaks.

Truthfully, I don't know why. I got it my first night in Australia. Craig and I went for drinks at the bar. When I returned to my flat, I pulled the letter out of my pocket, rereading the numbers again and again, trying to figure out what she meant by them.

I guess I thought if I inked them on my flesh, I'd understand them better. Fucking stupid if you ask me.

I don't tell her this.

Instead, I distance myself from her touch, put my shirt on, and ignore her.

"It doesn't have to be like this," Bellamy protests.

"Bullshit." I turn to face her. "You're here, and you were prepped for an interview from day one, which means you knew I was your assignment. You knew you'd see me. In fact, you probably wanted to see me."

She doesn't argue.

"Let me guess. You spent three years in the same job, and nothing's changed. You have a lot to prove, even if it's across the world from your tiny New York cubicle. Even if you have to see the guy you fucked over."

"You sound bitter."

"Maybe I am. *You* left me. *You* ended this."

"I did it because—"

"I don't want to hear your excuses, Bellamy. They're the last thing I want to hear."

She opens her mouth to speak, but nothing comes out. A minute and five sighs later, she says, "Well, I'm here for a week. It can either be an awful week, or we can agree to a truce."

"A truce." I toy with the word, wondering if I can stomach it.

"Yeah," she challenges, a glint in her eyes. "If you're no longer in love with me, if I no longer matter to you, it shouldn't be a problem. People only hold grudges when they care, right?"

Her eyes dare me to argue, but I have nothing to say to that.

She's right.

I still care.

Hell if I'd ever admit that.

"Right," I say. "A truce."

6

Bellamy

There's a koala glaring at me.

Liam and his teammates don't hold back their laughter, very much at my expense. We spent the past few hours volunteering at the local koala rescue. It's dark out now, but there's still a crowd of press here, taking photos of our every move.

Our.

It's too easy to forget that I'm part of the press, too.

My truce with Liam has lasted the past three days, where he has been nice but distant. I miss us. Having him in front of me without being able to touch him, confide in him, and love him is pure torture.

Liam's laughter sobers, almost as if he's just realized he's supposed to hate me. He hands the koala he's holding to a volunteer and heads to the back room. I look around to make sure no one, particularly Tyson and the media, is paying attention to me before following him.

When Liam sees me, he makes a show of washing his hand, so he doesn't have to talk to me. I study him from the doorway, cataloging every feature of his. His bright blue eyes. His buzzed hair. The filled-out muscles. That nose that's a bit too crooked, probably from breaking it all the time. Neanderthal.

"How'd you know this back room is here?"

"I'm here often," he says but doesn't elaborate.

I don't expect him to. It hits too close to home, where we'd sneak into the local zoo and stay overnight.

Instead, I joke, "You expect me to believe you normally spend your free time nursing kangaroos back to health? This isn't some ploy to impress me?"

"Impress you? You're full of yourself."

We're smiling at each other now, and the air feels lighter.

"Skepticism is hardwired in me." I lift a shoulder. "I'm a journalist."

The reminder sobers us. I chose the internship over him.

"Right," Liam mutters and backs away. He shakes his head, levels me with a look I can't decipher, and leaves.

As soon as I think he's out of earshot, I bring my fist to my mouth and scream out five days of frustration. Scratch that. Three years of anger, pain, and unrequited love.

You can do this, Bellamy.

I'm not too sure, but I exit the back room with the fakest smile on my face.

"We're trapped," Liam says when I'm near him.

"What do you mean?"

"Everyone left." He gestures to the gated entrance. "I tried the door. It's locked from outside."

"Can you call someone?"

He shoves his phone in his pocket and mutters a curse. "Phone's out of battery. You?"

I'm silent for a minute before I make a decision. "Same." I sidle next to him, my shoulder brushing his. My eyes flutter closed. I savor the brief contact, and it's so pathetic I almost feel bad for myself. "I was on my phone all morning and drained it. What do we do?"

His shoulder lifts, another flash of contact that flips my heart in my chest. "There's nothing to do but wait."

7

Liam

"Tell me the truth. Do you like it here?" Bellamy asks.

She's lying on the grass, using my sweatshirt as a pillow. It reminds me of when we used to sleep next to the koala enclosure at the Clifton Zoo, only this time, we're inside with the koalas. One of them is curled up to her hip. Another lays on my chest with its fist wrapped around my wrist.

"Yeah. I love rugby, I love the people here, I love the community I've built around me, and I love this country."

"But?"

"Why do you assume there's a but?"

She hesitates before saying, "Because I know you."

I could argue, but I don't, because she's right. There *is* a but. "But I miss my family."

I miss you.

There.

I fucking said it.

In my head, but still...

I'd managed to force out as many thoughts of Bellamy as I could the past three years. I blocked her number. Blocked her social media accounts.

Stopped coming home. Got a new phone without a million pictures of her on it.

Because I knew—if I saw her, if I talked to her, if I *remembered* her, I'd let her hurt me again.

Look at you. Five days together and you're already letting her in.

She sighs, pets the koala on her, and whispers, "Three."

"Three?"

"The amount of years I promised us. Before I came after you again."

"What?"

"Two. Mom says that's how old we were when I first told you I love you. Dad had finished the tree house, and your parents brought you over. My dad and mom helped us into the tree house. She says I turned to you and told you I love you. That those were the first words I ever said."

I'm silent. Speechless. Reeling, because I see where this is going, and it's like a train wreck waiting to happen. And I'm standing in front of the train, willing to take the hit. Even if it kills me.

"One," she continues. Ruthless. "The number of people I've ever loved. The number of people I'll only ever be in love with. In three years, there has been no one else. It's never been an option, because I'll only ever love you, Liam."

"Three. Two. One," I whisper. "Your letter."

"Yeah." She swipes at her eyes. I want to turn to her and maybe do something crazy like press my lips to hers, but there are koalas clinging to us, which is probably the most ridiculous sentence I've ever thought. "It was my promise to you. I tried to write more in the letter, but I knew if I did, I wouldn't be able to leave. You'd never let me give up the internship, so you'd turn down your rugby dreams. I just... I felt like I had to. I needed you to follow your dreams. I know it's selfish, but so is love. It's why you would have followed me to New York, knowing the fact that you gave up your dreams for me would have slowly killed me."

I don't know what to say to her.

I accept your unspoken apology?

Or maybe I'm the one who's sorry.

It's like she has flipped the past three years upside down, put them in a blender, and is trying to tell me it's Jamba Juice.

Bellamy doesn't give me a chance to speak. "Love is selfish and ruthless and ugly. If you think otherwise, you're deluding yourself. But we still want it, even if it leaves the deepest scars, because the scars love gives us are beautiful. They remind us what it's like to live."

This is her telling me she still loves me.

Maybe I'll give in. Maybe one more night won't break me. Maybe she'll leave, and I'll be okay.

Because the truth is, I miss her. I want her. I love her.

If she keeps this up, I'll give in.

8

Bellamy

Sweat is sexy.

I try not to think about it as I watch Liam add another weight to the bar he's lifting. A bead of sweat trails down his forehead, past his cheek, down his chin, and onto his bare chest. It should be illegal to be this hot.

If he stood in the middle of traffic like this, he'd cause a dozen car accidents and be liable for manslaughter, I swear.

"You're staring again," he says, a cocky smirk tilting the corners of his lips up.

"It's my job to observe you working out." I clear the huskiness out of my voice. "You know. For the article."

"Right," he deadpans. "The article."

I don't bother responding. I'm too busy following the bead of sweat down his chest, past the cut V I want to lick, and into his shorts.

"Fuck," Liam curses, and then his hand is around my wrist, and he's dragging me out of the weight room; past Tyson, who is busy tying his shoelace; and into a small closet.

I don't know who moves first, but his lips are on mine and hands are everywhere. I claw at his chest, climbing his body. My legs hook around his back. I grind myself against him, moaning when his lips hit the curve of my neck.

He swipes his tongue out. I grab his neck and push him back to my lips. The kiss is fast, rushed, delicious.

It's home.

A knock on the door startles us. I flick a glance back, noting that Liam must have locked it.

"Anyone in here?" Tyson calls out. "I'm looking for Liam."

Liam's hand dips below my shirt, his thumb swiping a path at the edge of my jeans. I moan. His other hand comes up to cover my mouth.

"Hello? I hear you! Liam, is that you?"

The hand at my jeans brushes my panties, pulling at the front until they press tighter against my clit. I clench at the feeling, needing him.

"Liam! I'm supposed to watch you!"

"Fuck," Liam mutters and sets me down. He rests his forehead against mine, fanning his minty breath across my face. "He won't stop. In my locker, there's a spare set of keys to my house. I'll text you the address. Meet me there, and I'll find an excuse to leave early."

I nod, struggling to clear the fog of lust. He adjusts my shirt, his thumb brushing against my nipple over the fabric. I laugh when he groans, and then he's gone, muttering some excuse to Tyson about finding a towel to clean his shoes.

Tyson peeks behind Liam and sees me, but I don't care.

I'm here for Liam.

He might not know it yet, but he will.

* * *

The first thing I notice inside Liam's bedroom is a small frame beside his bed. It's lying facedown, but I prop it back up. I nearly drop it when I realize what it is.

9

The note I left him.

He kept it.

"Bellamy?" Liam calls out.

I didn't even hear him enter.

"I'm in your room!" I set the frame down and sit on his bed.

If he notices the frame faceup when he enters, he doesn't say anything. Instead, he stares at me from the door, arms crossed and hip propped against the frame.

Finally, I break. "What are you looking at?"

"You. Only ever you."

He strips his shirt and meets me at the bed. I lift my fingers and run them down his spine, where the tattoo is.

I am his, and he is mine.

How we survived the last three years apart is unimaginable.

Liam's hand drags my shirt up, eyes lighting with satisfaction at the sight of my bare chest. He lowers himself to his knees, so he's level with me, and wraps his lips around my nipple.

I grip his shirt and tug until he's over me and my back is pressed against the bed. His fingers thread through my hair, teeth grazing my lips. I slide my pants off at the same time he does, eyes skimming our naked bodies pressed against one another.

He flips us, so I'm on top, guiding me onto his erection. And for the rest of the night, Liam Conners shows me just how much he's missed me.

He shows me just how much he loves me.

Neither of us talk about how this is the seventh day.

The last day.

10

Liam

Six seconds left in the game.

The ball feels heavy in my hands. I press it to the side of my chest and dodge a set of players, fake left, and lunge right. Then, I'm off, sprinting faster than I've ever sprinted. When I lower the ball to the grass, the stadium erupts in a roar, chanting my name.

"Liam! Liam! Liam!"

The victory is empty.

The thrill less noticeable.

She's gone.

I woke up to an empty bed with. No note. Only, there's no one to be mad at this time. Seven days. That's all we had. I knew last night would be our last.

She had a meeting with the team's GM this morning, and I'm sure she's on a flight back to the States by now.

But a part of me thought she wouldn't leave.

Fuck.

A few of my teammates clap me on the back. I shake hands with players on the opposing team, greet the other team's coaching staff, and make my way to the sea of reporters that begin to storm the field.

I must be hallucinating when I see rainbow hair.

I blink.

Once.

Twice.

Three times.

She's still there.

There's a press pass around her neck, but she has no microphone or camera following her. It's just her. And me. And I don't even wait before I run to her, pick her up, and kiss her in front of the cameras.

Hundreds of camera clicks sound around us, but I. Don't. Care.

She returns the kiss eagerly, wrapping her arms around my neck and pressing her entire body against mine. Her fingers meet my spine, right on top of my tattoo. She runs her fingers across it above the fabric.

I would strip her down and remind her exactly why she shouldn't leave if I didn't think she'd be opposed to starring in Australia's first rugby sex tape.

Instead, I set her down, press my forehead to hers, and ask, "What are you doing here? What about your job?"

She laughs, and it's so carefree it reminds me of everything I've ever loved about her. "I didn't come to Australia for my job, Liam. I came here for you."

EPILOGUE

Bellamy

One Year Later

"Are you sure this is okay?" I hold Liam's hand as we break into the koala sanctuary, hidden by the darkness of the night.

"No," he admits. "But I don't care."

"My boss will fire me if I'm caught."

"You can say you're working on a story."

I arch a brow. "About koalas?"

Lately, my stories have been about corporate cover-ups, elections, and the sacrifices Australian and international volunteer firefighters have made to fight the bushfires.

Nothing and everything has changed in the past year. Liam is still Rugby Player of the Year, to no one's surprise. But I'm a journalist at the top newspaper in Australia. That, I didn't expect.

When I left New York for Australia, I knew it was a one-way trip. I didn't care about my career. The people I left behind. My apartment. My life in New York.

All I knew was that my life was empty without Liam.

"Yes." He opens the gate to the koala enclosure, closes it behind him, and sets a blanket down in the center. "You can tell your boss a confidential informant fed you a story about teenage mutant koalas living in a sewer beneath the sanctuary while receiving training in martial arts from an old rat."

I sit beside him on the blanket. "America has Teenage Mutant Ninja Turtles, and Australia has teenage mutant koalas. Classic."

He pulls a remote from his backpack and presses it. Around us, lights strung across tree branches light up. I squint a bit and read what they say.

"Liam…"

"Three," he begins, his eyes fixated on me and fingers pinched around a ring. "The number of years I've had this ring. Even when I tried to forget you, even when I tried to move on, even when I told myself I was healing, I still loved you. I was in Perth, walking around after a match when I saw this in a window. The gem is made from tourmaline, the same rainbow as your hair."

He slides the ring on my ring finger, and I'm too stunned to speak. To even move. Three years… that was after I left him.

"Two," he continues. "The number of times I tried to quit the team when you were in New York. It's a running joke between me and Coach. I'd miss you and run to Coach, begging him to release me from my contract. He never did, but fuck, I tried. And finally, one—the number of people I want to spend the rest of my life with. Bellamy Davis, will you marry me?"

3. 2. 1.

The best promise I've ever kept.

"Yes."

* * *

VIRGIN RIDE

A SHORT STORY

A.L. JACKSON

1

Kelsey

A crack of thunder boomed overhead, and a bright burst of lightning flashed at the windows before the electricity to my little house flickered off and on.

Nerves prickled the nape of my neck, that electricity burning through the air, and my stomach tightened in anticipation.

I had this.

I rushed toward the little kitchen that sat just behind the living room, skidding around the edge of the counter, almost slipping in my socks as I hit the tile.

I jerked open one of the drawers, and I started pulling things out and setting them on the counter.

Flashlight. Check.

Candles. Check. Check.

Matches. Check. Check. Check.

Whew. I was set.

But wait.

Food.

Yes, food.

I whirled around and jerked open the pantry.

Stocked.

Of course, it was. It wasn't like I'd personally Hoovered through three months' worth of food in two days.

But double-checking never hurt a thing.

I blamed my father for my neurosis.

He owned a chain of local grocery stores and was basically as paranoid as could be.

He'd taught me to be prepared for any situation. To always have the things I needed within arm's reach because you could never anticipate what life was going to land at your front door, and it was your responsibility to be ready for it.

I rolled my eyes as I spun back around.

So that was kinda ironic considering he hovered over me like I was three and not nineteen. Overprotective to the extreme. The entirety of my schooling private and just about every outing I'd ever made supervised, not that I'd had a whole lot of those.

If I were being honest, there'd been like ... two. Maybe three. A few girls from school who'd taken pity on me and my awkwardness and invited me to their parties.

Which only turned out to be a disaster when the dumb chaperone I had to take everywhere with me would be lurking like some kind of creeper from where he stood three feet away, privy to my every conversation.

What was the use of that kind of freedom when it wasn't freedom at all?

Which was why I'd finally put my foot down three months ago. No more bodyguards. No more rules made up by my daddy. No more existing under his watch.

I was ready to live.

You know, hidden within the walls of my tiny house with the four deadbolts on the door.

No biggie.

Thunder splintered through the air, and the lights flickered again.

A tiny shriek left me, and chills lifted on my arms.

Sadie, my cat, jumped off the couch.

Her tail waved high in the air as she went down the hall.

Clearly annoyed.

I pursed my lips at her.

At least my faithful beardie was still chilling on the back of the couch. "You still love me, don't you, Beast? You are a sweet little dragon, aren't you?"

I gave him a scratch on his throat, the one part of him that wasn't covered in spikes, my little lizard as sweet as could be.

He lifted his little clawed hand and held on to my finger.

Adorbs.

I started to pick him up, only to freeze when I heard the low rumble coming up the street.

My heart kicked into overdrive, and I instantly felt myself start to sweat.

Oh goodness.

I listened as the massive bike rounded the corner at the four-way stop, and then I was climbing down onto my hands and knees and crawling across the floor to the window.

So maybe I did need some kind of supervision considering I was being the creeper, or maybe some medication or just a quick smack to the back of the head to knock me out of it, but I couldn't help myself.

Couldn't help but peek out from the side of the drape and watching the headlight on the heavy, scary-looking motorcycle come up the street.

The man riding it was even more intimidating.

Bad and mean and every single thing that would send my daddy straight into an overprotective tailspin.

Not that I could blame him.

That man was clearly bad news and probably about ten years older than me.

Oh, but was he ever pretty.

Long waves of blond hair flying out behind him. His beard thick and his eyes intense. Body completely covered in tattoos, something I knew because he liked to come out to smoke a cigarette way late at night without wearing a shirt, when he thought no one was looking.

I mean, not that I noticed or anything.

Rain poured outside, and the headlight on his bike glared through the deluge. He slowed and eased into the driveway exactly opposite of mine. Placing both booted feet out to the sides to keep the motorcycle upright, he killed the engine and kicked the stand before he lifted his magnificent body from the bike.

Hulking.

Imposing.

Wearing a tee and jeans, a chain swinging out where his wallet was tucked in his back pocket, the man completely soaked.

I gulped.

He swiveled his attention toward my house.

Panic hit me, and I dropped to the floor, pulse racing out of control and my stomach tightening in a way I didn't know it could do until the first time I'd seen the stranger across the street.

I counted to ten and then did it again, not allowing myself to peek back out until I'd counted to ten three times.

Carefully, I peeled the drape back the barest fraction, watching him from just a sliver.

He'd turned away and was striding up his driveway, raging as fiercely as the storm. He reached up and punched a number into the keypad that would lift his garage door.

Lightning flashed, lighting him up, but it was my heart going kaboom at the sight of him.

Intrigued and wanting all the things I shouldn't want.

The man my perfect fantasy.

A perfect dream.

But it wasn't like he'd ever take the time to look at me.

When his garage door didn't lift, he punched in the numbers again. He tried twice more before he sent a shout sailing into the rain.

A curse of the heavens.

He whipped his long hair around, the length drenched, his body soaking. He dialed someone on his phone, irritation burning through him, frustration radiating out.

As if he didn't know what to do.

He seemed to war with himself, looking around before he looked directly across at me.

It almost sent me toppling back. I needed to stop watching. I knew it, but I couldn't do anything but stare while he shifted back and forth on his feet, his shoulders vibrating with energy before he seemed to snap and finally come stalking across the street.

Oh God, oh God, oh God.

He was coming up my walkway, his boots splashing in the puddles of water that had gathered.

The air left me and my nerves went scattering, and another flash of lightning was blanketing the sky as he made it to the top of the walkway.

The man white-hot lightning, his blue, blue eyes shining orbs in the night.

I dropped the drape like it'd burned me, and I held my breath, nearly jumping out of my skin when a fist banged on the door.

I pressed my hands to my chest like it might keep my heart from stampeding right out.

I knew I was supposed to be prepared for anything. But this? This was one thing I could never have anticipated life would drag to my doorstep.

But isn't that what my daddy always said? Life would always shake us up. Slam us with something new when we least anticipated it.

Another rapping at the door and I hopped up onto my shaky legs, fumbling through the locks as quickly as I could. I left the chain at the top, opening it an inch so I could peek out.

"Hey," the man grumbled, rushing a hand through his wet hair, his voice so low I could feel it shake me to my bones. "I ..."

Warily, he glanced over his shoulder at his house. "I'm your neighbor across the street. Apparently, the storm knocked out my garage pad, and I don't have my key."

Oh yeah, like I didn't know he was my neighbor.

Nope. I so had not been watching him like a weirdo for the last three months.

"Oh, um ... would you like to come in?" I asked, stuttering all over myself because how could I not?

Not when a god had just descended on a peasant's door.

He looked pissed. "You're just going to invite me in? You don't even know me."

"And you're the one standing in the rain at my door." It was almost an accusation. I mean, seriously, what did he want me to do here? Slam the door in his pretty face?

He gruffed out a frustrated sound. "You should be more careful than inviting complete strangers into your house."

I almost laughed. Oh, him, too, huh? I'd just finally gotten out from under the fussy watch of my daddy. "You're not much of a stranger considering you've been living right across from me for the last three months. And I'm pretty sure I can make that decision for myself."

No, we'd never met.

And yeah, he was clearly trouble.

But I didn't think ... I didn't think he would hurt me.

"Do you want to come in or not?"

"Shit," he cursed toward his boots before he finally looked up. "Fine. Yeah. I'd like to come in. It's dumping buckets of piss out here."

I unfastened the chain and widened the door, and the man stepped through the threshold onto the mat right inside.

Shivers raced at his proximity.

I'd always known he was massive, but I was pretty sure he was close to having to duck his head to stand inside.

Fidgety as all get-out, I shut the door and latched the locks and turned around to look at the man.

Dripping wet, jeans stuck to his legs.

Shirt hugging every inch of his gigantic, towering body.

His chest heaving and his shoulders wide.

My eyes kept traveling, drawn all the way up to those potent, powerful eyes. I snapped my mouth shut when I realized it was hanging open. Then I promptly began to fall all over myself.

"Let me ... let me get you a dry towel."

I raced down the hall, careening into the small bathroom, gasping for any sane breath I could find. From under the counter, I grabbed a towel from the perfectly folded stack. Okay, it was for him, but I pressed it to my face to cover the scream.

Oh God. Oh God. What was I gonna do?

Nerves rattled, and I gave myself a fifteen-second pep talk.

I could do this without making a complete fool of myself.

I lifted my chin and forced myself out and down the hall, sucking in a staggered breath when he came into view when I got to the end.

It just wasn't fair that one person should be bestowed all that beauty.

I moved that way, trying not to shake with the ridiculous amount of attraction screaming from my chest.

"Here," I told him, shoving the towel at him.

He took it. "Thank you."

He pressed it to his face and rubbed it through his hair, but I knew it wasn't going to do a whole lot of good when the rest of him was soaked. "Take off your shirt. I'll put it in the dryer."

I itched all over, reaching for him and then yanking my hands back and then waving them erratically without touching.

Oh yeah, that pep talk worked all right.

Something scraped from his throat at the proposition.

Was ... was that a groan?

Oh, whatever that sound was, it made my belly flip and my head spin.

"It's fine," he gruffed.

"You're going to catch your death."

"Yeah, that's what I'm afraid of," he grumbled under his breath.

"Give me your shirt, would you?"

He hesitated. "You sure you don't mind?"

"God no."

So that flew out of my mouth way too fast.

"I mean, I-I," I stammered, trying to correct the blunder. "It would be rude of me not offer."

There we go. A perfectly normal response.

Blue eyes narrowed, watching me before he reached back and tugged the shirt from the back of his neck.

Watching him do it, I shook so hard I thought my teeth might have chattered.

On all things unholy.

Double unholy.

Tattoos covered him entirely, the man nothing but dark, dark art. Shoulders so wide and his waist narrow, all those designs disappearing under the band of his jeans.

I'd seen him in the distance before, but there was no experience like getting to see him up close and personal.

There wasn't one thing about this man that was soft.

Too bad I was a puddle.

Trembling, I took his wet shirt, just standing there for a beat while I watched him start to dry off.

I wanted to lick him.

He cut me a sharp look.

"Oh, yeah, right ..." Awkwardly, I jumped back, pointing behind me. "I'll just be ... I'll just be back here. Why don't you take off your boots?"

You should probably get rid of those pants, too.

I managed not to say it out loud.

Yay, me.

He grunted acknowledgment, and I hesitated again before I kicked myself into gear and went racing back down the hall. I shoved his shirt into the dryer and tossed in a dryer sheet for good measure, saying a thousand prayers that I could make it through this night without doing something stupid like climbing the man like a mountain.

I mean ... he was a mountain, anyway. Hiking him wouldn't seem all that odd, would it?

A blush rushed to my cheeks, and I bit down on my lip to stop the pictures that invaded my mind.

Nothing like spending months deluding yourself with a one-sided affair.

I was nothing but a naive little girl with big, big fantasies. How many times had I imagined him knocking at my door and for entirely different reasons than getting locked out of his house?

So maybe I was hooked on Hallmark.

Sue me.

My lonely heart sure wanted to.

Once I had the dryer running, I ducked back out, taking the hallway at warp speed, only to trip on my feet when I found him bending over to put his shoes and socks near the door, the damp towel wrapped around his neck.

His backside ... well, it was just as good as the rest of him.

He stood back up and turned around. "I'm Danny Ridgelaine. Friends call me Ridge."

I gulped around the knot in my throat. "I'm Kelsey. And I don't have any friends."

I popped off the joke, realizing how uncomfortable it was when his eyes narrowed rather than him laughing.

Awesome, Kels. Just keep roasting yourself.

Then I jumped when he shrieked. "What the fuck is that?"

I whirled around, heart racing like mad, looking for a serial killer sitting on my couch.

Nope.

It was just my Beast.

I scowled over at Ridge, tsking. "That's my bearded dragon. You're going to hurt his feelings."

"That thing does not have feelings."

"Yes, he does," I cooed at my beardie as I gathered him up and planted a kiss on his soft throat. "Yes, yes, he does, don't you, sweet boy?"

"You're a psycho," Ridge grumbled, still looking like he might want to bolt out the door.

"He doesn't bite. He's a lover, just like me." More cooing.

Ridge looked at me. Completely horrified.

I rolled my eyes and walked Beast to his cage that sat along the far wall. "There you go, buddy. It's sleepy time." I slid shut the glass and turned back around, and Sadie came prancing down the hall, swinging her tail, no doubt needing to check out what was going on.

Curiosity.

She was a cat, after all.

I leaned down and gave her a pet.

Ridge just watched me, clearly worried he might need to take me to the mental ward.

I got anxious, started stammering, "I just, I just like animals better than I like people. That's all."

So there went a flash of something soft through his expression.

"More trustworthy," he said.

I nodded in agreement.

"Though I think you'd do better with a guard dog."

I giggled, then quieted, and for a second, we just stood, staring at each other.

I couldn't tell if it was in discomfort or comfort.

Maybe both.

I finally pointed toward the kitchen. "Can I get you something to drink?"

"Sure. I shouldn't be here long. Put out an S.O.S. Hopefully it won't take too long for one of my crew to bring me a spare key."

I shook my head as I passed him. "It's no problem. You can stay for as long as you need to."

I opened the fridge and leaned in so I could give him a rundown of the options.

He made another one of those rumbly sounds that sent shivers racing through my body.

I could feel the warmth of him blazing from behind, the man standing right there, so close to touching, looking inside from over my shoulder.

Tension raced.

I could almost feel his confusion when he saw that I basically had one can of every drink in existence. "My daddy always taught me to be prepared,"

I explained in spite of myself. "I have one of everything in case I might have a guest. You're my first, so you get the best selection."

There I went again. Another lame, lame joke. This guy had to think I was pathetic.

I slowly turned around when I realized he'd stepped away, taking that warmth with him. I wanted to reach out and demand it back.

Every cell in my body clenched in embarrassment when I read his expression, my brow drawing tight. "Don't feel sorry for me. I just … I'm not good at getting out and making friends. That's all."

I hugged my arms over my chest.

Protectively.

Feeling exposed.

"Not feeling sorry for you. Just think a girl your age would be out on a Friday night and not hiding out in her house by herself."

"Well, I prefer to read. Way more interesting."

He contained a small laugh. "Is that so?"

"Yep. Way more interesting. And much, much sexier."

My eyes went wide when I realized what I'd said.

I wanted to clap my hand over my mouth.

But he laughed. Laughed this low, disbelieving sound, and I took it all back.

That was the sexiest thing.

His plush lips that were hiding under his beard tugged in the smallest grin. "Okay then, Kelsey, I'll have one of those beers, that is if I don't bore you too much."

Ah, a tease.

I raked my teeth over my bottom lip.

He made that sound again, his abdomen flexing.

"What was that?"

"I'm not bored … not bored at all," I rushed, and then he was staring at me in a different way, and oh my God, I was sweating all over the place.

I whirled around before he caught me drooling. "Any particular brand?" I asked with my face buried in the cold air of the refrigerator.

"Surprise me."

I sifted through the bottles until I found one that I thought fit him. I grabbed an Imperial Stout.

It looked dark and intoxicating, just like the man. I spun around and passed it to him.

He took it, our fingers brushing, fire streaking up my arm.

His potent gaze slide over me like he was searching for a clue. "How did you know this is my favorite?"

I rubbed my palms on my shorts. "You're just saying that."

"I'm not."

We got locked in a stare down, and God, why did someone so out of my league—so completely out of my stratosphere—make me feel like this?

Trembly and shaky and needy.

I guess they say we always love to chase down the contradictory.

And this man was exactly my opposite.

I cleared my throat, sidestepped him to get to another drawer, and dug around to pull out the bottle opener. "Here."

"Thank you." He popped the cap, eyeing the supplies I had out on the counter.

"Like I said, I'm prepared."

This time, there was no questioning his grin.

I eased back across the small kitchen, three feet separating us where I leaned against the refrigerator and he leaned against the counter.

Heat blistered in that space. Something more intense than I'd ever felt before.

Of course, the chance that I was hallucinating it was precisely one-hundred percent.

He took a long pull of the beer, lifting the bottle high, and my mouth watered as I watched his thick throat bob as he swallowed, his chest bare and his abdomen rippling.

Yep. That was it. I was gonna die in a puddle right here.

He dropped the bottle and swiped his tongue across his bottom lip to gather a dribble.

My tongue followed suit, sweeping across mine.

I couldn't help it.

Every single time I read someone licking their lips, I did the same.

An impulse I couldn't tame.

I guessed it applied in real life, too.

His eyes flared when he caught me doing it.

Shit.

I pressed farther back into the cold surface of the refrigerator, wishing it could swallow me up.

I was such a stupid, stupid girl.

"What was that?" he demanded low.

"I ... I don't know what you're talking about."

He took another long drink, watching me carefully, and I tried not to tremble. Not to fall into a pit of desire that was rising up to my knees.

Okay, I was liar. I was already drowning in it.

He dropped the bottle. "That ... right there. What were you just thinking, Kelsey?"

"I don't ... What do you think you saw?"

There.

He had to tell me first.

"I don't think you want to know."

"Oh yes, yes I do. I mean ... definitely. Definitely I want to know."

My head nodded emphatically.

He almost chuckled at the word vomit, except his eyes were doing that crazy thing again.

Like ... like maybe ... he wanted me.

No.

Impossible.

"I think you've been thinking about me the way I've been thinking about you." The words were low, threaded with caution.

My mouth went dry, and my hands were clammy, and my heart was beating out of my chest. My fingers were flat behind me, clawing for something to hold on to.

"And how have you been thinking about me?" I asked, my voice close to gone, nothing but a whisper.

Carefully, he set the bottle on the counter, the glass clanking as he did, those blue eyes burning a hole through the middle of me. Slowly, he inched across the floor, the man towering.

A fortress that had me wanting to climb him again.

He set his big, big hands on each of my cheeks, and he leaned in.

And ... and ... and he kissed me.

Kissed me so soft. Just the mere brush of his lips against mine.

So tender I couldn't have imagined he'd be capable of it.

Oh God.

My heart thundered and my stomach almost felt sick I was so excited. How was I going to ask him for what I wanted without completely passing out?

He pulled back, still holding on to my face when he murmured, "Like that, Kelsey. I've been thinking about you like that."

I was thinking him admitting it was cause for celebration, but regret moved through his gorgeous, masculine features.

"Fuck," he muttered low. "Fuck. What did I just do? I'm sorry."

Panicked that he was going to walk away, I gripped him by both wrists. "Don't. Don't apologize. You …"

Spit it out Kelsey, or he's gone.

"The only thing better than spending a Friday night reading would be spending it with you."

There.

Did he get it?

What I meant?

My gaze dropped, and I gnawed at my bottom lip, chewing so hard I was sure I was drawing blood. Searching through my shyness to where I was brave. I barely cut a glance back to him, eyeing him from the side. "I imagine you, you know?"

I shrugged like it didn't matter.

But Ridge was making that grumbly, needy sound again.

And oh God, I liked that name, and I liked that sound, and I knew I wanted him touching me forever.

"This is a terrible idea, Kelsey."

"I think … I think it's a great idea. I mean, I've been imagining us a lot … so it couldn't be all bad, right?"

He laughed out a self-deprecating sound. "You're gonna be the death of me, Kelsey."

"Then maybe we should stop talking," I whispered, and I lifted my chin to expose my neck, puckering my lips. "Do you want me, big boy?"

There it was. My one single ridiculous attempt at seduction. So maybe I'd ripped it right out of the pages of one of my books, and I was praying I didn't look like a disfigured duck.

I felt giddy when it worked.

Because Ridge groaned the deepest sound, and he was easing forward, pinning me flat to the refrigerator, his big body covering mine. "It'd be wrong for me to touch you, sweet girl. So wrong."

My head shook. "No, no it wouldn't, not if we both want it." My tongue darted out again, wetting my lips. Maybe that was when I realized this was real.

Like ... real, real, real.

He might actually want me.

This wasn't one of those fantasies I was so good at playing out.

Nerves rattled through me like the warning of a rattlesnake.

But I refused to be afraid.

I gathered up all the confidence I'd been saving for an important time.

"Show me, Ridge ... show me all the things you've been thinking about."

I could see it in his eyes, the war, the desire.

A rumble of something echoed through his chest, and suddenly I was no longer on my feet.

Swept up and into his arms.

The man carried me like I was a five-pound sack across the small kitchen to the table set up at the tiny nook in the back.

Windows surrounding us. The blinds shut, rain pelting at the glass and closing us in.

He set me on the edge of the table, and he pulled up a chair in front of me.

Shivers raced, and I was a quivering mess when he sat down and placed his hands on my knees.

Oh yeah, this was real all right.

"Where do you want me to start, baby, because you probably don't even want to imagine all the things I've been dreaming about doing to you." Something dark passed through his expression. "We do this, and I won't be able to take it back."

"Don't take it back. Just ... take everything."

"Kelsey," he whispered.

"Please." I got brave and threaded my fingers through the long length of his still-damp hair, the pieces sticking to his glorious chest, weaving with the patterns he had painted there.

His eyes dropped closed, and then he was leaning forward, running his mouth up the inside of my leg.

So slow.

So soft.

Handling me like I was glass.

Like he was going to break me.

Chills spread and my heart raced, and I struggled to keep it together.

His tongue barely peeked out to taste my flesh, his nose nuzzling along the hem of my white shorts, then he was heaving out a breath when he ran his mouth over the seam and leaned back to let his fingertips tease at the button.

He looked up at me, his jaw held in stone. "Are you sure?"

I scrambled around in my brain for something to say that wouldn't send him running.

But for once, I just wanted to be honest.

Trust someone with knowing me.

"I know you don't know a thing about me, but I've gotten to make so few choices in my life, Ridge. Let me make this. And I might be awkward and a little shy and I can't get one thing out of my mouth without sounding like a fool. But I need you to know this ... I want you. I want you in this crazy way that I can't understand. So please ... just please."

I blew out a defeated breath.

No question, he was gonna run. Think standing in the lightning would be a much safer bet than dealing with me.

He flicked the button.

Sharply, I inhaled.

Oh.

I was so unprepared for the onslaught of need that went pummeling through me.

And I realized right then, there were some things you really were never going to be prepared for. Some things that would shock you and you just had to go along for the ride.

I could hardly believe it was with him.

This moment too surreal.

I eased my butt up a fraction so he could pull down my shorts. He took my plain cotton panties with him as he went.

Holy cheese and grapes.

We were actually gettin' naked.

Nerves scattered and something brand-new surged through my being.

Emotion locked up in my throat.

I was really gonna do this … with this man that I'd barely hoped to imagine would be looking at me.

Cool air blasted my skin, and I'd never felt so exposed or so beautiful or quite so powerful in all my life. Because the man was looking at me like I might be the best thing he'd ever seen, and he was holding me by the outsides of my thighs, his warm breath spreading all over me.

"This. This is what I've been thinking of, sweet girl." He nudged in, barely brushing his lips across my center.

I jerked.

Whimpered.

Pleaded.

"Oh wow. I like that. I really like that."

There I went, rambling away.

On a low chuckle, he tucked me closer to the edge of the table, and he devoured me. Kissing into my lips, his tongue pushing deep into my pussy, the air growing thin.

Heat lifted and the storm raged and the man sucked and licked and elevated me to a place that I'd never, ever been.

My fingers curled in his hair, and I knew I was tugging too hard, demanding too much. Oh, this burn. It was more than I thought I could handle.

I felt like I was searching for something but didn't know how to find it.

Everything too much and not enough.

"Oh God, Ridge. Please. I need … I need …"

I was rambling. Incoherent. Losing sight except for the feeling that was taking me over. He licked me up and down, teasing my hole with two fingers.

The most embarrassing sound escaped my throat, somewhere between pain and pleasure, when he pushed both inside.

"Oh wow."

"Oh yes."

Oh wait, I'd said both of those things aloud.

I struggled to get closer, to move away. A blaze of pleasure tore through me, prowling my nerves, stretching me thin.

He drove his fingers in and out and sucked my clit into his mouth.

That pleasure shattered.

Streaking and sailing and I was crying out his name.

Probably crying a little bit, too.

I was never, ever, ever going to be the same.

My eyes opened.

My world rocked.

He lingered there, leading me through, whispering sweet things that I couldn't make out while his face was still buried between my thighs.

"Sweet girl, sweet girl."

"Ridge," I whispered, and I was sliding off the table and onto his lap, going for the button on his jeans. "I like you, Ridge. I like you so much."

I mean, I figured it was a little early for me to go professing my love. But I did. I did, I did.

"Let me—"

He clamped his hands over mine.

"Not a chance." It was a moan. Restraint. Pain.

I was kissing his face, nipping into his beard at his neck, chasing down his mouth.

It felt so nice. Touching him this way.

My tongue begged for his at the seam of his lips, and I writhed on his hardness.

How was it possible that feeling was already sweeping through me again?

He moaned.

"Please," I said, and his hands were on my back, slipping under my shirt, peeling it over my head.

"You're going to destroy me."

"That's okay because you already did me. Like ... really ... I'm done for, Ridge," I murmured, and I was fumbling around behind me to get to my purse, tipping it over and dumping the contents out.

A mint and some gum. A few quarters and a one. Tampons. Aspirin. A condom.

That's me.

Prepared.

I snagged the foil wrapper, and I edged back as he was pushing down his jeans.

My eyes got round as saucers.

Oh my bejesus.

If I thought the rest of him was big ...

"Baby, you don't have to do this."

"I really, really want to. Don't you?"

I peeked at him.

Nervously.

And I knew he could feel me shaking like a leaf all over his lap.

He tore open the condom.

My stomach tumbled and shook, and I needed him in a way I hadn't needed anything, just as much as I needed to make this choice myself.

Unprotected from my little world I'd always been sheltered in.

"Can I …?" I slipped my hands over his, and together we covered him.

He took me by the hips. That gaze on me.

"Will you fit?"

His jaw ticked in restraint. "If you want me to."

Oh, heck, yes I did, even though I was terrified, and I curled my arms around his shoulders. "Do it."

"You wrecked me the first time I saw you, Kelsey," he murmured into the side of my head. "I just … need you to know that first."

My head nodded frantically, and I held on tighter, and then tears were streaking from the corners of my eyes as the heat of him burned and seared and he filled me up to the brim.

No place left.

He'd taken it all.

And I was never ever gonna be the same.

Rest in peace, Kelsey Lynn.

I held on to him as tightly as he was holding on to me.

A moment of silence given for what we'd just done.

He edged back a fraction, his hand on my cheek.

"That was a blood oath, Kelsey." The words were a promise. Some kind of threat.

Confusion twisted my brow into a frown, and I wanted to ask him what that meant, but he leaned in and kissed me. Kissed me hard and kissed me slow and showed me all the things we'd both wanted from afar.

That one-sided relationship a farce.

The two of us a fact.

He led me, and I moved, my thighs shaking like crazy, my frantic groans filling the air as I lifted myself up and down, riding him, my fingers desperate as I fought to feel him everywhere.

He grunted, wrapping an arm around my back, holding me against him while he shifted us to the floor.

The man above me, thrusting and taking.

I hoped he didn't mind that I begged him for more.

Cold tile on my back and warm, gorgeous man on my front.

Rising up to support himself with one hand, he slipped the other between us, touching me again.

I erupted in a chaos of pleasure, not sure that I could even recognize myself anymore. The second I did, he took me by the back of the knee, shifting my leg to his shoulder, the rock of his hips erratic and his kiss the sweetest thing I'd ever felt.

And I was dead.

Gone.

Sure this man had just made me a fiend.

Too bad I was only ever going to want it with him.

I felt it when he came. The way his body jerked and his heart went crazy and he kissed me like he meant it.

Like this was something more than a one-night stand compliments of a raging storm.

He collapsed on me, and I held on to that fantasy as tightly as I could, gave myself that moment.

And I promised myself I would never, ever forget how I felt right then.

Ridge

Rain pattered at the window. Her room was darkened, her naked body tucked close to mine where she slept.

Kissing the back of her head, I held her as tight as I could, wondering how the hell in a span of an hour we'd ended up here.

Dread thundered.

She'd wanted her freedom. Her father would never let her have it.

I was there to watch her.

Protect her.

Let her think she'd gained her own independence.

She didn't know she was a Pelligro Princess.

Her father was one of the most powerful crime bosses in the west, one my bike club owed a debt.

I'd been the one assigned to fulfill that obligation. It should have been an easy repayment.

Keep an eye on the spoiled little girl.

Except she was everything I'd never expected.

Awkward and shy and the sweetest thing I'd ever seen. Girl thinking I didn't have the first clue she'd been watching me the whole time.

I never should have let my mind start racing that direction.

Never should have given in.

Never should have fallen in love with the girl across the street.

But I did.

And I'd just signed the warrant for my own death.

* * *

Do you want more of A.L. Jackson?

One click A STONE IN THE SEA now!

DARE TO DREAM

PREQUEL TO DARE TO RESIST

CARLY PHILLIPS

1

Austin Prescott sat in the offices of Dare Nation, the newly minted sports agency he'd opened with Paul Dare, a man he'd grown up considering like a father to him. Instead he and his siblings had recently discovered that *Uncle Paul* was their biological dad courtesy of sperm donation. Life was crazy. But then in the Dare world, it probably fell under the definition of normal. Family came in all shapes and sizes.

And in Austin's family, he was to be the kidney donor for Paul in two weeks, which meant his need to find an assistant was urgent. He tapped his foot impatiently, in no mood to deal with yet another interview. He'd spoken to enough women in the last week to make his head spin, and he still hadn't found the right fit.

He needed someone who could keep up with negotiations and someone who could sit at the fanciest restaurants with players and their wives who thought their shit didn't stink, all while being smarter than anyone else in the room. Except for him, of course. And someone who could handle the office while he was out on medical leave.

So far he'd interviewed Ivy League graduates with attitude and average students with MBAs who just wanted an in to meet and fuck a sports star. And Austin had plenty of experience with the latter. Hell, since his Division One NCAA days followed by his NFL career, he could bed any female he wanted, but he had to admit, easy lays were getting old. He wasn't ready to settle down, but his days of picking up women every weekend were becoming fewer and farther between. Not that he was a monk, far from it. A man had needs.

He lifted his phone to let Bri, his publicist sister who'd been helping him out until he could find an assistant, know that he wanted to cancel whoever was left for the day and start over tomorrow, when a knock sounded on his office door.

"Come in!" he called out, wondering why his sibling felt the need to knock.

"Mr. Prescott?" an unfamiliar feminine voice that went straight to his cock asked as she stepped inside and blew his mind. "The woman at the desk outside said I should just knock."

A gorgeous vision in a slim black skirt and a white blouse that should have looked like a uniform but instead had him wanting to bend her over his desk stepped into the room.

His gaze slid down to black pumps with enough of a heel to elongate those sexy tanned legs. Legs he wouldn't mind having wrapped around his waist as he fucked her senseless. Because from the tips of her toes to the top of her shoulder-length raven-colored hair, she epitomized class and perfection. The red lipstick merely added to her appeal.

"Mr. Prescott?" she asked, causing him to realize he'd been staring.

"Yes. I'm sorry. I wasn't expecting another applicant this afternoon. Ms...."

"Quinnlyn Stone, but everyone calls me Quinn."

He rose to his feet, hoping she didn't notice the tent in his pants. "Nice to meet you, Quinn." He extended his hand as she stepped forward. No sooner had she slid her cool palm against his than a jolt of unexpected electricity sparked between them.

Shit. This was bad. Very, very bad. He could not desire a woman who might work for him.

"Have a seat," he said in a gruff voice, gesturing to the dual chairs across from his desk.

"Thank you." She lowered herself into one, sliding her legs to one side.

Like he thought, classy, unlike the many women who'd deliberately crossed and uncrossed their legs in an effort to draw his attention to their ... assets.

She reached into her bag and pulled out a sheet of paper. "My résumé, in case you didn't have a copy in front of you," she said.

"I appreciate you being prepared." And since he hadn't been paying attention to who his next candidate was and had hoped to cancel, he really did need the information. He accepted the résumé and read through the page. "University of Miami undergrad and business school," he said, impressed with her education. "So where are you from?" He met her emerald gaze, held captive by the depths of those green eyes.

"Florida born and raised. I couldn't go far from home. My family needed me," she said somewhat cryptically.

"I see." It wasn't his business to ask why, though he was intrigued.

"I went on partial scholarship. As you can see, I graduated cum laude."

He'd noticed her honors degree. "And before this, you had a position with the Panthers," he said of the minor league team where she'd been an assistant to an assistant.

She rolled her shoulders. "It's called the ladder to success for a reason. I had to start somewhere. I have my letters of recommendation here, too." She leaned down to reach inside her purse again.

"No need. I'll look them over eventually. So you like sports?"

She nodded. "I come from a big family on both sides. A lot of siblings, cousins, uncles, everyone's a sports fan. I learned early."

He rolled a pen between his palms. "I hear you. My family was and is big on sports as well."

"You think? Two NFL players, an MLB star, a sports publicist sister ... it's impressive."

The first candidate who'd truly done her research. He was impressed right back. "So why do you want this job, Quinn? Better yet, what qualifies you over the other equally competent applicants I've seen today?" He hoped she'd stutter over her words or in some way give him a reason not to hire her so he could ask her out instead.

A wry smile pulled at those sexy lips. "Well, let's see. I'm organized, efficient, and I can corral a band of preschoolers, which means I'm certain I can handle arrogant athletes."

He raised an eyebrow. "Stereotype much?"

A pretty flush rose to her cheeks, but she didn't duck her head or look away. "If the shoe fits..."

He liked this sassy woman. "So you're saying because I played football..."

"And were a Heisman Trophy winner, Rookie of the Year for the Miami Thunder, and three-time Super Bowl winner that you're arrogant? Yes. Or else you wouldn't be the man sitting behind that desk today." She folded her hands in her lap and waited for his reply.

Not only had she done her homework, she looked him in the eye and was unafraid to stand up to him. "You're hired."

She blinked in surprise. "I'm sorry, what did you just say?"

He rose to his full height. "I said, you're hired. When can you start? Because I'm having major surgery in two weeks and I need someone to hold down the fort while I'm gone. Keep the clients calm and all that."

Those red lips he had plenty of uses for, in his imagination anyway, opened and closed twice before she composed herself and stood. "I can start whenever you need me. And thank you, Mr. Prescott."

"We're going to be working closely together, so call me Austin."

"Thank you, Austin."

He inclined his head. "We'll see if you're still thanking me once you've dealt with many of the juveniles I call clients. Your assessment of arrogant wasn't far off the mark."

She laughed, the sound one that would be a bright light in this office. Jesus, he was in trouble.

He strode around the desk and came up beside her. "You can talk to Bri outside. She'll take you down to our office manager, who will have you fill out paperwork and get you settled. Can you start the day after tomorrow? That'll give us time to get you up to speed before I'm out for at least five weeks. Maybe six." It sucked but his body needed to adapt to having one kidney. The doctors had warned him about exhaustion most of all.

He glanced at her, and she was still in shock. Since the salary and benefits had been laid out in the job description, he didn't need to go over those details.

Finally she nodded, her eyes wide, her expression brimming with excitement. "I'm looking forward to it. Thanks again." She spun and headed out the door, leaving him behind in a floral haze of lust and need for a woman he wouldn't be able to touch.

As long as she worked for him, his motto would be hands off. Or hands on his cock, since he had a feeling he'd be jerking off to thoughts of Quinnlyn Stone at least once or twice before he got his inappropriate need for her out of his system.

Austin glanced at his Rolex, one of the first gifts he'd bought for himself once he signed his original NFL contract, and counted down the minutes. It didn't take long for Bri to let herself in without knocking.

"I thought you were taking Quinn to meet with Lindsay," he said of their office manager.

"Already handled." His sister was the fixer of the family, mediating arguments among the four Prescott male siblings and occasionally their father, Jesse, when he'd been alive, like a pro. Her becoming a sports publicist was a natural choice after dealing with her family for years.

Bri plopped into the chair Quinn had been seated in earlier. "So that was a fast hire. What did you see in her that was different? Beyond the fact that she's gorgeous and exactly your type?" Bri waggled her eyebrows. "Since I know you wouldn't misbehave at work or hire her because you're attracted to her."

"Wiseass," he muttered. "Quinn has the balls to handle the job," he said bluntly.

"And handle you?"

He grinned. "She called me an arrogant athlete and proceeded to back up her claim. I'd say she's perfect for the job."

"Great! Now are you ready for surgery?" Bri leaned forward, resting her elbows on the desk. "We all got tested to be Uncle Paul's donor, but you drew the lucky straw." She shook her head. "Do we still call him Uncle Paul? It's all so weird."

She bit down on her lower lip, a habit he remembered from childhood.

"Yeah. We had a father." Jesse Prescott, who'd died when Austin was twenty-one, had been a decent parent to Austin, the natural-born athlete, to Damon, also a football talent, and to Bri, the only girl.

But to Jaxon, who'd preferred baseball to a contact sport, and to Bri's twin, Braden, the brain of the bunch and now a doctor, Jesse Prescott had been a hard-ass and often mean. Which meant they were all processing the sperm donor/biological father news in different ways. But there'd never been a question that if any of them were a perfect match, they'd donate a kidney to the man who had always been there for them in ways their father hadn't.

"I can handle a little surgery," he assured her.

"It's not little, Austin." Bri looked up at him with a worried expression.

"It'll be fine. Go check on Quinn. Make sure she has all her questions answered before she leaves for the day."

"Worried about her already?" Bri asked.

He rolled his eyes. "Go!"

Bri popped up from her seat and headed out. "I'll be around for you if you get nervous or anything, you know?"

He glanced at the sister he loved. "Yeah, Bri. I know."

* * *

Quinn sat alone in a conference room as she filled out myriad forms, shocked she could focus on anything after being alone with Austin Prescott and all that testosterone. She'd thought she'd been ready to meet him. After all, she'd done her research, googling him before she arrived for her interview. She hadn't lied about her family's interest in sports, but the bulk of her current knowledge came from digging around online about Dare Nation's clients and Austin Prescott himself.

But the online photos hadn't prepared her for the man in person. He had chiseled features and tanned skin. Dark lashes framed unique indigo eyes. He had full lips she could imagine kissing and a strong, built body beneath his suit, making him the whole package.

"Whew." She waved a hand in front of her still-flushed face. Her entire body heated in an inappropriate response to her boss.

She swallowed hard and filled in her social security number on the iPad with the forms the office manager had supplied, reminding herself this was her dream job. One she wouldn't mess up because her boss was hot. She'd grown up being a pseudo-mom to her bucketload of siblings and cousins. If not for her scholarship, she'd have attended college and business school wholly on student loans because her parents couldn't afford to send all five of her siblings to school on their salaries.

She had no intention of being a nanny, despite how well qualified she might be. She loved office work, and she intended to make the most of this prime opportunity. She'd pay off her student loans and have an independent life she could be proud of.

Besides, even if she'd met Austin under normal circumstances and had the same intense attraction, he wasn't the right kind of guy for her. Austin Prescott was a player and not just on the field. In his NFL days, he'd been the consummate ladies' man, never having a girlfriend, always seen with a different gorgeous woman on his arm. Actresses, models, perfect-looking females who fit his alpha-male image. Now that he was an agent to the stars, he was more discreet but no less discriminating in taste.

Quinn wasn't vain. She'd been told she was pretty, but she didn't work at it the way Austin's typical woman did. And she had no reason to be thinking about herself and Austin linked in any way at all except professional, she thought, and continued to fill out the employment forms.

* * *

Austin wasn't shocked when Quinn arrived at the office at eight a.m. on her first day. He'd said nine. She obviously wanted to make sure she had time to settle in before he put her to work. So far so good. No complaints on his end except for how much he desired her, but he knew better than to act on it and make her uncomfortable.

She obviously favored those slim skirts that showed off her ass and legs, and her silk tops wrapped perfectly around her curves. So, yeah, his head was on things other than work, but he had to get his shit together.

He'd been talking to his sister about his upcoming surgery and time off, and returning to his office, he passed Quinn's desk and paused. "Everything okay?" he asked her.

She nodded. "I'm doing as you suggested, reading through client files and getting to know about them."

"I have lunch with my brother Damon at twelve thirty, more business than personal. Join us. You can meet your first arrogant athlete," he said with a grin. "Other than me."

She shook her head and blushed. "You're not going to let me live that down, are you?"

"Probably not." He chuckled and headed into his office to go over a current contract that had already been vetted by the firm's lawyer.

An hour later, they were standing at a table. "Quinn, this is Damon, my youngest brother. Damon, my new executive assistant, Quinn Stone."

When Damon first looked at Quinn, his eyes opened wide with approval before he quickly schooled his features. Their mother would kick both their asses if they treated any woman with less than complete respect.

"It's nice to meet you, Quinn. How are you managing working for this guy?" Damon jerked his thumb toward Austin.

"I just started, but I'm enjoying myself so far."

Austin held out a chair, and she settled into it.

"So Austin tells me you play football," she said. "And from what I've read, you're a wide receiver for the Tampa Breakers?"

"Best there is. But I'm up for contract renewal at the end of the season, so I need this year to go well. And I need my agent to kick some managerial ass and get me the contract I deserve." Damon followed his words with an arrogant smirk.

At the thought, Austin met Quinn's gaze and grinned. "Does he fit the mold?"

"To a T," she said, laughing.

He liked the sound.

"Why do I feel like I'm the only one not in on the joke?" Damon asked, looking from Quinn back to Austin.

"Quinn thinks she's got us athletes pegged, and you, my friend, just proved her right."

"Can I get you something to drink?" a waitress asked, leaning in very close to Austin. So close her breast brushed against his sport jacket.

It was typical when they were out. Women picked one or the other brother to flirt with. Austin had seen her assessing them from behind a support beam, making her choice. Given the nine-year age difference between them, Austin at thirty-four, Damon at twenty-five, the woman had to have a type in order to choose. That and she looked a little older than the typical groupies who picked Damon.

Quinn's eyebrows lifted high. She wasn't used to how blatant the come-ons could be. If she was going to do her job, she'd get accustomed to seeing it.

"Excuse me but I'd like to order, too?" Quinn deliberately called the woman's attention away from Austin, and he had to wonder if she was doing him a favor or if there was a touch of jealousy involved.

The waitress straightened and barely glanced at Quinn, clearly annoyed by the interruption.

"Quinn, what do you want to drink?" Austin asked.

"A club soda with a splash of cranberry juice. Thanks." She treated him to a genuine smile.

"And you, gentlemen? What would you like?" the waitress asked in a syrupy sweet voice.

They both ordered Pellegrino. Austin was keeping his body clean for the organ donation, and Damon was in training.

They made small talk for a little while, Quinn holding her own on discussions of the game, plays, and positions.

After they ordered their meals, Quinn placed her napkin on the table. “If you’ll both excuse me, I’ll be back in a few minutes.” She rose and headed for the ladies’ room, and as he expected, Damon watched her go.

He waited until she was far enough away before letting out a low whistle. “Damn, bro. You should have fucked her, not hired her.”

Austin narrowed his gaze. “Watch how you talk about her, asshole.”

“Whoa.” Damon raised his hands in a gesture of peace. “Hey, I didn’t mean anything by it. Since when are you so damn sensitive about any woman?”

Austin forced himself to relax. Damon was right. Unless someone insulted the females in his family, he was usually calmer than this. Something about Quinn fired up his protective instincts, not that she needed him to look out for her. She could clearly hold her own. But he didn’t like the sound of his brother demeaning her in any way.

“So she’s different.” Placing his hands behind his head and stretching, Damon met his gaze.

“Yeah. But she’s off-limits.” Austin pinned his brother with a steady stare, making sure the kid knew he meant *back off*.

“Message received.” Damon looked past Austin and gave a short incline of his head, letting him know Quinn had returned.

She rejoined them at the table, and they had an enjoyable lunch. One where he was damned glad the tablecloth blocked the view of his dick, because everything about her did it for him. Her laugh, her stories, her expressive words, and the full pink mouth. He didn’t care what color lipstick she wore, he wanted to taste her. To feel her lips around his cock.

This hiring was going to be the test of a lifetime.

* * *

Quinn had been on the job for three weeks, and Austin had been out for the last seven days following surgery. She drove up to the house where he lived. It was more like a mansion, located in an exclusive neighborhood in South

Beach. She asked herself what she was doing here, and the answer was simple. She wanted to reassure him she had things under control.

In the time she'd spent by Austin's side, becoming familiar with clients and learning the office, she'd discovered she liked the man she worked for. He was demanding, which she could handle, didn't put up with shit from his young clients who thought they were God's gift to whatever sport they excelled in, and was a whiz at negotiating and putting someone in their place. She admired him and could learn a lot from watching him.

That was the professional Quinn.

Quinn the woman still had a huge crush on her employer and admired the fact that he was donating an organ to a family member. But she would never act on her feelings, and the job, as she'd hoped, was perfect for her.

Austin treated her with the utmost respect, and never in the time they'd been together had he crossed any boundaries or treated her like a woman he desired. She had, however, caught him looking at her with a slow simmer in his eyes more than once and convinced herself she was imagining things. It was for the best that they remain professional.

Needing something to hold when she walked in to face him, she'd stopped on the way and found the perfect item along with a package of Tim Tams her friend had brought home from Australia.

She headed up the long driveway filled with cars and across the walkway. The door was partially open, so she pushed the doorbell and walked inside.

Bri greeted her immediately with a warm hug. "It's so nice of you to stop by." She glanced at the bag in Quinn's hand. "Aww, you didn't have to bring the patient a gift," she said with a grin. "Come meet everyone."

Quinn followed Bri through a marble entryway into a hallway filled with people. The men all had a distinct family resemblance, not to mention the same requisite amount of testosterone, and wow, those Prescotts were hot.

Bri proceeded with introductions, doing a rundown of each and what they did for a living. The talent in the family ranged from the intellectual, from Braden, Bri's twin, being a doctor but also muscular and hot, to more alpha athletes — Jaxon, a baseball player, and Damon, the football player she'd already met. Austin's mother, Christine, was a warm woman who seemed to appreciate Quinn coming by. Quinn cataloged the information about them all for future reference.

Before she could process much more, Bri pulled her past the guys who'd, for whatever reason, ended up in the hallway and into a big family room, where Damon sat in an oversize reclining chair drinking from a can of soda and watching television while Austin lay on the sofa.

"Your highness, you have a visitor," Bri said, causing Quinn to chuckle. Bri turned her gaze to Damon. "You. Out. Let them catch up so Austin stops asking what's going on at the office. I'll go feed the rest of the crew," she said.

Damon smirked at Austin, then headed out. Bri's voice rose as she shepherded the family into the kitchen, and the din of voices grew lower.

Austin gestured for her to come farther into the room. He looked good in a pair of gray sweats and a navy T-shirt as he leaned back against a suede oversize sofa that was located in front of the massive large-screen. The beard on his face suited him, and those gorgeous indigo eyes stared at her, a slow grin forming on his sensual mouth.

"To what do I owe the pleasure?" he asked.

"I wanted to see for myself how you're doing. And here. I brought you something."

She handed him the bag, watching and suddenly embarrassed as he pulled out a stuffed horse, the Thunder mascot, wearing a jersey. "I love it," he said on a low, sexy laugh.

"I didn't want to come empty-handed."

"What's this?" He held the Tim Tams in his hand.

"You've never had Tim Tams? They're only the best Australian cookie *ever*. Chocolate biscuits surrounded by a chocolate cream filling." She moaned at the thought of the cookie she'd had this morning, remembering the taste that had exploded on her tongue.

His eyes dilated at her unintentional sexual sound. Shit. She cleared her throat. "You should try one."

An amused smile lifted his lips. "I will. And thank you, Quinn," he said in his rumbling voice. "Have a seat. I can't stand or I'd be a gentleman and do the right thing my parents taught me."

Grinning, she sat with a good amount of space between them.

"I've never seen you in jeans," he said.

She blinked in surprise. "No, I guess you haven't. But I wasn't going to come here dressed for the office."

His gaze drank her in. "Well, I like the casual look on you."

"I ... thank you."

He blinked and shook his head. "Sorry. That was inappropriate. So how have things been at the office? I've tried to check in, but my family has been alternating as babysitters, making sure I don't do much as per doctor's orders. Another five weeks of doing nothing and I may lose my mind."

She smiled, knowing how much he thrived on work. "Everything is fine. Quiet. You can relax and heal."

"Can we go over some of the new endorsements that have come in? I know Bri's helping you as is Rex King." He referred to the main agent who was directing her in Austin's absence. "But I hate being out of the loop. So show me those papers I know you slipped into your bag."

He winked at her, and damned if her panties didn't grow damp. For sure, the man was potent.

She shot him a mock glare and pulled out a bunch of offers from her purse. Drawing a deep breath, she slid closer until her thigh touched his and his body heat radiated through the soft denim. She swallowed hard, doing her best to ignore his warm, masculine scent that smelled so good.

He perused the documents, going over each by athlete, giving her his opinion, and placing the finished ones on his other side. She took notes, offering her own two cents deal by deal, but she saw him fading fast. Bri had told her he'd been warned about the exhaustion part of the recovery, hence his inability to return to work for a total of six full weeks and no heavy lifting at all.

She pulled the papers out of his hand. "You need to rest."

He frowned. "Dammit. The doctors said the fatigue could last a good three months while my body gets used to filtering through one kidney."

"Well, behave yourself. Do what the doctors say and you'll be back in no time." She glanced across his lap and reached for the papers he'd put aside.

Her arm brushed the bulge in his pants, and she sucked in a breath. He stiffened and grabbed her wrist with one hand. Seconds passed with just the sound of their harsh inhales and exhales echoing between them.

"Quinn," he said in a gruff voice.

She turned her head. Big mistake. Her gaze met his, and his lips were way too close.

"You should move away," he said, not making an effort to shift his own head at all.

"I know," she whispered. But she was frozen in place, the desire to kiss him, to feel the beard that now covered his face against her skin overwhelming.

His grip on her wrist tightened. And still she didn't turn away. So he closed the distance between them and sealed his lips over hers. Her lashes fluttered closed, and she met him halfway, accepting the kiss. His mouth slid over hers, causing her body to come alive. Flutters took up residence in her stomach, and yearning slid like honey through her veins. He might be lacking stamina, but his kiss was strong enough to consume her whole.

He parted his mouth, his facial hair tickling her lips as his tongue speared inside and tangled with hers. She groaned and his free hand came up to her neck, gripping her tight and holding her in place as he continued the delicious onslaught.

If not for the recent surgery, nothing would stop her from climbing into his lap, settling herself over the hard erection that was still pressing into her arm, and grinding against him while he continued the deep, drugging kiss. His lips played with hers, theirs tongues tangled and teeth clashed, and she knew he wanted *more*, just as she did.

"Jesus Christ, Austin. You just had major surgery. Can't this wait?" a male voice asked.

Though Austin released his grip on her neck, he didn't seem nearly as disturbed as she was, and she jumped back, mortified.

"Calm your shit, *Dr. Prescott*. I haven't moved an inch. No violating doctor's orders," Austin said in a desire-laden voice.

She closed her eyes, wanting the floor to swallow her whole. She peeked over and saw Braden shaking his head at his brother.

"I'm sorry." She jumped up, kneeling for the papers that fell to the floor.

"Quinn—"

Austin said her name, but she ignored him, gathering the documents.

Braden stepped over and helped her. "Relax," he said in her ear. "He's perfectly fine. I'm just making sure he doesn't pull his Steri-Strips."

She shook her head. "No. This shouldn't have happened. I work for him." She stood and shoved the documents into her purse.

"Braden, give us a minute," Austin said.

His brother left the room, and she forced herself to meet Austin's concerned gaze.

"I shouldn't have kissed you. If I made you uncomfortable, I'm sorry," he said.

"You didn't. Make me uncomfortable, I mean. I wanted you to kiss me. It just can't happen again. I need this job." She had student loans for what her scholarship didn't cover. Hell, given the way she was raised, taking care of every baby in her family, siblings and cousins, she needed this job to validate who she was as a person. "I love this job. And I'm not going to risk it by getting involved with my boss."

Especially not with a playboy who could pick up any woman he wanted at any random meal of the day. And she'd certainly seen females be less than circumspect, slipping him their number, rubbing against him, and being outright rude to Quinn, pushing her aside when they were out for business.

"I value you, Quinn. I don't want to lose you either."

She managed a nod.

"So we're good?" he asked.

"We're fine." Even if her body was still quivering inside from the best kiss she'd ever had.

* * *

Quinn left like the flames of hell were licking at her heels, and Austin didn't blame her. What the fuck was he doing, acting on his deepest desire and kissing the best assistant he'd ever had? Even in the short time she'd been working for him, he knew she could handle him. His demands. His clients. Their tantrums. He couldn't afford to lose her.

"Bro, damn, what were you thinking?" Braden sauntered into the room and slid into the chair Damon had occupied earlier.

"I wasn't," he muttered.

"Oh, you were, all right. Just with the wrong head."

Austin rolled his eyes. "Shut the fuck up," he said without heat.

He missed his brother when he was abroad, working for Doctors Without Borders, and Austin was glad he had Braden home for a brief time now.

"Holy shit, are those Tim Tams?" Braden flew out of the chair and planted his ass next to Austin, grabbing the cookies from beside him and opening them without asking.

"Hey! Those are mine."

"And you can share them unless you want me to run off with them, leaving you with none. It's not like you can chase me." Braden rolled a shoulder.

Austin shook his head. Jesus Christ. Siblings.

His brother pulled open the crinkly package and snagged a couple of biscuits, handing the rest back to Austin. “She must really like you if she gave you these.”

“She works for me. What you saw was a slip. It won’t happen again.” *It couldn’t happen again.*

His brother chuckled. “Keep telling yourself that. I saw how you two looked at each other.”

“What are you, the expert on relationships now? I thought you were single.”

Braden was the sibling closest in age to Austin, so they were tight. Always had been. “Let’s say there’s someone with possibility.” His eyes gleamed, and Austin knew his brother was in deep.

“I’m happy for you. As for me, I’m going to heal and get back to playing the field. After all, it’s what I do best.” He would put Quinn in the off-limits zone and keep her there.

He had no other choice.

* * *

Do you want more of Carly Phillips?

One click DARE TO RESIST now!

A REAL MAN DOWN UNDER

A REAL MAN SHORT STORY

JENIKA SNOW

SYNOPSIS

I'd loved him for the last fifteen years. I'd given him glances, had heated fantasies of all the things he'd do to me if I just told him how I felt.

And I hadn't known he felt, thought, wanted those same things with me.

Until we were finally honest with each other. Then everything fell into place.

A passionate night of uninhibited desires, feelings, and needs led to finding the one person I was always meant to be with.

Big.

My husband.

My best friend.

The one man who consumed me.

His name said it all. He was larger than life, possessive, territorial... obsessed with me. He let me know, had me feeling those things every single day until I was drunk off them. And here we were, ten years later, spending our anniversary on the beach during an Australian summer.

And there was nothing I wanted more than to let my very own mountain man show me exactly how feral he was with me, one touch and lick at a time.

LANDRY

I felt fifteen years younger in that moment as I lifted my arms and ran my fingers through my hair. Sweat coated my body, this light sprinkling of droplets that made me hot and cold all in the same breath. And as I swayed my hips to the music, danced to the beat, and rubbed my ass against his crotch, all I could think about was how much he wanted me.

He was hard, thick, his hands moving over me as if they had a mind of their own. And his mouth was on my neck, his tongue moving over my damp flesh. He growled against me like some feral animal.

"I could come right here, right now." He nipped at my throat and I moaned. But no one could hear me. The music was too loud, the atmosphere too sexual. Everyone here was seconds away from fucking on the dance floor.

I reached around and wound my arms around his neck, stretching my body out, feeling a slight breeze moving along me. But it was warm, humid. It was sexually laced.

"Fuck, I want you, want to slide my cock deep into you and feel how wet you are."

I moaned, and he turned me around in his arms, gripping the back of my neck tight enough I gasped. But I wanted more.

"Just take me then," I whispered, opening my eyes and seeing his half-lidded gaze trained on me. He slid his hand along the side of my throat and gripped my chin.

"Watch it, baby girl. You know how possessive I get. I don't want any of these motherfuckers seeing what's mine." He had his other hand on my ass, squeezing the flesh painfully hard, so hard I groaned. "I already want to beat some fuckers down for even breathing in your direction."

My body hummed at his words.

"You're playing with fire, Landry."

I grinned slowly. "Don't you want to get burned?"

He tipped my head back even more and pulled my bottom lip down with his thumb. He stared at my mouth, and I felt my heart thundering even more at the dominant look on his face. He let the flesh go, and it snapped back in place. I felt blood rush to the surface, and on instinct, I licked my lips.

I heard him groan right before he dipped his head and kissed me... mouth-fucked me right in front of everyone.

I knew what he was doing.

Big was staking his claim, marking his territory.

"Let's get out of here," I murmured against his mouth, not thinking about anything but being alone with my husband. He gave my ass one more powerful squeeze, and I felt a fresh gush of wetness soak my panties.

"If I take you out of here, I'm going to have to fuck you, Landry."

God, he was driving me insane, and I wanted to be that way. I wanted to let the alcohol I'd consumed make my inhibitions go out the damn window. And it was doing a pretty good job of that already.

And the knowledge that Big wasn't drinking, that he was staying sober to make sure I was okay, that no one fucked with me, turned me on even more. Because knowing he was this worked up without having any liquid courage, that he was this hard and ready for me, made me feel... powerful.

I let him lead me out of the club, bodies pressed together, the smell of salty sweat and beer in the air. The feeling of sex was thick all around us. I kind of liked it. It made me even more aroused. A guy bumped into me, and I heard Big growl low, reach out to push the man away, and bark out to "watch where the fuck you are going."

I tipped my head back and knew my grin was sappy and aroused. My big, strong husband was willing to do whatever to make sure no one so much as looked in my direction. It had a fire burning deep inside me.

We found ourselves on the beach, and I stopped to unhook my heels. Big took them from me and wrapped his other hand around my waist, keeping me close. My bare feet dug into the grainy sand. It felt good. Free.

But nothing felt as good as the man I was currently pressed up against.

He kept leading me away, farther down toward an outcropping of rocks, a personal little mountain, a private island. I didn't fight him, not when I wanted this just as much.

"You're drunk," he said gruffly, and I nodded, laughing softly. My cheeks were on fire.

I was intoxicated, and it felt good.

Yeah, I'd had one too many drinks, because the feel of a summer Australian breeze moving over my body was incredible. Maybe it was the scent of the salt in the air or the sound of the waves crashing against the shore.

I was halfway around the world, so out of my comfort zone, yet having the sensation like I was right where I belonged.

Everything ignited my senses.

Or maybe it was him.

Big.

My husband, who'd taken me to this incredible country for our wedding anniversary.

A man who worshipped the ground I walked on.

A man I loved more than anything else in the world.

He'd gotten out of his comfort zone, put his cabinet-making business back home on hold, and we'd packed up for a week of wanderlust.

This trip was glorious, surreal, and dreamy in every sense of the word.

Then we were sitting on the beach, the smell of the salt water thick in the air. I lay back, closed my eyes, and just felt myself fade away.

The feel of his hands on me then made me anxious to see where this was going. The way his calloused fingers skated along my body had me moaning.

"We shouldn't. Someone will be able to see us," I whispered, but truthfully I didn't care. After ten years of being with my big and rough-around-the-edges mountain man, I still felt like I was that young woman who was too afraid to tell him how I felt.

"We really fucking should, baby," he said gruffly, and I dug my hands deeper into the sand on either side of me, as if it could station me and not let me float off from the pleasure.

He started whispering dirty things to me, slightly muffled, wholly consuming. His obscenity couldn't be tamed, but then again, Big was a force to be reckoned with. It was one of the reasons I loved him so much.

Here I found myself, intoxicated from the champagne bubbles, drunk off the feel of him, and desperately wanting more.

So much more.

Exhibitionism.

Sex on the beach.

Uninhibited desires.

Here, we had no worries, no responsibilities. We were just two souls experiencing life for the next week, as if we were in our own world.

And experiencing life apparently meant raunchy, obscenely hot sex on the beach.

And I was all for it.

I wanted to experience all of that right here, say screw it to anyone who saw us, who stumbled upon us in this little hidden cover on the other side of the world.

"Will you let me in?" he whispered, and I wanted to tell him yes, but all I could do was nod. I couldn't speak, couldn't breathe. He was bringing me higher, so high I was going to fall over that invisible thread of reality and tumble headfirst into insanity.

I nodded, the best I could do with how drunk I was on the arousal.

"I should take you to the hotel, lay you out on the sheets, eat you out until you come all over my face."

I opened my eyes and lifted up partially, resting my upper body on my elbows so I could look down the length of my abdomen at him. God, under the moonlight he looked impossibly bigger, so muscular, and wholly possessed by me. He was poised between my thighs... above the very intimate, wet part of my body.

All he'd have to do was push my dress up, pull my panties aside, and he'd be able to feel how hot I was for him, how wet and ready.

"What are we doing?" I whispered, finally able to speak.

He lifted his head for a suspended moment and just stared into my eyes. I could hear the distant sound of the music from the nightclub we'd been at. It seemed to make everything a little bit more erotic.

I licked my lips, waiting for him to answer. Without breaking his hold on my gaze, he pushed my dress up so it was pooled around my waist. On instinct I spread my legs even wider, my heels sinking into the soft sand as I opened for him. I was breathing hard and fast. I wasn't able to stop myself, couldn't.

"Big." I said his name on a soft moan when he slid his fingers along my inner thighs and rest right at the junction between my legs. And still he held my gaze with his own. "What are we doing?" I said those words again, but they were so soft I figured he hadn't heard me.

"We're fucking, Landry." He leaned in close, and I felt the warmth of his breath move along my pussy. And even though I had panties on, it scorched my sensitive flesh.

Fucking. Yeah, that's what he was doing to me.

"I'm about to eat my wife out on the beach in Australia, lap at her pussy cream, swallow her orgasm."

Oh. My. God.

I couldn't hold myself up any longer and let my back rest against the sand. I spread my arms out and closed my eyes, feeling the moonlight on me, the warm Australian breeze moving along my body over and over again.

He reached up and pulled the bodice of my dress down, my breasts becoming free, shaking slightly from the force. He had big palms on the mounds, squeezing them gently, running his thumbs along the stiff peaks.

I started undulating against him, needing his mouth on me, his tongue moving through my slit.

"What if somebody sees us?" I felt like I'd asked that question over and over again, but maybe that had been a thought in my mind, playing on repeat like a broken record.

I heard him grumble softly, felt the vibration down to my very core. "Let them see us, Landry. Let them see what they can't have, that you're mine. Only mine." And then he hooked his thumb along the edge of my panties, pull it to the side, and everything in me stilled.

My heart stopped, the blood rushed through my veins, and for a moment in time I was frozen there. I opened my eyes and stared up at the night sky, looked at the millions of stars above me. I gasped at the first feel of his tongue flattening against my pussy, and opened my mouth at the sensation of him dragging it up and then sucking my clit into his mouth. I was spiraling out of control.

Over and over he sucked and licked at me, lapped up the juices that he'd caused in me, my arousal that was only for him. He ate me out, made my flesh even more soaked. Big sent shock waves of electricity straight through my clit so it encompassed every single nerve ending in my body.

He licked at my pussy like a starving man.

And when he slipped a finger deep inside me, my inner muscles clenched around him, drawing in that digit, needing something more substantial.

I needed Big and everything he was.

Before I knew what was happening, I was pleading for him to fuck me, this mantra that I was saying out loud and in my head over and over again. And he gave me exactly what I wanted. He hauled me up off the ground, had me straddling his waist, my panties pulled to the side by his finger, and the hot, hard length of him only covered by denim pressed against my pussy.

I was frantic as I went for his belt, undid the button and zipper of his jeans. His cock was hard and thick, long and ready. I gripped the base and started stroking him from root to tip, gathering the pre-cum that dotted the crown of his head, and used it for lubrication as I jerked him off.

I stared at his face as I did this, his mouth slightly open, his eyes hooded as he looked at me. I rose up and placed the tip of his dick at the entrance of my soaking pussy hole. And then I slid down, my body engulfing him, becoming stretched so I could fit him comfortably inside me. And as I sank down inch by slow inch, my moans and his groans seeming to crash loudly around us like the water against the shore, I knew I wouldn't last.

I was already on the verge of getting off, of letting that pleasure take me over, pull me down deeper and deeper until there was no hope of me breaking through to the surface.

I rose on my knees and started lifting up and moving down. I rode him hard and fast, my hands on his abdomen as I bounced, as my body sucked at his cock. I felt his muscles clench beneath my fingers, his body so hard the manual labor he did day in and day out was evident in his physique. He had his hands on my waist, his fingers digging into my flesh. He helped me rise and fall on him, using me as his vessel.

"Fuck. Yes. Give it to me," he groaned and bounced me faster on his straining, thick erection.

I closed my eyes and let the pleasure consume me. I heard nothing but the waves moving against the shore, this natural pulling and pushing that took my desire higher.

"I'm yours," I was able to whisper back, surprised I had any strength to speak at all.

"I want you. I need you, Landry."

I found myself drifting away, letting that ecstasy, the eroticism of being with Big take over. This was how it was every single time—all the years that had passed, the children we'd had, hadn't dimmed any of it.

How I felt for him hadn't lessened in the slightest. In fact, I loved him more every single day.

"God, Landry." His voice was nothing more than a gruff whisper, the bass of the music that surrounded us and our identical breathing making an erotic cacophony. "You feel so fucking good."

I didn't need to rub my clit to get off. Just having him deep inside me, the friction, the wetness... just *him* was enough.

I tossed my head back, my hair moving along the bare skin of my shoulder blades sending little tingles throughout me. My tits bounced from the force of moving up and down. "God, I'm going to get off!" I cried out loud and long, heard him grunting, felt him pounding into me, lifting his hips to get as deep as he could.

And then I felt him come right at that moment, filling me up with his seed, making me take every last ounce of it.

"I love you." I was vaguely aware he groaned those three words, but they were muffled by the sound of the blood rushing through my ears.

"God, Big." I breathed out hard. "I love you." And then I collapsed on top of him, my body spent, the tremors of my pleasure a rhythmic clenching around his shaft. I could feel how hard he still was, knew he'd be like that for a while.

He was insatiable when it came to me.

I didn't know how much time had passed, but when I finally rolled off, he refused to let me get far. He still had his dick buried inside me, his arms wrapped around me. I rested my head on his bicep, felt his fingers move through the hair that fell against my temple.

I slowly opened my eyes, blinked a few times. I was in this post-orgasmic haze, the moonlight washing over us, the silvery glow that made everything seem not quite real.

A fantasy.

But this wasn't something I'd conjured up. This was reality. Mine and Big's. And although this was a wonderful getaway, an escape for our ten-year anniversary, I knew once we were home, I would be just as happy. I'd be surrounded by our children, would have my husband by my side, and know that I was loved.

We were one family, one unit. He was my life and I was his.

And what we'd created was better than any fantasy I could ever come up with.

* * *

Do you want more of Jenika Snow?

One click BIG (A REAL MAN) now!

BASKET DAY

A LEGACY SHORT STORY

REBECCA YARROS

1

Bash

In Legacy, Colorado, no one fucked with tradition. In most cases, I was fine with that rather broad statement and sentiment. Today was not one of those days. Why? Because it was *basket day*, and my plane had been three hours late.

Three hours meant that instead of being a part of one of the hundreds of couples picnicking on the floor of the Chandler's enormous barn, I was standing on the edge, scanning the crowd like the tardy jackass I was. The whole structure was strung with party lights, and the heaters stationed at the edges staved off the spring chill.

"Didn't bid high enough, Sebastian?" Mrs. Anderson questioned, looking over her glasses at me as she reached for one of the dozens of lemonade pitchers.

"My plane was delayed, so I missed the bidding." Emerson was going to kill me. She was probably plotting my death right now. This was my first basket day after being gone for six years, after fighting like hell to get Emerson back since I'd returned home, and I'd missed it.

Her silver eyebrows rose as she tsked at me. "You should know better. Looks like it's going to be a lonely night for you."

“What about you? Who won the coveted Anderson basket?” I asked, my gaze still combing over the couples.

“Ha! I retired from basket day *years* ago. You know it’s only for the marriageable young ladies.”

“Because we all need our yearly dose of anachronistic misogyny,” Harper Anders, my best friend’s little sister, replied with a saccharine-sweet smile as she approached from my left. “Glad to see you made it, Bash, but I think you may have missed some incredible snickerdoodle cookies that I spied in a certain basket.”

I cringed. She’d made snickerdoodles? I was in so much trouble.

“Harper, you of all people know how important this event is to raise money for Hope House,” Mrs. Anderson chided. “I don’t even know what they’d do without the contributions basket day brings in.”

“Oh, I don’t know. Maybe we could all just donate money instead of baking and bidding on women disguised as baskets?” Harper shrugged, and I stifled a laugh.

“Who won your basket, Harpy?” I asked, having scanned at least half of the floor.

“Miles Ryan,” she answered, waving over her shoulder at the firefighter.

He nodded at her and smirked when he saw me standing there.

“Does your brother know you’re hanging out with a structure guy?” I looked sideways at the blond. The rivalry between the structure crew and the hotshot crew was legendary around here, but hey, not everyone could be a hotshot like we were.

“Like Ryker cares,” Harper snorted. “He knows I’d never get serious with a guy from basket day, or any firefighter, really. Besides, he’s got bigger things to think about in Australia.”

Five of our crew had taken an off-season position on a crew in Victoria, and there wasn’t a day that I didn’t check in with them as they battled fires there.

“Right, and Knox? You know he and Ryan don’t exactly get along.”

“Knox Daniels has jack and shit to say about who I date. He’s not even *here*.” She ignored Mrs. Anderson’s comment about the swearing and took a smaller pitcher of lemonade back to her blanket.

True. Knox was still in California—where I had just come from—waiting until the last minute to move home to Legacy for the upcoming fire season, but I knew he’d make it in time. It had been an uphill battle to reestablish the Legacy Hotshots after all but one member of the team had died in the fire up the mountain ten years ago, but we'd done it to honor our fathers.

Another look toward the makeshift dance floor and I saw her. Emerson Kendrick was seated on quilt with Greg Roberts. Of course, he'd bought her basket. He'd been buying her basket every year since I made the giant mistake of leaving Legacy six years ago.

But I was back now.

"That girl—" Mrs. Anderson started.

"If you'll excuse me," I interrupted with a grimace and started picking my way through the couples.

Emerson laughed at something Greg said, and my stomach twisted. Did she have to look so damned beautiful tonight? Her dark brown hair was loose around her shoulders, and her blue dress hung on every curve as she reached into the basket, pulling out a cookie—a freaking snickerdoodle.

I passed one of the support pillars as she looked up, and our eyes locked.

Hers widened slightly before a devilish smile slid across her gorgeous, kissable mouth. A mouth I knew was going to lay into me about my lack of punctuality as soon as she had the opportunity. She arched an eyebrow and handed the cookie—*my freaking cookie*—over to Greg.

I stepped back with my hand to my heart, letting her see just how wrong that was as my jaw dropped. *Really?* I mouthed at her.

She lifted one shoulder and then pointed to the giant painted sheet that hung from the far rafters. It read, "Welcome to the 76th Annual Legacy Basket Drive!"

I settled back against the pillar, folding my arms over my chest as she began the next thirty minutes of ignoring me. That was fine. Patience was my strong suit, and I used the time to mentally list every single thing I was going to do with that very kissable mouth the second I had her alone.

I moved when she finally did, following her back across the crowded floor to the lemonade table.

"You're seriously on a date with Greg Roberts?" I asked as I came up behind her, barely brushing my body against hers.

"You seriously missed basket day?" she retorted as she reached for a pitcher.

"Not that one. I saw Bobby Parker spike it." My lips skimmed the shell of her ear. "And I can't help it when my plane is three hours late."

"And I couldn't let a perfectly good basket go to waste," she answered with a shrug, putting that pitcher back and picking up another one, giving it a sniff before nodding. Then she turned to face me, brushing the back of her hands over my stomach as she carried the pitcher. "Now, you'll have to excuse me, Mr. Vargas. I happen to be on a date with Mr. Roberts. It's bad manners to keep a basket-bidding man waiting."

A spark of pure challenge rose in those chocolate-brown eyes, and it took every ounce of willpower I had not to send the lemonade sloshing to the floor and carry her out of that barn.

"Don't feed that guy all my cookies," I teased, catching her elbow as she sidestepped to get around me.

Her eyes widened in feigned shock. "*Your* cookies? He bought them fair and square. In fact..." She glanced down at my watch. "For the next two hours and thirteen minutes, they're quite legally *his* cookies."

I bent close enough to take in the scent of her bergamot shampoo. "How much did he pay?"

"A lot." She raised her face so our lips were merely inches apart. "He really likes the cookies."

My eyes narrowed slightly, and my body tensed, reacting to hers just like it always had. Some things didn't change just because you left for a few years. Hell, I burned for her more now than I ever had when we were teenagers. "I'll pay double."

She smiled, and my heart stopped. "I bet you would have...but you weren't here." She broke free of my light grasp and grinned at me over her shoulder. "Thanks for the tip on the spiked lemonade!" She crinkled her nose at me and then walked back to Greg, leaving me speechless and empty-handed.

"And that, my friend," River Maldonado said as he smacked my shoulder, "is why I know better than to travel on basket day."

I glared down at the younger hotshot, but he simply laughed and headed back toward his Avery.

One more lingering look across the barn at where Emerson sat with Greg, and I took myself home. I knew when to abandon the battle so I could win the war.

2

Emerson

I parked my car in the garage and took the basket from the passenger seat before heading inside. The house still smelled like construction—like new paint and new beginnings.

Dropping the basket in the mudroom, I hung my keys on the little hooks I'd installed a couple of weeks ago and put my coat away in the closet before heading toward the only light shining in the house—the kitchen.

Candles flickered on the granite, covering every surface but the island, where another basket sat. I ran my hand along the dark wicker, and a small shiver raced down my spine as I heard his footsteps behind me.

"His two hours and thirteen minutes are up," Bash growled as he set his lips to my neck. I grasped the edge of the counter to keep upright. Damn, that man knew exactly where my trigger spots were, and he wasn't being merciful.

"Bash," I groaned, tilting my head to give him better access. The things he could do with that mouth should have been illegal.

He cupped my cheek and turned my face toward him, then kissed me deep and hard, parting my lips with a sure thrust from his tongue. He tasted like home and sin and everything I loved—because he *was* everything I loved. His fingers were strong but tender, holding me so I could only receive his kiss, only take what he was willing to give.

This was the price for teasing him mercilessly at the barn, and I was more than willing to pay it. He kissed me senseless, taking me hard, then retreating when I arched back at him for more, where I felt exactly how much he wanted me. He toyed with me until my breaths came in choppy bursts, and when I couldn't take the passive stance a second later, I nipped at his lower lip.

He hissed, then spun me to face him, lifting me to the counter at the same time. The basket slid down the length of the granite as I parted my knees around his hips. His hands gripped my thighs, spreading them wider as he yanked me forward, lining us up at the edge.

"I missed you," I managed to say before he was kissing me again, erasing the seven lonely days I'd spent without him while he was wrapping up business in California.

"I thought about you every second I was gone," he promised against my lips before sliding his hands up my thighs—and under my dress. Funny how I'd gone six years without seeing the man, but now seven days was apparently my limit.

My fingers tunneled through his dark hair as my heart thrummed in the way it did when he was near. "You know Greg and I are just friends, right? I was just playing with you at the barn."

His hazel eyes had that green tinge to them I loved when he tucked my hair behind my ears. "I know." His hand slid down my arm until his fingers brushed over the diamond on my left hand. "He knows it, too. I wasn't worried. Jealous, maybe, but not worried."

"Because that says I'm yours?" I teased, running my hands down his long-sleeved shirt with the Legacy Hotshot logo on it.

"Because it says *I'm* yours," he answered. "I'm sorry for missing the auction, Emmy. I tried to get back." He didn't need to verbalize his apology. I'd seen it in his eyes earlier and felt it in his touch now.

"I know," I assured him. "Now make it up to me." I slipped two fingers into the waistband of his jeans, right above the zipper, and tugged.

He answered with a drugging kiss that left my head spinning. We were a tangle of arms and clothes, both of us desperate to get closer to the other. I yanked his shirt overhead and then traced the lines of his washboard abs with my fingertips as I kissed his chest, tasting and testing his skin, following the patterns of his tattoos.

"Fuck. Emerson, baby," he growled when I unsnapped his jeans and dragged his zipper down. "Do you know how badly I wanted to kiss you in the barn? To pick you up and carry you home so I could get my hands on you?"

"Show me."

He slid my dress up my hips, and I kicked off my heels so I could wrap my legs around his waist. The best thing about Bash was his heart. He loved me fearlessly, recklessly, with utter abandon. His mind came in a close second—the man was legitimately brilliant. But his body was the icing on the freaking cake. He was shredded—all hard planes and velvet-covered muscle, and he never failed to turn me on with a simple look.

I raised my arms, and he sent my dress to rest with his shirt on the floor, leaving me in the black lingerie I'd worn specifically to work him up during what I thought would be our basket dinner tonight.

"Damn." His eyes raked over me. "You've been wearing this all night?"

I leaned forward, raking my teeth lightly over the shell of his ear and relishing in his shudder. "Just waiting for you to take it off."

"Happy to oblige." He made quick work of the bra, and it fluttered to the ground as his mouth closed over my breast.

I whimpered at the pleasure, arching against him for more. He licked and teased my nipple into an impossibly stiff bud before giving the same treatment to the other. His hands shifted to my ass, pulling me tight against him as he worked me over.

"Bash," I urged him on, touching whatever parts of him I could reach.

He answered by sending his fingers up my thigh, then grazing over my underwear with his thumb. "Do you want me, Emerson?"

"What do you think?" I rocked against him, seeking the friction my body craved.

He groaned as his thumb slid under my thong and stroked me from opening to clit. "I think you're fucking soaked."

I moaned when he began to stroke and tease, knowing exactly where to apply pressure to make my legs quiver. "Please," I begged when he showed no signs of moving this along.

I wanted him deep inside me, moving with me, both of us so lost in the other that we forgot ourselves.

"In a hurry?" He grinned, stepping back just long enough to drag my panties down my legs, leaving me completely naked on our kitchen counter.

"I want you." I gripped the back of his neck and yanked him to me, kissing him with abandon, sucking his tongue into my mouth.

"Not nearly as much as I want you." He swore as his fingers found my core again.

I was on fire for him, my blood pounding a relentless beat that demanded the completion that only he could give me. We'd been apart for too long—not only the seven days he'd just been gone, but the six years he'd stayed away from Legacy. He'd only been home eight months, and we were still ravenous for each other.

He entered me with one finger, then two, pumping me with sure strokes as he rubbed at my clit with his thumb, his mouth drinking in my cries as he sent that pleasure spiraling deep within me. My mind spun as the tension gathered, winding tighter and tighter as he fucked me with his fingers, holding me captive with another hand at the base of my neck.

"Right there. God, you're right at the edge. So fucking beautiful, Emerson." His praises were hot puffs of air on my lips, but he didn't kiss me, even when I raised my head to his.

"Sebastian!" I framed his face with my hands as my entire body tensed, my orgasm beating at the doors.

"I've got you," he promised, then pinched my clit, sending my body into orbit as he gave me the kiss I craved.

The orgasm hit me hard, ripping a scream from my throat as pleasure washed over me in waves until I was limp. He replaced his fingers with the head of his erection, sliding inside me the first inch, then pausing.

My eyes flew open to see him staring at me with the kind of intensity that sent another aftershock of my orgasm through me.

"Now, God, Bash, *now*," I begged, gripping his hips to pull him closer.

"Say it," he demanded, sweat beading on his skin from the effort it took to hold so still.

"I want you." I kissed his bottom lip, but he still didn't move.

"Emerson," he pleaded, his arms turning to steel bands around me.

"I love you," I whispered softly, then repeated it against his mouth. I said it over and over as he slid into me, stretching my walls as he pushed deep. The feel of him was more than incredible—it was mind-altering.

When he was seated to the hilt, so deep inside me that I felt him throbbing with his own need, he kissed me gently. "I love you. You own every inch of me. Every single molecule that makes me who I am. It's all yours."

"Bash." I swirled my hips because it felt so damned good, and he groaned.

With one hand at the nape of my neck and the other at my ass, his hips began rolling, taking me over and over with steady, deep thrusts, vowing his love with his body. We moved together with single purpose, drawing out every ounce of pleasure we could in each other.

He took everything I gave and still kept going, taking us higher and higher, until our muscles strained and our skin was sweat-slicked. When that same pleasure wound within me, coiling like a spring, he adjusted his angle and sent me flying again, his name a cry from my lips as this orgasm hit deeper, even more consuming than the first. Then he fell right over the edge with me, his breath deliciously heavy against my neck as he recovered.

He kissed me, soft and gentle, then helped me down from the counter. A few minutes later, we were cleaned up—him shirtless because I'd chosen that particular item of clothing instead of my dress, and both of us barefoot on the kitchen floor.

"Don't you want to know what's in the basket?" he asked, wrapping his arms around me from behind.

I reached forward and pulled it close enough to open the hinged lid and then laughed. "Oh my *God*. Are those all spearmint Tic Tacs? How did you get them all here?" I turned in his arms, looping mine around his neck. The man knew my weaknesses, that was for sure.

"I ordered them weeks ago," he admitted. "I was going to break tradition and put my own basket up for bidding today." His grin was contagious, and soon my cheeks hurt from smiling so wide.

"I love you, Sebastian Vargas."

His smile fell. "Greg ate my cookies."

I rolled my eyes and pushed out of his arms so I could open the bread box in the corner, back by the toaster. "You mean these cookies?" I held up a Ziploc bag.

His eyes danced as he pulled me against him. "You made me extra cookies?"

"Guilty."

"You really are the best." He kissed me again, tossing the cookies to the island before sweeping me into his arms. He always made me feel so light, but he really was just that strong. "I'd rather have you for dessert," he said, carrying me out of the kitchen.

"I thought you just did," I teased as he headed up our stairs.

"I'm just getting started."

"I like the sound of that." My lips found his neck, and I kissed a path up to his jaw.

"I promise I won't miss basket day next year," he vowed as we reached the second floor.

"I bet not."

"But you can't miss it, either." Was that a slight note of panic in his voice?

"I wasn't planning on it." We'd made it to our bedroom door.

"Good. You're going to bid on me, right?"

I shrugged. "If Mrs. Anderson doesn't outbid me."

His outraged face sent me into a fit of laughter as he tossed me unceremoniously onto our bed. "You're going to pay for that."

I was still laughing when he climbed in next to me, quickly turning my giggles into full-out moans with his kisses. Laughter and kisses—that's what I'd get to spend years experiencing with this man.

Not just years.

We had forever.

* * *

UNTIL NEXT YEAR

ANNABEL JOSEPH

For M and L

1

Amara tiptoed over coarse sand, too shy to look up, although she knew he was there. Her floral-printed skirt skimmed almost down to her ankles, yet she felt naked. She always felt naked when she met Patrick. He affected her that way.

She might have been any beachgoer, except that it wasn't beach season. Still, she wore sandals, and her hair was twisted up in a bun to prevent frizziness and tangles from the salted, humid air. She wore a short-sleeved shirt because it was warm enough, even in October, and a lightweight skirt...

The first time she'd met Patrick here, she'd had on a long black skirt. A wearable pall, because she'd been so miserable, so dead inside. She still wore skirts every year because she liked the way they blew in the breeze and billowed around her legs, but she didn't wear black ones.

Sometimes the wind at Danger Beach was light, like today, a calm, soothing whisper. Once, two years ago, it had blown nearly as hard as it had the first day they met, when the tropical storm ripped shingles from the stilt-perched beach homes behind them and blew deck chairs out to sea.

Patrick had arrived before her, as always, to wait on the pile of rocks beside the pier. They'd sat there together on this exact day five years ago, and now this had become their day to meet at Danger Beach and remember the storm and everything that had come after.

He was rugged and beautiful, as Australian men were. He'd moved to the

US as a child, but the accent was still there. She teased him about it sometimes, about his folksy, unfamiliar turns of phrase, but the truth was, his deep, broad "down under" accent thrilled her way more than the clipped Mideastern syllables of the lame guys back home.

He watched her come, as he had that first day, although he'd been in the water then, up to his waist in cold, rough waves. Patrick's hair was pitch-black, dark as her own, his eyes a more forgiving light brown. She'd found him attractive from the start, although it took her time to realize it with everything else going on—that storm, both inward and outward, and that danger the beach was named for.

His shoulders were broad and muscular but not too muscular. His light, fitted tee revealed a sculpted torso. Yep, still working out. Amara wasn't a tiny thing, a skinny bitch, but when she was with Patrick, she felt light as a fairy. Such was his presence, his height, his vitality.

When she got close enough, his lips curved up in a smile. His strong features weren't cute or handsome. No, they were striking, but that might have been due to his inborn intensity. Now that they were steps apart, mere feet, he drew her in like a tractor beam. The day they met, he'd stared at her, almost angry in his need to know *how* and *why* and *what now*?

Today his stare was a little bit softer, but only just.

"What are you doing here?" she asked. It was a tradition. So much of this was tradition. Same stretch of beach, same day every year.

"What are *you* doing here?" he asked in return. "What the fuck are we doing here?"

She laughed and sat beside him on the rocks. Funny, how you could feel happy and wrought up and horny as hell all at once.

"You made it," he said. "I always wonder."

"If I wasn't going to be here, I'd have told you."

"I know, but I still always wonder. Or worry." His gaze softened, as much as Patrick could be soft. "I'm so glad you're here."

They took each other's hands without thinking, and even though it had been a full revolution around the sun since she'd last seen him, her fingers fit into his just right. They stared out at the waves together, at the horizon that was brighter today than it had been in some time. She knew they both pictured the rain and wind of their first meeting, though, the rumbling thunder and flashing lightning. Chaos, like end times, and it had somehow, over five years, turned into this.

After five minutes or so of this silent observance, he turned to her and squeezed her hand. "What do you say, Amara? Shall we move to drier land?"

"Yes," she said, holding his gaze.

They walked across the beach hand in hand, past a squat, waterlogged lifeguard station. It wasn't manned now. No one came here at this time of year, no families, no honeymooners, no beach-bum retirees. Few came in the summer, either.

Danger Beach was a mess of driftwood, broken shells, and riptides, and ugly cottages built high off the ground because so many storms brought floods. They retreated to one of these, a rental even smaller and uglier than the others. It had first been booked five years ago, by a young, dark-haired man who'd been seeking danger to help him forget the tragedy in his world.

As for Amara, she'd found this beach—and Patrick—by accident, escaping a family destination wedding one town over, where the beaches were prettier, and crowded, and not as dangerous.

"It looks the same," she marveled aloud as they walked beneath the house to a set of crooked stairs. Same anemic potted palms, same faded *Welcome* sign, same rusting Sea-Doo hunched against one of the concrete pillars that kept the cottage from being swept into the sea.

"It always looks the same," he agreed.

Small talk. So strange, when beneath her skirt, her body was coming alive. Her nipples tightened only from his nearness, his big, capable masculinity. He took the stairs two at a time and pushed open the door for her. His bags were on the floor. He'd probably gotten in yesterday so he could make everything more comfortable for her, air out the musty house and run the water until the sulfur smell disappeared. Those were the kinds of things Patrick did.

Oh, just a few of the amazing, wonderful things Patrick did.

As soon as the door closed behind them, the air and water meant nothing. *They* were the air and water, and everything on earth. He reached for her just as she melted against him. A year to wait for this, a year to remember the last time and anticipate the next. His lips crashed against hers, his hands wrenching her even closer than her own panicked press against him.

He smelled faintly of the sea, but more of Patrick, fresh soap, subtle cologne. She grasped his face, running fingertips across his stubble that never really went away. She caressed his square jaw, his soft curls, the muscles beneath his ears, his back, his clenching shoulders. As she felt all these parts of him and experienced all the memories embedded in her mind, he did the same.

He ran fingers through her hair, traced along her ears, thrust his tongue into her mouth to taste her. There had been others—a few others—but only Patrick ever kissed her this way, like he had to know and have all of her.

Once the initial reacquaintance was out of the way, the collecting of familiar scents and textures, they moved to the bedroom like sleepwalkers, not needing to see, only needing to walk, to get there. Amara's body felt electrified by his energy. When he took off her clothes, each brush of his hands or fingers against her skin was excruciating. Her nipples ached. Her pussy...

Her "down under," he called it, joking, sometimes. She always thought of it that way now. Her down under craved her man from Down Under, and he was here, alive, eagerly stripping off her clothes.

She did the same to him, feeling the familiar rush of emotion. They'd barely exchanged words, but it didn't matter. There'd be time for that later. First, lust, fascination, relief.

Ritual.

"Oh God," he whispered as he bared her to his gaze. Her nipples were tight as hard beach pebbles, and her skin was lush, damp from the humidity. When he stroked her arms, her waist, and her stomach, his fingers slid over her like she was made of silk. He made her feel valuable and priceless.

She made an impatient sound. He was still dressed. Why? She pushed up his shirt, though he had to pull it off himself because she wasn't tall enough to do it. The muscles of his chest moved, and his abs were carved, sliding with power. She reached for the waistband of his jeans. Other guys might stop her there. *Wait, let's take our time.*

Patrick never made her take her time, take any time. They both knew time could get away from you, be lost forever if you weren't careful. Time was here; time was now. Time was not for going slow.

They fumbled together, both trying to undo his button at once. Zipper down. Ah, there he was, her commando. His rigid cock fell into her hands, impossibly stiff and big. This was where she lost it, every time. There was too much of him, too much desire, too much need.

But this was where he grounded her, every time. He took her to the bed, half leading, half pushing, and covered her with his body. As she squirmed under him, he made soothing sounds, telling her everything would be okay, that he would take care of her. One palm smoothed over her arm, massaged her shoulder, settled against her neck.

"Shh," he said. "Shh, it's all right."

Her mouth fell open as he exerted the most careful pressure there, on her neck, where he might caress or kill her. She gasped softly, captured. *Shh, it's all right.*

He kissed her, squeezing, massaging, making her focus on him and the closeness they shared. He could grab her by the neck, and she'd let him. He'd done it that first day they slept together, and it had been the most powerful, most frightening experience of her life.

It's all right.

Shh.

Her legs spread beneath him, a natural, eager response to his power and command. Her hips rose to press against his cock. When he released her neck to grasp one of her breasts, she thrust that at him too, wanting him to have all of her. He sucked her throbbing nipple, teasing her, driving her mad. When the suck turned to a bite, she arched in agonized lust and tried to push him away.

He grabbed her hands and trapped them over her head. "Shh," he said again. That *shh* might as well have been a tongue over her clit. It made her wild. It made her helpless and wanting and alive.

"Please," she said, writhing under his gaze.

But he wasn't done, and wouldn't be done on her schedule. He kissed and sucked her other breast and bit her other nipple so the stinging, delicious pain matched the first. He let go of her hands and grabbed her thighs, and kissed her pussy even though it made her wail from the overload of sensation. He knew she couldn't bear it, but he did it anyway.

"No," she begged as he licked her. "Please not that."

"Suck me then."

He rearranged himself, pushed his cock in her face. He was on top, always on top. She mouthed his balls, then opened wide to take his length into her mouth. Who needed breathing? She gripped his cock to get a better angle, took it as deep as she could. In the end, he couldn't take any more of that frustration than she could. Mouths were nice, sweet, and sexy, but they both needed *more.*

He drew away from her exuberant lips and covered her with his body a second time. No need to fumble for a condom. With others, yes, they were careful, but they were fluid-bonded to each other by agreement and necessity. There could be no barrier, no matter how slick and thin. They couldn't stand for anything to come between them, not after the private storm they'd weathered together five Octobers ago.

Patrick's hips pressed right against hers, bore down hard on her, like he was holding her against the tides. She waited a year for this, an endless year to feel the tip of his cock nudge into her, demanding entrance despite its daunting girth. She arched to him, wet as the ocean. When he pushed inside, both of them died a little before they came back to life. They died, they waited, they felt the blood in their veins before they could move and do something about it.

And then they moved.

"Oh Jesus," Patrick muttered. "Jesus, Amara, the way you feel."

Shh, she wanted to say. *Shh, it's all right.* She couldn't though, because all her breath was used up in gasps and sighs and getting accustomed to having him inside her again.

That day five years ago, she'd felt so many things she couldn't name. To this day, she couldn't name the feelings, but every year she felt them the same again, so many overwhelming thoughts and realizations. *You're inside me. I feel you. I'm still alive.*

He was big. He hurt a little, but that turned her on. She got so wet that he could fill her deeper than anyone else. She held her legs wide, tilted her hips to him, taking all of him, because he could never hurt her as much as she'd almost hurt herself. The more he filled her, the more she wanted. When his hand returned to her neck, she groaned for him to press harder, to fuck her deeper, to make her scared and then make her feel okay.

He kissed her forehead, he kissed her eyes, he fucked her and fucked her. *Yes, yes, yes.* Sometimes he held her down. Sometimes he let her go and she grasped at him instead, at his neck, his flexing shoulders.

In the end, though, they always came the same way. When she couldn't hold off her orgasm any longer, when the gasps and moans and groans turned into one long, clenching whine, Patrick held her. He wrapped his arms around her and held her so hard she could barely breathe for his closeness. His presence was everything. His presence was the thing that made her climax go on and on as he rocked inside her.

Then, when she was safe, limp with relief, clutched in his arms, he would come inside her, pounding, trembling, his face pressed against her neck.

After that, they would be still, as still as they'd been when they sat on the rocks looking out at the tropical storm, except now they were still and safe with one another. He rested inside her, and she clung to him, and everything, truly, was all right.

Every year the same, but different, because every year they knew each other a little more. Today the sun shone hard, so when they came to life again, nuzzling their cheeks together, there was more to see, more to admire in each other's eyes. They shared a soft, lingering kiss, then another before he pulled away. She loved the breathless noise he always made when he eased out of her, gratified and spent.

"You all right?" he asked, touching her forehead.

"I'm perfect. Thank you."

They laid together, as close as two people could be, nearly as close as their enveloping embrace at climax. The first day they'd met, she hadn't known what to say after he'd come inside her like that. Now, things were more comfortable, less surprising. There weren't as many questions.

The day they met, there hadn't been many questions either, just so many feelings. It was an afternoon she'd never forget.

"I'm glad you're here, Amara," he said. "It's so good to see you."

"Yeah," she answered. "I'm so glad both of us are here."

2

They're on the beach again, later. Time has passed, time enough to make love twice, to shower in the cottage's sandy bathroom, to unpack a little, then make love again.

The sun's not quite gone, but it's a little colder now. They huddle together, once again staring out at the horizon, at the orange-gold water and the low, rickety pier. They speak of the day they met, every year. It's not easy, but they have to do it. It's ritual. Sacred duty.

"It's so calm," said Patrick. "Not like that day. That storm was crazy."

"That's what brought us here, wasn't it? The storm drew us like a magnet. Miserable people..."

Her voice trailed off. He picked up the thread, drew it tighter.

"When you're miserable, you look for ways to fuck yourself up. You collect the ideas in your head. Ways to destroy yourself."

That October day five years ago, both of them had ended up on the same deserted stretch of Danger Beach as a tropical storm buffeted the coastline, rocking the houses and kicking up sand and debris. She hadn't noticed Patrick when she got there. She'd been so spun up in her own loneliness and misery, in her black pall of a skirt, she hadn't seen anything but the pounding, oversize waves.

"I had a good year," she said, shaking away the memory of those waves, their rushing sound, their frenzied whitecaps. The waves were calm this year. "I accomplished a lot of things."

"You got a job." He gave her a congratulatory pat on the back. "You're a working journalist."

"You finished your residency. Being a doctor is more impressive than reporting on local politics."

"Local politics are important. You're important. Don't put yourself down."

He sounded like her therapist. Well, he was her therapist, and she was his, because they'd made a pact to always look out for each other. They spoke online almost every day, even when they weren't together. They kept up with each other's busy lives, with the small victories and irritating defeats, as well as the big victories, like her new job or his triumphant finish to his residency. He was a licensed doctor now, ready to save people in emergency rooms. She was a reporter who could be a voice for transparency and integrity in government.

"What a difference five years makes," she said.

"What a difference," he echoed. "We're lucky."

Five years ago, she'd kicked off her shoes on a stormy, gusting beach and walked into the water, right here, right along this shore. The water was cold that day but not freezing. Not cold enough to jolt her out of her suicidal stupor. She'd tried to off herself before, half-hearted attempts that failed, but now, she thought, she had nature on her side. Once she swam out far enough, she wouldn't be able to get back if she tried, not with the currents and the wind, and the lightning flashing overhead. The family wedding had been the last straw. *I will never find love. I don't belong. No one loves me. The world would be better if I wasn't here.* All the things a person's brain mutters when they stop taking the medicine they're supposed to take.

She hadn't seen Patrick as she waded into the water, but he saw her. He watched as she fought through the brutal surf to get out, out, out beyond safety.

He was on the same stretch of Danger Beach that day, for the exact same reason. He was failing out of medical school, running out of money to continue. His mother had died of cancer, and his father had stopped caring about life, caught up in a haze of alcohol and grief. Patrick wasn't strong enough to help him, not smart enough to be the doctor he'd always dreamed of being. He couldn't do anything, fulfill any of his dreams.

But he loved the water, he'd told Amara later. He loved the beach. When his family lived in Brisbane, when he was a boy, they went to the beach almost every day. So when the storm came, blowing in on an unthinking, unfeeling weather system, he'd thought, *Why not?*

Then he saw her, saw her start flailing and going under, and thought, *Why?*

He'd abandoned his bid to sink beneath the waves because he couldn't bear to watch her struggle. He'd swum over to her, two hundred yards or more through stormy, choppy waters—unlike Amara, he was a very strong swimmer—and he'd grabbed her hard. This was the part they both remembered together, because it happened to both of them. He grabbed her arms hard and jerked her from the current and started dragging her toward the land.

"What are you doing here?" she'd sputtered, breathless. Shocked.

"What are *you* doing here?" he'd shouted back, furious. Furious that she'd drawn him from the brink of his own disaster. "What the fuck are we doing here?"

The storm had been at a fever pitch then. Across the beach, shingles flipped like clumsy turtles, blown off the roofs of the shoddy beach cottages. Rain pelted them so hard they could barely see. They half walked, half stumbled to the pile of rocks beside the pier, not ready to leave the beach yet, to abandon what they'd psyched themselves up to do.

"What the fuck?" he'd yelled at her as they collapsed together on the wet rocks.

"I don't want to live anymore," she'd shrieked over the wind. "I'm all alone. I'm tired of being alone."

They disagreed over what happened next. Patrick thought that lightning hit the pier. He said the boom was that close, that he could smell the burning wood, even in the rain. Amara thought it hit farther out to sea, but either way, they started to run. He scooped her up and made her run, and they found their way through the rain and shells and seaweed and shingles, bare feet sinking into sodden sand. A deck chair flew from nowhere, skidding across the beach.

"We have to get inside," he yelled over nature's careless din.

"Inside" was the cottage he'd rented to try to get his head together, the cottage they returned to on this day every year. He'd pulled her up the stairs and through the door, and then there had been peace, if not silence.

The storm had been so strong that day, it made the cottage tremble on its stilts. The ceiling fan above them in the living room had rocked so violently it creaked. Amara burst into tears and cried harder than she'd cried in her life. Her life that had almost ended...but now she wasn't alone. The stranger, this man was holding her, squeezing her, crying himself, weeping in the terrifying, croaking way that men weep when they have never allowed themselves to cry.

They'd almost died, the two of them. Almost left this world, alone, but here they were, holding one another, keeping one another safe. That was early afternoon, when they clung to each other in a sort of rebirth. At some point, when she calmed enough, Amara took off her cold, gritty clothes and left them in a heap, and put on clothes that Patrick gave her. There was leftover pizza in the refrigerator, pizza he'd barely eaten because he'd decided to die. They shared it now, staring at each other in a kind of shock.

Their friendship, five years old now, began with tentative words. Explanation, grief, regret, excuses, anger, remorse, confusion, depression, gratitude. The talking grew easier, the relief grew greater, and as the storm blew by, angst was replaced by euphoria. *Here we are, two survivors.*

Amara told Patrick that he'd saved her life. He told her that she'd saved his. They'd made love as night fell, as the storm abated to silence and the ceiling fans stopped rocking over their heads. They'd spent three days together afterward, getting their land legs again. Getting strong enough to try again, to take their second chances and make something of them.

Before they parted, they made a pact to see each other again in a year.

Now here they were, five years later, on the rocks by the pier. Five years could make a world of difference. Five minutes could make a world of difference. She rested her head on his shoulder. He pulled her closer, squeezing her hand.

"What are you thinking?" he asked.

"So many things. Whenever I'm with you, I think about so many things, but not in a bad way. It's like...you help me. Being with you makes everything clearer and more comfortable."

"Yeah, for me, too. I feel the same."

"Maybe because we saw each other at our worst, at the very lowest points of our lives, and we were still okay with each other. It's not as easy for me to be comfortable with anyone else."

He made a soft sound, a chuckle. “Still dating all the guys? Trying not to be alone?”

She sat straighter and shook her head. “No, I’m over that.” *Because none of them measure up to you.* “I’m trying to just be a healthy me, you know? New job. New hobbies.”

“Scuba lessons, huh? I saw the pics.”

“Well, I knew you were into it.” She grinned at him. “Might try to see that Great Coral Reef one day.”

“Ooh.”

“I happen to know an Australian guy. He said it was pretty cool.”

The wind blew up for a second, capturing his laugh. “I’d love to scuba with you, Amara.”

“Maybe we can meet up there next year, instead of here. Or go on some scuba cruise together…”

“Mm. Maybe,” he said, noncommittal.

She bit her lip. Coming here, sitting on these rocks, it held a lot of meaning for both of them. Maybe it was too soon to abandon Danger Beach for more exciting activities. “Or whatever. Whatever you want to do.”

Patrick sighed and turned to her, his dark hair tousled by the sea air. “I don’t know. I’ve been thinking about this, and… Well, this ‘until next year’ thing is getting hard for me. I mean, we needed those years to get our shit together, yes.”

She stared down at the sand. “I like it, though. Meeting up every year to reconnect.”

“I like it, too. It’s just…” He rubbed his neck, the muscles straining against his palm. “I have my shit together now.”

And I’m ready to move on. If he said the words, they would crush her. She’d find a way to get on with her life, but…

“And I look forward to these yearly meetings with more than anticipation.”

“What?”

While she’d been freaking out, he’d kept talking. She turned back to him, met his intent gaze.

“Here’s the thing, Amara.” He paused and blinked, and glanced out at the water, just for a moment. “It’s getting too hard for me to wait a year. I see you in October and I’ve got my fix for a few months. Then it wears off and I’d like to see you again, but there are months yet to go. Being online with you isn't the same as being here, in person, where I can touch you and see you and feel you next to me."

He took her hands and held her closer, as if to shelter her from the wind.

"I thought you were going to say you didn't want to come anymore." Her fingers curled within his. "Now that you're through your residency, looking for a job."

"I want to get a job somewhere near you. I'm a doctor. I can work anywhere. If we lived closer..."

The panic inside her leaked out in a sigh. "Wow. Yeah. I could work anywhere, too. There are local politics everywhere."

"Do you see what I'm saying, though? Why are we doing this? It's been five years now. I think we should be together all the time. We've had our years apart to do what we needed to do, to get stronger and more stable, and we had those years because of each other. I wouldn't be here without you."

"I wouldn't be here without you, either. You saved my life."

"But there's more between us," he said. "When I'm not with you, I want you. I miss you. Every year, when I see you walk across the beach, I feel like I can take my first deep breath in months. 'Until next year' isn't enough for me anymore. You're here with me now, and all I can think is how happy that makes me and that I don't want to wait until next year to have this again."

He held her arms like he didn't want her to get away. It reminded her of the way he'd grabbed her in the water that day five years ago. She'd looked at his face, the face of the person who wouldn't let her flow into eternity, who thought she ought to try again. His eyes had been so intense, holding the force of an entire world. His expression had frightened her, but she'd known to give in and trust him, and let him drag her ashore.

So much had happened in those five years, so much for the better, but one thing hadn't changed, and that was the trust between them.

"I love you so much," she said, clinging to him as she had that day. "I don't want to wait until next year either."

It was settled then. They kissed on it, a tender, wondering kiss that went on and on. They could make more plans later, but for now they embraced as the sea breeze whispered past them. *You're safe*, it said. *You're safe.*

Even if the wind blew like a storm, like a hurricane, she knew she'd be safe with him.

"Let's walk down the beach," he said. "It's so beautiful today. More beautiful than ever."

They left the rocks and joined hands and set off on the first steps of a future together, a future that, maybe, was always meant to be.

* * *

Do you want more of Annabel Joseph?

One click WAKING KISS now!

MAL + ANNE + 1

A STAGE DIVE SHORT STORY

KYLIE SCOTT

1

"Pumpkin? Anne? You all right?"

I groaned, rubbing my lower back and various other parts of my body because oh my God. Four in the morning was such an awesome time for the baby to go to town kicking my bladder and various other internal organs. Sleep all day, party all night. It was fun to be a rock star's progeny.

"Time to pee," I mumbled. "Again."

He clicked on the bedside light, bathing the room in a soft golden glow. Tussled blond locks stood out in every which direction. Damn the man for making bed hair look good. "Anything I can I do?"

"No. Go back to sleep, Mal."

"Okay."

Killer, our Boston Terrier, stirred in his little doggy bed and gave me a disinterested look. Snacks and treats weren't given at this hour, so there was no point in getting up. He cuddled with his latest chewed-up Converse (another one of Mal's) and went back to sleep. Life was simple when you were a pupper. Especially a spoiled one like him.

I waddled toward the bathroom. Pregnancy was such utter bullshit. Don't get me wrong, the first six or so months weren't too bad once the morning sickness stopped. But then you just get bigger and bigger and bigger. They called it a baby bump. Damn liars. More like a baby blimp. No position, sleeping- or sexwise, was comfortable. A pity because I enjoy both resting and banging my husband. I can't even remember the last time I saw my toes or put socks on without contorting myself in some weird manner. Lower back pain was my new friend, and maternity yoga pants and oversize T-shirts were about the only things that fit me anymore. I don't care if people had been doing this since the dawn of time. All that mattered was that for me, right here and right now, pregnancy sucked. Thirty-nine weeks in and I just wanted my baby already. Now.

And then it happened. A stream of water shot out from between my legs, arcing up gracefully before descending and splashing all over the polished wooden floor, like I'd turned into a fountain or something. For a moment, I just stared, bewildered.

"Um, Mal?"

A sleepy grunt from over on the bed.

"I think my waters just broke."

An almighty rustling of blankets and sheets came from the general direction of the bed. "What? Are you serious?"

"Don't see how it could be anything else. Can you get me a couple of towels please?"

"You bet." In a show of dexterity, the man leaped from the bed and ran toward the bathroom. Unfortunately, he was in such a panicked rush that he made straight for the puddle, slipped and fell. Crash, boom, bang. Killer barked and danced around us. He stopped and sniffed the puddle once before going back to barking. This was all apparently very exciting for a pupper.

"Fuck," muttered Mal from the floor.

"Are you all right?"

"Yeah."

"No concussion?"

He rubbed the back of his head. "I got a pretty thick skull."

"That's true. Maybe we should calm down and not panic."

"Let's not be too hasty. The more we panic now, the better the stories we'll have to tell later."

"That comment sums your life philosophy up perfectly. But I think in all fairness you should have told me that was your motto sometime before you made me complicit in reproducing your gene pool."

"I'm serious. Now we have a great party story to tell about how I slipped and almost killed myself when your waters broke, and then swam manfully through the stuff to get you some towels." Writhing pathetically across the floor, he managed to get to the bath towels on the wall.

"I can't help thinking this story will be rather different depending on which of us is telling it."

He arrived back with the towels, sopping the floor around my feet. "True. I'm too busy being heroic to even notice how hot my mostly naked body must look to you right now."

"I know, right. All slick with amniotic fluid. What a turn-on."

His work mostly done, he grinned up at me. "I love you, Pumpkin."

"I love you too."

"We're going to be parents."

I nodded. "Yep."

"Solely responsible for a tiny little person who will communicate mostly by screaming at us. Or that's what Jimmy said."

"Well, he and Lena have twins. Hopefully just one baby won't be so hard to manage," I said. "Why don't we worry about that later and get to the hospital now?"

"Good idea."

Nice and slow, he got back to his feet and grabbed another towel off the wall, passing it to me. With the towel pressed against my crotch, I grabbed a change of clothes, etcetera, then got busy cleaning up. Mal appeared in a T-shirt and jeans, his hair dark from a ninety-second shower. He looked at me and I nodded. The time had come. I was in labor. Okay. We could do this.

TWENTY HOURS LATER

"I can't do this."

Mal tenderly wiped the sweat and tears from my face with a wet cloth. "You can. I believe in you."

"No," I wailed. "What do you even know anyway?"

Mal opened his mouth to answer, but Lizzy got there first. "Just breathe, Anne."

"Here comes another." Breathing in pants, I pushed as the pain took me over from head to toe. "Oh God."

Dr. Garcia, the OB/GYN, smiled encouragingly from where she stood between my legs. Fuck dignity. It had no place here. And while everyone was being so supportive, I was the only one who could push this behemoth baby out. Talk about unfair. I'd been so damn brave putting off having an epidural until it was time to push and therefore too damn late.

"The head is crowning," said Dr. Garcia. "That's it, Anne. You're doing great."

"Everyone is here for you. They can't wait to meet your baby." Lizzy smiled. Dark circles sat beneath her eyes. Fair enough considering we'd been at the hospital trying to bring this baby into the world for approximately seventy-two years and counting. Or that's what it felt like.

"It hurts. Oh man, it hurts so bad." Woe was me. "Wait. Who is humming the tune from *Rocky*?"

Mal pursed his lips. "Sorry. Just trying to be supportive."

"New rules." I pushed a strand of sweat-damp hair back off my face, focusing on the matter at hand. "No tapping out drumbeats on my belly while I'm in labor."

"I was saying welcome in Morse code."

"It's a baby, Mal," said Liz. "Pretty sure they don't come into existence already knowing Morse code."

"Since any child of mine, and of my awesome and right now particularly beautiful wife, is bound to be a prodigy, I don't think we can rule anything out at this point." Liz glared at him, and his shoulders sagged in an exaggerated fashion. "Fine."

"No snapping selfies that include me when I'm in the middle of a contraction and posting them to Instagram."

"I'm just so proud of you, and you know how much my two-point-one-million-more-than-Jimmy-has followers love you. Well...apart from a few of them. The more overly possessive, slightly fucking strange ones."

"No photos, Mal."

"All right, Pumpkin," he said in a resigned tone. "Though in my defense, I did tell the documentary crew they couldn't come in."

"You did one thing right. Yes."

At this, he high-fived himself. "Is that all the rules?"

"No humming inspirational movie themes during labor," suggested Lizzy.

"And that," I agreed.

He scratched his stubbly chin. "But what about the love theme from the *Titanic*?"

"They die. No."

"How about we skip movies entirely and just go for 'Bohemian Rhapsody'? Pretty sure I could hit the high notes."

"Mal..."

"Some Nirvana, maybe?"

I said nothing.

"Fine." He looked to heaven. "Whatever. But you're sucking all the fun out of this. I thought we could all have a little nitrous oxide, kick back and relax. But no, you had to make this labor all about you. Way to share, Anne. You're setting the baby a great example."

Give me strength. "I'm going to pretend you didn't say any of that because I don't even have the energy to threaten to kill you, let alone hit you with something right now. How the hell do people do this more than once?"

Lizzy shrugged. "No idea. You won't see me rushing back for another anytime soon, and Lena said she's done."

"See how you feel once you've got your baby in your arms," said the midwife, Gaylin. She was nice. Having had children of their own, both her, Lizzy, and Dr. Garcia understood my pain.

Mal did not. "I thought we'd settled on three?"

"Then you figure out a way to carry and birth them," I snapped. Being in extreme pain while you lay half-naked with your nether regions exposed to the world and your feet up in stirrups does not tend to put you in a great mood. Funny that.

"Yes, Pumpkin."

Liz snickered. "Good answer."

"Here it comes." I gripped Mal's and Liz's hands brutally tight, pushing with all my might as another contraction hit me. "Get it out. Get it out. Get it out."

"Nearly there, Anne," said the doctor. "That's it. Here comes the head."

"Breathe, baby. C'mon, Pumpkin. You got this."

"Push, Anne. Push." I don't even know who said that, but I pushed for all I was worth and then some. I pushed my goddamn heart out.

Not to be resentful of my not quite born child or anything, but this baby's head was ginormous. Quite possibly even bigger than their father's ego, and that was saying something. Another mighty push accompanied me yelling out cuss words like it was my job, and the baby slipped from my body and into the doctor's waiting hands. Holy hell.

"It's a boy!" Mal pumped a fist into the air. "We have a son, Pumpkin."

My smile was a trembling, weary thing. Yet the joy swelling inside my chest was off the charts. "A boy?"

A cranky cry filled the air. I'd never been so relieved to hear anything in my life. I didn't quite understand how worried I'd been about basically everything until I heard that noise.

"A healthy baby boy by the sound of things." Gaylin, the midwife, smiled and clamped the cord and so on. "Congratulations."

With our son wrapped up in a white blanket, Mal carried him over to me. "Come and meet your beautiful, brave, and all-round wonderful mama," cooed Mal. "You made a baby, Pumpkin. Fucking amazing."

"Hello, Tomas David Ericson." I'd never smiled so hard in my life. Nothing could have prepared me for the rush of love I felt for him. Nothing. Little fists waved in the air, still rather annoyed about the whole being-born thing. And his features were so tiny and perfect. Big blue eyes gazed vaguely in my direction. What with being used to the tiny terrors that were Lena and Jimmy's twin girls and my own very excitable nephew, Gibson, the baby's cry didn't seem all that loud after all. "Hello, my baby. Hey, Tommy."

"That's his name?" asked Liz, taking a peek at the baby.

Mal nodded. "Tommy for the drummer from the Ramones, the musical by The Who, and Thomas Hardy, who is apparently some writer dude Anne likes but nobody else in the real world has actually heard of."

"Hi, Tommy," said Liz in a gentle voice. "Hey there, baby. And to think, this is the kind of amazing you can produce while being annoyed by crazy pants here the entire time. My big sister is a talented lady."

"Puh-lease." Mal scoffed. "I only annoyed her because it distracted her from the pain. I knew what I was doing the whole time."

I scrunched up my nose. "No, it… Actually it did, didn't it?"

"Huh," said Lizzy.

"You're welcome." He gave me a grin, gently rocking our son in his arms. "The doctor wants to look him over. I'll bring him back in a minute. I love you."

"I love you too."

"Having trouble writing something other than your signature?" Liz's voice roused me from my dozed state.

"What?" Mal was leaning against the wall, a clipboard and pen in his hands. He sounded defensive. "No. It's just that the birth certificate is an official document. I had to make sure to get the spelling right and everything. Some things you can't rush. It's all good."

"Hand it over." Liz squared off in front of him, arm outstretched.

"Dammit." Mal scowled and handed the clipboard over.

"*Godzilla Velociraptor* Ericson!"

"Mal!" I shrieked.

"No, Liz, it's *pronounced* Tomas David Ericson. Or Tommy for short. But it's spelled Godzilla Velociraptor Ericson."

Liz stalked off in search of the nurse. "Can we have a new certificate to fill out please?"

"You guys are no fun. Imagine his first day of school."

I groaned and tried to get my exhausted brain to wake the hell up. I hadn't meant to doze off in the first place. We had visitors, after all.

Flowers and soft toys filled just about every available surface while the members of Stage Dive and their partners filled the chairs. The hospital room was large and luxurious, which was nice. And it smelled divine like a florist's shop. All other deliveries and congratulations would have to go to our apartment in Portland's Pearl District. We were out of room here. As for safety, Bon and Ziggy stood guard outside the door.

"A lot of press downstairs," warned David, the lead guitarist. His wife, Evelyn, sat on his lap, carefully holding Tommy. Both of them appeared enamored, and David's finger looked huge wrapped in the baby's small fist.

Having recently been fed, Tommy seemed content to give being on the outside a chance. Or at least, the crying had stopped for now. Since he'd arrived just after midnight, it was still the day of his birth. We'd all gotten some much necessary sleep during the day. Though we were both still tired. From what I'd heard and seen, however, that's just the way things would be for a while. Outside, the city lights stained the darkness.

"Agreed." Mal hovered near the baby, constantly on guard. It was sweet and hot to see him all papa-bear protective in his ripped black jeans and faded long-sleeve Henley with his long blond hair tied back. “We’ll put out a statement later. Something vague.”

David nodded. “The less they know about our private lives the better.”

“Right, no posting pics of him to Instagram, Jimmy,” said Mal. “That’s not cool.”

“How are you feeling, Anne?” asked Lena, cutting off her husband’s inevitable retort.

I smiled. “Sore. Tired. But fine.”

The twins and Gibson played with coloring books and crayons on the floor. A newborn baby wasn’t all that interesting to small children, apparently. A kids’ TV show played quietly on a tablet set next to the trio, and juice boxes and snacks were to hand. I couldn’t imagine Tommy being that big in a few years. He was so small in comparison. Though he hadn’t felt small coming out. Guess none of them did. My poor innocent vagina.

“Killer is enjoying his visit with us.” Evelyn grinned. “We left him curled up on the couch with a chew toy.”

“Thank you for that,” I said.

“Anytime.”

“My turn,” announced Lena, carefully lifting Tommy from Ev’s arms. “Hello, I’m your Aunt Lena. I have lots and lots of toys at my house. You’ll be interested in them when you’re older. Oh, he’s so light. I’d forgotten how small newborns are. And the twins were even tinier at first.”

“Do not get clucky.” Jimmy set his ankle on his other knee, watching his wife hold the baby. “I mean it, Lena.”

“Clucky? Please. You were the one suggesting another baby wouldn’t be so bad.”

“No. I suggested practicing making another baby wouldn’t be so bad.”

From his seat in the corner, Ben snorted.

Lena stuck her tongue out at her husband.

“At least when you put them in their bed at that age, they stay there.” Ben watched his son with a faint smile. “Gibby keeps trying to climb into our bed at night.”

“Do not,” said the child in question.

“Oh yes, you do. Aunty Martha said you even tried it at her and Uncle Sam’s house.”

Gibby gave his father a withering look before returning to his coloring.

The big bass player just smiled. "You and Anne have a lot of fun times ahead of you."

"They still have the nappies, puking up sour milk, and incessant crying to go through before they hit the good stuff." Lena stopped and sniffed the baby. "Speaking of which, time for a change of pants for you, my friend. Here you go, Mal."

Mal's eyes widened in alarm. "Uh, he needs to be changed? But you're good at that. You should do it, Lena. It'll be like bonding time."

"Forget it, pal. You're changing your own son's nappy."

"You haven't done one yet?" asked Jimmy with a scowl.

"He hasn't been out that long!" Mal protested, taking back his now crying son. "Sorry, Tommy. Daddy didn't mean to raise his voice. He was just being picked on by our evil, nasty friends. Yes, he was. Poor Daddy."

"Are you okay with him?" I asked, sitting up a bit farther. Ouches.

"I'm fine. I can do it."

"And he will." Ben rose from his chair, following Mal and the baby over to the change table.

"I don't need you looking over my shoulder," hissed Mal.

"Figure you need someone watching who has a clue."

"Whatever." And Mal got busy. Since the table had sides, I couldn't see much. Tommy's little hands waved in the air and a not so nice smell came from his general direction. Mal and Ben fought quietly over how to get him out of his gray-and-white stripe baby suit. Then Mal reared back in horror. "Oh good God. My son. What have you done?"

"Black and tarlike for the first few days, then it goes more normal," said Ben.

"Don't try and sugarcoat it, Ben. It's obvious that my child is the demon harbinger of the apocalypse. From the moment Anne got pregnant, we all knew this was a possible result."

"Wait until he does a power poop right up his back." Liz retied her long blonde hair in a low ponytail. "Those are truly special events."

Jimmy blew out a breath. "In all honesty, some of those onesies I just threw out. There was no getting all the poop off them. It had gone everywhere. I didn't even want to try to deal with the mess."

"You did not. That's terrible." Lena laughed.

"We were surviving on next to no sleep with two very demanding baby girls. Sacrifices had to be made."

"C'mon, Mal. Keep going," said Ben. "You got to get the job done or his little legs are going to get cold in this air-conditioning."

"Yeah, yeah." Mal nudged a strand of hair out of his eyes with the back of his hand. "This is like diffusing a bomb. Please stop crying, Tommy. Daddy's trying his hardest here. But your poop is really weird and sticky, bro. There you go, I think you're clean now."

"Do you need help?" I asked.

"Anne, you're supposed to be resting." Ev raised a brow. "He's a big boy. He can handle it on his own."

"He needs to learn sometime. Might as well be now," said Ben. "That's it, just slip the new one underneath him. No, position it a little higher. About there'll do."

"Brain surgery can't even be this hard," mumbled Mal. "Oh God, I've got poop on me."

"Stop being so precious." Lena crossed her arms, a smirk on her lips. "At least he's not peeing on you."

"Yet." Ben shot her an amused glance.

Ev bit back a smile. "How many millions are your hands worth again, Mal?"

"Don't mock me, child bride." Mal, tongue sticking out in thought, fit the baby's feet back into his suit. Not so easy to do since Tommy was kicking. "You just might be here facing this dark and perilous quest one day."

"Oh, please. I already know how to change a nappy."

"Me too," added Dave.

"Way to have my back, man." Mal pouted. "It's just you, me, and Mommy, Tommy. Everyone else is against us. And...you're done. Yes! Victory!"

"My turn." Ben picked Tommy up off the change table, narrowing his eyes on the baby's face. "He looks like Anne and Liz. Got the same shaped face. Very similar to Gibby when he was born."

"And me." Over at the basin, Mal turned on the taps and soaped up his hands. "Mostly me. Because I mean, he's so good-looking, right? The kid is ridiculously handsome. So it's got to be me."

"Whatever, man. Hey, Tommy. Welcome to the world, my friend."

"There's enough second-generation Stage Dive babies to start a band now," said David, arms wrapped around Ev's waist, drawing her back against his chest.

"Nuh." Jimmy shook his head. "Twins will probably be a duo like The White Stripes. Fierce girl-power rock 'n' roll."

Ben lifted a still-crying Tommy to his shoulder, positioning him carefully before rubbing his back in small circles while he did a back-and-forth movement. "Gibby will probably be a solo act. He's not that big on sharing, and Adam is his current hero."

"God help us all if he takes after Adam," said Lena. "Did you hear the latest story about him from Martha? He trashed a hotel room!"

Ben frowned. "I'm going to have to have a talk to that boy."

"Rock star's gotta do what a rock star's gotta do. There's a fine tradition of trashing hotel rooms and riding motorcycles through hotel lobbies for us to live up to." Hands clean, Mal started doing a slow-motion lap of the room with his hands in the air humming the tune from *Rocky*. Again. "I have conquered the nappy of death and ruin. Woo-hoo."

"Good work." I gave him a thumbs-up. "Is Tommy hungry again, do you think?"

"With babies it's always a guess," answered Ben, never stopping the gentle back-and-forth rocking motion and back rubbing. "But I think, if we turn the lights down and lower our voices, he might just go to sleep."

"Quiet voices," whisper hissed Gibby.

Ben smiled. "That's right."

Since his third victory lap took him by the light switches, Mal turned off the bulk of the lights, giving the room a shadowy, intimate atmosphere. And the swelling, amazing joyful feeling in my chest seemed so big that it might burst right on out of me *Aliens* style. Messy, but potent. Just as Ben had prophesised, Tommy's cries gradually quieted down to almost nothing at all. A hiccup and a whimper and the baby fell asleep.

"Do you want us to leave?" asked Ev in a whisper.

I shook my head. "Not if you don't want to."

"You all right, Pumpkin?" Mal slid onto the bed beside me. "Looking suspiciously teary there."

"Probably hormones," said Liz with a smile. "Though you've gone through a lot in the last day and a half."

"No." I shook my head, wiping a tear from my eye. "I love our family. That's all."

Mal smiled, planting a kiss against my forehead. "We do have a pretty great one. And now with Tommy as well..."

"Yeah. It's perfect." I turned my head and kissed him on the lips, soft and sweet. "Absolutely perfect."

* * *

Do you want more of Kylie Scott?

One click REPEAT now!

WALTZ WITH ME, MATILDA

TAMSEN PARKER

1

"Oh, Tilda, no. Honey, no."

I slumped and my eyes watered as Alvaro corrected my form. Again. For what must have been the fiftieth time tonight. Which might have been okay. I was good at taking direction. It was one of the things that made me a fine consultant. I was even better at listening to what my clients *thought* they wanted and giving them something that wasn't what they asked for but fulfilled the function they needed it to, and making them feel like it had been their idea. That was what made me a *phenomenal* consultant.

I didn't know enough about goddamn ballroom dance, however, to pull my usual tricks, and it was frustrating as all hell.

I had anticipated some frustration when I signed up for this class, was in fact counting on it, but I'd also had some misguided fantasies about what would happen when I showed up to begin my lessons. There was supposed to be some six-foot-five Prince Charming who could spin me around the studio for an hour before I went back to my empty apartment. Or hell, I was not picky. I would've taken a man of any height as long as he wasn't intimidated by me, knew what he was doing, and would lead. That's what I wanted; that's why I'd come here.

But as per usual, because I was six fucking feet tall and not a model-thin waif, I got assigned the male part. I was expected to take charge, to lead. It perhaps hadn't been fair for me to expect some random dude to take on the weight of my needs and expectations, but I was bordering on desperate and I just...

I wanted to be touched, held, guided, and then I wanted to go about my everyday life where I kicked ass and didn't take names because I had a goddamn assistant for that. And wow had my plan backfired. Real hard.

Alvaro was nudging my elbows, poking at my back, grabbing my hips and squaring them. I sighed apologetically to Polly, who was a far better dancer than I was but who had arrived late to class today and so ended up partnered with me. She gave me a tightly annoyed smile as I mouthed, *Sorry*.

"Again, ladies. You're both magnificent and proud. You don't lack for coordination—this should be lovely. Again!"

Then he spun off, counting, clapping, stomping, trying to turn his class of ugly ducklings into swans. Except I felt more like a goose. A very ill-tempered goose.

* * *

I hauled my carry-on and laptop bag up the stairs to the entrance of my apartment building, feet and shoulders sore after my long flight and class since I hadn't had time to come home and change after touching down at the airport.

Out of habit, I stopped to check my mailbox, the corner of my mouth tipping up as opening the spring-loaded door revealed an empty metal box. Not because I didn't have mail—I would—but because Bastian had remembered I was due back after the mail had come, and so he'd checked both our mailboxes again today.

Bastian Sydney Balter was my hot, reclusive neighbor. I traveled a ton, and he worked from home. He had also appointed himself as some sort of caretaker of my affairs because he thought I was a flake.

I wasn't—not really—but I did have a habit of forgetting my keys in my door. And I didn't always remember to have the post office stop my mail when I traveled, which was why he had a key and would do it for me when I was away.

In return, he would occasionally ask me to make him a spreadsheet or explain something about tech or taxes—things he seemed to believe I was competent at. And if he hadn't asked me for anything in a while, I'd bake him cookies. He liked my snickerdoodles. Which was not some kind of euphemism. Unfortunately.

Bastian was difficult to read, but I was pretty sure he thought of me as a force for chaos that he did his best to keep orderly so as not to disturb his world overmuch. Which was unfortunate because the guy was like six-six and the kind of handsome it was fundamentally wrong to keep cooped up in an apartment building all the time.

Wide-set baby-blue eyes that sloped down at the outside corners, making him seem as though he was perpetually giving bedroom eyes, sandy-brown hair that had volume to die for, and his beard was...well. Let's just say I wouldn't mind riding that ride if I thought he was at all interested. Which he wasn't, so we were cordial. Maybe friendly, on a good day.

Once I reached my apartment, I dropped my shit, petted my cat who Bastian had already fed, of course, as per his neatly printed note he left stuck to the food container. He was very concerned about Sheila and how irregularly I fed her even though my vet had assured me it was fine.

It was getting late, so I didn't bother to change before I wandered back out and down the hall to Bastian's apartment and knocked softly on the door. He wouldn't be asleep but he might be writing and I didn't want to disturb him if he was.

He was a very successful self-published sci-fi author, and while he mostly treated his work like any other kind—sitting down at his computer at eight thirty and writing until he called it quits at five—I knew he sometimes had fits of inspiration that he would take advantage of, headphones clapped over his ears and typing away late into the night, sometimes through the next morning. That's how he'd written the book that was on its third week on the USA Today list, and I didn't want to be held responsible for breaking his artistic trance or whatever it was.

But it was only a few seconds before the door was cracked open and he was standing there with a couple of reusable totes in his hands, brimming with the contents of my mailbox from the past three days. What can I say, I have a little catalog shopping issue.

He handed them over wordlessly, and I offered him a small smile through the exhaustion that had just hit me like a truck.

"Thanks," I murmured as I took them from his hands, enjoying too much the warmth of his skin as our fingers brushed.

A tiny wrinkle formed between his heavy brows, and he crossed his arms over his broad chest as he leaned against the doorframe.

"You okay, Tilda?"

I swallowed, trying to ignore the tightness in my throat because the truth was that I was not okay, and the rumble of his deep voice was not helping anything. Nor were the corded muscles of his forearms, nor was his being sort of effortlessly caring in his remote way, and—as much as I hated to admit it because I didn't want to be that kind of girl—him being tall.

I'd be lying if I said I didn't sometimes fantasize about Bastian while I got myself off. That his stoic silence and intense but inscrutable gazes were actually signs he was desperately in love with me. That one day when I was showing him the updates I'd made to his income and expense tracking spreadsheet, that he would rest his big hand over mine before circling his strong fingers around my wrist, tipping up my chin with his other hand and saying, "Tilda, let me take you to bed. And if you're game for it, I'd love to top you. I know you're strong and sharp and savvy and a goddess with a pivot table—that's one of the reasons I'd like to tell you what to do, tie you up if that's okay. It would be the greatest compliment of my life if you thought I was worthy of taking you over, if only for a few hours."

Yep. But real-life Bastian spoke maybe half-a-dozen words at a time and had never given even the slightest hint of having anything but a vague responsibility for me and my hectic existence. Like, yeah, he would check my mail and feed my cat and stock my fridge when I came back from a long trip. That wasn't because he *liked* me; it was because it pained him to think of anyone living so chaotically.

"Mmhmm, yep, sure am," I said with as much chipper energy as I could manage, and then biting down hard on the inside of my cheek so I wouldn't cry.

The wrinkle between his brows deepened, and I almost thought his mouth might be pulling into a frown, but it was hard to tell under all that beard.

"I know I'm not supposed to say this, but you maybe seem like you aren't?"

I took a hard swallow because what I wanted was to drop my mail on the floor and take a few steps until I was pressed against his big body, shock him into putting his arms around me and making me feel safe and cared for if only for a moment.

"You could come in and...talk? If you wanted to."

I must've looked worse than I thought if the poor guy was grasping at straws to try to make me feel better. As if he would be able to tolerate me breaking down into tears on his couch, as if he'd have any idea what to do as I tried to explain how I felt and what I wanted and how I was never going to have it. How I was incredibly slow-witted to have thought that dance lessons of all things were going to make me feel better.

Except...Bastian liked to take action, have concrete tasks. He might not listen to me talk or cuddle me or tuck me into bed and pet my hair until I fell asleep, but he liked to *do* things. And I had a problem maybe he could solve.

"Um, no, thank you. But..."

His brows lifted and the wrinkle disappeared. Curiosity? Hope? Impatience? Goddamn him and his enigmatic face.

"Would you come with me to my ballroom dance class next week?"

If Bastian were a dog, he'd be a German Shepherd. I'd thought about this a lot—probably more than was healthy—so I was very sure. Highly intelligent and loyal, also kind of uptight and needing to feel like he was working, being useful. *Well, dammit, Bastian, here's your chance to be useful. Take it.*

"I...I don't dance," he hedged.

"Neither do I."

"Then why do you go?"

It was a fair question but also not one I was eager to answer. Because I was a foolish girl who wanted a fairy tale? Because I was tired and I wanted someone to take charge in a way that was physically intimate but I could still tolerate?

I shook my head. "Never mind. Forget I asked, it was silly."

Then for the first time in my memory, he touched me. Not a brush of fingers as we exchanged parcels, not an accidental bump of shoulders as we sat close in front of his computer, but a purposeful, firm grip of his fingers above my elbow.

"It's not," he said. "Tell me."

It took my breath away.

The quiet firmness of his voice, the restrained power of his hold on me, how precise the pressure was, how big his hand was to be able to wrap two-thirds of the way around my arm. And honestly, oxygen deprivation is the only reason I can think of why the dam broke.

I did drop the bags of mail on the floor then, and one of them tipped over, catalogs and envelopes creating an avalanche of post-consumer recycled paper all over the carpeted floor.

“I don’t have a lot of time to meet people. Almost everyone I know, I work with, and I don’t date colleagues and definitely not clients. And I thought...” I swallowed, hard. “I thought maybe I could meet someone. Someone who might want to control me, be in charge of me sometimes. Like, yeah, in bed, but sometimes out of it too.

“And even if I couldn’t, then I could touch another person without it being weird because that’s what we were supposed to do. And I could rely on a man to lead even though that is usually the last thing I want. Definitely not at work. I’m tired and I’m stressed and I wanted someone to take all of that away for a little while so I could relax, so I could put my trust in someone for an hour a week. I still want that. But the thing is, I’m too tall. I’m too big. There are too many women in the class, so I have to be the man, I have to lead, and I hate it. It’s precisely the opposite of what I was looking for and I would quit but I don’t quit and...”

“And you thought I could be that person?” he asked slowly, looking at me as though that was the wildest thing he’d ever heard. Perhaps it was. Because not only had I spilled a whole bunch of highly personal information, I was also insinuating things about him that could very well not be true, that I had conjured out of thin air with all my wishful thinking. How mortifying.

That’s when the tears started, and I tried to stop them but instead ended up hiccuping and choking and wiping my eyes with my sleeve.

Bastian seemed to realize he was still holding my arm and let go. And that was... Well, that was it. I had said too much, I had let my chaos spill all over this orderly and reserved man, and now he was sorry for every time he had showed me kindness, every time he’d tried to right my erratic orbit.

I sputtered some apologies and gathered up my mail as well as I could from the floor. It was hard with the tears making my vision blurry, but I was pretty sure I got everything when I stumbled back down the hall to my apartment and shut the door behind me, half hoping Bastian would come, even though it would have embarrassed me. Even though it would be awkward.

But an hour later as I was settling into bed, Sheila curling up between my head and my shoulder and purring like a dirt bike, he still hadn’t come, and the mortification burned so hot in my chest that I couldn’t even bring myself to rub one out before I went to sleep.

* * *

After a weekend with some friends I'd had planned forever, I was off at another client's office, doing what I do best, which is help businesses set up the most effective systems to track and manage their financials.

I threw myself into it, not wanting to think about whether I would come home to a ton of mail shoved into my small post box, Sheila crying because she'd run out of food the day before, and dead plants. Because why would Bastian keep managing those things when I'd been such a heap of awkward and inappropriate? I didn't think he would.

I was usually glad to come home, if only for a night, after a trip. I loved my apartment, had made it cozy and comfortable, and if it was messy, then it was. It was my mess.

My heart lifted slightly when I opened my mailbox and it was empty. Okay, so I hadn't entirely alienated the man, that was good. Maybe we could forget what had happened the other day. Bastian did have an excellent poker face. While I did not, I was very good at brazening things out, and at some point my mortification would go from red-hot flames emanating from my cheeks to dully smoldering coals. Had to. Or maybe I'd just move.

In my apartment, Sheila greeted me by weaving through my legs and purring, and she had food and water in her bowls. Because Bastian was a good person and he wasn't going to abandon what he felt were his responsibilities even if I was a walking disaster. That's why he'd made these things his business in the first place, right?

But all the good feelings fled when I saw the pile on my dining table.

A stack of envelopes, catalogs, and packages. I always picked up my mail from him, and now he'd left it in my apartment. So he didn't have to see me. So he didn't have to subject himself to the disaster in person.

Well, that was fine. It's not like he'd been a big part of my life. We hadn't actually been friends, after all. Only neighbors who did each other favors and helped each other with things we weren't great at, who rounded each other's sharp edges. It was completely fine that I wouldn't see him anymore since he rarely left his apartment. Totally fine.

I turned on some music and started sifting through the mail, recycle bin at the ready. Ordered a new dress from one of my favorite shops. There was a catalog from the dance studio that I discarded because, yeah, no, wasn't going to be going back there after this session was over. I'd find something else to do. Maybe pottery. Maybe shooting things. Ax throwing was pretty hot at the moment.

But for now, I still had to go to dance class. Would in fact have to go for the next six weeks because I had committed, and I had paid for it. I was a lot of things, but I wasn't wasteful.

I showered because I'd be close to another human but didn't bother to pretty myself up. Even thinking about it was depressing, made me feel naive and narcissistic. I wasn't going to find a partner there of any sort so why aim any higher than basic human decency and acceptable levels of hygiene. Maybe I'd wallow with a bottle of wine when I got back in my too-tiny bathtub, my knees and breasts and shoulders poking awkwardly out of the water. For now, I had to grab my shoes and get to the studio.

* * *

Alvaro clapped his hands together to get our attention.

"Polly is out sick this week. We're supposed to have another student joining us tonight but they're obviously not here yet so you'll be with me to start, Tilda."

I nodded and attempted a smile that probably came out more as a grimace. I liked Alvaro a lot, and hey, I'd probably get to dance the women's part tonight. But we'd also look ridiculous, because Alvaro was handsome but in a delicate, petite way. He was maybe five-four, and yes, strong but svelte and elegant, not tall or hulking. At least I wouldn't have Polly glaring at me when I stepped on her foot again. I'd no doubt have the new person glaring at me instead. Yay.

"We're going to be working on the waltz this week. Does anyone know anything about the waltz?"

A few of my peers raised their hands, but instead of Alvaro calling on one of them, a familiar voice sounded behind me.

"Gaining popularity in Europe in the late eighteenth century, it's a rotating dance usually in triple time and performed mostly in the closed position. It was considered quite scandalous at the time of its introduction, given the physical intimacy required by partners."

I whipped my head around so hard and fast I almost sprained my neck. Would've been worth it, too, to see Bastian walking toward me in dress slacks and a button-front shirt. In contrast to the jeans and T-shirts—a hoodie if it was cold—I usually saw him in, this was...nice. His hair was more orderly than usual, although only just, and the whole package—him being here, looking like that—was throwing me for a loop. He came and stood in front of me, settled one of those big hands at my waist.

"What are you—"

He cut me off by leaning down, planting a kiss at the juncture where jaw meets ear that made my knees buckle, and murmured, "I'm sorry. For so many things. I'll explain later, I promise, but I'd like it if you'd conditionally accept my apology and agree to be mine for the next four hours. Please, Tilda."

I should have been angry, should have pushed him away and asked how dare he. Should've done and said so many things, but instead I nodded mutely and was rewarded with another kiss, a squeeze of his hand at my waist, and a soft "thank you."

"Ah, Mr. Balter, good to have you join us. And yes, you are precisely correct about the waltz."

Alvaro kept talking, but it was hard to focus because Bastian had pulled me into his side and then run his hand that had been at my waist up to the back of my neck and rested it there. He wasn't holding me hard, but there was a quality to the position, the weight of it that made something inside me loosen and tighten all at once.

My shoulders dropped, and everything got a little fuzzy, like one of those super-flattering soft-focus camera lenses. I'd thought it would take more than a single hand on me to make me feel dominated, controlled, at ease, but I'd been wrong.

At the same time, that specific tension that comes from being aroused was on the rise, and I could feel it curling in my body, winding its way around my erogenous zones and making me want to wrap myself around Bastian like he was a stripper pole.

I wouldn't though, because this was how he wanted me, and I wanted to enjoy it, settle in it, revel in it.

It was difficult to pay attention to Alvaro's instructions with everything that was going on in my head and in my body. When he told the class to pair off so we could get started and clapped to dismiss us, I felt only vaguely prepared.

But Bastian slipped his hand to the small of my back, led me to a free corner of the room and then pulled me to face him.

At first I went automatically to the lead position, and Bastian shook his head, gently but firmly arranged me so he was in the lead.

"I'm in charge right now, not you. Understood?"

My lips parted at the authority in his voice, and I blinked at him.

"Tell me, Tilda. Say my name."

"Yes, Bastian."

"Good girl."

He said it softly, but it hit me like a punch. How could two little words have such a visceral effect? And who was this imposter who looked like my handsome neighbor but didn't sound like him and sure as hell didn't act like him? I mean, I liked it, very much, but it was disconcerting to have my fantasies come to life right in front of me, be holding me in a dance studio after I thought I would literally never see him again. Surreal was the only way to describe it.

Alvaro put on music and I could hear him speaking, the low chatter of my classmates, but it seemed almost like white noise. The only thing I could see was Bastian's face, so close to mine. Slightly craggy nose, square jaw, and I noticed for the first time all the different shades of brown that made up his hair and his beard.

"Breathe," he instructed, a corner of his mouth tugging up, and I did.

We started moving and it was lucky we'd learned the basic box step in class before because otherwise there would be no way I was making this happen. I doubt I would've been able to move at all, never mind in some semblance of order. One of his hands in the center of my back with his fingers extended to cover some of my ribs, and the other gripping my hand and for once in my life making me feel small.

"You said you don't dance."

"I don't."

He said it easily, as though he wasn't very competently leading me in a perfect box step.

"Then what are you—"

"I have watched many, many YouTube videos on the waltz in the past several days. Alvaro was kind enough to tell me what you'd—what *we'd* be covering in class today. Made me laugh. Waltzing Matilda."

I snorted. "You know that's not at all what the song is about, right?"

His response was to clutch me closer to him, put his cheek to my own where I could feel him smile as he said, "I know."

The rest of class proceeded much the same way: Bastian's hands and lips on me, sweetly, possessively, his voice in my ear praising and so certain. It felt so much like a dream it was hard to concentrate. But I managed to focus enough because I didn't want to disappoint him. I wanted to please him, make him proud. Wanted him to claim me and tell me I was good.

At the end of class, Bastian helped me into my coat, even went so far as to button it and tie the belt at my waist, which made me flush. Dressing me? Which is when I remembered something he'd said when he'd first arrived.

"Class is only one hour. Why did you ask for four?"

"You'll see," he said slyly, taking my hand and heading toward the door.

We were about to walk out when a couple of my classmates cut us off. Jason and Alexis were a young engaged couple here to learn to dance for their wedding reception. Sweet, but I hadn't spoken with them much.

"I'm sorry, I don't mean to bother you, but..."

The man looked at his fiancée, and she made a go-ahead gesture with her hands while raising her brows.

"Just ask," she hissed.

"Yeah, okay. Um, are you Bastian Sydney Balter? The author?"

"Sure am."

The stars in the guy's eyes got even bigger, twinklier. I couldn't imagine he could see.

"Oh, wow, you're like, our favorite author. I love your books so much. Could I... Will you... Oh, man, I'm usually more articulate than this, I swear. If you'll be here next week, would you mind signing a book or two for me?"

"Yeah, of course. Bring however many you want, I'll come packing my best Sharpie."

I'd known Bastian was kind of a big deal, but I guess I hadn't realized quite how big? He was a total celeb. It didn't change how I felt about him, but it was nice to see that he was kind and humble with his fans.

"Uh, would you mind—"

Jason was trying to thrust his phone into my hand, no doubt to ask me if I could snap a pic of him and Alexis with Bastian, but then he stopped and looked at me, eyes narrowing, head tilting.

"Wait a second." Jason pointed a finger between me and Bastian, and I had no clue what the fuck was going on. Then a lightbulb seemed to go off over Jason's head, but I was still in the dark. "Oh my god, is Tilda the inspiration for Mireia from the Sentinel series?"

Bastian shot me a look. I could've been wrong, what with his beard and all, but I could've sworn he was blushing.

"Yes."

What?

"Oh, man, that is the coolest. Hey, could we get a picture with both of you then? Alvaro, would you mind?"

Jason and Alexis gathered us up and Alvaro snapped a few pics and then Jason and Alexis left, squeeing excitedly all the way down the hall. I still didn't totally grasp what had just happened, but that wasn't my most immediate concern. That would be Bastian settling his hand on the back of my neck again and guiding me out of the studio.

It felt nice and safe and warm and I was...happy. Confused, yes, but happy. I thought we'd head to the bus stop since that's how I'd gotten here, but apparently Bastian had driven and showed me to his car.

I'd seen the dark blue roadster before since our assigned parking spots were next to each other, had admired it, but had literally never seen him drive it. He handed me into the passenger seat, and I buckled in. When he'd pulled out of his spot, I had to ask.

"So are you going to explain all this now?"

"Would you mind if we waited until we got back to the building? This is going to take a while, and if we start now, it'll be all choppy."

"Sure."

So instead we made small talk. He asked me how my trip had been, and when we stopped at lights, he rested his hand above my knee. It was almost as if we'd been doing this for forever and not for barely an hour. I felt drunk on it.

It didn't take long for us to make it back to our building and to step into the elevator. When we stepped out again, Bastian looked at me with that intensity I'd never felt from him, and now I had to wonder whyever not. It practically radiated off the man.

"I'd like you to come to my apartment, but if you're not comfortable with that, I'm fine coming to yours."

I would've shrugged but his hand that was once again cuffing the back of my neck made it feel like a strange gesture. So I simply agreed.

"Yes, that's fine, Bastian."

I swear every time I said his name, something happened to him. He looked as though he wanted to bite his fist—perhaps to keep from biting me.

He didn't do either of those things, though, just walked beside me to his door and let us in.

And then his hands were cradling my face, his thumbs drawing across my cheeks.

"Unless you tell me not to, I'm going to kiss you now."

There were very few things I wanted more, so I stayed silent and after a few seconds of searching my features for a sign of resistance he wasn't going to find, Bastian pressed his lips to mine. Much like how he'd held me during our lesson, his kiss was firm and possessive, and I liked it. Allowed my body to sway toward him until not just our lips met, but all the way from our chests to our pelvises, and oh, he felt good.

His biceps swelled under my hands as he growled into my mouth and wrapped his arms around me tightly, one hand grasping my ass in a way that made me whimper. I wasn't used to being manhandled like this, and it was intoxicating. I didn't know what to do with it. And apparently Bastian wasn't entirely sure either.

He pulled away, his eyes wild and his breath coming heavy. "I'm sorry. I didn't mean to do that, I hope I didn't scare you."

"Scared is not what I'm feeling," I told him with a smile that verged on a grin.

"Okay. Good." He gathered himself then, picking up the pieces of the in-control man who had led me through a respectable waltz less than an hour earlier. "How do you feel about feet?"

Feet?

"Um, fine I suppose. I have neither fetish nor phobia."

"Come, then."

He brought me into his living room and told me to wait while he went into the bathroom. It was only moments until he was back, toting a basin of steaming water and a few towels.

"On your knees," he directed, and gestured with his chin.

Then he set the basin in front of me and sat on the couch, his thick thighs spread so his feet were on either side of the basin.

I hadn't been lying when I said I had neither fetish nor phobia about feet, but I couldn't deny that my hands itched to untie his shoes and slide them off his feet, peel off his socks, roll up his pant legs and...wash his feet. Feel my hands on him as I knelt and he watched me service him. The very idea of it made me wet, and I shifted on my heels where I sat. I hadn't been told what to do, so I clasped my hands in my lap and waited, barely breathing.

Then Bastian's fingers were gripping my chin, tilting my head up until I met his gaze.

"Do you like this?"

I rolled my lips between my teeth and nodded, swallowed. I couldn't explain why exactly. If any of the men I worked with tried to get me to do anything like this, I'd knee them in the balls. But this? This felt right, and I was enjoying myself, truly.

"Good. I hadn't planned to start this way, but after that class my feet are killing me. I don't know how you did it backward and in heels. Why don't you start and I'll give you that explanation I owe you."

I didn't need any more encouragement than that to get to work on stripping him to the shin and slipping his feet into the hot water.

He groaned when I did, and it sent a pulse of want straight to my cunt as I imagined him making a sound like that while he was inside me. Like that except hungrier, more desperate.

I thought of it as I plunged my hands into the water and allowed my fingers to wander over the bones of his ankles, the veins that rose blue under his pale skin, and the layer of hair dusted over his calves. Rubbed at his arches, dug my thumbs into the soles. I was so absorbed in my task, in touching him, that I was almost startled when he started talking.

"I owe you an apology. For a lot of things, but mostly for the other day. I was...stunned is not an excuse, and you'd think a writer would be good with words, but the thing is, the ones I send out into the world I get to delete, write again, move around, agonize over, try and try again, and that's not true in person. So I froze. Have been frozen, actually. Haven't written for days. Which is not your fault—see? Not good with words."

He scrubbed his hands over his face and into his hair, then settled his elbows onto his knees and took my face in his hands again. Made me look at him, which was almost too much. He was almost too much. I didn't know what we were starting here or if, indeed, something *was* starting, but whatever it was, it felt like I was on the precipice of a lot. Of dreams coming true, of finding myself waking in visions I'd conjured—had apparently manifested.

He bent to kiss my forehead and, when he pulled back, smiled at me so kindly, so gently that I was flooded with warmth, pleasure. I felt so good I wanted to wiggle; I couldn't even contain that much joy in my body. And he held me there as he spoke.

"The truth is...you have been my muse. We talk far more about my business than the books I write, which is fine. And it meant I never worried about you discovering that one of the heroines of my current series is basically you. That's what Jason was talking about. I hadn't realized exactly how obvious it was until he said something. But she's tall and strong and has ash-blonde hair and brown eyes with a ring of gold on the outside."

His fingers wandered into my loose locks, rubbed my hair in between them before he pushed some errant strands off my forehead, beckoned me to scoot around one side of the basin and rest my head on his lap, which I did, practically purring like Sheila as he stroked my hair, my hands resting on his feet still in the hot water. It was better than any story time I'd ever had.

"When she's not planning and executing military assaults on the bad guys, she's running her team's tech. She's beautiful and uses that shamelessly, and she doesn't take shit from anyone. While I've paired off most of my main characters and given them partners who will make and keep them happy, I could never conjure someone who would be good enough for Mireia, someone who would be her perfect fit. Despite fans clamoring for it—I get more messages about Mireia than anyone else—I couldn't figure it out."

That wrinkle appeared between his brows again as pensiveness overtook his features, as though he still couldn't figure it out despite having puzzled over it for... Well, he'd been writing this series for three years now. Had he honestly been thinking about this—about me—for three years? I opened my mouth to ask but he shook his head and I wouldn't interrupt. I could wait. I liked this story, the sound of his voice, how he petted me during the telling. I was in no hurry to be anywhere besides at his feet.

"In fits of vanity, I thought perhaps Mireia might like someone like me, but the more I thought about it, the less I could imagine that being true. She, like you, is a bright spark and outshines everyone. And also like you, I'd decided that though it would disappoint my fans—and frankly me—Mireia didn't need or want anyone. The two of you are so vibrant, what would a partner do except dull you? Force you to compromise? Be less than what you are?"

I was having a hell of a time seeing where this was going. I was beautiful? And impressive? But doomed to be alone? Thanks? But I stayed silent in hopes that he'd come to a different conclusion. Would I be here if he hadn't?

"When you came to my door the other night, and you were so...human. I realized I'd been unfair. To you, and perhaps to myself. You are as incredible as your avatar in my books, but you also have wants, needs, soft spots that render you vulnerable. That doesn't make you any less than what I thought you were. That you *are*. It just means shining that bright takes a toll."

I bit the inside of my cheek because yes, that expectation to always be on, to always have the answer, to always be the one people looked to—it was great and I loved it, but it was also exhausting.

"I like taking care of my partners. But I also like for them to hand themselves over to me. As you said the other day, in bed and sometimes out of it. And as beautiful as I've always thought you are, as articulate and funny, and how much I admired the way your mind works—most of the time—"

He smiled at me, a small teasing thing, and I smiled back, giggled and rubbed my face on his knee. Yes, the keys and the mail and the plants and the cat, I knew.

"I couldn't see you submitting to me. And I can't give that up. I've tried for women before, and we both end up hurt. So I didn't pursue you at all. Just let myself have pieces of you that hopefully wouldn't show how much I actually wanted you. When you said all that, the other day, it was like my world had turned upside down. Nothing made sense anymore. And I wasn't as quick as you or as brave to tell you outright, there and then, or even later. I picked up the phone a hundred times to call you while you were away, but I didn't want to tell you over the phone. I wanted you here. I wanted my hands on you, wanted to study your face, your body language..."

He trailed off, and I could practically feel the heat of his gaze as it traveled over my face, my body. It was kind of surprising that my clothes hadn't burned clean away, to be honest.

"I wanted to give you what you'd asked for. Because I want you, Tilda. I've had days to think about what this could be like and I was worried I might show up to your studio and you'd tell me to fuck off, but there wasn't anything else for me to lose. I still have two hours, and I'd like to show you what it would be like, for us to be together. Not all the time because I don't want you to be a different person. I like you just the way you are. But sometimes...sometimes when you say it's okay or when you need it. Or, I'm hoping, if I needed it, that we could be this way together too. You can say no anytime, and I promise I'll stop. Will you try?"

It was like falling. Exhilarating and dangerous at once, but I had to jump, had to try, had to see if I could in fact have what I had been craving, starving for. Could the hermit down the hall be my succor? God, I hoped so.

I nodded. And there was that gentle smile again, making me feel as though I was the best girl in the world.

* * *

I dried off his feet, and when I was done, he tugged me to standing and kissed me again, circled his fingers around my wrist and bundled me into his master bathroom. His apartment had a slightly bigger footprint than mine and apparently that included a narrow but deep soaking tub I immediately coveted. I only barely stopped myself from bouncing with glee when he started the faucet and let it run into the deep, wide tub I'd actually fit in.

Bastian undressed me, piece after piece of my clothing hitting the floor. Though I had been self-conscious about my body before, knowing he'd been so taken with me for years that he'd made a fictionalized version of me a heroine in his books eased some of that. Let me be proud of my long limbs, thick with hard-earned muscle, the curves that filled out my clothes. He thought I was powerful, beautiful. He had pined for me. And I was a mix of grateful and exasperated that he couldn't believe a woman like me would submit to a man.

I wouldn't. Not just any man, anyway. But for him, who I already knew to be kind, loyal, and responsible? Someone I respected and enjoyed being with? Someone who liked the hard-driving parts of me and wouldn't expect me to soften my whole self, make myself smaller so he felt better about himself? That could work.

If he'd told me this before...we could have done this years ago. And we were going to have to have a talk about what "kind" of woman wanted to be submissive in bed. Any and all kinds. That axis of your desires didn't have anything to do with anything else. But I could scold him later. For now, I was enjoying the way he looked at me, studied me, walked around me and pulled my naked back to his clothed front. How he circled my throat with his hand and locked me against him.

"You're so lovely, Tilda. Are you going to be a good, obedient girl for me?"

"Yes, Bastian."

I shivered as I said his name, and he held me tighter, hand at my throat, arm banded around my hips.

"Good. I like well-behaved girls. Like to spoil them, cherish them, dote on them. Would you like that?"

He kissed my neck, licked and sucked at it, sank his teeth into my trapezius, and I nodded convulsively, my throat dry. "Yes, Bastian."

He handed me into the bath, and I sank into it, groaning much the way he had when I slid his feet into the water. He poured water over my hair, shielding my eyes with his hand, and then washed it, strong fingers massaging my scalp and neck, working up a luxurious lather before rinsing it. I felt so adored, so relieved I could've cried.

Instead I let him repeat the motions with conditioner and then melted into his touch as he soaped up and massaged every inch of me until I was warm, sleepy, and so pliable I could've slipped down the drain.

I didn't though. I did, however, let him arrange my body so I was on all fours, my head was resting on a towel at the edge of the tub facing away from him, and my hips were above the waterline. Entirely indecent but I was deep under his spell now and I didn't care. All I cared about was the next touch, the next caress, the next way he'd tell me I was precious to him.

"I want to make you come, sweetheart. Are you okay with that?"

"Oh yes," I breathed, and I felt his chuckle as a vibration through his hands resting on my hips more than I heard it.

"Spread your legs, then. That's my beautiful girl."

And I felt beautiful. The way he hummed his approval as he slipped a single finger and then two into my pussy.

"You're so wet. So wet and so hot, god."

"For you," I said, and he groaned again, working his fingers in and out of me until I was thrusting back at him and he planted his other hand at the small of my back.

"What a squirmy, eager girl you are. But I've got a treat for you and you have to stay still for it."

I whined because between the penetration of his thick fingers and the rocking motions of my hips, I was on the edge even without any stimulation on my clit, and he laughed. Followed by a slap to my flank that made me jump and then dissolve into giggles.

"Do...do I get spanked if I'm naughty?"

I'd always been curious about how that would feel, and I was delirious with possibilities. I didn't think Bastian would tease me or be cruel if I asked for anything, but I was still shy, even in my frenzied state.

"You'll get spanked if you're naughty. You'll get spanked if you're good. You'll get spanked if I feel like it or if you need to be."

My cunt clenched hard around him, and I almost came then, thinking about being draped over his lap and subjected to that.

"I'm not going to spank you now, though. Now I want to taste you."

I expected him to remove his fingers so he could eat me better, but he didn't. Oh no. His tongue started where his fingers speared inside me and then licked...up. That small strip of sensitive skin and then a jolt of understanding followed quickly by a kick of ecstasy as he continued up to tongue my hole.

The feeling of it was like nothing else I'd ever experienced before—filthy and gorgeously intimate, sending shocks of bliss through nerve endings until between his fingers still working my pussy and his mouth loving on my asshole, I came. Harder than I'd ever come, gasping and panting and swearing, shaking and thrusting and crying out, collapsing and having Bastian ease me back into the water where he soon joined me after stripping off his clothes, letting some of the water drain out of the tub so we wouldn't slosh it all over the floor.

"I love seeing you come apart. So fragile, so precious. Better than I'd dreamed of, and trust me, I've dreamed of you a lot."

The way I laughed with him wasn't like the way I laughed with anyone else. Unguarded and filled with true joy. I snuggled back into him, relishing the thick hardness of his erection at my back, brought his fingers that had been inside me to my mouth, sucked the taste of myself off them and then lightly bit the tips of each and every one.

I turned around and straddled him, wanting my lips pressed to his, wanting to feel his hunger for me with my mouth. I wanted to guide his big, hard cock into my cunt and get fucked until we both came. But as senseless as I'd become, I still knew better than that. I was on the pill, yes, but that wasn't foolproof and it didn't do a damn thing to prevent STIs.

"Bastian, I want you to fuck me. Please."

I rubbed against him, frustrated by only being able to feel his length against my clit, against my entrance and not inside me. Not that delicious stretch that came from being penetrated by a substantial cock, and I wanted it.

"What a demanding girl you are," he said, kneading my ass with vicious fingers that dug into my flesh and made me want him even more. Not only his sweetness and care but also his marks upon my skin. "Who do you think gets to decide whether you get fucked? You or me?"

It wasn't feminist and it wasn't progressive. It wasn't what all the women who had agitated for sexual revolution would be proud of, or what I believed with every brain cell I had, but it sure as fuck pushed some elemental button in me.

"You. You, Bastian. You decide."

"That's right. And you're in luck because I want to see you come again, and come on my cock."

And then he did the most remarkable thing. Something I never would have dreamed of, something I never would've asked for because it had seemed impossible for so long. I knew he worked out at the gym in our building, but I'd clearly underestimated how much time he spent there because he stood in the tub, holding me to him as water sluiced down our bodies.

He set me down outside the tub and then climbed out himself, grabbed towels off the rack and wrapped me in one first before he tucked his own around his waist. He'd barely soaked up the drips before he was towing me out to his room, pushing me onto the bed and prowling over me, the muscles of his arms and chest in stark relief even in the low light. Strong, covetous, and coming for me. I arched my throat in surrender because I wanted him to possess me, wanted him to take me over.

He straddled my hips and reached to tug open a drawer of the bedside table, pulled out a strip of condoms and checked the date before ripping one off the end and tearing it open. I rested my hands on his thighs while he sheathed himself, dug my fingers into his strong muscles to keep from stroking his impressive erection.

A split second later, he was in between my legs, levering himself over me and taking my wrists one at a time above my head and then holding them both with one hand while he used the other to angle himself to slip inside me.

I arched and moaned when he'd worked in a couple of inches. Bastian was big, thick, hard, and hot. I wanted all of him at the same time I was worried I might not be able to take it. Not only the pure physical size of him but too the emotional, psychological impact of fulfilling this fantasy of mine, being held down and controlled, feeling a delicious kind of helpless while having the security of knowing I could stop it in a word.

"Bastian, please, I want more of you. Need more of you."

I tried, oh did I try to take it, but he was too strong, too solid, too determined.

Through clenched teeth with sweat beading at his hairline he gritted out, "Not until I say so."

I got the feeling he was testing himself at least as much as he was testing me, if not more. I was writhing underneath him, chanting my pleas and nearly in frustrated tears by the time he took pity on me and plunged his full length inside, bottoming out and stealing my breath.

He pressed his forehead to mine, and his forearms pinned mine down as he thrust into me—drawing out and sliding back in over and over, gaining speed and force until I was overwhelmed with the sensation of being taken, of being had. It was glorious. Powerful and powerless all at once, a sweet confection of everything I'd always wanted—I never wanted it to stop. Except I did because that would mean I'd found the peak of pleasure, that he'd dragged me to the top and shoved me over the edge, and oh how I wanted to fall because that would feel like my freedom and my undoing. Much like the hand he closed carefully around my throat.

"Come on, sweetheart. I know you're close. Come on and come for me. I want to feel you come on me."

It took a few more of his deep, hard thrusts for me to get there, but when I did, I saw stars. Bright white explosions behind my eyelids as I cried out his name, cried out my satisfaction, and had every ounce of pleasure wrung from me as our bodies worked against each other, his climax following not so long after mine with a few brutal thrusts and his teeth sinking into my shoulder in a way that made me cry out again and prolonged the aftershocks of my orgasm.

Bastian held me tight to him, kissed the top of my head, murmured soft, sweet things into my ear and made me feel for the first time in a very long time that I was safe and contained, that I wasn't too much and that he was someone I could trust with both my strength and weakness, someone who would cherish all of that about me.

When I came back from the bathroom, he held me just as tightly.

"Sleep in my bed tonight, Tilda."

"Yes, Bastian."

He squeezed me tighter for a beat and stroked my back. "Is there anything you want? Need?"

There was something I wanted, but I didn't know how he would feel about giving it to me. After all we'd done, after everything we'd been through, it seemed small and yet impossibly intimate and significant.

"Tell me about her. Tell me about Mireia."

Was it perhaps a little desperate and self-centered to want to listen to him talk about a beloved character he'd modeled after me? Perhaps. But he didn't sneer, didn't laugh. Simply said, "I'll do better than that. I'll read you her story."

I fell asleep that night with one ear to his chest, listening to the strong and steady beat of his heart, and the other hearing his rumbling voice reading his own words that told me how he'd felt about me for years. We would write the rest of her story together.

* * *

SANGUINE

SIERRA SIMONE

BASTIEN

I generally like priests, even when they're trying to kill me.

But I'm really not in the fucking mood this morning.

I can feel the warm kiss of the sunlight through the open folding doors, and I can hear the gentle churn of the Coral Sea outside—it's time to *sleep*, not deal with holy men scratching at my gates, and anyway, the whole reason I rented this place on Hamilton Island was so I could have a few months of peace, which I think I've earned, and I've especially earned the right not to be vexed by a self-righteous butcher, and all I want to do is sleep curled up in this sunbeam like a cat, and is that so much to ask?

After the buzzer rings the third time, I reach for my phone and open the security app to answer it. "Fuck off. And if you're here to kill me, extra fuck off."

"I'm not here to kill you." The voice on the other end of the line is impatient, as if *I'm* the problem here, even though he's the one rudely waking me up to murder me.

"I don't believe you," I say crisply. "Now please go away."

"We both know," the voice says, "that I can be inside the house in the next five minutes anyway. Unlike you, I don't need an invitation to enter, so you may as well let me in."

I think about this for a moment. The house is surrounded with stone walls and gates, but they're more to limit the gaze of tourists (and their smartphones) and paparazzi (and their cameras) than to stop serious intruders. Or priests on a mission.

"I can call security," I say.

"You can," the voice agrees.

It's Australian, that voice, although not broadly so. Just some pleasantly relaxed vowels and a slight lilt to the end of his sentences.

Damn that friendly accent, I can't tell whether he's telling the truth or not.

"*Ugh*," I say—not into my phone, just into the warm, sea-scented air.

I came to the Whitsundays to relax! To splash around in the water! To drink some nice Australian wine! And yes, fine, to bite the suntanned necks of happy tourists, but that's really immaterial to the point. Don't I deserve a vacation? Don't I deserve an infinity pool with ocean views?

"Fine," I say irritably—to the priest this time, not just my room. "You can come in. But maybe I'll kill *you*, have you ever thought of that?"

"I'm not here to kill you," the priest repeats, mostly without inflection, although I still hear the thread of impatience in his voice. Like he's already late for an appointment and taking the time to kill me is making him even later.

Ugh, fuck this guy. I have stuff I'd rather be doing too! Like sleeping!

I mutter a pissy noise into the phone—not strictly necessary, but I want him to know how annoyed I am—and I press the gate button. As it opens, I pull up the camera view to get an idea of his size. Not that I've ever had a problem fighting off priests—a tribe of paper-skinned elders and their scrawny, still-pimpled pupils—but it's good to know one's enemy and all that.

But I'm too late with the camera view. I just get a glimpse of silver-white hair as the priest moves past the gate and onto the narrow path crowded by exuberant tropical plants. An old man.

Please go away, I think as I push myself out of bed and tug on some linen pants. As grumbly and tired as I am, I still don't want to kill anyone. I've never liked killing, even when it was necessary, and I certainly don't like killing priests. Or old men.

Maybe I can scare him enough that he won't come back. Although if I know priests, I know that he will come back, and that's—sigh—a thing. A real thing that would be close to a problem, and I'm so very tired of problems.

Don't make me kill you, old man.

I pad to the door and open it before he can knock—and then freeze. Because I am not looking at an old man.

There're a few lines around his eyes, but that's not surprising for someone with fair skin as sun-kissed as his. The hair—the hair *is* near-white, but up close, I can see it's a very particular shade of blond, and it hangs to his shoulders in a sort of careless tousle that I like very much.

And his face ... it's the face of a man past true youth and into his prime—but not by very much. Stubble shadows a square jaw, a shallow cleft winks from his chin, and bright amber eyes stare at me from beneath heavy brows. He can't be much more than thirty-two or thirty-three, but those eyes look at me with the weary acceptance of someone three times his age.

Although as he takes me in—my face, my exposed chest and stomach, my bare feet—the expression in those haunting eyes changes somewhat. Heats into something less weary that could be lust or could be loathing, it's hard to say. I often inspire both in people.

The Australian priest is big, massive, a rock wall of a man—six and a half feet, shoulders filling the doorway—and I find myself appreciating the brutal, holy hulk of him as I take a step backward onto the balls of my feet. I'm very strong—I was before I changed, being not too much shorter than the Viking in front of me, and now I'm an apex predator anyway—but even I might have trouble with this one.

He sees my movement, and his amber eyes flash from my feet back up to my face. "I told you I wasn't here to kill you."

"I've heard it before, priest," I say, a tad crankily. (But I really have heard it before. Usually before the stake and mallet come out.)

For the first time since I opened the door, he looks surprised. "I'm not a priest."

I don't even have enough scoffs to scoff properly at that. "Please. I could sense you all the way from the gate."

His lips part. They are wonderful lips, as firm and sculpted as the rest of him, with two well-defined peaks and the shallowest possible curve to the bottom lip. All grim geometry, this priest's face. It's very hard not to want to lick it.

"You could ... *sense* me?" he asks, sounding unnerved.

I decide he's probably not going to kill me immediately, and also that a holy man in my house at this bright hour calls for something to drink, so I turn on my heel and stride into the kitchen. "You know what I am, and yet you're asking me this question?"

He follows me to the kitchen—first closing the front door, which I find a rather touching commitment to manners, all things considered—and then stands across the glistening expanse of kitchen island from me as I start chopping fruit for a nice sangria. He looks around before answering me, and while his face stays unreadable, there's no disguising the quick, saccadic movements of his eyes as they log every detail of this paradisiacal nest.

The house is a lovely, open-plan type thing, with one central kitchen-cum-dining-room-cum-living-room, and it spills out onto a shaded terrace, which then extends out to the infinity pool. As I have since I first came here, I have all the windows and folding glass doors open, letting in the breeze and ceaseless spill of the ocean outside. Dent Island is rucked up around the horizon, like a dark green quilt kicked to the bottom of the bed, and cottony clouds waft above like overfluffed pillows, and the pool is a rippling, Impressionist painting of it all, a painting set right into the lush, emerald lawn.

Everything inside the house is gleaming wood and generous furniture; it's tailor-made for a billionaire and their paramour, or maybe a celebrity and their entourage, but of course I'm knocking about in it alone, wasteful rake that I am. And the priest doesn't hide the moment this registers with him. "You're by yourself," he says.

"And you never answered my question." I finish chopping the lemons and oranges and move to the apples. "You know I'm a vampire, and yet you don't know we can sense priests? How have you survived this long?"

I'm genuinely curious. He's not surprised to see me moving through sunlight or popping the occasional apple chunk into my mouth, which means he knows more about vampires than most people. He knows we're mammals, not magic, and that our eyes are better suited to hunting at night, so while we skew nocturnal, the sunlight doesn't hurt us any more than it hurts a cat or an owl. He knows the combination of electrolytes, glucose, lipids and iron in human blood is the only complete meal for us—but we still eat and drink other things too.

"I'm not a priest," the man repeats. And then pauses. "Anymore."

"Aha!" I say through a bite of apple, pointing my knife at him. "J'accuse!"

Those eyes flash again. A thrill runs right down my spine, as if a lion had just locked stares with me. I'm not the only predator in this room, and I'd put my not inconsiderable money on him having been a vampire hunter in his time. Some self-destructive part of me idly wonders what it would be like to see those eyes flashing up at me as I pinned him to my bed ... or as he crawled over me, so big he blocked out all the light except whatever was reflected from his gaze...

"That chapter of my life is closed," the man says. "It was a long time ago."

"I bet it won't seem like a long time to me, and also, I don't care what Rome thinks, you're still a priest."

A growl rumbles in his chest as he takes a step forward. I think I feel that growl from the nape of my neck to the lazily stirring length in my drawstring pants.

"I'm. *Not.*"

I set the knife down and find a glass pitcher. "Do you know how vampires suspect a priest is near?" I grab an opened bottle of red wine and pour it in. An obnoxious *glug glug glug* noise fills the kitchen. "We have superior senses in almost every way. Truly superhuman. I can smell fear, for example, and I can hear lust—and in your case, I can perceive in every single possible way your clarity, your faith, and your devotion. It brightens the air around you, and it makes the space near you hum. I can taste your faith, and it tastes like"—I close my eyes and savor him on my tongue for a moment—"ironically, it tastes like communion. The wafers, I mean. It's the serotonin in your body. The dopamine too. It's so close to being sweet, but the moment you apprehend the sweetness, it dissolves. Beckoning you back, urging you to take more. Begging to be chased. Much like God Himself, if I may say so."

I open my eyes and get back to the sangria, adding the orange juice.

The man stares at me, lips parted again.

"None of that has gone away," I tell him, adding the fruit to the wine and then hunting for some brandy. "Maybe you no longer wear a collar, but inside, you're still a man of God. I'm not sure why you left the Church—or why you were kicked out—but lack of faith wasn't the reason." I find a cinnamon stick, swirl it in the pitcher with some flair. "Ta-da! Do you want some? Of course you do, you're Catholic and there're only golf buggies on this island, so who cares about drinking—here's a glass now, stop being so shy."

The ex-priest sniffs at the glass, then raises those wonderful eyes to mine. "It's only wine? Nothing ... else?"

I roll my eyes. "This isn't Gilded Age Paris, mon ami; I'm not stocking my cellar with casks of human blood in between visits to the opera. It's just wine."

"Hmm."

"You have to admit a priest worried about blurred lines between blood and wine is *deeply ironic*."

"Hmm."

"Also can I just point out the Latin root of 'sangria'? From 'sanguis,' meaning blood. So in a linguistic sense, we are drinking blood, am I right?"

I don't think I've ever seen anyone as serious as the man in front of me, even after being exposed to the full force of my linguistic wit.

But he does take a tentative sip, then licks his lips after, which sends my already interested cock into *very obviously* interested territory.

And then when he takes a real drink, and I watch the swallow work its way down his throat, I nearly have a heart attack. If I had my lips on that neck, if I had my teeth there ...

I have to move around the corner of the island so he doesn't see the needy erection currently pressing against my pants. They're loose enough pants but they're also thin, and also—this isn't to brag, it's honestly just true—it's a very noticeable cock when it's in the mood.

The man sets the glass carefully on the counter, as if one drink of wine will be quite enough, thank you very much. "You're not how I thought you would be," he says after a minute.

I'm trying not to think about his throat. Or the way a drop of wine lingers on his lower lip, begging to be sucked off. "And how did you think I was going to be?"

He shrugs. "I've met some vampires before. They weren't as...blithe...as you are."

"Blithe?" I echo, a smile growing across my face. "*Blithe*? That's the word you picked?"

The man grunts, and if I'm not mistaken, there's color coming up on his cheeks. "It's a real word," he mutters defensively. "I've read it before."

"First of all, can we just acknowledge that not using 'sanguine' was a real missed opportunity for you, given our discussion five seconds ago about Latin root words?"

"I like blithe," he says. Stubbornly.

I'm shaking my head and laughing. This silver-haired giant looks like he could crush rocks with his bare hands—and then out he comes with *blithe*.

"Got any other thesaurus words for me? Jocund, maybe? Mirthful? Merry? Gladsome? Gay?"

The word *gay* makes his cheeks go even pinker. Interesting.

"Let me ask you this, Mr. Ex-Priest: were you a hunter? Because if the only vampires you met were vampires you killed, then that probably explains why they weren't so blithe when they met you. When we're not fighting for our lives, we do tend to be a fairly sunny bunch. Get it? *Sunny?* You're not laughing. You're one of those austere Latin Mass priests, aren't you? You're the antonym to blithe, my friend, the actual living antonym."

"I was a hunter," he says, ignoring my excellent joke. "But I left because I didn't want to be anymore."

"So you're not hunting me now?" I ask.

He shakes his head. The ends of his silvery-blond hair brush distractingly over his shoulders. They're *big* shoulders, big and hard, and I wish I could squeeze them. From behind.

While I pressed slow and slick into his muscular body.

"I didn't come to hurt you," he says, and when he looks at me this time, there's a sort of earnestness underneath the grim sphinx thing he has going on. Like he wants me to believe him. "I came because I saw you last night, and I—" He clears his throat, pauses, clears his throat again. He looks very uncomfortable, and I'm already guessing why.

"You saw me hunt," I say. Flatly. "And even though it's not your job to stop me anymore, you feel like you need to—what? Chastise me for it? Threaten me away? Chase me off?"

"No," he says, more quickly than he's spoken all day. "Nothing like that. You didn't kill him—and you took so much less than you needed."

"I never kill, not if I can help it," I inform him, my blithe mood gone. (I'm a little sensitive about this, if you can't tell). "I haven't killed since—well, okay, it was Gilded Age Paris actually—but that was *provoked* and everyone I've told the story to agrees with me, if you must know. I just want to drink and then let my victims go, no worse off than if they'd donated blood. Which, I mean, really is what it amounts to if you think about it."

The pink is back in his cheeks. I blink at him, wondering why seeing me hunt last night would be embarrassing for him—*oh*. Ohhhhhhhh.

Oh yeah. This priest is getting very interesting indeed.

I give him my wickedest, most louche grin. "You saw more than the drinking, didn't you? You saw the *kissing*."

"Do you—" He clears his throat again. "Do you always kiss them? Your victims?"

"When they want me to." I fold my arms across my chest, suddenly back to enjoying this morning very much. All this delicate blushing on such a big, bleak man—it's a combination of delights, enticing and carnal. I wonder if I could bite that blush sometime, just a little nip, just a sharp, little kiss. "Why do you ask, my sullen priest? Are you in the market to be kissed? Or bitten?"

He shifts, and although his body ripples with unconscious grace, I can also sense his uneasiness. A light lace of adrenaline and cortisol in his blood, making the air around him taste faintly acrid—smoky and earthy, like a good Islay scotch. It's not unpleasant, but it does have wariness tickling at the nape of my neck again. I still don't know why he's here.

"Why are you asking me about kissing and biting? Why were you watching me? More importantly, *why are you here*?"

"I was working up to that!" the ex-priest grumps, shifting on his feet again, and I realize that I've completely misread him from the start. He's not impatient at all.

He's *nervous*.

I slowly uncross my arms and watch as he takes a step forward, and then a step back, and then turns to face the ocean, and then turns back to me. And then finally he says, "I came to see if—maybe—if you're not busy or anything —and only if you'd like to—I mean, only if you *felt* like it—if you'd like to get dinner. With me. Sometime." The last words he grates out like they're physically painful to speak, and that proud face dips down to the floor as if he's considering curling up into a miserable ball after this display of vulnerability.

Everything I was feeling—the petulance, the suspicion, the amusement —everything is replaced by a drowsy, dulcet bloom of tenderness in my chest.

Well, okay, not everything. There's still a heady cocktail of sangria-fueled lust coursing through my veins, but it's not at odds with the tenderness at all. Instead the two feed each other, making my heart thump for this shy, nervous man as I throb elsewhere.

I take a step toward him, deciding that if he wants to get dinner, he's probably not going to be bothered by the state of my erection. "So you saw me kissing and biting someone last night, and instead of killing me like a good vampire hunter, you want to take me out on a date?" I say it lightly, but the words are blunt. I need to be sure.

He looks at me through eyelashes the color of angry rain. "I'm not a hunter anymore," he says simply.

"But you were watching me last night. That wasn't hunting?"

"I have a new job this week, private security on the island. Midnight patrol."

He is such a big motherfucker that I'm not actually that surprised. His size, plus the way he carries himself—like a man who's taken lives—would be enough of a deterrent for most touristy troublemakers, I'd imagine. Still though. "Priest to private security—not exactly adjacent vocations, my friend."

His shoulder moves the slightest bit—the world's smallest shrug. "Finding work after the Church has been hard. The ... nighttime ... has stayed with me. The peering into shadows, the walking silently under the stars. It's a habit I can't break. So patrolling someplace in the dark seemed like a natural fit. I honestly wasn't looking for vampires. Just drunks or buggy thieves."

"But you found me anyway."

He blinks as if remembering. "I found you anyway. You were—you are—beautiful." He flushes again, looks away.

Beautiful. I've been called many flattering things before (because there's lots of flattering things about me, that's just facts) but it's been a long, long time since I've been called beautiful.

I study him as he looks out the window, the strong lines of his jaw and nose, the impossible color of his hair. The shy press of his full lips. I don't know this man's name, I don't know his secrets or his hopes or where he's from or where he sleeps at night or what he thinks about when he's alone. I only know that he's a bashful, grunting hulk of a man; I only know he used to kill my kind ... but for some reason, has chosen not to anymore.

I only know that he saw me kissing and biting someone last night, and instead of hunting me down out of a lingering sense of duty to humankind, he's here awkwardly asking me out on a date. Telling me he thinks I'm beautiful while I fuss at him over sangria.

The tenderness I'm feeling toward him is practically an undertow now. I'm being sucked into the deep.

"What's your name, former priest? And do you know mine?"

His expression is careful when he looks at me. Guarded. "You go by Bastien."

Bastien is, in fact, my real name, and only someone who knows how to burrow into layers of paperwork would have found it on my lease here. "You were a hunter indeed," I murmur.

He nods, but he doesn't apologize, which I respect. And maybe even like? I have to admit, after centuries of prowling after people, it's rather nice to be prowled after myself.

"And I'm ..." The man hesitates, and I realize it's because he's unused to saying his first name. It makes me wonder how recently he's left the Church. "My name is Aaron."

I've wandered close enough to him that I could touch him now, if I wanted. I don't, but I do enjoy the way his eyes rake down my taut stomach to where my pants hang low around my hips. He yanks his gaze back up as if embarrassed to be caught looking, but I don't miss how he angles his body ever so slightly away as if he doesn't want to frighten me with his body's response to mine.

I have never met a priest or hunter like him. A quiet brute who just wants dinner and maybe kissing. Maybe more ...

Maybe waking up this morning was a good idea after all.

"Okay, Aaron," I say softly. "I'll go to dinner with you."

AARON

When I was a young priest learning how to hunt vampires, our teachers warned us how beautiful vampires were, how beguiling, how they could bewitch the senses and thwart good sense just with a smile.

Well, here I am on a date with a vampire, utterly bewitched. Good sense thwarted past reckoning.

"More wine?" Bastien asks, tipping the bottle to my glass and topping it off before I can refuse. The fading sunlight limns him in red and pink and gold, and I'm trying not to stare, but it's impossible. His face is almost too lovely to be real—a Pre-Raphaelite composition of full lips and long eyelashes, large eyes and a Greek nose. His jaw is finely carved and his cheeks and forehead are aristocratically high, and he is all contrasts—sculpted features with soft, inviting lips, ivory-pale skin with dark eyes and hair.

He looks like a painting. Like he would have been in a painting when he was mortal.

"We're quite a sight, aren't we?" Bastien observes, setting the bottle down and picking up his own glass by the stem. His vowels curve with an accent I can't quite place—nearly French, nearly British, a fleeting glimpse into lifetimes he's spent on other shores. "A vampire and a priest, breaking bread."

Old habits have me glancing around, although we're in the far corner of the covered restaurant patio and well out of earshot of any other diners. When I look back to Bastien, his mouth is curled up at the edges.

"Worried the villagers will come knocking with torches and crosses later?" he asks, amused.

I make an affirmative grunt, and then I look down at my wineglass. "I didn't need any more wine."

"Yes, you did," Bastien says, the smile still toying at his lips. "How else will I get to know your deepest, darkest secrets?"

He's got a point. We've made it through the walk up to the restaurant and ordering our meal with me barely speaking at all. Because of one very embarrassing fact that I decide is best to confess to him now. "I don't have secrets. Or things to talk about. I'm not—I'm not interesting. Like you." I look down at the sunset-colored ocean below us as I say this, so I don't have to see the moment he decides this is a terrible, boring date and he's going to leave.

But he doesn't leave. And when he finally speaks, his richly musical voice is pitched very low and very soft, in a way that sends heat licking in my belly. "A former priest—a former vampire hunter—who saw a vampire being wicked and decided to get closer to wickedness instead of further away ... that sounds very interesting to me."

Closer to wickedness ... I almost shudder with the accuracy of his words. When I saw him kissing that man last night, when I saw the pleasure on the man's face as Bastien held him close and buried his mouth in the man's neck, I'd felt longing like I'd never felt it before. I'd felt the first real jolts of arousal since I left the priesthood.

I wanted it. I wanted kisses and biting. I wanted this vampire to do to me what I'd vowed I'd never let any vampire to do me, and drink my blood. In fact, I'd even worn a long-sleeved sweater—very, very thin, mind you, because even with the constant breeze, Hamilton Island is warm—because it has a low rounded collar that completely exposes my throat. I don't have the words or eloquence to tell Bastien what I want, but maybe he'll know it without me having to tell him. Maybe he'll take it without asking. Maybe he'll pin me in some dark corner somewhere and make me moan with pleasure the way he did to the man last night.

I dare to look back at Bastien. The smile is still there, but it's no longer a signal of amusement. It's a signal of something else ...

An invitation, maybe?

Or maybe I'm just seeing what I want to see. Maybe it's pity. Maybe I'm pitiable and pathetic, a clumsy, eager fool who wanted to get closer to something dangerous and beautiful and who's now made himself ridiculous.

I suddenly wish I'd worn a collared shirt. I look like a vampire's version of a tart.

Bastien sees I'm lost in my own mind, and he reaches for my hand. It takes me a minute to understand—it's been so long since I've been touched in kindness—and then even longer to accept. Bastien sees my hesitation but attributes it to something else. "We're safe here," he says softly. "I won't let anything happen to you."

His meaning is clear; this bright, touristy place does feel very safe, but safety is always conditional on whose hand you're holding, and where I grew up, this could still be dangerous. It's a particular kind of fear I didn't have to feel as a priest, but now it's here, as real as my desire for Bastien. I didn't realize I was afraid until he offered to help hold the fear with me.

I look down at our hands as he speaks, and then I have to look away. The sight of our fingers and palms—big and square and obviously male—touching is the most wonderful and the most terrifying thing I've ever seen. And his words ...

"Thank you," I manage to get out. The warmth and pressure of someone holding my hand, promising to keep me safe, is making my throat ache, and the words come out rough. "I'm not used to someone thinking they need to protect me. Because I'm so big," I add in order to explain, and Bastien laughs.

"I can see that. You are *very* big."

The words are flirtatious enough that I feel myself blushing. He laughs some more.

"You're very easy to tease, you know," he points out. "I've made you blush like a virgin all day, and it's starting to make me wonder how long it's been since you've been on a date."

"I've never done this before," I admit in a mumble.

He grins, eyes sparkling. "A date with a vampire? I imagine not."

"No, Bastien. *This.*" I look down at our hands and then to the wine and the table and the view.

A small line appears between his brows. "Aaron. Please tell me I'm not your first date."

I can't tell him that, so I don't say anything at all.

Bastien's grin fades, but his eyes remain intense. "Are you a virgin?"

I make a noise that could mean anything, but Bastien doesn't let me wriggle out of answering.

"I know it's an invasive question, but I'm a vampire, so humor me. How untouched is my laconic priest?"

The possessive *my* in *my laconic priest* makes my pulse thud a little harder, and Bastien's eyes rove over my exposed neck as I reply honestly. "Very, um, untouched," I admit.

He lifts his eyes back to mine and tugs his hand free. "Well then."

I stare down at my now-empty hand, feeling stupid, and I slowly pull it back into my lap. Maybe he doesn't like virgins. Maybe he doesn't like the reminder that I was a priest. Maybe—

"What do you say we skip dinner?" Bastien asks, interrupting my panicked self-recriminations. "I'll feed you at my house."

I blink at him. "What?"

He leans forward, a lock of hair tumbling over his forehead and his dark eyes flashing with some strong emotion I can't identify. "Aaron, I'm sitting across from a strapping ex-priest who's been flaunting his naked throat at me all evening, and now he tells me he's a virgin. The reins of my control are understandably snapping." He digs out some cash for the wine and tosses it on my table, and before I can say anything, he's taking my hand and hauling me easily to my feet and tugging me out the door.

Confused but also flattered and also hoping this means what I think it does, I follow Bastien, trying not to look like I'm getting dragged off to slake a vampire's obscene needs. My dick gives a heavy twitch at the thought, stirring and lengthening until I'm swollen enough that I have to adjust myself so I don't look like a walking teen-movie gag.

"When did you leave the priesthood?" Bastien asks once we're on the footpath back to his house. He's in a white button-down shirt, and the setting sun outlines all those flat, dense muscles underneath the fabric. He's built lithe and lean and graceful, and I have the sudden image of him crawling over me like a huge cat, eyes hot with hunger.

I'm too distracted to answer him. "I—what?"

Bastien sighs. "Look, I know learning you're virginal in the extreme should make me *more* careful with you, and probably we should have, like, five more dinner dates and some long talks about intimacy before I even think about touching you, but I'm a vampire, okay? I'm sorry, but I'm one of your sexy grunts away from taking your virginity in between some shrubs while the wallabies watch, and it's been a century or two since I've needed to fuck like this, and I'm barely hanging on, so what I need to happen right now is I need you to help distract me until we get back to my house and I can at least give you some privacy before I put my mouth all over you. Got it? Good. Now talk to me. When did you leave the priesthood?"

Too many feelings for me to process are crowding my chest and stomach. Lust and shyness and gratitude and fear and more fear.

So I just try not to think about all that and give him what he wants instead. It's easy, in a thrilling kind of way, to surrender to his bossiness. "I was officially dismissed from the clerical state four months ago. The Church was ... reluctant, I guess. There are not so many of us left now that they can easily let even one go."

"Not so many priests?" Bastien asks.

"Not so many priests who are trained as I was," I clarify.

"Ah, in the Order of Saint Marcellus, you mean," Bastien says, and I'm surprised.

"You're not supposed to know that name," I tell him.

Bastien makes a scoffing noise. "Vampires aren't supposed to know the name of the ancient order sworn to hunt them down?"

"It's supposed to be secret; we're forbidden to whisper it to anyone outside the order, even in the throes of death. Who did you learn it from?" I frown, thinking of all the reasons a priest of the Order might break his vow. "Did he tell you under duress?"

"You mean, did I torture it out of someone?" Bastien asks dryly. "No. I earned that knowledge honestly. How long were you a priest?"

"Ten years. What do you mean you earned it honestly?"

A wallaby hops across the road, stopping to look blankly at us and then moving along after a moment. Bastien watches it, his face growing distant. "I earned it a long time ago," he says finally, which doesn't really answer my question. "When I was mortal. Why did you become a priest?"

There it is again, that urge to do as he says. I answer him without worrying that I sound grunty or stupid or overeager, even though this is the most I've spoken aloud at one time in the last four months, and it feels strange. "I grew up in a small town an hour outside of Toowoomba. There're as many churches as there are houses, or so it felt like. Praying was in my blood, but so was fighting, and it felt like there was nowhere good a big, hot-blooded boy like me would end up, but my childhood priest wanted to help.

He sent me to his mentor in Brisbane, and they promised if I went to seminary and was ordained, they'd find the right place for me. And that's how I ended up in Rome, inducted into the Order."

"Hmm," Bastien says. A warm breeze ruffles up the road, and when I look over, his shirt is clinging to every contour of his torso and chest. And his trousers are clinging too, and I see the distinct outline of a large erection—the same one I did my best not to gawk at this morning. Bastien wasn't lying about wanting me. And I want this vampire to want me. I want him to touch me and make me bleed and make me come. I want it so much my body hurts trying to hold all the wanting—and the terror of *who* I want—inside it.

"I think," Bastien says, "you've just explained the *how*. And not the why. Don't forget I can taste your belief, Aaron. You became a priest because you wanted to, not because it was the only choice you had, and I want to know why."

I grunt a little, not sure how to answer this. Somehow I know he won't settle for the short and easy answers I gave when I was in the process of ordination—the *I feel called* and *I want to serve God as much as I can*, the kinds of answers that are as expected as they are reductive. And I can't make a fool out of myself more than I already have.

I decide to give him the truth, as intimate and ephemeral as it is.

"I always knew I loved God," I explain, "because I always knew He loved me. When I was a boy, I would go out to my family's cotton fields and watch the sky at night. We were way out in the bush, and there weren't any lights, and the sky was dripping with stars. So many stars that it felt like I could hold out my hand and they'd fall into my palm like rain. Like all I had to do was ask and God would fill my heart with stars like He filled the cisterns and wells and lakes with water, and who wouldn't want to serve a God like that?"

"Who indeed," Bastien murmurs, something tender and awed curling into his words. "Do you still believe that? About the stars? That God will fill your heart with stars if you ask?"

"Yes."

"So the boy on the farm became a priest because he grew up with stars raining light on him night after night, and it felt like God Himself was covering him in a net of pure love." Bastien's voice is still tender, but it's tight too, as if he's upset. "There are many worse, and cheaper, reasons to become a priest, Aaron. My hat is off to you."

We turn onto the narrow road that leads to the expensive houses celebrities like to rent—a road I've patrolled a few times since starting my job here. Bastien doesn't say anything as we approach the discreet gates of his home, and I'm starting to feel like I've said something wrong.

"Bastien," I say, feeling clumsy with my words, as usual, "did I make you angry with me? By talking about God."

Bastien lets out a huff, and I almost smile. He's so *funny*, this bloodthirsty painting of a man, he's so open. It only took me ten years of vampires and death to become a silent gargoyle, but that he's managed to live lifetimes and still be funny and honest and adorable—it's astonishing, really.

He punches in the code to his gate as he huffs some more, and then as he impatiently ushers me through, he says, "I'm not angry, Aaron."

"You're not?"

A self-deprecating puff of air. "I'm a little ashamed is all."

"Ashamed?"

"It's one thing to scent your earnestness," he says as we walk down the path to the door. Cockatoos ruffle and bitch as we walk by, but they sense in their animal way that Bastien is a predator, and so they give us a wide berth, fluttering from a distance. "But to hear it—to know it—Aaron, I don't think you appreciate how good you are. And if I weren't already going to hell on account of being an immortal cannibal, then I'd be going to hell for the mere fact that your goodness incites me to badness. It makes me want to do very, *very* depraved things with you. To you, actually, very much to you."

I don't think I can breathe. I want those depraved things so badly, but when I open my mouth to tell him so, all that comes out is a low noise of acknowledgment.

Luckily, Bastien doesn't seem to mind my taciturnity. He keeps going as he opens his front door. "I want to fuck your goodness. Do you understand how odd that is? I want to bite it. I want to drink these wonderful, earnest secrets of yours down as you shudder for me. I want to make you feel every dirty thing you've earned by being so good; I think you're too pure to be truly debased, but my God, I want to try."

The door swings open, and we step inside, and before I can react—which means it happens too fast for *any* human to react—I'm shoved against the wall and Bastien's mouth is on mine.

He pins me there with a forearm against my throat, his free hand roaming shamelessly around my body, sliding over my stomach and hips and then delving right past my waistband, sending my back arching far off the wall.

"Whoa, there," he says like I'm a stallion he's trying to break, and fuck if that doesn't get me hotter. All my life, my size has been something to be afraid of, something to be contained, but Bastien seems ... *delighted* by my bigness. *Pleased* by it. Aroused by it. Like it's thrilling for him to have a massive, wild male grunting and snarling at his touch. And for some reason, that makes it thrilling for me. He isn't scared of me, and he's just as strong, if not stronger. I don't have to worry about hurting him or scaring him, no matter how much I thrash or no matter how many snarls I make.

And I am snarling now as his clever fingers find my erection and squeeze before pushing lower to cup my testicles. His mouth on mine is firm and persuasive, coaxing me to open in between my growls, his kiss turning possessive as he strokes along my tongue and licks at the inside of my lips.

"What can't I do to you?" he whispers against me. His hand in my pants is wicked, and I've never felt anything like it, not even the times I've done this to myself. "Tell me, mon prêtre. What can't I do to you?"

I know he's honestly asking, and so I give him an honest answer. "Nothing."

"That's a dangerous thing to tell such a one as me."

"I watched you take care of a total stranger last night. You only took a little, and when you were done, he was conscious and smiling and safe. And you have every reason to hate me because of what I used to do, and yet you're still asking me permission now. I trust you, Bastien."

He goes still against me, and after a second, he pulls back enough that he can meet my stare, pulling his hand free from my pants too, which has me arching again. His eyes are so dark, so unreadable. His breath is warm against my kiss-damp mouth. "You truly trust me?"

"I do."

He closes his eyes. "Maybe you shouldn't."

"Are you going to kill me?"

"Jesus!" His eyes fly open. "Of course not, Aaron! What the *fuck*."

"Then I trust you," I say, shrugging against the wall. He lowers his forearm and takes a deep breath, running a hand down his face.

"Okay. Okay. I'm going to fuck you and I'm going to bite you and I'm going to play with your cock and maybe suck it too—not all in that order, obviously, I'm having a hard time thinking right now. It will feel good when I bite you and I won't take too much, but I need you to tell me if it's still too much or if it hurts. I mean, hurts in a bad way. You know what I mean."

Seeing this noble vampire all flushed and flustered—because of me—is gratifying beyond measure. "I trust you," I repeat simply. "As long as you don't mind that I—I don't know what I'm doing."

"Jesus Christ," Bastien mutters to himself, running another hand down his face. "Do I mind that this giant farm-boy-slash-priest is a virgin and trembles whenever I so much as hold his hand. *Jesus*."

He presses back against me, one hand deftly unbuttoning my pants and freeing my erect organ. I hiss the moment it hits the cool air, and he hisses along with me as he looks down and sees I'm already wet at the tip.

"Am I the first person to touch this cock?" he asks me, his voice low and sounding more French than ever. "I think I must be. You're about to go off in my hand, and I haven't done anything yet. Fuck, that's sexy. Jesus, are you about to come right now? You really are. *Fuck* fuck fuck fuck—"

Bastien's husky wonder is the soundtrack to my first orgasm with someone else; all it takes is looking down and seeing him wrap those elegant fingers around my length and I am done for. He doesn't even squeeze me, he doesn't even stroke me—he *holds* me and I come immediately.

We both watch as thick ribbons of white spill from the tip and over his fingers, my erection visibly jerking with each and every surge. I'm ashamed, I'm so ashamed, but there's no stopping it, no stopping the heavy spurts desperate to leave my body. And even in the midst of my shame, it feels so *fucking good*, so good that I don't care how lewd I'm being, how I'm dirtying Bastien's hand and dripping onto his floor, I don't care, if someone tried to stop me before I was finished, I'd rip them in half, because I need to finish more than I need to take my next breath, that's how urgent and necessary this is.

Not that there's any possibility of stopping anyway. The surges are a mindless, animal pleasure, hooked deep into my belly, and by the time I'm spent in Bastien's hand, I barely know my own name. I couldn't have torn myself away from this moment even if I'd had bands of brother priests to help me, and it isn't until the uncivilized spilling stops that I realize I was grunting and pushing into Bastien's hand.

I go silent and still, feeling like a dirty beast.

Bastien looks up at me with something like shock, and I'm wondering if maybe he's never had a clumsy virgin come all over him before, and maybe he's disgusted by it—

Before I can even finish the thought, he's kissing me, devouring my mouth with skillful, pressing strokes, driving every other thought and worry from my mind. Between us, my exposed cock gives an eager kick, and he pulls back, lips swollen and pupils blown.

"I have to fuck you now," he says hoarsely.

"Okay," I agree, and then he grabs my hand and yanks me toward his bedroom. I manage to sort of tuck myself back together as we go, although the horse is rather out of the barn as far as pride goes at this point, given that I just came all over his floor after he did nothing more than hold me in his hand.

"That was the sexiest thing I've ever seen," he says, partially to himself as he tugs me along. "And I've seen a lot. My God, how am I going to do this. A *virgin*. Think, Bastien, think." He lets go of my hand to flap his own in a sort of vague, horny distress.

"Bastien," I say as we reach his bed.

"What?"

"I'm very big."

"I *know* that, Aaron, I just saw how big you are. Why do you think I'm in such a state?"

It's never occurred to me before that a vampire could be, well, cute, but there's something very cute about how fussy he is when it comes to his reactions to me. "No, I mean, I'm a strong bloke. Sturdy and tough, you know? And the Order—" I won't mention the grim endurance tests of pain and strength, because even in my limited experience, I know it wouldn't make good bedroom talk, so I settle for, "The Order made me even tougher. You can't hurt me." I think of the stranger Bastien drank from last night, his eyes fluttering in ecstasy as his hips mindlessly rolled against a vampire's. "I want you to be at your wickedest. *Please*."

For a moment, Bastien looks almost young. Helpless with his own wanting. And then he's all vampire again, hungry and heavy-lidded. Very, very wicked as he unbuttons his shirt and lets it fall to the floor. The wickedest as he toes off his shoes and removes his socks and unbuttons his pants. The ruddy head of his erection peeps out above his zipper, swollen and dark against his pale stomach, and the fading sun over the ocean bathes his perfect form in pink and purple-hued light as he walks toward me.

"Clothes off," he says, not bothering with *please* or *thank you*. "Let me see this priest who needs to sin so badly."

With shaking hands, I do as he says, peeling off my sweater and shoes and pants. The bedroom has large glass doors that fold open, and the breeze comes right up off the water, sweet and soft and somewhere right between warm and cool. Shadows move through the room as the trees and shrubs outside rustle in the breeze, and by the time I'm naked, Bastien is in front of me, running appreciative hands all over my body like a shadow himself, like the actual darkness is beckoning me into an embrace.

And I go willingly.

"Down, sweet priest," he whispers, guiding me onto the bed, onto my back. "Down, down. Let me have a taste."

I expect his mouth on mine after that, or maybe even on my neck, but it's my stomach where I feel his kiss first, hungry and quick, and by the time I tense and gasp underneath it, he's already moved down to my navel, and then down the trail of hair to the base of my cock.

I'm not ready for it, not ready for how soft his mouth is, how wet, how it's almost like tickling but it's not, tickling isn't the right word at all.

"What can't I do to you," Bastien murmurs, almost to himself.

"Nothing," I whisper to the ceiling. And then his fangs sink into my erection.

It should hurt, and for the first instant it does, a spark of pain sizzling up my spine, but it's replaced immediately with pure, delicious pleasure as Bastien begins to suck. It's indecent, yes, so indecent, a vampire *there* doing *that*—it should be the ultimate boundary for a priest sworn to destroy vampires. But I'm not a priest anymore, and my body is aching down to the marrow for his sharp, bloody kiss. I don't know what kind of magic vampires possess—or if it's some biological mechanism designed to help them catch and keep prey—but his fangs feel *good*. An invasion, yes, but an invasion like his tongue in my mouth is an invasion, an invasion like his dark eyes in my mind are an invasion. And each suck—the *suck*—oh my God, it's almost better than coming itself, it's like Bastien is yanking pleasure out of my body, like he's drawing the very heart of me out through his bite.

And that it's on my cock ...

"Fuuuck," Bastien says, wrenching himself away, his mouth bloody in the dark. I can feel the wet smear of where he was sucking me on my dick, and I'm harder than fucking ever. "*Fuck*. I could do that forever, do you understand? I could drink from your cock every night and never get sick of it. What are you doing to me? No, don't try to answer, I know you'll just grunt at me and then I won't have any more information than before you grunted. Don't move."

It's nearly dark outside, with only the last lavender blush of dusk and the pool lights outside to light the room, and so it's his silhouette I watch as he goes to a table by the bed and pulls out a small bottle.

"In case you don't already know, vampires can't carry human infections," Bastien says, coming back to the bed. "So we don't need protection."

"You're not worried about getting me pregnant?" I ask, and Bastien pauses between my legs, his head tilted.

"Aaron, did you just *make a joke*? You did! You made a joke! I'm so proud, I'm like your joke-father, except not really, that would be creepy, unless—I mean, if you want to call me *daddy*, I am not opposed to that at all, I'm just saying, I think I could get used to Daddy Bastien if we worked on it."

I'm smiling at him, at the ebullience of him even with his dick jutting out from his hips and his mouth still wet with blood, and that's when I hear the bottle click open and then feel the slick press of his finger.

I grunt as my blood-smeared cock gives a leap. A hot feeling knots itself tight in my belly, low down, and it cinches my balls up to my body.

"My virgin priest," Bastien croons, adding another finger. He does something—presses somewhere—and a groan tears out of my chest. My hips leave the bed as I follow some unknown instinct and try to fuck up in the air, needing more, needing to fuck or be fucked or anything really, so long as it's *more*.

"I'm giving you my cock now, mon prêtre. Open for me—yes, like that—do you feel me against you? That's it, yes, breathe, breathe, my wonderful seeker of wickedness. Oh, I love how you squirm, I love how those powerful hips buck for me. Yes, almost there, breathe, breathe. Do you feel me, sweetheart? I feel you, and you feel like a hot fist clenched around my shaft. I'm not going to last long, not with you, you sweet, brutal man. Fuck."

It's like being split in two but in the best possible way. Bastien is so much bigger than his fingers, and the power behind each and every stroke is enough to make me grunt even though he's going slow. He moves between my thighs with sleek, near-cruel strength, but I love it. I'm throbbing into the cool ocean air with how good it feels to be underneath this vampire, and each stroke is hitting me someplace deep inside that has my grunts getting louder, longer, lower.

"It's happening again," I moan. "It's gonna— I'm gonna—"

He lunges forward, fangs shining in the shadows, and right as I begin the shameful spurting again, his face is in my neck and he's biting me and drinking me down. The sheer, intoxicating pleasure of his bite coupled with the possessive invasion of him inside me—I feel ridden, I feel owned, I feel dirty and wild and seen. I feel like I want this forever, this exact moment, Bastien buried inside me, both fang and cock, while my own cock throbs and spills between our stomachs.

And it's as he's drinking me that his own orgasm begins jolting inside my arse, as if the pleasure of tasting me has pushed him over the edge, and he sucks his fill as his hips keep fucking and fucking and fucking, shoving into me with a desperation that drives my own climax further and further on, spattering again and again between us both.

Minutes go by, and then hours. Eternities. Both of us caught in a dizzying world of bleeding, primal orgasms. Until finally Bastien lifts his head and hisses his deep, predatory satisfaction into the dark.

The sound warms up the inside of my chest. I satisfied him. I've felt more alive tonight than I have in years, I've found the wicked ecstasy I came here looking for—and yet the thing that has me smiling at the ceiling is that I've pleased him.

He notices. "You like being my toy?" he murmurs, nuzzling into my bloody neck and kissing it, licking it clean. "My personal priest toy? Hmm?"

"Yes," I grunt. I turn so he has to look at me. "I—I want to do it again."

He laughs a little, kissing my lips and then draping himself on top of me. "We need to wait a while before I drink from you again. Maybe a day or two. But everything else ..."

Hope is scarier than being bitten by a vampire, but I let myself feel it. "You want to see me in a day or two?"

Bastien's ribs heave against mine, and I can't tell if he's laughing at me or if it's one of those self-deprecating laughs for himself. "Aaron," he says, "I don't want to frighten you, but I'm already trying to figure out how I can marry you, or at least keep you locked up naked for my pleasure for the next decade. Yes, I want to see you in a day or two. And a month or two. And a year or two. I have nowhere else to be, and you're the best thing I've found in more than two hundred years. So by all means, consider yourself penciled in."

"Oh," I say. It's about all I can say. I'm feeling too many things to say anything more. Except. "I was a priest in the Order, Bastien. I want this more than you can know, but ... our pasts ..."

Bastien kisses my chest, his hips beginning a gentle war of pressure and friction as he does. "I'll tell you a secret, mon prêtre," he murmurs. "I was a priest too."

For a moment, there is only the sound of the ocean outside. I can't think. I can't even breathe, I'm so stunned. "You were a priest?" I manage.

He doesn't stop his kisses or the sweet thrusts of his hips below. "I joined during la revolution," he says between presses of his lips to my skin. "Because I was terrified. I was the pointless, wastrel son of a comte, and I felt certain I'd be thrown in prison or worse, so I left the Second Estate for the First for no better reason than I was scared of my own bloodline and what it meant. I was asked to join the Order not long after, which I did, and was sent back to Paris to hunt vampires. There were many there that decade, drawn by the slaughter, and there were many vicious, murdering ones that I still don't regret killing. But all it took was one faster than me, one cleverer, and then I was at her mercy, and she drank from me, of course, that unforgivable sin for the Order. She gave me a choice, after—she could let me go back to the Church, where I would have to lie for the rest of my life about being bitten, or she could turn me. I only knew panic then; I was still chasing after some idea of safety. I didn't know I would be trading a short, lonely life for a long, lonely one, or I might have chosen differently, you see."

Bastien falls into silence then, and my chest hurts for him. I wrap my arms around him and brace my heels, and flip us over, so I'm caging him in.

"Christ, you're big," he mutters, but it's with delight as he runs both his hands over my bum and hips and back. My cock likes it when I'm patted and stroked like a prized stud, I guess, because it's all the way hard again, aching a little but ready for more. I rub it against his fresh erection, and we both groan.

"Bastien, I don't want you to be lonely," I say.

"It was maudlin of me to phrase it that way. I'm not lonely right now."

"No." I try again, searching for better words. "I'm not going to let you be lonely. Starting now. I want—I want to be tied to your bed. Married to you. I want your teeth in my neck whenever you're thirsty. I want it, and you've said that I've earned every dirty thing I want by being so good, so I've earned this and I'm taking it."

Bastien's eyes glitter in the dark. "So you are, mon prêtre. So you shall." He sounds happy and hopeful and just as scared as me, and yes, it's undeniable now, I'm falling in love with a vampire. "And if you are to be mine for all these months and years, what shall I do with you next?" he asks.

I rub my cock along the length of his, making us both shiver. "I think I have a few ideas," I tease.

"Look at you," Bastien says proudly. "One day with me and you're making jokes and smiling! You're no longer the antonym to blithe; you are the absolute definition of it. Blithe beyond belief."

I lean down to kiss his beautiful mouth, and I can still taste blood between us. "I think you mean *sanguine*," I say, and then as we're still laughing, Bastien reaches for the bottle and the night sharpens once again into wonderful, wicked desire.

And it doesn't escape my notice that as Bastien worships me into sweet oblivion, the stars outside are raining down light over the sea.

* * *

LOVE YOU FOR ALWAYS

WILLOW WINTERS

ANA

He's already dressed, skipping breakfast and heading out the door. Every weekend has been like this. I barely see my husband in the blur of busy days and tired nights.

I wish we could go back to the Golden Coast. To barefoot walks on the sandy beach and times when kisses came easily. Nearly a decade ago, back to the days when Tristan always held my hand. We slept in and cuddled in bed, which always led to more.

Back to the days I was shy to kiss him before brushing my teeth—because back then we would kiss first thing in the morning.

"You're already going?" I ask Tristan as he pours from the pot of coffee into a thermal tumbler with the company logo on it. I blame his work for all these emotions that keep me up at night, his side of it cold and empty.

Standing in our kitchen, the granite counters clear of clutter except for a single pile of mail, mostly containing bills, and a vase that's been empty since Valentine's Day last year, my husband looks up at me. Sympathy echoes in his piercing blue eyes, and when he swallows, the cords in his neck go tight. It makes the stubble on his jaw look all the sexier. "I have to, honey."

I'll always melt at that nickname.

I'm a sucker for him. He had me the first night he ever laid eyes on me. Tall, broad shoulders that make even a plain white T-shirt look divine on him... I never had a chance with this man.

"I made you coffee though," he offers as if I'd rather have a cup of joe than him. My bare feet pad on the dark gray tiled floors as I make my way to him. They're cold and that makes me all the warmer when he holds me in his arms. Nestling my head against his shoulder, I take in the smell of his cologne and the feel of his muscular chest as he kisses the crown of my head.

"I wish they'd never sold the company," I say just beneath my breath.

Four years ago, his company sold to another. Nearly everyone lost their jobs. We were the lucky ones because they transferred my husband. He kept his job, but it moved him three states away for most of the week.

My heart squeezes when he doesn't say anything other than, "Me too."

I hate how little I see him. I hate that I'm stuck here, with a teaching job I worked my ass off to get, so I barely see my husband. I should be grateful, and for a while I was. But distance makes things harder, and time can change anything.

"Are you sure you have to go?" I question him when he releases me. I tighten the sash on my robe and fold my arms over my chest.

Years ago, at the Golden Coast, he held my hand on our honeymoon and told me he'd love me forever. I love this man with everything in me, but I don't know how much longer we can survive this.

"I have to. I wouldn't leave if I didn't have to."

My throat's tight when I nod in understanding.

It's a Saturday and I'm in nothing but a robe, while he's fully dressed in a slate-gray suit. I want to sleep in and kiss him and love him, to feel him in ways I've desperately been missing. And he says he has to go to work.

"Will you be home for dinner?" I question, finding it hard to keep his questioning gaze.

"Of course." His answer comes out with a careful cadence. Like he knows something's wrong. "You okay?" he questions.

"I miss you," I admit, my voice cracking, but he already knows I miss him. It's gotten harder to be away from him, not easier.

"Let me take you out to dinner tonight," he offers. "A date night. Like we used to do."

Hope flutters in my chest, and a smile slips onto my lips until he adds, "I just have a few things to wrap up."

Late nights and constant work comes with who Tristan is. He's always been this way.

"I'll see you tonight then," I answer, closing the distance, getting up on my tiptoes to plant a kiss on his lips.

I don't expect his hand to splay on my lower back, keeping me pinned to him, or for him to deepen the kiss. But, oh how I love it. His teeth scrape gently against my bottom lip until I part my lips for him, granting him entry. The warmth spreads through me, from my tippy toes all the way up to my cheeks where I can feel a blush blooming.

When he breaks the kiss, he whispers in the air between us, "Love you for always."

I love him for always too. That's why this hurts so much. It wouldn't if I didn't love him the way I do.

ANA

College is supposed to be where you sow your wild oats, or at least that's what my grandmother used to say. Back then, when I first laid eyes on Tristan at a pub on main street at the university, I thought he'd be a fun time.

And I thought that's all it would ever be.

We burned hot together. The casual glances that held on a little too long, the small touches with the passing drinks as a football game played in the background that neither one of us seemed to care about although the rest of the bar roared with excitement or disappointment every other play.

He was tall, dark and handsome. I was wearing my tightest jeans and a flowy top that gave away a little too much cleavage. I thought the moment he leaned down to kiss me, his lips tasting of pale ale and all male, my hand gripping his bicep through a polo, that we'd have a wild night together. One to remember.

I didn't expect him to call me the next day and tell me he was taking me out that weekend. He didn't even ask me. He later told me he was terrified I'd say no if he asked. So he took a risk.

That night I wore a red dress, red is supposed to give you more confidence. And a matching shade of red on my lips for lipstick courage. Complete with my best black heels and a little clutch.

That was the first night he told me I looked beautiful.

A week later was the first morning he made pancakes before I woke up and told me I wasn't allowed to sneak out in the morning like I had been.

A week after that, he told me he had feelings. Seeing each other every few days turned into every other, which turned into us spending fairly equal time, always together, at each other's place.

A month went by before I told him I loved him and he told me he knew, before admitting he loved me too.

I remember it all. Every moment we had. First kiss, first night, first date, first everything.

Each one felt like I wasn't worthy. It's scary to fall in love.

He's the one who said, "I love you for always," first.

In the kitchen, at our first apartment together, he brushed his nose against mine while we were making dinner together, and he said it.

I believed him because it felt like it was meant to be. Like we were simply made for each other.

My phone vibrates on our bed and I barely hear it, the distant memories of our past still lingering, but I do. As I toss the red chiffon dress onto the bed, I don't know why I was crying. I guess it's the pregnancy hormones and the fact that I don't know how I'm going to tell Tristan. We didn't plan it, and I don't know how to tell him. But I have to.

How did we get like this? To the place where we have another first we've both wanted since we got married, but I have no idea how to tell him?

Taking the phone in my hand, I smile at his text: *I'll pick you up at seven.*

TRISTAN

Red is Ana's color.

Something about the shade just suits her. The allure of it, the strength in such a bold choice; she wears it with elegance, even if her fire has dimmed.

As I turn up the radio in the car, it doesn't go unnoticed that she's barely spoken to me. Nervousness pricks its way along the back of my neck. I know she's unhappy and she's been that way, but I'm doing everything I can and tonight I can finally make her happy again.

"You look stunning, honey," I compliment her over the hum of the radio.

I still think I have her, she's still mine because every compliment still makes her smile, that beautiful blush coloring her cheeks to be nearly as dark as the clothes she wears.

"You look pretty darn handsome yourself," she whispers, and it's then that she places her hand on my thigh as I keep driving. I was waiting for that. Her little touches are everything. I've missed them so much.

With my left hand on the wheel as I slow at a red light, I lift her hand with my right and kiss her knuckles, one by one, and then turn her hand over, giving her wrist a kiss before the light turns green.

Her small hum of satisfaction and the way her shoulders relax is everything that I needed.

"Where are we going?" she asks me, and I tell her it's a surprise but she won't have to wait much longer.

"Oh"—she perks up in her seat, a wide smile on her face—"the Blue Grill."

"Our first date as a married couple was here," I remind her.

"How could I forget?" she answers with a smile, her hand still on my thigh as I park the car.

"We sat at the bar because it was so full..."

"My hand may have slipped up your skirt a time or two," I complete the thought for her as I put the car in park and lean over to kiss the crook of her neck. She squeals with delight, and I love it. I love everything about her. What we had and, more importantly, everything to come.

We walk side by side, hand in hand through the large double doors of black glass into the elegant foyer of the restaurant.

When I give my name to the host and he leads us to the private back room, she squeezes my hand and whispers, "What's back here?"

The wooden doors open to a private room with a single round table in the center, the chairs seated close together. The white tablecloth is already laid out with candles, a vase with red roses, and a note on one of the plates. A note I wrote for her.

"Tristan." Ana's voice is tight with emotion, and I simply kiss her cheek and pull out her chair for her.

As she scoots in, I take my own seat and rush things more than I wanted to do. I'd planned to make her wait. To wine and dine her like I used to before telling her. But the look on her face, seeing her break down like this, I can't wait. I have to tell her. She's been through enough. These years apart have been so much harder on her, and I need her to know that we don't have to do it anymore.

"Read it," I whisper as she stares at the crisp white envelope. "I'm not much of a poet or anything, but I have something to tell you."

She reads the note out loud, her eyes watery, so she dabs them first with the corner of the cloth napkin.

I hope you know I don't take you—or us—for granted.

I miss you every day.

When I said I will love you for always, I meant it because that's all I want to do.

I've only worked so much to get back home to you.

. . .

The moment she reads *back home to you*, her hazel eyes widen and she whips her gaze to mine. "What does that mean? You're coming home?" Nervousness and hope wind together in her voice.

Strands of brunette hair fall from the elegant bun on the top of her head. I brush them behind her ear and keep my hand there, cupping her cheek as I tell her.

"I got a job offer in the city. Only forty minutes from our home." Her gasp is covered by her delicate hand. "I've had a few interviews the last few weeks I've been home. That's what I've been doing, but I didn't want to tell you. I didn't want to get your hopes up until I knew for sure. I know this has been hard on us, and I can't be away from you anymore."

I knew she would be happy, but I didn't expect the tears. I didn't realize she was so emotional about it all.

"I never would have stayed away if I'd known it made you this upset." At my admission, she shakes her head, reaching out to my cheek and cupping it like I am hers.

With the tip of her nose brushing against mine, she steadies herself, giving me a peck on the lips before looking back up at me.

"I'm glad you're coming home, because this baby is going to need both of us."

The moment she says *baby*, her hand moves to her belly, and shock and then elation hit me harder than I could ever imagine.

"You're pregnant?" I question her in a single breath, and her wide smile is joined with a nod.

I hug her and she hugs me back, both of us clinging to each other, both of us surprised in the best of ways.

There are ups and downs in marriage, there are good times and there are bad, but moments like these and all our other firsts that we've shared and will share in our lives are so worth every dip on this wild ride.

"I love you," I tell her and kiss her, crushing my lips to hers before she can even say it back.

I love you for always.

* * *

Do you want more of Willow Winters?.

One click HARD TO LOVE now!

CAROLINE'S SURPRISE

SUSAN STOKER

EDITED by KELLI COLLINS/Edit Me This

Caroline thinks her husband, Matthew "Wolf" Steel, is taking her out to dinner for their twenty-fifth anniversary, but he's got a bigger surprise in store.

AUTHOR NOTE

If you read the short story I wrote a few years ago called "The Boardwalk," you already have a clue about what Caroline's surprise is going to be on her twenty-fifth wedding anniversary. But even if you haven't read that other story, you'll hopefully swoon with delight at reading about a man's devotion and love for his wife.

1

Caroline Steel sighed in exasperation as she looked at her husband. She and Matthew "Wolf" Steel had been married for twenty-five years. Today was their anniversary, in fact. They'd checked into a fancy hotel by a beach near their Southern California home, and she'd been looking forward to dinner at one of the finest steakhouses the city had to offer.

But her *dear* husband had just informed her that he wanted to take a walk on the beach before they ate.

"This dress you bought me yesterday isn't exactly appropriate for a beach walk," Caroline protested.

"You look beautiful," Matthew told her.

Caroline loved when he complimented her, but at the moment, she was too irritated to appreciate his comment. "These shoes are going to be impossible on the beach," she told him, trying to think of another excuse that would get her out of his crazy idea.

Her husband loved the ocean. Loved everything about it. The way the wind blew on the coast, the smell of the water, the salt in the air that you could actually taste on your lips. Normally, Caroline did too, but she'd just spent an hour doing her hair and makeup, wanting it to be perfect for their dinner. They'd gone shopping yesterday, and Matthew had bought her the most beautiful floor-length pink dress. It had little cap sleeves and flared out from her waist, making her feel like a princess.

At fifty-seven, Caroline knew she was too old to be considered pretty. The fact of the matter was, she'd *never* been a beauty. She was plain. Boring. But Matthew had always said that, from almost the second he'd seen her, he'd known she was the woman for him. They'd met in an unconventional way, on a plane that had been hijacked by terrorists. Because of her background as a chemist, Caroline had been able to help save everyone on board. But then the people behind the hijacking had come after her...

She didn't like to dwell on that time in her life, but it had brought her Matthew, so she didn't regret one second of what had happened.

Matthew was sixty-one, and instead of looking like a wrinkled old man, he seemed to get more distinguished with age. His hair was sprinkled with a healthy dose of gray, but he kept it cut short, just as he had when he was a Navy SEAL. He'd lost the bulk of the muscles he'd had as a younger man, but Caroline was still just as attracted to him today as she'd been twenty-five years ago when they'd gotten married.

There had been some hiccups on their wedding day—namely, they'd never made it to the church because of a car accident involving their friends—but that hadn't stopped them. They'd ended up saying their vows in the emergency room, surrounded by all their loved ones. Caroline had never regretted not having a traditional wedding; she was too thankful to have Wolf as her very own.

But, there were times when her husband drove her crazy. Like now.

He had no idea what walking along the boardwalk would do to her hair. It would blow all her hard work to smithereens. By the time they arrived at the restaurant, she'd look pathetic, and Matthew would probably look just as polished and handsome as he did right this minute.

He was wearing a pair of jeans and a navy polo. And while some people might think it odd that he was wearing denim to a fancy restaurant, Caroline loved that he did what he wanted, wore what he wanted, and could get away with it.

"Matthew, seriously, I want to look good for you tonight, and if we walk along the ocean, I'm going to be a mess."

Matthew walked toward her and took her head in his hands. Tilting it up so she had to look in his eyes, he said lovingly, "You always look beautiful, Ice. I don't care if you wear your pajamas or this beautiful dress. You're the love of my life, and I'm always proud to be by your side."

She shivered in delight when he called her Ice. He'd given her the nickname back when they'd first met, and it always made her go gooey inside when he uttered it. "Matthew," Caroline complained, "I love you, but sometimes you're clueless."

"Just for a little bit," Matthew cajoled. "We won't stay long, but I have it on good authority that there's something you're going to want to see on the beach this evening."

Caroline sighed, knowing when she was beaten. When Matthew's voice got low and he gave her those puppy dog eyes, she couldn't deny him anything. "Fine, but if we're late for our reservations, I'm blaming you."

Her husband beamed. "Deal." Then he leaned down and kissed her. The kiss started out tender and light, but soon morphed into something much more passionate. They might be older and not have the stamina they used to, but their sex life was still active and intense.

Caroline pulled back and put her hand on her husband's cheek. "I love you," she told him.

"I love you too. And I plan on showing you how much tonight when we get back here to our room."

"I can't believe you got the honeymoon suite," Caroline said with a shake of her head. "I would've been perfectly happy with a regular room. This one is way too expensive."

"Nothing is too expensive for you," Matthew said. "I might not be able to buy you a brand-new Lamborghini, but I can splurge every now and then on a nice hotel room with some extras to make sure you know how much you're loved."

"Like the dozen roses?" Caroline asked, peeking over at the gorgeous bouquet on the table next to the bed. She'd wanted them as close to her as possible so she could smell them all night, even while she was sleeping.

"And the chocolate-covered strawberries, and the champagne," Matthew said with a smile. "Now, come on, we need to get going," he told her, grabbing hold of her hand and pulling her toward the door.

"I swear, if there's a volleyball tournament with scantily clad women jumping around, I'm gonna have to hurt you," Caroline mock threatened.

"Maybe they're guys wearing banana hammocks," Matthew teased.

"Ewwww. Gross," Caroline said on a laugh. She adored that her husband still made her laugh after all these years. When they were on the elevator on the way to the lobby, Caroline leaned into Wolf. "If I forget to tell you later, thank you for the best twenty-five years of my life."

He kissed the top of her head. "I think that's my line."

The doors opened, and Matthew exited slightly in front of Caroline. It was one of the small ways he was always protecting her. Always on the lookout for people walking too fast who could run into her, or ruffians who might think they were an easy mark because of their ages. Matthew had surprised more than one person with his strength and determination to keep her safe.

They walked through the lobby, and Matthew nodded at the concierge as he passed. Then they were on the street walking toward the boardwalk nearby. It wasn't much of a boardwalk, really, more like an old wooden walkway along a stretch of sand. It wasn't very long, but Caroline liked the benches the city had placed along the route, and the fact there were people out and about, from young to old, enjoying the fresh ocean air.

She and Matthew walked hand in hand, and Caroline had to admit that this was a great idea. Her husband held her shoes in his left hand and held on to her tightly with his right. "I can't decide which beach is my favorite," she said easily. "I mean, I love Southern California, and we've spent most of our time here, but there was something so magical about the beach in Alaska."

"Magical?" Matthew asked. "It was damn cold if you asked me."

Caroline laughed. "Well, at least you didn't have to swim in it."

"Not *that* time, I didn't," he retorted.

Caroline didn't know all the details about the missions her husband had gone on as a SEAL, but she knew that's what he was referring to. She squeezed his hand, trying to let him know how proud she was of him, then went on with her thought. "The boardwalk in New Jersey was fun. All the stalls with food and arcade games. I liked that beach too."

Matthew grunted. She knew that hadn't been his favorite vacation, but he'd gone because she'd wanted to experience it.

"I think Hawaii was my second favorite," she went on. "Not Waikiki, there were too many people there to truly enjoy the beaches, but the North Shore was amazing. I can't believe how big those waves were. The surfers were insane! But there's one beach I keep hearing about that I'd love to visit."

"Where's that? I'll get a ticket tomorrow," Matthew said.

And Caroline knew he wasn't kidding. He would totally go online and buy them tickets to wherever she wanted to go. Leaning against him, she wrapped her arm around his waist, enjoying the feel of his own around her shoulders. They kept walking down the boardwalk at a slow and steady pace. People easily passed them, walking, running, biking, and riding scooters, but neither seemed to notice.

"Australia. I've never been there, but everyone I've talked to who's visited has said the people are lovely. I even went and looked up famous beaches over there."

"You want to go to the Great Barrier Reef?" Wolf asked.

Caroline shook her head. "No. I mean, yes, I'd love to see it, but I think I'd like to visit Bondi Beach. It's only about thirty minutes from downtown Sydney, and there are a ton of great restaurants in the area. The history of it is fascinating. Bondi was originally Boondi, which is an aboriginal word meaning 'surf' in English. It's iconic, and I'd love to see it someday."

Matthew stopped abruptly in the middle of the boardwalk, and Caroline looked up at him. "What's wrong?"

"Nothing's wrong. If you want to go to Australia, I'll take you to Australia. I'll make sure you see kangaroos, koalas, and echidnas. We'll go to a show at the famous opera house and have dinner with the Sydney bridge in the background. And yes, we'll go to Bondi Beach. I'll even swallow my pride and take you to Manly Beach."

Caroline giggled. "Is that really what it's called?"

"Yup. But don't get your hopes up, the only man I want you ogling at Manly Beach is me."

"That's a given," Caroline said, snuggling up to her husband. "And thank you for indulging me."

"I'd do anything for you," Matthew said. "Come on, the thing I wanted to show you is just ahead."

Caroline had already forgotten that Matthew wanted to show her something. She assumed it was maybe a sandcastle building contest or something. She'd always been fascinated with the detailed sand creations people could make.

They walked farther down the beach until Caroline saw a large group of people gathered on the sand ahead of them. She couldn't see what was going on, but figured that was where Matthew was taking her.

Caroline wasn't paying attention to where they were going, too busy daydreaming about Australia and holding a cute koala bear, when Matthew stopped and turned toward the beach.

She finally focused—and gasped in surprise.

She *knew* the people on the beach. They were their friends.

All of Matthew's SEAL teammates were there with their wives. Abe and Alabama, Cookie and Fiona, Mozart and Summer, Dude and Cheyenne, Benny and Jessyka, and his old commander with his wife, Julie, too. Even Tex and Melody were there.

Not only that, but many of the other SEAL men they'd gotten to know over the years were also there with *their* wives. Children were everywhere, the older ones looking after the younger ones.

And every single person was wearing white. White shirts, dresses, pants. It was as if a cloud of white had descended on the beach...and it was beyond beautiful.

There were also rows of chairs set up in the sand facing what looked like an altar.

"What? What's happening?" Caroline asked, looking up at Matthew.

"I'd go down on one knee, but we both know I'd probably make an ass out of myself trying to get up since my knees are shot. I'm sorry you missed out on your beautiful church wedding twenty-five years ago, Ice. I thought you might like a do-over of sorts, and we could renew our vows right here."

"*Now?*" she asked stupidly.

Matthew grinned. "Yeah. Right now. All our friends are here. I'm sorry, but I lied about dinner at that fancy steak place. I promise to take you there later. The hotel here"—he gestured to a large hotel behind them—"is catering a reception right on the beach after our ceremony."

Caroline wanted to cry. Matthew wasn't the most traditionally romantic man. The roses and chocolates back in their honeymoon suite were the most traditional things he'd done in a very long time. But he showed her every day how much he loved and cared about her. Filled up her car with gas, made dinner most nights for them, took the garbage out, held her hand everywhere they went. She'd always take Wolf exactly the way he was, without the over-the-top romantic gestures.

But this...this was the most amazing thing that had ever happened to her. She knew how much work went into planning something like this. From talking to the hotel to getting all their friends to coordinate their schedules. "Was this what you were doing all those times I caught you being all secret-like?"

He looked a bit sheepish. "Yes. I prayed you wouldn't think I was cheating on you or something. All those late-night phone calls and the extra time I was spending on the computer. I just wanted this night to be perfect for you. I'd give you the moon if I could swing it."

"I love you, Matthew. So much."

"And I love you too. So? What do ya think? Shall we do this?"

"Yes!" Caroline exclaimed.

They walked hand in hand toward their friends, and Caroline noticed that Matthew had even hired a professional photographer who was clicking away on his camera as they approached the group.

As soon as they got close, they were surrounded by their friends. Everyone wanted to give their congratulations and crow about how they'd been able to keep this a secret from her.

Caroline accepted their teasing and knew she was smiling like an idiot. She had no idea where Matthew had put her shoes, and was well aware that her hair—which she'd worked so painstakingly to put up—was blowing out of control, but she no longer cared one bit.

After fifteen minutes of saying hello to everyone and thanking them for coming, Matthew whistled sharply. "Okay everyone, enough chitchat. Time for me to marry my wife...again."

Everyone laughed. It took a few minutes to wrangle the children, but soon everyone was sitting and gazing back expectantly at Caroline and Matthew at the end of the makeshift aisle in the sand.

"You ready?" Matthew whispered.

"For you? Always," Caroline told him.

Then they walked slowly down the aisle toward the justice of the peace Matthew had hired. Caroline barely held it together as he welcomed everyone. He spoke of everlasting love and friendship. His words were heartfelt and resonated within Caroline.

She and Matthew gazed into each other's eyes while he was talking, and she'd never felt closer to her husband.

Soon, it was Matthew's turn to speak.

Caroline blinked in surprise and realized that she was going to have to come up with something romantic and witty to say on the spur of the moment. She wasn't ready! Had no idea what to say.

But then...she couldn't think about *anything* but Matthew's words.

"Twenty-five years ago, I took you as my wife. I thought it was the best day of my life, but I was wrong. Every day that followed was the best day. I believe in our marriage, in us, more strongly today than ever before. You never wavered in your support of me. Every time I said goodbye and went on a mission for the Navy, you never showed your fear. Never did or said anything to let me know you were feeling anything other than support and love for me.

"But I know you were scared. Terrified that you wouldn't see me again. You did what you needed to do, and that made our reunions all the more sweet. I love you, Caroline Steel. You've made me a better man in every single way. I stand here in front of you today, with our friends as witnesses, to renew my original vows to you. Through sickness and health. I will protect you, stand by you—and in front of you, if needed. I will put you first, because you spent much of our marriage putting my wants and needs ahead of your own. No matter where life takes us in the next twenty-five years, know that I will always be there for you."

Caroline was crying ugly tears. The kind that made her eyes red and puffy, but she couldn't help it. She never would've thought she could be as happy as she was right this second—and Matthew had kept her pretty damn happy the last twenty-five years. When she'd first met him, she'd been at a weird place in her life. Wanting to find someone who would appreciate her for who she was, but not thinking it would ever happen. She'd been overlooked by just about everyone. But after a rocky start, Matthew had *seen* her. And had loved her anyway.

"Your turn, Ice," Matthew said with a small smile. He reached out and wiped the tears off her cheeks gently, then tucked a lock of hair behind her ear.

"I'm not sure I can follow that," Caroline said honestly. "But I'll try. There *were* times over the last twenty-five years when I wasn't sure I could do this. Be married to a Navy SEAL. To a man larger than life like you. I was afraid I'd fade into the background and be lost in your shadow. But from day one of our marriage, you refused to let that happen. Through your strength and love, I blossomed. You gave me the gift of friendship with your teammates, and I gained sisters through their wives.

"I love you more today because of all that we've been through. I promise to be by your side when you're sick, hurt, or in need of comfort. I promise to make sure you know how appreciated you are every day for the rest of our lives, no matter how long that might be. I'm not scared to live to be a hundred and ten, because I know you'll be by my side, loving me, protecting me, and giving me the best life you can. I love you, Matthew. I can't wait to see what the next twenty-five years has in store for us."

"I love you," Matthew whispered as he leaned close.

"I think you're supposed to wait to be told to kiss her!" Dude yelled from the audience, but Matthew ignored him.

Caroline grinned before her husband kissed her as passionately as he had the first time they'd gotten married. It might make some of the younger kids on the beach wince, but she couldn't wait to get Matthew back to their honeymoon suite and show him how much he meant to her.

As if he could read her mind, Matthew whispered against her lips, "Reception first, Ice, then bed." He pulled back, turned her to face their audience, and held up their clasped hands. "Married...again!" he yelled.

Caroline knew she was smiling crazily but didn't care in the least. When Matthew was happy, she was happy.

Once again, they were surrounded by their friends, everyone congratulating them and telling them how beautiful the ceremony was.

They all walked up to the hotel as a group, and Caroline gasped at the setup. It was both elegant and laid-back...which fit the setting perfectly. There were beautiful flower arrangements on every table with candles she knew would give the area a romantic glow after the sun went down. The tables were placed right in the sand, and a huge buffet was arranged off to the side.

Matthew led her to the front of the line and proceeded to pile her plate high with food.

"Matthew, I can't eat all that!" Caroline protested, laughing.

"You can try," he told her.

"Why are you always trying to get me to eat?" she grumbled as he led the way to one of the tables.

"Because you need the vitamins," he said with a smile. "Gotta get the proper nutrients in you when I can. If it was left up to you, you'd eat nothing but doughnuts and other junk food."

Caroline smiled because he was probably right.

"And before you complain, green beans are good for you," Matthew told her. "And...you know I'll eat what you can't finish."

She *did* know that. Matthew had been eating her leftovers for as long as they'd been married. It was kind of their thing. Of course, he wasn't a Navy SEAL anymore and had to watch how much he ate, but they both loved the tradition they'd started so long ago.

The meal was delicious, and Caroline didn't even mind the wind blowing her hair in her food or how the seagulls were standing watch only feet away, waiting for a child to leave their plate unattended, or the chance to snatch a dropped piece of bread.

When the staff brought out dessert, Caroline wasn't surprised to see what Matthew had chosen.

"German chocolate cake?" she asked with a laugh.

"Yup. It's our favorite."

"*Your* favorite," she corrected.

"Yup," he agreed again, not looking abashed in the least.

Caroline didn't mind. He deserved an extra-large slice of his all-time favorite cake for pulling off this surprise. Everything had been perfect as far as she was concerned. And she loved Matthew all the more for putting it together.

She ate as much as she could of her cake and grinned when Matthew pulled her unfinished portion over in front of him.

As he polished off the rest of her slice, Caroline rested her head on his shoulder. A waiter brought over a tea kettle filled with hot water and a bag of Earl Gray tea. She smiled at her husband.

"Now that's really *your* favorite," he said with confidence.

"It is," Caroline agreed. "You spoil me."

"I'd do anything for you," he told her.

After she'd finished her tea, Wolf stood and held out his hand to her. Caroline took it and he led her to the middle of all the tables, where there was a small space in the sand. He pulled out his phone and clicked on it a few times until the sound of their wedding song filled the air around them.

"May I have this dance?" Matthew asked.

Caroline nodded as he took her in his arms. They swayed back and forth in the sand as "Come To Me" by the Goo Goo Dolls played. It was an unconventional wedding song, but she'd never forget how he'd changed the lyrics twenty-five years ago to perfectly fit their situation and their courtship. She'd loved him then, and she loved him now. More than she could adequately put into words.

When they finished their dance, Caroline realized that most of their friends had stood up and were swaying back and forth as well. There was so much love around them, Caroline almost felt overwhelmed.

"The sun's about to set. Come with me," Matthew said, pulling her toward the ocean. Caroline went without a fuss.

Matthew stopped just beyond where the waves reached the sand on the beach and turned to face her. He put his arms around her waist, and she rested her palms on his chest.

"I'm sorry I lied to you," Matthew told her. "I really wanted this to be a surprise."

"You can lie to me about things like this all you want," she replied, grinning. "No one other than you has ever made me feel so special and loved."

"You *are* loved," Matthew said seriously. "Everyone was thrilled to come today. We might not have had kids, but everyone here thinks of you as their second mother."

"I know. Remember that time I thought it would be a good idea to have thirteen of those little stinkers over at the same time so their parents could have some time alone?" she asked.

"Don't remind me," Matthew said, mock shuddering.

"Do you regret not having kids?" she couldn't help but ask.

"No." His answer was immediate and firm. "I've loved having you to myself. I know that makes me a selfish bastard, but there ya go. Besides, we've practically helped raise our friends' kids, I don't feel as if we've missed out."

"But we don't have anyone to take care of us when we get old."

"Some people would say we're *already* old," Matthew said without a hint of worry in his tone. "Besides, you've got *me* to take care of you, and you'll take care of me. We'll be fine."

Just then, Tex's granddaughter, his daughter Akilah's firstborn, crashed into Wolf's legs, almost knocking him over. She was only four but already quite smart. "Tag, Uncle Wolf, you're it!" the little girl yelled, then dashed away.

Matthew looked back up at Caroline and quirked his eyebrow. "Not have kids?" he asked dryly with a grin.

Caroline threw her head back and laughed until her stomach hurt. He was right. She may not have given birth to a child, but she'd definitely done her part in raising the young men and women who'd shared their special day. And now those kids were having their own children. The cycle of life would continue, and both she and Wolf had more than enough family to take care of them if they needed it when they were older.

"Look," Matthew said softly, turning her to watch the sun go down beyond the horizon.

Caroline was always surprised at how fast it happened. One second the sun was there as an orange ball in the sky, and the next it was just gone.

Life was like that. One day you were happy and living the best life you could, and the next you were gone. But never forgotten.

Everyone left a legacy behind, and she hoped she and Matthew would leave a good one.

As they made their way back up to the reception area, the photographer —who'd followed them without their knowledge—showed them a picture he'd taken. It was of the two of them standing by the ocean, the sun setting behind them. Caroline was laughing with her head thrown back, and Matthew was looking down at her, smiling.

"Oh my God," Caroline gasped as she looked at the picture on the man's camera. "I'm totally framing that."

The man smiled. "Yeah, I think it's my favorite of the night, and that's saying something, because you have a beautiful family."

Yes, they certainly did.

* * *

Later that night, Wolf slowly unzipped the beautiful pink dress and slipped it off Caroline's shoulders. He couldn't believe how beautiful his wife still was. She had more wrinkles than she used to, and she complained that her skin sagged in all the wrong places, but all he saw was perfection.

She went into the bathroom to get ready for bed, and he did the same in the second bathroom the luxury suite provided.

They met back in the bedroom, and Caroline climbed on the bed and opened her arms to him. Wolf quickly joined her, pulling her into his embrace. He inhaled deeply, loving the smell of salt and the fresh ocean air that lingered on her skin.

Neither of them were young anymore, but that had never stopped them from loving each other. Wolf eased his way down Caroline's body, excited by the look in her half-closed eyes as he spread her legs and settled himself between them.

After he'd sent her soaring with an orgasm, he climbed back up her body and eased himself inside her. He made love to his wife slow and easy, never taking his eyes from hers. He didn't last long, never did anymore, but that didn't matter to either of them.

Closing his eyes and memorizing the feel of Caroline under and around him, Wolf exploded.

He gathered his wife into his arms again and covered them both with the sheet. She snuggled into him just as she had for the last twenty-five years.

"What's your favorite memory from our life together so far?" Caroline asked sleepily.

"You waking up next to me, and seeing the love in your eyes when you open them and see *me*," Wolf said without hesitation.

"Really?" Caroline asked. "Out of everything we've done, that's your favorite?"

"Absolutely," Wolf told her. "What about you?"

"It's impossible for me to narrow it down to one thing," Caroline said with a small shake of her head. "It's the way you always make me feel as if what I say matters. The way you listen...really *listen* to me. When we look at each other, and it's like we're thinking the same thing, like we share a brain."

"I love that," Wolf admitted.

She was quiet for so long that Wolf thought she'd fallen asleep, but then she surprised him by saying quietly, "I think the reason I wake up looking at you with love in my eyes is because I always sleep well, knowing you're watching over me."

Wolf felt his eyes misting. He wasn't a crier. Never had been. Being a Navy SEAL had pretty much assured that. He'd seen and experienced too much to cry at the drop of a hat. But her words struck him hard.

"I'll *always* watch over you, Ice. No matter what happens in the future. You can count on me."

He'd expected a loving reply, but all he got was a light snore.

Chuckling softly, Wolf closed his eyes and tightened his grip on his wife. He and Caroline were a matched pair. And while he had no idea what was in store for him and Ice in the future, he knew without a doubt he'd do whatever it took to make the next half century just as great as the first twenty-five had been.

* * *

Do you want more of Susan Stoker?

One click SECURING CAITE now!

BAD REUNION

A JEZEBEL COVE PREQUEL FICLET

ROBIN COVINGTON

1

I wasn't in Melbourne anymore.

I had a million things to do and the countdown clock to the grand reopening was ticking down to go time, but I had to take a minute and soak in the fact that I was standing in the middle of my bar.

My. Bar.

Not the bar I was managing for someone else. Not the bar where I was working as many shifts as they would throw at me to get the tips. Not the bar where I was training to learn how to pour drinks and manage the weekend crowd. Not the bar where I used to have go in and drag my father and brothers out when Mom got tired of waiting on them at home.

No. This was *my bar*. Well, it was mine as long as I kept making payments to the bank, and there would be nothing and no one who would stand in between me and making this place one-hundred-percent mine.

There was still lots to do, and the workers would be back here bright and early tomorrow morning to complete the tasks of installing fixtures and refinishing floors and tiling bathroom floors in time for the final inspection. But right now it was just me, the crates of glasses ready for me to put them away, and Halsey on the Bluetooth speaker.

I wouldn't have had it any other way.

If someone had told me twelve years ago that I'd be back here, I would have taken that bet and not felt bad at all about taking their money. With my prom dress balled up on the floor of my room, I'd beat feet out of Jezebel Cove and signed on as a crew member on the boat that would take me as far away from here as possible. The massive yacht on its way to Australia had been my ticket to ride and leave my shitty family situation and a lifetime of judgment and pity behind me.

The nautical miles, each one sliding away under the waves the boat left in its wake, had given me room to breathe and space to think about what it was I wanted. Australia had given me time and opportunity to flex my muscles and stand on my own two feet and figure out who Twila Parsons really was. Not the daughter of Harlan Parsons, career criminal and drunk. Not the sister of Billy and Joe, two brothers determined to follow-on in the family business. Not the girl who'd needed hand-me-downs out of the bin at the Methodist church.

It had been the right thing to do, the only way to save myself, and I regretted nothing.

Well, almost nothing.

I'd left unfinished business behind. Not because I'd wanted to—but it had been me or everyone else who hung expectations and needs on my shoulders and my heart. Things that had been too heavy to bear, too much to carry with me.

No matter how much it had broken my heart to leave ... him ... them behind.

I shook off the emo bullshit, moving toward my phone to change the playlist to something with less regret and more kicking ass. Lizzo popped up on the screen, her voice filling the space and bouncing off the hardwood ceilings as I shimmied my ass to the beat, grabbing the towel to polish the glasses that wouldn't get on the shelves by themselves. Opening Twilight and tackling the mountain-sized task of making my business successful had to be my focus, my future. Nothing would be accomplished by dwelling on a past that most people had forgotten over the past twelve years.

What had to be accomplished was the hiring of the few remaining staff and starting the training sessions. Serving drinks and food wasn't rocket science, but I had definite ideas about how I wanted my place to function. Jezebel Cove wasn't the big city, but we had a pretty even mix of locals and tourists and both had money to burn for a good meal, generous drinks, and a place to see and be seen. I had the cook and the location near the cove, and everything else would be built on good service and word of mouth.

Coming back home hadn't been my first choice. I loved Melbourne and I had built a life there but I'd always known that I would have to return one day. And then a call from my brother and I'd known it was time. Dad and Billy had run one job too many, and it looked like they were going away for a long time. Mom needed me. Billy's wife and kids needed me. Family was family ... no matter how many miles you put between them. So, I had come home, and here I was.

"Hello the house!"

The deep voice, echoing off the walls and floors of the relatively empty space, scared the crap out of me, and I let loose a shrill whoop of surprise as I jumped and braced myself behind the bar. I hadn't locked the front door of the building, and that had been a really dumb oversight because while this guy didn't sound like a serial killer, the problem with most serial killers is that they didn't sound like one when you first met them.

I instantly regretted listening to so many true crime podcasts, but I was glad that I'd taken those self-defense classes in Melbourne. My phone was on the other end of the room, but I had plenty of things behind the bar that I could use as a weapon if necessary. I pocketed a steel corkscrew and peered around the ladders, stacks of chairs, and crates of glassware to see who my first potential future customer was.

The guy was big enough to live up to the voice. Dark hair peeking out from under a baseball cap, broad shoulders, and large hands carrying the large box that obscured his face.

"We're not open yet," I said, rising up on tiptoe to try and get a look at him. He was tall, and while I wasn't tiny, my five feet four inches wasn't enough to grant me a glimpse of his face. At this point I still couldn't tell if he was friend or foe.

"That's okay. I'm just here to drop something off for Jagged Arrow Distillery." He stopped in the middle of the floor, neck craning to get a look around and feet shifting uncomfortably. "This box is heavy and full of bottles of bourbon and I don't want to drop them so..."

"Oh shit," I said, realizing that he wasn't here to murder me but to deliver the case of locally distilled and famous whiskey I'd ordered for the bar. I swept my arm along the bar top, clearing a pretty big spot where he could dump his package. "Here, walk straight ahead and put the box on the bar. It's all clear."

I heard a deep rumble of a laugh from behind the box, and then I watched as he shuffled forward a little bit at a time as I motioned him towards me with gestures there was no way he could actually see.

"You're there. Another two steps. You got it. Just lower the box straight down and you're good."

He grunted when some part of his body hit something but the box didn't waiver and he slowly lowered his package to the bar with the barest clink of the glass bottles contained inside. I dived into the parcel, opening the top to pull out a bottle and admire the deep, caramel-amber liquid inside and the all-too-familiar label on the outside.

"Twila, is that you?"

I looked up, my heart thudding in my chest as it recognized the voice before my brain could catch up. His face looked the same but different, stronger and leaner. He was taller, broader, his eyes the same deep color of the bourbon his family made. His mouth, lips full but currently not twisted in the smile that had made my stomach flip and my body flush with heat. His hair ... it was so different. Short and austere, nothing like the way he used to wear it flowing over his shoulders and down his back. It had been a source of pride for him. A connection to the ancestors of his mother, his tie to the Cherokee nation. And now it was gone.

He wasn't the boy I'd left behind, but my body would have known this man anywhere.

It was Jake. Jake Blackstock. My Jake.

My one and only regret.

2

I was going to kill my brother.

I'd have to figure out a way to hide the fact that I had strangled the living shit out of him from my parents, but I would bet hard-earned money that Riley had planned this moment. He was probably at home right now laughing his ass off. The ass I was going to kick all the way to the next county as soon as I figured out why the-one-that-got-away was standing in the newest bar in town looking good enough to eat.

"Twila?" I was repeating myself, but honestly I was trying to verify that she was real. God knows I'd seen her enough in my dreams over the years.

"Jake?" Twila stood there, the bottle in a white-knuckle grip in her hands. Her expression was a cross between *what the fuck* and *somebody catch me*, but I couldn't think of a damn thing to say.

For two people who had once had everything to say to each other, it was painfully clear that we had nothing to say to each other right now.

The bottle slipped, almost in slow motion, and that broke the stalemate of silence between us as we both lunged for it at the same time. I was too slow around the end of the bar to really have any chance of catching it, so I closed my eyes in relief when Twila caught it in midfall, stopping its progress a few inches from the floor.

We both huffed out a burst of laughter, kneeling on the floor and grinning at each other like the first two idiots who had discovered fire. The almost-disaster had sucked the suffocating awkwardness out of the room, and what was left felt like it was manageable. My mom always said that the first few minutes of any new situation was the worst, and while I didn't always give a thumbs-up to the stuff she said, I was going to run with this one.

"Jesus, that was close."

"And your stuff isn't cheap. If I had broken that bottle, I would have cried on the spot."

"Riley would have comped you a bottle."

"And I would have let him," Twila said, reaching up to place the bottle on the counter above us. I rose to my feet, offering her a hand, and was shocked when she took it. It wasn't an immediate—she hesitated for a couple of long seconds and then put her hand in mine with a brisk shrug of her shoulders.

The contact was immediately charged with something sharper than electricity. It surprised me and it shouldn't have. This was the girl who'd had me hooked from the first time I'd set eyes on her. And here I was, right back under her really inconvenient spell.

One touch and I remembered every time my fingers had caressed her skin and stroked her body. I knew that her eyes closed when she came, her body releasing a sigh as she came down from the high. She liked to ride me, controlling our pleasure and dragging it out until we were both wrung out and empty. Twila loved it when I kissed her after I'd gone down on her, relishing the taste of her on my lips. I remembered it all in vivid, excruciating, body-tightening detail.

And from the rapid-fire pulse of her heartbeat just under the skin of her wrist, Twila remembered it all as well.

She stood and we stared at each other for several long, heavy moments before she closed her eyes and swallowed hard. I mirrored her actions, desperate to reclaim my own balance. Twila took a step back and tugged out of my grasp, putting enough distance between us to break the inconvenient rebirth of stuff that needed to stay buried in the past. When she opened her eyes again, her voice was clear.

"I was expecting Riley to bring the delivery. When we talked on the phone, he said he wanted to come by and check it out."

I let out a breath, glad that we were both going to act like we didn't have an elephant-sized past sitting in the corner booth of the bar. I wasn't one to run from conflict, but damn, I needed a minute for this one.

"He was dealing with some shit at the farm. I was free, so I told him I'd bring it by." I looked around the space, taking in the changes she's made to this place. "Wow. This looks different from when Al had it. This is amazing."

Twila looked around the room, her smile genuine and so much like the one I had spent hours coaxing out of her a lifetime ago. I'd lived for that smile. Hell, I'd lived for this girl.

"Thanks. I think it's going to be okay." She shot me a look that was now equally threaded with doubt, giving away just how much she had on the line with this venture. Twila didn't give much away; she kept most things to herself, or at least she had. I didn't really know this woman. "I'm busting my ass to make it work, so it won't be because I didn't try."

And she'd been busy. The inside of the old warehouse-turned-pub was a mix of the old wood and nicer seating and fixtures. The new lighting made it cozier and sexy instead of scary and suspicious. If the food was good and the booze prices were decent, then she'd be packed every night she was open.

I waved her off, mentally cataloging what I knew about the current state of business in Jezebel Cove. There were a lot of pluses. "You've got a great location near the the cove to grab the tourists, and people have always come down here to hang out. The fact that the place will be updated to the current decade is all good."

"From your mouth to God's ears," she said, crossing her fingers.

"I'm guessing you know how to run a bar?" I asked and knew the minute it passed my lips that I had asked the wrong thing if we were trying to avoid the past. No, my question was like inviting a vampire in the door: once you did it, you couldn't take it back.

"Yeah." Twila drew out the word, clearly thinking through her response. I had a feeling that this conversation was going to answer a lot of the questions that had gone unanswered the last twelve years. Her family had refused to tell me anything. "I ran a few bars in Melbourne."

"Melbourne."

"Australia," she clarified.

I let that sink in for a minute. "You went to Australia?" I took a breath, but the anger was right there on the surface and I did my level best to not give in to it. Twelve years of pissed off wasn't what I needed to let loose right now. Or ever. I wouldn't give Twila or any of the Parsons the satisfaction. "Wow. I didn't realize that you had to run across the world to get away from me."

Her eyes narrowed, arms crossed over her chest in frustration. Wrong thing to say. Again. But I didn't care.

"That's not fair, Jake," Twila hissed, pointing up at me, her expression all kinds of furious. "It wasn't about you."

"Hard to tell when you cut me out of your life." I leaned over, our faces inches away from each other. "I had no idea where you were. None."

"I left a note!"

"All it said was, 'I can't stay. Don't hate me.'"

"Did you hate me? Did you, Jake?"

The question hit me from out of the blue, but the smallness of her voice didn't stop me from unleashing my anger on her.

"Yes. Yes, I did."

Jesus. If I could have taken it back, I would have. Not the truth of it but the way it slammed into her. I saw the impact of my admission on her face for a split second before Twila lurched backward, twisting away from me and careening toward the bar. Her arm caught a couple of glasses on the bar top and sent them flying, and there was no Hail Mary catch to save them from shattering on the hardwood floor.

"Fuck!" Twila growled out and dropped into a squat, reaching out with unsteady fingers to clean up the mess. "Fuck. Fuck." She picked up a large shard of glass and dropped it almost as quickly, blood running down her fingers. "Ow. Fuck."

"Damn it, Twila." I knelt down next to her on the floor, and took her bleeding hand in my own. She pulled back, but I held on tight, reaching behind me to grab a roll of paper towels. I tore a few off and pressed them against the cut, glaring at her when she tried to pull away. "Stop it. I want to see if you need stitches."

"This is your fault, Jake."

"Guilty as charged. Be still." I sighed, pulling off the towel to get a better look at the cut. Not too deep. She wouldn't need stitches.

"Give me my hand back."

"Hold on a minute. I need to put pressure on it again. I almost have the bleeding stopped."

I tugged back on her arm, and Twila fell into me, her body pressed against mine. I could feel the swell of her breast, the soft brush of her hair against my cheek, the hot exhale of her breath on my mouth. We stared at each other, gazes locked in anger and dissolving into something more like regret. Whether it was for the current situation or the past, I didn't know.

"I didn't hate you, Twila." The confession was easy to give. It was the truth.

She sucked in a breath, her exhale shaky and wet with emotion that she blinked out of her eyes. "I don't know why not. I would have hated you."

I shook my head. "I never wanted to hate you."

"I wanted you to." Twila's voice dropped into a whisper that I had to lean in to catch all of it. "I hoped that you hated me. It's easier."

"Nothing about it was easy."

"Jake."

Her voice broke on my name, and that broke the control I'd fooled myself into thinking I had gained over the last twelve years. When it came to Twila Parsons, control was a myth.

Kissing her was as natural as breathing. I had no idea who made the move first and it didn't even matter because we met in the middle, our lips brushing against each other's in a firm, deliberate press that had one purpose: to learn each other again. Mouths opened, tongues collided, and the wet, slick heat of her was more addictive than any of the drinks she would serve in this bar.

Twila moaned against my mouth, her hands gliding up my chest to wrap themselves around my neck and drag me down to her. She took control for the moment, deepening the kiss with long, languid pulls that deprived us both of oxygen and left us both panting and aching for more. I tangled my fingers in her hair, the silky strands cool against the rapidly rising heat of my skin. I soaked her in, the scent of her body warmth and sweet perfume making my head spin. Leaning in closer wasn't just an option, it was vital, the only thing keeping me tethered to this moment.

"Twila. So damn beautiful," I murmured, my lips skimming across her cheek before pulling back to look down at her. Her dark eyes were hot, pupils blown with her arousal, and my body responded to Twila in the only way it knew how. She knew it was coming, and when I dived back in and claimed her mouth, she opened to me, demanding for me to take what she offered.

I was ravenous, barely taking time for ragged breaths in between the frantic joining of our mouths. I teased her, teased myself, alternating between possession and tender exploration, making her groan and clutch at my shoulders. I read her response as an invitation and dragged her onto my lap, breathing a sigh of relief when she straddled my hips and ground her pussy into my hard cock. It was an electric, sharp-edged arousal that teetered on the fine edge of pain and pleasure. I wanted this. Craved it. My body remembered how good we were together, and it wanted another chance to find pleasure in with her.

"Jake. Yes."

"Jesus. You're sweet." I lowered my head and bit along the curve of her shoulder, bared to me because of the slim straps of her tank top. I rubbed my hands up her arms, exploring her body, one slipping down to palm her ass and drag her pelvis even closer to me.

I cupped her breast with my free hand, stroking her nipple as I reclaimed her mouth with a wet, hungry kiss. She ground down on me, making us both shudder with the promise of even greater pleasure if we could just get rid of all these damn clothes.

"Twila, I want you. Let me fuck you, baby." I kissed the edge of her mouth, tongue dipping in to tease, entice. I needed to feel her around me, riding me slowly until we both collapsed from bone-deep satisfaction. "We know how good it can be."

She stared down at me, lips swollen and wet from our kisses. Twila examined my face, and whatever she saw there, whatever she planned to say was cut off by the sound of my cell phone ringing in my pocket. And I could tell by the ringtone that it was the station.

Cursing under my breath, I shifted her on my lap and pulled out my phone. "Sorry. It's the station. I have to take it."

She nodded, eyebrows scrunched in confusion and her eyes glued on the badge hooked onto my belt loop as she climbed out of my lap. I scrambled to keep her there but she was too fast and I needed to take the call. I couldn't do both.

"Blackstock." I listened for several moments, cursing as it became clear that I was going to have to go in. Whatever had been happening here wasn't going to continue, and that was a good thing. The right thing. So much more than our past stood between Twila and me. I had temporarily forgotten it, but the call of my duty brought it down like a ton of bricks. Or more appropriately, a cold shower.

Twila stared at me, leaning against the bar as she slowly wrapped her cut finger in a Band-Aid. Her expression was wary, cautious. Eyes often focused on my badge.

I ended the call and rose to my feet, sliding the phone back into my pocket.

"I've got to go," I said, motioning toward the door. I wiped a hand across my mouth where I could still taste her on my lips. It was a good thing that we'd been interrupted. It was a bad idea. Full stop. "Twila, we need to talk."

"What do you do, Jake?"

"Twila."

"What do you do for a living, Jake? It's not a hard question."

I looked down to where the badge rested at my waist. I had forgotten it was there. It was just a part of me now. It was who I was.

"I'm a cop, Twila. I'm a detective with the city police."

She nodded, her mouth pressed in a hard line as she shook her head in angry disbelief. "And?"

I knew what she was asking. Twila wasn't a stupid woman. And I wasn't a stupid man. I knew what my answer would mean for me. For Twila. For us.

But the truth was the truth.

"I was the man who arrested your father and your brother. I'm the reason they went to prison."

* * *

Do you want more of Robin Covington?

One click RUSH now!

KING OF LIBERTINES

PAM GODWIN

I met him on a hot and rainy day.

The clouds hung low. The sea swelled high, and his eyes glinted the stormiest shade of gray.

The moment he stepped onto my ship, his arrogant scowl confessed two things. One, he was rakishly, offensively handsome. Two, he wasn't impressed to find a woman captaining the fifty-gun galleon.

Not that I cared a whit what any man thought.

It was the summer of 1719. The British had just defeated the Jacobites. The French had laid their beloved Jean-Baptiste de La Salle to rest. The Governor of the Bahamas had granted the king's pardon to my old friend, Calico Jack. And a rare few women—yes, the gentler, *weaker* sex—were joining the echelons of seafaring, hell-raising ruffians who plundered the West Indies.

I wasn't the first lady pirate who feared neither God nor man nor death. And I wouldn't be the last.

With rain slanting off my wide-brimmed hat and soaking through my linen corset and trousers, I blew a blonde curl from my face and cast a fleeting glance across the upper deck.

And stumbled into surly gray eyes for the hundredth time.

Tall and ruggedly lean, the stranger braced his boots shoulder-width apart, flexing power through his warrior stance. Leather straps and steel blades dangled about a trim waist. Brown breeches molded around long legs and tucked into black boots. Within the *V* of his open shirt, a sculpted, sun-bronzed chest attested to the physical demands of a life at sea.

Oh, he was one of the Brethren of the Black Flag, to be certain. A fearsome pirate, through and through. But there was more to him than violence and mayhem.

The sinuous curve of lips, the casual drape of an arm over the rail, the predatory eyes that tracked my every move… Even at a distance, he positively radiated seduction.

But I didn't need a companion to warm my bed. I had plenty of those waiting in every port. What I needed were more gunners.

He'd boarded the ship with another man, looking for work. Between the pair of them, there was enough well-thewed muscle and youthful stamina to take on the king's navy from a gun deck. By God, I bet they could feed twenty-pounders into the snouts of iron guns all day without breaking a sweat.

They loitered along the larboard bow, waiting to meet the ship's captain. I wouldn't make them wait much longer. But first, I had to deal with the disobedient crew member staring down at me.

Saunders stood three hands taller than my female height. Despite his oily hair and crooked, sun-blistered nose, he wasn't an ugly English tar. Just lazy and unmindful sometimes.

Today's dereliction earned him a fist across the face as I shouted with all the fury of a disappointed captain. He tucked his bearded chin to his chest and wrung the hat in his hands, his mouth a grim slash of shame.

Further chastisement wasn't needed. He wouldn't be falling asleep during his watch again.

"When this rain lets up," I said, "I want the decks swabbed until they shine like new."

"Yes, Captain."

His eagerness to please injected steel into my spine as I strode through the rain toward the two potential recruits. Keeping my eyes on my boots, I measured my steps to avoid a slip on the wet planks.

Tropical showers fell briefly and often in the West Indies, but never with such churning energy in the air. It gathered like a lightning storm and skated prickling frissons across my skin. When I looked up, a gasp escaped me.

Close enough to touch, I stared into a face that could've been chiseled from rich marble. The shadow of stubble didn't blunt the squared angles. Nor did the fringes of lashes soften the intensity.

This close, his eyes shocked my heart. So pale and luminous, the irises were startling, inhumanly colorless.

His hair fell wildly about his shoulders in hues of brown, the top half braided with shell beads and scraped back into a leather queue, lending him an exotic air. Add to that the wide pillar of his neck and a physique stacked with foreboding strength… I'd never met a man as intimidating and beautiful as this one.

It took multiple swallows to clear my throat. "Welcome aboard *Jade*."

"*Jade?*" His forehead beetled as he glanced around, giving the galleon a closer look. "Edric Sharp's *Jade*?"

"She's *my* ship." Uneasiness swelled in the space between my heart and stomach.

Numerous galleons cruised the high seas, but none so notorious as this one. My father had seized it from a Spanish treasure fleet. *For me.*

Removing the figurehead, flags, and other distinguishing features made it less identifiable. Hopefully, less of a target for the Royal Navy, pirate hunters, sea marauders—anyone seeking to capture Edric Sharp's only child.

I'd willfully signed up for this life, one that put me on the run. Murder and piracy came with the territory, and I owned that. Just like my father before he died.

Grief trickled through my chest, and my hand fell to the compass at my hip, the last thing he'd given me. I missed him desperately, with an ache that would never fade. But I buried it, deep down beneath the calm of a windless sea, forbidding any vulnerability to show.

"I'm Bennett Sharp."

"The legendary daughter?" Silver eyes narrowed into disbelieving slits. "I thought you were a fantasy, invented by lonely, maniacal men."

"Perhaps I am." I shrugged. "And you are?"

"Priest." He leaned against the ship's rail, scrutinizing me. "Priest Farrell."

I almost laughed. "Does your name reflect your purpose, Priest?"

"Only men who are virtuous serve the Lord."

"You strive to cheat God, then?"

"God, Man, and Devil." His lips flattened. No hint of humor.

"Since I'm none of those three, shall I presume you won't cheat *me*?"

Now he smiled, canines sharp and white, tensing my stomach.

Charming.

And therein lies the wolf.

The man he'd arrived with made a grunting sound. "He'll bed you, Captain. *Then* he'll cheat you."

He could try.

"I beg your pardon, madam." Priest held up a finger. "This will only take a moment."

In the next breath, he swept out a leg and had the other man on the deck beneath him, pounding his fists into flesh. The defendant countered with his own punches, and a heartbeat later, they exploded into a full-fledge scuffle.

During the span of the past five years, I'd seen enough bloodletting and carnage to numb the senses. If these miscreants were part of my crew, I would end the dispute and punish them justly.

But since I didn't know them, this was a fine opportunity to appraise their endurance, pain tolerance, and fighting skills.

May the best man win. *And perhaps earn himself a job.*

I stepped to the side as they rolled, lunged to their feet, and swung again. Each man absorbed and delivered hits in turn. Grunts rent the air. Blood sprayed the deck. But not once did I sense a loss of control. They seemingly fought, not to maim or injure, but to prove a point, as if this was how they established boundaries between them.

They jabbed and dodged, charged and parried, flowing together like water, like they'd done this a million times. Were they friends? Or kin?

Similar heights and builds. The skin on their palms and beneath their collars, where the sun didn't often reach, had a European pallor.

The second man wore his hair unfashionably short, cropped up the sides, leaving a rebellious brown stripe from forehead to nape. Six gold rings adorned the curve of his ear. Not a whisker on his hard jaw.

In snug-fitting breeches and a black tunic, he was as wickedly handsome as Priest. Only, when he stole glances at me, my blood didn't heat as if I'd been pumped full of rum.

Unlike Priest, whose intoxicating gaze made my limbs go limp, my stomach flutter, and my thoughts slide into drunken chaos.

It didn't matter who won this fight, I couldn't invite a distraction like Priest Farrell into my life.

All at once, the rain dried up, and the men broke apart. Chests heaving, knuckles bleeding, they returned to their reclined positions against the rail as if nothing had happened. There was no clear winner, but I sensed they'd just settled some private dispute.

"Back to work, lads." I waved off the few crewmates who had gathered to watch the action.

As they dispersed, I became uncomfortably aware of the sun that now baked through the thinning clouds. Or maybe it was the sweltering heat emitting from the two men staring at me.

I focused on the one with short hair and brown eyes. "Your name, sir?"

"Reynolds Farrell."

Same surname. Same accent.

I flicked my gaze between them. "You're brothers."

"We share the same father." Priest spat a glob of blood over the gunwale. "Nothing more."

They didn't look alike. But they spoke the king's English in the same mesmerizing lilt, making the vowels sound rounder, sexier.

My mother came from England, my father from Ireland. But those weren't the only accents I knew. "You're Welsh."

Reynolds nodded. "And you're from the colonies."

Carolina, to be exact. But none among my crew knew my upbringing. I'd left my mother's landlubbing life behind to follow my father's love for the sea.

I shifted my gaze toward the shoreline of New Providence that lay a hazy distance to larboard. As recent as last year, it had been the home base for over a thousand pirates. But now, even Nassau was no longer safe for my kind.

"Where were you before anchoring in Nassau?" I asked.

"I spent these past eighteen months serving as a quartermaster on a Dutch expedition." Reynolds crossed his arms. "We've been exploring the coastline of New Holland. Have you heard of it?"

My breath caught. "You mean the Southern Land? Terra Australis?"

"Aye."

"That's on the other side of the world!" I couldn't believe it. "What's it like?"

"The land stretches to the ends of the earth, and the creatures... It's like nothing you've ever seen." His eyes glimmered. "There are deerlike beasts that stand as tall as a man and hop on large hind feet, and they have these pouches..." He gestured at his abdomen. "To carry their young."

"Truly?" I shook my head, trying to imagine it.

He dazzled me with stories of colorful birds, lethargic bears, and indigenous peoples who hunted with curved throwing tools that spun through the air and returned to the hunter as if guided by magic.

Then I asked him about his duties as quartermaster, absorbing his answers with blooming excitement. My current first mate was long in the tooth, riddled with health issues, and itching to retire. I might have just found his replacement.

Priest remained silent throughout the conversation, his elbows braced on the rail at his back, and his gaze never straying from mine.

"Why didn't you join the expedition with Reynolds?" I squinted at him.

"I'm a raider." He scoffed. "Not an explorer."

"Yet you don't have a ship?"

"Not presently. When the need arises, I take one under my command."

I heard his meaning loud and clear.

Pirates acquired ships through terror, cannon fire, and invasion. If a raider was well-spoken and authoritative, he could inspire any crew to overthrow their captain and vote himself in.

Priest oozed cunning and authority. God knew I could use his strength on my gun deck, but not at the risk of losing command of my ship.

Decision made, I turned to Reynolds. "If you wish to sail with us, I need a new quartermaster. Wait for me in my cabin, and I'll have you sign the articles."

If I had any concern about where his loyalties would fall—with his brother or his new captain—it vanished the moment he strode toward my cabin without a backward glance at Priest.

No love lost.

I nudged up the brim of my hat and raised my face toward the other man.

Priest met my regard. Then he stole my breath, my voice, and perhaps my very sanity.

He was, quite impossibly, even more gorgeous than five minutes ago. Shafts of Caribbee sunlight bore through the clouds, drying his hair and gilding his skin. The bumps and scrapes swelling on his face only added to his rough-hewn allure.

Definition of muscle, tendon, and bone drew my gaze along his body, every inch so enticingly masculine and perfectly sculpted. Those long legs.

That serious mouth. Those stormy gray eyes... Sweet sisters of the child Jesus, his stare went deep. Devouring. *Dangerous.*

He pushed off the rail and erased the distance in two prowling strides. When he stepped into my space, my sharp inhale flooded with the tangled scents of leather, ocean, and something spicier, darker... Something uniquely, sinfully *him.*

Leaning closer, he curled the heat of his body around mine without touching. My palms slicked. My heart racketed, and a deep swelling throb flared between my legs.

Never had a man's proximity affected me so swiftly and completely.

Get rid of him, Bennett.

"Since I don't wish to be bedded or cheated, I have no need for your services." I leaned back to meet his eyes. "Remove yourself from my ship, if you please."

He stared down the length of his nose, not a trace of surprise or disappointment shining in those beautiful features.

Then he shifted, angled his head beneath the brim of my hat, and drew closer. So close his lips brushed my cheek as he spoke.

"When you change your mind..." His voice was smooth, rich, and deliciously dark. "Reynolds will know where to find me."

I shivered through a rushing torrent of heartbeats.

He turned, swung over the gunwale, and descended the ladder to the waiting jolly boat.

When he vanished over the side, all the air—and its unsettling energy—went with him.

* * *

The next evening, I sat behind the desk in my cabin, staring hard at my compass as if I could unlock the blasted thing through sheer will alone.

When my father gave it to me, he said it was a map to the wealth he'd accumulated through two decades of pirating. He also alluded to a key, suggesting that when I was ready, I would figure it out.

Well, it had been five years, and I was no closer to breaking open the compass than I was at age fourteen.

With a weary sigh, I set it on the desk and hunched down to study it from a different angle.

"Is it broken?" Reynolds sat across from me, writing in his notebook.

Over the past twenty-four hours, he'd settled seamlessly into his role as the new quartermaster. After filling that notebook with a list of the day-to-day operations of the ship, he spent the morning recruiting men for the gun crew and handling the collection of food, water, and wood for our impending voyage.

Now, I just needed to figure out our destination.

"The compass works." I rotated it slowly and tilted my head, examining the polished brass edges.

My crewmates understood this instrument meant more to me than anything in the world. But they didn't know it was a map to Edric Sharp's treasure. They didn't even know the treasure existed. I trusted no one with that information—especially not a man I met only yesterday.

But as my quartermaster, he would need an explanation for why I spent so much time in my cabin, attempting to break apart a perfectly good compass.

"My father gave this to me. It's some kind of puzzle."

His eyebrows knitted. "What does it solve?"

The location of unfathomable plunder. Riches beyond what my crew could ever want or need in a lifetime.

More than that, I hoped it led me to a letter from my father, parting words of love, something from him I could absorb into my soul.

"I don't know." I rubbed my head and sat back. "Whatever it is, I need it. *We* need it."

"May I see it?" He held out a large hand.

My hackles bristled, and everything inside me screamed protectively. I kept my expression neutral, however, and passed it to him with feigned indifference.

He lifted the lid. Fiddled with the dial. Swiveled north to south and back again. "Is there a key?"

"Yes. But I don't know if it's a physical object, a lever, a code, or something else entirely. There's no visible keyhole."

"You're certain it's a puzzle?" He handed it back.

"I'm certain it's more than a compass." I marked the flash in his eyes and his quick attempt to empty his expression. "What are you not saying? Do you know how to unlock it?"

"No, that's not..." He rolled his bottom lip, making me wait through an agonizing pause. "I know of an inventor, a magician of instruments, someone who could decipher whatever that is."

"You say?" I jumped to my feet, my heart racing. "Who? Where is he?"

"*She...*" He gave me a stern look. "Will not see you."

"Why not? I'll pay in coin. Whatever she wants. Where can I find—?"

"You're not hearing me, Captain. She's extremely private and suspicious. Her interactions are done in secret, and she surrounds herself with viciously loyal guards. *I* have never met her. I don't even know her name, and if I stepped onto her turf, she would have me killed simply for knowing where she lives."

"If she's such a mystery, how do you know so much about her?"

"I just do." He rose from the chair and paced to the windows behind my desk.

"Someone you know must have access to her. Who?"

With a hand braced on the pane above his head, he pinched the bridge of his nose. Perturbed. Uncomfortable. Definitely avoiding eye contact.

Then it dawned on me with harrowing clarity.

"Priest." I slumped into the chair and groaned. "She receives him."

In more ways than one, I suspected. Any woman with a pulse wouldn't turn away Priest Farrell.

Except me. I'd sent him off my ship, and now... God confound me, I had to find him.

And see him again.

And ask for his help.

At what cost?

My stomach sank. "There's no one else? No other blackguards she'll speak to? What about other inventors?"

"None that I know." He shifted, leaning his back against the windows. "Is this really that important?"

"I've been trying to decipher this thing for five years." I grabbed the compass and stood, my insides buzzing with rising hope. "Where is Priest?"

He closed his eyes through a resigned breath. "I'll take you to him."

* * *

Reynolds took me to a brothel.

Beneath a velvet sky of stars, Nassau seethed in the humidity. The stink of unwashed bodies choked the streets. Music and laughter vibrated the air. Horses whinnied in the distance. A fisherman vended his daily catch, and a painted woman lounged on an overhead balcony, her rouge melted and eyes glazed with rum.

Dread twined through my stomach. "He's in *there*?"

Reynolds followed my gaze to the woman and nodded at the door beneath her balcony. "This is his home when he's not at sea."

I'd left a crew of one-hundred-and-twenty men waiting in the harbor so I could barter with a rogue who lived in a bawdy house.

His own brother had warned me against him, claiming he would cheat me. *After* he bedded me.

I intended to pay for Priest's help with coin. If he wanted more, I would find another way to unlock the compass.

Island heat rose from the ground in waves, making me sweat beneath layers of skirts and stays. I wore modest attire. No visible weapons. No implication of wealth, crime, or notoriety.

Posters, proclamations, and folklore had immortalized my name. But whenever I went ashore, I ensured no one recognized me as the pirate Bennett Sharp. Very few knew what I looked like. Hell, Priest hadn't even believed I was real.

A grin pulled at my mouth. "How does Priest elude the governor while he's here?"

"The girls in there keep his comings and goings a secret." He glanced up at the two-story building. "They're very protective of him."

"Hiding behind whores. I can't decide if he's brilliant or spineless."

"Word of warning, Captain. He's outsmarted and outlived every person who underestimated him."

"That's the second time you've warned me about him."

"As your quartermaster, it's my duty to protect you."

I took care of myself just fine, but no need to be cocky. "That's why you're going to stay out here and keep watch. If the governor's men come sniffing around—"

"I'll get you out of there." He leaned a shoulder against the door and fixed me with a sobering look. "The king of libertines."

"What?"

"That's what they call him." He gestured at the door and held my gaze. "Don't sleep with him."

I snorted. "Trust me to have more dignity than that."

"You're not the one I don't trust."

Someday, I might be able to return Reynold's trust. But not today. With a brace of pistols under my skirt, a blade strapped to my thigh, and four daggers in my boots, I was prepared to be betrayed.

And I'd stalled long enough.

With a steadying breath, I left Reynolds on the street and opened the door.

A short hallway led to a large interior courtyard packed with tropical flora, seating areas, and half-dressed women. They lolled on satin settees, draped over banisters, and played cards at the tables.

The fragrance of herbs, perfumed oil, incense, and loam tickled my seafarer's nose. So feminine, those scents. So peculiar. I couldn't recall the last time I'd been surrounded by women rather than a rowdy lot of sweaty men. Perhaps not since childhood.

A second-story mezzanine overlooked the courtyard on all sides. To the left, a curved staircase led to the upper level, where dozens of closed-off rooms stared down over the balustrade.

As I stepped into view, every pair of kohl-smudged eyes shifted in my direction. I didn't have to wait for the madam to announce herself. She emerged from a lush chair in the corner, shimmering head to toe in a beaded gown of burgundy.

The bodice cut deep enough to tease out the tips of pink nipples. Ironed black ringlets piled high on her head, and the red stain on her lips accentuated her porcelain skin.

About a decade older than my nineteen years, she was pretty in a delicate way. But I recognized the toils of a hard life behind those green eyes.

"I'm Harriet." She held out a dainty hand, palm down, expecting me to kiss it. "Welcome to the Garden."

I refused her limp wrist and took in the surrounding greenery and blooming petals. A garden, indeed.

When I turned back, I found her examining me with an unnerving expression. "What are you looking at?"

"My apologies, but you are so..." She trailed a finger down her neck and toyed with her velvet choker. "Beautiful doesn't properly describe you. Heavens, you possess a..." She blinked slowly, staring. "A rare, natural, untamed beauty."

I raised my brows. "Um—"

"Your hair goes on forever. All those curls... Like golden fire. Oh, and those ocean eyes, graceful neck, tiny little waist... Mercy God." Her hands fluttered, stroking the air around my body. "You're magnificent beyond what any man could ever imagine a woman to be."

A soft smile made its way to my lips before I caught myself. "I'm not here to work for you."

"No, of course not." Her cheeks flushed, and she pushed back her shoulders. "For you, I would offer the best flower in the Garden."

Though I'd taken a woman to bed a time or two, I preferred men. And I never paid for companionship. "I'm looking for Priest Farrell."

"Aren't we all, my dear." She made a tittering sound and coughed into a gloved hand.

"Which room is his?" I hardened my voice, scanning the circle of balconies overhead.

Calm and collected, she didn't tense, blink, or give anything away.

I spun toward the staircase, resolved to search every room until I found him. But before I made it across the courtyard, a throng of women beat me there.

They stood together, blocking the stairs. More spilled in from the top and gathered on the steps. In various stages of dress from nude to fully clothed, they stared silently, stoically, united in their purpose.

I could remove a blade and cut my way through the horde. But once they saw the weapons beneath my skirts, my anonymity would be compromised. The moment I spilled blood, they would alert the governor.

I also needed to consider Priest. Terrorizing his pretty whores probably wouldn't incite him to help me.

Flexing and releasing my fists at my sides, I turned back to find Harriett's expressionless face inches away.

"I'm here to request his help." I plucked a coin from a hidden pocket and pressed it into her hand. "I mean him no harm."

"Who?" She stared at her palm, unmoved.

I gritted my teeth. "The king of libertines."

She smiled at that and tucked the coin between her breasts. "Left at the top of the stairs. Third door on the right."

A mix of relief and aggravation coursed through me. If his pet name was a code word, Reynolds should have just said that.

I went up the stairs.

The women returned to their business, disappearing within shadowed rooms. When I reached the third door, it opened.

A blond woman stepped out, clutching a blanket to her nude body. Smears of rouge and lip stain ran across her cheek, and her hair tangled into knots around pale bare breasts.

Her gaze flew to mine, and she smiled with a shyness that didn't belong in this place.

A shiver of disgust clenched my stomach. But there was something else, something irrational and unwanted tightening my chest.

I couldn't think about him touching this woman.

Or any woman.

No, that was absurd. Expecting to find him alone in his room was absurd. Feeling anything for this man was horribly, embarrassingly absurd.

He lived in a brothel. They called him the goddamn king of libertines, for Christ's sake. Jealousy was so far out of the realm of reality. What the devil was wrong with me?

The blonde scurried away, leaving the door cracked open.

I slid a dagger from my boot, if only because I needed something to squeeze. Then I strode into the bedchamber.

Darkness engulfed the perimeter. The aroma of rum and sex invaded my nostrils. A candle glowed on the bedside table. More flickered on the dresser and windowsill, casting dim light across the bed.

Two nude bodies lay tangled amid the twisted counterpane. Slender, soft, female bodies.

Several paces away, a chair faced the bed at an angle, and in it sprawled the king of libertines.

I couldn't help but shudder in the presence of the shirtless, silver-eyed rake. The chiseled *V* of his chest offered so many ridges, valleys, and shadowed indentations I had the sudden urge to run my hands over him. And my lips. My tongue.

A flash of heat struck low in my belly.

His legs stretched out before him, long and muscled, encased in tight breeches that stopped at the calves. With no boots or woolen hose in sight, it felt strangely intimate to gaze upon his bare ankles and feet.

I was no blushing virgin, but my encounters with men rarely involved the removal of clothing. A quick poke against a wall or over a table suited my needs. I never had a desire to see a man in only his skin.

Until now.

The front flap of his breeches lay open, revealing a trail of dark hair that led to the long, thick outline of him beneath the fabric. I wished the covering was completely untied so I could glimpse that impressive bulge in the flesh.

As it were, I saw enough. His waist was lean, his abdomen hard and flat. With the chest and arms of a gladiator and the silken lashes of nobility, he was entirely too pretty to take in all at once.

The corner of his mouth crept up. A mouth Prometheus must have fashioned from satin and sin. His smirk emanated sheer masculine arrogance, and I felt myself tensing, my heart thrumming hotly as if preparing for battle.

No matter how much he rattled me, by God's teeth, I refused to look away.

Neither did he.

The languid dip of his eyes put me in a trance. Everything else faded to black—the room, his whores, my rationality—until all that remained was him and me and the shimmering, scorching energy between us.

After the span of several heartbeats, his brow pleated, and his lips slipped into a frown. Whatever this was, he felt it, too. And he was as confused by it as I was.

"Are you the reason he hasn't touched us since his return?" A husky voice drifted from the bed, breaking the spell.

"I beg your pardon?"

"It's been two days." An auburn head popped up from the tangled bedsheets. "He's only watched us from that chair with his beautiful cock in hand." She pouted her lips. "We knew *something* was wrong."

"She's the reason, all right." The other woman sat up, her eyes huge and round as she ogled me. "Look at her, Cheri. Isn't she the most stunning creature you've ever seen?"

"As ethereal as a sea queen." The redhead crawled across the bed toward me, wearing only stockings. "Won't you join us, love?"

"Get out." I tightened my grip on the blade and pointed it at the door.

The women exchanged looks. Then they turned to Priest.

He rose from the chair and tightened the laces on the front of his breeches. "Good night, Cheri and Amelia."

His large hand slipped around mine, and in the next breath, I was being pulled from the bedchamber. Caught in his iron grip, I stumbled to keep up with his long-legged strides.

Was that not his room?

Cruising along the mezzanine banister and veering off around the corner, he dragged me to the back of the building. I could've freed myself with the blade at any time, but curiosity kept me compliant. For now.

From a small table, he snagged a lit candle in a tin holder and carried it into the last room. I staggered in with him, whirling and breathless.

The tiny windowless space struggled to accommodate two trunks and a single mattress that didn't seem big enough to support his muscled frame.

Backing up, I bumped the farthest wall in three steps. "This is where you sleep?"

Alone?

"Yes." He closed the door and set aside the candle.

I held my breath, waiting for the words, *I knew you would come,* or something equally condescending. But he remained silent, reclining against the wall, watching me with those silver hawk eyes.

Would he stop me if I tried to leave? He wasn't blocking the door or setting off my instinct to fight or flee. Instead, he regarded me with such intense focus I couldn't remember why I was here.

"Are you planning to use that?" He glanced at the knife in my hand.

"That's up to you."

He grunted, a deep, sexy sound that made my insides feel weightless. "Cheri and Amelia are right."

"About what?"

"All of it. Jesus Christ, Bennett, you're gorgeous. Astonishingly, unreasonably so." He studied me from beneath the heavy mantle of a perplexed brow. "Looking at you brings me more pleasure than anything I could experience in this house."

Assuming he'd sampled every flower in the Garden, he'd probably grown bored and thought I would be an entertaining challenge.

My blood simmered, and I glowered at him, trying to maintain my anger. But I couldn't. He seemed genuinely baffled by his reactions to me.

"Tell me why you're here." Suspicion threaded through his Welsh inflection.

Lowering onto the narrow mattress, I propped a boot on the wall and sheathed the blade. Then, for no logical reason, I let my skirts drift a little higher, recklessly showing skin above my knee.

His gaze homed in, and his jaw set.

Don't tease the wolf.

I straightened the hem.

From my hidden pocket, I removed the coin purse and compass and set both on the pallet beside me. "I want access to your instrument inventor."

Gray eyes sharpened. Then they widened, and in an abrupt transformation, he threw back his head and roared with laughter.

The rumble heated through me, arousing me, and that pissed me off. "Care to tell me what, pray tell, is so damned funny?"

"When you followed me in here—"

"You dragged me here."

"Just so. There's only one reason a woman puts herself in my bed."

I sprung from the mattress so fast my head hit the wall. "Damnation!"

Another gravelly laugh, his eyes shining with amusement. "You are delightfully unexpected, Bennett Sharp."

What was it about this man that made my skin hot and my knees weak every time he smiled?

"On the ship..." Blood pounded through my temples. "You thought I would change my mind and seek you out because I wanted to *bed you*?"

"Women are woefully predictable." He pushed off the wall and leaned over me. "But you came here for something else, hm? An inventor?"

"Yes."

The room was too small, and he was standing too close, smothering me with his addictive male scent.

My lungs constricted, and I inhaled through my mouth. "How do I convince your...the inventor to receive me?"

"You can't. She despises women." He grabbed the compass, inspecting it top to bottom. "Why did you bring this?"

"It's a puzzle." I walked him through the same story I'd given Reynolds, keeping the details short and ambiguous.

He tinkered with the dial and hinges and handed it back, his stare disconcerting. "Is it a puzzle or a *map*?"

"What do you mean?" I pretended ignorance as my gut twisted into knots.

"Your father celebrated a long, illustrious career of raiding. Where is his plunder, Bennett? Are you hiding a ship full of riches? Or did *he* hide it and give you an encrypted map of its location?"

Sickening dread spiked through me. "He lost everything when he died."

Could he read the lie on my face? I met him stare for stare, relaxing my features into a mien of apathy.

Whether or not he believed me, he let it slide. "The woman you seek is reclusive, distrusting, and exceedingly particular in matters of detail. But I know her demands, and she always receives me."

"Where?"

"She inhabits a small island off the southern coast of Hispaniola." He lifted the coin purse from the bed, poked through the gold pieces, and gave it all back. "Take me to her, and I'll get your compass unlocked."

As tension fell from my shoulders, new worries piled on.

"Is this not enough coin?" I held out the purse.

"I'll handle her payment."

"How? What does she want?"

"Nothing you can give."

My attention dropped to his groin and flicked away, my stomach souring. "You sleep with her?"

"She requires one night." His gaze caressed my face, burning, penetrating.

Gnawing unease gathered at the base of my spine. "You trust her?"

"I've used her several times to decipher a tabula recta, a scytale, and various other tools designed to protect secrets. When I find a strange device among the spoils I take, she's the only one who can open it. She's discreet, and she's never cheated me."

In my mind, I pictured a withered old crone hunched over a stone table in a cave. Then I imagined him bedding her, and the visual shattered apart.

"Is she...?" I toyed with the tie on the coin purse. "Is her price tolerable?"

"She's beautiful."

He said it without lust in his voice or heat in his eyes. No eagerness. No passion. I searched his expression for abhorrence or dread and didn't find that, either. He seemed oddly indifferent about it all. As if sex with this woman was just a means to an end.

It bothered me. Worse than that, I wanted to call the whole thing off. But if he didn't mind the cost of her services, why should I?

"What about *your* payment?" I shoved the coin purse against his chest.

He didn't grab it. "It'll take a week to sail there. We should get going."

Bending over his sea chest, he fished out a cutlass, shirt, boots, and multiple daggers. The weapons went on his waist, strapped in place by leather belts. Then he donned the boots, the linen shirt.

Watching him dress in the confines of his bedchamber, I couldn't have moved if I'd wanted to. Powerful muscles flexed with his movements—the bulges along strong arms, the squared bulk of shoulders, the ridges of ribs and abs. There was so much man within my reach. I swear my skin was shrinking too tight, and my nipples threatened to rip through the corset.

When he finished, he stood in the candlelight like a bronzed, battle-ready titan. My limbs went weak.

It was impossible to not think about the pleasure that body could bring when he looked like that. When he looked *at me* like that. Like he could turn my entire world inside-out with just one thrust.

Liquid curls of heat rolled between my legs.

"I'm not paying you with sex." I proffered the coin purse again.

"Do you pay your other crewmates with sex?"

"You say?" Indignation steamed from my pores. "Absolutely not!"

"Do you pay them with coin?"

"When we take a prize vessel, each man receives a share of the spoils as his due. You know how this works."

He pushed away the hand holding the coin purse. "Then why, madam, are we having this conversation?"

Because he was the most confident, sexually charged, uncommonly handsome libertine I'd ever met. The raw, uninhibited magic I felt with him wasn't one-sided, and I didn't know if I was strong enough to keep this partnership out of my bed.

Returning the purse and compass to my pocket, I breezed past him and out the door. The sound of his footfalls followed, slow and graceful, shivering up my spine.

I'd come here to request his help, and he agreed to give it without compensation. But in truth, he'd procured precisely what he'd sought aboard my ship yesterday.

A position on my crew.

I just hoped this transaction wasn't more than either of us bargained for.

* * *

The next morning rode in on a tropical trade wind. My hair whipped around my arms as I leaned against *Jade's* mighty foremast, watching the whitecaps sweep by and feeling damned excited to have a destination at hand.

After we weighed anchor last night, Priest met with my African helmsman, Jobah. Over a spread of maps, lobster chowder, and ale, they chartered our course to Hispaniola.

The din of bare feet padded behind me as the crew scrubbed away the night's spume. Overhead, canvas danced in the wind, and beyond the oaken bows, the sunrise reflected against the water in ripples of salmon and silver.

Glittering silver. Like his eyes.

It could be argued that Priest was the most alluring, extraordinarily handsome man on the planet. But it didn't matter. Within a week, he would be in another woman's bed. It was in my best interest to stop thinking about his eyes, his beauty, and his gravelly Welsh cadence.

"Did you raid the cabin boy's wardrobe?"

I froze. And melted. God, that voice—dark and silky and so very near. I didn't need to turn around to confirm his proximity at my back. I felt him there, his heat enveloping me like an embrace.

My blood hummed, and my breaths wheezed as if I'd scaled the shrouds a dozen times. As my head tried to float away, I registered the question he'd asked.

Cabin boy's wardrobe?

I wore faded brown trousers cut off at the knee, black boots, and an ivory blouse tucked into a leather belt. The only impractical accessory was the choker at my neck, fitted with the jade stone my father had given me.

My attire made it easier to climb ratlines, scour decks, and swing my cutlass in battle. No one, especially not this man, could make me feel inferior for dressing how I wanted.

I whirled on him. "If you have a problem with—"

"Christ, you're fierce." His gaze traced my face, fixating on my mouth as a primal sound vibrated in his chest. There was so much longing, so much *danger* in that growl, it tangled my thoughts. "Fierce, ravishing, glorious in ways no other woman could duplicate... That doesn't begin to illustrate the sight of you."

I dissected his words, looking for trickery. "What are you doing?"

"Enjoying the view." He prowled around me.

"Stop."

"Stop enjoying?"

"Stop looking."

"You realize every man on this ship spends a great deal of time looking and enjoying and pleasuring himself to images of your arse in those trousers."

If that were true, they never let it reflect in their interactions with me. They respected me.

The only eyes that leered on this ship were stormy gray and rude as hell. If I exposed a scandalous curve or hint of flesh, those eyes homed in and stared.

The wind snatched a tendril of his masculine scent and teased it past my nose, further irritating me.

"Damn your eyes, you indecent bastard." I shifted to the starboard bow and leaned against the rolled-up hammock that protected the deck from enemy shellfire.

He joined me there, forearms on the rail beside mine, his body angled toward the sea. "You walk around with a perfect round backside in tight breeches, and you call *me* an indecent bastard? You're torturing your crew, Captain."

Silence stewed between us while I debated knocking him into a cocked hat.

Then an unrepentant grin stole across his lips.

He was teasing me?

My muscles loosened, and I stifled my own grin. "You aren't supposed to notice a captain's arse."

"Is that right?"

"Of course. Everyone knows a superior arse of any shape or size is meant to blend in with the overall power of a captain's impressive authority."

He blinked. His mouth twitched, and there it was. That seductive smile with all its lethal teeth, sculpted curves, and mesmerizing twists.

This man was going to ruin me.

I let that sink in, sobering as I recalled Reynold's warning. "How do you plan to cheat me?"

"I changed my mind about that."

"Really?" I said dryly.

"I boarded this galleon with the intent to overthrow her captain and take her command. It's what I do." A frown formed on his forehead as he watched me with quiet appraisal. "Then I met you and lost interest in taking your ship."

"Because I'm a woman?"

"No."

"Because I'm Edric Sharp's daughter?"

"No."

"Then why?"

He caught a wisp of my hair and rubbed the strands between finger and thumb, his expression pensive.

"I want to know you." He let the wind tug my curl from his hand. "I want to see your command as a captain and hear your mind as a woman."

He could've said anything else, any variation of excuses and falsehoods to explain away Reynold's warning and make me feel comfortable about his presence here.

But his answer scared me. Shook me to the core.

That was how I knew he'd spoken the truth.

"Captain," Reynolds said behind me.

I turned to find my quartermaster glaring at Priest. My attention darted between them, my senses picking up on their usual hostility. But Reynolds remained silent, the moue of displeasure on his face fading away. If he'd heard Priest's confession, he accepted it as I had.

"If you're ready to break your fast," he said to me, "the cook prepared a meal in your cabin."

"Thank you." I looked at Priest. "Have you eaten?"

Over the next hour, the three of us shared a hearty breakfast of salt fish, buttered eggs, and ship biscuits while discussing Nassau's political atmosphere and the downfall of the king's pardons for pirates.

No matter our backgrounds and motivations, we agreed wholeheartedly on the value of rebellion over the traditions of society. It was the pirate way. While Nassau succumbed to British rule, we would never surrender with it.

Reynolds eventually left the cabin to oversee the operations of the ship, leaving Priest and me deep in discussion. We talked about our adventures at sea, our favorite ports, and our bloodiest battles. We talked about many things, so incredibly riveted in what the other had to say neither of us seemed capable of pulling away.

And so began our voyage.

As hours rolled into days, our conversations grew closer, looser. Effortless. We talked over shared meals, laughing and arguing about everything. We talked when I made my rounds on the upper deck, strolling side by side in the salty air.

Each night, he left me at the door of my cabin and slipped away to sleep in the crew's quarters, only to return before dawn with breakfast and more conversation.

By the fifth day, I knew more about Priest Farrell than any person I'd met in my lifetime. I knew where he came from, who his parents were, his childhood, his biggest regrets, greatest fears, deepest desires, and somewhere along the way, I shared all of that with him, too.

We weren't that much different, he and I. He regretted the deaths of friends, feared the loss of freedom, and desired companionship with people he could trust with his life.

The more we talked, the more I was drawn to the man beneath the gorgeous face. I'd never felt compelled to tell anyone about my upbringing, my grievances, and my darkest thoughts. Yet I found myself divulging the strangest things, craving every conversation, and missing him the moment he left my cabin at night.

He never touched me sexually. But I sensed the need in him, the desire to know me in that way.

As the days passed, I craved him, too. I ached for him to kiss me, restrain me, and claim me whether I consented or not. I couldn't stop my thoughts from going there, plunging into the darkest places while he sat beside me day after day, looking at me the way he did.

He needed to just put himself inside me, into the hungry wet heat of me, and stroke himself there until this tarnal infatuation went away.

But we didn't talk about that. Nor did we discuss the woman he would bed when we arrived at our destination.

On the sixth night, *Jade* reached landfall beneath the escort of a pale, bloated moon.

The sight of the small island's shoreline should have filled me with unbridled excitement. I'd never come this close to discovering the secret of my father's compass.

Instead, the looming finality of my time with Priest sat like a hot boulder in my stomach.

He walked beside me on the upper deck, hands clasped at his back, lost in his own thoughts. But his gaze never strayed far, always shifting in my direction, reaching, touching, *knowing*.

"You're quiet." As he tipped his head, moonlight pooled on the planes of his chiseled face.

"So are you." I rested a hand on his forearm, bringing our stroll to a stop in the shadow of the mainsail. "We need to talk about tomorrow."

"Why?" His mouth flattened into a hard slash, the anger in it taking me by surprise. "Are you going to turn this ship around and forget about the compass? Or do you want to hash out the details of what I'll be doing in her bed?"

I jerked away and pressed a hand against my constricting chest.

He gripped my chin and forced my eyes back to his. "We can't discuss tomorrow without talking about us."

"Us?"

"This." His hands slid into my hair, bringing our foreheads together. "Our connection. The mysterious alchemy of it. The goddamn energy crackling the air."

My breath hitched as he grabbed my hips and hauled me against him, lining up all our intimate parts. Paralyzing heat spread downward, fanning through my body with diabolical precision.

"I know you feel it, Bennett. I perceive its effects on you—the desire, the uncertainty, and most of all, the fear of this thing we're becoming."

We were becoming one. A single, inseparable unit. A mating of souls.

And I was sending him into the clutch of another woman's body.

Chaos erupted between my ears as I tried to rein in my jealous rage. "You and I... We just met. This is—"

"It's terrifying, I know." He dipped his head and set his mouth upon the crook of my neck, roving at leisure, his tongue leaving wet trails of heat on my skin. "I never would've believed what could change in a week in your company."

"What changed?"

He stared down at me, flexing a strong, irritated jaw. The intelligent eyes that seemed to see straight through me said what his mouth didn't.

Everything had changed.

Our mission.

Our motivations.

Him and me together.

A rollicking song broke out behind us. The deep voice, thick with drink, sang in tune while stringing together verses with improvisations. A fiddle joined in, probably the young sailor I always saw trailing after Reynolds. When a bone whistle struck the chorus, the decks boomed with life and commotion, every seaman singing along, many of them dancing.

Their gaiety melted the numbness in my feet, and soon, I was smiling with them, humming along with the rhythm.

Without warning, a muscled arm hooked around my back, and I lost my breath as Priest twirled me across the deck. He caught my hand in his and yanked me close. Then we spun again, moving to the music, stomping our boots, and laughing uncontrollably.

Rowdy tars gathered around us, clapping and chanting. Even Reynolds got caught up in the revelry, singing at the top of his lungs.

Over the past week, the crew had taken a liking to the king of libertines. It shone on their faces whenever they talked to him, and now, as they encouraged him to swing me faster across the planks.

We danced through several more songs, pounding our boots until the seam on his ripped.

He stopped, bending at the waist and laughing as he pulled his boots off in pieces.

When he straightened, half-lidded eyes found mine. We panted from exertion, our heavy exhales mingling, coming faster, harder, building toward *more.*

"You need new boots." I grasped his warm hand and turned toward the hatch to my cabin. "Come with me."

Down the ladder and through the passageway, I didn't slow until I reached my chamber. He followed me in and leaned against the closed door, watching me with a guarded expression.

He wore no boots, no gold jewelry, no fancy clothing or extravagant accessories. He didn't own a ship. Didn't keep the prize vessels he stole. I'd seen the teeny space in the brothel where he slept. It barely accommodated a pallet, let alone a trove of riches.

I leaned a hip against the desk and crossed my arms. "Why do you raid if you don't care about wealth?"

"This lifestyle offers..." His focus darted through the room as if searching for the answer. "There's a promise of...this journey into the unknown that..." His gaze landed on mine. "I'm only now beginning to appreciate."

"You *are* an explorer."

"I'm not interested in the geography of the world."

"No, you're looking for the *meaning*."

So was I.

Could it be that we found that meaning right here, sparking in whatever this was that drew us together?

My lungs tightened, and I turned away, contemplating his boots and the reason I'd led him down here. After an endless minute of inner conflict, I stepped to the armoire and removed an old pair of jackboots.

"These belonged to my father." I set them in his arms. "If they fit, you can have them."

He blinked slowly, staring at the worn leather, knowing full well what the boots meant to me. Throughout our conversations, I'd shared stories about my father, my memories of him in those boots, and the details of how I acquired them when he died.

His hands caressed the leather and laces with reverence as he pulled them on, adjusting them around his knees.

"They fit," he said, his voice beautifully husky, silver eyes questioning.

I nodded, my chest warming with the rightness of it.

"Bennett..." He moved fast, too fast, coming right at me.

Fear and desire crowded in, and I stumbled back, my hands flying up in defense. He caught them, pinning my arms to my sides.

"Be calm." He made a shushing sound, trapping me with muscle-corded heat as he flattened my body against the wall.

Then he lowered his head and traced my lips with the tip of his tongue, teasing, tasting, and bursting pleasure through my belly. Warmth tingled through my limbs, my fingertips, and into my breasts, hardening my nipples.

He pressed deeper, opening my mouth fully, his hand cupping my head, his other at my waist, and I fell into heaven. With a kiss that decimated all others, he plundered my lips, caressing and licking and driving me mad with yearning.

I came alive. Everywhere our bodies touched, I burned. Burned beneath the bruising pressure of his mouth. Burned against the hard length of his need. Burned with the knowledge that I shouldn't, *couldn't* go through with this.

He'll bed you. Then he'll cheat you.

Don't sleep with him.

But not even Reynold's warnings doused the fire consuming me. I was lost in this man, my hands clawing muscle as need sang through my breasts and pooled between my legs.

My entire being clung to the slide of his hot mouth, to the weight of his sculpted body, to this inexplicable connection that sank through flesh and bone and bound our souls into one.

"Weigh anchor and hoist the mizzen, Bennett." He fisted a hand in my hair and kissed the corner of my lips. "We're leaving this island."

I went still, panting against his mouth. "The compass..."

"It comes with a price." He released me, his hands falling to his sides as he glared with all the condemnation of an enraged god. "Have you forgotten what I must do to unlock your precious puzzle?"

"You know it's not just a puzzle."

"Edric Sharp's plunder..." he breathed, eyes wide. "So it *is* a map?"

"You didn't know?" My hands fisted. "You were bluffing?"

"I was *guessing*."

"A plague take you, Priest." I groaned, pulling at my hair. "God, you make me crazy."

"What happens when you find his loot?"

"I've dragged this crew across the West Indies for five years looking for a treasure they don't even know exists. If we find it, we'll split it, just like every other prize. Since you're part of this crew, you'll get your share."

A week ago, I entered into a partnership with the king of libertines. If this was a romantic relationship, I would never share him with another woman. But it wasn't, and I refused to stand here and demand commitment and monogamy from a man I just met.

Maybe he did care about wealth. Perhaps he was looking forward to bedding this beautiful, reclusive woman again.

I unhooked the compass from my belt and handed it to him. "The choice is yours."

He stared at the instrument, curling his fingers around it. Though it looked small and delicate in his huge palm, it'd been the biggest, heaviest thing on my mind since I took command of my father's ship. It still was. Only now, it was no longer the most important.

Gray eyes locked on mine, holding me in place, making me wait. I fought an exhausting mental war, trying to interpret the minute shifts and tics on his face before he broke eye contact.

His expression shuttered as he wedged the compass into his waistband. Then he turned and left the cabin, shutting the door with quiet, heart-breaking finality.

* * *

I cried myself to sleep. It was a very un-captain-like thing to do. But dammit, I was a woman first and foremost, and my heart wanted something greater than chests of gold and bloody battles.

I wanted Priest Farrell.

As the first rays of dawn brushed the windows of my cabin, I pondered my selfishness with a clearer state of mind.

Choosing Priest meant choosing my own desires over that of my crew. But if I didn't fight for him, what was the meaning of all this? Why fight at all, if not for each other?

If I let him go, I didn't deserve him in the first place.

Hot, silent determination saturated my soul as I slid from the bed, still dressed in yesterday's clothing.

At the door, I found Reynolds on the other side with a platter of salt fish. "Is Priest awake yet?"

"He's not here."

"What?" My blood turned to ice.

"He left for the island last night." Stepping around me, he set the food on the desk. "I thought you knew."

No, no, no. He was supposed to leave today. Why would he sneak off in the dark?

She requires one night.

God help me, he'd gone to her—worked up from our kiss and angry from our conversation.

I was too late.

Was he still in bed with her now? Waking her with his beautiful mouth and talented hands?

Nauseating pain crashed through me. I staggered backward and spun toward the windows, hiding the anguish on my face.

How could he do this? After the profound week we shared together, how could he run into the arms of another woman?

No. This was my fault. I'd shown him my grief over losing my father, poured out my heart about the compass. Priest didn't bed her because he was a lusty, shameless rake. He did it because he knew how badly I needed that map.

I couldn't even let myself imagine the possibility of him running off with the compass with no intention of returning. He wouldn't do that. Not to me.

Pushing down the agony, I squared my shoulders and strode through the cabin. "When did he leave?"

"A few hours ago."

Only a few hours? He hadn't been with her the entire night? My pulse quickened. Maybe I still had time.

"For what it's worth," Reynolds said from the doorway, "he wasn't himself when he left. He seemed…troubled."

My stomach hardened as I strapped on my cutlass, pistols, and daggers.

"What are you doing?" He leaned against the door, tugging on his earring.

"I'm going after him." I stormed toward him, bracing for a fight. "Don't try to stop me."

"I'm not." He smirked, stepping to the side. "I'm getting out of your way."

By the time I reached the upper deck, the sun was cresting the eastern edge of the island. I raced to the larboard bow, frantically scanning the dense foliage that fringed the shoreline.

"Did Priest take a jolly boat?" I asked a nearby seaman.

"Yes, Captain."

I squinted at the shore, unable to see a boat beached on the sandbar. Where the devil did he go?

We carried other boats on *Jade's* stern, so I hurried to the ladder there and swung a leg over the gunwale to start my descent.

"Captain!" Reynold's voice rang out behind me. "You're not debarking alone!"

I didn't need a damned guard. Shifting my weight, I stepped onto the top rung.

And stopped.

Far down below, a boat rocked in the water beneath the ladder, and it wasn't empty.

Stormy gray eyes stared up at me. Eyes that glowed with an intensity that scorched my skin, even at this distance.

I felt like an iron cannon was perched on my lungs. I couldn't breathe, couldn't move. I couldn't do anything but hold his gaze as he leaped onto the ladder and scaled his way up.

My heart hammered as he grew closer, the details of his appearance growing sharper. Red stains oozed from multiple tears in his shirt. Blood dripped from a cut on his cheek.

Needles pricked my throat. What happened to him? How badly was he hurt?

When he ascended into hearing range, I shouted, "Are you okay? Hurry!"

He took his time, devastating my nerves with his silence. Then he finally reached the top. "I'm fine, Captain. Just a few scratches."

I threw myself around him, hugging his massive shoulders and trying to haul him onto the deck. The effort ended with his arms holding me up as we stood together, chest to chest, locked.

"I couldn't do it." He stared down at me, his face frozen and bleeding. "I didn't even try."

I opened my mouth, failing words as my insides rose and fell in little dips.

"I didn't want her hands on me. I didn't want...*her*."

"Priest..."

"She's not you, Bennett." Quiet fury whispered through his accent, laced with bewilderment. "I don't want anyone but you. I'm sorry." His gaze shifted, dropping to my weapons and my position near the ladder. "What were you doing?"

"I was going to stop you." I stood taller and gripped the collar of his shirt. "I was going to fight for you like I should have done last night."

I caught a flash of a grin before his mouth crashed over mine. He kissed me right there in front of my crew, his tongue thrusting past my lips and his hands molding around my backside.

Whistles and cheers exploded around us, and somewhere near the forecastle, Reynolds barked orders to set sail.

Priest didn't release me, his breaths panting thickly against my mouth. I felt his desire in the muscled arms around me, in the flexing strength against my body. I tasted him, pressing into him, aching to feel the rigid length of his arousal again, wanting it inside me, craving the delirious pleasure I knew it would bring.

As if reading my mind, he gripped my hand and strode in the direction of my cabin. The crew scrambled around us, towing in the anchor and preparing *Jade* to sail.

"Why are you bleeding?" I jogged to keep up with his ground-covering gait.

"She didn't like my offer." He stopped at a barrel near the hatch and lifted the lid.

Confused, I peered inside and gasped.

Why was my compass in there?

He reached in and grabbed it. Then he was moving again, dragging me along behind him.

"You didn't take it with you?" I huffed, chasing him down the ladder and through the lower level.

"Too risky. I went there to barter with something other than...*myself*. Gold coins, ornate artifacts, exotic gems... I even offered her a share of the prize if she unlocked the puzzle." He reached my cabin and ushered me inside. "But I didn't tell her that this was the puzzle." He held up the compass and set it on a shelf. "Now she'll never know what it looks like."

"But what if she'd agreed to your offer?" I shut the door and leaned against it, captivated by his mind.

"I would've returned to the ship and retrieved the payment and the compass."

"Instead, she attacked you?" I stepped toward him and prodded at the cut on his face. "Because you wouldn't sleep with her?"

His shoulder gave a careless shrug. "She didn't want to let me go."

"*I* don't want to let you go."

"Then don't."

He closed in, and I retreated, taunting him. With a flash of teeth, he pulled off his shirt and kept coming. My back hit the door, and my lungs emptied.

The next breath was his, warm and delicious, on my face, my neck, my lips. His dark aura pressed in, and I welcomed the wildness of it, silently begging for everything he intended to give me.

"You are a unique, stubborn, beautiful woman, Bennett Sharp." He yanked my hips to his, grinding me against his arousal and making me wet. "I look forward to worshiping you, serving your body, and feasting on your cunt until we're both drunk on pleasure."

"You better not—"

"Resist all you want. It won't do you any good." His lips moved so close to mine I felt the heat of them.

"I was going to say…" I grinned. "You better not stop."

Our mouths collided, exploding in a battle of lashing tongues, clicking teeth, and hungry breaths. Our hips met. Our eyes held, and our hands mauled.

Weapons dropped. Boots tumbled. Clothes ripped. Then we were sliding together, nude and gasping, flesh on flesh, touching, exploring, kissing, rocking as one, and miming the movements of sex.

Spirals of sensation coursed through me, trembling up my legs. "Need you."

"Patience." His palms covered my breasts, squeezing.

Then his hands roved, touching me everywhere before he put those wicked fingers in the place I needed him the most.

"Soaked." He circled my entrance, groaning. "For me."

"Yes, we know. You can gloat about it later. Right now, just…" I cried out at the slide of his touch. "Put it in."

His fingers thrust, stroking me into a vortex of unimaginable pleasure. I moaned and threw my head against the door, riding his hand and needing more.

"This, Priest." I reached between us and gripped the heavy, rock-hard length of him. "Put *this* in."

He grunted, kicking his hips, his gaze never leaving mine.

"You're going to scream." He lifted me, hooking my legs around his hips and pinning my back to the door.

"Definitely."

He took his cock in hand and met my eyes. Then he fed his thick length into my body.

"Oh, Gahhhhhd! Oh, God. Oh, God," I screamed, liquefying around the unholy intrusion.

The groan that escaped him sounded animalistic, matching the feral lunge of his thrusts as he pounded me against the door.

"Christ almighty, you're perfect." He slammed himself into me, kissing and biting my lips between gasping words. "Made for me. For me alone."

The deep, gravelly noises he made spun me higher, hotter, wetter. Our bodies slapped together. Our breaths shook, and our hands dug in, climbing deeper, closer, trying to swallow each other whole.

And the best part? His eyes.

Glowing and dilated, they burned into me, never losing focus, never straying from mine.

He watched me as he took us to the highest peak. He didn't look away as we fell over the edge together, groaning and panting and shaking as one.

And he wasn't finished.

Before I caught my breath, he had me laid out on the desk with his face between my legs. Then he took me in the chair, on the floor, against the windows, and finally in the bed.

Entangled in sweaty limbs, stripped to the skin, and deeper still—deep enough to expose our hearts—we were buried so far inside each other there would be no unraveling.

After that, we slept. We ate. We made our rounds with the crew. Then we fell back into bed and into each other.

Over the weeks and months that followed, Priest and I didn't give up on my father's compass. We plotted together, studied maps together, and became addicted. *Together.* Insatiable. Inseparable. We couldn't keep our clothes on, our hands to ourselves, or our hearts closed off.

What began as an unstoppable explosion of passion forged into something pivotal, essential, and *more.*

And that was how I fell in love with the king of libertines.

Now, if you think this is where the journey ends, I should warn you. This was only the beginning.

Our love story takes a devastating turn, ripping and drowning and dragging our hearts through the darkest depths without quarter.

* * *

THE VOW

A RIVERS WILDE SHORT STORY

DYLAN ALLEN

HAYES

"What's wrong, Hayes?" Confidence asks when I flop face-first onto the massive four-poster bed in the center of our hotel room.

I groan as the firm but accommodating mattress forms a supportive cradle around my travel-weary body.

"We're on vacation. You can't be tired," she informs me and nudges my foot.

I don't respond.

Maybe, if she thinks I'm asleep, she'll let me lie here until I really am.

She touches my foot again, this time not to jostle it but to stroke it. "I was hoping we'd be making up for lost time. We haven't had sex in almost a month."

I'm instantly alert. I roll to my back and find her standing next to the bed, peering down at me with a soft, indulgent smile on her heart-stopping face. She's bathed in a ray of sunlight that turns her corn-silk blonde hair into ripples of champagne that brush her bare shoulders.

"Come here," I growl and make a grab for her. She giggles and dances out of my reach.

"Ohhhh, did I say the magic word?" she drawls with wide-eyed innocence.

"Yes, you did, and now my magically awoken dick expects you to make all its dreams come true." This time when I reach for her, I get my arm around her.

She slides her arms around my neck and kisses me.

"I will, but I want to shower first."

"Why?" I frown and draw back a little.

"Because I'm sweaty." She grimaces for emphasis.

"I like your sweat," I divulge before I press a hungry kiss, an open-mouthed kiss to the side of her throat.

She scrunches her shoulders up and leans away, her grimace deepening. "Pregnant sweat is different from normal sweat, Hayes. My dress is going to stick to my ass permanently if I don't get it off soon." She slips out of my arms completely and heads to the bathroom. "I'll get a head start. Can you order us some food?"

Disgruntled by my now-empty arms, I give her a disbelieving frown. "You're hungry already? We stopped for those sandwiches on the way here," I say and pat my full stomach for emphasis.

She gives me a squinty-eyed glare. "I'm carrying your son, Hayes. And he's always hungry." The note of accusation in her voice makes me chuckle.

"By the time you're done, I'll be all nice and clean and you can come join me. Please?" she adds when I don't answer right away.

"You're a tease," I quip but sit up. I can't say no to her. Not even when it means saying no to my dick.

I'm just in time to catch a trailing flutter of mint-green fabric as she disappears into the bathroom. That dress, low-cut and thin strapped, has been making me crazy all day. The light fabric clings to every single glorious curve of her body. Her spectacular shoulders, arms, chest, and braless breasts have been on full display for me and every other fucking pervert she's walked past today.

I'm not like some of the men in my circle of acquaintances. They think of their wives as prizes and get off on other men ogling their trophies.

Confidence is absolutely the most beautiful woman I've ever laid eyes on. But she isn't arm candy. She's an entire trove of rare treasures, and I don't want anyone else to lay their covetous eyes on her.

But, it's summer in Houston. That means hundred-degree weather every day. Far be it from me to tell my pregnant fiancée to cover up. I've spent the entire month glaring at men who don't give a shit about the ring on her finger or the child growing in her belly.

It's not as hot here in Cabo, but I know she only packed bikinis and things to wear over them for the weekend. Just the thought of the men ogling gives me a headache.

"We should have rented a private house," I call, loud enough so she can hear my disdain all the way in the bathroom.

"It's a five-star diamond resort," she announces, her voice full of indignation that's aided in its effectiveness by the bathroom's excellent acoustics.

"Yeah, so we're surrounded by rich strangers," I mumble under my breath.

She sticks her head out of the door and glares at me. "What was that?" she asks with a telltale quaver in her voice. Her pregnancy has brought about a lot of changes. One of them being how easily she cries.

That's the last thing I want. I smile. "I said, I wonder if they have cheeseburgers. I can't find the menu."

"Oh, so I guess it's a good thing I have that weird little habit, huh?" she gloats. I usually tease her for memorizing menus.

I roll my eyes. "Just tell me."

She beams and clears her throat as if she's about to make a speech. "They have a few kinds, but I think you'd like the cast-iron burger. I want the Baja chicken sandwich and ask them to put bacon on top. Oh, and I want fries instead of the pasta salad thing it comes with. And you're welcome." She smiles sweetly and shuts the door.

A few seconds later, the shower starts.

I wonder if she's taken her dress off. I picture her naked but for a scrap of lace fabric she calls panties barely covering the full petallike lips of her pussy.

My dick jumps at the visual.

Fuck, I need to get this food ordered so I can finally satisfy my hunger, too.

Restraint is my middle name. For a man like me, who lives such a public life, impulsive, emotion-driven behavior is a liability. So when it's just me and her, I let loose completely. From how we talk, to how we fuck—everything is intense, loud, and reckless.

Or, it used to be.

Settling into life in Rivers Wilde, and with me, hasn't been easy for her. It was bad enough that my family made her feel so unwelcome. But then her job got crazy, too. I shudder at the memory of being arrested for getting between her and a coworker who went what she calls "postal."

It was an ordeal. But it made us the team we are now. Things settled down, and we started focusing on our future. I was looking forward to a nice long stretch of peace. For a few weeks, we had it.

Then, we started talking about the wedding.

We had drastically different ideas about what that day would look like.

I suggested we'd gather our friends and family at a private beach in Galveston and say our vows at sunset next to the water. Something simple, easy, and private.

Confidence wanted the whole circus. White dress, packed church, and a fancy party for two hundred of our closest frenemies. I balked. She said, "I'm not getting married in the middle of the night as if I've got something to hide."

That made no sense to me, but uncharacteristic tears followed the declaration. So, I nodded like I understood and told her to have whatever she wanted.

The wedding is in a few weeks and instead of relaxing and letting our planner do her job, she's more and more involved with it. For the last month, she comes home from her day job and locks herself in her home office to work on "wedding stuff." By the time we're ready for bed, she's exhausted and passed out before her head hits the pillow.

I'm not a jovial person at the best of times, but after a commercial flight, standing in the customs line for almost an hour and fighting our way through a sea of men trying to sell us time-shares at the airport, I'm cranky and tense.

I remind myself that we're going to spend the rest of the weekend in relative solitude. And once we get settled, I'll finally get to relax. I need to fuck, shower, and eat—in that order.

I walk over to pick up the phone and press the button marked *service*.

It's answered immediately.

"Buenos tardes, Mr. Rivers, and welcome to Pueblo Bonito," a young, upbeat male voice trills at me. "I'm Roger, your private concierge for the weekend. My priority is to make your weekend remarkable. How may I be of assistance, sir?"

"I'd like to order lunch and have it brought up to our room." The promise of excellent service has made my tone less biting, but it's still several degrees less upbeat than Roger's when he responds.

"An excellent meal is the perfect way to start your stay. The menu is right next to the phone." He takes an audible breath as if he's pausing and waiting for some signal for me before he continues speaking.

"I've got it, I'm ready to order."

"Hayes, baby? Can you ask if they have sweet and sour sauce?" Confidence calls from the doorway of the bathroom.

"Yes, we have sweet and sour sauce," Roger says chirpily, and I make a mental note to remember that sound travels across the room.

"Good. We'll have two bottles of mineral water, the Baja Chicken sandwich with bacon on top and fries instead of the pasta salad." I scan the menu for myself before I realize that she was right about what I'd want. Like she always is. "I'll have the cast-iron burger with vinegar chips."

"Excellent choices," Roger sings in praise. "Could I entice you to add a few slices of bacon to your burger, too? It's thick cut from pork that is brought in by a local farmer. It's delicious."

The bathroom door opens to reveal a naked, dripping wet, smiling Confidence. My eyes linger on her fuller than normal breasts and their peaked nipples and the fat lone droplet that clings to one honey-colored tip. My mouth goes dry. With a groan, I rise to standing and start toward her.

"Mr. Rivers, is everything okay? You sound distressed?" Roger's anxious chirp in my ear reminds me I'm still on the phone.

"Send the food," I say before I hang up and throw the phone down on the bed and stalk toward her.

She takes a step back into the bathroom, her smile turning coy as she disappears behind the door.

My dick is hard as a rock by the time I make it to the bathroom.

"The water's perfect, just the temperature you like it. And you have too many clothes on, Mr. Rivers," Confidence drawls and then steps under the spray.

I pull my T-shirt over my head and step out of my shorts before I follow her. She's standing in profile under the rainforest-style spray, her head tipped back, eyes closed as the water runs over her face.

I stop and take her in. She's the kind of beautiful that overshadows everything else when she walks into a room. The kind that inspires men to take up arms and fight to be her champion.

But the best part is that, as awe-inspiring as she is to look at, it's nothing compared to the wonder of her brilliant mind or the fierce loyalty that is the drumbeat of her love.

I won't lie, though. I'm fucking glad all of that is wrapped up in such a beautiful package. I feast my eyes on the rest of her body. When they trace the swell of her belly, where my son is growing, my heart skips a beat. Neither of us wanted to wait to find out the sex, and ever since we found out we were having a boy, my stomach has felt like a flock of wild geese have made it their home.

As if she knows what I'm thinking, she covers her belly with her left hand. The diamond ring I gave her as a token of my promise glints on her finger. I've got everything I ever wanted, right here. I bask in that knowledge for three more heartbeats before I lean back and nudge the door closed with my foot.

Her eyes pop open, and a wide grin parts her lips.

"Hey, baby, come here. The water feels so good," she drawls.

She opens her arms wide in invitation, as if I ever needed one, when I step into the large shower stall. I draw her flush against me with one arm around her waist and press the other to the wall right over her head.

The slide of her skin, smooth as satin and soft as gold dust, slick and warm, against mine is incredible. Her fingers dance up my arms, slip over my shoulders and cup both sides of my neck. She presses featherlight kisses all over my chest and throat. I close my eyes and savor the unhurried, lingering pace of her progress while the perfectly warm water cascades over us.

I've been dreaming about her like this, and I don't waste any time making the most of it. Her hard nipples press into my chest wall, and I draw my hand down her back in a slow caress until I reach the rounded curve of her perfect ass and I tilt her forward until my cock nestles tight between us.

A month ago, I would have hoisted her up, slammed into her and pounded her into that wall. But then her belly popped. Overnight, she went from looking like she'd eaten too many tacos to looking like she'd swallowed a small human.

The undeniable evidence of a human being, a tiny, soft-headed, fragile person growing inside her, scares the shit out of me. What if I hurt him? So, I started dialing it back. Even after the doctor assured me there was no way I'd hurt him, I just... don't see how that's anatomically possible.

So, I'll wait until we're out of the shower to get inside of her. But I'll get a damn good head start now.

I slide my hand into the thick, damp hair at her nape. I curl my fingers to form a fist and pull her head back until the angle is right for me to kiss her.

Her sweet lips are soft and pliant under mine. I move us back until our heads our free of the spray, and then I press my tongue into her mouth, where hers meets it stroke for stroke. I take my time, rediscovering the texture and taste of her.

We're as easy and lazy as the white wafts of steam that surround us. Her hands move—one up to cradle my head, the other down to roam my body. She kneads the muscles in my neck, my shoulders and my back and a groan of satisfaction rumbles up my throat. I break our kiss to let it out, throwing my head back as little ripples of pleasure rush over my entire body and the lingering tension leaves me.

"That feels good?" she asks rhetorically, and I look down to find her smiling like the cat who got the cream.

I nod and give her ass a good squeeze before I reach behind me for a washcloth from the stack right outside the shower.

"Sit down," I order her, nodding at the bench seat lining the left side of the massive stall. She smiles, bites her plump bottom lip the way she does when she's excited, and lowers herself gracefully onto the white and gold marbled stone seat.

I pour the golden-honey-colored soap, the same hue as the pearl-sized nipples she's twirling between her fingers, into the washcloth and kneel in front of her.

I take my time, washing every crevice and dip before I move up to her ankles, up her calves, behind her knees and then over the front of them. She relaxes against the wall, her eyes closed, her lips slightly parted while I pamper her.

I skip the valley between her thighs and focus on her belly. I put the washcloth down and fill my hands with soap for this part. She's almost seven months pregnant, and he's still got a lot of weight to gain. But, anatomically, he's fully formed, and sometimes if my hand is in the right place during one of his sinuous rolls, I can distinguish his limbs, right under her skin. I press a kiss to the center of her belly, whisper hello to him before I take her breasts in my still-soapy hands and rub them gently, drawing circles around her puckering nipples.

Her posture changes from relaxed to assertive. She presses into my hands, her thighs fall open and her hips jut forward. She's ready. And, so am I.

I take her nipples between my thumb and forefinger and squeeze. A husky, melodic moan bubbles out of her, and she slides a hand between her thighs and strokes herself.

I love watching her. I learn the pattern of her pleasure more intimately each time she does this in front of me.

I reach up, grab the showerhead hanging on the wall and turn it on. I test the temperature on my arm before I turn it on her and rinse her clean of the soap I've spread all over her.

"Time to taste my handiwork," I try to quip, but my voice is rough with need and it comes out like a groan. And when I finally get my lips around her stiff, fragrant nipple and get the first feel of it on my tongue, it's like tasting heaven. She moans, spearing her hands into my hair and holding my head close. The scrape of her nails on my scalp nearly undoes my control. Savoring and going slow instantly loses its appeal.

I'm ready to fuck.

But, I left her pussy unwashed so that when I ate it, I'd still be able to taste and smell her and not whatever was left behind after the soap rinsed away. And I'll be damned if I let that go to waste.

I spread her thighs so my wide shoulders fit between them, and open her to me. Her pink, wet, perfect cunt glistens up at me, and my mouth waters. I use my fingers to pull her even wider and press a small kiss to the hood of her clit. I pull back to look at it one more time.

"Hayes, don't tease me," she says in a desperate voice.

I chuckle at the impatient frown on her face before I give my queen what she wants.

I lick her, lapping up all the slick evidence of how much she's enjoying herself. I coat my tongue with her musky honey and push it inside her, groaning at the way the greedy muscles grasp at it. I want to feel more and push two fingers inside her.

She's so tight. She's going to feel so good gripping my dick. I pull her clit into my mouth, nibbling a little before I suck it, soft but fast, the way I know she needs it. She goes off, her thighs shaking on my shoulders and her fingers clenching rhythmically in my hair as she trembles in the seat.

When she's done, panting and boneless against the wall, I slip my arms under her knees and lift her up into my arms and carry her into the bedroom dripping wet and smelling good enough to eat---again.

The view is spectacular, but my full attention is on my throbbing dick as it brushes the firm muscle of her backside with each step I take.

"Oh baby, I need you inside me," she says and drops hot, wet kisses to my shoulder and neck. The first drop of pre-cum seeps from the head of my cock, and I pray for the strength it'll take not to bust a nut the second I'm inside her.

I lay her on the bed, and she arranges herself on her side. I lie down facing her and lift her leg over mine. The head of my dick is one big pleasure nerve, and as I glide through the wet slit between her thighs, lubing myself up, the sensation is explosive.

"Tesoro, God, I need to fuck you." I pant in her ear, and she shudders.

The phone's loud ring cuts through the air. And Confidence jumps like someone walked into the room. She out of my arms and scrambling across the bed before I can register that she's going for the phone.

"Sorry, babe, but this could be important."

What the fuck?

I take four strides to walk around the bed and get to the desk before she's even off the bed.

"Hold the line," I blurt out and lift the phone up over my head just in time to keep the phone out of her reach.

"Give it to me," she whispers and stands up on her toes, grasping at my arm to try to pull it down at the same time.

"We were about to fuck." I take a step back.

"Hayes, they can hear you," she says in a harsh whisper.

I shrug. "And?" Not hiding my irritation, while I wait for to explain.

She looks between me and the phone, torn between wanting to argue and not wanting the person to hang up. Finally she lets out a huff of exasperated breath and glares at me when I smile triumphantly.

"You are so nosy. I was trying to surprise you. Give me the phone, let me take care of this and then I'll tell you everything," she says in resignation.

"Please hold for Ms. Ryan," I say into the speaker and hand her the phone.

"You're also annoying," she grumbles before she stalks naked into the bathroom.

"But, I'm effective," I say, and she glares at me before she slams the door and punctuates the end of that scene with an unmistakable, "Fuck off!" I start after her when there's a knock on the door.

Excellent timing. I pat my suddenly rumbling stomach. Fucking with Confidence is always good for my appetite.

"Coming," I call and slip on my sweatpants before I pull the door open.

I find a young man with dark, pomade-slick hair and dimples piercing both cheeks even though he's not smiling, panting and sweating as he leans against the doorframe for support.

He straightens and his expression goes from winded to confused.

"Is this Ms. Ryan's room?" he asks.

He's wearing the hotel's marron-colored livery, but the absence of a food cart behind him tells me he's not here to bring me our order.

I narrow my eyes in suspicion.

"Who's asking?" I ask him, squaring my jaw.

His eyes widen, and he takes a defensive step back.

"Ah—I'm from the restaurant. There is a problem, and Ms. Cara hasn't arrived. Is Ms. Ryan available?" He looks over my shoulder into the room.

"Did you say Cara?" I move to block his view, and he gulps and leans away.

"Yes, Ms. Ryan's friend. She was supposed to be there by ten, but it is already almost noon and she hasn't arrived. We don't have a cake."

I blink in confusion. "Arrive?" I say stupidly.

"My manager sent me to see if Ms. Ryan could come down to speak with the bakery."

I have no idea what this man is talking about. Cara? Cake? Bakery? What is going on here?

The door to the bathroom comes flying open, and Confidence walks out, fully dressed again. This time in a white T-shirt and shorts with the word *Queen* embossed in black and gold all over.

"I have to go downstairs," she says and then comes to a halt when she notices the young man. She groans, rubbing her temples as if she knows he's bearing bad news.

"Oh my God, what now?" she asks no one in particular.

"What else? Who was on the phone?" I ask, and this time, I'm not smiling or cajoling.

A pained expression crosses her face, and she sighs in exasperation. "There's a problem with my mother's room."

My heart thuds uncomfortably, and I rub my chest.

"Your mother is here, too? On our vacation? The one we took so we could be alone?" My hopes that she'll laugh and tell me how absurd that sounds die when her eyes dart away and she nods.

"I need to go downstairs and deal with whatever is going on. I'll tell you everything as soon as I get back," she says, a fretful expression I don't like one bit creasing her pretty brow.

"Yeah, that would be a good thing, baby. I hope whatever you've got to say starts with, 'I didn't invite my best friend and mother on our vacation, Hayes,'" I deadpan.

She bites her lip. "Try to have an open mind, please?"

"Yeah, that's a tall order when I've got blue balls and an empty stomach," I say flatly.

She frowns, she doesn't respond before she slips out of the door.

CONFIDENCE

I grew up trapped between my abusive, alcoholic father and the merciless, unpredictable flood waters of the Mississippi delta. I only made it out of my town because my mother forced me to believe that I had something to offer the world. I stepped into the arena known as Big Law with my mother's dreams for me and my naivete as my only shields.

They threw me to the wolves. I was at rock bottom, trying to claw my way back, when I met Hayes. I spent the last of my savings to travel to Italy with Cara for a friend's wedding. The minute I laid eyes on him, I could tell he was the kind of man that could change a woman's life. My intuition was spot on.

Our whirlwind romance, our dramatic and sudden engagement and his family's unbelievable public drama earlier this year all led to a swirl of press attention that I wasn't prepared for. But I'm a fast learner and things... are settling down.

Now, we're a just a few weeks away from the wedding I've always dreamed. I wanted this trip to be one he'd never forget.

Hayes hasn't said a word since I got back and "explained" as much as I could without spoiling the surprise. His jaw ticks as he unlocks the door to his new suite and shoulders it open.

"I was trying to surprise you. I'm sorry everything got so messed up," I say as soon as the door closes behind us. I can't bear the silence anymore.

Hayes looks at me, his face fixed with that serene smile he's been wearing since I told him my mother and Cara needed to stay in our room tonight. Their room has a broken thermostat.

The hotel was at full occupancy, with not a bed to spare – save for the one I booked . So, instead of surprising him like I planned, I had to tell him that his brothers were here. Dare's room had two queen beds, and Hayes would bunk with him for tonight.

"I told you, it's fine. If you're happy, so am I," he says. As easy and sincere as he's trying to seem, his smile doesn't make it all the way to his eyes. When he turns away to unpack, his jaw is still ticking.

"You don't have to say it's fine if it's not," I say.

"I know," he returns easily. His smile is wearing thin, but it's there.

Then, he flings the clothes in his hand haphazardly into the drawer and slams it shut.

A giggle erupts from my throat with no warning. I clamp a hand over my mouth and stare wide-eyed at him. His facade of calm slips and his eyes narrow. It takes herculean-level strength to remove all the humor from my face. "I'm sorry. I know it's not funny. I'm not laughing at you."

"How strange then; that's exactly what it looks like," he rejoins in a dry, unamused voice.

"It's just... it's obvious you're pissed." I point helplessly at the half-shut drawers with clothes spilling out of them.

He gives his workmanship a disdainful glower. Then, with a weary sigh, he turns away from me and starts straightening the mess.

I know he'll be fine once the evening is over. But, I feel a surge of guilt that he's unhappy now. This was all supposed to go differently. I toe the thin grout line on the caramel-colored tiles laid in a stunning geometric pattern on the floor.

I'm not good at subterfuge. I knew that. But, I'm determined to pull this off. It's not my fault he's so hard to shop for. What do you give the man who has everything?

The answer came in a stroke of inspiration: He's laid the entire world at my feet. I wanted to give him his heart's desire. It was crazy to plan in such a short time. I've worked on planning this weekend in every spare moment I had. It's meant that I've barely seen him. But, the look on his face when he finally realizes why we're here will make it all worth it.

I'd planned to fuck him, feed him and get him a drink to make sure he was nice and loose and relaxed. Then I would let him hang out with his brothers while I got to work.

Instead, I spent the last hour sorting out my mother's room and getting the cake figured out. I have other fires to put out, and I still need to pick up my dress from the mail room downstairs. But I can't leave Hayes until I know he's okay.

"They'll have a room she can use tomorrow. I know it's annoying, but it's just one night. And they're all leaving the day after tomorrow, so we'll be on our own for the rest of the week."

"Stone lives in Colombia. He came all this way for a weekend?"

"He's why I picked this resort. He's here for a conference and it's really nice, so I figured it was a good place to meet," I tell him.

He eyes me suspiciously, and I have to bite the inside of my cheek hard to keep from laughing at his naked skepticism. I'm grateful my plan stayed airtight so long. If he'd a whiff of what I was planning, he would have hounded me until I told him everything.

Thank goodness, I only have a few more hours to keep this secret. So I lay it on thick one more time.

"I just wanted to give you a nice weekend with your family. You've been working so hard. We both have. I brought you to paradise, and all I've done is stress you out."

He walks over and grasps my chin, forcing eyes to his.

"I'm not stressed. It'll be nice to spend time with them. And paradise is wherever you are. So, I'm fine."

My heart squeezes. I love him so much.

"Oh, baby, I—"

The loud rumble of his empty stomach cuts me off, and I rear back in horror.

"Oh my God, I didn't even let you eat before I kicked you out of the room. Wait here and I'll get the food cart from the room." I give him an apologetic smile and turn to go. He grabs hold of my ponytail and I stop.

He winds it around his fist, pulls backward, turning me until I'm facing him. His eyes are dark and intense.

"Fuck that food, I want to finish eating you, Tesoro." He nibbles my lips before he kisses me long, and wet, and slow again. It's been an hour since we were in the shower, but I taste myself on his tongue. My thighs clench at the memory of the magic his hands and mouth worked on me.

I tip my head back and gaze up at his striking, bold-featured face. He's not classically handsome, but he's nothing short of beautiful. His dark chocolate-brown hair hugs his head in a crown of short waves that give him the look of a roman god. His lush lips are parted slightly as he looks down at me. His eyes glitter like fractured amber behind the thick crescent of lashes that frame them.

"I planned to spend all day balls-deep inside of you. Stay with me. Whatever you were going to do, it doesn't matter."

His mouth, sinfully full, stung and soft from my kisses, beckons me to stay and indulge.

It's a testament to how much I love him that I find the presence of mind to remember my ultimate mission and pull away.

"We'll be together tonight, King," I say and hope the hotel's promise to fix thermostat today holds.

His eyes flare with heat at the endearment.

It's the one I only use in our most tender moments.

When he's making love to me and my body is lit up with emotion and sensation that turns me into a boneless, throbbing mush.

When his lips are on mine, devouring me like my kiss is his oxygen.

In those moments, just like now, when my soul is on fire with love for him, he's the king of my heart. And I call him by his name.

"Say it again," he drawls in his honey-coated baritone, his heated gaze fixed on my mouth.

"You're going to fuck me all night, King." I enunciate each word.

He cups my breast through my shirt.

"You've been braless all day." He thumbs my nipple and then drops his head to suck it through my T-shirt. I clutch his shoulders and moan from the friction of his tongue and the cotton of my shirt.

His hand slips inside my shorts, and then his fingers are snaking around my panties and pushing inside of me. I cry out at the delicious collision of pleasure and pressure that blooms and spreads like wildfire through my entire body. His fingers pump and stroke and take me higher with each touch.

"Take my dick out," he orders, and I reach between us and start to unbutton him. My hands move with a clumsy desperation. The door to the suite chimes and then opens. I freeze. Hayes lifts his head from my breast and puts a possessive arm around my shoulders, keeping me from turning around.

"Get the fuck out, Dare," he growls.

I cover my face with both hands and groan.

"No, Hayes, I've got to go. I'm sorry." I cup his jaw so I can stroke his closely cropped beard while I kiss him.

My cheeks flame as I turn to face his little brother, Dare. I cross my arms over my chest to hide the wet spot his mouth left.

"Hey." I stop to press a quick kiss to his cheek. He looks just as embarrassed as I feel.

When I get onto the elevator, I can still feel the brush of Hayes's beard against my fingers. I can't wait to feel it between my thighs later. First, I've got a dress to pick up.

* * *

"What do you mean, it's not here? Can you check with the delivery service again?" I ask, unable to keep the panic out of my voice. This can't be happening.

She taps her watch. "It's 5:05 p.m.; they close at 5pm. I'm so sorry," she says, her expression genuinely apologetic before she turns away and disappears into the dark recesses of the hotel's package room.

"I need that dress," I say under my breath, but watch her go without trying to stop her again. She can't do a thing to help me.

"Confidence Ryan?" The woman's voice is smooth and tight as a silk rope, and I turn around and stare in disbelief at Regan Wilde-Landel in all her stunning glory.

"What are you doing here?" I ask, gawking at her. She's our neighbor in our Houston neighborhood, Rivers Wilde. Her family founded it.

But it's not just the sheer improbability of seeing her that has my jaw on the floor. It's that she's the walking definition of stone-cold, drop-dead gorgeous. She looks the way we tell girls "no one" looks without airbrushing and Photoshop.

I know she has three kids, but her figure is a master class in how to look like a Victoria's Secrets Angel. Her bikini is white swaths of fabric covering just the bare necessities and showing off every single perfect line and curve of her body.

Her hair is the richest dark chocolate-brown and falls in beautiful spiral curls all over her head and shoulders. I've never seen her hair like this. I know her mother is Jamaican, but her hair is always bone straight. I assumed that's how it grew. Her skin is as flawless as the rest of her. Smooth, golden brown from the sun with not a line, blemish, freckle or scar to be seen anywhere.

"What's wrong?" she asks, her imperious tone drawing my attention back to my crisis.

"I had a dress delivered here to wear tonight, and it wasn't. So, I don't have anything to wear."

She looks at the gold Cartier watch on her delicate wrist and then up at me with an arched eyebrow. "Hmmm, The boutique on site just closed, but..." she purses her lips thoughtfully .

"Do you think they'd open for me?" I ask, hope lifting my voice an octave.

"I don't know. We enforce pretty strict hours to make sure our staff aren't here too late. Some of them live far away," she explains.

"*You*r staff?" I repeat dumbly.

"Yes, this is my husband's property." She says *property* like she's talking about a house and not this five-mile stretch of luxury resort on the Pacific Ocean.

"It is? Wow. It's incredible. I had no idea."

"So, what's the event?"

"A beach wedding. At sunset, It's a surprise, though so if you see Hayes please don't say anything."

She eyes my shorts and T-shirt with a conspiratorial smile. "Your secret is safe. But, t won't do for you to wear that. Come with me," she commands and starts walking away without waiting for me to respond.

I have to take two steps for each one of her to keep up. But I'm so happy she's helping me, I barely notice.

"Is your family here, ?" I ask when we stop in front of the store.

Her smiles falls away and her eyes shutter. But not before I see the flare of panic in them. "It'll be a little tricky given that belly, but I think I've got just the thing." She turns away and ignores my question. She unlocks the door and we slip inside.

She lets me try on four dresses, but I end up with the first one she picked out.

"Thank you so much, Regan." I'm nearly giddy with relief at how random and fortuitous it was that I saw her. I give her an impulsive hug in thanks.

She stiffens slightly but then hugs me back. After years of acrimony between her family and Hayes, this moment feels like a harbinger of good things to come for us when we get back home.

"We'll be at the beach in two hours. You should come. I'd love to have you. Bring your husband and kids."

She smiles, but sadness flickers in her eyes.

"Oh, that's a terrible idea, darling. But, thank you. And good luck. It's wonderful that you're so in love with your future husband. Make sure you stay that way." She presses a kiss to each of my cheeks before she walks away.

HAYES

"Why the fuck are you smiling like that?" I nudge my brother, Stone, with my elbow.

He immediately stops smiling. "I don't know what you're talking about." He says and I eye him in the mirror, but drop it. He's always been a private person and I know that pushing him is the surest way to talk.

I turn back to the mirror and run a brush through my hair. I feel him watching me and dart an inquisitive glance in his direction.

"How do you *know*?" Stone asks, and our eyes meet in the mirror.

"Know what?" I ask and run my fingers through my hair one last time.

"That you want to spend the rest of your life with her."

"Well, for one, I'm in Mexico when I want to be home. And. I'm sharing a room with my brother instead of finding another hotel altogether. And, I'd rather swallow hot lead than disappoint my girl."

Speaking of her... I haven't seen my woman since she walked out of my room earlier that day, and I'm fucking grouchy about it.

Stone laughs, and I freeze.

"I haven't heard you laugh in at least three years," I say.

"That's not true." he scoffs, and a smile plays on his lips.

"Has there been an invasion of body snatchers? Who the hell are you?"

"Fuck off, Hayes. You haven't seen me in two years. A lot has changed."

"I saw you two weeks ago on FaceTime, and you looked like the same miserable fucker you've always been. Last time you looked like that, you were eating one of those lemon muffin things you used to be obsessed with."

He purses his lips in a self-satisfied smile and nods. "You don't say..."

"Are you two peacocks done hogging the mirror?" Beau shouts from the bedroom. I stick my head out of the bathroom. He's lounging on the bed, and Dare is nowhere in sight.

"Where'd he go?" I ask and eye Dare's bed. It's strewn with more clothes than he could possibly need for a weekend, hair products, his laptop, two cell phones, and several wads of cash. I push away the unfair flare of suspicion as I take in his things. Dare has been home from rehab for two months. He's doing well. I can see the change in him. I just need to accept that his lifestyle is less traditional than mine.

I clap my hands together both to refocus my thoughts and to get my brother's attention.

"Listen, whatever C is up to, I want you guys to promise me you didn't let her rope you into anything crazy."

"Too late. That little blonde Napoleon you're handcuffing yourself to can't be reined in," Beau says cryptically and grins. He hops up and saunters to the small bar by our balcony.

He hands me a glass and another to Stone and raises a toast.

He makes a lewd joke about marriage and balls in vises. I laugh even though it's not really that funny. I'm happy. I've missed my brothers.

I was fifteen when my father died; I went to live with my Aunt Gigi in Italy until I came of age. We haven't lived in the same place since. But we're still as close as ever. Even Dare and I, though we butt heads—literally, at times.

We're scattered all over the place, and it's been too long since we got together outside of the holidays.

Confidence never ceases to amaze me. They told me she made it clear that she wouldn't take no for an answer when she called them to plan this. Even though I've missed her this afternoon, it been nice to spend the afternoon with them. —I feel bad that I didn't thank her before she went off on her mysterious errands.

A simple and easy day is the best gift anyone has ever given me.

In my family those kinds of words—*simple* and *easy*—were met with suspicion. I'm the new head of my family's business. It's an energy and real estate dynasty that's older than the state of Texas. My grandfather made sure

I understood that my first duty was to the preservation of the legacy I'd inherited.

He thought of himself as the alpha of a wolf pack. When his children turned out to be disloyal, dishonest and unprincipled people, he did what any good alpha would do. He turned them against each other and waited until the strongest of the litter eliminated the weaker ones.

His oldest, my Aunt Gigi's marriage was a misalliance, and she was disinherited.

His younger son Thomas was expelled from West Point after a scandal involving grade fixing and cheating, and my grandfather refused to even consider him.

My father, Jason, his quiet and unassuming middle son, became heir by TKO.

My grandfather was a relentless, calculating, and ruthlessly strategic businessman. In the thirty years that he was at the helm, he took Kingdom from a dinosaur of an oil company to a real estate investment business that spanned the globe.

He loved the strong and useful. Everyone else was a waste of space and good oxygen. My biological mother died from complications after childbirth. I was just seven years old when he told me my mother's death was the consequence of natural selection. "You were born with a killer instinct, son, leading this family is your destiny," he told me.

When he died, my father stepped into his shoes.

Jason Rivers may not have had a killer instinct, but he had a very human one.

He was under no delusions about his capability for leadership. He became chairman in name only. With my grandfather's right hand, Swish, and him acting as it's figurehead, Kingdom thrived. It was a beautiful partnership.

I could not say the same about his marriage to my stepmother. He started dating Eliza a few months before my grandfather died. She was a beautiful whirlwind of mayhem and chaos. Her three children had three different fathers. The youngest, Dare, was less than six months old when she moved in.

The elder Rivers had made it clear that she would only become his daughter-in-law over his dead body.

She made sure there was a special toast made to his memory at their wedding.

Living with her was only made bearable because of the boys who became my brothers. Dare was one. Beau was two, Stone was three when their mother married my father.

"Okay, let's go. Everything is ready."

Beau's abrupt declaration startles me. "Ready for what?" I ask. Confidence has been cryptic and said we were having dinner at the beach at sunset.

"For you, dumbass. That's all I'm allowed to say," he adds when I start to press him for more.

I turn to Stone, who is distracted by whatever he's reading on his phone.

He's smiling, again.

This time, with teeth.

My curiosity about the evening is forgotten. I give him a suspicious once-over.

"Don't get me wrong, I'm glad to see it. But, why the fuck are you smiling at your phone?"

He flushes, and his eyes get an almost dreamy look, one I've never seen. Even before five years ago.

"I think... I'm in love."

"Wow." I can't hide my surprise.

He smiles wryly. "I know. It's a little complicated, though."

"How so?"

"She's married. Don't say a fucking word. Not to anyone," he orders.

Then, he claps me on the shoulder and follows Beau out the door. I put my shoes on and grab my wallet and hurry after them.

The elevator doors open on our floor just as I'm catching up with them.

"Good timing," Beau mutters as we step onto the crowded car.

Conversation is impossible, but I catch Stone's eye and give him a look that he knows means that I'm not done with him.

He smirks and shrugs.

I smirk back and plan my attack as we descend.

When we step off the elevator, I pounce.

"I forgot my phone upstairs," I lie.

"Aww, shit. Hayes. If you're late, Confidence will fucking kill me," Beau whines.

"Then you go get it. And Stone can escort me to whatever this is."

"Good idea. I'll be five minutes behind you," he says and then turns back for the elevators.

"That's not a little complicated." I fall into step beside a speed-walking Stone.

He scoffs. "It is. She won't be married for much longer. Now that I know for certain she could be mine, I'm just going to wait for everything to align and make my move."

"I thought you had a girl in Colombia," I ask.

"I do. But this woman... she's my endgame."

"Are you hers?" I ask. When he doesn't respond, I glance at him and find his attention is on something on the other side of the lobby.

I follow his gaze and glimpse ... someone who shouldn't be here.

"Is that... Regan Landel?" It's a rhetorical question. Of course, it's her. No one besides her twin brother, Remi, looks like that.

"Yes, that's her," Stone says. His voice has an odd tone, and I turn away from Regan, who appears to be directing staff, to look at him.

He's watching her the way I watch Confidence. Devouring every detail like his life depends on it.

A very terrible foreboding knots my stomach.

"Stone, no. Please tell me...it's not her," I groan and nudge him to start walking again.

"It's not her," he deadpans, glancing over his shoulder at her as we walk away.

"Are you out of your fucking mind? She's our neighbor.. Her husband is my friend. And he's completely crazy about his wife. You can't—"

"I absolutely can," he says in an unequivocally resolute voice.

"Stone—"

He shakes his head and points at the restaurant we're standing in front of. "We'll talk later. We're here. It's showtime."

CONFIDENCE

The minute I lay eyes on Hayes, my nerves make a roaring comeback.

Dressed in classic white pants and a pistachio-colored linen shirt, he looks every bit like a tycoon vacationing in Baja.

He has a fearsome reputation. But the real Hayes is nothing like the cold, cunning man he plays for the world. He's confident but so humble. Ambitious but not blindly so. Generous without being frivolous. Possessive without being overbearing. Principled but pragmatic. All of that alone is a potent aphrodisiac. Add to it how he enhances every scene he steps into with his magnetism and dark, brooding intensity, and he goes from eligible to certifiable unicorn.

As some members of his family remind me every chance they get, men like him marry royalty or women with pedigrees and last names like Rothschild. Not a nobody from nowhere, with nothing to her name but determination and love.

If I didn't have his ring on my finger, I wouldn't believe that he'd chosen me to share his life.

But, I do have his ring on my finger. And he didn't just choose me. He claimed me and then fought for me.

I cross the room toward him. He's standing patiently listening to whatever my mother is saying. A hush falls over the small group I've gathered tonight. Cara grabs my hand for a quick squeeze as I pass her. His brothers huddle and watch with solemn but pleased expressions on their handsome faces.

I tap him on the shoulder. He turns right away, his eyes already lit with a smile I know is just for me.

My heart skips an entire beat.

"Wow," he exclaims as he takes in my dress and makeup. "I would launch a thousand ships to make you mine, Tesoro. You look amazing."

If I were my feelings, I'd be a puddle of sweet, sticky love. "Thank you, baby. So do you." I beam up at him.

"The sun is setting," Dare calls, and Hayes glares in his direction. Then does a double take when he realizes everyone is watching us. He makes a slow 360 turn to look around the "restaurant."

I lower myself onto one knee.

"What's going—" His voice trails off as he pivots around to face me again.

"If I had to choose one person to see, touch, and love forever, it would be you. Loving you is more natural than breathing. Hayes, will you marry me?" I ask, rushing the words out before he can interrupt me.

"Am I in the twilight zone? I already asked you this," he responds, a stunned expression on his face.

"Now I'm asking *you*.," I tell him, trying to suppress a laugh of delight at having caught him so thoroughly off guard.

"Yes," he says hurriedly before he cups me by my elbow and pulls me back to standing. "What's all this?" he asks, as wide-eyed as I've ever seen him.

I'm smiling so hard my cheeks hurt.

"My present to you. A wedding at sunset, on the beach with just our friends and family."

"Tonight?" he asks, his expression dazed as he looks around the room as if he's seeing it all again for the first time.

"If you'll have me, yes." I hold out my hands to him, and he lets me lead him around the room where we've set up the tables to the small private beach where we'll have the ceremony. The rest of our guests, including his two best friends from college, are waiting.

We walk up the small aisle hand in hand.

I make a note to tell Dare's that he's going to have to find somewhere else to sleep tonight. No way am I spending it without him.

We exchange simple vows. I put my ring on his finger. We seal the officiant's declaration with a kiss, and with the crash of the Pacific Ocean behind us and the sun's final salute on the horizon, we become the sum of each other.

HAYES

Confidence gives the best head. But it's the sight of the platinum band on my finger as it fists in my wife's hair that makes my knees weak.

I pull out of her mouth and coax her up to standing. Her lips are puffy and wet from her very impressive blowjob, and her eyes are glassy with lust.

"I don't want my first nut as a married man to be in your mouth."

"I wouldn't mind, but I'll take your dick however I can get it," she says as she straddles my thighs and sinks down on me. Finally.

I take one of her nipples into my mouth and thrust up into her soft pussy and groan at the tight fit. She glides down easily, like her body was made just for this purpose.

"We're married," she sighs, her head falling back as she gazes up at the star-spangled twilight sky. Her smile is voluptuous with gratification. I release her nipple and pull her head down so I can look into those radiant blue eyes.

"Yes, you little terror, we are." I nip her lip and grab her hips and rock up gently into her.

"Hayes, I won't break..." she says and sucks my bottom lip.

"I know you won't ... El bambino, though." I trace her tummy.

She rolls her hips, grinding down on me before she lifts up. I look down to watch as my dick comes into view, coated with her. She drops back down, filling herself to the root again.

"Hayes, I need it hard, I need you deep, please."

What the fuck is wrong with me? Why am I making my queen beg for what's hers?

I move fast, and she whoops as I flip us over. I slide my hands under her knees and lift her legs over my shoulders.

"Is this deep enough?"

She smiles, wicked and bewitching beneath me as I thrust deep.

"It's a good start."

I see her challenge and raise it. I drive down, hard, fast, deep until her thighs are trembling against my shoulders. She takes it and owns every single second of it.

And when she comes with my name on her lips, I feel like a king.

I like my mountains steep and skyscraping. My motto is, the harder the climb, the more rarified the reward at the end. And thank fuck for that because I inherited a mess the size of Mt. Rushmore.

We got off to a rocky start, quite literally. But, loving her has shown me that steep, sheer, difficult aren't words that should ever describe a relationship.

Cohort, spotter, catcher, life raft, trench-warfare comrade, teammate, and confidante—Confidence is all of those.

She is a living vessel of my future. More than the legacy I inherited, loving her love feels like my birthright. And it's that crown I wear like a king.

* * *

Do you want more of Dylan Allen?

One click THE LEGACY now!

THE BOOGIEMAN

MARY CATHERINE GEBHARD

1

It was without a doubt the worst moment in time to be turned on. I was supposed to be providing grief counseling, not getting hot and bothered by memories of her and her dead husband. I couldn't help it. I'd been expecting woeful lamentations about how she missed his scent in bed, the way he said her name, the way he smiled.

What I got was leather. And whips. And chains.

Mrs. Adams wiped a stray tear from her cheek. "Today is laundry day. One time I forgot to do the towels, leaving them unfolded. The last time I did that... The last time..."

Mrs. Adams started to wail.

"The last time you did that?" I prompted. Did I sound too eager?

"Jared came home and immediately took me over his knee. I remember I was so turned on I was already wet all down my thighs. I thought my red butt was going to be enough punishment, but Jared made me lay out the towels. He fucked me on them, pulled out, and then came all over me and the towels." Mrs. Adams took a deep breath and just in time. My own breath was clenched, and I held my pen so tight I thought it might break. "He still wasn't finished punishing me. I remember him reaching down and rubbing my pussy raw until I came all over the towels. They were ruined. I had to go out and buy new ones."

I'd always been a vanilla cupcake kind of girl. I never asked for sprinkles.

I never mixed in strawberry. There had always been this part of me that wondered what other bolder flavors tasted like, but all I'd ever ordered was vanilla. Now, as Mrs. Adams recounted her story, I couldn't help but wonder again: was I vanilla because I liked vanilla, or because I'd never tried any other flavors?

Just as Mrs. Adams opened her mouth to, presumably, continue, my phone vibrated.

Time's up.

Thank God.

"Please hold on to that thought," I said, standing up. "I promise if it were any other day, I would let you continue, but I have a standing appointment."

I quickly shuffled Mrs. Adams out of my private office, into the blustering snow.

It took me over an hour to drive to my appointment, and by the time I arrived, I was rushing.

In my home of Lake's End, Colorado, not much happened, but drive some miles north and the most deadly and dangerous criminals are housed in the world's only super-max prison. Lucky me, I got to play doctor to them.

No, really, lucky me.

I went to school just for that.

A gust of wind blew, and my papers scattered across the ground.

"Shoot!"

Even though it was spring, snow was still falling in big, puffy flakes, and a few of my papers got wet. Colorado never really gave a fuck about seasons, and Lake's End really liked to give the middle finger.

When I stood up, my heart stopped. Froze in my chest like his icy-blue eyes.

I was face-to-face with the most intimidating man I'd ever seen.

He was so tall I had to crane my neck back to see into his striking eyes. His thick, corded muscles were covered in tattoos and scars. He had a full, blond beard, and one side of his head was shaved, the right side falling across his eye wildly and somehow elegantly.

I worked with murderers and serial killers, unapologetic psychopaths who delighted in trying to make me squirm with terrifying and disgusting words, but something about him made my spine tingle like when I ate too much sugar.

It wasn't his height that made me clench my papers and force myself to look beyond him at Aaron, the guard. It was his easy smile, like he knew something I didn't.

Because all I could think about was Mrs. Adam's story.

I immediately shuffled past, pretending I hadn't seen him.

Pretending the redness in my cheeks was from the cold.

2

Today my psychopath was skittish. I call them my psychopaths because that's what it feels like. In some twisted way, they belong to me.

I'm the only one who really talks to them.

Who understands, without judgment.

Today he was convinced someone was coming for him.

"You're in one of the most heavily guarded places on the planet."

He shook his head. "Not from the Boogiemen. Not even the police know his face. One minute alive...the next dead. No one left alive to remember their faces."

"The boogieman?" I tilted my head. "The one who goes bump in the night?"

This man was normally a very calm person. I didn't know a lot about him because most of his information had been redacted. I'd gleaned he was one of those "hands-clean murderers." Probably had thousands of deaths on his hands but always made sure the blood was covered on someone else.

In here, I've seen his kind crumble after he meets the guys who really enjoy getting blood on their hands.

His brow knit and he said quietly, "Seven."

"There are seven of these boogiemen? What do they want with you?"

He closed up, and after that, no matter what question or how I phrased it, he wouldn't speak. I couldn't stop thinking about it, though.

I knew it was most likely paranoia, and I made a note to adjust his meds. But earlier… Mrs. Adams' memories were twisting in my gut with this mythical boogieman. It was weird, right? You shouldn't get turned on by the thought of some dangerous myth. *I* was weird, though. I was someone who wasn't afraid of death but fascinated by it. My bucket list was filled with illegal and immoral experiences. Ones I knew I'd never do but loved to fantasize over anyway.

It was dark when I finally left. I waved goodbye to Aaron and started my drive home.

Boogieman…

I don't know why the blue-eyed beast of a man popped into my head.

3

I was at my mailbox getting my mail when I heard the soft crunch of snow behind me. I spun, finding a man with a knife. The blade glinted silver in the night. Terror and adrenaline seized my gut in knotty twists.

I took a step back. "I don't have any cash on me."

I went through a mental list of people at the prison I could have pissed off. There were so many. They always told me I got too close to the prisoners.

"I—" I broke off.

The knife fell limp from his hand to the soft snow. I peered closer, and all-out terror seized my veins. There was *another* man behind the guy with the knife, a giant shadow in the night. I fell against my mailbox with a gasp, grasping the snowy metal.

The new man held the guy with the knife up by the neck—a *broken* neck—then let him go. My would-be attacker fell to the snow in a heap.

Quick. Simple. Vicious.

I held on to my mailbox for dear life.

Did I thank this man? Thank him for killing my would-be attacker. The words stuck in my mouth, eyes flicking from the new threat to the old one making a deathly snow angel on my front porch.

The new threat picked up the man's cigarette and stuffed it into his pocket, then his eyes landed on me. It only took two steps for his massive body to reach me, arms outstretched.

I opened my mouth on a scream just as he covered my mouth. Everything went black.

4

I woke up sideways, my hands bound. My seat vibrated—I was in a car. It felt like leather. I smelled something delicious and spicy, like expensive cologne. The last thing I remembered was...the attack.

Being saved.

I think.

I saw a sideways vision of the man driving. Tattoos snaked up the back of his neck. Blond hair fell to one side of his shaved head. He drove casually with one arm.

I slowly sat up.

Had he really saved me to kidnap me?

I had no idea who he was, but I didn't know the other guy either.

"If you want money, I don't have any."

Silence. Not so much as a head tilt.

I had no idea how long I'd been out, no idea where we were going. I was bound but not painfully so. I wasn't gagged, which meant when we stopped, no one would hear me if I screamed.

"Are you going to kill me?"

More silence.

He was driving at an incredibly fast speed. Nighttime Colorado—if we were still in Colorado—blurred into a starry black.

"Are you going to rape me?" I whispered.

He slowly lifted his head, eyeing me with one raised brow through the rearview before looking back at the road. "You wish, darlin'."

I couldn't help the laugh that escaped me. "Okay, well, that's mighty presumptuous of you." Maybe it's being surrounded by psychopaths all day, but I've kind of lost my...sense of self-preservation. Like, big deal, you murdered a bunch of people.

The guy before you ate their faces.

To my surprise, he smiled. It lit up his shockingly handsome face.

Humor stained his low, gravelly voice, like he'd just drunk a bunch of whiskey. "Shouldn't you be screaming?"

"Shouldn't you be making me scream?" I countered. This time he broke out in a full-on grin. He ran his tongue across his top teeth, and I was glued to that.

"I don't think you know what you're asking for." His eyes were animalistic. Looking like he wanted to eat me. Driving so, so fast but refusing to take his eyes from mine.

I swallowed and stared forward.

When they joke back, it isn't because they're on your side. I was a mouse trying to play with a cat.

It was silent for two hours. I kept track. Then the car jolted in quick successive bursts, and a loud rattling noise filled the silence. We came to a stuttering, halting stop. My savior/kidnapper pulled the car to the side of the long stretch of road as smoke billowed from the hood, seeping into the stars.

Those heart-stopping eyes met mine in the mirror again.

"This is the luckiest day of your goddamn life."

5

The luckiest day of my life was apparently watching, hands bound, as my kidnapper fixed his broken car. It was nice, too. One of those really expensive ones I can never remember the name of but I know cost as much as a house.

We were surrounded by woods on all sides, and the road stretched into darkness. I kept looking for moments to escape. I might not fear death, but I won't stick around and buy it coffee. The night smelled of wet pine, and the trees behind us were tall and black, entirely eclipsing the sky.

He was such a hulking beast of man, who didn't seem at all at odds with the grease and darkness. A large, silver gun was set next to him as he worked, so easy to grab. I wondered if he was taunting me.

He reminded me of a Norse god, a bloody Viking. Meanwhile I was still in my soft work clothes, and the air was bitter and biting.

"Why am I here?" I asked.

"There was a dangerous man outside your house."

"Clearly." I gestured with my chin to my surroundings. "Are you implying you were saving me? Then why are my hands tied?"

"You have a massive death wish," he growled.

"Maybe," I admitted.

He lifted his head up from behind the sleek black and blue car, eyes darkening in a way that made my belly pancake.

"Aren't you afraid of me?"

I leaned closer, just a little. "Should I be?"

He nodded slowly.

"I'll keep that in mind."

He grinned, shaking his head, before his brutish, beautiful blond head disappeared beneath the hood again.

"So...I should be afraid of you. What happens when you fix the car? I die?" No response. I couldn't figure out why he would save me only to kill me.

Seemed a little inefficient.

But...I'd had weirder patients. Maybe this guy just didn't want someone else killing his prey.

I looked around again, trying to see if there was any way I could make a run for it.

"You could try and run." His easy drawl drew me back. "I'd hate to have to throw your hundred-pound ass over my shoulder."

He still had his head buried beneath the car, and I only saw his muscular biceps and triceps, the way sweat glistened along his inky tattoos.

"One hundred pounds? Add at least forty to that, pal." My weight was a sore spot with me. I wasn't overweight, but I was always five pounds away from it. The fact that I couldn't lose ten pounds was a niggling thought in the back of my mind. Each time I reached for a cookie, or a brownie, or what-the-fuck-sugary-thing-ever, I remembered that I only had five pounds to spare. Did he really think I was one hundred pounds, or was it just one of his mind games?

My bet was mind games.

"Maybe you keep those extra pounds in your tits and ass." He paused and lifted his head, raking his gaze over my body. "Yep," he concluded with an easy, low laugh.

Heat rushed through me, but I quickly tamped it down.

If I had a nickel for every time one of my psychopaths said dirty, filthy things to try and get a reaction from me...well, I'd be pretty fucking rich.

"Where are you taking me?"

Silence.

"Are we still in Colorado?"

More silence.

"Why were you at my house?"

More. Silence.

"I've seen your face. I've seen your car. You're not exactly someone who blends in…"

I swore I heard a laugh from beneath the hood, but it was too low to tell. "Do you *want* me to kill you?"

I made a sound like *ehh*.

"I don't care what you hear or see, Octavia. Does a lion care about the fly that rests on its back?"

"Depends on the fly."

"If you tell anyone about us, we'll know. If you come looking for us, we'll know."

Us? I looked up and down the desolate road, wondering if we'd be getting company.

"What if I think about you?" I whispered.

His eyes flamed, and blood rushed wild in my ears, dripping between my thighs. Which was probably why I didn't do well on those dating sites. They don't have a seeking-partner-with-death-wish option.

He leaned forward and my breath caught.

"I'll know."

As instantly as the air sizzled between us, it died. He went back under the hood. I shifted around on my feet, then straightened my shoulders. He'd said my name earlier.

"How do you know my name?"

He leaned to the side enough to toss a glance at my name badge, the one that said Octavia Bell PhD.

Oh. Right.

"Well…what's your name?"

Silence.

Of course. Like he would really tell me his—

"Seven."

"Seven?" I perked up. "Your name is Seven? Like the number?"

"That's what they call me."

There are seven of these boogiemen?

No…it was just a coincidence.

Still, I shifted on my feet more. I didn't believe in coincidence or fate. Had my psycho been referring to the boogieman's *name*?

"So you say you're not killing me…" I swallowed. "What are you planning to do to me?"

"I'm just another psycho. Once I get my car fixed, I'll throw you into a hole and get that lotion for you."

I tried to stop the smile from breaking my lips. It sounded like a complete joke, and I liked it. I'd never met anyone who joked like I did, laughing at the darkness.

But I should probably take him seriously.

He *had* kidnapped me.

"I can help," I lied. "I know a lot about cars. My...brother...taught me."

He stepped back, wiping the grease on his hands onto a cloth, eyeing me. Sizing me up.

"I'd just need to be untied." I turned around, holding out bound hands.

Seven pulled out the biggest knife I'd ever seen, even bigger than the other guy's, then grasped my wrist, tugging me back against his body.

Heat.

He smelled like clean sweat and smoke and something else, something rich.

"You look good in your bindings. Submissive." He reached out, tugging on one of my curly, strawberry-blonde strands just as he sliced through my restraints. "Shame."

I rubbed out my wrists.

He handed me a flashlight, and I got to work, shining a light on the metallic engine as he worked a wrench inside the car. My heart pounded, waiting for the right moment to make my move. Maybe I could slam the hood on his head.

I eyed the gun, wondering if I could grab it.

"You could try," Seven said as if reading my thoughts. I snapped my gaze from the gun to his, and he was grinning. "You'd lose...but the struggle is the fun part." My mouth went dry, and he laughed, going back to work.

"Just tell me what you were doing outside my house. Please."

Seven exhaled. He rested carved, tanned arms inside the car, tilting his neck, giving me a flash of his bored blue eyes. "You're not gonna like it, Doc."

"Try me."

"I saw something I wanted, so I took it."

Rationally, I knew that could mean *anything*. To play with. To torture. I'd heard those words spoken so many times before. But my thighs throbbed at the lazy heat with which he spoke them.

Seven turned back to the car, and seeing my split-second opportunity, I slammed the hood on his head.

6

I sprinted until my lungs gave out, but I wasn't even feet inside the shroud of trees when I was hurled into the air and slammed onto a shoulder. I fought him, trying to get off his back. All I succeeded in doing was cutting my forehead on a stray branch. His shoulder dug into my stomach as he walked with powerful strides back to the car.

"People will notice I'm gone," I said as he placed me next to the car. "They'll worry."

He ignored me, tying my arms *and* legs this time, at the ankles. His eyes landed on my forehead, and then he thumbed my forehead, pulling away blood.

"Stubborn fucking woman. You should be thanking me." He stood up, disappearing around the back of the car.

"Thanking you?" My jaw nearly fell off its hinges.

"You'd be a chalk outline right about now if it weren't for me, darlin'." He reappeared with what looked like a first-aid kit.

Instantly I was wary.

Even more so when he opened it and dropped down before me like he was going to clean me up or something.

"A normal person would have called the police. Not...this." I lifted my bound arms and legs. He shot me a deadly look, the only deadly look I'd received from him.

Was he the Boogieman?

If he was, then I was getting my cut in my forehead cleaned by the Boogieman. No—not *the* Boogieman; that didn't exist.

There was no such thing as a mythical man that went bump in the night.

The Boogieman.

It wasn't real. It was a delusion inside my paranoid patient's brain. Yet, this man was the most terrifying person I'd ever met. Even down, bending on the soles of his feet, he towered over me.

"You don't normally do things like this, do you?"

He dabbed lightly at my forehead with his massive hands. "Kidnap annoying women?"

He seemed like someone who thought things out.

This wasn't thought-out.

It was rushed and hasty.

"Do things without thinking."

He shot me another deadly look.

Which once again made me wonder *why* he'd taken me.

He dabbed the cut on my forehead with something that stung, and I winced.

"Does it hurt?" he growled.

Weird, right? This guy just snapped someone's neck; why does he care if a little alcohol stings?

"You could have left me to die. Instead you put me in your car."

"Kidnapped," he corrected.

"And cleaned my wound."

"Don't like stains on my leather."

I quirked my head. "Do you plan on killing me?"

He slowly pulled away, a bloody cotton swab in his hand. His knuckle lingered on my jaw.

"You're not gonna find what you're looking for, Doc."

"What's that?" I whispered.

"A soul. I kill and I like it."

Run. Run away. Run from the man who says he loves to kill, who might be the most feared killer *of all*. Don't focus on how his blue eyes pulsed in the night, how his knuckle still caressed my jaw.

"You're not gonna find what you're looking for," I replied softly.

He arched a brow, waiting for me to elaborate.

"Fear."

Something flickered in his eyes; then he turned and slammed the first-aid kit shut. Leaving me on the ground, bound and tied.

I watched Seven work. He'd lit a cigarette and from my angle, I could see most of him.

"Are you the Boogieman?" I asked, eyes plastered on his every movement. "Is it true? What does it mean?"

"It means I never should've put you in my fucking car."

"So it's true." The realization fell like a lead weight.

No one gets out alive.

I looked at the little wisps of smoke still spiraling from the engine into the sky.

He was right.

This was the luckiest day of my goddamn life. What happened once he fixed whatever was broken?

"Why does the Boogieman want *me*?"

"You ask too many fucking questions."

I shrugged. "It's my job."

Why would the Boogieman want someone like me? Why would he *save* me?

"Don't start thinking you're special." He slammed the hood of the car. "Stand up, Doc."

"Wait." I stood up, scrambling away, struggling not fall backward in my bindings. "Just hold on."

I'll be dead by morning. There was so much I wanted to do.

I never went to Australia.

Saw the Great Barrier Reef.

"Is this the part where you beg for your life?" he asked, bored.

My mind flashed back to this morning, the things Mrs. Adams had said. All the dirty things I'd always wanted to do. The illegal and immoral part of me that I kept caged, pretending I could feed it by playing with other monsters.

My eyes landed on the monster before me. The killer. The thing that haunted the other boogiemen's dreams.

"Have sex with me," I blurted.

7

"Shouldn't you be crying? Begging?" he said, humor tinging his dark voice. "You want to fuck?"

"You're going to kill me. I...want to know what it's like."

His face twisted like I'd spat in his food. "You're a virgin?"

I rolled my eyes. "I want to know what it's like to fuck someone like you."

His eyes darkened. "Once again, darlin', you don't know what you're sayin'." I noticed he had a slight southern drawl, but it only came out occasionally. He took a step to me, blue eyes gleaming. More than intrigued, a wolf that had just found a doe all alone in the woods.

"I work with psychopaths. I know exactly what I'm saying."

"I'll break you within the first two minutes, Doc."

I swallowed, but when I spoke again, my voice was rough. "Promises, promises."

I continued. "I know how it works. No one gets to see the Boogieman and live. Fuck me. I'm giving you permission."

"Do you think I need your fucking permission?"

He grabbed the gun off the car, then pressed it to my head before I'd blinked.

"Have you ever used one of these before?"

I swallowed and slightly shook my head, afraid to jostle the gun.

Not even to go hunting.

His impassive laughter dripped down my neck.

I was playing with fire, I knew. I wasn't ever one to back away from a guy. I usually asked them out first. This wasn't some guy; he was the Boogieman. There was a reason I worked with psychopaths, though. Play with fire enough, eventually you crave the burn.

Adrenaline. Excitement. It made a heady cocktail in my head.

I couldn't die without tasting the dark side.

The thing that kept me up at night.

He spun me around, forcing my chest flat against the side of the car.

"What gets you hot? Is it knowing you're going to be fucked by the guy killing you?"

He shoved the gun down my pants, pressing the cool metal to my hot flesh. His lips came to my neck, hot, possessive. I arched into it, a sigh like steam falling from my lips.

"Yeah, that's it. I'm the most dangerous person you'll ever meet. You're hot for it."

He rubbed the gun against my naked flesh, up and down, until I could hear the slick sound. I grasped the top of the car as he pushed into me. He consumed me, forced his whole self into me until his muscular chest burned his heartbeats into my back, his beard scraped against my skin, and the gun would bruise.

"You'd let me do whatever the fuck I want to you? The guy that just kidnapped you?"

My toes were curling. A jagged moan fell from my lips. Seven had that same predatory intrigue staining his words as before, like he was getting off on the realization as much as I was. The dirty, dark truth I'd just discovered.

But then all at once he pulled the gun out, stepping away.

"Take a mental picture, Doc, because you'll never get a night with a man like me."

The sudden distance was jarring, and I all but fell against the car.

Rejection and shame branded me.

I couldn't die like this.

So I laughed. "I've got you pegged. You're just like every other psycho out there. You didn't save me. You, what? Saw someone in your space and got territorial or something. So you're going to murder me and make a big show of it here? Probably gonna do something real original and dress me up like a doll or some shit."

Teeth flashed like daggers. "Careful, Doc, you sound a little heated."

"You wouldn't understand." I slid to the cold ground. "My client thinks you're some mythical being with superpowers but you're just like every other man I've interviewed, and men like you never understand."

"And what are 'men like me'?"

"Cowards." I bit out the word like it was acid on my tongue. "Hiding behind your own demons."

He bent down, jeans flexing over his knees, until he was eye level.

I made sure to match his stare, and he seemed surprised.

"I may be a lot of things, sweetheart, but I'm no coward."

"No, of course not." I smiled, but my eyes remained hard. "You're big. You're tough. Nothing fazes you... Except maybe a little emotional attachment." I started to laugh. "I've been treating men like you for years. Figures I'd die by one."

He grabbed my chin, forcing me close until my lips were a thread width from his, and my neck strained from it, as if he wanted to possess every thought, every breath.

"Sweetheart," he said, "let's get one thing straight. You may think you've met men like me before, but you have never and will never, meet anyone like me."

I was so fucking sick of these assholes. Day in and day out they taunted me and I had to play good little psychiatrist, when sometimes you just wanted to—

I spat in his face.

There was a split second when I realized the extent of my actions, when it registered in his eyes as well. Raw. Untamed. Like he couldn't believe I'd done it.

I couldn't believe I'd done it.

He growled. "Fuckin' death wish."

Then he ripped my lips to his.

8

Seven pulled me off the ground, and shoved my back against the hood of his car. It gave with a dent. He claimed my mouth in a ruthless, savage kiss. Adrenaline rushed like fire through my body. He made me feel like I could be eaten at any moment.

He gripped my pants and tugged them past my hips, just enough to expose me. The material scraped down with his savage pull, leaving little red striations on my skin.

"What are you doing?"

His answering grin was savage and wild. "Whatever the fuck I want."

A second later he ripped my panties.

Bare.

Bare before the man about to kill me, on the car he'd kidnapped me in. Cold Colorado air whispered along my naked lips, spreading goose bumps along my skin. Seven leaned over me, elbow punching the metal of his expensive car, caging me.

"What kind of sex does a guy like me have?" he asked, roughly palming my pussy. There was no foreplay, no buildup. He played with my pussy like he owned it. Like he'd always owned it and had a right to do whatever he wanted with it.

I gasped at the heat building, already arching into his hand.

"Is it dirty and fucked up, Doc? Do we use chains and shit?"

I couldn't breathe, his deep blue eyes piercing.

"Or is it the thought of dying that's got you dripping all down my fucking hand." He knifed one finger inside of me as if to punctuate his point, blindingly fast. "Or are you wondering what my hands can do after I just killed a man?"

God, *yes.*

I shouldn't, but just the words had my back arching off the car's hood. My eyes found his as a wicked moan left my lips. He watched me with a bored disinterest, and I felt like a toy beneath him.

Somehow that got me hotter.

He rubbed my pussy, then spanked it. Over and over again, until I was raw, gasping, breathless. A car whooshed past us, and the moment broke. Shame and fear leaking in. I should jump up. Scream.

Seven gripped my chin, dragging my eyes back.

"Not finished with you, Doc."

He shoved my panties into my mouth, gagging me. He pulled the silver gun out, and it glinted in the starry light.

"Scared now, Doc? This is what you want, right?"

No. Yes.

He pressed the cool tip to my lips, spreading me with the blunt head of the gun. He was testing me. He didn't think I'd go through with it.

I shouldn't.

But I arched into it, needing this like I've never needed anything before. His blue eyes flashed, and his easy, lazy demeanor vanished, giving way to possession, like he needed me to do this too. When he spoke, his growl was jagged, rough.

"Spread your fucking legs."

It was hard, my pants weren't even past my knees, but I did. I opened them as wide as they could go, hips aching. Seven pushed the shiny, metallic tip deeper inside me.

I gasped and Seven shoved the panties harder into my mouth until I gagged on them, at the same time shoving the gun deeper inside me.

"Are those wet with you? What do they taste like? Like a whore? A dirty whore who likes to be fucked by psychos?"

I gasped, arching up.

"Do you want me to hurt you, Doc?"

My eyes widened at the thought.

"If I called you a good girl, would you let me fuck you hard with this gun, shove it up your ass?"

My body melted and slacked at his words, and a vicious grin speared his lips.

"Holy shit. You would. You'd do anything." His words were knowing and savage. He fucked me harder with the gun, greedy. I became weightless, boneless, swallowed in the truth of his words.

"If I said you were so fucking good coming on my hand right now, you'd do whatever the fuck I asked."

He bent down, pressing his chest against mine and forcing my back hard against the metal. "You think you have me pegged?" he whispered viciously. "I had you figured out at the fucking prison."

His brutal hands turned soft and coaxing as the gun slid another millimeter inside me, and his lips came to my neck, worshipping and reverent.

"I'm not gonna fuck you, Doc. You haven't earned that. You haven't even come close to earning my cock."

The cool metal slid all the way into my pussy as another car zoomed by. They could see me spread eagle on the hood of his car. Wanton. His massive body hid *what* he was putting inside me, but for all intents and purposes, I was open. Open for the world. Open for everyone.

And I'd never been more turned on.

He laughed.

His tongue licked a line of fire along the lobe of my ear before he bit it, *hard*. "You want a murderer to fuck when he's done killing, use ruthless hands all sweet on you. I know your type."

His hands turned viciously gentle, as if to play out the scenario. A scenario of *him* coming home to me after brutally killing someone.

It was so wrong. So twisted. I moaned through the now wet fabric in my mouth, and Seven ripped the panties away, replacing them with his lips. He kissed tenderly. Passionately. His tongue weaving with mine, commanding me, consuming me in a way I'd never been owned before.

I fell apart into his mouth.

He laughed as I came, arching the gun deeper, more fully inside me.

"I could press the trigger," he said against my mouth, swallowing my moans.

He could press the trigger while he was kissing me tenderly, sucking on my lips and tongue. I didn't think I could get hotter. My orgasm fractured at the thought, exploding into a million, jagged pieces.

He kissed me softly, whispering ruthlessly, "Yeah, that's what you want. I've got you pegged."

He slowly slid the gun from my body, and a trillion aftershocks of pleasure followed in its wake.

"You want your own little monster to play with, Doc." He spanked my already bruised pussy before twisting my nipple through my shirt on a pinch.

"No," I moaned through the fabric.

I was a good person. I was *good*. Right? This was just a fantasy I needed to play out before I died.

Another vicious, mind-melting twist.

"The monster in me sees the monster in you. Nobody wants to admit they're the villain in their own story, Doc. But once you do, it's pretty liberating."

He dived for my lips, and I kissed him back with abandon. I swear I saw a softness in his eyes, an almost *aching* look, but then I realized the stars were growing fuzzy above him.

The air too warm...

The world fading...

To black.

9

I woke up alone, in my bed. Immediately the night before flashed through my mind in short, searing bursts.

The monster in me sees the monster in you.

It was a bad dream. A nightmare. I couldn't have done those things with a complete stranger—a criminal.

Not me. Not Octavia Bell, PhD.

But then I saw my panties, the ones I'd had shoved into my mouth as he gagged me and fucked me with a gun, set prettily on my nightstand. Next to them was a letter.

You don't have everyone pegged, darling. - Seven.

* * *

Do you want more of Mary Catherine Gebhard?

One click TIED now!

SHOPPING FOR MORE

A SHANNON AND DECLAN SNIPPET

JULIA KENT

1

Featuring Shannon and Declan from my *New York Times* bestselling Shopping for a Billionaire series.

"You're killing me, Shannon," Declan says over the Facetime video chat we're having. He's in Australia, on a quick layover for some meetings with a resort chain that might carry our coffee. A few years ago, as a wedding present, Declan bought me Grind It Fresh!, a regional coffee chain with the best coffee I'd ever tasted. Some men would buy their new wife a necklace, a fancy bike, or a favorite memento.

Mine went a little overboard.

We co-own and co-manage it. I handle on-the-ground issues at our headquarters here in Boston. He's the road warrior. His trip to Indonesia to negotiate fair trade coffee deals was a big success, but he's been gone for three entire weeks.

Three weeks.

Three weeks of no sex. Three weeks of no kisses. Three weeks of no one to turn to for a silent hug, a quick smile, a simple vent. Yes, we have phones and texts and video chats, but it's no replacement for your lover's hot breath on the back of your neck as he initiates what you've been wanting, too.

The red garters had to come out, even if all we can do is have virtual sex.

"How about I kill you with my thighs wrapped around your face?" I tease.

His hand goes to his belt, pants unbuttoned, fly unzipped, one part of his body *very* much alive. Declan has eyes the color of heathered emeralds, framed in a strong face, broad cheekbones, with thick, dark hair. He holds his shoulders straight and tall, with a confidence that comes naturally. Unruffled and unraveled before me, half-naked and breathing with a rough edge that speaks to desperation, I watch him on-screen, a small smile teasing my lips.

In public, he's an impenetrable wall, a steel fort, an airtight container of business might and financial savvy.

In private, he's *mine.*

And I'm the one who brings him to the point of panting, holding his erection in one fist, staring at the red garters that made him lose his mind a few years ago and imagining plunging into *me.*

"Those damn garters. I'm imagining you in my office that day. Remember? On my desk?"

"How could I forget?"

The sound of his ragged breath makes me feel less silly. Since having our baby last year, Declan's travelled significantly less, but running a global coffee brand doesn't lend itself to a lot of time at home. We manage. Declan and Ellie have a standing date for Facetime video calls, and he reads her bedtime stories every night, even if it means he does it with his morning coffee from halfway around the globe.

We chat constantly, dealing with business issues, weaving in personal life conversations.

But no video camera, no Internet connection, no unlimited data plan is a substitute for having my husband naked in bed with me.

None.

"Are we really doing this?" I giggle.

"Pretty sure I'm done," he says, but I can see he is definitely not. It's dark here, late at night, which means it's lunchtime there.

I guess I'm having a nooner at midnight.

I move my face as close as possible to the camera.

"Shannon, what are you doing?"

"Put it right by your camera."

"Put... what?"

"You know."

I can't see anything, because my mouth is right up against my video lens, but I sure can hear.

"What the hell are you—oh, no. No. *No*." That last *no* sounds like a growl.

"What? It's the closest I can get to simulating."

"First of all, that's not even *close* to what your mouth feels like. Second of all, you're asking me to put my junk on a glass screen and... what? Move it up and down?"

"You can't exactly poke it at the screen and pretend it's a hole."

"This thing is so hard it might *make* a hole."

"Declan!" My cry of outraged hilarity makes me stop, mid-sound.

I realized I've gone and done it.

You know that movie, *A Quiet Place*? The one where monsters track humans by sound and kill them if they even snap a twig?

That's one big metaphor for parenting a small child, let me tell you.

"Mama? MAMAMAMAMAMAMAMAMAMA," Ellie cries from her bedroom next to ours.

"NO!" Declan grunts, then lets out an aggrieved sigh. "Damn it."

"No sex," I say with a sigh.

"Makes me feel like I'm right back home."

I wince. He's not wrong. But it hurts, anyhow.

Toddlers are the OG cockblockers.

Shoving the sash of my bathrobe together as I stand, I tie it off, looking back up at the screen to find Declan looping his belt.

"I'm sorry."

"Me, too." He looks at his crotch. The thick outline of his erection is obvious, even across video.

"MAMAMAMAMAMA! Wan up! Wan up!"

I close my eyes, trying to shut out the spike of immediate reaction her cries generate in me. Shifting roles from sex kitten to mother isn't second nature for me, so I feel weirdly exposed as I look down at my loose top, breasts uncovered for Declan's viewing. These same breasts feed my child.

It's my own mind that controls how I feel about how they're used by others.

Pulling my robe around me, I grab the tablet and shove it into the wide front pocket on the robe. The robe is new, a Christmas present from my husband, one he selected just for this purpose.

Can you tell we've done too many of these Facetime calls? We're the Facetime Family.

My throat aches a bit at the thought, stinging with emotion.

"Up! Uppy!" she calls again, only this time the tone is less frantic, giving me a chance to take a true, deep breath and feel my lower ribs press against my inner arms.

"If we had a live-in nanny, you wouldn't need to do this," my pocket says.

I tap the back of the tablet's case and say loudly, "If we had a live-in nanny, you'd get less sex, because I can't make love with you when someone else is here."

Running into Ellie's room, I find her red-faced, eyes teary and wide. Her little arms reach for my neck, and soon, she's clinging to me, little ribs racked with aftershocks from crying. I pull my tablet out to show her Daddy.

"Shhhhhhh," I say as I sway-walk back to my bedroom, where Declan stares back at us, the image cutting him off at the waist on the display screen.

"Hi, Ellie!" he coos, instantly in Awesome Dad Mode, making me smile. My father and Declan are about as different as two men can be, but in this—parenting and loving their child—they are one and the same.

"Dah-dee!" Ellie squeals, touching the screen. "Whatcha doon?"

"I am in Australia!"

"Stray-lee!"

"Yes! Good! I am coming home tomorrow."

"Morrow. Wan swings whichoo."

"Swings! Of course. How many pushes?"

"All da pushes!"

A wistful look takes over his face. I know that look. It's the expression of a man who would rather be here than where he actually is. Ambition is in his DNA, but loving his daughter takes precedence.

"All the pushes, sweetie," he says as Ellie kisses the glass screen.

"Wan milk, Mama," she says. "Chocka mick."

"How about water?" I offer. Sexy times are over. Parenting mode engaged. "Water and some cantaloupe."

"Catnayope!" she crows, toddling off to the kitchen in her footed sleeper. As she leaves, Chuckles pokes his head into the room. He spots Declan, and I swear the cat smiles.

"Want me to put Chuckles on? He can kiss the screen for you."

A huff, then a long sigh. "I'm not sure I want this anymore."

"Want what?"

"This." He motions with his hands as if gesturing to the whole, wide world. "All the travel."

"You can build a coffee empire without it."

"No, Shannon. I can't."

"You can come home and focus on other aspects of the business. Or you could retire."

"Retire? I'm not that old!"

"Retirement isn't just for old people."

"But I love what I do. I just hate being away from you and Ellie."

"You're the boss. Change it."

A wry grin spreads across his face. "You're right."

"I am?"

"I've been gone from you for too long. I miss you."

"I know. Three weeks without sex is a long time."

"No—not the sex. I miss you. I miss my friend. I miss hearing you laugh. Your breath on my face. Your cold feet against my calves. How you smell in bed. Moving furniture around because you want to make a play area in the living room for Ellie. Going to vintage shops and buying weird sculptures."

"They're not weird!" I bring the tablet into the kitchen with me, where I find Ellie on the floor, the tub of precut cantaloupe in her lap, each little fist clutching an orange piece.

The fridge door is wide open, casting a sci-fi glow over her.

"You bought a gnome drinking coffee out of a toilet, Shannon."

"For next year's Yankee Swap!"

"The gnome had a frog on a leash."

"It's supposed to be funny!"

"And when you press the button, it sounds like an octopus being choked to death."

"Your point is...?"

He makes a grunting sound worthy of Geralt of Rivia.

"Fine," I inform him as Ellie thrusts her sticky fingers into the venting grate under the fridge. "Next time we go to a thrift shop, you get to find something better."

"I'll just send Dave."

"You cannot send your executive assistant to find a Yankee Swap present!"

"Of course, I can."

The silence is what makes me suspicious.

"Declan?"

Another grunt.

"You—you had Dave shop for you this year, didn't you?"

Another grunt.

Suppressing the impulse to sing the first line of *The Witcher* song and toss a coin his way, I turn the video camera on Ellie instead.

"Say hi to Daddy!"

"Hi, Daddy! Wan catnayope?" She shoves a grayish, half-chewed piece, smearing it on the glass where Declan's mouth is.

"Mmmmmm," he pretends. "Yum!"

My two minutes of talk with my husband, time spent not monitoring her, has led to a twenty-minute cleanup.

"Daddy likes da catnayope!"

"Nice sentence!" he says, grinning.

"She's been saying four- and five-word sentences all week," I tell him.

His face falls. "She has? I missed it." Voice going gruff, he turns negative. "Damn."

"Damn!" Ellie repeats.

"Shit," he mutters.

"That doesn't help!"

"I mean, I like it!" Overenunciating, he does the time-tested technique every parent tries.

"I yike it!" Ellie repeats.

Magic.

The man has magical powers. If I said the S-word, Ellie would repeat it ad infinitum, and always in the worst possible places. At the pediatrician's, at the yarn shop Mom loves where the woman running it looks like a church organist—you get the picture.

Declan does it and *bam*—crisis averted.

Chuckles pads up to the screen and starts licking Declan's face. When I try to pet him, I get a condescending sniff.

Dec laughs.

Chuckles runs off.

"I miss being home," Declan says. Squaring his shoulders, he nods to himself. "And it's entirely my fault."

"Your fault?"

"Which means it's utterly under my control."

"Huh?"

"If something is a person's fault, there's a cause-effect relationship. You can't be held accountable for something you can't control. I can control being away from my family."

"Yes, you can. You're the boss. The owner. The CEO. What you do with your time is completely your decision," I affirm.

"And I've been deciding to be away. It felt like it was inevitable, but it's not. Not if I say no."

"Say no to yourself?"

"Say no to the idea that in order to be successful, I have to do it like this." Eyes the color of an Irish hill meet mine. "I choose. I have the power."

"You always do."

"And I don't want to lose these years with you. With Ellie. With our other children."

A tingle forms in my belly. "Other children?"

"Shannon, I—" A distinct buzz cuts him off. "Damn it."

"JAM IT!" pipes up a little voice behind me. I turn and look down.

Ellie's using a potholder to smoosh cantaloupe pieces into the grout between tiles.

"I have to go. Some sort of problem with air travel out of Australia because of the fires."

"Oh no!"

Ellie looks at me, eyes wide, reading my emotions.

"It's fine. It's not fine, of course. The fires have been horrible. But my plane will leave. I'll be home in two days. No matter what."

"Good!"

"MAMA!" Ellie screeches, holding up a red finger. "I got a boo-boo!"

"Let Daddy kiss it," Declan says as I hold her finger to the screen.

"Mwah!" says my billionaire husband, being as goofy and lovesick with his daughter as I've ever seen him.

"Dat better, Daddy!" She gives him a very sticky kiss.

I blow him one. You think I'm kissing that screen now? Ewww.

"See you soon. I love you."

"I love you, too, Dec."

"And I mean it. I'm redefining how I build Grind It Fresh! There is a better way, and I'll find it."

"I know you will. You'll find your way home."

* * *

Two Days Later

It's three a.m. and Ellie, who is cutting yet another molar, is finally asleep, her slumber the steady sound of the ocean lapping at the shore. It's hypnotic, really, a sound I could listen to for the rest of my life and never tire of it. How do toddlers do that? When awake, she's a whirling dervish, needing constant attention.

In slumber, she draws me in, too, a work of art to behold.

Dec texted me earlier, told me he'd be home around five a.m. If I hold out, I can greet him at the door, but the long yawn that follows as I move into our kitchen tells me that's not happening. Sleep is the currency of parenthood at this stage of our lives.

I'm not spending it all on the hope he'll be home on time.

A brewed cup of chamomile helps me unwind. So, too, does the lovely photo album my mother and father put together for us. Mom's going through all our old family photos, and Dad took eighteen years of digital camera archives and printed the best shots. Between the two, they created cherished albums, custom-made for me and my sisters.

Cameras, in my childhood, were pulled out for special occasions, and a photo of a group was meant to be carefully arranged. You had twenty-four takes on a roll of film, and for my parents, who barely scraped by so Mom could stay home with us, you didn't waste film.

But once they got their first digital camera in 2002 in a Black Friday deal Dad still talks about (the tent in front of the electronics big-box store, the record low temperature of eleven degrees, the glares as he got the last camera at $99...), that was it. Photos became memories on a drive, hard or flash or thumb, and suddenly all our memories were there but not in front of us.

This present? This is pure gold.

I already have my baby book, the late '80s photos stamped on the back with *York Photo*, a mail-order service that kept the cost of developing film down. Mom and Dad never, ever used the photo huts or the place in the mall, where prices were higher.

The baby book beckons, on the end table, right under the new album.

Mom, pregnant with me, my older sister, Carol, in her arms. Dad, his ear against Mom's belly, with Carol on his shoulders. All four of us, me in utero, in front of our house, which would have been new to them.

Then.

Now it's paid off.

I turn the page to see brand-new me, Mom, hovering as little preschooler Carol holds my eight-pound form in spindly arms, a big grin testimony to how excited she was to be a big sister. Mom and Dad, standing in front of a hospital, me in a car seat.

Close-ups of me in a crib. In Dad's arms. On Mom's shoulder.

I'm sure Carol's baby book is longer, better, more detailed. Our younger sister, Amy, never fails to complain bitterly that hers is nothing more than black-and-white photos from the Chuck E. Cheese booth and school pictures.

Not quite, but she has a point.

I take a sip and stare at the fireplace, a gas stove insert we added for warmth and fun last year.

Ellie is my first. She's my Carol.

The next child we have will be my equivalent. Declan's a middle child, too.

We've produced an oldest.

When is it time to produce a middle? We know we want more than two. Four makes me a little nervous.

Three feels just right now that we've had one.

As I page through the albums, I find Dad cutting wood, Mom planting a vegetable garden with a baby in a carrier on her back. Every photo is simple, all at local parks, the house, and occasionally in Syracuse, where Dad's extended family is from. No trips to Disney, no shots in Paris, no big vacations.

I see tents. Backyard staycations. Remodeling projects and homegrown fun.

So different from what Declan and I can give to our children.

A tug at my heart makes me choke up as I look at the newer pictures. My nephews being born (no crotch shots, so no worries). Pictures of my ex-fiancé, Steve. Mom cut him out of almost every single one, so careful it's like a surgeon did it.

But he's in larger group photos, in profile.

So is Carol's ex, Todd.

My nephews' father.

Years of change roll out as I turn the pages, eighteen of them, all passing like blinks.

"You're right," I whisper to Declan, though he's not here. "You're missing out."

I couldn't tell him that on the Facetime chat. It felt cruel. Ever since Ellie was born, I've wanted more of him than I wanted before.

Strange, right? Because you'd think I'd want less, given the addition of a child. That the wanting of my husband would recede a bit.

No. It's only intensified with time.

Not just to have him here to build a life with our child.

To build a world with just me. Just us. Making decisions, supporting each other, being intimate, sharing this journey. No one knows why we're here on this planet, but I do know this: I wouldn't spend this lifetime partnered to anyone else.

Declan is it. He's my soul mate, my reincarnated partner, my energy lifeline, my core. Whatever you call it, whatever you believe, he's how I figure out who I am.

My husband is a witness to my growth.

And an instigator, too.

Stifling a yawn, I realize the chamomile did the trick, my eyes resting on a picture of me and Dec, taken the first time Mom and Dad met him, the day he came to the apartment I shared with my sister, Amy, a one-bedroom walk-up above someone's garage in a town about a half hour from our parents. Dad sat on a dead mouse Chuckles brought home to us, and Declan got a glimpse of Mom's crazy.

He didn't bat an eyelash.

Okay. Maybe one or two. Mom's crazy can't be understood with a quick look.

But he stayed anyhow.

Someone surreptitiously caught him on camera, in profile, chatting with Dad before the Great Dead Mousecapade, Chuckles nosing up against Dec's shin. Chuckles hates everyone, but not my husband.

Cats *know*.

The polite smile on Declan's face makes me wonder what he and Dad were talking about as I got ready for that first date. Second date? We'd already gone out for a business dinner that, to this day, I swear was *not* a date.

But Declan does.

His argument: we kissed. He brought me a corsage. It's a date.

My argument: well, how can I have one when he's that romantic?

The clock on the stove reads 3:47 a.m. as I yawn, Chuckles climbing off the pillow next to me with a sniff and a liquid motion that makes me wish I could be a cat for a day. What does it feel like to have bones that are jelly when you need them that way?

My bed feels so good, if cold and empty. A comfortable mattress is worth its weight in gold, but the warm body of a man in love with me is priceless.

Before my mind can race through all the things I have to do tomorrow, I'm out.

* * *

The kiss in my dream has a taste, like coffee and mint, like strawberry and relief. As I roll over to wrap my arms around Declan's neck, I halt.

This isn't a dream.

"Dec?" I whisper, fuzzy and half out of it, his elbow pressing my hair against the pillow.

"Mmm," he says as he kisses me again. "I'm home."

His erection taps against my thigh like a door-to-door salesman selling dildoes. "I can tell." A rush of heat pumps through me, his closeness a thrill. After three weeks of distance, this is almost too much, more than I could hope for.

He's home.

He's here.

And we're both so, *so* horny.

"How about a quickie?"

"It's always a quickie with Ellie around," I hiss as he pulls my panties down, in me before I can finish blinking, his mouth on my neck, tongue flicking the spot under my ear that drives me crazy. My legs are around his naked waist, the man completely bare, his ass familiar and strangely new as I reach around him and squeeze as he thrusts long, slow, dangerous strokes into me.

"This is the best welcome I could possibly have," he murmurs in my ear as I make a sound of agreement.

"When did you get home?" I ask, the words turning into a gasp as I arch my hips toward him, the full sensation closing an open need in me.

"Thirty seconds ago."

"Took you that long to get naked? Slacker."

He laughs, the movement pressing his pelvis into me, my walls clenching tight in response. The amused rumble in him turns into a low groan, the kind that makes me wetter and hotter, my hands on the end of my nightgown, pulling up.

Until I realize I've buttoned it high.

I am completely naked, every inch of me from the neck down pressed up against nude Declan, but my face is covered by the nightgown.

"Is this some role-play thing you've been hiding from me, Shannon? Because you don't have to cover your face."

"Ghosting is a new kink I forgot to mention, Dec," I say as he laughs and tightens his thighs, moving his knees so he has his hands free to unbutton the button holding me hostage.

"I thought ghosting is when you disappear on someone."

"My mouth disappeared."

"I would never, ever want your mouth to go away, Shannon. Never ever. Your fucking amazing mouth."

"Then help me get unstuck," I mutter, the cloth in my mouth.

"Kissing you through cotton isn't nearly as good as this," he murmurs as the cloth pulls my long hair up over my head, his mouth on my jawline, tongue dancing against mine as he resumes his rhythm.

After so many weeks without sex, our climaxes are quick, hard, simultaneous, and almost perfunctory. The emotion is there, but the need overrides sentimentality. Plus, we have a toddler.

Get your orgasms in while you can the first time.

There's never a guarantee of round two, and sometimes even round one is called on account of...

Toddler.

I curl up in the crook of his arm and hear his heart go from a steady gallop to a simple beat, until he sits up, crawls out of bed, and paws through a small bag.

"What are you doing?"

"Getting your present."

"Now?"

In his hand, he holds a brown, crinkly pack of—

"TIM TAMS!" I gasp as my stomach lets out a gurgle so loud you'd think an alien is about to pop out of it.

Declan shakes his head as I open the box. "Sorry they're crushed."

"Crushed, intact, they all taste the same!"

"You can buy them here in the US, Shannon. Dave can get them for you anytime."

"They don't taste the same."

"But they're—"

I shove a cookie in his mouth.

We crawl back under the covers, both of us listening for Ellie.

"I want another one," Declan says suddenly.

I hand him a cookie.

"No—not that. Those are for you."

"Oh. Good. Because I wasn't going to be stingy, but..."

"I want another child, not another Tim Tam."

"Of course, you do. We've talked about having more." I shake the container, sad to discover I really am eating the last one.

"I'm ready to start. Now."

"*Now?* Don't you need a little time for your refractory period to finish up?"

"Not right this moment. But... I think it's time for you to go off birth control. Ellie is sixteen months old. If we're lucky, the new baby will be a little more than two years younger. That seems reasonable."

I stroke his cheek. "It doesn't have to be reasonable."

"It doesn't?"

"You don't have to make a case, Declan. No flowcharts or PowerPoint decks required. You can appeal to me with emotion."

"I want this," he says, voice low and hoarse. "I want us. I want you. And I want my family. Our family. The one we build together."

"I do, too."

He kisses me.

"And I want a house," I add.

"A house?"

"Yes."

"You don't like the condo?"

The bedroom door nudges open a few inches, making me realize that in Declan's rush to make love, he didn't close it. Ellie's almost at the point where she can crawl out of her crib. Since becoming a mother, I've found myself more modest. Less impulsive about sex. Not that I don't want it—I certainly do—but it's taken on a mystique. A holiness. A sense of reverence.

We used sex to make a human being out of love, lust, an egg and a single sperm.

Something so powerful *should* be taken seriously.

As I'm about to answer Declan's question, Chuckles leaps up onto the small bench at the end of our bed and settles in, mouth turning down, little fangs poking out as he closes his eyes and sighs.

"I want a garden," I start to explain.

"A garden?"

"You know—tomatoes and cucumbers and carrots and—"

"I know what a garden is. Why?"

"And goats."

"You want goats?"

"Chickens, too. Maybe ducks?"

"DUCKS?"

"Their eggs are really good." I'm not even going to *mention* the llama.

"Where are we going to keep all these animals?"

"In the barn. On our land."

"You want to move out of the city and have a farm?"

"How about we start with a house and a dog and a garden?"

At the word *dog*, Chuckles lifts his chin off his paws and glares at me.

"*You* say the word 'dog' next time," I whisper to Dec, cheek against his chest. "He'll take it better from you. Right now, I'm pretty sure he's plotting how to steal my breath in my sleep."

"How about we start with the baby part and move on to the house after."

"You can't multitask?"

He laughs. "I see how this negotiation is going."

"Promise me we'll have a house before the next baby is born."

"Promise. Where do you want to move?"

"Wherever you are."

"Well, that's easy. I'll always be with you." He stiffens. "You don't want to move to Mendon, do you? Near your parents?"

"Not that far outside of Boston."

"Then where?" Before he finishes the words, he groans. "You want to move to Weston, don't you? Near my brother and Amanda."

"She *is* my best friend." I frown and look at him. "Wait a minute. This whole having another baby thing. Is this inspired by Andrew having twins? You want to catch up to your brother?"

He bristles at the words *catch up*. "No!"

"You two are so competitive."

"We are," he admits.

"I'll bet *he* brings home *two* containers of Tim Tams whenever he comes home to Amanda."

"You're not going to let this go, are you?"

I reach under the sheet and grab something else. "Nope." Signs of life appear. "Hmmm. You seem to be recovering nicely."

He yawns. "My jet lag has jet lag."

"*This* has no lag."

"You have to do all the work if you want another round."

I climb on top of him, straddling, easing him in with a comfortable stretch that makes us both groan with pleasure.

I kiss him, then pull back, hair in his face, his eyes shining in the moonlight.

"Just like pregnancy. I do *alllll* the work."

"I would have a baby for you if I could."

"This one will be born in a hospital," I say firmly. "Not an elevator."

"Ellie's birth was a freak accident."

"Emphasis on *freak*."

"So was meeting you," he says as his nudges his hips up.

"I was doing my job evaluating the cleanliness of that men's room in your bagel shop!"

"This is not the kind of dirty talk I imagined we'd do in bed while I was gone, Shannon."

"Then find something else for my mouth to do, Declan."

The kiss that answers me is lush and roaming, genuine and authentic, a slow, long, wet ramble through the layers of me he feels but can't name. When you've been with someone for enough years, you choreograph how you touch them. You don't realize it, but it's there, a series of patterns that fall into place without conscious thought.

The waist touch. The shoulder stroke. The love pat on the ass. The arm around shoulders or waist. Hand in hand or fingers threaded? Head on a shoulder or tucked into a chest? Chin on her head or her ponytail resting against your collarbone?

Palm on your knee while you drive? An arm under an elbow for support on outdoor deck stairs? A hand up out of a recliner while she's pregnant? A hand down on stairs to give him extra help?

And then there are the intimate connections, the endless variations of kisses and touches, of bare flesh against flesh, of tongues between legs and mouths of velvet. The push and pull, the up and down, the side to side and back to front and the heady insolence of all the ways you can use your body to love another person with all your heart, heat, and humanity.

Humor, too.

By the time Declan's finished kissing me, our second round of love-making well underway, I hear a little voice in the other room, babbling away like Ellie does.

See? Round two is never, ever a given.

Soon, she'll call out for Mama, and when Daddy comes to pick her up, she'll shriek with laughter, arms extended for a hug she has come to rely on.

She knows he's there for her.

And that's really all anyone can do for anyone else, right?

Be there.

Because presence *matters.*

This snippet, featuring Shannon and Declan McCormick, is just a taste of their world. My *New York Times* bestselling Shopping for a Billionaire series has fifteen books you can sink into. Read ... now.

* * *

Do you want more of Julia Kent?

One click SHOPPING FOR A BILLIONAIRE now!

TENACIOUS BOND

A HOLLY WOODS FILES SHORT

EMMA HART

Before the babies and the wedding, even before the engagement...

There's a surprise party to pull off, so the last thing Noelle and Drake need is a dead body in the park.

Naturally, that's exactly what they get...

1

"This is the stupidest idea in the world," I say, huffing as I lug a boxful of decorations into the function room of the Inn.

Drake grunts from behind the three he's carrying. "Yeah, I'm sure you're really struggling there with your one boxful of balloons and banners."

"You're the one who wants to be a hero, honey." I put my box down, then take the top two from him. "That'll teach you."

"I have to. I'm in trouble with your mom after I cut that cheesecake."

"I told you not to do it."

"Can't you talk to her?"

"Did you bring me a slice of the damn cheesecake?" I raise an eyebrow, knowing the answer was no.

Because the asshole had the gall to steal a slice and not even think about his poor, hungry girlfriend, stuck in her office while he was on his day off.

"It's really all Nonna's fault. If she hadn't demanded those shelves be put up and guilted me into it, I wouldn't have even been there."

I nudge his arm as we step outside. "She'll be over it in ten minutes when something inevitably goes wrong here."

"Don't you dare jinx it, Noelle Bond!" Mom snaps from the back of Dad's truck. "This is bad enough as it is trying to keep this stupid party a secret from that awful woman!"

Ah, Mom and Nonna's stunning relationship is on full display today.

"I don't know why she needs a surprise party," Mom went on, pointing at a box for Drake to pick up. "Nobody throws me random parties for my birthday. It's not like it's a milestone birthday!"

"Honestly, Mom, every birthday she reaches is a milestone. Mostly because it means it's another year that one of us haven't killed her yet," I say dryly.

"Are you arguing with me?"

"No, I was agreeing with you."

"Mmph. Take that box in and start blowing up balloons."

I open my mouth to argue that I have to work, but she sends me such a scathing look to be quiet that I slap my lips together and take the box she's shoved in my direction.

"Looks like I'm not the only one on her shit list," Drake mutters.

"Oh, shut up," I shoot back. "It might be your day off, but it's not mine. This has been a two-hour-long lunch break. She's lucky I have no appointments this afternoon."

"I have to admit, I'm happier with you here. At least I know you're not tracking a murderer."

"Well, honey, if you did your job, I wouldn't have to find them for you, would I?" I sniff and open the box that holds all the balloons.

Holy shit. There are like a hundred in here! She doesn't really expect me to blow all these up by myself right now, does she?

I glance over my shoulder where I can just catch a glimpse of Mom through the door.

She does. She expects me to do all of these.

"This is ridiculous," I say, looking to Drake. "Why do I get stuck with the crappy job?"

"Because you'll complain anyway?"

"Oh, I love you, too." I grab the first balloon and stretch it out. "Looks like these balloons are the only things getting blown today."

He moves lightning fast and grabs a handful of them from the box. "I'll help."

"I bet you will." I snort and secure my lips around the first one to blow it up.

"Why-a are-a you here?"

Both Drake and I freeze. The sound of a trunk being slammed shut echoes through the air, and we both turn to see what the hell Nonna is doing here.

"Why are you here?" Mom snaps back. "Aren't you supposed to be at the doctor?"

"Bah! No-a doctor can-a help-a me!"

Well, she isn't wrong. Maybe a psychiatrist, but I'm not even sure Nonna knows what one of those is.

"Where-a is-a Noella?"

What the hell does she want with me?

"I have-a a date for-a her."

"A date?" Drake says, lips twisting to one side. "Is her age getting to her? Or does she really think there's someone else out there who's crazy enough to fall in love with you?"

"Jerk." I punch him in the arm and move toward the door.

"Noelle is dating Drake," Mom answers before I get there. "She doesn't need a date."

"Oh. I heard-a that-a they had-a broken up."

"And you thought you'd get me a date instead of seeing how I am?" My eyebrows shoot up. "Thanks, Nonna."

Nonna turns her piercing gaze onto me. "You are-a almost-a thirty. You are-a running out-a of time."

Ah, it's always so nice to have a walking, talking ovary reminding you of your age.

"Drake and I are fine," I say. "I do not need your date."

She sighs. "Just-a as well. Nobody other than-a him is-a crazy enough-a to-a date you."

"Told you!" Drake yells from inside.

I mean it. The balloons really are the only things getting blown today. He might get murdered if he's lucky.

Not that I have any intention of wishing any more murder on Holly Woods. We have more than enough, thank you.

Drake's phone rings from inside, but I can't hear what he says because Nonna instantly goes into a tirade in Italian, demanding to know why everyone is at the Inn.

"We're helping with a delivery," Mom says, leaning against the truck. "And you're going to the doctor. Your appointment is in ten minutes."

"I will-a stay with-a Noella."

"You sure as hell will not."

"You-a invoke-a hell like-a that, you will-a go-a to Hell," she warns me.

"I'll see you there, then," I mutter, digging in my pocket for my phone. There's a new message from Bek, and I open the text.

Bek: Dead body in the park

Oh, sweet baby Jesus.

That explains Drake's phone call.

He appears in the doorway with a frown on his face. "Gotta go. There's a body in the park."

"I'm coming," I say quickly.

He glares at me.

"I'm coming," I repeat, moving toward his truck before he can say a word. "I'm not getting roped into taking Nonna to the doctor."

It's Mom's turn to glare at me, but I get into Drake's truck anyway.

"You're going to be the death of me, woman," he mutters, starting the engine.

"Ah, well. At least you'll die happy."

2

There's really nothing pleasant about seeing a dead body.

I've seen far too many in my life, really. Between my time on the Dallas police force and moving home to Holly Woods to open my private investigator business, I don't want to think about how many I've seen.

This one is no different.

He looks like he's middle-aged, but that's about all I can tell.

He's hanging from a tree, after all, using a belt as his noose.

I'm simultaneously filled with a mixture of sadness and relief. Relief that this doesn't appear to be a murder, and sadness over a man who felt like taking his own life was the only way out.

"Pretty cut-and-dried, don't you think?"

I peer at my younger brother, Brody. "Suicide?"

He nods, putting his hands in his pockets. "There was a note in his pants pocket wrapped around his license. Bit strange that he's totally naked, mind you."

Well, I have been trying to ignore that part.

"He used a belt," I reply. "He's a stocky kinda guy. Maybe he likes to be naked, so he stripped off before he did it."

"Mm."

"Do you think it wasn't suicide?"

"He's being a brat," Trent, my eldest brother, says as he joins us. "All his injuries so far are consistent with suicide. We need to get him down and send him for autopsy before we can say for certain."

Like I don't know how it works.

"Why is he naked, then?" I ask.

"I don't know. I can't ask him, can I?"

"Your sense of humor is weird." Bek muscles in between me and Trent. "Ouch. That's unfortunate."

"What are you doing here?" Trent demands. "How did you get back here?"

"There's nobody guarding the line." She cocks her thumb over her shoulder in the direction of the police line that Drake and I had crossed on our way here. "Is there supposed to be? Because I passed Jessica in the parking lot and she looks like she's planning on marching up here."

"Let her. She can't handle dead bodies. She'll soon go away." Brody laughs.

I fold my arms over my chest at the mention of Drake's ex-fiancée. "She comes up here, and you're gonna have two dead bodies."

Trent rolls his eyes. "Brody, go and hunt down those useless morons who are supposed to be guarding the line, and tell them that under no circumstances does anyone cross it. Understood?"

"Yes, Dad."

I bite my tongue as Brody salutes him and jogs in the direction of the line.

"Bek? Why are you still here?" Trent demands.

"Oh." She looks at him. "I'm just nosy."

He opens his mouth, then pauses. "I have no idea why I allow you two anywhere near my crime scenes."

"You don't. Drake does. And he outranks you." I grin.

"I wouldn't say I let you," Drake drawls, joining us. He looks to Trent. "They're going to cut him down now. Can you make sure they get him back to the morgue without any issues? I'm going to speak with the family and see if they can tell us anything."

"Can I come?"

Drake meets my eyes. "If you promise to wait nicely in the car."

"Fine." I roll my eyes and turn around. "Let's go."

"Did she just agree to something without demanding a cupcake?" Bek asks.

"Fuck off," I call over my shoulder. "Well, Drake, are you coming?"

* * *

"That was rough." Drake gets into the truck and runs his hand through his hair. "Apparently none of them had any idea that he was struggling. He hid it really well. His note doesn't give anything away, either."

I reach over and rest my hand on his thigh. "I'm sorry."

He places his hand over mine and smiles tightly at me. "The daughter took it the worst. She was adamant there was no way he did it because they were going to the cinema this weekend."

Sadness wells inside me. That poor girl. I can't begin to imagine what she's going through right now—what the whole family is going through.

"Is that it, then? Is it all over?"

"It will be when Tim's done the autopsy. We should get an idea of exactly what happened tomorrow morning, hopefully." He squeezes my fingers. "Shall we get something to eat? Then I'll drop you off at the office and head to the station."

I nod, and he starts the engine.

"Hey, mister!"

Drake frowns and rolls down his window. "Hey, kid."

A kid—well, teenager—runs down the path from the house Drake himself just left and stops at the side of the truck. His face is red and blotchy from crying, and he rubs his nose with his sleeve.

I pull a tissue out of my purse and hand it to him, leaning over Drake to do so.

The kid smiles gratefully as he takes it and mumbles a, "Thank you, ma'am."

"Can I help you?" Drake asks.

He nods. "I didn't want to say this in front of my mom, but my dad was having an affair."

Holy shit!

"I caught him and he said it was over, but I think he was lying. I wanted to tell you in case it will help you figure out why he did this."

Drake reaches out and touches his shoulder. "Do you have any idea who the woman was?"

"Um. I think her name was Paula. Blonde hair. I saw her in a Starbucks uniform, so I think she works there."

"Thanks, Jack. That helps a lot. You go back inside and look after your mom, okay?"

He nods and turns. When he's halfway down the path, he stops and looks back at us. "It wasn't our fault, was it? Any of it."

I feel the exact moment Drake's heart breaks.

"No, buddy. None of it was any of your fault."

Jack nods once more and resumes his return to the house, this time with his head held a little higher.

Drake blows out a long breath and pushes the button to roll his window back up. "Nothing is ever simple in this town, is it?"

"Do you think this other woman had anything to do with it?"

He shrugs as he pulls away from the side of the road. "I don't know, Noelle. I'm ninety-nine percent sure Eugene committed suicide, but only because I never say one hundred percent."

"But if she can help you figure out why he did it, then you'll pursue her until you collapse."

"You know me too well."

"I do. Now, where's the nearest Starbucks that has a Paula working for them?"

3

Apparently, we can't just barge into all the Starbucks within a fifty-mile radius because that's "unprofessional."

This is exactly why I left the police. I suck at rules. And I mean I suck hard.

Now, I'm stuck in the office blowing up balloons that Mom had my brother, Devin, drop off. I should have really known better than to think she'd let me get out of it just because there was a dead body.

In a family of cops, life doesn't stop just because someone else's has.

Which is why I'm blowing up balloons and not investigating all the nearby Starbucks.

I sigh as I tie off my five hundredth balloon. A slight exaggeration, but that's what it feels like. I throw it on the floor to where the rest of them are and sigh again when I realize I'm going to have to put them all in trash bags and somehow get them to the Inn.

It's going to take me ten trips, isn't it?

Dang it.

My phone rings, and I reach over and hit the button. "Bond P.I., Noelle Bond speaking."

"Wanna take a trip?" Drake's voice crackles through the speaker.

"I can't. I'm in balloon hell."

"I promise not to tell your mom."

I tie off another balloon. "Where are we going and why?"

"I found Paula. She works at the Starbucks closest to GiGi's in Austin."

I pause. "Does that mean you'll buy me cupcakes, too?"

"Yep, and Brody has been roped into taking all those balloons to the Inn so you don't have to. Are you coming?"

"A mistress and cupcakes? You bet your ass I am."

He laughs. "I'm pulling in now."

"So soon?"

"I know you well, Bond. Get down here now. I'm not going to wait all day for you."

"All right, give me two minutes."

"You're not wearing your shoes, are you?"

"Nobody wears Louboutins to blow up balloons, Drake." I hang up at that stupid comment and slip my feet into my shoes beneath the desk. I grab my phone and purse and pull my door shut behind me, then head out after asking Gia to take my messages.

Just like he said, Drake is waiting in his truck with the engine still running. I climb up into the passenger seat—never an easy feat for me—and grin at him.

"Amazing. Cupcakes really is all it takes to bribe you," he muses, pulling out of the Bond P.I. parking lot.

I roll my eyes. I'm not even justifying that with a response—he should already know that cupcakes are my kryptonite.

If he doesn't, who the hell has he been dating?

Idiot.

The drive to Austin goes quickly, and we pass GiGi's on the way to the Starbucks where Paula works. Apparently, someone has already called ahead and confirmed she's definitely working right now, so I'm not surprised when Drake rolls his shoulders and goes into Cop Mode the second he steps out of the car.

"Do the Austin PD know you're here?" I ask, knowing how much of a dick some of those guys can be.

"Yep. They gave me permission to chat with her."

"Has Tim done the autopsy yet?" I question as we approach the door.

He shakes his head, but that's all I get from him before we step inside. He bypasses the line with authority and goes to the counter. After a small apology to the next person in line, he says, "I need to speak with your manager."

The girl behind the counter raises an eyebrow. "You'll have to wait in line like everyone else."

He pulled out his badge and put it on the counter. "I need to speak with your manager. Now."

Her eyes widen into saucers, and she almost trips on her way to get the manager.

Drake smiles warmly at the line. "Nice day for a coffee, isn't it?"

Goddamn it, Drake.

I shake my head as I step up next to him. "Not the time," I hiss.

He chokes back a chuckle, sobering the moment he sees a tall, blonde woman walk toward him. His eyes flick to the name tag moments before my own do, and we see the name of the person we're both looking for.

Paula.

As Drake introduces himself, I look her over. She looks about my mom's age, with lines in all the right places, indicating she's a big ball of laughter and happiness.

"And this is my colleague—"

"Sasha," I say, holding out my hand. "Sasha Daniels."

Drake shoots me a look but says nothing. "Is there somewhere private we can talk?"

"Of course. Come on through to the back." Paula motions for us to follow her through the door, and we do. She leads us to a small room tucked in the back. We take the offered seats, and she says, "To what do I owe the pleasure of this visit, Detective Nash?"

"I understand you're acquainted with a Eugene Phillips."

Panic flashes in her eyes. "I'm familiar with the name."

"I understand you're familiar with more than just his name."

She sags, sinking into the only empty chair left. "What do you know?"

"We've been informed you've been having an affair with him."

"That's true," she admits, shame coloring her heavily powdered cheeks. "I'm not proud of it, you understand. I'm in a very unhappy marriage."

Yeah, you and every other cheater, lady.

"I'm not here to judge you, Paula," Drake says gently. "I just want to know about your relationship with him."

Her eyes narrow. "Why? What does this have to do with anything?"

I share a look with Drake. I know he didn't want to tell her so soon into the conversation.

"Paula, I'm sorry to tell you this, but Eugene was found in the park in Holly Woods this morning."

She pales. "What do you mean, found?"

"We believe he committed suicide overnight. We'll know more when his autopsy is complete."

"No." She clutches her hands at her chest. "Oh, my God. That's why you're here, isn't it?"

"We informed the family this morning," Drake confirms. "I spoke to his son, who told me about your relationship."

"We're trying to find out what his motivation may have been," I say softly, reaching out and touching her arm. "His children are heartbroken, and we'd like to give them some answers."

"Of—of course." She brushes her hands over her face. "Of course. I'll tell you anything you need to know."

Drake steps in. "Tell me about your relationship."

Paula's hands shake as she sets them in front of her on the table. "I, uh—it's been nine months. We met in a bar, became friends, and it went from there."

"Was it physical or emotional?"

"Both," she replies. "Physical at first, but it recently became emotional."

"Did his wife know?"

"No. Neither did my husband."

I glance at her left hand. "You're not wearing a wedding ring."

"I often take it off for work." She wrings her hands together, fiddling specifically with her fourth finger on her left hand.

I look pointedly at that movement. "Are you sure about that?"

"I think I know when I do and don't wear my ring, Ms. Daniels."

Drake flits his gaze my way. "Paula, would you give us a moment?"

I follow him out of the room, and the moment he shuts the door, I say, "She's lying. The girl behind the counter was wearing an engagement ring. She doesn't need to remove it to make coffee."

"Noelle—"

"She's lying," I repeat. "When have I ever steered you wrong on this? She. Is. Lying."

He draws in a deep breath, nostrils flaring.

"Give me sixty seconds and I'll break her."

"You know I can't do that."

"So go to the bathroom." I shrug. "You have no idea what I'm asking her."

"Jesus, woman." He runs his hand through his hair. "Sixty seconds. I know nothing."

I grin, pat his chest, and head back into the room.

Paula looks up the moment I step inside. "Your name isn't Sasha, is it?"

"You heard that?"

"I heard him call you Noelle."

I sit down in the chair opposite her and cross one leg over the other. "I'll reintroduce myself. My name is Noelle Bond. I used to be with the Dallas Police Department, and I now run Bond P.I., a private investigation company in Holly Woods. I'm trained in numerous things, notably body language, and I'm somewhat of an expert in it."

She doesn't move.

"I have sixty seconds, so I'll make this quick. I know you're lying about your wedding rings. You don't need to take them off to make coffee, and you touched your left ring finger when you were asked about them. Now, you can tell me the truth about your relationship with Eugene."

She swallows, her throat bobbing with the intensity of the movement. "I split with my husband a month or so ago. We're still living together, but only for the sake of our son."

Now we're getting somewhere.

"Did he know about the affair?"

"Yes. Eugene and I discussed leaving our partners. I told my husband before he told his wife. He promised me he'd tell her this week."

"Did he?"

"Not that I know of." Paula pushes her bangs from her eyes and looks between us. "If he did, he didn't tell me yet."

He hadn't told her. I'm sure of that much. If he had, Jake would have told us this morning.

"Did he ever say anything that might make you question his mental health?" Drake continues. "Were there any indications he was struggling?"

She shrugs one shoulder. "Nothing extreme, no. He was under some pressure at work, and I imagine our affair was a stressor, but I never imagined that he'd do something like this."

Emotion crumples her face, and Drake touches her arm. "We'll leave you alone, now. Do you have a number I can call in case I need to talk further with you?"

Paula sniffs and nods. She reaches for a small pad of paper on the table, scribbles down a number, and tears the sheet off for Drake.

"We're sorry for your loss," he says, folding the sheet up and putting it in his pocket.

I smile, but I struggle to put warmth in it. Yes, I'm sorry she lost someone she cares about, but that someone is another woman's husband. A father. Their own selfish needs ripped apart at least one family, and maybe contributed in part to his death.

It's hard to feel sympathy in a situation like this.

"What do you think?" Drake asks when we're back in the truck.

"I don't know. I think she jumped the gun on telling her husband about the affair and put him under unnecessary pressure to tell his wife. She'd already broken up her family. I doubt she cared about his." I peer out of the window as he pulls out of the lot. "But I think her husband knew before she told him, just like I think Eugene's wife knows."

"You would know," he acquiesces. "You think they all knew?"

I nod. "I really do."

His phone rings then, cutting off whatever he was going to say to respond. I take it from the center console and answer, putting it on speaker and holding it out. "It's Tim."

"Tim. What's up?" Drake says, addressing the coroner.

"Drake. I have news for you," Tim replies. "Are you sitting down?"

"I'm driving."

"Ah, well, try not to swerve off the road."

"Stop fuckin' scaring me and tell me," Drake bites out.

"Eugene didn't commit suicide. It was a setup. His injuries aren't consistent with death by hanging. He was strangled, but by human hands. The bruising is all there."

Well, holy fucking shit.

Drake says goodbye with a heavy breath. "I think I need to go and see the husband."

I agree.

4

"Just like that, he confessed?" I secure my earring in my ear and look at Drake. "That doesn't make any sense."

He shrugs on his suit jacket. "We went to the door to speak with him. Andy took one look at my badge and admitted it."

"Holy crap."

"Me and Trent interviewed him, and he came clean about it all. Said he knew about the affair before Paula told him, just like you said. He found out who it was through a friend who works at the coffee shop with her, and started to follow him. He wanted to know what Eugene had that he didn't. He admits that he became obsessive about it to the point he befriended him, and Eugene had no idea who he was." Drake slicks his hair back from his face and picks his keys up from the dresser. "That was how he lured him to the park. Andy said he told him that his wife was having an affair and he wanted to kill himself. Eugene went running to the park, and Andy hit him from behind, then strangled him. When he was dead, he hung him from the tree and hoped nobody would notice."

I frown as we head downstairs. "Wouldn't the blunt force trauma tip you off it was murder?"

"You'd think, but Tim couldn't find any evidence of it. Whatever he hit him with, it wasn't hard enough to do any damage. Just stunned him enough for Andy to pounce."

"He went to help a friend and ended up dying. That's kind of sad."

"It is. Still, Eugene's family are comforted knowing it was nothing they did, and his wife knew about the affair, too. She said she kept the peace for the kids, but she planned on leaving him as soon as Jack turns eighteen in a couple of years."

"Wasn't he going to leave her?"

Drake opens the door of the truck for me. "No. I asked her, but she said there was no way he would have left his kids. He may not have loved her anymore, but he wouldn't have hurt his kids that way."

"Makes sense." I get into the truck with his help and take my seat. "Maybe there was a semblance of good inside him after all."

He grunts as he gets in his side.

"How did Paula take it?"

"About as well as she could." He backs out of the driveway and heads in the direction of the Inn for Nonna's party. Mom managed to pull it off without our help, although I'm sure the two million balloons I blew up earlier helped. "She was heartbroken, of course. She essentially lost both her husband and her boyfriend in one day. Not to mention the guilt over the situation because she now has to explain everything to her son."

"That sucks," I agree.

"You still don't feel any sympathy for her, do you?"

I laugh, glancing over at him. "It's hard! She decided to cheat, and her and Eugene's actions caused this whole situation. I'm not saying either of them deserve what's happened to them, but it is a stark reminder of why people should keep it in their pants."

"I will quietly remind you that most cases of infidelity don't result in murder."

"I will quietly remind you that in my books, all cases of infidelity should end in murder."

"Remind me again why I love you?" he teases.

"Because my ass looks great in yoga pants—and I'm keeping your murder solve rate up. We all know you take the credit for *my* discoveries."

He reaches over and squeezes my knee, laughing his ass off. He releases me to pull into the parking lot of the Inn. It's absolutely packed, and it's great to see so many people here for Nonna's birthday.

Even if she drives me insane, people love her.

For some reason.

Drake helps me out of the truck and slips his fingers through mine. "Of course I take credit for them. I'm in charge."

"Yeah, at the station. Not in my office you're not."

"But I am in the bedroom." He winks, giving me a wolfish grin, and pushes open the door.

"Surprise!"

The word echoes off all the walls, making me jump backward. Drake's laugh breaks through it all as he pulls me against his side, and I stare around at everyone in shock.

A huge banner is hanging on the wall that says, *Happy Birthday, Bond. P.I.!*

"What is happening here?" I breathe, looking around at everyone.

"Bond P.I. is three!" Bek shouts, rushing forward to hug me. "And here's the best banner. It's your murder-solving tally." She points up to another one that reads *Noelle: 4. Holly Woods PD, 0.* But someone had crossed out the zero and written a *1* next to it.

"Why is there a one there?" I ask.

"We solved one today!" Trent calls from the other side of the room.

"He confessed!" Bek shouts back. "It doesn't count!"

Bickering immediately breaks out between all the members of my family and the police department, and I laugh, leaning into Drake's side.

"Can I take credit for this?" he murmurs into my ear.

I lean up and kiss him. "Just this once."

* * *

Do you want more of Emma Hart?

One click FRENEMIES now!

STITCHES

MELANIE MORELAND

IAN

I signed the last of the forms, checked all my patients had been discharged or sent on to other doctors, then stood with a tired smile. I handed off the last of the charts to the head nurse.

"I'm out of here, Gail."

She smiled, glancing at her watch. "Only three hours past shift change," she stated dryly. "Hot date somewhere?"

I laughed as I slung my messenger bag over my shoulder. "Yep. Me and my pillow. I'm planning a hot make-out session with it for the rest of the day."

She shook her head. "You need a life."

I pushed up on the counter separating us and planted a kiss on her plump cheek. "Still waiting for you, Gail. When you're ready to leave Marv for some hot action, I'm your guy."

"I'll meet you at sundown," she quipped.

"Done."

Her laughter followed me from the ER. Gail was old enough to be my grandmother, and I had a soft spot for her. She doted on her husband, and I loved teasing her about running away with me. She was a good sport and gave as good as she got, even making me blush with her innuendos. I often thought she was the closest thing I ever got to foreplay anymore. There was simply no time in my life for a girlfriend or even a non-serious relationship.

No woman in her right mind would want to take me on. Between my shifts at the hospital, my volunteer work, and my irregular sleeping patterns, I was far too much work. So, aside from my slightly inappropriate teasing with Gail and the occasional disastrous date, I was firmly single—my only constant companion in the romance department: my hand.

Cool, fresh spring air hit me as I walked out the doors. I stood breathing it in deeply, ridding my senses of the medicinal smell that lingered. I glanced around, noting the full ambulance bay and hearing the chaos that came from the inside every time a door opened. I had no doubt Gail would sort them out fast. She was an amazing charge nurse, and I was glad to work with her.

I stretched, my back and shoulders creaking and snapping in protest. It had been a busy night in the ER, and between nonstop patients and catching up on charting this morning, I was ready to head home.

I turned in the direction of the park, deciding I needed some coffee and a breakfast sandwich at the little café in the center. Being the weekend, it was busy, but I waited patiently for my sandwich and took it and a steaming cup of their cinnamon-laced brew over to my favorite bench. A little off the beaten track, it was quieter, less people around, so I rarely encountered anyone else when I went there. It was a great place to wind down after a long shift. I sat, stretching out my long legs and placing my messenger bag on the empty space beside me.

I sipped and munched, enjoying the quiet. Leaning back my head, I let the breeze ruffle my hair and the solitude settle into my brain. My shoulders loosened, and I began to relax. I finished my sandwich, wadding up the paper and stuffing it into the empty coffee cup. I was about to stand when I heard the sound of running feet and two distinct voices. I turned in the direction they were coming, the voices getting louder as they approached.

"Chloe! Come back!"

"No, Momma! I gots to find him!"

"Chloe! I said—" The voice cut off with a gasp, and suddenly, from the bushes burst forth a small child. She stopped short seeing me, her brown eyes large and startled in her round face. Corkscrew curls were a chaotic, riotous mass around her head, the color of wheat—bright, golden, and sunny. I judged her age as about four, maybe five. I smiled at her, wanting her to know she was okay with me.

I waggled my fingers. "Hi."

She startled me by racing over, stopping in front of me. She placed her tiny hands on my knees and tilted back her head, regarding me seriously.

"Hi. I'm Chloe. Have you seen my Stitch?"

"Pardon me?" I asked, immediately going into doctor mode at the word *stitch*. I cast my gaze over her, not seeing any open cuts or scrapes. "Stitch?" I repeated.

She nodded impatiently. "Stitch," she repeated. "My koala. I lost him. Mommy and me been looking everywhere!" Her voice rose to an almost wail, her chin trembling, and fat tears gathered in her big eyes.

"No, sorry. I haven't seen him. When did you last have him?"

Her brow furrowed and she wiped away her tears, leaving a smidge of mud on her freckle- covered cheek. She was quite endearing with her serious expression.

"He was with me on the monkey bars. And when I had juice," she added triumphantly, looking at me as if that should answer the mystery of the missing koala.

"Sorry, ah, Pumpkin. I haven't seen him." I glanced around. "Didn't I hear your mommy?"

She sniffed and looked behind her, clearly surprised not to see anyone. She whipped her head around, more tears racing down her face.

"Now I lost Mommy too!" she sobbed. Then in a move I hadn't expected, launched herself at me. Without thinking, I gathered her up, letting her little arms wind around my neck as she cried.

"Hey, hey," I soothed. "It's gonna be fine. Mommy's probably in the bushes looking for Stitch. "We'll go find her." I began to stand when a woman stepped out from the same place my little hugger had appeared. Although *stepped* might have been too strong a word. Hobbled was more like it. She gripped the small tree trunk as she stared, her mouth agape as she took in the sight of me holding who I assumed was her daughter. There was dirt on her cheek, and her face expressed pain. From the way she was awkwardly holding her foot, I understood the gasp I had heard earlier.

For a moment, I was speechless. She was the loveliest woman I had ever seen. Average height, with golden hair the same wheat color as her daughter's, swept up off her face. Her eyes were lovely. Large, wide, dark pools set in a face I could only describe as *captivating*. Rounded cheeks, full lips, and a stubborn chin that, at the moment, was raised in confusion. I cleared my throat and spoke.

"Look, Chloe, there's your mommy."

Before she could move, I hurried toward the strange woman, talking fast. "She was upset and jumped up for a hug. I wasn't—"

She cut me off with a wave of her hand. "I saw." She opened her arms. "Chloe, baby, come here."

I transferred my little hugger to her mother, frowning when she bit back a grimace of pain.

"Are you hurt?"

She shook her head. "I twisted my ankle. It's nothing."

Before she could protest, I dropped to my knees, peering at the appendage. It was slightly swollen over the top of her sneaker, and I frowned.

"You should let me look at this."

"And why should I do that?" she challenged, glaring down at me. Her brown eyes were filled with fire, pinning me with her gaze.

I stood, meeting her fire with determination of my own. "Because I'm a doctor."

"A doctor?"

"A pediatric doctor."

"I'm not a child," she stated dryly.

I didn't tell her I had noticed exactly how unchildlike she was. Instead I smiled. "Bones are bones. That never changes."

"S-S-Stitch," Chloe hiccupped.

"We'll find him," her mother promised, turning to leave.

"After I look at your ankle," I insisted, halting her departure by grabbing her arm gently. "Please."

She hesitated but nodded. As she tried to step forward, she made a low sound of pain. I stopped her forward motion. "Wait. Give me Chloe."

I'm not sure who was more surprised when Chloe didn't argue, but instead she reached out her arms. I placed her on my hip, then wrapped my free arm around her mother's waist. "Lean on me," I instructed.

We limped to the bench, and I set Chloe on the wooden seat, then helped her mother lower herself down. I bent over her foot. "May I?" I indicated her ankle.

"Do I have a choice?" she asked humorously.

I had to chuckle. "Of course, but I'd prefer you said yes."

She regarded me for a moment. "Thank you," she said simply.

I tugged off her sneaker, then examined her foot, taking care to move it slowly and gently.

"Not broken," I assured her. "But sprained."

"Okay."

I reached into my messenger bag and pulled out a tensor bandage. I didn't expect the sudden bark of laughter. I glanced up in surprise, mesmerized once again by the vision of prettiness in front of me. Her dark eyes were lit with amusement, and her smile was wide. Two deep dimples appeared in her cheeks. She was mesmerizing, and I found myself returning her smile.

"What's so funny?"

"You carry bandages with you?"

I winked. "Today, yes. Yesterday, I had some enemas in my bag."

"Guess it's my lucky day."

"Guess so."

Still chuckling, I bent over and swiftly bandaged her foot. After slipping her sneaker back on, I had her stand, and she took a few test steps.

"It feels better," she said with a sigh. "Supported."

I stood. "Good. Ice it. Try to stay off it. Keep it up. It should be fine in a few days."

"Okay. Thanks."

I turned to Chloe, who was watching us quietly, her knees tucked up to her chest. "Now, you, Pumpkin. This koala of yours. You had juice together? Then he disappeared?"

She screwed up her face, thinking. "Yes," she stated emphatically.

"Where was this juice fest?"

Chloe tapped the bench. "Here."

"Hmm." I scratched my neck. "I didn't see him, ah, her, when I got here."

"Him. Stitch."

"Stitch. Right."

I glanced at Chloe's mom. "With your permission, I'll walk around a bit with Chloe and we'll look for Stitch." I handed her my phone. "You take this and give me yours. I'll film where we go so you know I'm not trying to ah, *nab*, her or anything. You can track us. You stay off that ankle."

"On one condition."

"Sure."

"You tell me your name."

I held out my hand. "Ian. Ian Taylor."

"*Dr.* Ian Taylor?" she asked.

"Yes. Should I just call you Chloe's mom?"

That smile appeared again. The one that lit her face and brought out her dimples. "Samantha." As she spoke, she slipped her hand into mine. I closed my fingers around hers, feeling the warmth and softness of her skin. How well her hand fit into mine. I also noticed she didn't wear a wedding ring.

"Nice to meet you, Samantha."

There was a strange feeling of regret when her hand slipped from mine. I held out my hand for Chloe. She took it and tugged me away.

For some reason, I kept looking back at Samantha.

And every time I did, she was staring right back at me.

IAN

I sat dejected, the sounds of Chloe's distressed sobs still echoing in my ears, long after she and Samantha had walked away.

We had failed.

Despite our search, we never located Stitch.

I took Chloe everywhere she told me they had been that morning. The monkey bars, the swings, the slide. Even the café. We asked everyone we came across, Chloe's description of Stitch getting more detailed as the minutes passed. When Chloe got tired, I set her on my shoulders and we kept looking. She told me all about the adventures she'd had with her koala and how much she loved him. About his special place on her bed. His favorite food and color. His loose ear he got when she shut it in the door. How much he loved to wear the scarves her mom made him with scraps of wool. I even found out Stitch became her best friend after her dad left, so I had my answer to my unspoken question. With every word, I fell a little bit more under her sweet charm.

After an hour, we had to give up. We'd been everywhere they had been that morning. Chloe was quiet as we walked back to her mom, who was waiting with open arms for my little hugger. Chloe started to cry, telling her mom that Stitch didn't like the rain and it was cloudy and he'd be alone.

Samantha stood, holding Chloe. She handed me back my phone, took hers, her voice cordial but cooler than before. "Thank you, Dr. Taylor."

"I'm sorry I couldn't find him."

She shook her head. "You were very kind. I hope we didn't disrupt your day too much."

I didn't like the formal sound of her tone. I preferred her teasing, sweet one. I waved off her apology. "Not at all."

I stroked my hand over Chloe's wild curls. "Will she be okay?" The thought of her being sad bothered me.

Samantha nodded. "She will."

"Ah," I hesitated, wanting to ask for her number, but for some reason knowing she wouldn't give it to me. She had shut down, and I wasn't sure why, or how to ask her. Before I could figure out what to say, she offered me a tight smile, then turned and walked away, her limp still there but not as bad. Chloe lifted her sad face and waved before burying her head back into her mother's shoulder. I hated seeing the tears that clouded her eyes. I also hated the sudden change in Samantha's demeanor.

I sat, feeling strangely bereft. What had caused the sudden shift in Samantha's manner was a mystery. I picked up my messenger bag and headed toward home. My pocket vibrated with a reminder, and I realized I had missed a text. It was from Gail.

I'm done with Marv. Meet me later and we'll figure out our exit strategy. By midnight we can be in the Bahamas.

Normally her text would have made me laugh. No doubt, Marv had called her with some inane question or, heaven forbid, made a decision without her.

Except, I knew Samantha had seen the message. She had no idea it was a joke, and she thought—well, I had no idea what she thought, but it was wrong. I wasn't running away with anyone. She had no clue it was all in fun.

I shook my head in frustration and shoved my phone back in my pocket.

"Thanks, Gail," I muttered. "You're always going on about me finding someone, then you yourself cockblock me."

I passed a garbage can and remembered my cup and wrapper were in my other pocket from earlier. I stopped to shove them in the can, only to miss the opening. I bent to grab them when I saw it. A furry paw sticking out of the corner of the overflowing waste bin. I yanked on it and pulled out a koala bear, wearing a knitted orange scarf with a loose ear.

I found him.

Too late.

Samantha and Chloe were gone, and I hadn't gotten her number.

I somehow doubted she took mine after seeing Gail's message either.

I was about to stuff Stitch back in the garbage, but I hesitated, and for some reason shoved him in my messenger bag.

After all, it was going to rain, and Stitch shouldn't be alone.

* * *

I finished a chart and drained my coffee. I was having one of the unusual, rare days in the ER. We were steady but not slammed. I actually drank my coffee while it was still reasonably warm instead of ice-cold, and I was keeping up with charting. I glanced at the clock. Two hours to go and I was off for three days. I was looking forward to the time away.

I headed to the nursing station and glanced at the board. Only three new cases since I'd slipped into the lounge. And only one with my color highlighted, indicating a child.

"Non-urgent," Gail said, sidling up beside me. "Little girl fell in the park, her wrist is sore, but the biggest problem is a huge splinter that got lodged in her hand. I can help if needed. Exam room three."

"Panicked?" I asked. I hated walking into rooms with panicked parents. They often caused the child more distress than needed.

"No. Mother and child both calm. Cute pair, actually."

"I'm sure the man in their lives thinks so. Not in the market for a ready-made family, Gail," I declared dryly.

A flash of riotous curls went through my head, and I shook it to clear my thoughts. That wasn't ever going to happen. I had been back to the park every day and hadn't found my little hugger or her mother. That ship had sailed, although I still held on to Stitch.

I headed to exam room three and walked in, stopping short when I saw the "cute pair" waiting for me.

Samantha sat on the exam bed, holding Chloe. Chloe's hand was wrapped in a towel and she clutched it to her chest. There were traces of blood on the cloth. Her red-rimmed eyes met mine and widened. Samantha looked as shocked as I felt. It was Chloe's greeting that brought me back to the moment.

"Dr. Ian! Hi!"

I strode forward, pulling up the stool and sitting in front of them. I smiled at her. "Hello, Chloe." I glanced up. "Hello, Samantha."

She paused, then spoke. "Dr. Taylor, I didn't realize you worked here."

I nodded. "Guilty as charged." I focused on Chloe. "Now, Pumpkin, I hear you've been removing wood from the park and hiding it under your skin while doing acrobatics." I tsked teasingly. "Dangerous stuff."

She shook her head, her curls bobbing. "I was running. I fell."

I held out my hand. "May I see?"

Without hesitation, she let me take her hand, and I examined it, then looked up at Samantha. "Well, like mother, like daughter. The wrist is sprained. I need to get that hunk of wood out of her hand, though, and I might have to add a stitch. It's deep."

Chloe's chin began to tremble. "Will it hurt?"

I shook my head. "Nope. Promise. I'm really good."

Gail walked in. "Dr. Taylor is the best. And he always has a treat after if you're good."

Chloe's eyes grew round. "A treat?"

I nodded. "The cafeteria here has the best milkshakes ever. If you're brave, I'll get you one."

I could feel Gail gape behind me. Normally the treat consisted of a little toy we kept in a wooden chest. It was always fun to watch the child pick out something, forgetting for a moment what procedure had just occurred. But Chloe deserved a real treat.

"Okay," she agreed, although her voice was shaky. "Can Mommy stay?"

"Of course," I soothed. "She can hold you while I do my job. It won't take long, and you'll feel much better once that nasty piece of wood is gone."

Samantha was watching us closely, a small frown on her face.

"When was her last tetanus shot?" I asked.

"A year ago."

"Okay, good. I think I'll send her home with some pills. I'll clean it well, but I want to make sure there isn't any infection. Is she allergic to anything?"

"No." Her eyes grew misty. "It happened so fast."

Without thinking, I reached out and squeezed her shoulder in comfort. Her hair was down today, the same riotous curls as Chloe's, tumbling past her shoulders. The coils felt soft under my fingers.

"Kids and scrapes happen all the time. It's part of growing up. I'm glad you brought her here instead of trying to dig that out yourself." I'd seen that happen too often with disastrous consequences.

She nodded, not saying anything. I noticed her gaze drifted to my hand, and I wondered if she was looking for a ring, the way I had the other day. I knew I had to address the unspoken question between us. I just had to figure out how.

"Gail will get everything ready and she'll help me, so it goes fast. She's the best."

"I am," Gail agreed, moving around the room to get the supplies.

"I'll be right back. I have to get something," I informed them and hurried to my locker. I pulled out the koala bear that had taken up residence recently. Once I had gotten him home, I tossed him in the washer, cleaning him of the debris that had been dumped on him in the garbage can. I carried him with me for a few days in case I found the girls and could give him back, but finally I tossed him inside the locker after giving up. He was fluffy and smelled clean, and I knew a little girl who needed him as much as he needed her. It would help distract her while I dug that nasty wood out of her little hand.

Back in the room, Gail had everything set up. Samantha was holding Chloe, and Chloe's arm was on the table, a small draping set up so she wouldn't have to see what I was doing. Chloe appeared anxious, and I could see she was shaking with fear. Samantha was trying to comfort her, soothing her curls and talking quietly. I crouched beside them.

"Before I start, I have something I think you're going to like, Chloe."

"What?" She sniffed.

I pulled Stitch out from behind my back. "Look who I found after you left the park."

Instantly, her countenance changed. She reached for her beloved koala, one word escaping from her mouth. "Stitch!"

I stood and watched her love on her little bear. She petted and hugged him. Showed him to Samantha. Talked and cooed to him like a real live being.

"His ear is fixed!" she exclaimed.

"He was brave and let me stitch it," I explained, showing her the black thread.

"Did he get a milkshake?"

"Um, no, he got a bath instead."

"Where did you find him?" Samantha asked softly.

I leaned down close to her ear. "The garbage can. The bath was necessary."

She smiled. "No doubt. Once again, Dr. Taylor, thank you."

"Ian. My name is Ian."

"Ian," she repeated. "Thank you, Ian."

I straightened and addressed Chloe. "You ready, Pumpkin?"

She clutched Stitch close. "Yes."

"Okay, then."

* * *

"All done."

It had gone well. The worst part was the freezing, and Chloe handled it like a champ. Gail kept her talking, and she was so happy to have Stitch back, she grimaced but didn't move. After that, I was able to remove the deep wood swiftly, irrigate and clean it, and luckily, only have to glue it shut.

While working, I made small talk, casually asked Gail about Marv, and she took care of my problem by telling Samantha about her husband of forty years and how he liked to irritate her. She tilted her head toward me.

"This one insists he's waiting in the wings for me, but every time I try to take him up on the offer, he finds an excuse for me to stay with Marv. I'm beginning to think he's nothing but a tease."

I met Samantha's wide gaze with a wink. "Marv's a good guy. The only person you should run off to the Bahamas with is him. I'm actually boring."

"I doubt that," Samantha murmured.

Before I could stop myself, the words were out. "Maybe you can find out for yourself."

If her hands weren't full, I was sure Gail would have clapped in glee.

I wrapped Chloe's hand in a bandage and used a small tensor on her wrist. I looked down at Samantha's foot as I was wrapping it.

"How's the ankle?"

"Much better."

"Good."

Gail looked between us and cleared her throat. "Well, Dr. Ian, your shift is over, which works out well. You can take the girls for a milkshake with no worries. No time limit."

"Isn't that convenient." I smirked, knowing I had an hour left on my shift.

"Yep. We'll give Chloe a few minutes to relax while you finish the chart; then you're free." She winked. "All of you are free to enjoy a milkshake together."

I followed Gail to the door. "I know what you're doing," I whispered.

"I hope you know what *you're* doing," she replied smugly. "I got it all set up for you. Don't blow it. Your skills are lacking, you know."

I rolled my eyes, then glanced toward the girls. Samantha was snuggling Chloe, her head bent over, holding her tight to her chest. I couldn't tell where she ended and Chloe began with their bright hair so similar.

"I'll be back," I told them.

"We'll be waiting." Samantha peeked over Chloe's head.

Those words made me smile.

I hoped I knew what I was doing too.

SAMANTHA

Watching Chloe with Ian was fascinating. I had never seen her react to a man the way she had with him. The day we met him, when I had stumbled trying to catch up with her, and had watched her run up to him, desperate to find her beloved Stitch, I'd been worried. He was a stranger, and she was alone with him. I had pushed through the bushes just as she flung herself into his arms. His facial expression and reaction calmed me. He was soft-spoken and kind, and I could hear every caring word he said. He wasn't a danger to her. His reaction to my injured ankle proved that even more. His innate gentleness surrounded him.

He stood after bandaging my ankle and insisted on trying to locate Stitch. I couldn't believe we had lost him—he had been her constant companion since before Chloe was two. I had bought him for her just after Dan left us. She barely remembered her father, but Stitch was her world. I was so used to him being locked onto her little backpack. His Velcro-covered paws must have given away and he got left behind. I wasn't sure how Chloe would manage without him.

Ian questioned Chloe in a direct, calm manner. His hands were on his hips as he thought about her replies. He was tall—well over six feet, with sandy-colored hair and hazel eyes that twinkled when he laughed. An angular jaw covered in scruff set off full lips and a handsome face. His shoulders were wide, waist slim, and his smile was inviting and warm.

He seemed pretty perfect until I read that text and shut down. It hit too close to home, and when he returned with Chloe, empty-handed, I concentrated only on her. I'd already had my heart trampled on once. I wasn't allowing it to happen again—and I wouldn't allow my child to be hurt.

Except now, the teasing text explained and Ian sitting with Chloe on his lap, listening intently to her, and seeing how tender he had been with her earlier, my mind and heart were at war. When he had given her back her beloved friend, I almost wept. The rapturous joy on her face was a sight to behold. Since we sat down, Ian had peppered us both with questions, never rushing my answers but obviously interested.

My mind told me not to get involved. My heart whispered this man was different.

Which one could I trust?

IAN

Over vanilla milkshakes, I had found out a lot about Samantha and Chloe.

Chloe was five. Samantha preferred Sam—at least to friends. They had moved here to Grimsby last month from Toronto. “I wanted a smaller town for Chloe to grow up in,” she explained.

I was delighted to find out they lived in the same condo complex as I did—four floors above me. Given my odd hours, it wasn’t surprising we had never encountered each other in the building.

I planned to change that.

Sam was a book editor for a publishing house. She made her own hours, and as I realized, they rivaled my own at times.

She informed me she was divorced from Chloe’s dad.

“He left us for his secretary,” she clarified quietly. “He told me in a text—on his way to the Caribbean with her.”

I covered her hand on the table with mine. “No wonder Gail’s text spooked you.”

She lifted a shoulder. “I had no business being upset.”

“Is it wrong to tell you I’m glad you were? I was upset I didn’t get your number.”

She glanced at Chloe, now sitting beside me, busy coloring a picture for Stitch, to show him all he had missed in the past week, talking to him in her sweet little voice.

"Are you certain of that, Ian?" she asked. "It's not only me."

I thought of how I'd felt when they walked away from me in the park. How joyful I was, despite the circumstances, that I'd found them today in my ER.

"I am. But maybe I should ask you the same thing. My hours here are crazy. I volunteer at the local youth shelter twice a week. I get called in at odd hours. I'm paying off student loans, and I live pretty simply." I held up my hand before she could respond. "Dating hasn't gone well for me, to be honest. But as bad as all that sounds, I felt something in the park. Something again today when I saw you. Something that told me, maybe it was time to find a new priority in my life. That maybe that priority was you and Chloe."

She looked contemplative, then spoke low so only I could hear.

"My ex was wealthy and ignored us. Everything else came ahead of us. He walked away without a warning and blamed me for focusing on Chloe instead of him. She was then and is now my priority. She always will be. I don't need money and a fancy place. I need the person to be present, if that makes any sense."

"Understood." I took a chance and leaned forward, covering her hands on the table with mine again and squeezing her fingers. "But what if we agreed to carve out a little time for us and see where that takes us? If maybe we could be present for each other?"

She glanced at Chloe.

"We can take it slow," I insisted. "Friends."

"Friends?" she repeated.

"Well, friends who date." I grinned.

"Tell me, Ian," she murmured, bending low over the table. "Does this 'friends who date' thing include kissing?"

I dropped my gaze to her full mouth, unconsciously licking my lips. "Lord, I hope so. I mean, if you want it to."

"Yeah, I want," she breathed out, bending closer. "You're so sexy, who wouldn't want to kiss you?"

I grinned. She thought I was sexy. She wanted to kiss me. Date me.

What a great day. I moved closer over the table, caught in her spell, wanting to taste her lips.

Then Chloe piped up. Loudly.

"Mommy, are you *kissing* Dr. Ian? Is he your boyfriend now?"

We both pulled back. I was shocked how close we had been to each other.

Chloe was watching us with wide eyes. I met the curious gaze of a few colleagues. Sam blushed as she picked up her coffee cup.

"We'll talk about it at home, Chloe," she said.

Chloe shrugged. "It's okay. I like him," she replied. "So does Stitch."

I met Sam's embarrassed gaze with a wink. "There you have it. Approved by the koala. Guess I'm your boyfriend."

"Oh hush," she responded.

But she smiled. Dimples and all.

And it was a glorious thing to see.

SIX MONTHS LATER

IAN

I slipped into the condo, trying to be quiet. One of my fellow doctors had been called away on a family emergency, so I worked a double shift to cover him. It was almost five in the morning, and I knew my girls would be asleep, although Chloe would wake up in the next couple of hours.

It turned out the "friends who date" didn't work so well for us. Three days after Chloe's trip to the ER, I took Sam out, leaving Chloe in the capable hands of her sitter. The date had gone better than I hoped, and by the time I was finally able to kiss her good night, the sexual tension between us was through the roof.

I covered her mouth with mine, teasing and light, dragging my tongue along her bottom lip. "You gonna open up for me, sweet Sammy?" I whispered against her lips.

With a soft whimper, she did, and I slid my tongue along hers for the first time. Her warm breath filled my mouth, her taste overwhelming my senses. Sweet, minty, and Sam. Addictive. And somehow, right there, I knew, I would never get enough of her. Seconds later, she was pressed against the wall of her hallway, one leg wrapped around my hips. It was only Chloe's voice calling for her mom that broke us apart. It let common sense seep back into my brain, pushing out the lust and desire that had swamped me.

I set her back on her feet and kissed her full mouth.

"Duty calls."

She stared at me, her eyes wide with desire, her hand still clutching my shirt collar. I smiled at her. "It's just the start, Sam. I promise." I gave her one last kiss. "Goodnight."

She had nodded and whispered, "Night," and walked toward Chloe's room, her gait a little off. I let myself out, not wanting to go but knowing it was for the best. If I stayed when she returned, I'd have her under me on her sofa in five seconds flat.

I rounded the corner and stopped with a smile. Sam was asleep on the sofa, her laptop open, a cup of cold coffee sitting beside her. I knew she was against a deadline, and had no doubt taken advantage of the fact I was working to finish the manuscript she was editing.

I looked around the room, still amazed this was my life now. Once I kissed her, once I had made love with her, I knew I was never letting Sam go. Her gentle personality, her caring ways, her laugh, her smile, the way she mothered Chloe—everything about her drew me in. And I adored Chloe. The two of us were buddies and, along with Stitch, had many adventures in the park, the pool downstairs, and the playground.

We now lived together. I had been spending so much time in Sam's place, I hardly remembered what mine looked like. When a three-bedroom place opened up in the same building, Sam had slipped the listing in front of me, looking nervous. I had kissed her long and hard, then called the manager. There was no discussion needed. My girls were it for me and I was ready. We moved the following month, and my life became a dizzy calendar of all things Chloe, Sam, and me.

I knelt in front of Sam and gazed at her. I had some news to share with her, and I wanted to tell her before Chloe woke up. I slipped her laptop onto the table and leaned forward, nuzzling her mouth. I felt her smile as she woke, her lips moving with mine effortlessly.

"You're home."

"I am."

She cupped my face. "You must be so tired."

"I grabbed a nap. I see you've been working too."

"Yeah, I finished the manuscript and sent it back."

I quirked my eyebrows. "A dashing rake in this one? Or is he a duke?"

She grinned. "Both."

Sam edited the historical romance genre. I had discovered a guilty pleasure in reading the books she edited, often amused by the antics and turned on a great deal of the time. I loved it when she printed out a steamy section and left it on my pillow. We had re-enacted several scenes, and my favorite nickname for her was *wench*. She giggled when I would lower my voice and call to her.

"Come to me, my wench. Show your duke how much you love him."

"You'll have to tell me all about it."

She waggled her eyebrows, looking adorable. "I will. There is one scene I think you'll like. How do you feel about wearing a kilt?"

It was my turn to grin. "Bring it on, lassie." I kissed her, then moved away, knowing if I stayed close, there'd be no more talking, and Chloe would be up soon.

I sat across from her, taking her hand. "Did the package come?"

"Yes."

"Great. I'll give it to her today."

"You spoil her."

I kissed her knuckles. "She deserves it. You both do." I drew in a deep breath. "I have some news."

"Okay?" She looked anxious, her brow furrowing.

"I accepted that job at Urgent Care."

"You did?"

I nodded. "The salary is decent, my hours are set which means I'll have more time for us, and the benefits are great. Once I'm settled, if I want, I can pick up a few shifts in the ER."

"You love it at the ER."

I shrugged. "Yes. But a lot of that was so I stayed busy. I don't want to be so busy anymore. I want time with my girls. The Urgent Care facility is great. I met some of the staff, and I'm looking forward to the change." I sighed. "To be honest, with Gail leaving to retire, and some of the new heads they have at the ER, it was time. They were talking more cutbacks and extra hours. I don't want to burn out."

"Then it's a good decision."

I met her gaze. "Yeah, it is."

"I, ah, did something yesterday."

"Oh?" I asked, curious.

Sam looked nervous. Then she lifted her chin. "I paid off your student loans."

I blinked. Then again. "What?"

"I paid them off."

"Why-why would you do that? How?" I sputtered.

"I used some of my settlement." She held up her hand before I could argue. "Dan paid a lot to get rid of us, and I put most of it away for Chloe's education. But I wanted to do this—for you, for us."

I sighed heavily. "I don't want you paying my debts."

"I'm not. You can repay me at a much slower rate and with no interest. I figured it all out." She eyed me speculatively. "I wanted to do that, Ian. Please let me. Knowing it's less stress for you makes it less stress for me. Besides"—she flashed me a grin—"it would piss Dan off if he knew his money went to help you, so it's a double bonus for me. Please accept it."

I sat back, amazed at this woman. How lucky was I.

"I will pay you back."

"I know. I have it all documented."

"I love you."

She smiled, her dimples deep, her eyes glowing. "I love you."

Thumping, fast footsteps headed our way and broke the moment. Wild curls, slipper-covered feet, a saucy smile, and the ever-present koala came around the corner. "Daddy!"

She had started calling me that when I moved in. It just slipped out one day while we were snuggling. When she'd said it, I had looked at Sam, who was watching us with tears in her eyes.

"You are my daddy now, right? You live with us. You call me Pumpkin. That's a special name. So is Daddy."

Since Dan had nothing to do with her, and I loved her like my own, I nodded. "Yeah, Pumpkin, it's good. I am your daddy and proud to be."

Chloe jumped on my lap, and I let out a loud exaggerated groan. "You are getting too big!"

She giggled. "Mommy says I am sprouting like a weed."

I kissed her forehead. "Mommy is right."

With a grin, I pulled a box from beside the chair. "I got you something."

Her eyes grew round like saucers. Chloe loved surprises. She traced her name on the package.

"What is it?"

"Open it and see."

I helped her open the thick cardboard, then let her pull off the wrapping. She emitted a little coo when she saw the contents. Two new koalas.

"I thought Stitch might like some friends," I explained. The truth was poor Stitch was getting pretty worn out, and I worried what would happen when he was no longer up to the task of being hauled around everywhere. I had stitched Stitch up so often, I wasn't sure there was a seam intact anymore.

She touched the fur. "A mommy and a baby," she whispered.

"Stitch can be the Grandpa—like Papa Marv." Gail and Marv were like family to us and grandparents to Chloe. The adoration was mutual on all sides.

She slipped off my knee and gathered her new animals tight to her chest. "Stitch loves them! He has a family now—like me!"

Her words made my throat tight. "Yeah, Pumpkin, he does."

"I have to go introduce them to everyone!"

I chuckled. "Okay. What will you name them?"

She looked at me as if I was nuts. She held up the mommy. "This is Stitchy." Then the baby. "This is Baby Stitch."

I nodded sagely. It made perfect sense.

She ran down the hall, talking excitedly.

"That's her day, probably her month made." Sam stood in front of me, smiling.

I pulled her onto my lap. "Since you made my life perfect, it seems only right I can make her smile."

She kissed my jaw. "You make us both smile."

I tilted up her chin, kissing her. "Good."

She snuggled closer, and I wrapped my arms around her. I was surrounded by the sounds and scents of home. Chloe's little voice, Sam's body close to me, her curls tickling my lips as I nuzzled them. The feel of the comfortable chair that molded to my body. Knowing in a few moments Chloe would tear back into the room, and we'd move to the kitchen and have breakfast. That tonight, once she was in bed, I'd have Sam alone and we'd spend hours making love and talking about the future.

Our future.

I leaned down close to Sam's ear. "I'm gonna marry you one day."

She lifted her head with a smile, responding the way she always did when I said those words. "Okay."

"Soon."

She lifted her eyebrows. I had never added that word before. "Okay."

I ran my finger over her cheek. "Let's set a date, sweet Sammy. Make it official."

She grinned and nipped at my finger. "Anxious?"

"I want everyone to know you're mine. You and Chloe. I want to be a real family." I drifted my hand down to her stomach. "I want to make more Chloes with you."

Her eyes lit up. Her dimples came out and she smiled widely.

"Next week?"

I lowered my mouth to hers.

"Perfect."

* * *

SWEET CAROLINE

HERO'S PRIDE SERIES

AUDREY CARLAN

1

INK

I cannot believe I'm tattooing a fucking koala bear.

Adjusting my hold, I wiped the blood away from the saturated areas pooling at the woman's hip, then pressed the needle back to her pearlescent, previously unmarked skin.

A tattoo virgin.

Usually, I hated tatting a hot chick with their first tat. They tended to be too high maintenance. And I definitely didn't want to be tatting cutesy shit like koala bears, cartoon animals, rainbows and stupid crap people would regret later, but it wasn't my role to sway them from what they wanted, and I couldn't boot her to my employee, Kidd, because he was busy working a tat for my club brother's old lady.

I glanced across the room and watched with a grin as Kidd, one of my genius artists and a current Prospect for the Hero's Pride, worked on our Vice President's old lady. The biker princess of them all, Shay O'Donnell. Well, technically she was Shay Crawford, and had been for almost two years now.

Rex grumbled and crossed his massive arms, dipping his face near his wife's tits where my friend worked.

I chuckled and filled in the nose of the koala bear.

My canvas moaned a little in the back of her throat. My dick stirred to attention. Damn. Been a while since a woman moaning had given me a stiffy when I wasn't the one making her moan in pleasure.

"You okay there, Sunny?" I stopped the tattoo gun and waited for a reply.

She looked over her shoulder, and her golden hair fell in a straight sheet down her back as she cocked a brow. "Sunny?"

I gifted her one of my most sultry smiles. The one that usually got me into a girl's panties quicker than I could tattoo them. Then again, it usually wasn't that hard to get in a girl's panties if she went for the tall, tatted, unruly, motorcycle-club-member type. I had pitch-black hair, eyes a cerulean blue, and tattoos from neck to ankles. If tats weren't a woman's thing, I wasn't the man for them.

"Yeah." I gestured to her hair with my chin. "Like pure sunshine."

She preened and her cheeks turned a rosy hue before my eyes.

Nice.

Yeah, she was a pretty one.

Innocent and sweet.

"So why the koala bear?"

She smiled so big it was like the sun actually shone down on my dark soul.

As a patched-in brother of the Hero's Pride Motorcycle Club, I scored a lot of tail. Usually, however, they were women who knew the score. Not cotton-candy sweet, with a smile and hair as bright as the damn sun.

"Just got back from doing a summer abroad. I'm studying to be a marine biologist, but I was taken with the wildlife in Australia, obviously the most by the koalas, which are actually a marsupial, not a bear at all."

"Hmm. Interesting." I fired up the tattoo gun and worked on adding the perfect shading to the fur in the picture she'd provided that I then hand drew. At least I got to draw the thing freehand. That made having to use my gifts on a girly "marsupial" less lame. Not totally, but I figured if I had to do it, I'd make it as badass and realistic as possible.

"Goddamn it, Kidd! You touch my wife's tit again and you're going to lose that goddamned arm!" Rex growled and my canvas trembled.

"Hold up, Sunny." I wiped the area and set my tools to the side, hiking off the chair I was straddling and making my way to where my MC brother was hassling my employee.

I nudged Rex's beefy shoulder, making sure not to touch him with my gloved hands, and looked down at where Shay lay. Her shirt was off, huge tits encased in a sexy-as-fuck black lace bra. Under her right breast she was having the date of her wedding and the date her children were born added to her ribs. Ouch. The ribs were the worst, but she was taking it like the badass bitch I knew her to be.

"What's the problem here?" I cocked a brow at Rex, not my employee, because I knew Kidd. He was doing everything in his power to avoid touching an old lady's body in any manner. Especially the Vice President's wife. The President's daughter.

The men in the Pride took their relationship with their old ladies to a possessive, Neanderthal level. I could totally understand, not that I could relate. I didn't have an old lady as of yet but was keeping my eyes open.

"Kidd keeps pressing his hand and his forearm to my wife's tit," Rex grumbled, breathing fire like a dragon ready to strike.

"You realize in order to get to that area, so he can tattoo it perfectly, he'll likely brush up against and oftentimes have to press up against her breast. She chose the area, not Kidd. Brother, this happens every time your woman wants ink. Give the guy a pass. He's getting patched in next month. You think a brother would intentionally touch your old lady inappropriately? Think hard, man." I stared into his amber-colored eyes. His mouth twisted into a scowl.

"Fuck, just hurry it up." Rex pushed his fingers into his long waves of hair and turned around. The needle fired up again.

I gave Kidd an apologetic look followed by a snarky grin.

"Shut the fuck up, man. I keep telling you to stop having me do the old ladies, but no, you love messing with me."

I shrugged. He was right. I'd had enough razzing from the Hero's Pride MC when I was prospecting. It's part of the process. So, when a brother comes in and asks for ink for his woman or his old lady, I send them over to Kidd.

Honestly, it's usually pretty funny. When it's Rex, not so much.

I chuckled and winked at Shay as she lay there smiling like the sexy loon she was.

"You suck," Kidd mumbled and got back to work.

"Damn straight. Never had any complaints either." I laughed and made my way back to sunny and sweet.

Once I started work on Sunny's hip tat, I let everything fall away. Her pretty spun-gold-colored hair and big brown eyes, my brother, his old lady, and everything in between, and just focused all my attention on completing the most kick-ass koala the world had ever seen.

As I was about halfway through, I heard a strange moaning noise. The sound tingled along my nerve endings, causing gooseflesh to rise on my skin.

I shook my head and looked at Sunny. "You okay?"

Her cheeks were a fiery pink, and she bit her lip, then squirmed in her seat. "Um, I think that couple you were talking to, um, went to the back room to have a, uh, chat."

I narrowed my gaze and held my breath.

A crooning sound came from back office. "Jesus, baby, you're so hard, mmmm."

Fuck.

"Fuck yeah, gonna lick you clean, Pussycat," Rex grumbled low in his throat, and if I didn't know any better, I would have sworn they were going at one another five feet from me, not thirty-five feet down the back hall where the office was.

Sunny—who wasn't named Sunny, but I forgot her fuckin' name the second she asked me to draw a koala bear—trembled and gripped the table, her nails digging into the leather.

I started up the gun and got back to work, hoping that was the end of their shenanigans but knowing with everything inside of me there was no way in hell it was.

"Taste so good, like pure honey. I could eat you all night." I heard Rex's statement, and my dick hardened behind my jeans.

I adjusted my cock and balls and ran my forearm along my suddenly sweaty head and got back to work.

"Oh God, oh baby, oh my..." Shay's broken, alluring voice cut through the sound of the tattoo needle, the music playing in the background and my ability to focus.

"Shit," I griped and ground down on my teeth.

Sunny's body jostled along the table as she turned her head to the side and smiled, a little giggle leaving her glossy peach lips. "This is funny," she noted good-naturedly.

At least she wasn't one to bitch about the indecency of it.

I sighed. "Not really the time or the place, but I'm not gonna bother them because they have a pair of just over one-year-old twins at home. My guess, they don't get a lot of alone time to let loose." I went back to tatting the two opposable thumbs the bear had, wanting them to look as realistic as possible.

"Aw, that's sweet of you. You're a good guy, Ink."

"Yeah, I'm a regular do-gooder." I chuckled and finished one hand, moving to the other three claws on the bear's opposite hand curled around a gnarled branch with eucalyptus leaves, filling them in and then adding a little white for a reflection.

"Yeah, bend over, show me that sweet pussy and ass." Rex's voice reverberated through the tattoo parlor. Kidd at least had put his headphones on and was cleaning up his station, the closed sign on the door already in place.

Rex's command was followed quickly by a loud wail from his wife.

"Take it. You take your man's cock. All of it, baby. That's right, fuck yeah." Rex roared his triumph.

Sunny's body wiggled against the chair, so I placed my hand to her back, pressing gently. "Easy. Relax or you're going to have one wonky-as-fuck bear. Might look more like those dancing bears from the Grateful Dead, instead of a tribute to a country you loved," I teased.

She giggled and the sound went straight to my cock. I gripped between my thighs and squeezed the massive bulge.

"You're feelin' it too?" Her coffee-colored gaze was zeroed on my hand over my cock.

I smirked. "Kind of hard not to when you've got a live porno happening in the other room."

She licked her lips, and her pupils dilated. "Yeah," Her voice was breathy, and I wanted nothing more than to take her mouth with mine and taste her candy-coated tongue.

I swallowed, my throat suddenly dry as we stared at one another. And that's when the pounding started.

Skin against skin.

Body to body.

Carnal fucking.

If I had to guess, Shay was bent over the desk, her lush curves naked from the waist down. Rex would have his pants around his knees, his large paws on her hips while he hammered into her from behind.

"Taggart!" Shay cried out, using Rex's real name, moaning so loud I clenched my fingers, my knuckles turning a snowy white.

Sunny turned in her chair. Her tank top was twisted into a knot just below her breasts, and her yoga pants were pressed down low on her hips so I could have unfettered access. Her belly button was a tiny little slit against a flat abdomen I wanted to run my tongue down.

"More. Give me more, woman. Squeeze my dick. Fuck. So good. My wife so goddamned perfect." He continued to fuck Shay for all to hear.

Well, not everyone. Just me and Sunny, who was looking at me, licking her lips as though I were her next meal.

I glanced over at Kidd's table, and he was gone, the light in front of the store turned off, proving he'd left for the night and locked the front door when he did.

"We're alone?" she asked.

"Except for them." I nodded toward the back room where the fucking had ramped up even higher.

"You have a girlfriend?" she asked out of the blue.

I shook my head. "Nope."

"Got a condom?"

My heart pounded a rapid beat, and my palms started to sweat. "Yep."

"You want to fuck me, right here, right now?" Her gaze was half-lidded and filled to the brim with desire.

"Hell yeah. Drop your pants, Sunshine," I growled.

She stood and, without any further discussion, pushed her yoga pants and panties down to her ankles, then kicked them off.

I ripped off my gloves, tossed them on the floor, pulled out my wallet, grabbed a condom, tore it open, undid my pants and my cock sprang to attention.

"Wow. Nice." Her gaze was on my hard-as-stone shaft between my thighs.

"Glad you approve," I said while I sheathed my length.

"Harder! Harder, baby!" Shay screamed and Rex growled with a fiery intensity that slithered down my spine and settled hotly at my cock and balls.

"Hop on, Sunny." I leaned back.

She grinned. "I thought you'd never ask."

With sure movements, she straddled my lap, centered the flared head against her wet slit and slammed down until her ass met my muscled thighs.

Bliss. Pure fucking nirvana speared through my body, and I dug my hands into her thighs.

Her body arched, offering the column of her neck. I pressed my lips to it, then my tongue and ran it up the slender surface. She smelled of wild berries and tasted like heaven. I tunneled my fingers through her silky hair, gripped the roots in a fist and forced her mouth to mine.

She opened for me instantly, sucking my tongue while fucking my cock with her slick, tight, viselike grip. She tasted of the Orange Crush soda she'd been sipping earlier.

"Jesus, woman, you know how to fuck." I bit at her lips.

She grinned, wrapped her arms around my neck and used her legs to bounce up and down, riding my cock like a professional horse jockey.

I gripped her around the waist, plastering her form to mine. Her body rocked and rolled as though she were made to take my cock.

"Again, Pussycat! Wrap those legs around me. Yeah, like that! Come again, baby," Rex commanded from the other room.

A fresh bout of arousal slickened my woman's ride, making it easier to sway up and down on my length.

I lifted my arm up her back, curled one hand around the nape of her neck and yanked her down, lifting my hips, hitting as deep as possible.

Unlike Rex and Shay, I was able to keep my mouth over Sunny's, stealing her soft sighs and heady moans as she came undone in my arms, her body tightening, sweat misting along her chest.

She was a goddess.

Riding like the wind.

Her hair unbound, a tumble of brightness falling against my ink-covered arms.

I took a second to imprint the beauty that was her in my mind as her head tipped back, her body locked around mine and she offered the sky a silent wail of pleasure.

With quick movements, and her pussy clenching around my shaft, I clamped my mouth over hers, tasting her final moan on my tongue as she climaxed.

The telltale spark of release started at the base of my spine, swirling around the root of my shaft in what seemed like endless tantalizing circles until I gritted my teeth, ground her body down on mine, and let go inside of her.

For a couple minutes we sat there, kissing softly, intimately, as if we'd done this deed a thousand times before, when in reality, we'd only just met tonight and I didn't even remember her name.

I was such a shit.

With one last sweep of my tongue, I nibbled her plump bottom lip.

Sunny inhaled and exhaled, then languidly rose off my spent length.

I sighed and slumped back in my chair.

She grinned wide, slipped on her panties, then her yoga pants and darted to the bathroom.

I took care of the condom, tying off the end and putting it into a paper towel, then tossing it into the big trash bin that I'd take out with me this evening when I got ready to leave.

Sunshine came out of the bathroom, her hair falling into her pretty face. A dreaminess coated her expression as she turned to face the chair, pulled down her pants to her hips and hugged the leather.

I smiled and shook my head, put on a new pair of latex gloves and fired up the tattoo needle.

Fifteen minutes later, Rex led Shay through the hallway and out into the open parlor. Her long brown hair was even more wild than usual, her icy-blue eyes soft, her lips as bruised as the woman I'd just fucked.

"Shit, man, did we keep you?" Rex said with apology in his tone.

I ran a perfect black line around the foot of the koala, filling in the toenail claws one at a time.

"Nah, just finishing up Sunny's tat."

"Oh, I got a tattoo tonight too!" Shay gushed and swayed over to us to look at the bear. "Oooh pretty! Are you from Australia?" she asked as though we hadn't just heard them fucking the daylights out of one another so hard we ended up having a quick fuck ourselves.

"Nope. Just visited and was obsessed with the little buggers. Ink drew this one from scratch off a picture I took of my favorite furry friend."

"Cool, man." Rex admired the tattoo. "For a chick tat."

Shay swatted her husband's bicep. "Shush! Just because the rest of the world doesn't want to get snarling lion heads, reapers, skulls, and motorcycles doesn't mean they aren't important and just as cool."

"It's okay. I don't care if other people think my tattoo is cool or not. It's for me, not them."

And wasn't that just the best fuckin' answer in the world.

"Well, I call bullshit on my husband. He has our twin's footprints in the shape of a heart with their names tatted on his chest." She poked at said chest with a red-tipped finger.

"Woman, besides you, nothing is more important than my babies," he half snarled. The damn man was so balls to the wall every time he spoke of his wife and kids.

Shay blushed prettily at my brother. "Yeah," she gushed and wrapped her arm around her man. "We didn't, uh, bother you...um, did we?" Shay's tone was breathy but still concerned.

I pressed my lips together. "Bother us? Not at all. More like *inspired*." I chuckled.

"Hmm? I don't get it." Shay frowned and pressed her head to her man's shoulder.

"No worries, Princess. Get home to your babies. Kiss 'em from Uncle Ink, yeah?"

She smiled wide. "You got it! Don't work too late. Bye, Ink. Nice koala, chickee! Hope to see you again." She hooked her arm around her husband's waist. "We'll head out the back to the bike."

I waved with the hand not finishing up the last bit of white around the koala's furry neck.

"Those two always like that?" Sunny asked.

My hackles rose on instinct. I didn't take kindly to people judging my brethren or their old ladies. Those two, regardless of their lack of modesty, were two of the best people I'd ever known in my entire life. I'd die for either one of them.

"Gone for one another. I swear it was like cartoon hearts were popping up all around them like an aura," she teased.

I chuckled and exhaled, relief filling my veins as I realized how cool this woman really was. "Yeah, they are."

"Good for them," she hummed, and I finished the last of her tattoo and spread some petroleum jelly along the three-by-four-inch area.

"Go take a look." I slipped off my gloves and tossed them to the bin.

She scrambled up, now back to her sunny disposition, and took in her tattoo in the long mirror. "It's incredible. So lifelike! Thank you, Ink. I'll love it forever."

"Glad you like it. At first I was thinking tatting a koala bear was a little lame for a Friday night."

She pursed her lips and cocked her head.

"Or for anytime."

Her head tipped back, and she laughed heartily, crossing her arms over her abdomen.

"Then you proved me wrong. Don't suppose I'll ever forget you or see a koala bear without remembering what happened here tonight."

"Two memories for the price of one." She waggled her hips and danced a little in a circle.

The woman was endearing.

I cleaned up my space while she dug through her purse and got out the cash we'd agreed on before I started her ink.

I shook my head. "Can't take it."

"Why not?" She frowned.

"Babe, seriously? Fucked you. Tatted you. Want to fuck you again after I buy you a couple beers and a burger at O'Donnell's."

She put a hand to her hip. "I don't even know you and you want to take me out to dinner and drinks? Give me a free tattoo? Do you even know my name?"

"Woman..."

She bugged out her eyes playfully.

I liked this game.

Fuck.

I liked this girl.

"You say woman and what? I answer with *man*?"

"Get your shit. Taking you for burgers, beers, and another round of boning. This time preferably on a comfy mattress where I get to see and put my mouth all over you."

She ran her fingers through her hair and twisted her lips around. "Oh, I don't know...it's getting kind of late. Besides, how do I know I can trust you?"

I came to stand in front of her, hooked her around the waist and pressed her to my chest. "What's your name, Sunshine?"

Her lips twitched, and her nose crinkled. "Wouldn't you like to know."

"Gonna find out one way or another."

She shrugged. "Then I vote for another."

"Jesus. Crazy bitches with koala bear tattoos and hair that shines like the sun who ride cock like a goddess. I must have been hit in the head too many times as a wayward teen to want to move forward with this."

She snorted. Actually *snorted* with her laughter until she covered her mouth with her hand.

"I heard that."

"You didn't!"

"Babe, you just snorted like a piglet. Maybe instead of Sunshine I'll call you Piglet?"

Her eyes widened, and I steered her out of my shop to the back alley where my bike sat.

"You wouldn't dare call me that."

"I would if you don't tell me your real name..."

She groaned. "Fine. It's Clementine."

"Shut the fuck up?" I practically stumbled swinging my leg over my Harley.

Sunny grinned and bit her bottom lip. "No, it's not." She piggy-snort laughed again, and I couldn't help but lose the plot in response, laughing alongside her.

"Woman, get on the back of my bike."

She jumped up and down like a little girl and clapped her hands before putting her purse over her form cross-body. "We're going for three memories tonight, Ink. I've never ridden on a motorcycle." She put her arm to my shoulder and swung a long leg over the back.

When I got her settled, I started the bike and revved it so she could feel the power between her thighs in a way I would die trying to match in the bedroom tonight, after burgers and beers.

"What's your name, baby?"

"Caroline."

"Sweet Caroline, just like the song?"

Her lips pressed to my ear. "Just like the song."

We rode to O'Donnell's, where we met up with Riot, Mags, Holly, Tank, Shadow, and a few other brothers from the Pride. Whip was behind the bar sneaking kisses from his old lady, Anya, the local ballet teacher in town.

I pushed through the crowd and presented Caroline to my family.

"Hey, everyone, this is Caroline, but she goes by Sunny."

* * *

THE DATE ARRANGEMENT

A. ZAVARELLI

1

WILLOW

Smoothing my hair out in the reflection of my compact mirror, I take a deep breath and run through my mental checklist one last time. As an actress, I'm used to memorizing lines, but tonight I'll need to remember an entire backstory. It isn't for a character but rather a wealthy Aussie bachelor.

Daxon Blackwood. Thirty-two years old. Single. No children. Heir to Blackwood Vintage Estate, one of the largest wine producers in Australia. Rich, successful, handsome as hell.

That last detail I decided for myself after the photographs popped up in my e-mail chain with Daxon. His job proposal wasn't one I'd typically accept, but as a traveling actress, no two days are ever the same. When I received the request to "fake a date" with the handsome wine tycoon, I almost turned it down without a second thought. I am not an escort, and that isn't the type of "acting" I do. But the more I read through the offer, the more I considered it.

The conditions were laid out clearly. This was a fake date and nothing more. I would not be required to perform any public displays of affection other than casual flirting. It seemed easy enough, and the pay was great. Well beyond what I would typically expect for a few hours of my time. In fact, with this five-thousand-dollar paycheck, I could easily spend some time exploring more of Australia between jobs. There were so many places I wanted to see, and after reading the contract, I couldn't find a downside. What was one date with a handsome man and a bonus paycheck on top of it?

It came as no surprise that the event honoring Daxon's official takeover of the business was being held at the Blackwood Estate in McLaren Vale, South Australia. A stunning locale with vineyards as plentiful as the glittering beaches along the neighboring coast. The entire region is charming and idyllic, and I can't help being in awe of the passing scenery as I relax into the seat of my cab and rehearse my own backstory.

Willow St. James. Twenty-six. Single. No children. World traveler. Actress. Jane of all trades between jobs.

All of that is true, but I leave out the part about having no real family to call my own because at the end of the day, nobody wants to hear that sob story.

The taxi pulls to a stop, and a million butterflies take flight in my stomach as I peer out the window. Blackwood Vintage is nestled into the very heart of the McLaren Vale region, with views overlooking rolling hills and the most pristine lawns I've ever seen. Just on the cusp of dusk, the buildings and surrounding gardens are aglow with solar lights. It looks like a scene straight from a fairy-tale book, and immediately I am drawn to the magic of this place.

During the course of my research for this evening, I learned that the estate boasts a tasting room, cellar door, and several restaurants and cafés. It's a popular venue for weddings and parties, but the Mediterranean-themed winery is also recommended online as the perfect weekend getaway with plenty of neighboring accommodation.

"She's a beauty, isn't she?" The taxi driver peers out the window as he waits for me to retrieve the cash from my wallet. "Must be a party here tonight, I take it?"

"It's an event to honor Daxon Blackwood," I tell him. "And the winery is lovely. I'm excited to see it."

I hand him some cash, and he thanks me with a smile. "Have a good time."

Steeling myself with a deep breath, I exit the car and aim for a relaxed attitude as I take my first step toward the main building. But I don't even make it that far before two men approach me, glancing at my face and then back to each other as if to confirm their unspoken thoughts.

"Willow?" the guy on the left asks.

"Yes?" My brows pinch together in question. How does he know who I am? I know this isn't Daxon based on the photographs he sent me.

"Good to meet you." The stranger extends his hand, and I shake it out of politeness. "I'm Dave. This is Bazza. We're Daxo's mates."

"Oh." My shoulders relax a little. "Nice to meet you both. Are you here to show me inside?"

They share another look that spells mischief, and I don't like where this is going.

"We are. But first we just need to go over a couple things."

"Like what?" I frown.

"The contract you received explained your role tonight," Dave says. "But see, the thing is… Dax isn't exactly aware that we hired you."

"Are you kidding me?" I stare at them in disbelief. "I thought I was speaking to Daxon. Is this some kind of prank? Because I don't find it funny."

"It's not a prank." Bazza holds up his hands. "Listen, Dax is a very proud bloke. He works hard, and this estate means everything to him. He's a stand-up guy, and we wouldn't be asking this of you if it wasn't important."

"His ex-missus ran off with his best mate," Dave adds hastily. "And they're both going to be here tonight. It's the first time they'll all be together in one room since it happened. The wound is still raw, and we're just trying to look after our mate. That's all."

I curse under my breath as I turn back to find that my taxi is long gone. What I should be doing is marching straight out of this place to call another one. But I can't help considering what they said about Dax. They told me a story they knew would pull at my heartstrings, and even though these two boneheads have tricked me to get me here, I feel like their intentions were good.

"So, what exactly do you expect from me if Dax isn't even in on this scheme?" I ask.

"We were hoping you could just flirt with him a little. Keep his attention for the night. Ask him about the wines, the location, things of that nature. Just keep him talking and help him relax a bit."

"That's it?" I arch an eyebrow at the building, which is already bustling with people. "What if he doesn't take the bait?"

"Start with the wine," Dave advises. "If you do that, he can't turn you down."

They seem more confident than I feel about the entire plot, but I figure since I'm here, I may as well give it a shot.

"All right," I sigh. "I'll see what I can do."

2

DAXON

"Daxo!"

I tear my attention away from Twila and Matt to find Dave and Bazza waving me down. Between them, there's a woman I don't recognize, but her eyes are on me as they approach. It feels like a trap, and Bazza only confirms it when he introduces her.

"This is Willow." He throws me a wink. "She's a Yank."

I repress the urge to groan as I meet her gaze. Willow is pretty, with long auburn hair and pale green eyes. Exactly the kind of temptress who might have drawn me in only a few years ago. I have a notion that's the entire point as they subtly nudge her in my direction. But regardless of who she is or where she's from, I'm not interested. Full stop.

I offer her a disinterested nod as a greeting, hoping she'll get the point as I scan the room for a familiar face I might talk business with. Something to keep me distracted.

"You have a lovely place here," Willow says. "Mediterranean-themed wines, I'm told? It's unique. Would you mind me asking where, specifically, you've drawn your inspiration from?"

Her question surprises me, and when I study her face, it seems like she's genuinely interested, but it's difficult to tell. I once thought the same thing about Twila and look how that turned out.

"The Blackwood family has been in the wine business for well over a century," I inform her. "I can't take credit for the inspiration, but my great-grandfather was rather fond of Italy. In fact, he married an Italian woman. Their passion was the original inspiration. Now, we merely carry on their traditions and add a few modern twists as we see fit."

"Don't let his modesty fool you." Dave slaps me on the back. "Daxo's been working these fields since he was a youngster. He knows everything there is to know about the wine business, from the ground up."

Twila's laughter from across the room distracts me momentarily, and I adjust my collar, wishing I could step out for a moment to get some fresh air. It's been ten months since I've seen her, and that isn't nearly long enough. The same could be said for Matt, someone I once called a mate. Now she's wearing his ring, counting down the days until she can rightfully claim half of what's his.

"What would you recommend for a red?" Willow touches my arm with a familiarity that stirs some life back into my deadened soul. That feeling catches me off guard, and when I meet her gaze, I feel like I need to escape before it infects me further.

"Sangiovese is my favorite," I answer brusquely.

"Perhaps you could show her to the private tasting room?" Bazza suggests. "It's not often that we have a guest who's traveled so far to see the place."

I drag a hand through my hair and scan the nearest exit, wondering how many guests might notice if I slip out before the evening is over. It's a fantasy I can't indulge at the moment, but regardless, I have no intentions of giving Willow a private tour of the tasting room or anything else she might be after. She's a beautiful woman, but I'm not interested. I can't be. After the Twila situation imploded, I learned the hard way women only want one thing from me. To Willow and all the other wandering eyes in this room, I'm merely a checkbook in a nice suit.

"Pardon me, but perhaps another time," I tell her. "My grandfather is expecting me—"

"Expecting you to show this lovely young lady a good time?" the old man himself interrupts. "I heard she asked after a good red. Why don't you show her to the cellar?"

My jaw flexes as I meet my grandfather's gaze. I have nothing but love for the old man, but he is as stubborn as the day is long.

"Hello there." Grandfather extends his hand to Willow. "Pierre Blackwood. It's a pleasure to welcome you to the estate."

"The pleasure is all mine." Willow beams at him. "You have an incredible piece of paradise here."

"Thank you." He nods. "Don't mind my grandson here. He's all business, but he'd love to show you around the place, wouldn't you, Dax?"

He meets my gaze with a mischievous grin, and despite my irritation, I can't help caving in to his request, just as he knew I would. When it comes to my grandfather, there is little I would deny him. The man has raised me. He's given me a purpose and a passion and taught me everything I know, and now he's passing the estate into my care. It's an honor that comes with a lot of responsibility, and he knows I won't let him down. But he also can't seem to get it out of his mind that I need someone by my side, regardless of the countless times I've assured him things are fine just as they are.

"I suppose I could slip away for a few minutes," I concede, gesturing for Willow to follow me. "Come, let me show you the cellar."

3

WILLOW

Dax leads me around the cellar with a precision that proves he knows this place like the back of his hand. But beneath his cloak of civility, it's evident he'd rather be anywhere else right now. He's hardly even glanced at me, and if I were a woman with self-esteem issues, I might take it personally.

Unfortunately, I recognize Dax's hardened expression and his clipped tone all too well. He is emotionally closed off. Hard-hearted and bitter. And I can't even say that I blame him, considering the story his friends told me. But his jaded attitude can't dull the thumping of my heart as I study him. The photos really didn't do him justice. With his jet-black hair and dark brown eyes, he is the epitome of an Aussie heartthrob. Throw in his sun-kissed skin and the accent to die for and he'd be the perfect man, if only he didn't so clearly want nothing to do with me.

"Would you like to try a sample?" he asks over his shoulder.

"You don't have to do this." I pull the rip cord on this charade, and he turns to me with a puzzled expression.

"Pardon?"

"The tour." I gesture around the cellar. "It's lovely, certainly. And of course, I'd like to see it, but it isn't necessary for you to guide me if you have better things to do."

Bewilderment flashes in his eyes as he considers my statement. "Are you dismissing me?"

"I'm just offering you an easy out." I smirk. "I'm not here to ruin your evening, and it looks like that's all I'll be doing if I stay. So, if you don't mind, I think I'll just go."

I turn to leave, and he catches me around the arm. "Wait."

When I glance up at him, he's much closer than I remember him being. And at this distance, the intoxicating scent of his cologne is difficult to ignore. It's spicy and masculine, and I wouldn't mind sampling a taste of his lips right now, the way his dark eyes are boring into my soul.

"You're just going to leave?" He frowns as if the thought is unfathomable to him. The abrupt shift in his mood doesn't make any sense.

"I think that would be best," I murmur in complete contradiction to the fact that I can't stop staring at him.

He nods as if to say he agrees, but he still hasn't released me. When I glance down at his fingers, his gaze follows, and to my disappointment, his hand falls away.

"Good night, Dax." I force the words from my lips and head for the exit, only to be halted again a second later.

"Don't go," he requests in a gravelly voice. "You came here to see the place. Let me show it to you."

It isn't fair that I know his vulnerability and he knows nothing about mine. This whole night has been nothing but a disaster, and I'm certain the right thing for me to do is leave. But when I look at him, I also realize I don't want to.

"Stay," he commands, and involuntarily, I find myself nodding along.

Dax grabs a bottle and a couple glasses from the bar and pours two samples for me.

"Sangiovese." He hands me the first glass before pointing to the second. "Cab Sav. These are our most popular blends, but why don't you see what you think."

"I have to confess I know very little about wine." I swirl the liquid in the glass between my fingers. "I drink it on occasion, but—"

"All the better." Dax smirks. "I'd prefer you have nothing else to compare it to."

My cheeks warm as I hide my own smile behind the glass. I don't know what to make of this man. Cold one minute and hot the next. He's a mystery to me, but one I'd definitely like to unravel.

I dip my head forward, breathing in the aromas of the wine before I bring the glass to my lips. The flavors burst across my tongue, and I close my eyes, trying to identify exactly what it is I'm experiencing right now. But I don't know if it's the wine or the man serving it that has me so off-balance.

When I open my eyes, I'm surprised to find that his are on my lips. My wine-stained, cherry-red lips. The irises I thought couldn't get any darker pool with heat, and I feel it between my thighs.

What is happening right now?

"It's delicious," I murmur, trying and failing to find any other descriptions.

"Then let's just leave it at that," he answers with a rougher quality to his voice than he had just a moment ago. Or is that my imagination?

Dax swaps out my glass, and this time when I sample it, he goes on to point out some of the architectural features of the cellar. I listen with a keen ear, noting the passion in his tone with unadulterated admiration.

"You really love it here, don't you?" I graze my fingers over some of the woodwork as I examine the structure.

Dax pauses to meet my gaze again. "I do. This is my home. My lifeblood. This soil, the air, the sea, and the grapes. There is nothing else in this world like it."

"I'm inclined to agree." I peek down the hallway that leads into the garden. "I've seen a lot of places, but there is nothing quite like Australia."

"Would you care to see the lawns?" he asks.

"I would," I admit. "But only if it's no trouble."

"It's not," he answers with a note of regret.

I follow him outside, and he steers us toward the garden. It's a beautiful night for a walk, but the floral scent carried on the breeze only makes it more so.

"How long have you been here?" Dax asks.

"A few weeks." I pause to examine one of the roses. "I started my tour on the Gold Coast, but I only just came to South Australia a few days ago. I'm staying in Willunga."

"It's a nice area." He nods his approval. "There's a weekend market with a good selection of local produce, if you get a chance to check it out."

I can't tell whether he's inquiring how long I plan to stay or simply making an observation, so I just nod. But as we continue and Dax points out the different florals in the garden, I sink into a comfortable feeling I don't often have around others. On the occasions that we do fall into silence, I don't feel the need to fill those spaces as I normally would.

"You travel for work, I take it?" he asks as we wind our way into one of the vineyards. He no longer seems to have a destination in mind, but I'm content to follow him as we allow the noise of the party to fade into the background.

"I'm an actress," I confess. "It's not always a full-time job, but I get gigs in different places so I can travel. In between, I also end up doing a lot of odd jobs."

"An actress." He arches a brow at me. "I wouldn't have expected that."

"Thanks?" I laugh.

"I didn't mean it as an insult," he says. "It's just that you seem very grounded... and well—"

"You thought most actresses are divas?"

His lip tilts up at the corner, revealing a dimple in his cheek, and I can only imagine how hot he looks when he really smiles.

"Something like that," he admits a little sheepishly. "Don't get me wrong, I appreciate a woman who can dress up." His eyes roam over my black dress with a heat I know I'm not imagining this time. "But I also appreciate a woman who can get her hands dirty too."

"I've had my share of dirty hands." I laugh. "Farm work, fruit picking, stable work, cleaning. You name it, I've probably done it. That's the thing about being a perpetual backpacker. You end up doing a lot of the jobs nobody else wants."

Dax studies me, and in that moment, my entire world shifts. I don't know what it is about this man that makes me feel so tipsy. I've barely had a full glass of wine, but right now, I suspect I'm drunk on him.

"Don't you get tired of traveling?" he asks.

"Honestly?" I shrug. "Yes. But where do you go when nowhere really feels like home?"

I regret the words as soon as I say them, and Dax frowns. "Don't you have family somewhere back in the States?"

"I have an aunt I keep in contact with. We aren't very close, but she's the only real family I know."

"What about your parents?" His question surprises me, and when I look at him, I'm glad to see he isn't asking out of obligation but genuine curiosity.

"My father left when I was just a toddler," I admit. "And my mother wasn't around much when I was growing up. She dropped me off with whoever would take me for different lengths of time until eventually, she just didn't bother to come back at all."

"That's awful." Dax shakes his head, and he looks angry on my behalf.

"It wasn't great, but it wasn't horrible. I consider myself lucky I never had to go into foster care. But it makes it hard to feel connected to any particular place, you know? I got the travel bug when I was young, and I always thought I'd eventually find the right place to lay down roots."

"It's pretty bold," he says. "Traveling the world solo. It takes courage to do something like that. I took a gap year with a few mates, but I doubt any of us would have dared to try it indefinitely on our own."

"Well, you have no need." I smile up at him. "Everything you could ever want is right here, isn't it?"

He pauses to look around, and there's a peace that settles into his features I wish I could feel myself. But in a way, I do. Right here, in this moment. In this magical place. It's a balm to my soul.

"You're perceptive," he answers. "Not everybody sees it that way."

"They'd be crazy not to," I tell him.

He shrugs. "For some, this is just a machine. They see what it can bring them, not the land itself. The traditions or the pride or the hard labor and love that has gone into every bottle. There are some people who can only see the money."

His words feel like a test somehow, but I think it has more to do with his ex than anything else.

"The art of appreciation isn't for everyone," I concede. "But only the lucky few who can truly understand it."

Dax pauses again, and I feel his eyes on my profile, but I can't bring myself to look at him. This was supposed to be a fake date, but right now, it feels more real than anything else I've ever known. I'm not entirely sure what to make of it.

"Did you grow up on the estate?" I ask.

"Yes. My grandfather raised me after my parents died in a car accident."

"I'm so sorry," I offer, shaking my head. "That must have been really difficult."

"Losing them was the difficult part," he says. "But there was nothing difficult about being raised here. I had a good life. No complaints that I can speak of."

"He seems like a good man."

"He is. Albeit a little mischievous at times."

We both laugh at his implication, and then Dax leads us to a grassy hill with a seating pavilion nestled on top of it. The perfect place to sit and take everything in, which is exactly what we end up doing.

Between the comfortable silences, Dax asks me more about the places I've visited and my childhood in the States. We touch briefly on my time living with my aunt, and then I steer the conversation back to him.

"What about you? Any other tragic tales to put mine to shame?"

A shadow falls over his expression, and he shakes his head. "Nothing that's worth talking about."

I don't know why I say it. It's stupid and risky, and I have him at a disadvantage, but I want to hear the words from him.

"It seemed like you didn't really want to be here tonight. Like maybe there was someone you were avoiding."

His jaw flexes. "Was it that obvious?"

Guilt sinks into my gut like a rock. I can't lie to him. But I don't want to tell him the truth either. "It wasn't overly obvious. Just an observation."

"She's my ex." He leans back in the chair and studies the stars in the sky. "And the guy with her was my best mate. At least, he used to be. His family is in the wine business too. That's why they're here tonight."

"I take it they didn't wait until you were apart to um... hook up?"

Dax simply nods as if it's nothing more than fact now.

"Well, for what it's worth, I think it's very civil of you to have them at your party."

"I don't have much of a choice." He sighs. "We have to work together from time to time. Our families have always had good history. I can't let his indiscretions ruin generations of hard work and partnerships."

"That's a good attitude to have." I cross my arms and shiver. "Sometimes we just have to accept what isn't for us."

"Are you cold?" he asks.

"I'm okay." I shrug, and truly, I am. I could sit here all night staring up at the stars. The breeze is a little cool, but it's nothing compared to the beautiful view.

"Here." Dax shrugs out of his suit jacket and hands it to me. When he does, his arm brushes against mine, and we both freeze. Our gazes lock, and for a moment everything else slips away.

Dax frowns as if he doesn't quite understand what's happening between us. I'm glad I'm not the only one. When he helps me into the jacket, I curl into it with a contented sigh. It smells like him, and oddly enough, it makes me feel safe. It's not a feeling I'm accustomed to, and I'm not really sure how to handle that.

"I don't usually offer," he says. "But I could show you the main house if you'd like. It's probably a little warmer there."

"Don't you have a party to get back to?" I tease.

"It's my party." He glances down the hill. "I can leave when I want to. As long as the wine is flowing, I doubt anyone will even notice I'm gone."

I mull it over, trying to remember that I'm here for a fake date. *Not real.* And suddenly, I wish I weren't. I wish I had just come here and met Dax on my own without any contractual obligations or agreements that might muddle what seems to be happening naturally between us.

But how often have I felt this way? I can count the total of times on one finger, and that's including right now. It might be stupid, or reckless, or a million other things. But for the first time in my life, I decide to throw caution to the wind.

"I think I'd really like that, Dax."

4

DAX

Leading Willow down the tree-lined path to the Venetian-inspired villa I've called home for most of my life feels a little like walking into the eye of a hurricane. I'm not entirely sure why I wanted to bring her here, or why I'm studying her so closely as she takes it all in. When the full enormity of the structure comes into view, she halts completely, her head snapping up to mine.

"This is... your home?"

Her surprise catches me off guard.

"It is now," I concede. A fact I haven't shared with many people. "My great-grandfather designed and built it for his wife. Everything from the hand-cut tiles to the stained-glass windows, he had a part in."

"It's incredible," she murmurs. "Your life is like a fairy tale."

"I've been blessed with good fortune." I nod, but there's a hint of somberness in my tone, and Willow doesn't miss it.

It's ridiculous that I should feel lacking in anything, given her particular background. I have a family, a beautiful home, the best job in the world. Everything I could ever want or need. But I can't help feeling that there's still something missing from my life when I look at her.

"Does Pierre live on the property?" she asks curiously as I lead her up the stairs and open the door.

I shake my head. "When he decided to retire, he bought a boat, claiming he wanted to spend his days sailing. But truth be told, I think this place just had too many memories for him. When my grandmother passed, he wanted to start a new chapter. Not to forget her, just..."

"Somewhere he didn't feel so sad." Willow offers an understanding smile. "I get it."

And for the first time in many years, I feel like she's the only one who does.

"Let me show you around the place." I take her hand in mine, a gesture that seems to come naturally, and one she doesn't protest.

Over the next twenty minutes, I point out the architectural details I've come to love over the years. The gothic arches and stone accents. The cathedral ceilings and Palladian-style dome at the center of it all. Willow listens with interest as her fingertips graze over the smallest elements with an appreciation I often forget. Witnessing her fall in love with the artwork my great-grandfather created does something to my soul. And while she's busy admiring the hand-carved stone, I'm busy admiring her.

"It's so beautiful." She turns to meet my gaze. "But don't you ever get lonely here?"

I don't know what possesses me, but I'm caught up in the moment, and when my fingers graze her cheek, it feels right. When she inadvertently leans into my touch, I know she feels the same.

"It does," I admit.

She blinks, her eyes heavy and her gaze warm.

"It gets lonely here," I murmur right before my lips crash into hers.

She gasps and I swallow the sound as I take her into my arms. Somewhere in the back of my mind, I'm hoping she'll be the rational one. Maybe she'll tell me we shouldn't do this. Or that we just met. Or that I'm crazy for feeling this pull to her. But she only melts into me, kissing me back with a fire I don't want to put out. Not tonight. Not ever.

"This is insane," she sighs between kisses. "But it just feels so... *right*."

"I know." I discard the jacket wrapped around her and graze my palms over the curves of her shoulders as I drag her closer.

"I never do this," she adds. "I don't want you to think less of me—"

"I don't either," I admit as my mouth skates along the delicate arch of her throat. "There's something about you. I can't help myself."

"I thought it was just me," she breathes into the space between my neck and shoulder.

Our lips find each other again, and between frenzied gasps, I'm unzipping her dress while she fumbles over the buttons of my dress shirt. At the same time, I'm walking her backward, leading her toward my bedroom.

Logic has abandoned both of us. I was right about her from the moment I saw her. She's a temptress, and she has me under her spell. But right now, I simply don't give a fuck.

I shrug out of my shirt, and her eyes pause on the hard planes of my chest with an appreciation I'm coming to recognize well. She reaches out to touch my bare skin, tracing her fingers over the sun-kissed canvas that months of hard work under the brutal Aussie sun created.

When she presses her lips to my collarbone, she also breathes me in. A full-body shiver moves over her as I slide her dress off her shoulders. The fabric pools on the floor, and all that's left is a matching black lace bra and knickers. I'm so fucking hard I could blow right now just looking at her. I haven't been with a woman in the better part of a year. But Willow isn't just a woman. She's a goddess, and she doesn't even know it.

Her fingers skim the hard bulge in my trousers, and I shudder as she slowly tugs the zipper down. I don't know what I'm expecting from her, but when she sinks to her knees before me and kisses my cock through my briefs, it isn't that.

My fingers tangle in her hair, and she rubs the length of my arousal with her palm, teasing me through the cotton fabric. It's enough to make me forget what year I'm in or why I ever thought this was a bad idea to begin with.

When she tugs the briefs down and my cock falls out, she wraps her palm around the thick base and drags the head to her cherry-red lips. Fucking hell. She closes her lips around my shaft and pulls me deeper into the warmth of her mouth. The slow, tortuous assault of her tongue nearly brings me to my knees as the silky strands of her auburn hair tickle my fingers.

It would be so easy to let her keep going, but I'm not even close to done with her yet.

"I want to feel you." I tug her up into my arms and palm her between her thighs. "Here."

She moans into my mouth, and I walk her back to the bed as I unclasp her bra, freeing the most beautiful pair of tits I've ever seen in my life. Her skin is velvety soft, and when I dip my head to take one of her pink nipples into my mouth, she tastes sweeter than I ever could have imagined.

She bucks against me as I slip my fingers into her knickers and slide them through her arousal. When I find her clit, she curls her hands around my biceps and buckles onto the bed. I chase her, sliding her knickers down over her hips and kicking off my trousers. We're skin to skin when I thrust my cock against her wetness, and she pulls my face back to hers, devouring me like I'm what she really thirsted for tonight.

In the back of my mind, I consider that there was something I needed to do. But that thought escapes me as she arches her body into mine and spreads her legs, inviting me in. My cock is soaked in her want for me, and when I bump against her opening, I only have the intention of feeling her for just a second.

That second turns into a full minute when I bury myself deep within her warmth. Our lips and teeth clash with a fervor I haven't experienced even to a fraction of this degree. She squeezes my body against hers, her head falling back into the pillow as I thrust deep between her thighs.

My fingers find her clit again as I suck her breast into my mouth, flicking her sensitive nipple with my tongue. Tension builds, the only sounds between us the slapping of my body against hers, drowned out by our ragged breaths. When she begins to tremble around me, I increase my pace, driving her into the bed as I send her completely over the edge.

She digs her nails into my back and comes with a long, stuttered sigh. Her body milking my cock is too fucking much. The sight of her flushed skin. Her swollen lips. Her heavy-lidded eyes. Every detail pushes me past the point of no return. I'm merely a prisoner in my own body as I collapse into her and unleash my aching cock deep into her womb.

It's a fact I can't ignore. I took her raw, and I just came inside of her. The thought should terrify me. But when I open my eyes to meet hers, all I feel is a deep sense of satisfaction as she grazes the side of my face with her fingers.

"Dax?" she murmurs.

"Hmm?"

"Can we do that again?"

5

WILLOW

Sunlight filters in through the gauzy curtains of Daxon's bedroom, waking me with the natural rhythm of the earth. When I open my eyes, my heart jumps as I catch him watching me, his arm still wrapped around my waist.

We're both naked, curled against each other, and it's the most intimate night I've ever spent with anyone. It feels like a dream, and there's a part of me that dreads waking from it.

"Good morning," he greets me with a raspy voice.

"Good morning." I smile up at him.

Somewhere downstairs, the sound of a door shutting echoes through the house, and his brows pinch together before a familiar voice floats up the stairs.

"Oi, Daxo. You alive up there?"

"Shit." He scrubs a hand over his face and shakes his head. "That would be Bazza. Probably Dave too."

That one simple sentence is enough to douse me with ice water. *His friends.* The same friends that set this entire thing up. How could I so easily forget that?

Daxon has no idea what really brought me here, and suddenly everything feels like a lie. But how can I tell him that when he's looking at me the way he is right now?

"I should go deal with them," he grumbles. "They have a tendency to stop by often."

Before he's even out of bed, there's a knock on the bedroom door, and Dax throws the blanket over both of us as Bazza peeks his head in.

"Oi, did you hear me?" He startles when he sees me peeking out from beneath Dax's quilt. "Oh, good morning there, Willow."

A smile curves Bazza's lips, and he shakes his head. "Sorry for the interruption, mate. Didn't know you had company."

"I'll meet you downstairs." Dax looks at him sharply.

"I brought pastries." Bazza winks. "There's enough for everybody."

"Go," Dax orders pointedly, but his chest shakes with laughter the minute Bazza pops back out the door.

"Sorry about that." He leans in and kisses my temple as if it's the most natural thing in the world. "They're like brothers to me. Sometimes, they forget boundaries."

"It's okay." I force a smile as I consider how to spill the beans.

"Why don't you take a shower first," he offers. "I'll go downstairs and put some coffee on."

"Okay," I croak.

Dax slips into some track pants and a T-shirt and combs a hand through his hair before he throws me a wink and leaves me to get cleaned up. I drag myself into his palatial bathroom and spend the entirety of my twenty-minute shower trying to conjure up the best way to explain this situation to him. But the truth is, I'm worried it doesn't matter how I explain it. Dax has trust issues. That much is obvious to anybody. And I'm terrified that the second he discovers the facts, this will be over before it even begins.

I could run out of here with my tail between my legs and preserve this one perfect night in my memory for all of eternity. Or I could tell him the truth, which is what he deserves, and risk imploding it all. Either way, it feels like I lose.

The magic I felt upon waking up in his bed dissipates with every step as I make my way down the curved staircase to meet him in the kitchen. As I suspected, Dave and Bazza have both joined in on the morning's brunch, and from the looks of it, they won't be going anywhere anytime soon.

"Heya, Willow." Dave winks at me when I step inside the room. "Why don't you join us?"

I sit down at the table, and Dax offers me a plate with croissants and fruit.

He seems so much more open this morning, it almost kills me as I smile at him without betraying my nerves.

"How do you like your coffee, love?" he asks affectionately.

"Just some milk will do," I answer.

He brings me the necessary utensils and a cup before giving my shoulders a squeeze.

"Hope you don't mind," he says. "I already ate. I was starving."

"Not at all," I assure him as my belly rumbles in agreement. I think I know why we're both starving this morning.

"I'm going to take a quick shower," he tells us. "Be down shortly."

I nod and he disappears, and it takes Dave all of two seconds to bring up the elephant in the room.

"I can't thank you enough for doing this," he says. "Daxo looks bloody well satisfied this morning."

"I didn't anticipate anything happening last night." I narrow my eyes at him. "It just did. And I want to be clear, it wasn't because of our arrangement. In fact, I want to call the whole thing off. Please just forget you ever asked me."

"But I've already written you a check." He pats his pocket and drags the evidence out, sliding it in front of me. "A deal is a deal."

"The deal is off," I insist. "I don't want it. And I'm going to tell Dax the truth, just as soon as—"

"Tell me what truth?" Dax's voice startles me from behind.

My heart leaps into my throat, and Dave's face pales at the same time. We both try to reach for the check, but Dax gets to it first. When he sees my name scribbled on the recipient line, his entire body goes rigid.

"What the fuck is this?" he growls.

Nobody speaks. I don't know what to say, and I'm trying desperately to find the words when Bazza chimes in.

"It was just a harmless arrangement," he says. "It's no big deal, Daxo."

"What arrangement?" His eyes pierce into mine, and I know it has to come from me. I need to make him understand.

"They hired me to be your date last night," I blurt, and his face turns to stone. "But I had no idea it was your friends. I thought I was talking to you, and then I arrived—"

"You hired me a goddamn hooker?" He stares at his friends in disbelief before returning his arctic gaze to me.

"I'm not a hooker." The words tumble from my mouth with obvious horror. "I'm an actress. And I didn't expect any of this, Dax. What happened last night had nothing to do with what they asked of me. You need to know that. I planned to tell you everything this morning. Honestly—"

"I want you out." He gestures to the door. "Grab your shit and leave. Bazza and Dave, you can fuck off too."

Tears sting my eyes as he storms from the kitchen without waiting for a reply. As bad as I considered his reaction would be, this is so much worse. And my humiliation only intensifies as tears start to leak from my eyes.

"God, this was so stupid of me," I mutter under my breath as I stumble to my feet.

"Please don't go." Bazza stands up to help me. "He just needs a few minutes. Let him cool off—"

"No, he's right." I shake my head. "We tricked him. I should have never agreed to it. Please take your money; I don't want it."

They both protest as I exit the kitchen and flee toward the door, but it doesn't matter. I know in my heart, any chance I may have had with Daxon is completely ruined. I shattered his trust, and for that, I have nobody else to blame but myself.

6

DAXON

"Hey, Dax." Twila squeezes my arm with a familiarity she has no right to. "It's good to see you."

I grunt a response, focusing my gaze on the inventory list in front of me. I don't know what she's doing here, but whatever it is, it can't be good.

"It's been a while." She smiles as I finally meet her gaze.

"Not long enough, Twila."

Her eyes shine with emotion, and she nods. "I guess you've moved on. That woman from the event, I take it? I heard she's an actress."

Her observation pricks at the still-raw wound in my gut whenever I think of Willow. It's been three months, and I can't seem to forget her. Her scent still lingers on my suit, which I haven't brought myself to wash just yet. But it's the image of her tear-streaked face when I told her to leave that haunts my sleep and every waking hour.

I feel like an asshole, but every time I consider what she did, the pain is an excuse to justify my behavior. After all, that's the reason I said I didn't want another relationship. The lies, the manipulation, the schemes. I tell myself she's just like every other woman before her, but it feels less true over the passage of time.

Bazza and Dave have been insistent to remind me that she had no intention of taking the money, and in fact, she called the whole thing off. That may be true, but she still didn't tell me. She waited for it to implode before she confessed. And while I can't blame her for getting wrapped up in what she thought was an honest business deal, I can blame her for being dishonest.

"We aren't together," I answer Twila solemnly.

Hope shines in her eyes, and she dares to reach out and touch my arm again. And when I shrug her off, it occurs to me how indifferent I feel toward her now. At one point in time, I used to think she was beautiful, but now, I could pass her on the street without ever pausing to look twice. Because her hair isn't red, and her eyes aren't green, and she isn't the temptress who branded herself into my soul without me even being aware of it.

"Daxo." Dave inserts himself into the conversation, offering a pointed look at Twila. "We need you, mate. Big wine crisis down at one of the distributors."

I shut the logbook with a frown and offer Twila a dismissive nod before Dave drags me out of the restaurant and toward his car.

"What's going on?" I ask.

"I'll tell you on the way," he says. "Just get in. It's urgent."

I don't trust his version of urgent, and it feels like there's something amiss here again. But I've come to accept that Dave and Bazza are a little like the two stooges. They have the best of intentions, but things don't always go to plan. While I've forgiven them for the humiliation of three months ago, I still haven't forgotten.

Dave opens the passenger door of his Ute and practically shoves me inside before he races around to the driver's seat and fires up the engine. Thirty minutes later, he still hasn't told me which distributor is having the supposed crisis, and when we pull up to the airport, it becomes evident I've been played again.

"What the hell is going on?" I demand as he turns to me with a sheepish grin.

"I'm doing what your pride won't allow you to," he informs me. "Willow is boarding a flight out of Australia tomorrow. But if you get to Melbourne today, she has one last shift at her job. There's still time to catch her."

His announcement drowns out the protest I already had prepared for this argument. *Willow is leaving.* And I know as well as Dave does that once she gets on that plane, I'll never see her again. But that's what I wanted, wasn't it?

"This is your last chance," Dave tells me. "What are you going to do, Dax?"

7

WILLOW

“You can take off a few minutes early if you want,” my coworker whispers in my ear as I close the register. “I know you have to pack tonight.”

“Thanks,” I murmur. “I’ll just take this last customer first.”

It’s a grand intention until I look up to find the dark eyes that have haunted my dreams for the last three months.

“Daxon?” I blurt in disbelief. “What are you doing here?”

His eyes drift over my face, and his features pinch as he seems to come to a silent conclusion. “I was going to order a coffee,” he says. “But if you’re almost finished, I’d rather just speak with you.”

His offer catches me off guard, and I’m not sure what to make of it. What are the chances that he’d be in Melbourne, at the very same coffee shop I’m working my last shift in tonight?

I glance at my coworker, and she gives me a nod and a wink as I untie my apron and gesture to one of the seats in the corner. “I’ll meet you out there in a second.”

He nods and makes himself comfortable while I finger comb my hair and peek at my reflection in the shiny surface of the coffee machine. I wasn’t expecting to see him today, or ever again, and I am woefully unprepared.

“You look fine,” Sophie whisper hisses. “Now get out of here.”

I don’t feel as certain as she is, but I swallow down my nerves and meet Dax at the table. He’s dressed casually, in a button-down shirt and jeans. He looks as gorgeous as I remember, and it only makes the pain in my heart throb when I consider how we left things.

"You look tired," he observes with a frown.

"I am," I admit. "I've been working a lot."

Tension fills the space between us, and I'm not sure what else to say. Why is he here? What does he want to talk to me about? I have a million questions, but none that I'm brave enough to voice out loud.

"Willow." He clears his throat, and his eyes fall to mine. "Dave told me you refused the money. He also explained the entire scheme, and the only conclusion I keep coming back to is that I'm an asshole. A prideful one at that. The things I said to you that day—"

"I was going to tell you," I interject, my voice wavering with uncharacteristic emotion. "That morning, I had every intention—"

His features soften, and he extends his hand to mine. "I know. It was just easier to believe you were like everyone else in my past. I kept telling myself that so I wouldn't chase after you, but now I finally realize I was being incredibly stupid."

My head dips to hide the fact that I'm on the verge of tears. "What we shared that night, I can't even begin to tell you how much that meant to me. I haven't stopped thinking of you, but I knew I had to let you go. I have a plane ticket tomorrow, and I'm going back to the States."

"What if I asked you not to?" he pleads. "Would you stay?"

My throat bobs as I choke down my feelings. "It isn't that simple, Dax."

"Why?" He looks crestfallen, and I can't stand the thought of hurting him anymore. But he deserves to know the truth this time, without hesitation.

"My time for traveling and living my life on a whim has come to an end. It's time for me to grow some roots. And as much as I love it here, I can't stay permanently. There are visas and other things that complicate matters."

"We'll get you a new one," he says. "We'll make it work."

"Dax, I'm pregnant," I blurt. "We didn't use any protection, remember?"

His face pales, and he looks so shocked I rush to get the rest of my intentions out.

"I didn't want to ask you for anything. I didn't want you to think this was my way of tricking you into something. And I still don't. I can raise this baby on my own. I don't expect anything from you, honestly."

"No." He looks horrified by the idea, and before I can comprehend what's happening, he's dragging me up into his arms and forcing my gaze to his. "I can't... I don't want that, Willow."

"What do you mean?" I frown.

"This baby is ours, and it should be raised by the both of us. Here in Australia, with two parents and a real family. You can lay down roots here. We can lay them down together."

I smile because it's everything I could ever want, but I have to be realistic. "I don't want you to do this out of obligation. That isn't what I'm looking for."

"It isn't." He strokes my face beneath his palm, his lips lingering a breath away from mine. "I came here to get you back, and that hasn't changed. I have no regrets except for the time I already wasted. This baby is the start of something great. An adventure we can take together. I want to be with you; it's just that simple. The only thing you have to consider is if you want that too."

The restrained hope in his eyes nearly brings me to tears. I know this man has been hurt in the past. He's been betrayed, and this isn't an easy thing for him to do. But the fact that he's here, laying it all out for me, tells me everything I need to know.

"Okay." I smile up at him in confirmation. "Let's take this adventure together, Dax. If that's really what you want."

"It is." His lips crash into mine, and for a moment, I forget everything else around us. When we finally come back up for air, I feel drunk all over again, and I know he feels it too.

"You know what?" His fingers tangle in my hair as he brings his lips to my ear.

"Hmm?" I close my eyes and breathe him in.

"I think I was always meant to be yours."

* * *

TAKEN BY THE HOBO

KAYTI MCGEE

1

My every day is exactly the same. I wake up, take a quick shower, and swing by the coffee shop on my way to work. I know all the finance blogs say I should make coffee at home and save the money, but letting someone else do the work makes me happy. Four dollars a day worth of happy. There's always a busker outside of the shop, it being a corner that gets a lot of foot traffic, so I drop my change in the hat/bucket/guitar case of the day and head into my building to do another day's identical work of answering calls and filing paperwork.

Today's busker is better than normal. He's singing Bob Dylan and playing guitar. He's got soul. As evidenced by the pants he's wearing, covered in kangaroos. It takes a confident, soulful man to wear those pants. When I drop my dollar in his case, he looks up and gives me a huge smile. I notice two things at the same time. First, the facial tattoos. Terrifying. Second, the smile is adorable, and I float a little on into work.

He's still there when I leave for lunch, having moved on to Sublime covers. This time, I get a wink along with the smile. The tattoos under his eyes read *super* and *sleepy*, and you know, I feel that. I am too.

It's a real shame that he's clearly a homeless felon, because he looks like a good time. But only one type of person tattoos their face.

On my way back in, bag of food for the office in hand, he switches his song midway to "There She Goes," and I just about drop my bag of burritos laughing. I turn back, and he's singing directly at me. I'm definitely going to give him a second dollar after work.

But when I walk out into the waning sunlight at five, he's gone.

It's probably for the best. I can't afford to get attached to hobos, my coffee habit is expensive enough.

But lo and behold, the next morning he's back, wearing a koala-printed suit that was probably actually free from Goodwill it's so ugly. I don't know today's song, it's kind of hip-hop, but it sounds cool. Against my better judgment, I buy a second coffee and leave it next to the guitar case. He seamlessly transitions to "In Other Words" and does a flawless Frank Sinatra impression. It's such a shame he didn't pursue music professionally instead of tattooing *do not enter* above his right eyebrow.

Such a shame, in fact, that I find myself thinking about it multiple times through the morning. It's very disruptive, and I'm not happy.

I accidently file several pieces of legal paperwork under *H*. *H* for hot. *H* for hobo. *H* for heaven help me. It's just that I'm a little bit of a sucker for guitar players. Me and about ninety-five percent of the population, I know, but still. Surely that's the issue here. If he stops singing and starts talking, I'm dead certain I'll get over this creepy crush I'm developing. I always do. The guy who plays guitar at parties is never the guy you actually want to date.

So on today's lunch run, I grab extra for him. It's worth that seven-dollar value meal, too, to see the joy on his face when I walk up and set it down next to him.

"I *love* chicken tenders! How did you guess?" I blink at him as he happily puts the guitar down and looks at the sauce packet options.

"Just lucky, I suppose." Because it would be rude to say that he just looks like the type of person who enjoys fast food. Which is probably a little bit stereotypical of me, too. Homeless felons with facial tattoos might have exceptional taste in food for all I know. But this one... may not.

"Man, this is just what I needed today. Hey, how about I take you out tonight? Repay the favor?"

I'm stunned. Truly at a loss for words. Where would he take me? A soup kitchen? A Dexter kill room? And yet, I already know what I'm going to say.

"Okay. Did you... did you want to swing by mine first? You could take a shower, or whatever..." I trail off as he stares at me. Is this rude? I don't know what the etiquette is. I've only been a hobosexual for about twenty-four hours, this is all new.

"People always think I need a shower," he says, popping a piece of chicken into his mouth. "But I'll be fine. Here, let me write down an address for you, and you can just meet me there. Seven sound good?"

I'm nodding but also nervous. *He'll* be good, but will I?

I hustle back to the office, bagful of cooling chicken in tow. What have I agreed to? Curse my inability to say no to sparkly-eyed street urchins! No one speaks to me for the rest of the day, probably because I'm putting out strong vibes of some sort or another. Just before leaving at five, I knock on my boss's door.

She's my boss, yeah, but she's also my best friend.

"Hey, girl. Do you have a second?"

She looks up, grins, and beckons me in. "What's up? I have overtime if you want it. The Bentley case is shaping up to be a doozy, and I know you were hoping to save a little money this year."

"Actually, that would have been a much better decision. Next week?"

"Sure. What was your bad decision? You didn't have dairy at lunch, did you? Because you *know* better." She's already rummaging through her drawer for a Lactaid.

"No, no. I just agreed to a date." At that, she slams the drawer and opens her purse.

"Thank God. Here's a few condoms from my personal stash. Do you have a picture? Let's stalk him on social."

I take a deep breath.

"I don't know how to find him on social. I don't know his name. He's, uh... today's busker." I nod toward her window, which overlooks the corner he stands on. She tries to stand up to go look, but she's laughing too hard to actually get any momentum out of the chair.

"The one with tattoos on his face?"

I grimly confirm.

"Maybe double bag it, then. He looks like he just emerged from a rugby scrum of low-rent strippers outside the Taco Bell." I narrow my eyes. She isn't wrong. "That being said, there's sort of something about him, isn't there? When I walked in this morning, he was singing Elvis to a couple of old ladies. It was cute."

She isn't wrong there either. There *is* something about him. Which is why I've got to leave if I'm going to have time to both get cute and recharge my pepper spray.

"Anyways, I'm dropping you a pin so you can track my location. Please notify the appropriate authorities if I don't check in by midnight." There's no such thing as a graceful exit from this conversation, and her cackles follow me down the hall. I tuck the condoms in my purse before anyone else notices.

I mean. Just in case.

I get home with enough time to take a quick shower of my own and blow my hair out. I don't want to look *too* good for wherever he plans to take me. I play my outfit casual too, high-waisted plaid pants, a cropped T-shirt, and kitten heels. Just mascara and lip gloss on my face. It's good enough. I order a ride and type in the address he gave me.

"Wait a minute," I say out loud. "*Olive Garden?*" Welp.

He's already there when I get there, which is nice. I appreciate timeliness in a person. He's decked head to toe in another one of his suits, this one emblazoned all over with stills from the movie *Spice World*. I immediately turn into one of those memes where my brain tells my mouth, *Don't say it. Don't say it. Don't say it.* And then my mouth opens and tells him, "*Spice World* is my favorite fucking movie of all time, and I know every single word to it by heart."

He laughs and hands me a glass of wine that he's preordered. I choose to believe there will not be a roofie in it, based on absolutely nothing but the Spice Girls. No one who proudly wears their faces all over his body can be all bad.

"This suit brings a lot of joy," he says, running one tattooed hand over his French braid. "I hope you like Olive Garden. It's my favorite restaurant."

"I don't know if I've ever been," I have to confess.

"Oh, wow. You're in for a real treat. There is so much free stuff here!" And now it's starting to come together. Our server comes by with a giant bowl of salad and a basket of breadsticks, and my date actually claps. Our server turns bright red and bolts. He's probably intimidated by the tattoos, too. And the fresh coat of nail polish. And perhaps a tad by the French braid. Certainly not by the Spice.

He dishes out some salad for me, quite the gentleman. "So, what's your name, anyway?"

"Cady." I take a sip of the wine. It's very grape-y.

"Oh, cool, like in *Mean Girls*!"

Okay, hold up. He's got extremely bold fashion, Spice Girls joy, drinks wine, *and* knows teen movies? Maybe I won't need the condoms after all. But on the other hand, if he plays for my team, I might just be in love.

"I'm Dallas Mail, officially, by the way."

I shake his hand across the table. "Nice to meet you, Dallas, officially. You're very talented."

"Thanks! It's nice to get away from it all and just enjoy the music, you know?"

I nod like I know, but I don't. I'm an executive assistant at a law firm in a midwestern city. My idea of getting away from it all and enjoying the music is watching *The Voice* before bed. Besides, what's he getting away from—his parole officer?

Before I have the chance to think too hard on it, our red-faced server shows back up with a plate in each hand. "I know you like these," he squeaks out before fleeing again.

Wow, Dallas is really scaring the bejesus out of this poor kid. But the good news is, I just got... "Chicken parmesan, extra crispy! He *does* know what I like! Hey, do you want some more wine? We can get a lot more samples."

What the hell, I think. I haven't been on a date in over a year. Just because this one is thriftier than my grandma doesn't mean I shouldn't enjoy myself.

Besides, he's doing that giant grin again, and it's surprisingly hard to say no to that inked-up cute little face of his.

"Let's do it." Famous last words.

A bottle apiece later, I'm having the best date of my life. Dallas is hilarious. I can't imagine any of these stories are true, but who cares? Anyone who wants to make up a story of getting cursed by an evil ghost after touching the box it lives in is entertaining enough in my book.

"It's true! I was in a car wreck after that, then the robbery, then almost a plane crash... It was a crazy time in my life, man." I wipe tears of laugher away from my eyes. The restaurant is starting to close around us. How did time fly that fast? I take a deep breath and decide to just go for it.

"Do you want to come back to my apartment for a nightcap?"

He grins again and nods as he gets up to go pay.

"Don't worry. The curse is broken, so you're safe with me." And bizarrely, I do feel like that's true. Heaven help me if my mother ever found out what I've been up to. I covertly text my boss that we're headed back to my place and immediately put it on silent so I won't have to hear the inevitable barrage of texts back coming in. Then I order us a ride, because I'm certain this dinner has set him back quite a bit.

The ride back to my place is only about ten minutes, and he spends it singing along to the radio. It helps calm any of my lingering concerns about sleeping with a guy with face tattoos. Talent trumps tats, for sure.

I unlock my door and invite Dallas inside. He heads straight for the kitchen and opens the fridge to put our leftovers away. "If you don't want these, I will definitely eat them later. Oh, hey, Bud Light's my favorite!" I had completely forgotten I had those. I think they were left over from making beer cheese soup or something like a year ago. He happily pops one open, and then divides it among two champagne glasses he takes off my bar cart. I'm starting to think there's almost nothing that doesn't make him happy. It's very pure and wholesome.

We clink our glasses, and I lead him to my bedroom.

I set my glass down on the nightstand and help him take his *Spice World* suit jacket off. This close to him, I'm relieved to smell soap. He *has* showered recently. I rise up on my tiptoes, and he lowers his head and kisses me.

It's tentative at first, figuring out each other's rhythms, but it gets deeper and longer and his hands are on my cheeks and it's all very swoony. At some point we move to the bed, him kicking off his sparkly cowboy boots, and me pulling my shirt over my head. I scrabble around in my purse with one hand, looking for the condoms, while I keep kissing him. I wonder if he has tattoos on his dick.

A few minutes later, I am pleased to report that he does not, although, "I'm not ruling it out," he says.

I sort of assumed that a guy who looks like him would be into some weird kinky shit, but we end up in missionary, doing lots of kissing and hand-holding. It's all very cute and romantic.

I never pictured myself here, but life is full of surprises.

Like the one I have the next morning, after two more rounds of really good sex, when I offer to give him a lift to his corner.

"Oh, that's really nice, but I'm actually flying out today." I stare at him uncomprehendingly. He couldn't possibly have made that much money busking, could he? "Back home?" he tries again. "I have to start making the new record?"

Home?

Record?

And will I have to wait another year to get laid again?

My mind is swirling with questions, some more important than others.

"You really don't know who I am, do you?" He tucks his T-shirt into his Spice pants. "Haha! I thought you were just being discreet."

"Oh, God, are you on a wanted list?" That could explain a *lot.*

"Not exactly. I'm a Grammy nominee."

I'm highly suspicious. He pulls his phone out of his Spice pocket and does a search before handing it over for me to see the results. And sure as shit, under the name Mail Postone, he does appear to be a famous musician. I am *aghast.*

"Honestly, I just assumed you were a homeless felon."

"And you took me home anyways? I'm worried about you."

"Me too, Dallas. Me too. Well, I have to get to work..."

He pulls on his Spice jacket and takes his phone back.

"Same. I have to add up how much money I made on the street this week and write a check. I saw this picture of a koala with bandaged hands on the Internet, and I was like, man, I gotta do some charity shit for Australia. So I'm donating that money, and we shot some footage I can use for a video for the song I'm also donating proceeds from. Also, I have to write a song to donate proceeds from."

I am shook. You could knock me over with a feather, seriously. A honk sounds from outside, and he kisses me once more before running out to hop in the back of the limo that's currently idling in my lot.

My boss is going to *die.*

And a month later, I pretty much do too, because I open my mail to find a plane ticket and a note:

They opened a new Olive Garden by me, let's go get some free shit.

He didn't sign it but hardly needed to. I pull my weekend bag out of my closet and start filling it with clothes. I have a hobo to catch.

* * *

Do you want more of Kayti McGee?

One click SCREWMATES now!

PRESTON

TRINITY ACADEMY SERIES

MICHELLE HEARD

Australian finches were a big part of my life for twelve years.
My days were filled with taking care of them, and they provided me with so much happiness.

I'm dedicating this one to all the people out there working hard to save Australian wildlife during the devastating wildfires.
You're in my prayers.

ACKNOWLEDGMENTS

Sheldon, you're my everything.

The moment I got the email for Skye, I was beside myself with excitement. To be able to take part in this anthology is such an honor. I'm unbelievably thankful for this opportunity to help make a difference.

Sherrie, Sheena, and Leeann – Thank you for listening to me ramble, for reading and rereading the Trinity Academy series with me.

A special thank you to every blogger and reader who took the time to take part in the cover reveal and release day.

Love ya all tons ;)

SYNOPSIS

Nerd.

Four eyes.

I'm used to hearing the names.

Growing up, it bothered me, but not anymore.

I've done something most only dream of. At the age of twenty, I've become irreplaceable to the heirs of CRC Holdings.

I've aligned myself with the most powerful families in America, and it's starting to pay off.

People say money can't buy you happiness, but I beg to differ. A taste of wealth has brought me status, recognition, and friends. Being awkward, though, the only thing that still evades me is love.

That is until I cross paths with a crazy bird-loving girl.

1

Please Note: *This is a* ***stand-alone*** *spin-off from the Trinity Academy series.*

Preston

With my friends being away for the first two weeks of our summer break, I feel a little lost. The past year I've thrown myself into my mission to become an assistant to one of the monarchs of Trinity Academy. It's a coveted position I've managed to snag.

Technically speaking, I'm Lake Cutler's assistant, but I've been working with Falcon Reyes and even got to help out Mason Chargill. The three heirs of CRC Holdings have changed my life, and for that, they have my absolute loyalty.

I was just another geek with too thick glasses and an awkward personality to match before they became my friends. Helping Mason take revenge on Serena Weinstock and her corrupt father for trying to drown Kingsley, Mason's girlfriend, was the highlight of my year.

It has given me friends who would walk through fire for each other, and it's boosted my self-confidence sky-high.

Since I've been a student at Trinity Academy, I've learned I don't have to look like a supermodel to fit in. Not that I'm bad looking, but being atypical and gawky doesn't exactly help in the love department. Not that I'll know what to do if a girl showed interest in me.

My phone beeps in my hand, and a notification shows I have a message from Falcon.

A small grin plays around my mouth as I tap on the screen to open the text while walking toward the park near my parents' house.

Falcon: Wish you were here. You should come.

There's a photo attached of the Namib desert where Falcon and the group have traveled with their families.

Hitting reply, I let out a chuckle.

Preston: As beautiful as it looks, I don't think my sinuses would be able to handle all that sand.

Dots appear after Falcon has read my message.

Falcon: Excuses, excuses. Rest well while I'm gone. We have a lot of work to do once I'm back.

Preston: Yes, boss.

Something smacks into my glasses, and for a moment, I can only see a blur. The instant my eyes focus on the flapping feathers, I let out a screech and startle so badly my phone goes flying into the air.

"Ahhh... crap... help... get it away... crap..." I keep shrieking like a girl, not caring about my fragile image as I try to swat the bird away from my face.

"Stop hitting at it!" a girl yells, which has me freezing on the spot, staring wide-eyed at the feathered creature as it perches on the frame of my glasses. "Stay perfectly still."

Asking me to stand still right now while one of my worst fears is staring me right in the eyes, literally, is near impossible, but before I can yank my glasses off, a pair of hands reaches for the bird. I'm a squinting, shivering mess as I watch the girl pick up the vile creature, and then she cradles the damn thing like a baby while having the audacity to scowl at me.

"You could've hurt him," she snaps at me, the frown on her forehead deepening.

"Me?" I manage to gasp. "The thing attacked me."

Scoffing at me, she rolls her eyes. "Oh, please. Chopper is harmless."

Chopper? She named the beast?

"Certainly didn't seem harmless when it was trying to take out my eyes," I argue.

Remembering my phone, I glance around and then walk over to where it's lying on the path. When I pick it up and see the shattered screen, I hold it up so the girl can see. "Definitely not harmless, seeing as it broke my phone."

"Chopper didn't break your phone," she disputes, sticking her pointy nose in the air as she lifts her chin. "You broke it when you threw it."

Frowning at the girl, I shake my head. "Only because your bird almost gave me a heart attack. The thing scared the living daylights out of me. Shouldn't it be on a leash or in a cage?"

When the girl begins to walk toward me, my eyes widen, and the fear I felt a moment ago comes rushing back with every step she takes. "Chopper is completely harmless. See?" She shoves the bird closer to my face, and I blink a couple of times from delayed shock.

Beady black eyes stare at me from where it's perched on her finger.

Letting out an awkward squawk, I lurch backward. "Get that thing away from me!"

The girl instantly cradles the creature against her chest as if to protect it from me, then tilts her head. "You're really scared of birds?"

Looking up at the sky for divine intervention because it's too hard to talk to this girl, I shake my head. "I think that would be pretty obvious."

"I've never met anyone who's afraid of birds before. You should touch Chopper. I bet the moment you see he won't hurt you, you won't be scared anymore."

I take a deep breath to try and push the growing frustration down. "That's not happening in this lifetime. Give me your number or address so I can give you the bill for my phone once it's repaired."

She lets out a chuckle as if I said something funny. "You're kidding, right?"

"No." Shaking my head again makes my glasses slip down my nose a little. I shove them back into place before I continue, "Your bird broke the phone, so you should pay for the repairs."

"This is ridiculous, but okay. Do you have something to write my details down on?"

Shoving the broken phone in my pocket, I say, "Just tell me. I have a good memory."

She quickly blurts out her number and address then starts to walk away from me. Not being in immediate danger any longer, I begin to notice what the girl looks like. Other people would call her cute with her light brown hair cut in a bob around her heart-shaped face.

From over her shoulder, she calls, "By the way, I'm Katie."

"Oh... ahh... Preston. Preston Culpepper."

"See you around, Preston Culpepper."

2

Katie

I keep chuckling whenever I remember Preston Culpepper's reaction to Chopper.

"Like you could hurt a fly," I mumble to my pet budgie. I fell in love with birds when I visited my family in Australia five years ago. Since then, I've set up aviaries in my parents' backyard and have been breeding all kinds of species. This year was the first time I managed to breed with my tiny flock of gouldian finches.

While I was changing the water this morning, Chopper decided to fly off, and it took me a whole hour to find him.

"You gave your mother a big fright, little man. Don't fly off like that again. That guy could've hurt you," I croon lovingly while petting his yellow head. I caress a finger down his light green back then grin at him. "You're so pretty."

Checking right and left, I cross the road. I find myself glancing over my shoulder back at the park opposite from my house, but unable to see Preston, I slip in the side gate of our property.

"He was funny," I murmur while walking around the side of the house. "I wonder whether he'll really send me the bill?"

Chopper answers with a squawk before he takes flight. He circles the backyard a couple of times then lands on a tree stump I have set up outside of his cage. Preening his feathers, he forgets all about his impromptu adventure.

I pour fresh water into a bucket and open the gate to my gouldian aviary. Setting the bucket down, I begin to fill their water dispensers, and when I'm done, I glance up at the brightly colored birds all perched in the highest corner of the cage.

"Y'all need to start laying eggs for mamma," I say before I step out of the cage. I watch them all flock down to the fresh water and feel the familiar tinge of worry.

I only have four pairs left of the original nine pairs I had. Every winter, I lose a pair, and it's heartbreaking. Unfortunately, gouldians aren't the best of parents and sometimes just refuse to nest at all.

Letting out a sigh, I walk over to the next aviary where my bechinos are. They look like tiny owls which always brings a smile to my face.

It takes me two hours to fill all their water and seed dispensers, and when I'm finally done, I quickly mop up the mess they made the day before from the aisles.

"Katie, someone is here to see you," Mom calls from the back door.

"Send them out," I call back.

Stepping out of the last aviary, I empty the bucket and rinse the mop before I glance in the direction of the back door. Seeing Preston slowly walking toward me has me frowning, but I'm soon struggling not to laugh as he warily eyes all the birds.

"Cracker!" Chopper squawks from his perch before he swoops down from it, diving toward Preston.

"Oh, dear Lord," Preston shrieks and ducks down, ending up cowering on the grass.

I laugh as I call out, "Chopper, go get a cracker from Grandma."

Luckily, he listens and continues his flight to the back door. "Chopper. Cracker. Chopper. Cracker," he parrots the words until Mom comes out to feed him. She notices Preston, sitting in a crouching position in the middle of the lawn, his hands still covering his head.

"Katie, come on. That's no way to treat a guest."

"Sure is funny, though," I chuckle as I step closer to Preston. "It is safe to get up. I don't breed vultures."

"Could've fooled me," Preston grumbles. He first peeks around him before apparently deciding it's safe enough and climbs to his feet. Digging in his pocket, he hands me a slip of paper. "The cost of the repair."

My eyes widen. "Seriously, you had the phone repaired already?"

"Of course. I need my phone."

Tilting my head, I can't resist teasing him. "Are you one of those people who never look up?"

He frowns at me and shifts his glasses back up his nose before asking, "One of those people?"

"Yeah." I shrug and grin at him. "One of those people who never look up from their phone."

"I'm not here for you to judge me. Just give me the money so I can leave," he states, an upset look tightening his features.

I didn't expect him to get angry from my teasing, and it makes me really look at him. His brown hair is cut short and neat. His face is sharp and clear, and the way his green eyes keep dropping from mine tells me he's either shy or a creep.

"I was only teasing you," I explain as I begin to walk toward the house.

Preston doesn't say anything but follows behind me. Walking into the kitchen, I grab my bag and glance over my shoulder at him. "How much is it?"

"Two hundred and forty-nine dollars. The amount shows on the receipt I gave you."

Shocked, I frown at him, then glance down at the receipt in my hand. "Damn, is the thing gold plated?"

"No, it's actually cheap for an android phone."

"Could've fooled me," I mumble as I pull two hundred dollar bills from my wallet. "Mom, do you have a fifty I can borrow?" I call out.

"Check in my purse," she yells from deeper inside the house.

Grabbing the note, I hold the money out to Preston, but before he can take it, I snatch it back. "I feel like I'm being ripped off. I'll make you a deal. I'll pay you if you pet Chopper once."

"What?" Preston's face flushes, and he begins to stammer, "Ah... n...w... a..." Taking a deep breath, he squares his shoulders. "No."

"I promise he won't peck you. Just pet him once," I try to encourage him.

"What happens if the bird takes a chunk of flesh out of my hand?" he questions.

"You'll only bleed a little," I tease but quickly realize my mistake when Preston gives me a you-must-be-crazy look. "He won't bite. I promise."

Preston stares at me for a little while, which has me adding, "Chopper has never hurt anyone, and besides, he just had crackers, so he's not hungry."

"Like that's supposed to make me feel better," Preston grumbles. Pushing his glasses back into position again, he gives in. "Let's just get this over with. I have work to do."

Clapping my hands excitedly, I stick my head into the hallway and yell, "Chopper, come to Mamma."

"Mawma...mawma...mawma," Chopper squawks as he comes out of the living room and waddles toward me.

"Aww... you melt your mother's heart," I croon as I crouch to pick him up. Petting his head, I turn to Preston. "Come on, you can do it."

"This will probably be the biggest mistake of my life," Preston mumbles under his breath as he takes three cautious steps toward me. Fear wins out, though, and he stops with his gaze locked on Chopper.

"Just hold your hand out, and he'll fly to you," I say. Before Preston can refuse, Chopper pushes off from my hand and soars the short distance to Preston.

The moment he lands on Preston's shoulder, it looks like the poor guy's about to faint. I close the distance between us and place my hand on Preston's shoulder so Chopper can climb on my fingers.

"It's okay. He won't hurt you," I reassure Preston. With my free hand, I reach down for his and bring it up toward my budgie. I take hold of one of Preston's fingers and help him to softly pat Chopper's head. "See? It's not that bad, is it?"

Preston's eyes dart between me and Chopper, and he swallows nervously before he answers, "I'm not sure."

"Cracker," Chopper squawks, which has Preston yanking his hand back.

"Wanna feed him a cracker?" I ask.

"No." The word bursts from him, but then he takes a deep breath and says, "Maybe...?"

I grab a cracker from Chopper's stash and hold it out to Preston. As he takes hold of it, Chopper flies to his hand and perching on his finger, he begins to nibble on his favorite food.

Preston lets out a couple of deep breaths before the corner of his mouth lifts in a slight smile, which has me staring like an idiot.

How's it possible that a little ole smile can transform his entire face? A second ago, he looked like a robot, but now...

"Damn, you've got to smile more." The words tumble out before I can stop them. Preston's eyes dart to mine, and I see a flash of shock before he lowers them, looking embarrassed. Having already put my foot in it, I continue, "Your entire face lit up. You should really smile more. It makes you look attractive instead of closed off."

Preston begins to blink, and then he darts around me and heads for the front door, stuttering, "Ah... uhm..."

"Your money," I call out.

He stops and looking uncomfortable, he says, "Oh, right."

I give it to him, but when he takes another step forward, I ask, "You taking Chopper with you?"

It only frazzles him more, and it looks like he's about to short circuit. Taking Chopper from his hand, where he's still perched happily, I smile as I say, "Thank you for taking a chance on Chopper. I hope he's helped you with your fear of birds. You're welcome to come and spend some time with him whenever you feel like it."

I haven't even finished my sentence when Preston darts out the door. "Yes... okay... it's was nice meeting you... and Chopper." He waves nervously back at me as he continues walking toward the garden gate. "Oh, shoot!" He turns and brings me the half-eaten cracker. "Almost took his food. Sorry."

"See you around," I call after him, and it's only when the gate slams shut behind him that I think to ask him for his number. "Hey, Preston Culpepper!" I call out and quickly jog to the gate. "Wanna give me your number?"

"Why?" he asks, his eyes wide on me as if I might bite him.

"Because that's what people do when they meet. They swap numbers, and besides, it's only fair seeing as you have mine."

"Oh?" He shuffles his feet, and shoving his hands in his pockets, he blurts the number out before he darts down the street as if there are a hundred budgies chasing him.

"Shy," I mumble to Chopper as I watch Preston's retreating back. "He's definitely shy. I don't understand why, though. The guy sure is good-looking."

3

Preston

Feeling flustered, I keep walking until I'm well out of sight of Katie's house.

I slow down until I come to a stop and glance over my shoulder.

"What was that all about?" I mutter to myself. "I should smile more?"

No one has ever used the word *attractive* when it comes to anything regarding me.

I shuffle my feet and adjust my glasses, then glance back again.

'You should really smile more. It makes you look attractive instead of closed off.'

With her words playing over and over in my head, I slowly begin to walk again. By the time I reach my house, I'm confused as hell.

"Does she really think I'm attractive when I smile?" I slump down on the couch in the living room and stare at the floor. "Did that really happen today? A girl actually called me attractive?"

I pull a face and shrug. "Even though her sanity could be questioned, I have to admit it was nice to hear her say that about me."

My phone vibrates in my pocket, and pulling it out, I see that it's Mason calling.

"Preston Culpepper speaking," I answer, sitting upright.

"You can see it's me calling. Why do you keep answering the phone like that?" Mason asks, his tone abrasive like always. At first, I used to be scared of him until I got to know him better and realized it's just his way of talking.

"It's a habit," I explain. "Do you need me to do something?"

"Yeah, I know you're on break, but the IT team can't get a computer up and running at CRC. Can you go look at it?"

"Sure." I get up and grab my keys from where they're hanging on the key holder. "I'll go there now."

"Thanks, I owe you one. It's Director Wilson's computer. I'll let him know you'll be there soon."

"Okay. Enjoy the rest of your trip," I say as I walk to where my car is parked.

"Talk to you soon."

I tuck my phone back in my pocket before I climb behind the wheel.

Driving into town, my mind keeps going back to the morning's events. When I stop at a red light, the reality of what happened slaps me upside the head.

"I touched a bird," I say in awe. A smile grows on my face, and as I pull away, I sit a little straighter as pride fills my chest. "Wow, I actually touched a bird."

When I reach the CRC Holdings' impressive building, I park my car and rush inside. I take the elevator up and make a point of smiling at the receptionist before I go to knock on the director's door.

Entering the office, I say, "Good day, Sir. I'm Preston Culpepper. Mason asked me to check your computer."

"Son, if you can fix this thing, I'll buy you dinner," Director Wilson says, looking frazzled. "I needed to send off an important email an hour ago."

"I'll do my best, Sir."

Director Wilson moves out of the way so I can sit down, and I soon get lost in my work.

Ten minutes later, I reboot the harddrive and sit back. "That should do it. Would you mind signing in and checking that everything is still there?"

"It's fixed?" Director Wilson looks at me as if I've performed a miracle before he takes the seat I just vacated. He signs on and after another minute, lets out a relieved sigh. "Son, you're a lifesaver. Thank you."

"You're welcome, Sir." I begin to walk toward the door. "Have a nice day."

"Hold up," he calls, which brings me to a stop. "I owe you dinner. How does tonight sound?"

"You don't have to, Sir. I was only doing my job," I try to decline as nicely as I can. I don't fare well in social settings.

That's no lie. This morning is proof of it.

"Nonsense." He writes something on a piece of paper and holds it out to me. "This is my address. We sit down for dinner at seven. Please join my family and me."

Taking the paper, I shove it in my pocket. Not wanting to be rude to a director of CRC, I reply, "If you insist. Thank you for the invite, Sir."

* * *

"For someone with such a high IQ, you sure do stupid things," I grumble at myself as I park my car in front of Director Wilson's house.

Staring at the house, I ran from less than eight hours ago, I let out a defeated sigh. I never thought I'd be back here again.

Just my luck that Katie is the director's daughter.

I climb out of the car and adjust my jacket. Looking down at my suit, I'm thankful Falcon introduced me to his tailor and had suits made for business purposes, or I'd still be looking like a disheveled mess.

I stand restlessly in front of the house, unsure how I'm going to handle tonight.

How am I going to act casual around Katie?

What if I screw things up for CRC?

Shoot.

In need of advice, I pull my phone out of my pocket and dial Falcon's number.

"Hey," he answers a couple of seconds later.

"Hi, it's Preston."

"I know." He lets out a chuckle. "The caller ID showed your name. What's up?"

"Director Wilson invited me for dinner after I fixed his computer," I explain.

"Oh? That was nice of him."

"I suppose," I mumble, totally feeling out of my depth.

"Why do you sound worried?" Falcon asks, picking up on my dejected tone.

Deciding to just tell him the whole story, I launch into an uncomfortable ramble. "I met a crazy bird girl this morning... after her bird practically attacked me. You could say she's cute... or maybe even pretty... I'm not sure. My phone broke, and after having it repaired, I went to her house so she could pay for it. She made me touch the bird... it wasn't as bad as I thought it would be... he even ate a cracker from my hand."

I stop to take a breath and hear Falcon chuckling. He must've put me on speakerphone because I can hear Lake wheezing with laughter in the background.

"So, you met a girl?" Mason takes over the conversation.

"Yes." I quickly add, "And her bird."

"What's the problem? Did you fall in love at first sight?" Mason teases.

"No," I blurt out. "She called me attractive and well... right now, I have to go in for dinner, and I have no idea how to handle the situation."

"Wait. What does the crazy bird girl have to do with you having dinner with Director Wilson?" Mason asks.

"Oh, I forgot to mention that part. Director Wilson lives at the same address as Katie, so I'm assuming she's his daughter," I explain.

There's a moment's silence before Mason replies, "Just so I understand," he takes a breath before continuing, "Katie is Director Wilson's daughter, and because she called you attractive, you're standing outside the house worrying because...?"

"Because I don't know how to handle this situation," I answer a little impatiently. "A girl has never called me attractive before."

"Oh, now I understand," Mason says, and I can hear the smile in his voice. "Let me ask you one thing."

"Shoot."

"Do you like, Katie?"

"Huh?"

"Preston, is the attraction mutual between you and the girl?"

"What attraction?"

"God, help me. Lake, can you stop laughing so you can explain it to him? You're better at these things than I am."

"I can try," I hear Lake wheeze and roll my eyes even though a smile is already forming on my face. "Preston, you there?"

"Where else would I be?" I answer, which has Lake chuckling again.

"Okay, listen up. Remember when Mason and Kingsley met, and they hated each other?"

"I was too busy studying to pay attention," I explain.

"That's true. Fine, tell me how you feel when you're around Katie."

"A little worried about her sanity, but mostly scared of the birds."

A burst of laughter sounds over the line, and a couple of seconds later, Falcon is back on because evidently, Lake can no longer breathe.

"You guys are really enjoying this, aren't you?" I ask, trying to sound stern even though them laughing always brings a smile to my face.

"Do you like Katie?" Falcon asks directly.

"I don't know her well enough," I answer, a slight frown forming on my forehead.

He shoots another question at me. "Would you like to see the girl again?"

"With or without the birds around?" I ask.

"Damn, dude. Without the birds."

"I think it would be nice to see her again," I admit.

"Thank fuck, we're finally getting somewhere." Falcon lets out a tired sigh. "Go in there and just be yourself, Preston. If she's interested in you, she'll make a move. The worst that can happen is you enjoy a nice dinner."

"Do you think a girl could be interested in me?" I ask, still not sure about this whole dinner thing.

I hear the laughter die, and then Lake's voice comes over the line, "Preston, any girl would be lucky to have you. You're smart, good looking, and loyal to a fault. Go in there and sweep her off her feet."

I swallow hard on the compliments Lake just gave me.

Before I started at Trinity Academy, I was nothing more than the nerd the jocks would bully.

"I'm not sure I can sweep a girl off her feet," I admit.

"You can. I have all the confidence in the world in you. You're badass, Preston. You saved Kingsley's life. You took down a senator. You can do this."

"I can do this," I repeat Lake's encouraging words.

"You can do this," Falcon and Mason call over the phone. "Go in there and get the girl."

"Okay. Okay. Okay." I take a step toward the garden gate while sucking in deep breaths. "I'm going in."

"Put away the phone first," Lake calls out.

"Okay. Bye." Before I hang up, I blurt out, "Thanks, guys."

4

Katie

When the bell rings, I get up to open the front door. Dad said someone from work is coming over for dinner, so I took extra care with my appearance and even put on some makeup.

Opening the door, I'm surprised to see Preston so soon again. "Hey, you're back?"

"Ah... yes." Slowly a smile pulls at the corner of his mouth as his gaze quickly scans over me. "You... uhm... you look nice."

The compliment makes a smile appear on my face. "Thanks, we're expecting a guest for dinner."

"Right."

Preston keeps looking at me until I ask, "Why did you come over?"

"Katie, was that the doorbell I heard?" Dad calls from inside the house.

"Yeah, it's just a friend," I yell back.

When I look back at Preston, he's still staring at me with an expectant expression on his face.

Dad comes up behind me. "Preston, please come in." Turning to me, Dad frowns. "Why didn't you invite him in?"

It takes me a second to put two and two together. "Wait, Preston is your guest from work?"

"Yes." Dad glances between Preston and me, then asks, "Do you know each other?"

"We met earlier when Chopper flew the coop." I move out of the way so Preston can come in.

I'm beginning to wonder whether I summed him up all wrong.

Mom comes out of the kitchen and smiles when she sees Preston again. "Would you like something to drink?"

"Water would be nice," he answers, his posture even stiffer than it was this morning.

"Come in. Let's sit in the living room for a little bit before we eat," Dad says, instantly monopolizing Preston for himself.

Usually, I would go help Mom, but my feet have a mind of their own as I follow the men into the living room. When Preston takes a seat on the double-seater across from Dad, I sit down in the open space next to him and ask, "What do you do at CRC?"

"Oh, I don't actually work for the company," he explains.

Confused, I look to Dad for an answer, which has him explaining, "Preston is currently a student at Trinity Academy and also Falcon Reyes's assistant."

Shut the front door!

If he's a student at Trinity Academy, it means he comes from an important family.

A very important family seeing as he's Falcon Reyes's assistant.

Crap, I should've been nicer to him earlier.

I try to remember whether I did anything that could get Dad in trouble at work.

Mom comes in with a tray of drinks. As she sets it down on the coffee table and hands Preston his water, she asks, "I overheard the conversation. How do you find studying at Trinity Academy?"

Preston first takes a sip of his water, then sets the glass down before he answers, "I'm enjoying it. They're accommodating and letting me finish my four-year degree in two years."

We all blink at Preston, and Dad is the first to recover from the surprise. "Isn't it hard doing a four-year degree in so little time?"

Preston shakes his head, and smiling self-consciously, which seriously looks endearing and hot at the same time, he admits, "I got in on a scholarship because I have a high IQ. My photographic memory also helps a lot."

I stare at the man beside me, totally swept off my feet. He sounds so humbled and nothing like the conceited and arrogant guys I've known in the past.

A warm feeling enfolds my heart, and I wonder if it's possible to fall for someone so quickly.

"Oh really," Dad says, sounding almost as impressed as I am. "And how did you get into business with Falcon Reyes of all people?"

Preston shifts as if he's uncomfortable, and the closed-off look settles over his face again. It seems like he hates being in the spotlight.

"Dad, should we move to the dining room?" I ask so Preston doesn't have to answer the question.

"Oh, right." Dad lets out a chuckle.

We all rise at the same time, but when Preston takes a step forward to follow Dad, I grab hold of his hand and whisper, "Hold up a second."

I watch my parents leave before I look up at Preston. "You don't have to answer any questions you're not comfortable answering. Whenever you need me to jump in and distract them, tap my leg or grab my hand or clear your throat. Just give me a signal."

Preston tilts his head, a slight frown line between his eyes. "You want to help me?"

"Of course." I smile brightly until I realize I'm still holding his hand.

Our eyes drop to our joined hands, and I expect him to yank away any second now, but instead, he gives my fingers a squeeze.

"Thank you, Katie."

I try to shrug it off, but hearing him say my name only makes my smile grow bigger.

5

Preston

Katie's holding my hand.

What do I do?

What would the guys do?

They would probably have the guts to kiss her.

You're in her family's home, idiot. Her mother and father are in the dining room.

I give her hand another squeeze before I pull mine free from the hold.

"Let's eat," she says, and it takes my legs a moment to work before I can follow her.

I've never met a girl who literally makes me weak in the knees, and the feeling is strange but exciting at the same time.

When I'm seated next to Katie at the table, we all load our plates with food. Even though I come from a happy home, my family never sits together for dinner. We usually grab our plates and scatter in different directions. Dad watches the news while Mom goes to sit out on the patio. Whenever I'm home, I'll eat in my room.

After taking a couple of bites, Director Wilson asks, "Are you studying IT?"

I shake my head while I swallow the bite of food. "No, I'm busy with a degree in economics."

There's a look of surprise on his face. "What made you choose that direction?"

I place my fork on the table and rest my hand on my thigh. "I'm already good with computers and thought the degree would help me in the business world."

"I'm sure it will. You're already doing great for yourself," Director Wilson compliments me.

I clear my throat feeling uncomfortable with the direction the conversation is heading. I'm a private person, especially seeing as I'm a friend to Falcon, Mason, and Lake. People are always trying to get information on them from me, and I have to be careful that I don't say something that will reflect badly on them.

* * *

Katie

Glancing down, I watch Preston fist his hand on his thigh. I reach in under the table and place mine over his, then say, "I think another one of my gouldian pairs are going to lay eggs."

"Oh, really?" Dad says. "How do you know?"

"I've put in some nesting materials, and it's all used up. I'm totally taking it as a good sign."

"Gouldian?" Preston asks.

I'm about to explain when he turns his hand over beneath mine and weaves our fingers together.

Feeling surprised but excited at the same time, I begin to ramble, "I went to Australia when I was thirteen. After I saw all the birds there, I studied everything I could find on Australian finches, and Dad helped me set up the aviaries. You should come again during the day, so you can see what they look like."

"So, all the birds I saw out back this morning are from Australia?" he asks, really looking interested.

"Yeah, while I was there, we helped the Australian Wildlife Conservancy count goudlians. It's so sad, there are less than two thousand five hundred left in the wild. I've been hoping to breed some in captivity, but I've only managed two chicks over the past five years."

"Wow, that is sad." Preston seems to be deep in thought. "Is there anything I can do to help?"

Surprised, I smile up at him. "I'm sure AWC could use help. We should check out their website."

"We can do that," Preston agrees.

Silence falls over the table, and when I glance at my parents, they're both grinning at us.

"What?"

Mom's the first to move, and grabbing her plate along with Dad's half-eaten one, she says, "Nothing. Time for dishes. Daniel, come help me."

I watch my parents clear out of the dining room and then begin to chuckle.

"Did I miss something?" Preston asks.

I shake my head and smile up at him. "No, they're giving us some privacy."

"Why?"

I tilt my head and unable to stop the words, I admit, "Because they like you, and more importantly, I like you, Preston Culpepper."

Shock ripples over his face, and for a moment, it looks like he's going to bolt for the nearest exit, but then he squares his shoulders. I feel his fingers stir between mine as he locks eyes with me.

"You like me?" he asks.

"Yeah." Wiggling my eyebrows at him, I tease, "I think you're a catch. Wanna try dating?"

His eyes widen, as he mumbles, "You're very direct."

"Is that a bad thing?" I ask, hoping I'm not too pushy.

Preston thinks for a short moment before he answers, "No. I actually appreciate that you're straight forward." He shifts in his chair, then admits, "I'm not good with people."

"I'm not good with people either," I say to make him feel comfortable again. "That's why I prefer spending time with birds."

The corner of his mouth curves up, and he glances at me. "It could've been any animal, but you had to pick birds?"

I let out a burst of laughter. "Once you get used to them, they won't seem so scary anymore."

6

Preston

I'm still in shock after everything that happened yesterday.

We held hands.

I never thought of myself as a person who would like to be touched, but after today, I learned that I actually liked holding hands with her.

I like Katie.

It's weird. Two days ago, she wasn't in my life, and today I find myself looking forward to seeing her again.

Hoping I'm not making an idiot of myself, I walk the short distance to Katie's house.

Never thought I'd live to see the day I'm willing to be around birds for a girl.

My phone starts to ring, and pulling it from my pocket, the caller ID shows Falcon's name.

"Preston... ah... Hi," I answer awkwardly, trying to get used to answering the phone casually.

"You're going to get it right one of these days," Falcon chuckles. "You're on speaker. Tell us how it went last night."

"Uhm... Hey, guys," I greet Mason and Lake as well before I continue, "I think it went okay. We held hands. That's a good sign, right?"

"Aww... you've made your dad proud," Lake croons. He's always joking about how his friends are more like children to him. It's the first time he's included me, though, and it makes me smile.

"That's a very good sign, Preston," Mason says.

"I'm on my way to Katie's house now," I mention, feeling anxious. "What if she changes her mind about liking me?"

"Then you take it as a learning curve and move on to the next girl," Mason gives his piece of advice.

"Next girl?" I almost choke on the words. "I can hardly handle this girl."

"You seem to be doing well, so don't sweat it," Falcon encourages me.

Reaching Katie's house, I shuffle my feet and adjust my glasses. "I'm outside her house. I better go inside."

Lake's voice comes over the line. "Let us know how the date goes."

"Date? Is this a date?" I ask, feeling stupid, which isn't something I'm used to.

"More like a second date," Mason corrects Lake.

"True, it means you can totally go for the kiss today," Falcon adds.

Kiss.

I clear my throat and glance at the house.

"Kiss?" I whisper, scared someone will hear.

"Just pucker your lips and go in for the kill," Mason offers, which doesn't sound like good advice to me.

"Seriously? Pucker his lips?" Falcon asks. "Don't listen to Mace. You have to first frame her face with your hands and stare deep in her eyes, then you slowly lean in for the kiss."

"You're both scaring the shit out of Preston," Lake grumbles. "Dude, just let it happen naturally. Don't force yourself."

"Uhm... okay." I draw my bottom lip between my teeth with worry.

"Damn, and here I thought you looked best when you smiled," Katie suddenly says.

My eyes snap up and then widen with surprise as I watch her lean against the front gate to her house.

"You should definitely bite your lip more. Totally hot move," she continues.

"Is that her?" Mason asks.

"Of course that's her, dumbass," Falcon chuckles.

"Kill the call," Lake laughs. "Give the guy some privacy."

The line cuts out, and I lamely tuck my phone back in my pocket. Clearing my throat, I can't stop my eyes from darting everywhere other than at Katie.

"So... are you coming in or what?" she asks, opening the gate.

"Ah... in?" I ask stupidly, then quickly add, "If that's okay?" Feeling nervous as hell, I begin to ramble, "I should've called first."

"Get your sexy butt in here already, Preston," Katie chuckles.

I take a couple of steps forward and close the gate behind myself.

Suddenly Katie closes the distance between us and places her hand on my shoulder. Standing on her tiptoes, she presses her mouth to my cheek, and for a moment, all I can do is blink while my breath rushes from my lungs.

"I'm glad you came over," Katie says as she pulls back, and taking hold of my hand, she begins to lead me toward the side of the house. "I can't wait to introduce you to all my children."

Feeling that I need to say something, I say, "It's nice to see you, too... again."

When we near the aviaries, Katie points to one of the cages that is filled with colorful birds. They're much smaller than Chopper, who isn't anywhere to be seen at the moment.

"These are my gouldians," Katie states with pride.

"They're pretty," I admit. Glancing at the next aviary, the corner of my mouth lifts in a smile. "Those must be the bechinos. You were right, they do look like little owls."

"Cute, aren't they?" Katie asks.

"Yeah."

"Katie, is Chopper out back with you?" Mrs. Wilson calls from the kitchen door. When she sees me, she adds, "Oh, hi, Preston."

"Hi, Mrs. Wilson," I call back.

Katie glances around, then says, "He's not out here."

"He didn't come for his cracker when I called," Mrs. Wilson states, then adds, "You think he flew the coop again?"

Katie begins walking toward the side of the house. She's still holding my hand, so I follow right behind her.

"I'll go check the park. He's probably somewhere close by," Katie calls to her mother before we head for the front gate.

"Does he fly away often?" I ask as we cross the road to the park.

"Not that much. He's only flown to the park four times," Katie explains.

She begins looking in trees, so I do the same, hoping Chopper doesn't fly into my face again.

7

Katie

It's been almost two hours since we started searching for Chopper. Worry and despair claw up my spine, and my eyes dart frantically from one tree to another.

"Chopper, come to Mamma," I call out. "Chopper!"

A lump pushes up my throat, and my eyes begin to sting from holding back the tears.

"Chopper," I try to call, but it comes out sounding like a whimper. Bringing my hands up, I cover my mouth as my breath hitches. "Where are you?"

I move my hands up to my hair and grab two fistfuls as I turn desperately in a circle, praying I'll see my budgie in one of the trees.

"Found him!" Preston calls, and I quickly turn in the direction of his voice. Seeing him hurrying toward me from the opposite side of the park, cupping something to his chest, makes me break out in a sprint to get to him.

When I see Chopper peeking through Preston's fingers, I reach out and take him. Holding him to my chest, I can't stop the tears from falling as relief washes over me.

"My little man. Mamma was so worried," I croon as I pet his head.

A thankful smile forms on my face, and I take a deep breath to try and calm my rampant emotions. Looking up at Preston, I'm so glad he was here to help me.

Not thinking, I stand on my tiptoes and press a kiss to his mouth. "Thank you so much," I whisper when I pull back.

I glance down at Chopper, then back up at Preston, who seems to have frozen from the impromptu kiss.

"Sorry, I shouldn't have done that." I try to rectify my mistake, worried I moved too fast for Preston.

He takes a couple of breaths, then tilts his head as if he's thinking hard about something. The next moment he reaches up and framing my face, he steps closer to me, caging Chopper between our bodies.

"You kissed me first," he says, his eyes locking on mine with such an intensity it makes my insides do cartwheels from anticipation.

When he begins to lean forward, I close my eyes, the smile never leaving my face.

* * *

Preston

Frame her face.

Look into her eyes.

Go in for the kill.

I keep repeating my friends' words over and over until I finally press my mouth to Katie's.

At twenty years old, I've never wanted to kiss a girl before. I never used to worry about what my first kiss would be like.

All my life, I was only interested in computers and my studies.

Until a crazy bird-loving girl entered my life.

I don't know if I'll be any good at dating.

I have no idea how to have a relationship.

But as my lips touch Katie's, none of those worries bother me.

Let it happen naturally.

Remembering Lake's advice, I close my eyes and immerse myself in the moment. Katie pushes up on her toes to get closer, and I tilt my head to the side as I move my lips against hers.

When I feel her tongue against my bottom lip, all reasoning ups and leaves me. I part my lips, and when our tongues touch, the entire world fades until there's only this girl.

The first girl I've ever kissed.

The first girl to make me feel.

It's like I'm waking up from a deep sleep.

Kissing Katie makes me want to explore more, to learn everything there is to know about falling in love.

My breaths speed up, and when I try to step closer, Chopper squawks, "Cracker."

Feeling breathless, I pull back, and my eyes dart between the bird and Katie's flushed face.

"Wow," she breathes, and then a beautiful grin forms around her mouth. "I get a feeling there's a lot about you, I don't know, Preston Culpepper."

That makes two of us, Katie.

There's a lot about myself I don't know, and I can't wait to find out what it is.

Feeling ten feet taller, I gather up my courage and place my arm around Katie's shoulders. We begin to walk back to her house, and then she leans her head against my shoulder, a happy smile on her face.

My life has changed so much in the past couple of months. Who knows what else lies in store for me.

I tighten my hold on Katie's shoulders and smile down at Chopper in her hands.

Thanks for slapping me upside the head, little man.

If you loved this introduction to Trinity Academy, then be sure to read...

* * *

THE CANDY ACQUISITION

CELIA AARON

1

Stella

I chase Teddy until I drop to my knees and flop over in the grass, my heart pounding as I hear the thud of his footfalls and the crinkle of fall leaves.

The noise abruptly stops. “Mommy!”

“I’m too old. Go on without me.” I wave a hand at the passing clouds as a cool wind blows past. “Save yourself.”

The crunch of leaves resumes, but no thudding.

He blocks the sunlight as he stands over me, his hair forming a dark halo around him. “I won.”

“You won.” I reach out, grab his ankle, then yank so he falls on his back beside me.

“Hey!”

I roll over to face him. “Don’t let your guard down.”

“Not this again.” He huffs.

“You’re still little. You don’t get it.” I brush a leaf from his hair as he frowns at me. “But when you’re older, you’ll see that it’s important to always protect yourself. Always be thinking about what the other guy is doing, going to do, or already done.”

“You sound like Dad.” He wrinkles his nose. “Besides, I’m not that little. I’m seven.”

"Practically a man." I grin and try to hold in the emotion that wants to bubble up. How did he get so big so fast?

Footfalls approach, and I'd know that cadence anywhere. Another dark angel blocks the sun, but this one makes my heart thump not with wistfulness but desire.

"What are you two doing out here?" He reaches for me and pulls me to my feet.

"Racing." Teddy pops up and jets toward the house where Rebecca and Renee stand on the front porch, both of them in matching pink princess costumes.

"Princesses again this year?" Sinclair asks.

I shrug. "They'll grow out of it."

"They need to think bigger. Queens or nothing."

"Is Teddy coming?"

"He's already at the town house with his new girlfriend." He looks up and sighs. "I don't remember this one's name."

"You never remember any of their names," I only half scold.

"Why should I waste time on meaningless women when I have you in my clutches?"

"Your *clutches*?" I smirk.

"Would you like a demonstration?" He runs a hand through my hair and pulls my head back, angling my mouth in his favorite position—and mine. When Sin kisses me, I grasp his shirt, loving when his grip in my hair verges on pain.

"Save it for the bedroom. We've got business," Lucius calls from the front door.

The twins turn and rush him, both of them demanding he pick them up at the same time. He does. Because he's a total pushover for whatever my redheaded devils desire.

"Will he ever stop being a cockblock?" Sinclair grits out.

"Never." I get on my tiptoes and kiss his angular jaw. "Happy Halloween."

"Mommy, come on!" Rebecca calls. "We want candy!"

I roll my eyes. "As if I don't have a bag of candy inside they could eat until they were sick."

He tilts my chin up until I look him in the eye. "It's not the same. The chase is the fun part. Working for what you want. Tracking it down and claiming it. Far different than having it simply handed to you."

"Predator."

"Always." He kisses me again to a variety of groans from the front porch.

"I'll eat you up later. At the witching hour." He grunts, then leans over and hoists me onto his back, carrying me to the house with one hand gripping my ass while I try not to giggle.

2

Sinclair

The parish is appropriately festive, ghosts in the trees and jack-o'-lanterns on porches. We pull into the driveway of the town house, a three-story home done in white and black with ornate wrought-iron railing and balconies that are the perfect spot to watch the Mardi Gras parades.

"The wisteria bloomed again." Stella raises her brows at the purple flowers climbing the trellis all the way up to the roof. Her patchwork dress costume and stitched lines on her arms are particularly unappealing, but that doesn't stop me from wanting her. Nothing ever will.

"This late in the year, that's a bad sign." I lean over and kiss her. "Trouble is coming."

She nibbles my lip. "Trouble is already here."

Lucius pulls up behind us, his Range Rover purring as we get out. Little Teddy is already poking the koi pond with a stick, and the girls rode with Lucius, so their squealing will begin soon enough.

Irritating children, a mouthy wife, and brothers I can't scrape off no matter how hard I try—this is the good life. The one I thought I'd never get to have. But here I am. I rest my hand on Stella's ass as we walk up the stairs to the porch.

A jack-o'-lantern already burns here, the face carved with the precision of a surgeon. My brother Teddy's work, no doubt. I adjust the collar of my ridiculous costume. Stella informed me that I'm "Jack Skellington" and she's "Sally," but that was after I told her I didn't want to dress up this year—which I tell her *every* year and she ignores *every* year.

She waves the girls over. "Come on, princesses, you need to have a snack before we go trick-or-treating. You too, Teddy."

"I've already had a snack." The elder Teddy opens the front door for us, and a nondescript brunette on his arm flashes her teeth at us as we walk in.

"Hi." Stella is far warmer than she should be with strangers. But that's her way. I've tried many times to spank and choke it out of her, but here she is greeting Teddy's girlfriend instead of treating her like the stray cat she is.

I walk past and into the kitchen. Our housekeeper, Vivian, has already laid out cheese cubes, grapes, and a plate of fairy bread. She always dotes on our children with little bits of her culture—which, perversely, includes bread slathered in butter and decorated with all sorts of sprinkles.

Rebecca and Renee follow me, and I scoop them onto the counter as they giggle.

"Who let you get so big?" I stare down my nose at Renee. Of the two, she's by far the one with the most mischief.

"You did, Daddy." She goes straight for the fairy bread with the bright pink sprinkles.

"And what about you?" I soften my voice for Rebecca. She's sensitive like her mother.

"Mommy?" she asks and takes a grape.

I kiss them both on the crown as Teddy runs in and grabs me around the legs.

"Daddy, I think I killed a fish!"

"Wonderful." I help him onto one of the stools along the granite island. "Eat some snacks so you won't lose your mind walking the neighborhood."

He reaches for a juice, and I swipe it from him and insert the straw precisely before he can stab it through the entire container and make a mess. Little Teddy has my hair, my eyes, and my love for the darker things in life.

I look around at my brood, satisfaction hitting me in the chest like a well-timed punch. I'm complete. And for a man who could've counted the happy days of his childhood on the fingers of one scarred hand, I'm getting far more love and contentment than I ever thought possible.

"What are you doing?" Stella hugs me from behind.

"Feeding these savages." I ruffle Teddy's hair. He's wearing a grim reaper costume. Good man.

Lucius walks in and starts partaking as well, though I suspect he may have a bottle stashed somewhere on him. Sobriety is a narrow road, and he's never been known to walk a straight path. Even so, he's better than he used to be.

I reach back and grip Stella's waist, then jerk my chin at Lucius. "Watch them for us."

He raises a brow as I take Stella's hand and pull her with me down the back hall.

"Sin?" Suspicion coats the word on Stella's tongue.

As it should, because I intend to do things to her that may be illegal in certain states, including ours.

I pull her into the bathroom. "Does this ridiculous dress come with underwear?" I lift her onto the vanity as she gives me a scolding look.

"I'm a married woman with three children. Of course I'm wearing underwear. And I made this costume myself."

"The former is unfortunate." I hike her dress up, grip the sides of her panties, and rip them off. Eyeing her shapeless patchwork dress, I add, "The latter is, too."

She tries to act perturbed, but her look changes when I free my cock from my own silly costume.

"Spread for me." Not waiting for her to obey, I push her knees wide apart, then position myself at my second-favorite spot before pushing into my first-favorite.

I scoot her to the edge of the counter, sinking deep into her as she grips my shoulders. With a yank, I pull her dress down and run my tongue along the vine tattoos that match my own and snake along her pale skin. Her moan is a symphony of lust as I nibble her collarbone.

"You'll have to be quiet, my sweet little Stella." I start a rough rhythm, just the way we like. "Touch yourself. We're coming together. Soon."

Her hand slides to her pussy, and her fingers go to her clit.

I look down, the sight of her fingers against her sweet pink flesh sending another jolt of need straight to my cock. Riding her harder, I tongue her throat, sucking and biting as the sconce next to us bounces from the force of my thrusts.

Her thighs begin to shake, and then she makes that one sexy gasp that tells me she's on the edge. I grip her throat and squeeze while my other hand leaves bruises on her hip. When her breath stops and I feel her slick walls bearing down on me, I shove hard and deep inside her. Slapping my hand over her mouth, I let her milk me until I can't resist any longer. I stifle my groan as she moans into my hand, her eyes locked with mine as I spend inside her, giving her every bit of me, marking her as mine.

A knock sounds at the door. "Hey, I need to piss."

Stella rolls her eyes.

I would commit murder if I weren't firmly embedded in my true love. "There are seven fucking bathrooms in this house. Go find another one!"

Lucius laughs. "I know. I just wanted to fuck with you."

3

Stella

"You can't eat all that." I try and swipe away some of Teddy's haul from the counter.

He reaches for a Blow Pop and snags it. "Let's go again."

"Again?" I sit on the stool, my feet aching in these ridiculous Sally shoes that I now realize were utterly unnecessary. Regular old flats would've worked fine.

"Yeah, I need more." He grins, and he looks so much like his father that I can't tell if it warms my heart or breaks it.

"Go on. Take him for one more round." Sinclair cocks his thumbs at the twins. "I'll put them to bed." Rebecca is already sleeping, her face on her arm and a smear of chocolate on her cheek.

"Brush their teeth." I give in and toss Teddy his empty bucket.

"Sure I will." Sin kisses me on the mouth, then lifts Rebecca into his arms and shoos Renee toward the stairs.

"Seriously, brush them," I call.

"Yeah. Going to get right on that."

I smirk at his retreating back and allow Teddy to pull me out into the night one more time.

"How many houses are we going to have to hit?" I grumble and look back at our house, the brightly lit windows promising comfort and maybe hot chocolate.

"Just a few." Teddy strides ahead of me.

I catch up when he breaks off to knock on the door of a house I could swear we've already visited. But the lady that comes to the door doesn't notice or doesn't mind, because she gives him a big helping of candy.

"That enough?" I ask.

"Mom." He shakes his head like he's disappointed in me.

I laugh and drape my arm across his shoulders. He's getting tall. Soon he'll be bigger than I am, and then he'll start breaking hearts. I dread those days of crying girls and rebellions and hormones. For now, though, everything is serene. Calm. Peacef— My scream cuts through the cool night.

Teddy and I are grabbed and dragged off the street and into a small lane between two large houses.

"Scream again, and I'll hurt you." The first one speaks in a gruff voice, a ghoul's mask over his face.

The other is huge and easily holds Teddy with one hand. They press us against the side of the brick house.

I try to stay calm. "I don't have any money on me."

"We don't want money." The man holding me presses his forearm against my throat. "We came for *you*."

4

Sinclair

I twitch the front curtain for the hundredth time. Stella and little Teddy haven't returned, and I'm on the verge of going out looking. After all, we may be years away from the Acquisition, but there are still those who remember —and those who wish to see it rise again.

"They'll be back soon." Teddy has his arm around his girl, though I've noticed she seems to watch Lucius far more than her date.

Lucius takes a small swallow from his flask, then stuffs it back into his pocket. "Have faith."

"I have faith. What I don't have is patience. They've been gone for an hour."

"Half an hour," Teddy's date chirps.

I finally turn and look at her full in the face.

She meets my gaze for only a sliver of a second before she blanches and shrinks into Teddy's side. I'd order her out of the house, but I have bigger problems.

"That's it. I'm going after her." I grab my coat from the peg by the door and stride out into the night that's growing more blustery.

"I'm coming." Lucius follows.

"Me too." Teddy walks out and stuffs his hands into his pockets. "Carrie, hang here and watch the girls." He closes the door, then rolls his eyes. "She's so clingy."

"You weren't saying that when she was riding your face about five minutes before we got here."

Teddy wipes his mouth. "How'd you know?"

"You know, for being a goddamn almost-doctor, you sure are a dumbass sometimes."

Teddy shrugs. "I can't be awesome at everything, just most things."

Lucius ruffles his hair the same way he does to little Teddy. "Come home more often, asshole. It's been too long."

"I know. Just trying to get done with my residency."

"If you two are done, I'd like to focus on finding my wife and child," I grit out.

A handful of older children wander past, their outfits ranging from whimsical to dark. Most of the smaller children are already in for the night, their parents hurrying them to bed to try and stifle the sugar high and resulting tantrums.

"They can't be far." Teddy splits off and takes the other side of the street.

Lucius peers down alleys as I keep my gaze ahead. They would've come this way. Our house is close to the square, and most of the residences are along this part of the street. It wouldn't make sense for them to have turned in the other direction.

"I can check the square." Lucius seems to read my mind.

"Go." I quicken my pace as his steps disappear behind me.

Teddy and I stop at the next street corner, and he shoots me a questioning look.

"Check there." I point down the cross street, and he turns and hurries away into the dark.

Continuing straight, I cut past a park with old oaks and a line of tall, narrow row houses. When I take the next turn, acid churns in my gut. I know this street far too well. It's the one where Stella used to live, where she and her father holed up in a worn Victorian mansion with a buckling roof and skeletons in the closet. It's gone now, the house razed and only a vacant, weedy lot remaining.

I head straight for it, my steps quickening right along with my pulse. If anything has happened to my wife or son, I will rain down hell on whoever had the audacity to touch them. Just the thought of them in danger has me flexing my hands into fists.

A sound floats on the cold wind. A whimper. And it's coming from the vacant lot. I break into a jog and cut through the yard of the neighboring house, my steps silent on the damp grass as I hurry into the backyard.

"—told you I don't have any money." Stella's voice, and there's fear in it.

"And I told *you*, this isn't about the money." A man's voice, overly gruff, as if he's trying too hard to sound aggressive.

I slow and peek through a twist of brambles between the properties. Two men. One huge. The other wiry. Both in Halloween masks. Teddy and Stella appear unharmed, but he holds tightly to her.

She holds a hand out to ward them off. "Just let Teddy go. Okay?"

"Not a chance." The thin one shakes his head.

I creep closer and try to get a look at what sort of weapons the men have. No guns, from what I can see in the moonlight. Good. Reaching back, I pull out my pocketknife and flick it open.

Stella leans down and whispers to Teddy.

"Hey, what are you doing?" The wiry one's voice lightens a little.

I stand up straighter.

"You aren't going to hurt me or my mom." Teddy steps in front of Stella, his little fists up.

The big one laughs.

That sets Teddy off, and he runs, but he wisely takes on the smaller man, using his fist in a direct crotch shot.

"Motherfucker!" He doubles over as Stella rushes the big guy.

I stow my knife and watch, a smile ticking at the corners of my lips.

5

Stella

Feinting to the left, I circle the big guy, then dart toward him and jam my foot into the back of his knee. He staggers and reaches for me, so I throw myself out of his reach.

He growls in frustration and stomps toward me as I scramble to my feet and cast a glance at Teddy. His eyes huge, he's watching.

"Run!" I wave him away. "This is the part where you get to safety."

"Come closer, *Krasivaya*." Giant hands grab for me, and I narrowly avoid them, moving farther into the weeds along the side of the property.

The thin one starts to recover, his gut-wrenching coughs subsiding. Teddy is still paralyzed with fear.

"Run!" I yell again and launch myself at the giant.

He catches me, and I try to jam my fingers into his throat, but he grabs my wrist and squeezes the air from my lungs with his other arm.

"Let go of my mom!" Teddy rushes him and grabs his leg.

When Dmitri yells and drops me, I land with a thud and see that Teddy has sunk his teeth into the big man's thigh.

I snort a laugh on accident.

"I didn't plan on having children, but I don't think it's an option anymore." Alex dry heaves and pulls his mask off, his bright pink hair almost fluorescent in the night.

Teddy lets go of Dmitri's leg. "Alex?"

"Hey, buddy." He waves. "It's your mom's fault I'm a eunuch now. Don't blame yourself."

Dmitri pulls off his mask, too. "*Molodoy*, how big you're growing." He lifts Teddy into his arms.

"Dmitri?" Teddy turns to look at me. "Mommy, what's going on?"

"Your mother has some explaining to do." Sinclair strides from the tree line, his dark gaze fixed on me.

I scramble up from the ground as Sin rushes toward me like a cyclone of fury and intensity.

He grips my chin and pulls my face to his, then kisses me rough and deep while pulling me tight against him. I melt for him. Like I always do. Like I always will. Wrapping my arms around his neck, my feet don't touch the ground as he lifts me.

"Always with the hetero affection," Alex complains. "Standing right here, Sin. Where's my kiss?"

Dmitri grunts a laugh as Sin puts me back on my feet.

Teddy has already climbed onto the huge Russian's shoulder and drums on his close-shaved head. "I beat you!" He grins. "Alex didn't stand a chance."

"Not when you aim for the goods. Damn." Alex steps gingerly, wincing as he goes. "I'm done here. Where's the house? I need a drink and some ice."

Sin peers down at me, never looking anywhere else. "You did this?"

"I needed Teddy to feel what real trouble is like. It'll keep him safe." I shrug. "We were never really in danger."

His eyes narrow. "And you couldn't have told me about this little plan?"

"I could have, but then you'd be hovering and bossing and overbearing."

He smirks. "Me? Surely you're thinking of someone else."

"Absolutely not." I stretch up onto my tiptoes and brush another kiss against his full lips.

"Good. Because if you were, I'd have to kill him." He wraps his arm around my waist as Teddy and Lucius come crashing through the trees, both of them stopping short when they see all of us.

"What the hell?" Lucius shakes his head. "I should've known there was some bullshit afoot." He pulls out his flask. "Greetings, *suka*." He toasts to Dmitri, who then drops into a litany of Russian curses so vile they would probably kill a small child.

I reach up and take my son's hand. "You did well, Teddy. But next time, you run for safety, okay?"

"And leave you?" His dark brows draw together.

"Yes, you need to—"

"No. We protect each other. Always. Your mother protects you, and you protect her." Sin takes Teddy from Dmitri's shoulders and hugs him tight. "We look after our own."

"I was going to kill them for Mommy!" Teddy throws his little arms around his father's neck, adoration in the movement.

"That's the correct answer." Sin pats his back.

We walk off the old property and head toward the new one. Teddy walks between Sin and me, one of his little hands in each of ours.

"Daddy?" He looks up at his father.

"Yes?" Sin gives his usual cold stare right back.

Teddy skips a step, his feet kicking joyfully. "Does this mean I can get the tattoos now?"

We laugh the rest of the way home, and once the house is asleep, Sin makes good on his promise. At the witching hour, my spider eats me up until there's nothing left, and that's just the way I want it.

* * *

Do you want more of Celia Aaron?

One click COUNSELLOR now!

MINE FOR TONIGHT

BRIGHTON WALSH

INTRODUCTION

Summary

Paige Bennett thought all she had in store for the night was some girl time with her besties, but when they bail early—on her and on the evening—she catches a ride home with the one guy she knows she shouldn't want. And if that isn't bad enough, she invites him in for a whole different kind of ride.

Though Mine for Tonight *is set in the Reluctant Hearts world, this short, utterly filthy story can be read as a complete stand-alone.*

1

paige

When I went out tonight with the sole intention of helping my best friend, Tessa, get over an awful breakup, I didn't intend to end the evening in a car with a fuckhot guy I barely know. I can't remember which one of my so-called friends suggested the horrible idea that he drive me home, but whoever did is on my shit list because now I'm stuck in a too-small car with Adam Reid. Adam Reid of the smoking body and amazing hair and brilliant blue eyes and scent that makes my mouth water just at the idea of getting a taste.

And, of course, it's all happening when I've had just enough alcohol to quiet the voices telling me what a bad idea it would be to sleep with someone so entwined in my best friend's life. Especially when I only do one-night stands, and I only do them with men who know the drill. Adam is definitely not one such man. Adam's a relationship guy through and through. He's a keeper. Just not someone kept by me.

It's quiet in the car, only the sound of my restless thighs against the leather of the seat. He doesn't even have the music on. It's like he's enjoying seeing me squirm. And that just pisses me off more. Men do *not* make me squirm unless I want them to.

"How long are you home for?" I ask, desperate to fill the silence.

Although reminding myself that he's not sticking around in town, and thus the perfect man to scratch a temporary itch with, probably isn't my best idea.

He glances at me before returning his gaze to the darkened, snow-packed road in front of us. "Just through New Year's. I head back to Colorado on the second."

I nod, staring out the window just to avoid looking at him. Has it really been that long since I've gotten laid that the sexual tension between us is thick enough to cut with a knife? He's said approximately twenty words to me the whole night, but it's not his words or lack thereof that have me shifting in my seat, my jeans pressing right against my swollen clit. It's his looks...those hungry stares he gives me, his eyes so full of passion I'm surprised my clothes don't disintegrate right off my body.

Thank God no one else is going to see how fucking drenched my panties are. I mean, honestly, he hasn't even *done* anything. And maybe that's what's drawing me to him? For once, not having a guy pounce on me immediately is cranking my interest up to a thousand.

Well, my interest can just settle the fuck down, because the only action I'm going to see tonight is from B.O.B., my battery-operated boyfriend. He's the only cock I've let stick around for more than a week, and that's because he doesn't do anything but please me. No gross habits, no annoying conversation, no smothering. Just cock.

Adam parks in front of my apartment building, and I shoot out of the car like a cannon, calling a quick, "Thanks for the ride!" over my shoulder before I shut the door and hustle toward the building's front door as fast as I can in my heeled boots and amidst the scattered snow covering the walk. If I have any hope of avoiding jumping Adam's bones, I need to run away and not look back.

But instead of staying in his car like I assumed he would, he shuts off the engine before getting out and following me up the walkway to my building, the crunch of his boots on the snow-packed sidewalk echoing through my body.

"What're you doing?" I ask, shuffling through my purse for my keys.

He slides me a look, his hands in the pockets of his wool peacoat. Honestly, no twentysomething has any damn right to look that hot wearing a businessman's jacket.

"I'm making sure you get into your apartment okay, Ms. Drunk."

I narrow my eyes at him. "I am not drunk."

He cocks a brow at me. "You shoved a finger in Jase's face and told him there were no penises allowed tonight."

And I'd do it again in a heartbeat. The guy who broke my best friend's heart deserves a whole lot worse than my finger in his face. "You obviously don't know me very well. I just did that last week at girls' night before I had even a single drink."

The corner of his mouth tips up in an almost-not-quite smile, and my panties go up in flames. "Yeah, well. I'm still making sure you're getting into your apartment safely."

I stare at him for a long moment, our breath puffing out between us in the cold December night. If he follows me inside, there's no telling what will happen. But he's not backing down, his fixed stare on me proving that he's not budging.

With a sigh, I shoulder my way through the front door, then head down the stairs to my place. What I should tell him is that if walking me to my door is his way of angling for an invite into my place, it's not going to happen. Nope, because I'm going to stand my ground, no matter what my lady parts are begging me to do.

Instead, I say, "Do you want to come in?"

Shit. Fuck. Shitfuck.

He glances down at me where I'm standing with my back against my door, the knob clutched in my hand, simultaneously praying he says yes and that he turns around and leaves without a word. Leaving without a word would definitely be the better option for both of us.

Okay, that's not true. And there's really only a tiny part of me that hopes he says no. A tiny, miniscule, insignificant part. One that realizes if he follows me inside, this night has the possibility of blowing up in my face. But, as I stare at his gorgeous ice-blue eyes and that dark hair begging for my fingers, the rest of me doesn't care. Doesn't care that Adam Reid isn't one-night stand material. Doesn't care that I don't fuck guys who have a penchant for relationships. We're two adults who can do what we want.

"Is that *you* asking me to come in, or the alcohol?" he finally asks.

I roll my eyes and reach out to press my fingers against his hard chest, biting my lip as I follow the path they walk down over his rigid abs before I tuck them into the waistband of his jeans. And sweet Jesus, but there's either a very large surprise waiting for me behind his fly, or he's walking around with a water bottle in his pants. "I'm not drunk, Adam."

I don't tell him I'm still a little tipsy—just tipsy enough to allow me to ignore the fact that this isn't a good idea—because he's the kind of guy who won't let anything happen if a girl isn't one hundred percent cognizant. And I want something to happen between us. I really, really fucking do.

He swallows, dropping his gaze from mine and allowing his eyes to rove over me. And the way he takes me in, the way his eyes sweep over me from head to toe, is like a caress on my skin, heating me up all over again. He can't even see my breasts through the layers of my clothes and my down-filled coat, but my nipples still perk up at his attention and my clit is doing the damn salsa inside my panties, hoping, *praying* he says yes and pays both of them a little attention tonight.

He's quiet for what seems like an eternity, and I hold my breath, waiting for his answer. When he lifts his eyes to mine, they're hungry, boring into me as if he can't wait to devour me, and I have to swallow a moan.

"Open the door, Paige."

2

adam

This is a first. I may be twenty-five, and I've had my share of sex, but I've never taken a girl home with the sole purpose of fucking her. And definitely not when I wasn't in a relationship with her—hell, Paige and I haven't even been out on a single date. And yet, I'm here, cock hard as steel, desperate to get inside her. Because, shit, Paige Bennett is drop-dead gorgeous, and as soon as she assured me she wasn't drunk, all bets were off. I'd be a fucking idiot to say no to a night with her—even if it is only a single night. And I'm not a fucking idiot.

She stares at me for a moment before twisting around and fumbling with her keys in the lock, her rush to get inside apparent. Stepping up behind her, I pull her long, blonde hair to the side and brush my lips against her neck, breathing her in. She moans—too loudly for the shared space we're currently standing in—and drops her head back to my shoulder, her hands pausing in their quest to open the door.

From everything I've heard about Paige, we're as different as night and day. Accepting her invitation to come inside is probably a bad idea. Actually, there's no probably about it. But fuck... It's been a long damn week being home for Christmas and finding out exactly how much trouble the family business is in. Trouble that I'm afraid is going to fall to my shoulders, despite the fact that I live half a country away.

So, no. This may not be my best idea, but that's not going to stop me. Not when I desperately need to get lost in another body. And Paige's body is one I could spend days...*weeks*...getting lost in.

"Open the door," I say again, sliding my hand around to press flat against her stomach and tug her back to me. Straight into my cock that's been hard since she slid her gorgeous ass into my car.

She reaches back and digs her fingernails into my thigh, her breaths coming out in pants, and I haven't even really touched her yet. Haven't filled my hands with her perfect breasts or cupped her pussy to see if she's as hot for this as I am. "If you want me to get us inside, you need to stop doing that."

I nip at her ear, taking the lobe between my teeth and tugging gently. "How about this—you open the door and get us inside, or I'll fuck you out here."

"Oh Jesus." She sags against me but finally rights the key in the lock and twists the knob, sending the door banging back into the wall inside her apartment.

She barely has time to slam the door behind her and drop her purse to the floor before I'm on her, ridding her of her coat before I toss mine aside along with it. I grip her hips, dragging kisses along her exposed neck as she rests her head against the door, her fingers thrust in my hair. Christ, she smells good. Sweet. Her scent is probably the only thing sweet about her, which may be why I can't seem to say no to this.

Sweet is my MO, my fallback, my standard. The kinds of women I'm normally attracted to are sweet to the very core, but there's no denying the hardness currently pressed against my zipper, fighting to escape. And there's no denying I'm hard strictly because of Paige and everything she brings to the table. And I'd bet my last penny there's nothing sweet about it.

"You and I won't work." She pants against the top of my head as I kiss my way down her chest, tugging the deep V of her sweater even lower until her braless tits pop out. *Fuck me.*

Without hesitation, I flick my tongue against a hard nipple before engulfing it in my mouth. I let it go with a pop before lifting my eyes to hers. "Feels like we're working just fine to me. You want me to stop?"

"Fuck, no, keep sucking." She presses against the back of my head, guiding me closer to her breasts, the cherry-tipped beauties begging for my attention.

So I give it to them. I suck and lick, bite and tug until Paige is a mess of incoherency. She's slumped against the wood, her legs barely holding her up, and I don't have to reach into her panties to know she's fucking soaked.

Satisfied with the state she's in, I pull back, feeling a smug sort of gratification seeing her eyes glazed over, her tits flushed pink, and her lips parted with panting breaths. I undo my jeans, keeping my eyes locked on hers, before I reach into my back pocket and pull out my wallet to grab the condom stashed there. I send up a little prayer in hopes that Paige has more, because I've only got the one, and I already know once isn't going to be enough with her.

"Take off your pants." My voice comes out rough and low, full of need, and I can't even bring myself to worry about showing my desperation to be inside her. There's no point when my cock is hard and throbbing, the thick shaft jetting out to her as soon as I free it from my boxer briefs.

Her gaze drops to it as I roll the condom down its length, her tongue licking along her lower lip as if she wants nothing more than to get a taste. Later. It'll have to be later, because right now I want nothing more than to sink inside her pussy.

"Take off your shirt," she counters. Like she isn't just as desperate for contact as I am. Like she's not the one three seconds from coming thanks to nothing more than my mouth on her tits and watching me stroke my cock.

Without hesitation, I grip the neck of my shirt and yank it off, tossing it to the side before I lift a brow at her. "Now, Paige."

"Didn't take you for the bossy type," she says, but she does as I asked and lowers her jeans, toeing off her boots so she can pull them off.

"Guess you just bring it out in me," I say, my eyes caught on the apex of her thighs, her pussy hidden behind pale blue panties. "Sweater, too."

She rolls her eyes but reaches down to grip the hem and lifts it over her head. "Just so there's no confusion here, the only reason I'm doing what you tell me to is because I want that cock inside me."

Said cock jumps as I get my first full look at Paige in all her gorgeous, nearly naked glory. Fuck me, she's a wet dream come to life, all long, strong legs and full, tight tits, thick hips perfect for gripping. My gaze drops to her pussy, still covered by her panties, and I cock my head to the side, narrowing my eyes to get a better look.

A low chuckle rumbles out of my chest. "I definitely wasn't expecting these," I say, reaching out to trace the top band of her underwear.

"No? What were you expecting?"

I shrug, my gaze caught on the soaked-through cotton. "I don't know. Silk. Lace. Nothing at all. Definitely not cotton panties with a bear print all over them."

"Um, ex*cuse* you. They're *koalas,* Adam. Have some goddamn respect."

I chuckle, lifting my eyes to hers. How she can look intimidating while she's mostly naked and wearing kids underwear for all intents and purposes, I'll never know. "Should I see myself out?"

She sniffs, crossing her arms under her breasts, presenting them to me like pink-tipped gifts. "No. You can make up for offending me with orgasms."

"I see. And how long do I have to give you these makeup orgasms?"

"I haven't decided yet."

"Well," I say, taking a step back and crossing my arms to match her stance. "I better get to work then, huh? Take them off."

She rolls her eyes, but she doesn't object as she drops her arms, her fingers tucking into the sides of her panties as she works them down her legs. And then she stands to her full height and I get my first complete look at her gorgeous, naked body, her pussy pink and glistening even in the low light. Christ, I could stare at her all day. I *want* to, just so I can memorize every inch and call back the details anytime the urge strikes.

"You just going to look, or are you actually going to fuck me?" she asks, her full hip jetted out to the side, hand resting there.

I lift my eyes to hers for the briefest moment before I'm on her, gripping her under her ass and lifting her up against me, my body sandwiching her between myself and the door. She gasps as I bite down on the fleshy part of her breast, no doubt hard enough to sting, before I lave it with my tongue.

"Are you always this mouthy?" I ask, my voice rough, my cock straining to sink inside her.

"Yes." She pants against my ear, gripping me tightly to her as I guide my cock to her pussy.

I swipe the head through her slit, groaning at how wet and hot she is. "All the time or just during sex?"

She laughs, the throaty sound puffing along my skin and sending a shudder through my body. "What do you think? Now, get inside me."

Fucking a woman against a door isn't my style. Neither is diving straight into sex without more foreplay than some brief nipple action. And yet, somehow, I find myself doing both as I notch my cock at her entrance and drive inside without hesitation, not giving her a second to catch her breath before I start a frenzied, unrelenting pace.

"*Jesus*, Paige." I groan, lowering my gaze to where I'm disappearing inside her. "Fuck..."

"That's—" She whimpers low in her throat, seeming to lose her train of thought as she wraps her legs tighter around me, her fingers threaded through my hair and tugging hard enough to sting. Clutching my head to her chest, she moans, the sounds of her pleasure a constant cadence in the room, punctuating the rhythmic slapping of our bodies coming together.

And fuck me, but my balls are already drawing up tight, ready to go off. I grip her under her ass, digging my fingers into her as I lift her up and down on my length, clenching my teeth to ward off my orgasm. But even reciting the first thirty-five digits of pi is only going to hold it off for so long, especially when her pussy is gripping me like I'm sinking straight into heaven. I need her to come, and I need her to come now. "You feel so fucking good. Are you close?"

"Uh-huh," she says, nodding vigorously as she guides my head down to her tits.

I take her clear, unspoken order and curl my tongue around one distended tip, glancing up at her to meet her eyes. My muscles are burning, sweat beading down my back, the urge to come so strong I can nearly taste it. But I'll be damned if I go off before she does. "Rub your clit for me, Paige. Get yourself off on my cock."

"Oh Jesus," she says, her eyes squeezing closed before she snaps them open again, locking them on mine. She drops one hand, sliding it down her stomach and not stopping until she reaches where my cock is disappearing inside her. Her fingers slide on either side of my pumping shaft, her answering moan throaty and deep.

"Fuck. *Fuck*. I said to rub your clit not my cock." I bite down on her nipple in punishment, but from the way her pussy ripples over my length, it wasn't much of one.

She moans, her fingernails digging into the back of my neck as she continues driving my cock crazy with her other hand. "Do that again. Oh God, Adam, I'll come if you do it again..."

With a growl, I dive in, sucking her nipple hard into my mouth before sinking my teeth into it and tugging. She comes with a scream, her head tossed back as she shakes in my arms, her pussy squeezing my cock until I can't take it anymore. I drive deep, spilling inside her as I come with a harsh groan.

We stand there for long moments, both of us trying to catch our breath. Jesus, I can't believe I fucked her against the goddamn door. Didn't even take the time to get undressed completely, my jeans hanging loosely off my hips. Hell, I still have my shoes on.

This isn't me. I'm not uncontrollable. I'm never so ravenous for a woman I can't wait the thirty seconds it'd take to make it to a bed.

And yet my cock is already growing hard again inside Paige, desperate for round two, and I'm not sure we'll get to a bed this time either.

3

paige

I barely managed to catch my breath before Adam had me laid out on my dining room table, my legs over his shoulders and his mouth on my pussy. Jesus, who *is* this guy? I thought I knew him from the stories Tess had told me over the years, but the picture she painted is so completely different from the guy whose tongue is buried inside me, I can't help but wonder if they're even the same person.

"Oh my God." I reach down, threading my fingers through his thick hair and tugging. I don't even need to guide him where I want him, because this walking, talking dream come true already knows. He's only been down there for five minutes, but he's already managed to figure out the direction, speed, and rhythm I want my clit licked and sucked. And he's exploited every goddamn detail, drawing out my impending orgasm, making me desperate with want and crazy with need. "Adam. *Adam.*"

He hums against my flesh, his bright blue eyes connecting with mine as he pumps two fingers into me. Jesus, I should be embarrassed by how wet I am, how the sound of my excitement echoes around the room, but I'm not. Fuck me, but I'm not. All I care about now is coming harder than he made me come against the door—which will be a tall damn order. But with as good as this guy eats pussy, I'm confident he's up for the challenge.

Pumping into me with sure, steady strokes, he curls his fingers inside me, stroking the spot that only B.O.B. ever seems to be able to find. He pulls back just enough to blow on my clit. Just enough to say, "You gonna let me taste all that sweet come?" before he's back on me like a starving man.

Fucking *hell*. My orgasm slams into me so fast, I don't even have time to scream before my body is pulsing against his fingers and his mouth, his groans of approval only taking me higher, extending my pleasure.

After the last wave crashes through my body, I slump against the table, my arms and legs like lead weights. I can't move, can barely breathe, and I wasn't even the one doing all the work. Adam, on the other hand, stands from where he was kneeling on the floor, swiping a thumb over his wet lower lip. Wet from me. Jesus, this man is hotter than sin, his broad shoulders blocking out the light behind him, his cock standing proudly at attention once again.

Sometime between when he took me against the door and when he dived face-first into my pussy, he stripped himself the rest of the way, and now he stands in front of me completely naked, making me wish I could memorialize his perfection with a picture. Something for me to pull out long after he's gone when it's just me and B.O.B. seeing to my needs.

"Condom?" he asks, his voice throaty and deep.

"Who said you get to fuck me again?"

He doesn't even dignify that with a response, just stares at me, his hand going to his cock and gripping hard. His fingers wrap around his thick shaft, tugging, stroking, and the sight sends bolts of electricity straight to my clit. I don't know what it is about Adam, but I can't get enough of him, can't help but want more. Everything he does pushes me a little further, makes me a little more desperate. Never mind that I've already fucked him. Never mind that he's already made me come twice. I want more. I *need* it.

"In my purse."

He grabs my bag from where I dropped it next to the door and holds it out to me without a word, his gaze never leaving mine.

I've never hunted for a condom faster in my life, but I find it with ease and hold it between two fingers, lifting a brow at him. "What now, Captain Bossy Pants?"

He chuckles low in his throat and drops his gaze to my pussy, still on display for him. As if he's desperate for another taste, he licks his lips. "Now, it's your turn."

"My turn?" My turn for what, exactly? The orgasm count is two to one in my favor. It should be *his* turn.

"Show me what you want. What you like." He braces his hands on the table on either side of my shoulders, leaning over my body until our noses are nearly touching. "Show me how you want to get fucked again, Paige."

If words alone could get me off, Adam would've made me come a dozen times by now. But of course, I can't tell him this. Can't tell him that he has me just as desperate for him as he seems to be for me. Instead, I press my hand to his chest and push until he backs up, before I slide off my table and stroll into my living room as if I don't want to drop to my knees right where he stands and take him into my mouth.

I glance at him over my shoulder to see if he's following me, but he's not. He's rooted in place, one hand gripping his cock as his gaze appears to track the sway of my ass. To test the theory, I stop at the couch, hands braced on the arm, and bend over, giving it a little shake.

His eyes snap up to mine, and there's so much hunger in their depths, it nearly steals my breath. He rips open the condom packet before rolling it down his shaft, his purposeful strides eating up the distance between us. "Hope that's where you want it, because that's where you're getting it."

In response, I shake my ass again and grin when he groans low in his throat. The smile falls away when Adam comes up behind me, the rough hair of his legs scraping against my thighs as he lines up his front to my back.

Leaning over me, he presses a hand to my stomach and tugs me into him, his lips against my ear. "You want to get fucked hard, don't you, Paige?"

What I want to say—or moan, actually—is, *God yes*. What I actually say is, "What gave me away?" I turn my head and catch his jaw with my teeth, lifting my ass until I'm pressing against his length.

"Hold on tight." He doesn't even get all the words out before he slams into me, his cock gliding easily inside me despite his size.

With one hand gripping my hip, he wraps his other fist around my hair, tugging my head back as he fills me over and over again. "Is this what you wanted? What you needed?"

I bite my lip to stifle the words that threaten to pour out. *Yes*. A thousand times yes. In answer, I reach back and dig my fingernails into his pumping ass, trying to take him deeper, trying to guide him faster.

He grips my hip harder, his fingers digging into my flesh, and growls into my ear, purposely slowing his pace. With aching slowness, he drags his cock in and out of me, pulling a whimper from my throat. His lips curve up against my shoulder as he brushes their softness over my skin. "*Fuck*, I'm not ready for this to be done yet. Can you can feel every inch of me filling you up like this?"

"*Yes*," I practically whine. "But I want it faster. Fuck me *faster*."

He nips my jaw, one hand sliding up to cup my breast. "Nah. I'm going to fuck you exactly how I want to, and you're going to love it. You already do."

"I never said that," I say, attempting to steady my quavering voice.

He chuckles low, his teeth scraping against the side of my neck. "You don't have to—your dripping pussy tells me everything I need to know. It tells me exactly what you like and how you like it."

He's not wrong. Wetness coats my thighs, and there's no end in sight to my reaction to him, because he does seem to know exactly what I need. Exactly what I want. He pushes his cock into me again, the thick head dragging along my G-spot. I shudder against him, my eyes fluttering closed on a gasp.

"Don't be quiet now. All the neighbors already know what we're doing. Might as well tell them how much you love riding my cock."

My mouth drops open, all air leaving my lungs as he exploits that magical spot inside me until I'm coming again and again, my throat hoarse from screaming.

"That's it," he says, his voice tight, his movements frenzied and wild. With my orgasm still flowing through me, he pumps into me with abandon, his cock driving deep over and over again until he stills inside me, finding his release.

Resting his head on my shoulder, his panting breaths ghost down my back, creating shivers in their wake. He releases my hair, running that hand down my arm as his grip on my hip loosens, his fingers brushing softly against my skin where I'm certain he's left marks.

"How many condoms do you have?" he asks, his voice breaking the silence in the room.

I'm still trying to catch my breath, residual waves from my orgasm still crashing through my body. I glance at him over my shoulder. "A box."

"Good," he says, his lips brushing my nape. "Let's see how many we can get through tonight. Because I'm not done with you yet."

I'm not done with him yet, either. Not by a long shot. Which, in itself, is new and unprecedented for me. I love sex, and I love men, but I get bored or annoyed quickly, and I have no time for needy assholes who think I owe them something. I've always been able to count on that.

But with Adam, he's not any of those things. And I'm not sure one night is going to be enough.

* * *

Thank you for reading *Mine for Tonight*! If you loved the beginning of Paige and Adam's story, be sure to check out *Paige in Progress* where they take their relationship from frenemies to so much more!

Relationship-phobe Paige Bennett knows exactly what she wants. Her dream job is finally in her grasp, and she's not letting anything—least of all a man—distract her. Which is why one-night stands are perfectly satisfying. She just never expected one to show up right across the hall.

Adam Reid escaped his hometown as fast as he could, but he's returned to help with his parents' struggling business. And he managed to land himself a hot neighbor while he was at it. Relationship guy through and through, he knew having Paige once would never be enough. He's bound and determined to win her over, no matter what it takes.

Adam's in town for only a short time, which gives Paige what she needs—amazing chemistry with an expiration date. But despite her only wanting right now, Adam's sights are set on Paige. And he's playing for keeps.

* * *

ONE WILD RIDE

CHELLE BLISS

1

Gigi Gallo

I didn't expect this year's college Spring Break to be any different than the last, but I was wrong.

My cousin Tamara smirks as soon as our eyes meet. "Look who decided to come up for air."

Pike's next to me, arm slung around my shoulder, nose buried in my hair as I face my cousin for the first time since I left with a total stranger. "Hey, Tam."

Lily's staring at me like I'm an alien. "I was so worried," she says, always the mother hen of the group.

Mallory's lips twist as her eyes rake over me before swinging to Pike. "Bitch did it. Didn't think she had it in her."

"Never underestimate me," I tell Mallory, unable to hide my smug grin. She challenged me. Told me I was a prude and didn't have the balls to walk up to a total stranger, the hottie now draped over me, and leave with him.

It was a totally stupid thing to do. I could've ended up dead, but I got lucky. Pike was nothing but a complete gentleman...well, at least when I wanted him to be.

"Leave her alone, Mal," Mallory's sister, Mary, says, slapping her sister on the shoulder. "Not everyone has to be as loose and free with their body as you are."

Mary and my cousin Lily are so much alike. They're both bookworms, obsessed with school, and never seem to care about guys. The last thing either of them want is a quick hookup and meaningless sex.

I thought I was going to get a one-night stand, but after spending one day with Pike, I know I want more. I have a few more days of vacation left before reality and classes start again. For now, I plan on holding on to the badass biker and riding him for as long as I can.

"Jealous bitches," Mallory mutters, still eyeing my man like she wants to rip him away from me and claw my eyes out.

I slide my arm behind his back, resting my head on his chest, and curl my fingers into his T-shirt. "There are plenty of guys here waiting for you, Mal. Why don't you get busy and show us how a real woman does it?"

Her entire face contorts as she pushes herself up with her hands flat on the table. "I think I will. I'm bored with you guys anyways." She stalks away, pushing her tits up, readying herself for whatever major spring break conquest she's about to have.

"Sit." Tamara pushes the chair Mallory had just occupied out farther, dipping her chin toward the seat. "I want to hear all about it."

"Um." I glance up, meeting Pike's eyes. "Can I have a few minutes with my girls, babe."

"Babe?" Tamara giggles, elbowing Lily. "Aren't they so cute together?"

"Cute?" Pike grumbles at my side. "Take your time. I'm going to catch up with my friends."

"Okay," I sigh, sounding like a lovesick puppy, smiling up at him. "I'll be here." I pitch my thumb toward the table, unable to take my eyes off his.

He leans his face forward, grabs my ass with both hands, and kisses me. Not a small peck either. A long, deep, demanding kiss filled with so many memories of last night and the promises ahead. When he pulls his lips away, I sway in his arms, barely able to stand.

He gives me that sexy smirk that drew me to him to begin with. "Don't take too long, darlin'. I'm not a man who likes to wait. I want you to meet the guys too."

"Okay," I whisper, saying the same thing I said before. It's like he zaps my brain, causing even the simplest thoughts to become impossible.

He peers over my shoulder, staring at my girls. "Bring the chicks if you want. I'm sure the guys would like them."

I turn, looking at Tamara, Lily, and Mary, knowing full well only one of them would fit in with his friends. "I don't know," I mumble, catching the deer-in-headlights look on Lily's and Mary's faces.

Tamara's lips pinch. "We'll be there in a few," she tells him, ignoring my apprehension about introducing them to a group of rowdy bikers. "All of us."

Pike grunts, brushing his lips against my cheek, scraping my face with his beard. "Just as long as your fine ass is by my side, I'll be a happy man."

I grin. "Okay," I whisper again, silently cursing myself for being a bumbling idiot. I stand there, watching him walk away, loving the way his jeans hug his ass.

"Well, fuck me," Tamara says, punching me square in the thigh, causing me to flinch. "You did it! You fucked a badass biker dude."

I glance around, but the music's too loud and people are too busy partying to overhear what my cousin decided to shout as loud as she could. "Shut up, Tam," I tell her, narrowing my eyes as I slide into the chair next to her.

She waves me off, smiling so big I can practically see all her teeth. "Tell us everything. We want details."

"You want details," Lily corrects her, staring down at the paperback she brought with her. Who does that? Brings a book to read on spring break at a bar filled with hot guys? My cousin. I swear to God she's one of the most boring human beings on the planet, but I still love her.

But then I glance at Mary and she's doing the same thing. Face buried in a book, not living in reality. Maybe life's easier that way for her with a sister like Mallory, always ready to jump on her case for not being fun enough.

I never gave Lily shit about her reading or awkward social skills. She is who she is. A bar filled with bikers during spring break, which just so happened to also be Daytona Bike Week, wasn't exactly her cup of tea, but she came anyway.

"You look different," Tamara says, studying my face as I sit back in my chair, feeling my body finally start to relax. "Fuckin' a biker agrees with you, babe. You're glowing."

I cover my face with my hands, hiding my smile. "It was only supposed to be a night."

"Disappeared for two damn days so far. Got a few more left too. You stayin' with us tonight or that tight-assed hottie of yours?"

"I don't know, Tamara. I should probably come back to the hotel tonight. I'm already in too deep with this guy. Staying with him longer will just make it harder to say goodbye."

Lily finally glances up from the pages of her book. "You're falling for him?"

I shrug. "I don't know what I am." I hold my head and take a deep breath. "I'm just so..." I sigh. "So."

"Happy?" Tamara asks. "'Cause from what I'm seeing..." She points at me, wagging her finger. "You look happy. I haven't seen you this chill in a long, long time."

I peek over my shoulder, catching the green eyes across the bar. He's staring at me, watching me even though he's talking to the guy next to him.

"He hasn't taken his eyes off you," Tamara tells me. "Don't come back with us. If he makes you happy, ride that happiness for the rest of this week. You never have to see him again after that. You can leave with nothing more than happy memories that'll last you a lifetime."

Mary snorts, finally entering the conversation as I turn back around. "Be careful or you'll leave with more than memories."

I wrinkle my nose, wondering what's always up Mary's ass. If anyone in the world needs to get laid, it's her. She has a perpetual pout on her lips, probably because her sister is such an asshole.

"Shut your face, Mary. Read your damn book," Tamara tells her, pushing the book closer to Mary and rolling her eyes.

"Was he a gentleman?" Lily asks, always curious even though she's never had sex.

"Completely." I smile, being half-truthful.

"Well, that's disappointing," Tamara adds. "I figured he'd be a wildcat in the sack."

I laugh. "Oh, he was, but he was a gentleman too."

"Babe," Tamara snaps. "You're talking out of your ass."

"Maybe you've just been with the wrong type of guys, Tam." I smirk, knowing my cousin shares her love freely with just about anyone she deems worthy.

"There's a hottie next to Pike. We should go say hi," she says, pushing back from the table. "You two in?" She glances at Lily and Mary, who are hiding behind their books, slinking down in their chairs.

"You two have fun. We'll just stay here and read."

"Sounds like a great time," Tamara teases. "Don't get too wild."

"Leave them alone," I tell Tamara, waving her off. "I'll text you tomorrow, Lily, and give you an update again."

"Wait." Tamara freezes, narrowing her eyes as she presses her hand to her chest. "You didn't text me."

"Thanks, Gigi," Lily says, ignoring Tamara.

"Come on, Tamara." I grab her hand, not really having to force her to go over to the long-ass table of badass biker guys. Men, especially rough-looking ones, are her kryptonite. "We'll go talk to the guys, but I swear to God, if you embarrass me..."

"I won't," she says in my ear, pulling her hand from my grip. She fixes her outfit before wiping the corner of her lips. "How do I look?"

I glance down, taking in her short shorts and tube top. "Perfectly slutty."

She smiles, proud of my answer. "That's exactly what I was going for tonight. Between Mary and Lily, though, they were killing my cock mojo."

"Cock mojo?" I gape at her, wondering how we can be related.

"Yeah." Her smile widens. "It's a thing. Trust me."

I shake my head, turning back to face the table of no less than twenty men, eyes all on us and hungry for more than food.

"See," she whispers, leaning over in my ear. "Cock mojo. You got cock mojo too, sweetheart. His cock is probably doing backflips right now watching your tits jiggle."

"Shut the hell up, Tam. Seriously, you're ridiculous."

But when my gaze meets Pike's deep green eyes, I know what she's saying is true. He's not looking anywhere else in the bar. Not at any other woman, just me. It's like no one else exists except the two of us. No one else matters in his eyes.

The man next to him is talking to Pike, gaze flickering between Tamara and me.

"I'm taking that one to bed tonight," Tamara announces like I'm competition.

"Whatever you want, Tam."

"I want to climb that man like he's a tree."

I ignore her, keeping my gaze locked on Pike as we make our way through the crowd until I'm in front of him.

Pike's legs jut out, his boots catching me behind the knees. I tumble into his lap, my face almost colliding with his chest before his arms are around me, moving me into place. "Missed you, darlin'," he whispers in that deep, rough tone that sends tingles down my spine.

My belly flips, and I know I'm in trouble. No man has ever made me feel this way. No one has ever made me feel as special or wanted as he has in the last few days. "Missed you too," I say, my voice unsteady and small.

"Well, who do we have here?" the man next to Pike asks, staring at my cousin like she's the most delicious thing in the world. "Aren't you a beauty."

Tamara extends her hand, offering it to the man. "I'm Tamara, Gigi's cousin." She dips her head my way and smiles at the handsome stranger.

"The guys call me Koala."

Tamara gives him a flirtatious smirk. "That's kinda hot," she tells him, still holding hands with him. "I was just saying I wanted to climb you like a tree, but maybe you wanna climb me, baby."

I roll my eyes so hard I'm surprised they don't become permanently lodged in the back of my head. "So embarrassing," I mutter as Pike tightens his arms around my body, laughing his ass off.

"Eh, the guys like girls like her."

Girls like her. Easy girls.

Hell, I have no room to talk. A few days ago, I marched up to Pike out of the clear blue and asked if he wanted to fuck. In reality, I'm not different than her even though I wasn't a professional at the banging game like my sweet dear cousin.

"Wanna get out of here?" he asks her, acting like no one else is around and that she and I aren't here together.

"Do you know him?" I ask Pike, glancing between my cousin and this man I don't know from Adam.

"He's the Disciples Australian chapter. He's only in town for Bike Week to take care of some business. We only see him a week a year, but the little I know him, he's a good, solid guy."

"Gigi," I say, earning me a hand to the face. "Don't ruin this for me. You got yours. Now I'm getting mine."

The tall, leggy biker steps over everybody to stand in front of Tamara. He towers over her, covered in muscles and tattoos. "Come on, sweetheart. I think I know what you need."

"Don't you want to meet the rest of the guys?" I ask, pleading with her without actually begging for her not to go.

"I'm good," she says, smiling up at Koala as he slides his arm around her shoulder. "Better than good, actually. I'm fan-fucking-tastic."

"Let's get you off those feet but not out of those heels." He waggles his eyebrows, staring at her like she's nothing but dessert.

"They're gross," I mutter, snuggling into Pike's chest like I've been doing it my entire life.

"So, Gigi," another man a few seats down says, drawing my attention away from my cousin, who's on her way out of the bar. "Where ya from?"

"Um, south," I say, being cagey.

"South?" His forehead crinkles. "As in Miami?"

I nod. "Yeah. How about you..."

"Eagle," he says, pointing to the patch on his vest. "I'm from everywhere."

He's cagier than me, which I find endearing in a weird way.

"You want a drink?"

"Tequila, please." I smile at the older man, soaking in his rough, weather-worn face.

"No, darlin'. Only beer for you."

I gape at Pike, ready to pout because beer makes me feel bloated and gross.

Pike's hand tightens on my thigh. "I need you conscious tonight for what I have planned."

"Beer it is," I say, staring up into his green eyes, melting into his touch like a big puddle of needy goo.

He lifts my chin, finger against my skin, bringing my lips to his. "Trust me, darlin'. I'm going to give you something to remember."

My stomach flips, and my inner freak does a somersault, celebrating the evening to come. "I don't think I can ever forget you," I murmur against his lips.

"I'm going to make sure you don't," he whispers, his eyes locked on mine, hungry.

I know I'm fucked. I've never done this. Never had a fling with a man I wasn't in a relationship with. Pike was the exception. A spring break tryst and nothing more.

But I already know walking away from this man isn't going to be easy. In a handful of hours, he had me wrapped around his little finger, begging for every touch, kiss, and thrust of his cock.

I wasn't in love.

No.

I was in lust with the badass biker.

I promised myself I'd never fall for a bossy alpha like him, but here I am, falling hard and fast for someone just like my father.

His hands move to my ass, both palms groping me as his tongue pokes through my lips, sweeping inside my mouth. I moan, loving the way he kisses me.

Never have I ever felt so wanted and needed by a man before. It's like he sucks the air right out of me, trying to soak up everything that's me.

Pike pulls away as my eyes flutter open, wondering why he stopped. "Want to get out of here?"

"Yes," I whisper, grinning because I know that means sex and orgasms.

Pike taps my ass, signaling for me to move. I stand quickly, gawking at him like he's the most handsome man I ever met. In all actuality, he is. He throws down a twenty, covering the beers we aren't going to finish.

"Guess you're out," Eagle says, laughing with a smirk.

"Got a woman to please," Pike tells him.

Heat creeps across my face, and I turn my head to hide my embarrassment. Being with a man so open about sex is refreshing and terrifying at the same time. But there is no disrespect. This isn't college, and these are grown men after all.

We start to walk away when a hand comes out of nowhere, wrapping around my wrist. "Do I know you?" the stranger with the Disciples cut asks me.

I shake my head, snatching my hand from his. "No, sir. You don't know me."

"You look so familiar." He eyes me warily.

"She's mine, Morris. Hands off," Pike barks behind me, looming over me like an eclipse.

"Not trying to take your piece, man. Chill. I swear I know her from somewhere though." He studies my face again, and I take a step forward, scurrying away from his watchful eyes.

What if he knows me? Does he know my family? Fuck. He could cause a whole bunch of trouble I don't need right now. We lied to our parents when we told them we were staying back at the dorm for spring break. The last thing I need is for some badass biker calling my dad or my uncles, ratting me out.

"You don't know her," Pike tells him, his voice deeper this time. "If you do, forget her. You hear me?"

"Forgotten," the stranger mutters as I keep walking, almost running toward the door.

When I step outside, I see Tamara in the lap of the biker, Koala, sitting atop his bike. They're making out, hands moving over each other's body as she straddles him.

"Should we..." I point toward the two, who could probably be charged with lewd and lascivious behavior in almost every county of the state of Florida by the way they're pawing each other in public.

"Leave them be," Pike tells me, throwing his arm around my shoulder. "We have other things to do, darlin'. More important matters to attend to tonight."

"Orgasms?" I swallow, my mouth dry.

"Lots of orgasms," he promises with a wicked twinkle in his eyes.

Best spring break ever.

Thank you for reading One Wild Ride. If you're interested in finding out what happens to Gigi & Pike, pick up FLAME, now available everywhere.

* * *

LIFELINE

WILLOW ASTER

With so much love for my Australian family

1

The plane bounces to a stop, and I check my watch *again*, willing it to freeze long enough for me to make my connecting flight. The attendant warned me earlier that we probably wouldn't make it in time, but I hoped LAX was struggling with the same computer glitch as MSP and I could make it; otherwise, the next flight to Sydney, Australia, doesn't leave until tomorrow night at seven.

Everything about the day has gone wrong. Scratch that, everything about the past *two* days has been topsy-turvy. So here I am, sweating in the crowded plane and willing everyone to move faster so I can run to see if my flight is still here. I'm not a patient person on a normal day, and when the guy in the row behind jumps ahead of me, I nearly headbutt him into oblivion. I imagine a domino effect, everyone going down and me walking across all of them.

I pinch the bridge of my nose and take a long, deep breath. *Keep it together, keep it together. This is a vacation, Violet! Just relax.*

My calming thoughts don't do much to help, and when the people in front of me finally start moving, I step out and get elbowed in the back. I don't even turn around to glare at the person for what I'm sure is accidental. Let's hope. *Zen, zen, zen, that's me.*

Somehow I get off the plane without telling anyone off and check the monitor to see what my options are. It's still here. Oh my God. I can't believe the plane is still here, two and a half hours past the time it was supposed to take off. The new departure time is in two minutes. Oh God, I'll never make that.

LAX is swarming with agitated flyers; the lines are backed up at every gate. I take a quick look around and sprint as fast as I can to my gate, which of course, is at the farthest point from where I landed.

I'm two gates away when the crowd thickens even more. In looking at the screen behind the attendant to see if the plane is still here, I hit a boulder and land on my backside. A face bends down to peer at me; I blink to make sure I'm not dreaming this perfect face, but no, his intense brown eyes are drilling into me.

"You were on a mission," he says, and if I weren't already on my ass, he'd have knocked me back down with his swoony accent.

"I'm so sorry. I—" I shake my head and he holds out his hand and I take it. He lifts me up like it's nothing, and I feel as if I'm diving headlong into a full-body blush, especially when I stare up at him while he still has my hand. "I was afraid I'd missed my flight."

"My apologies as well. I would normally be on full alert when a beautiful girl is running straight for me, but—" His shoulders shake with laughter, and if he weren't so incredibly hot, I'd smack him. I mean, hello, cheese, but I can't fault any man when he calls me beautiful. Not with that accent. Weakness. "The flight to Sydney is about to board," he adds.

My shoulders sag in relief, and I shakily release his hand. "I can't believe I made it."

"They're warning us already that the plane is an older one—you'd think they'd stay quiet about that sort of thing, especially with this technological mess..." He shrugs and I stare at the way his arms fill out his shirt, not to mention that chest. I force myself to look into his eyes, but then I'm blushing again. He's talking and I can't even focus. "It's got the first-class passengers yabbering about it before they get on..."

"What?" I swallow hard and he frowns.

"Are you sure you're okay?"

I nod and he seems satisfied with that. I feel the warm sweep of his eyes as he takes me in. I already know I'm a wreck. My hair is in two high buns, so it'll be harder to mess it up on the plane, but I'm sweaty, I'm wearing an oversize sweatshirt that is not flattering and leggings that my mother suggested I throw away a year ago. He grins and my breathing falters. I want to say wow, but I just barely hold it in.

"Lachie Conn," he says, holding out his hand again.

I stare at him in confusion, and he repeats it. "What?"

"We seem to have difficulty understanding one another," he says with a smirk. "Lachie Conn," he repeats, and then his eyes widen as he seems to wait for me to say something. I still have no clue what he's saying. "And...will you tell me your name?"

"*Oh*, that's your name? I'm so sorry...I thought that was some sort of Comic Con or something...do you have those in Australia?"

He laughs again and I die. I *die*.

I take his hand and shake it. And again there's a jolt between us. His eyes are crinkling at the corners with his grin, which it turns out is another great weakness of mine. I never knew.

"Violet Abernathy."

"It's very nice to meet you, Violet Abernathy. And yes, we do have Comic Con. No relation..."

I'm too flustered to say anything, but I nod and laugh just as they announce that we will begin boarding. He picks up his bag and nods back, then turns and walks away. I'm sad to see him go, but he was wrecking my insides being that close. Everyone lines up, and it's a madhouse. I don't bother pushing my way forward at this point—I have my assigned seat, and the thought of being on the plane for close to fifteen hours is already messing with my head. I can wait a few more minutes to get on and maybe regain my strength after that near-death experience with Lachie Conn, god of the muscles and crinkly eye grins.

* * *

When I give my ticket to the gate agent, she smiles and a little ticket prints out. She hands it to me and says, "You've been moved up. Take a look at your new seat."

"Oh, okay. Thank you."

Maybe this is their way of trying to right the wrongs. I got to the airport yesterday practically bouncing with excitement for this trip of a lifetime. I'd been saving for two years, and not once in my planning did getting to the airport and them telling me my flight was canceled for twenty-four hours ever enter the vision. I pleaded with them to find another flight, anything to get me started, but no. Nothing was available. They told me to go home and come back the next night and we'd try again. It was a depressing, cold Uber drive back to my apartment. I'd been leaving arctic Minnesota for the summer heat—I hadn't brought my coat.

When I got back to the airport earlier tonight, the flight was delayed several times due to the computer mess, and they said I might have to spend the night in the LA airport if I missed my flight. I didn't care. *Get me one step closer...*

But here I am, not only getting on my flight but moved up to the seat right behind first class. I look longingly at the amazing little cubicles they have, but the seats past this are even tighter than my new section. This is a marked improvement, and I'll happily take it...even though I'm in the middle seat. Ugh, I didn't think to check that. I wonder if I could change back to my original aisle seat back in the dregs.

"Ms. Abernathy, is that you?" I look up, and Lachie is standing there, smiling. He puts his bag in the overhead compartment and sits down next to me. "I hope you don't mind. I had your seat upgraded."

2

Well, color me speechless. I don't even know what to say. Wow comes to mind again, but clearly my brain cells are already on vacation.

"You...what? Wow." I sigh, clearly disappointed in myself.

"I apologize for the presumption, but I hoped *maybe*..." He turns from me and looks down at his hands.

When he doesn't finish right away, I clear my throat. "Maybe what?"

"Maybe you wouldn't mind getting to know me better too. It seemed like an incredible opportunity wasted, *in my opinion,* if this whole flight went by and I didn't get to know you."

Wow. Thankfully, I keep the word in this time.

An older woman stops at our row and hollers, "I'm by the window there." She points at the seat next to me.

"Righto," he says as we both stand to let her in.

"I'm Alma," she says. Or maybe that's what she says—it sounds like a cross between Alma and Almer, so I'm not positive. "And this is the last you'll hear from me." She leans in like she's going to whisper, but her voice makes me jump when it comes out. "Took a sleeping pill that should be kicking in shortly. Can't wait." She cackles and I can't help but laugh with her. "Feel free to try to wake me when they come around with supper, but don't bother if it's just Vegemite. I might be the only Aussie you meet who can't stand the stuff. Although you really should try it if you haven't," she adds. She sniffs and pulls out a chunk of material that she proceeds to blow up until it's a neck pillow.

I still haven't said a word, haven't had to, but she peeks over at me expectantly once she gets it around her neck. It looks uncomfortable from this angle, but she leaves it on.

"The two of you are lookers. Been together long?"

My eyes widen, and I look at Lachie. He grins and puts his hand on my arm, giving it a pat. I shiver and his grin widens.

"Six years," he says, leaning in closer. "High school sweethearts."

Alma's eyes narrow, but then she smiles when his hand slides down my arm and weaves his fingers through mine. I stare at our hands in shock, first of all that he's got the balls of a steel dragon to put on this act with a stranger—*me! I'm the stranger!*—and second and craziest of all...his hand is the perfect fit for my long fingers.

"You remind me of me and my husband, Alan...coming up on sixty years. Bet you didn't think I was old enough, did you?" Her cackle is infectious.

"Sixty years. That's incredible. I hope Violet and I can say the same one day." Lachie's voice is so sincere that I turn to stare at him. When he gives me a slight wink, I can barely hold back a cackle of my own.

"You're off to a good start...six years," Alma says with a smile. She then turns to face forward and closes her eyes. "Nighty night, lovebirds. I'll see you in the morning."

I pull my hand away from his, giving him a look as I do.

"Aw, why do you want to ruin the fun?" he asks, that smirk ever present.

"You're a cheeky thing, aren't you?" I say it haughtily, but if he looks closer, he'll see my lips tripping over themselves to not crack into a full-blown beam.

"Someone's been practicin' their Aussie lingo. Sounds good on you. Although I do prefer this accent you've got going. Where are you from?"

"I live in Minnesota."

"*Minnesoooota.* Aren't you supposed to say 'dontcha know' with that?" His *know* sounds like the woman on *Fargo*.

"Aren't you supposed to say 'sheila' every five seconds?"

"My dad will when he meets you," he says, laughing harder when my eyes widen.

My face warms, and I have to look away. "I have an uncle who says 'dontcha know' too." I lean my head back and give in to the laugh that's been building.

A loud snore comes from Alma, and we haven't even taken off yet. The seat-back instructions are read as we start moving, and Lachie and I are quiet since the attendant is standing right by us. She makes deliberate and dare I say, sexy—with the way she lowers her lids and then licks her lips twice—eye contact with Lachie the entire time she recites her lines. What the hell. I flush for her sake, even though she's hot and I'm sure it works for her...but jeez, she's nervy. I look at Lachie to see if he's noticing, and catch him looking at me. He grins like *oops, caught*.

And I grin back, going for a nonchalant, easy grin while hoping this foreign *I'd marry you and have your babies* feeling inside is just because I haven't slept properly all week. That and the fact that he's the most beautiful person I've ever seen in real life. And Minnesota has hot men. We're a hearty, healthy bunch with strangely good skin due to being frozen half the year.

I yawn, then clutch the armrest when we take off.

"Have you ever been on an international flight?" Lachie asks.

"No, first time."

"What made you choose Australia?"

"I'm going to see my friends, Christine, Kell, and Kate. We're meeting for the first time actually...but I feel like they're my family already."

"Wait, back up. You've never met? Then how do you know each other?"

"Books. We met over books online."

"I'm so confused, but we have all night." He grins and his eyes drop to my lips.

I press mine together and feel my chest get all fluttery. It's hard not to just stare at him, and I'm somewhat relieved and devastated when the lights go out.

"Why would they want to wreck my view?" Lachie mutters. He leans closer, and I feel his breath in my ear. "You know...if we were on a date, this could technically count as date number four or five by the time we land."

"But we're not," I say, turning toward him and then hastily facing forward again. He was even closer than I thought. "We just met."

"Right, but a man can dream. Are you a crusher of dreams, Violet?"

Now, I'm glad it's dark so he can't see my smile. "I hope not," I whisper.

"So you're a book lover?" he asks.

"Obsessed."

"And how do you meet other obsessed book lovers online? Is it a porn-type site except with books?"

"No!"

He chuckles and I shake my head, again happy for the dark so he doesn't see my red face.

"Someone's a little touchy. Tell me how it works." His voice is a low, sexy purr, and the accent...way more of an aphrodisiac than any food or drink I've ever had.

"Well, I know it sounds crazy, but we met in a Facebook group. My friend, Kell, has a book group, and somehow I found it. They love so many of the same books as I do, so it was an instant connection."

"What is this group? Could I be part of it?"

I frown at him, trying to see if he's making fun of it, but he looks serious.

"It's probably not the kind of books you're into," I tell him.

He starts grinning wider. "So it *is* like a porn-type site except with books. I knew it!" When his laugh gets louder, I clamp my hand over his mouth before I can stop myself. The whites of his eyes shine in the dark, and we both crack up. He holds both hands up for mercy, and I drop my hand. "My sister will love you," he says under his breath, still laughing.

I love how he keeps saying things that make it sound like I'll meet his family, even though the thought is ridiculous. I'll never see him again after this plane ride, but it's fun to play along.

"What if you guys don't get along in person?" he asks once we've both stopped laughing.

"Impossible. I talk to them every day, and I've never been closer to anyone! I think Australians are my people."

I realize how he'll run with that as soon as I've said it, and he leans in, his face so near I could just barely lean in and we would touch.

"Pretty sure you're right about that," he says.

My heart thuds so hard, and for a moment I get the craziest feeling like he might kiss me.

3

Four hours later...

Lachie and I sit face-to-face, whispering to one another while everyone around us sleeps.

"So how do you spend your days?" he asks after we've eaten weirdly rectangular pieces of chicken and salad.

"I have a roommate and she's a bit antisocial, so when I need it noisier, I go to my parents' house. They have three foster kids right now, and there's always something fun going on over there." I pause and yawn, my eyes watering. "What about you?"

"You're so tired. I should let you sleep." He reaches out and traces my forehead and eyebrows, and my eyes shut with the sensation. When I open them again, he's smiling at me.

"I don't want to waste a second of this flight sleeping," I whisper, and his fingers trace down to my cheek and the dimple that's on my right side.

"I don't either," he whispers. "You're so beautiful it hurts."

I think I stop breathing for a few seconds.

"No girlfriend then," I finally manage to say.

"I wouldn't be making sure you're in this seat by me if I had a girlfriend. And I wouldn't be doing this..." His fingers drop off my face and settle on top of my hand, looping between mine. My heart takes another lap around the plane and comes back winded. "I've just signed a deal with the Richmond Tigers..."

"Oh, what is that?"

"Football." He leans back against his seat, still turned toward me, and his face gets the most serious I've seen it. "It's what I've always wanted to do. Can't believe it's happening really."

"That's amazing. Congratulations."

He nods. "Thank you. Have you ever heard anything about Aussie rules? Our game is a bit different than yours."

I shake my head, and his eyes light up. He lets go of my hand, pulling out his phone. He takes a minute to find what he's looking for and then holds it up for me to see. It's a video of a game, and I spot him within seconds...just in time to see him catch the ball and then do a flying leap over another player, bouncing the ball as he runs, and then he kicks it into the end zone, if it's even called that.

"I know so little about the game, but I know *that* is like our football on *speed*."

He laughs. "Yeah, it's a good time."

"How are you not in pain all the time?"

"We're a tough breed." He grins and I laugh out loud, then rush to cover my mouth.

I turn back to look at Alma, and she's still out. I face him again, and he's putting the phone away.

"What's it like, getting ready to do what you've always wanted? Are you nervous at all? What if it isn't as great as you expect?"

I'm still a bit shook by him flying in the air with the ball. It's freaking crazy.

"I think it will be worse and better than I'm expecting."

I nod. "I know what you mean."

"You never finished telling me how you spend your days," he says.

"Oh, I was hoping to avoid that." I smirk and he lifts his eyebrows and motions for me to keep going. "I write. Kell reviewed my first book and contacted me...that's how we all started talking."

"So you're saying it was *your* book you bonded over..."

"Among others! But yes, I've written a few and...they seem to...go over well," I end awkwardly.

"You are adorable." He leans in closer. "I've never met a novelist before."

"I've never met a professional football player before."

The tension is thick as we stare at each other. He reaches out and takes my hand again.

"You know, I think we'd be around the third date by now," he says.

"Took us a while to get to the careers."

"Well, it took us forever to cover all our favorite foods. You have an extensive list." I love his voice when he's teasing; it takes on a husky sound that I feel all the way to my toes. "And you still have some catching up to do... You know what, I'm going to see if they have any Vegemite on this flight. Maybe the only thing Alma is wrong about."

I laugh and crinkle my nose. "From what I've heard of it, I'm good. Thanks, though."

"It's not a real trip to Australia if you don't have Vegemite."

Three hours later...

We've managed to scoot even closer together, with the pesky armrest between us lifted, and are sharing a blanket. We've covered our families, our recent graduations from college, what his upcoming schedule will be like, I've told him outlines for three upcoming books, and we've covered all our favorite parts of the Harry Potter books. I've never been able to talk to someone like this, ever. I still can't believe it's happening. It feels like a dream.

"So tell me again, three days in Sydney, then taking your time driving to Melbourne with stops along the way...what about Brisbane?"

"I don't think so. Next time, I guess."

"I don't want to take your time from your friends, but I'd love to meet them. I'm heading to Melbourne in a few days too."

"Really? They'd love to meet you. I can already imagine them swooning over you."

"Swooning, huh?"

"Oh, don't act like you don't know you're swoonworthy."

He laughs. "Swoonworthy, really? Is this *you* swooning?" He reaches out and touches my face; this time his thumb swipes over my lips, and I can't think straight.

"This is definitely me swooning," I whisper.

He closes the distance between us, and when his lips touch mine, everything in me jolts to life. I've been staring at his mouth all night, and it feels even better than it looks, which is saying a lot. My eyes fall shut and my God, his tongue. He pulls me closer, and my hands grip his shoulders, his hair, his face. He groans into my mouth, and my stomach drops into my feet as we explore one another. It feels soon, and yet, it feels like a lifetime has passed. Or at least three dates. I smile against his mouth with that thought and wish no space were between us, that I could climb into his lap and forget that we're on a crowded plane. I reluctantly pull away, breathing hard, and lean my forehead against his.

"I'm not going to want to let you go. You know that, right?" he asks. "This is crazy, but real. Right?" He grips my face and looks at me, his chest rising and falling fast. "I've never had such an immediate—" He leaves it hanging, and I want him to finish his thought because it sounds like he's feeling exactly what I'm feeling...but that really *would be* crazy. Wouldn't it?

"There's no rush for you to go home, is there?" He grins. "How about you stay at least long enough to see the whole country... It'll take a while, but since you've come all this way..."

We both laugh because we know it's ridiculous, and yet...I do have a job that I can do anywhere. And bonus: I can call it research.

"How about we think about dinner with my friends for now...see how that goes?"

He leans in and gives me another scorching kiss. "That'll be date seven by then. I think we're on a good trajectory. On date ten, I'll take you to meet my family. Or week after next, if that sounds good to you."

"I should've known you were trouble the moment I ran into you."

"And yet, you flew into me like you were home." His face grows serious when he says those words. "Wow," he whispers.

"I know."

4

Three hours later

After we're served breakfast, I can't stop yawning. I don't want to sleep, but the exhaustion is winning out. My head and heart are full from all the stories we've shared throughout the night, and now that I've eaten, I can hardly keep my eyes open.

"Come here," Lachie says.

He pulls the blanket closer around us and pats his chest. I sigh as I nestle into his neck and rest my hand on his chest. It's perfect—solid, warm, and—out.

* * *

The captain telling us we're getting ready to land jars me out of sleep, and I sit up, blinking. *No! How much time did I miss?* Lachie blinks sleepily back at me, his smirk especially sexy when he's just waking up. I get a sharp pang in my gut; the thought of saying goodbye in just a few minutes *hurts*. That seems stranger to me than the fact that I cuddled with a man I just met fifteen hours ago.

Lachie squeezes my hand, and I can't help myself—I tuck back into the crook of his arm and enjoy the way his chest feels a little bit longer. People around us are waking up, and the sun is shining throughout the cabin.

"I put all my information in the outside pocket of your bag," he says.

I jolt at his voice. We whispered for so long, it feels nice to hear him.

"I can't stand the thought of not seeing you again, but I also don't want to be the arsehole cutting in on your time with the girls. Say the word, and I will be there." He kisses my head, and I blink back the tears building. One drops on his shirt, and I hurry to wipe my face before he sees. "My offer stands about you extending your trip. Think about it."

"I will. I can't believe this—" My voice breaks, and I don't try to finish. I think he knows exactly how I'm feeling.

A few minutes later, we have to lower the armrest, forcing us to sit up and get our things together for landing. Lachie goes to the bathroom, and I do too, not the same one—mind out of the gutter!—and I brush my teeth and stare at myself in the mirror. Even with how heavy I feel about telling Lachie goodbye, my cheeks and eyes are bright. I look happy. I smile at the thought of him wanting me to stay, and decide I'll take each day as it comes. This is already a trip of a lifetime; why not believe it can be life-changing in every way?

When I get back to my seat, Lachie's standing in the aisle, and Alma smiles up at me.

"Well, that's the best night of sleep I've had in sixty years!" Alma laughs. "My Alan can snore with the best of them," she adds. Her face drops when she sees my eyes filling. "Oh, what's got you looking so glum?" She glances at Lachie and squeezes my hand. "Listen to this old lady when she tells you that life is too short to waste a moment doing anything other than what makes your heart happy. If someone who's lived as long as I have can say that, it's the truth." She gives my hand a pat and leans in closer. "I saw when the two of you collided at the airport and knew I was witnessing a great love story in the making." She winks and laughs so loud she turns heads. "Alma could work for a baby boy or girl, I'd say..."

Lachie laughs almost as loud as her, and it's mesmerizing. I have to peel my eyes away from him to look back at her and say with a straight face, "It's a deal. You're invited to the wedding and all of baby Alma's birthdays...both you and Alan." I turn and grin at Lachie, and the look in his eyes makes my chest flutter. I'm glad I'm sitting or the man would take me down *again*.

Eventually there's no more avoiding it. We've landed and have our carry-ons and are walking off the plane. When we step off, I hug Alma and remind her my number is in her phone and that I'd love to hear from her. She invited us to come over for dinner, but I'm not sure if she's just being nice or if she really plans on following through. She seems like someone who follows through, and I really hope it works out.

She walks away, and it's just Lachie and me. He looks down at me with sad eyes and a smile.

"I'll stay with you until your friends come," he says.

I nod, too torn up to say anything. He shifts his duffel bag on his shoulder, and I roll my carry-on behind us. He grabs my hand, and my skin heats just from that little contact.

How is it possible to miss him already?

As we're walking, he pulls me to the side, out of the way of everyone hustling through the airport, and sets his bag down, pulling me to his chest. I let go of the handle of my bag and wrap both arms around him, hugging him as hard as I can.

When we pull away, he lowers his head and puts both hands on my cheeks, tugging my face to his. We kiss like we'll never see each other again, and when the tears start falling down my cheeks, I don't even care.

I do eventually gasp for air and then laugh at how dramatic I'm being, crying and kissing him. I'd internally roll my eyes hard over anyone who told me this had happened to them. It's too unbelievable.

"I remember my friend Adri telling me something one time, about when she went to Russia and spent one night in a tiny town as far north as you can go. It took her twenty-four hours one way to get there. She spent the night and had two meals with a family she'd never met before, sang a few songs, and only was able to speak with one person there who interpreted to everyone else." I wipe my face and look to see if he's still with me. "Not a great way to interrupt a kiss, sorry. But..." My eyes start filling again, and I bite my lip to keep it from trembling. "When she left the next day to take the twenty-four-hour train back to Moscow, they came to the train station, and the men and women all wept as they hugged her goodbye. They stood there waving until she was out of sight." I sniff and Lachie reaches out to wipe a tear. "I get it now. Sometimes it only takes a moment with a kindred soul to make a permanent mark. I'm afraid you've done that to me."

His mouth crashes into mine, and he lifts me up until I'm level with him.

This kiss is too passionate to be bittersweet, too fiery to be heartbreaking, as we stand there in the airport saying goodbye.

Someone whistles, and we reluctantly break apart. He still holds me in place and looks at me with such intensity, I shiver.

"I'd be afraid if I hadn't left a permanent mark...because you've done the same to me. Please see me again. If you can't stay here, it'll be some time before I'm able to visit the US again, but I'll have a few breaks here and there. If you'll have me, I'll be there."

"How about both?" I whisper, leaning my forehead against his. "I'll extend my trip a little bit...we can see if we really get along or it was just a plane haze, and then...you come meet my family if, you know...there's a chance."

"God, I want there to be a chance," he whispers, giving me one more kiss.

"I mean, Alma called it, so...I think there really might be."

* * *